THE COMPLETE CHRONICLES OF THE JERUSALEM MAN

BY THE SAME AUTHOR

King Beyond the Gate
Legend
Wolf in Shadow
Ghost King
Waylander
Waylander II
Last Sword of Power
The Last Guardian
Knights of Dark Renown
Quest for Lost Heroes
Lion of Macedon
Drenai Tales
Dark Prince
Stones of Power
Morningstar
The First Chronicles of Druss the Legend
Bloodstone
Ironhand's Daughter
The Hawk Eternal

THE
COMPLETE CHRONICLES
OF THE
JERUSALEM MAN

Wolf in Shadow
The Last Guardian
Bloodstone

David A. Gemmell

Published by Legend Books in 1995
Am imprint of Random House UK Limited

Random House Australia (Pty) Limited
20 Alfred Street, Milsons Point, Sydney
New South Wales 2061, Australia

Random House New Zealand Limited
18 Poland Road, Glenfield,
Auckland 10, New Zealand

Random House South Africa (Pty) Limited
PO Box 337, Bergvlei, South Africa

Random House UK Limited Reg. No. 954009

© David A. Gemmell 1995

First published in 1995 by Legend Books

The right of David A. Gemmell to be identified as the author of this work has been asserted by him in accordance with the Copyright, Designs and Patents Act, 1988

This book is sold subject to the condition that it shall not by way of trade or otherwise, be lent, resold, hired out, or otherwise circulated without the publisher's prior consent in any form of binding or cover other than that in which it is published and without a similar condition including this condition being imposed on the subsequent purchaser

Printed and bound in Great Britain by
Mackays of Chatham PLC, Chatham, Kent

ISBN 0 09 966341 4
0 09 967661 3 (export only)

Contents

Wolf in Shadow — vii
Foreword — xi

The Last Guardian — 327
Foreword — 329

Bloodstone — 611
Foreword — 613

Wolf in Shadow

This novel is dedicated to the memory of 'Lady' Woodford, who believed in love, courage, and friendship, and gave those who knew her fresh insights into the meaning of all three. Sleep well, Lady.

And to Ethel Osborne, her sister, for a lifetime of love and care.

ACKNOWLEDGEMENTS

Nothing is created in a vacuum, and I am grateful to many people for their help in the creation of WOLF IN SHADOW. My thanks to Elizabeth Reeves, my editor, for bringing me out of the mist; to Peter Austin, for the wagon-master; and to Jean Maund, Stella Graham, Tom Taylor, Ross Lempriere, Ivan Kellham and Tony Fenelon for invaluable assistance.

Thanks also to Jeremy Wells, for loyalty and friendship, in a world that rarely understands either.

Foreword

Of the many characters I have created over the years, few have captured the imagination of readers as powerfully as Jon Shannow, the Jerusalem Man.

Alan Fisher, the award winning author of *Terioki Crossing*, and a fan of the film Casablanca, has a phrase that sums up characters like Shannow. 'They walk out of Rick's Bar, fully formed and real. The author doesn't have to work on them at all. There is no conscious act of creation. One moment they don't exist – the next they stand before you, complete and ready.'

I remember the moment Shannow walked out of Rick's Bar.

It was at the end of a miserable, wet day in Bournemouth at the start of autumn in 1986. I was the group managing editor of a series of newspapers stretching from Brighton to Portsmouth on the south coast. The previous week I had a call from my father to tell me that my mother was in hospital and that surgeons feared she had terminal cancer. They were right. A year before she had suffered the amputation of her right leg, and fought back to make a dramatic entrance at a Christmas Dance. This time there would be no fightback.

I had visited her in London, and then driven to Bournemouth for a business meeting, concluding it at around ten that night. I was staying in a small hotel of remarkable unfriendliness. The kind of place – as Jack Dee once said – where the Gideons leave a rope! I hadn't eaten since the previous evening and I called the night porter. He said the kitchen staff had gone home, but there was a plate of olives someone had left at the bar. Nursing the olives and a very large glass of Armagnac I returned to my room and opened the Olympia portable typewriter.

I was at the time preparing a Drenai novel, featuring the Nadir warlord Ulric, which my publishers had commissioned. According to the contract the book was to be called *Wolf in Shadow* and was, loosely, a prequel to Legend. I had completed around sixty pages. They weren't good, but I was powering on as best as I could.

Sitting by the window, looking out over Bournemouth's glistening streets, I tried to push the events of the week from my mind. My mother was dying, I was was waiting to be fired, and staff, who had joined my team in good faith, were facing redundancy. After the fifth large Armagnac I decided to continue work on the book. I knew I was drunk, and I also knew that the chances of writing anything worthwhile were pretty negligible. But forcing my mind into a fantasy world seemed infinitely more appealing than concentrating on the reality at hand.

The scene I was set to continue had a Nadir scout riding across the steppes. The intention was to follow him to the top of a hill and have him gaze down on the awesome army camped on the plain below.

I focused on the typewriter keys and typed the following sentences....

The rider paused at the crest of a wooded hill, and gazed down at the wide, rolling empty lands beneath him. There was no sign of Jerusalem...

The walls of the mind came crashing in as I typed the word *Jerusalem*, thoughts, fears and regrets spilling over one another, fighting for space. There followed a bad hour, which even Armagnac could not ease.

But after midnight I returned to the page and stared down at it. It called out to me. Who is he, I thought? What is he looking for, this Jerusalem Man?

And suddenly he was there. Tall and gaunt, seeking a city that had ceased to exist three hundred years before. A lonely, tortured man on a quest with no ending, riding through a world of savagery and barbarism.

The story flowed in an instant, and I wrote until after the dawn.

Through all the despair that followed in those next painful months I found a sanctuary in the company of Jon Shannow. Through his eyes I could see the world clearly, and understand how important it is to be strong in the broken places.

As a result Shannow will always be one of my favourite characters.

For a while back there he was the best friend I'd ever had.

David A. Gemmell   Hastings, 1995

Prologue

The High Priest lifted his bloodstained hands from the corpse and dipped them in a silver bowl filled with scented water. The blood swirled around the rose petals floating there, darkening them and glistening like oil. A young acolyte moved to kneel before the King, his hands outstretched. The King leaned forward, placing a large oval stone in his palms. The stone was red-gold, and veined with thick black streaks. The acolyte carried the stone to the corpse, laying it on the gaping wound where the girl's heart had been. The stone glowed, the red-gold gleaming like an eldritch lantern, the black veins shrinking to fine hairlines. The acolyte lifted the stone once more, wiped it with a cloth of silk and returned it to the King before backing away into the shadows.

A second acolyte approached the High Priest, bowing low. In his arms he held the red ceremonial cape which he lifted over the priest's bald head.

The King clapped his hands twice and the girl's body was lifted from the marble altar and carried down the long hall to oblivion.

'Well, Achnazzar?' demanded the King.

'As you can see, my lord, the girl was a powerful ESPer, and her essence will feed many Stones before it fades.'

'The death of a pig will feed a Stone, priest. You know what I am asking,' said the King, fixing Achnazzar with a piercing glare. The bald priest bowed low, keeping his eyes on the marble floor.

'The omens are mostly good, sire.'

'Mostly? Look at me!' Achnazzar raised his head, steeling himself to meet the burning eyes of the Satanlord. The priest blinked and tried to look away, but Abaddon's glare held him trapped, almost hypnotized. 'Explain yourself.'

'The invasion, Lord, should proceed favourably in the Spring. But there are dangers . . . not great dangers,' he added hurriedly.

'From which area?'

Achnazzar was sweating now as he licked dry lips with a dry tongue.

'Not an area, Lord, but three men.'

'Name them.'

'Only one can be identified, the others are hidden. But we will find them. The one is called Shannow. Jon Shannow.'

'Shannow? I do not know the name. Is he a leader of men, or a Brigand chief?'

'No, Lord. He rides alone.'

'Then how is he a danger to the Hellborn?'

'Not to the Hellborn, sire, but to you.'

'You consider there is a difference?'

Achnazzar blanched and blinked the sweat from his eyes. 'No, Lord, I meant merely that the threat is to you as a man.'

'I have never heard of this Shannow. Why should he threaten me?'

'There is no sure answer, sire, but he follows the old, dead god.'

'A Christian?' spat Abaddon. 'Will he seek to kill me with love?'

'No, Lord, I meant the old dark god. He is a Brigand-slayer, a man of sudden violence. There is even some indication that he is insane.'

'How do these indications manifest themselves – apart from his religious stupidity?'

'He is a wanderer, Lord, searching for a city which ceased to exist during Blessed Armageddon.'

'What city?'

'Jerusalem, Lord.'

Abaddon chuckled and leaned back on his throne, all tension fading. 'That city was destroyed by a tidal wave three hundred years ago – by the great mother of all tidal waves. A thousand feet of surging ocean drowned that pestilential place, signalling the rein of the Master and the death of Jehovah. What does Shannow hope to find in Jerusalem?'

'We do not know, Lord.'

'And why is he a threat?'

'In every chart, or seer-dream, his line crosses yours. Karmically you are bonded. It is so with the other two; in some way Shannow has touched – or will touch – the lives of two men who could harm you. We cannot identify them yet – but we will. For now they appear as shadows behind the Jerusalem Man.'

'Shannow must die . . . and swiftly. Where is he now?'

'He is at present some months' journey to the south, nearing Rivervale. We have a man there, Fletcher. I shall get word to him.'

'Keep me informed, priest.'

As Achnazzar backed away from his monarch, Abaddon rose from the ebony throne and wandered to the high arched window, gazing over New Babylon. On a plain to the south of the city the Hellborn army was gathering for the Raids of the Blood Feast. By Winter the new guns would be distributed and the Hellborn would ready themselves for the Spring war: ten thousand men under the banner of Abaddon, sweeping into the south and west, bringing the new world into the hands of the last survivor of the Fall.

And they warned him of one madman?

Abaddon raised his arms. 'Come to me, Jerusalem Man.'

Chapter One

The rider paused at the crest of a wooded hill and gazed down over the wide rolling empty lands beneath him.

There was no sign of Jerusalem, no dark road glittering with diamonds. But then Jerusalem was always ahead, beckoning in the dreams of night, taunting him to find her on the black umbilical road.

His disappointment was momentary and he lifted his gaze to the far mountains, grey and spectral. Perhaps there he would find a sign? Or was the road covered now by the blown dust of centuries, disguised by the long grass of history?

He dismissed the doubt; if the city existed, Jon Shannow would find it. Removing his wide-brimmed leather hat, he wiped the sweat from his face. It was nearing noon and he dismounted. The steeldust gelding stood motionless until he looped the reins over its head, then dipped its neck to crop at the long grass. The man delved into a saddlebag to pull clear his ancient Bible; he sat on the ground and idly opened the gold-edged pages.

'*And Saul said to David, Thou art not able to go against this Philistine to fight with him, for thou art but a youth, and he is a man of war from his youth.*'

Shannow felt sorry for Goliath, for the man had had no chance. A courageous giant, ready to face any warrior, found himself opposite a child without sword or armour. Had he won, he would have been derided. Shannow closed the Bible and carefully packed it away.

'Time to move,' he told the gelding. He stepped into the saddle and swept up the reins. Slowly they made their way down the hillside, the rider's eyes watchful of every boulder and tree, bush and shrub. They entered the cool of the valley and Shannow drew back on the reins, turning his face to the north and breathing deeply.

A rabbit leapt from the brush, startling the gelding. Shannow saw the creature vanish into the undergrowth and then uncocked the long-barrelled pistol, sliding it back into the scabbard at his hip. He could not recall drawing it clear. Such was the legacy of the years of peril – fast hands, a sure eye and a body that reacted independently of the conscious mind.

Not always a good thing . . . Shannow would never forget the look of blank incomprehension in the child's eyes as the lead ball clove his heart. Nor the way his frail body had crumpled lifeless to the earth. There had been three Brigands that day and one had shot Shannow's horse out from under him, while the other two ran forward with knife and axe. He had destroyed them all in scant seconds, but a movement behind caused him to swivel and fire. The child had died without a sound.

Would God ever forgive him?

Why should he, when Shannow could not forgive himself?

'You were better off losing, Goliath,' said Shannow.

The wind changed and a stomach-knotting aroma of frying bacon drifted to him from the east. Shannow tugged the reins to the right. After a quarter of a mile the trail rose and fell and a narrow path opened on to a meadow and a stone-fronted farmhouse. Before the building was a vegetable garden and beyond it a paddock where several horses were penned.

There were no defence walls and the windows of the house were wide and open. To the left of the building the trees had been allowed to grow to within twenty yards of the wall, allowing no field of fire to repel Brigands. Shannow sat and stared for some time at this impossible dwelling. Then he saw a child carrying a bucket emerge from the barn beyond the paddock. A woman walked out to meet him and ruffled his blond hair.

Shannow scanned the fields and meadows for sign of a man. At last, satisfied that they were alone, he edged the gelding out on to open ground and approached the building. The boy saw him first and ran inside the house.

Donna Taybard's heart sank as she saw the rider and she fought down panic as she lifted the heavy crossbow from the wall. Placing her foot in the bronze stirrup she dragged back on the string, but could not notch it.

'Help me, Eric.' The boy joined her and together they cocked the weapon. She slid a bolt into place and stepped on to the porch. The rider had halted some thirty feet from the house and Donna's fear swelled as she took in the gaunt face and deep-set eyes, shadowed under the wide-brimmed hat. She had never seen a Brigand, but had anyone asked her to imagine one this man would have leapt from her nightmares. She lifted the crossbow, resting the heavy butt against her hip.

'Ride on,' she said. 'I have told Fletcher we shall not leave, and I will not be forced.'

The rider sat very still, then he removed his hat. His hair was shoulder-length and black, streaked with silver, and his beard showed a white fork at the chin.

'I am a stranger, Lady, and I do not know this Fletcher. I do not seek to harm you – I merely smelt the bacon and would trade for a little. I have Barta coin and . . .'

'Leave us alone,' she shouted. The crossbow slipped in her grip, dropping the trigger bar against her palm. The bolt flashed into the air, sailing over the rider and dropping by the paddock fence. Shannow walked his horse to the paddock and dismounted, retrieving the bolt. Leaving the gelding, he strolled back to the house.

Donna dropped the bow and pulled Eric into her side. The boy was trembling, but in his hand he held a long kitchen knife; she took it from him and waited as the man approached. As he walked he removed his heavy leather top-coat and draped it over his arm. It was then that she saw the heavy pistols at his side.

'Don't kill my boy,' she said.

'Happily, Lady, I was speaking the truth: I mean you no

harm. Will you trade a little bacon?' He picked up the bow and swiftly notched it, slipping the bolt into the gulley. 'Would you feel happier carrying this around?'

'You are truly not with the Committee?'

'I am a stranger.'

'We are about to take food. If you wish, you may join us.' Shannow knelt before the boy. 'May I enter?' he asked.

'Could I stop you?' returned the boy bitterly.

'With just one word.'

'Truly?'

'My faults are many, but I do not lie.'

'You can come in then,' said the boy and Shannow walked ahead with the child trailing behind. He mounted the porch steps and entered the cool room beyond, which was spacious and well-constructed. A white stone hearth held a wood-stove and an iron oven; at the centre of the room was a handsomely carved table and a wooden dresser bearing earthenware plates and pottery mugs.

'My father carved the table,' said the boy. 'He is a skilled carpenter – the best in Rivervale – and his work is much sought after. He made the comfort chair, too, and cured the hides.' Shannow made a show of admiring the leather chair by the wood-stove, but his eyes followed the movements of the petite blonde woman as she prepared the table.

'Thank you for allowing me into your home,' said Shannow gravely. She smiled for the first time and wiped her hand on her canvas apron.

'I am Donna Taybard,' she told him, offering her hand. He took it and kissed her fingers lightly.

'And I am Jon Shannow – a wanderer, Lady, in a strange land.'

'Be welcome then, Jon Shannow. We have some potatoes and mint to go with the bacon, and the meal will be ready within the hour.'

Shannow moved to the door, where pegs had been hammered home. He unbuckled his scabbard belt and hung his sidearms beside his coat. Turning back, he saw the fear once more in her eyes.

'Be not alarmed, Fray Taybard; a wandering man must

protect himself. It does not change my promise; that may not be so with all men, but my spoken word is iron.'

'There are few guns in Rivervale, Mr Shannow. This was . . . is . . . a peaceful land. If you would like to wash before eating, there is a pump behind the house.'

'Do you have an axe, Lady?'

'Yes. In the wood-shed.'

'Then I shall work for my supper. Excuse me.'

He walked out into the fading light of dusk and unsaddled the gelding, leading him into the paddock and releasing him among the other three horses. Then he carried his saddle and bags to the porch before fetching the axe. He spent almost an hour preparing firewood before stripping to the waist and washing himself at the pump. The moon was up when Donna Taybard called him in. She and the boy sat at one end of the table, having set his place apart and facing the hearth. He moved his plate to the other side and seated himself facing the door.

'May I speak a word of thanks, Fray Taybard?' asked Shannow as she filled the plates. She nodded. 'Lord of Hosts, our thanks to thee for this food. Bless this dwelling and those who pass their lives here. Amen.'

'You follow the old ways, Mr Shannow?' asked Donna, passing a bowl of salt to the guest.

'Old? It is new to me, Fray Taybard. But, yes, it is older than any man knows and a mystery to this world of broken dreams.'

'Please do not call me Fray, it makes me feel ancient. You may call me Donna. This is my son, Eric.'

Shannow nodded towards Eric and smiled, but the boy looked away and continued to eat. The bearded stranger frightened him, though he was anxious not to show it. He glanced at the weapons hanging by the door.

'Are they hand pistols?' he asked.

'Yes,' said Shannow. 'I have had them for seventeen years, but they are much older than that.'

'Do you make your own powder?'

'Yes, I have casts for the loads and several hundred brass caps.'

'Have you killed anyone with them?'

'Eric!' snapped his mother. 'That is no question to ask a guest – and certainly not at table.'

They finished the meal in silence and Shannow helped her clear away the dishes. At the back of the house was an indoor water pump, and together they cleaned the plates. Donna felt uncomfortable in the closeness of the pump-room and dropped a plate which shattered into a score of shards on the tiled wooden floor.

'Please do not be nervous,' he said, kneeling to collect the broken pieces.

'I trust you, Mr Shannow. But I have been wrong before.'

'I shall sleep outside and be gone in the morning. Thank you for the meal.'

'No,' she said, too hurriedly. 'I mean – you can sleep in the comfort chair. Eric and I sleep in the back room.'

'And Mr Taybard?'

'Has been gone for ten days. I hope he will be back soon; I'm worried for him.'

'I could look for him, if you would like. He may have fallen from his horse.'

'He was driving our wagon. Stay and talk, Mr Shannow; it is so long since we had company. You can give us news of . . . where have you come from?'

'From the south and east, across the grass prairies. Before that I was at sea for two years – trading with the Ice Settlements beyond Volcano Rim.'

'That is said to be the edge of the world.'

'I think it is where Hell begins. You can see the fires lighting the horizon for a thousand miles.'

Donna eased past him into the main room. Eric was yawning and his mother ordered him to bed. He argued as all young people do, but finally obeyed her, leaving his bedroom door ajar.

Shannow lowered himself into the comfort chair, stretching his long legs out before the stove. His eyes burned with fatigue.

'Why do you wander, Mr Shannow?' asked Donna,

sitting on the goatskin rug in front of him.

'I am seeking a dream. A city on a hill.'

'I have heard of cities to the south.'

'They are settlements, though some of them are large. But no, my city has been around for much longer, it was built, destroyed and rebuilt thousands of years ago. It is called Jerusalem and there is a road leading to it – a black road, with glittering diamonds in the centre that shine in the night.'

'The Bible city?'

'The very same.'

'It is not about here, Mr Shannow. Why do you seek it?'

He smiled. 'I have been asked that question many, many times and I cannot answer it. It is a need I carry – an obsession, if you will. When the earth toppled and the oceans swelled, all became chaos. Our history is lost to us and we no longer know from whence we come, nor where we are going. In Jerusalem there will be answers, and my soul will rest.'

'It is very dangerous to wander, Mr Shannow. Especially in the wild lands beyond Rivervale.'

'The lands are not wild, Lady – at least, not for a man who knows their ways. Men are wild and they create the wild lands wherever they are. But I am a known man and I am rarely troubled.'

'Are you known as a war-maker?'

'I am known as a man war-makers should avoid.'

'You are playing with words.'

'No, I am a man who loves peace.'

'My husband was a man of peace.'

'*Was?*'

Donna opened the stove door and added several chunks of wood. She sat for some time staring into the flames, and Shannow did not disturb the silence. At last she looked up at him.

'My husband is dead,' she said. 'Murdered.'

'By Brigands?'

'No, by the Committee. They . . .'

'No!' screamed Eric, standing in the bedroom doorway

in his white cotton nightshirt. 'It's not true. He's alive! He's coming home – I know he's coming home.'

Donna Taybard ran to her son, burying his weeping face against her breast. Then she led him back into the bedroom and Shannow was alone. He strolled into the night. The sky was without stars, but the moon shone bright through a break in the clouds. Shannow scratched his head, feeling the dust and grit on his scalp. He removed his woollen jerkin and undershirt and washed in a barrel of clear water, scrubbing the dirt from his hair.

Donna walked out to stand on the porch and watch him. His shoulders seemed unnaturally broad against the slimness of his waist and hips. Silently she moved away from the house to the stream at the bottom of the hill. Here she slipped out of her clothes and bathed in the moonlight, rubbing lemon mint leaves across her skin.

When she returned Jon Shannow was asleep in the comfort chair, his guns once more belted to his waist. She moved silently past him to her room and locked the door. As the key turned, Shannow opened his eyes and smiled.

Where to tomorrow, Shannow, he asked himself?

Where else?

Jerusalem.

Shannow awoke soon after dawn and sat listening to the sounds of morning. He was thirsty and moved to the pump-room for a mug of water. Behind the door was an oval mirror framed in golden pine and he stood staring at his reflection. The eyes were deep-set and dark blue, the face triangular above a square jaw. As he had feared, his hair was showing grey, though his beard was still dark on the cheeks with a silver fork at the chin.

He finished his drink and moved outside to the porch and his saddlebags. Having found his razor and stropped it for several minutes, he returned to the mirror and cut away his beard. Donna Taybard found him there and watched in mild amusement as he tried to trim his long hair.

'Sit out on the porch, Mr Shannow. I am expecting some

friends today, and I think I should make you look presentable.'

With long-handled scissors and a bone comb she worked expertly at the tangled mess, complimenting him on the absence of lice.

'I move too fast for them, and I swim when I can.'

'Is that short enough for you?' she asked, stepping back to admire her handiwork. He ran his hand through his hair and grinned – almost boyishly, she thought.

'That will suffice, Fray Taybard . . . Donna. Thank you. You said you were expecting friends?'

'Yes, some neighbours are coming over to celebrate Harvest. It was arranged before Tomas . . . disappeared, but I told them to come anyway. I'm hoping they will be able to help me with the Committee – but I doubt they will . . . all have their own problems. You are welcome to stay. There will be a barbecue, and I have made some cakes.'

'Thank you, I will.'

'But, Mr Shannow, please do not wear your guns. This is still, in the main, a peaceful community.'

'As you wish. Is Eric still sleeping?'

'No, he is in the long meadow gathering wood for the fire. And then he must milk the cows.'

'Do you have any trouble with wolves or lions?'

'No, the Committee shot the last lion during the winter and the wolves have moved to the high country. They sometimes forage in winter, but they are not a great problem.'

'Life here seems . . . settled,' he said, rising and brushing the hair from his shirt.

'It has been – it certainly was when my father was Prester. But now there is Fletcher; we will not call him Prester, and I know that does not sit well with him.'

'You said last night that your husband was dead. Is that a fear or a reality?'

She stood in the doorway, her hand on the frame. 'I have a talent, Mr Shannow, for seeing faraway things. I had it as a child and it has not deserted me. As we speak, I can see Eric in the far meadow. He has stopped gathering wood and

9

has climbed a tall pine; he is pretending to be a great hunter. Yes, Mr Shannow, my husband is dead. He was killed by Fletcher and there were three with him: the big man, Bard, and two others whose names I do not know. Tomas's body lies in an arroyo, hastily buried.'

'Fletcher desires your lands?'

'And me. He is a man used to obtaining his desires.'

'Perhaps he will be good for you.'

Her eyes blazed. 'You think I will suffer myself to be taken by my husband's killer?'

Shannow shrugged. 'The world is a hard place, Donna. I have seen settlements where women are not allowed to pair-bond with a single man, where they are communal property. And it is not strange in other areas for men to kill for what they want. What a man can take and hold, he owns.'

'Not in Rivervale, sir,' she told him. 'Not yet, at least.'

'Good luck, Donna. I hope you find a man willing to stand against this Fletcher. If not I hope he is, as I said, good for you.'

She moved back into the house without a word.

Some time later the boy Eric came into view, towing a small hand-cart loaded with dead wood. He was a slim boy, his hair so fair it seemed white. His face was set and serious, his eyes sad and knowing.

He walked past Shannow without speaking and the man wandered to the paddock where the steeldust gelding trotted to him, nuzzling his hand. There was grass in the pen, but Shannow would have liked to give him grain. The beast could run for miles without effort, but fed on grain he could run for ever. Five years ago Shannow had won 2,000 Barta coins in three races, but the gelding was too old now for such ventures. Shannow returned to his saddlebags and removed the oilskin gun-pouch.

Pulling the left-hand pistol from its scabbard, he tapped out the barrel pin and released the cylinder, placing it carefully on the porch beside him. Then he ran an oiled cloth through the barrel and cleaned dust from the trigger mechanism. The pistol was nine inches long and weighed several pounds, but Shannow had long since ceased to notice the weight. He checked the cylinder for dust and then slipped it back into place, pressing home the wedge bar and replacing the weapon in its scabbard. The right-hand pistol was two inches shorter and brass-mounted with butt plates of polished ivory, unlike the dark apple-wood of the longer weapon. Despite the difference in barrel length it was this weapon that fired true, the other kicking to the left and unreliable at anything but close quarters. Shannow cleaned the pistol lovingly and looked up to see Eric watching him closely, his eyes fixed on the gun.

'Will you shoot it?' asked the boy.

'There is nothing to shoot at,' said Shannow.

'Does it make a loud noise?'

'Yes – and the smoke smells like the Devil. Have you never heard a gun fire?'

'Once when the Prester shot a lion – but I was only five. Mr Fletcher has a pistol, and several of the Committee have long rifles; they are more powerful now than any war-maker.'

'You like Mr Fletcher, Eric?'

'He has always been nice to me. He's a great man; he's the Prester now.'

'Then why is your mother afraid of him and his Committee?'

'Oh, that's just women,' said Eric. 'Mr Fletcher and my father had an argument and Mr Fletcher said the carpenter should live in Rivervale where the work was needed. The Committee voted on it. Mr Fletcher wanted to buy the farm but Father said no, I don't know why. It would be nice to live in Rivervale where all the people are. And Mr Fletcher really likes mother; he told me that, he said she was a fine lady. I like him.'

'Did . . . does your father like him?'

'Father doesn't like anybody. He likes me sometimes, when I do my chores well or when I help him without dropping anything.'

'Is he the only carpenter in Rivervale?'

'He was, but Mr Fletcher has a man working for him who

says *he's* a carpenter. Father laughs about him; he says the man thinks a dove joint is found on a pigeon's leg!'

Shannow grinned. The boy looked younger when he smiled.

'Are you a war-maker, Mr Shannow? Truly?'

'No, Eric. As I told your mother, I am a man who loves peace.'

'But you have guns?'

'I travel through the wild lands, Eric; they are necessary.'

Two wagons crested the skyline. 'That will be the Janus family and the McGravens,' said Eric.

Shannow replaced his guns in their scabbards and moved into the house, hanging the weapons on the hook inside the door.

'Your guests have begun to arrive,' he told Donna. The house smelt of fresh-baked bread and cakes. 'Is there anything I can do?'

'Help Eric prepare the barbecue fires.'

All morning wagons arrived, until more than twenty formed several lines inside the pasture. With three barbecue fires burning and almost fifty peeople moving about, Shannow felt uncomfortable. He wandered to the barn for a little solitude and found two young people holding hands in the shadows.

'I am sorry to disturb you,' he said, turning to leave.

'It's all right,' said the young man. 'My name is Janus, Stefan Janus. This is Susan McGraven.' Shannow shook hands with them and moved outside.

As he stood by the paddock, the steeldust gelding ran to him and Shannow stroked his neck. 'Almost time to leave,' he told the horse.

A woman's voice rang out. 'Susan! Where are you?' The young girl ran from the barn.

'I'm coming,' she answered. The young man joined Shannow; he was tall and fair-haired and his eyes were serious, his face intelligent.

'Are you staying in Rivervale?'

'No, I am a traveller.'

12

'A traveller who is uncomfortable with crowds,' observed Janus.

'Even so.'

'You will find the crowd less hostile when the people are known to you. Come, I will introduce you to some friendly faces.'

He took Shannow into the throng, and there followed much shaking of hands and a bewildering series of names which Shannow could not absorb – but the lad was right, and he began to feel more comfortable.

'And what do you do, Mr Shannow?' came the inevitable question, this time from a burly farmer named Evanson.

'Mr Shannow is searching for a city,' said Donna Taybard, joining them. 'He is a historian.'

'Oh,' responded Evanson, his face portraying his lack of interest. 'And how are you, Donna? Any sign of Tomas?'

'No. Is Anne with you?'

'I am afraid not. She stayed with Ash Burry; his wife is not well.'

Shannow slipped away, leaving them to their conversation. Children were playing near the paddock and he sat on the porch watching them. Everyone here seemed different from the people of the south; their faces were ruddy and healthy and they laughed often. Elsewhere, where Brigands rode, there was always a tension – a wariness in the eyes. Shannow felt apart from the people of Rivervale.

Towards the afternoon a group of riders came down the hill, six men riding directly towards the house. Shannow drifted back into the main room and watched them from a window. Donna Taybard saw them at the same time and wandered over, followed by a dozen or so of her neighbours.

The riders reined in and a tall man in a white woollen shirt stepped from the saddle. He was around thirty years old and his hair was black and close-cropped, his face dark and handsome.

'Good day, Donna.'

'And to you, Mr Fletcher.'

'I am glad to see you enjoying yourself. Any word from Tomas?'

'No. I am thinking of going to the arroyo where you left him and marking his grave.'

The man flushed deep red. 'I don't know what you mean.'

'Go away, Saul. I do not want you here.'

People were gathering around the riders and a silence settled over the scene.

Fletcher licked his lips. 'Donna, it is no longer safe to be so close to the edge of the wild lands. Daniel Cade has been sighted only eight miles south. You must come in to Rivervale.'

'This is my home and I will remain here,' she said.

'I am sorry, but I must insist. The Committee has voted on this. You will be paid handsomely for your home and comfortable quarters have been set aside for you and Eric. Do not make this any more difficult. Your friends here have offered to help you with your furniture and belongings.'

As Donna's eyes swept the group, Evanson looked away and many others were staring at the ground. Only Stefan Janus moved forward.

'Why should she go if she does not wish to?' he said.

Saul Fletcher ignored him and moved closer to Donna.

'There is no sense in this, Donna. The Committee has the right to make laws to protect its people. You must leave – and you *will* leave. Now!' Fletcher turned to a huge, barrel-chested figure on a large black gelding. 'Bard, give Donna a hand with her belongings.' As the big man moved to dismount, Jon Shannow stepped from the shadowed doorway and stood on the porch overlooking the crowd. Bard settled back in the saddle, and all eyes turned to Shannow and the guns he now wore. In turn he studied the men who had just arrived. He had seen men like these all his life – chancers, Brigands, war-makers. They all had that look – that stamp of cruelty, of callous arrogance.

'If Fray Taybard wishes to stay,' said Shannow, 'then that is the end of the argument.'

'And who are you, sir?' asked Fletcher, his eyes on the pistols at Shannow's side.

Shannow ignored him and turned to the riders, recognizing two of them.

'How are you, Miles?' he called. 'And you, Pope? You are a long way from Allion.' The two men sat very still, saying nothing.

'I asked you who you were,' said Fletcher, his hand resting on the walnut grip of a double-barrelled flintlock sheathed at his waist.

'He's the Jerusalem Man,' said Miles, and Fletcher froze.

'I have heard of you, sir. You are a killer and a warmaker. We will not suffer your kind in Rivervale.'

'No?' said Shannow mildly. 'My understanding is that you are no stranger to murder – and Miles and Pope were riding with Cade only a year ago.'

'That is a lie.'

'Whatever you say, Mr Fletcher. I have neither the time nor the inclination to argue with you. You may leave now.'

'Just say the word, Saul,' shouted Bard. 'I'll cut him down to size.'

'Yes,' agreed Shannow. 'Do say the word, Mr Fletcher.'

'Don't, for God's sake!' shouted Miles. 'You've never seen him.'

Fletcher was far from being a foolish man and he heard the terror in Miles' voice. He swallowed hard and then moved to his horse, mounting swiftly.

'Too many innocent people could suffer here,' he said, 'but there will be another day.'

'I hope so,' Shannow told him and the riders galloped from the yard.

The crowd remained and Shannow ran his eyes over them. Gone was the open friendliness, replaced now by fear bordering on hostility. Only young Janus approached him.

'Thank you, Mr Shannow. I hope you will not suffer for your kindness.'

'If I do I will not suffer alone, Stefan,' he said and walked back into the house.

The last wagon left just before dusk and Donna found Shannow sitting in the comfort chair.

'You shouldn't have done that for me,' she said, 'but I am grateful.'

Eric came in behind her. 'What did you mean about father's grave?' he asked.

'I'm sorry, Eric, but it's true. Fletcher had him killed. I'm sorry.'

'It's a lie,' he shouted, tears falling freely. 'You hated him! And I hate you!' He turned and fled the house.

'Eric! Eric!' she called and then began to weep.

Shannow went to her, and held her close until the tears and the sobbing eased. He could find no words to comfort her, and Jerusalem seemed so far away.

Shannow sat at the pine dinner-table watching Donna Taybard kneeling at the wood-stove, as she raked out the ash with even, thoughtless strokes. She was a beautiful woman, and he could see why Fletcher desired her. Her face was strong and finely-boned, her mouth full and made for laughter. It was a face of character, of strength in adversity.

'This talent,' he said, 'of seeing faraway things – how did you come by it?'

'I don't know. My father thought it was the Stone, but I'm not sure.'

'The Stone?'

'The Prester called it the Daniel Stone. It was from the Plague Lands and when held in the hand it glowed like sunlight behind ice. And it was warm. I played with it often as a child.'

'Why should he think the Stone caused your talents?'

She brushed ash from her hands and sat back. 'Do you believe in magic, Mr Shannow?'

'No.'

'Then you would not understand the Stone. When my father held it the sick would be healed. Wounds would close within seconds, with no scar. It was one of the reasons he became Prester.'

'Why was it called the Daniel Stone?'

'I don't know. But one day it refused to glow, and that was an end to it. It is still in my father's old house, where

Fletcher now lives. Ash Burry tells me that Fletcher is always toying with it – but it will never work again. The Prester told me its power had departed for ever.'

'But now you have powers.'

'Not of healing, or prophecy, or any real magic. But I can see those close to me, even when they are far away.'

For a while they sat in silence. Donna added kindling to the stove and lit a fire. Once the blaze was roaring she closed the iron door and turned to Shannow.

'May I ask you a question?'

'Of course.'

'Why did you risk your life with all those men?'

'It was not a great risk, Lady. There was only one man.'

'I do not understand.'

'Where there is a group, there is a leader. Nullify him and the rest count for nothing. Fletcher was not prepared to die.'

'But you were?'

'All things die, Donna. And I was pleased to repay your hospitality. Perhaps Fletcher will reconsider his plans for you. I hope so.'

'But you doubt it.'

'Yes.'

'Have you ever had a wife, Mr Shannow?'

'It is getting late,' he said, standing. 'Eric should be home – shall I look for him?'

'I am sorry. Did I offend you?'

'No, Lady. My discomfort is my own and no fault of yours. Can you see the boy?'

She closed her eyes. 'Oh, God,' she said. 'They have taken him!'

'Who?'

'Bard and some others.'

'Where are they?'

'They are travelling north-west, towards the settlement. They have hurt him and his face is bleeding.'

Gently he pulled her to her feet, then took her hands in his.

'I will find him and bring him home. Rely on it.'

Shannow left the house and saddled the gelding, heading him north at a canter. He avoided sky-lining himself on the crests of the hills, but still he rode with uncustomary speed. He had neglected to ask Donna how many men rode with Bard, but then the information was immaterial. Two or twenty, the plan would be the same.

He emerged from the trees above the raiding party and sat back in the saddle. There were five men, including Bard – of Fletcher there was no sign. Eric's unconscious body was draped across Bard's saddle. Shannow breathed deeply, trying to stem the red rage swelling within, his hands trembling with the effort. As always he failed and his vision swam. His mouth was dry and the Bible text flowed into his mind:

'And David said unto Saul, Thy servant kept his father's sheep and there came a lion and a bear, and took a lamb out of the flock.'

Shannow rode down the hill and reined in ahead of the riders. They spread across the trail; two of them, Miles and Pope, were carrying crossbows cocked and ready. Shannow's hands swept up and smoke and flame thundered from the right-hand pistol. Pope flew from the saddle. The left-hand pistol fired a fraction of a second later and Miles pitched to the ground, the lower half of his face blown away.

'Step down, Bard,' said Shannow, both pistols levelled at the giant's face. Slowly the man dismounted. 'On your knees and on your belly.' The giant obeyed. 'Now eat grass like the mule you are.'

Bard's head shot up. 'The Hell . . .' The left-hand pistol bucked in Shannow's hand and Bard's right ear disappeared in a bloody spray. The big man screamed and ducked his head to the ground, tearing at the grass with his teeth. The other two men sat motionless, their hands well away from their weapons.

Shannow watched them closely, then transferred his gaze to the two corpses.

Then he spoke: *'And I went out after him, and smote him, and delivered it out of his mouth: and when he rose against me I caught him by the beard and slew him.'*

The two riders glanced at one another and said nothing. The Jerusalem Man was known to be insane, and neither of them had any wish to join their comrades, living or dead, upon the grass.

Shannow edged his horse towards them and they avoided his eyes, for his face was set and his fury touched them.

'You will put those your friends upon their horses, and you will take them to a place of burial. You will not, at any time, cross my path, for I will cut you down as deadwood from the Tree of Life. Go collect your dead.'

He swung his horse, offering them his back, but neither man considered attacking him. They dismounted swiftly and bundled the corpses across the saddles of the horses standing quietly by. Shannow rode alongside Bard, whose mouth was green and who was vomiting upon the grass.

'Stand and face me, Man of Gath.' Bard struggled to his feet and met Shannow's gaze. A cold dread settled on him as he saw the eyes and the fanatic gleam. He lowered his head and froze as he heard the click of a pistol hammer. His eyes flickered up and he saw with relief that Shannow had uncocked the weapons and returned them to their scabbards.

'My anger is gone, Bard. You may live today.'

The giant was close enough to pluck Shannow from the saddle and tear him apart bare-handed, but he could not, even though he recognized the opportunity. His shoulders sagged. Shannow nodded knowingly, and shame burned in Bard's heart.

Eric groaned and stirred on Bard's horse nearby.

And Shannow lifted him from the saddle and took him home.

Donna Taybard sat with Eric for over an hour. The boy was shaken by his ordeal. He had awakened to see Jon Shannon and two corpses, and the smell of death was in the air. The giant Bard had been shaking with fear and Shannow had looked an infinitely more menacing figure than Eric could have imagined. He had ridden home behind Shannow, his hands resting on the gun hilts as they jutted from their scabbards. All the way home Eric could see the two bodies, one with half a face missing, the other lying face-down with a huge ragged hole in his back where shards of bone had torn through his shirt.

Now he lay in bed, the after-shock making him sleepy. His mother stroked his brow and whispered soothing, loving words.

'Why did they kill Father?'

'I don't know, Eric,' lied Donna. 'They are evil men.'

'Mr Fletcher always seemed so nice.'

'I know. Sleep now; I'll be just outside.'

'Mother!'

'Yes, Eric?'

'Mr Shannow frightens me. I heard the men talking and they said he was insane – that he has killed more men than the plague. They said he pretends to be a Christ-person, but that all the real Christ-people shun him.'

'But he brought you home, Eric, and we still have our house.'

'Don't leave me alone, Mother.'

'You know that I won't. Sleep now. Rest.'

Leaning forward, she kissed his cheeks, then lifted the coal oil-lamp and left the room. He was asleep before the latch dropped home.

Shannow sat in the comfort chair staring at the ceiling. Donna placed the brass lamp on the table and moved to the stove, adding fresh wood to the blaze. As his head tipped forward and he caught her gaze, his eyes seemed unnaturally bright.

'Are you all right, Mr Shannow?'

'*Vanity of vanities, saith the preacher, vanity of vanities; all is vanity. What profit hath a man of all his labours which he taketh under the sun?*' Shannow blinked and leaned back.

'I am sorry,' she said, placing her hand over his, 'but I do not understand you.' He blinked once more, and smiled wearily, but his eyes lost their glitter and he seemed mortally tired.

'No, it is I who am sorry, Donna Taybard. I have brought death to your house.'

'You gave me back my son.'

'But for how long, Donna? All my life I have been the rock in the pool. I make a splash and the ripples rush out, but after that? The pool settles and is as it was. I cannot protect you from the Committee, nor Eric. I can make no difference to the evil of the world – indeed, sometimes I think I add to it.'

She held his hand tightly, forcing him to look at her.

'There is no evil in you, Mr Shannow. Believe me, I know these things. When you first came I was frightened, but I have come to know you. You are kind and you are considerate, and you have taken no advantage of my situation. In fact the reverse is true; you have risked your life for Eric and me.'

'There is nothing to that,' he said. 'My life is no great treasure; I do not value it. I have seen things in my life that would have cindered another man's soul – cannibals, savages, slavery and wanton murders. I have travelled far, Donna. And I am tired.

'Last summer I killed three men, and I vowed never to kill again. I have been hired to rid settlements of Brigands and war-makers – and I have succeeded. But then the eyes of those who sought me turn on me, and I see the fear in their eyes, and they are glad to see me ride on. They do not say, "Thank you Mr Shannow, stay among us and farm." They do not say, "We are your friends, Mr Shannow, and we will never forget you." Instead they hand me the Barta coins and ask when I will be leaving.

'And when I go, Donna, the Brigands return and all is as it was. The pool settles, the ripples die.'

Donna stood and pulled him to his feet. 'My poor Jon,' she whispered. 'Come with me.' She led him to a room at the back of the house and in the darkness she undressed him, removed her own clothes and pulled back the blankets on a wide bed. He came to her hesitantly and where she expected him to cover her with fierce passion, instead he stroked her skin with surprising gentleness. Her arm moved around his neck, pulling his face down until their lips touched. He groaned then, and the fierceness followed.

He was an inexpert and almost clumsy lover, not at all as skilled as Tomas the Carpenter, yet Donna Taybard found a fulfilment with Shannow that transcended expertise, for he was giving everything of himself, holding nothing back – and at the end he wept, and his tears flowed on to Donna's face.

And she stroked his brow and whispered soothing, loving words – and realized these were the same words she had used to Eric an hour before. And Shannow slept, just as Eric slept.

Donna moved to the porch and washed the sweat from her body with a bucket of cool fresh water, then she dressed and wandered to the pen, enjoying the freshness of the night.

People would think her a slut for taking a man so soon after her husband's disappearance, but she had never felt less like a slut. Instead she felt as if she had just come home from a long journey to find all her friends and family waiting with open arms. The Committee could offer no terror tonight. Everything was in harmony.

Shannow's gelding wandered to her, thrusting his muzzle towards her hand. She stroked his face and neck, and wished she could saddle and ride him out over the hills; wished he had wings to carry her high in the sky under the moon and over the clouds. Her father had told her wondrous stories of a winged horse from Elder legends, and of a hero who rode him to slay demons.

Old John had kept the demons from Rivervale, and when the grateful people had wished to call him Leader he had opted instead for Prester, and no one knew its meaning, bar John, and he only smiled knowingly when they asked him. Prester John had gathered the men into a tight military unit, established watch beacons on all high hills, and soon the Brigands learnt to avoid the lands of Rivervale. Outside in the wild lands, amongst the wolves and lions, the new world endured a bloody birthing. But here there was peace.

But the Prester was only mortal, and though he had ruled

for forty years his strength failed him and his wisdom fled, for he allowed men like Fletcher and Bard and Enas to join the Committee.

Tomas had once told Donna that the Prester had died broken-hearted, for in his last days he opened his eyes and saw at last the stamp of the men who would soon replace him. It was even rumoured that he tried to oust Fletcher, and that the young man killed him in his own home. That would never be proved now, but not one of the Landsmen would call him Prester and Rivervale was sliding inexorably back to merge with the wild lands.

Fletcher had recruited many strangers to work his shallow coal-mine, and some of these were brutal and versed in the ways of the Outside. These Fletcher promoted, and one day – in late Autumn the year before – the people of Rivervale awoke to a new understanding.

Able Jarrett, a small farmer, was hanged by Fletcher and four of his men for consorting with Brigands. An old wanderer was hanged with him. At first farmers, ranchers and Landsmen got together to discuss ways of dealing with the Committee, but then Cleon Layner – a leading spokesman – was found beaten to death in an alley behind his home and the meetings ended.

The forty-year mission of Prester John had been undone in less than three seasons.

Donna clapped her hands and Shannow's gelding ran across the pen. If Shannow felt he was merely a stone in the pool, what would John have felt before he died, she wondered?

She pictured Shannow's gaunt bearded face and his haunted eyes, and compared him with her memories of Prester John. The old man had been tougher than Shannow and that made him less deadly, but otherwise there was much about Shannow that John would have liked.

'I miss you, Prester,' she whispered, remembering his stories of winged horses and heroes.

Chapter Two

For several days the little farm received no visitors. The Committee undertook no revenge raid, and Shannow spent his days helping Donna and Eric gather the small corn harvest, or picking fruit from the orchard in the west meadow. In the late afternoons he would ride the gelding over the hills and through the high woods bordering the farm, to scan the distant skyline for signs of moving men.

At night Shannow would wait until Donna invited him to share her bed, and on each occasion he reacted as to an unexpected gift.

On the fifth day a rider approached the farm in the hour after noon. Shielding her eyes against the sunlight, Donna recognized the ambling gait of Ash Burry's mule, even before identifying the portly saint.

'You will like him, Jon,' she told Shannow as the rider approached. 'He is another who follows the old ways. There are several saints in Rivervale.' Shannow merely nodded and watched warily as the tall, overweight man dismounted. He had wavy dark hair and a friendly open face.

Burry opened his arms and hugged Donna warmly. 'God's greeting, Donna. Peace be upon your house.' His blue eyes flickered to Shannow and he held out his hand. Shannow took it; the grip was not firm and the man's hands were soft.

'And greetings to you, brother,' said Burry, with only the trace of a smile.

'Let's not stand in the sun,' suggested Donna. 'Come inside. We have some apple juice cooling in the stone jug.'

Shannow remained outside for several minutes scanning the hills before joining them.

'There is still no sign of Tomas, I understand?' remarked

Burry. 'You must be very worried, Donna.'

'He is dead, Ash. Fletcher killed him.'

Burry looked away. 'Hard words, Donna. I have heard of your accusation and it is said to be unfounded. How can you be sure?'

'Trust me,' said Donna. 'You have known me all my life and I do not lie. I have a gift of always being able to see those close to me, wherever they are. I watched him die.'

'I know of your . . . gift. But once you saw the old Prester lying dead at the foot of a canyon – you remember? Yet he was alive.'

'That is not entirely just, Ash. I thought he was dead, for he fell a fair way – and I was right about that.'

Burry nodded. 'And yet not all gifts are from the Almighty, Donna. I cannot believe that Saul Fletcher would do such a thing.'

'He hanged Able Jarrett and some poor wanderer.'

'The man was consorting with Brigands . . . and it was a Committee decision. I do not condone the taking of life, Donna, but right or wrong it was in accordance with Rivervale law – the law laid down by Prester John.'

'I do not recall the Prester hanging a Landsman, Ash.'

Shannow pulled up a chair by the window, reversed it and sat facing the saint, his arms resting on the chair-back.

'Mr Ash, might I inquire the reason for your visit?' he said.

'The name is Burry, sir, Ashley Burry, and I am a long-time friend of the Prester's family. I baptized Donna many years ago, and though she does not follow the faith I regard her as my godchild.'

'So this is merely a friendly visit?' asked Shannow.

'I hope that all my visits are friendly, and that all who know me regard them as such.'

'I am sure that they do, Mr Burry,' said Shannow, smiling, 'but it is a long ride from Rivervale on a hot day.'

'Meaning, sir?'

'Meaning that you have something to tell Fray Taybard. Would you be more comfortable if I left you to speak with her?'

Burry rubbed at his chin and smiled to cover his embarrassment. His eyes met Shannow's and understanding passed between them.

'Thank you for your frankness, Mr Shannow. Yes, that would indeed be courteous.'

After Shannow had gone, Burry and Donna sat in silence for several seconds. The saint refilled his pottery mug with apple juice and then walked around the room, idly examining the furniture he had seen so many times before.

'Well, Ash?' said Donna.

'He speaks well, Donna, but he is a Brigand – and a known Brigand. How could you allow him to stay?'

'He follows your ways, Ash.'

'No, that would be a blasphemy. I do not kill wantonly.'

'He rescued my son.'

'That is not as I have heard it. Bard and the others found the boy lost and were returning him to you when Shannow arrived and killed Pope and Miles.'

'Nonsense. My son was beaten and taken from the north meadow, and they were half-way to Rivervale with him. And that was the same day Fletcher tried to force me from my home. Are you blind, Ash?'

'The man is a killer – they say his mind is unhinged.'

'Did you find it so?'

'That is not the point. He may be rational now, but he terrified Bard and the others. Did you know he shot off Bard's ear?'

'I wish it had been his head!'

'Donna!' said Burry, shocked. 'I think the man is possessed, and I believe that his evil power is affecting your judgement. Saul has spoken to me of you, and I know that he holds you dear. He has no wife, Donna, and he would be a good father to Eric.'

Donna laughed. 'We talk about judgement, Ash, and then you advise me to marry the man who probably murdered my father and certainly killed my husband! Let's talk of something else: how is Sara?'

'She is well, but she worries about you; we all do. The

Committee have passed sentence on Shannow and they mean to hang him.'

'I am going to prepare some food for you, Ash. And while I do it, I want you to find Jon and talk with him.'

'What could I say?'

'You can talk about your God, Ash. He at least will be able to understand.'

'You mock me, Donna,' he said sadly.

'Not by intention, Ash. Go and talk to him.'

Burry shook his head and rose from the table. Out in the sunlight he saw Shannow sitting on a white rock and watching the hills. The man was wearing the infernal pistols which had so brutally slain Pope and Miles and God knew how many others, he thought.

'May I join you, Mr Shannow?'

'Of course.'

'When will you be leaving Rivervale?'

'Soon, Mr Burry.'

'How soon?'

'I do not know.'

'What do you want?'

'I want for nothing, Mr Burry.'

'It is said that you seek Jerusalem?'

'Indeed I do.'

'Why?'

'To answer all my questions. To satisfy me.'

'But the Book answers all questions, Mr Shannow.'

Shannow smiled. 'I have read the Book, Mr Burry – many many times. But there are no pistols mentioned. Twelve years ago I saw a picture which had not been painted. It was like a frozen moment in time. It was a city, but it took me a long time to realize it was a city for the picture was a view from the sky to the ground. There is nothing like it in the Bible, Mr Burry. I met an old man once who had a special book, very old. In it were drawings of machines with wheels and levers; there were seats in these machines and men could travel in them without horses. Why are these not in the Bible? The old man said he had once seen a picture of a metal machine that could fly.

Why is this not in the Scriptures?'

'It is, Mr Shannow. You will recall that Elijah ascended to Heaven in a chariot of fire? You will also recall that there are many examples of angelic beings in strange machines.'

'But no pistols, Mr Burry. No guns.'

'Is that important? We know that Christ told his disciples that the end of the world was nigh, and we know that it happened. The oceans rose and the world was destroyed. Those of us now living are in the End-times.'

'But does it not also say, Mr Burry, that these are the times of the Anti-Christ, that men would wish they had never been born and that pestilence, plague and death would stalk the land?'

'Yes. And that has certainly come to pass.'

'And that a New Jerusalem would be built?'

'Yes.'

'Then I mean to find it.'

'Only God's servants will find Jerusalem, Mr Shannow. Do you honestly believe you serve the Almighty?'

'No, Mr Burry, I do not, though I have tried and will go on trying. I was taught that the world is young, and that Christ died three hundred years ago and his death caused the oceans to rise. Yet I have seen evidence that the Dark Age of our world lasted much longer than that. You know that there are some who believe that the Lord died two and a half thousand years ago?'

'Heretics,' declared Ashley Burry.

'I agree with you, yet I wonder if they are not closer to the truth than you or I. I have seen remnants of old maps which do not even show Israel, or Judah, or Babylon – or even Rome. There are names unheard of in the Book. I need to know, Mr Burry.'

'For what purpose? Are we not advised to ignore the seeking of signs and portents?'

'And yet when the clouds darken, do we not reach for our oilskins?'

'Yes, Mr Shannow, but what does it matter if the Dark Age after our Lord was long or short? We are here now. Does it matter if machines once flew? They no longer do so.

Does not Ecclesiastes say, "*There is nothing new under the sun*", and that everything that ever was will be again?'

'Have you ever heard of England, Mr Burry?'

'A Dark Age land, I believe. They preserved the Book.'

'Do you know where it might be?'

'No. Why is it important to you?'

'I once saw a scrap of paper with a printed verse that said, "And was Jerusalem builded here, in England's green and pleasant land."'

'May I offer you some advice, Mr Shannow?'

'Why not? Most people do.'

'Leave this place. Continue your search. If you remain, you bring only death and despair to this house. The Committee has declared you a Brigand and a war-maker – they will hang you, sir.'

'When I was a child, Mr Burry, my parents built a home for my brother and myself. It was by the banks of a beautiful river, and the land was rich and open and wild as sin. My father tamed that land, and it brought forth crops and it fed our cattle. Then some men came who wanted fertile land. They killed my father. My mother they abused before cutting her throat. My brother and I escaped, though I was speared and bleeding badly. My brother dragged me to the river and we swam downstream. We were taken in by a neighbouring farmer – a strong man, with four strapping sons. No one reproached the Brigands who had killed my parents. That was the way life was.'

'It is a familiar story,' admitted Burry, 'but times change.'

'Men change them. But I have not finished, Mr Burry. Both my brother and I were brought up to believe in love and forgiveness. We tried, but the same raiders – growing fat and yet strong – decided they wanted more land. One night they attacked our new home. My brother killed one of them with an axe and I slew another with an old musket. But still they won. This time it was I who rescued my brother and we escaped on an old stallion. My brother lost his faith then. Mine became stronger. Two years later I returned to the farm and put the Brigands to death.

'Since then I have killed many. I have never stolen, or cheated, or lied. Nor have I broken the Commandment: Thou shalt not do murder. I am not a Brigand, but I am a war-maker. I make my war upon the evil, and I am no danger to honest Landsmen. Only the ungodly need fear me, Mr Burry, or those who serve the ungodly.'

'What happened to your brother, Mr Shannow? Did he find his faith?'

'We both learned to hate. I hated the Brigands and the death dealers, but he came to despise the Landsmen who stood by and allowed the Brigands to prosper. No, Mr Burry, he did not find his faith.'

'You are a bitter man, Mr Shannow.'

'Indeed I am. But I am content with what I am and I do not compromise my principles. Now you, Mr Burry, are a man of God. Yet you come to this house to defend murderers, and you align yourself with the ungodly. Fletcher killed Fray Taybard's husband. His men are a pack of cut-throats. And even now, Mr Burry, you sit here as the Judas goat and death is waiting as we speak.'

'What do you mean? You are speaking nonsense.'

'Am I indeed?'

'Explain yourself.'

Shannow shook his head and smiled. 'There are three men hiding in the trees to the north. Did they come with you?'

'No, Mr Shannow, they did not, but you must realize that a sum of fifty Barta coins will be paid to anyone who brings in the body of a known Brigand.'

'I should have taken the corpses to Rivervale,' said Shannow. 'Both Miles and Pope were known murderers; they killed a travelling family in Sertace two years ago, and they also rode with Daniel Cade when he was raiding the south-west.'

'I do not believe, you Mr Shannow.'

'It is better for your conscience that you do not, Mr Burry.'

*

The meal was eaten in silence and Burry left soon after. Eric said nothing as the saint rode away but went to his room, shutting the door behind him.

'I am worried about him,' said Donna as she and Shannow cleared away the dishes and plates.

'He fears me, Donna. I do not blame him.'

'He is not eating, and his dreams are bad.'

'I think your friend Burry is right and I should be moving. But I fear for you – when I am gone, Fletcher will return.'

'Then do not go, Jon. Stay with us.'

'I do not think you understand the danger. I am not a man any longer, I am a walking bag of Barta coins for any who feel they can collect on me. Even now there are three men in the hills building their nerve to come for me.'

'I do not want you to go,' she said.

He reached out and lightly touched her cheek. 'I want only what you want, but I know what must happen.'

He left her then and walked to Eric's room. He tapped on the door, but there was no reply; he tapped again.

'Yes?'

'It is Jon Shannow. May I come in?'

A pause. Then, 'All right.'

Eric was lying on his bed facing the door. He looked up at the tall figure and saw that Shannow was wearing his father's shirt; he had not noticed that before.

'May I sit down, Eric?'

'You can do what you like. I can't stop you,' said the boy miserably.

Shannow pulled up a chair and reversed it. 'Do you want to talk about it?'

'About what?'

'I don't know, Eric. I only know that you are troubled. Do you want to talk about your father? Or Fletcher? Or me?'

'I expect Mother wishes I wasn't here,' said the boy, sitting up and hugging his knees. 'Then she could be with you all the time.'

'She has not said that to me.'

31

'Mr Burry doesn't like you and I don't like you either.'

'Sometimes I don't like myself,' said Shannow. 'That keeps me in the majority.'

'Everything was all right until you came,' said Eric, tears starting as he bit his lip and looked away. 'Mother and me were fine. She slept in here and I didn't have bad dreams. And Mr Fletcher was my friend – and everything was fine.'

'I'll be gone soon,' Shannow told him softly, and the truth of the words hit him like a blow. The pool settles, and the ripples fade, and everything returns to the way it was.

'It won't be the same,' said Eric, and Shannow could offer no argument.

'You are very wise, Eric. Life changes – and not always for the better. It is the mark of a man how he copes with that fact. I think you will cope well, for you are strong; stronger than you think.'

'But I won't be able to stop them taking our house.'

'No.'

'And Mr Fletcher will force mother to live with him?'

'Yes,' said Shannow, swallowing hard and keeping the awful images from his mind.

'I think you had better stay for a little while, Mr Shannow,' said Eric.

'I think perhaps I had. It would be nice if we could be friends, Eric.'

'I don't want to be your friend.'

'Why?'

'Because you took my mother away from me, and now I am all alone.'

'You are not alone, but I cannot convince you of that, even though I probably know more about loneliness than any man alive. I have never had a friend, Eric. When I was your age, my father and mother were killed. I was raised for some time by a neighbour called Claude Vurrow; then he too was killed and since then I have been alone. People do not like me. I am the Jerusalem Man, the Shadow, the Brigand-slayer. Wherever I am I will be hated and hunted – or used by "better" men. That is loneliness, Eric – sitting with a frightened child, and not being able to reach out and convince even him – that is loneliness.

'When I die, Eric, no one will mourn for me. It will be as if I never was. Would you like to be that lonely, boy?'

Eric said nothing and Shannow left the room.

The three men watched Shannow ride from the farmhouse, heading east towards the forests of pine. Swiftly they saddled their ponies and rode after him.

Jerrik took the lead, for he was the man with the long rifle, a muzzle-loading flintlock a mere thirty-five years old. It was a fine gun which had seen three owners murdered for owning it. Jerrik had acquired it as settlement for a gambling debt two years before, and had then used it to kill the former owner who was tracking him to steal it back. It seemed poetic, somehow, though Jerrik could not verbalize the reason.

Behind him rode Pearson and Swallow, men Jerrik could rely on . . . so long as all three were poor. The trio had arrived only recently in Rivervale, but had swiftly come under Bard's watchful eye. He had recommended them to Fletcher, and this task was their entry to the Committee.

'Hunt down and kill the Jerusalem Man.' The long rifle could handle that, given a fixed target, and Swallow was an expert crossbowman. Pearson was more of a knife expert, but he could hurl a blade with uncanny accuracy. Jerrik was confident that the deed could be completed without tears.

'Do you think he's leaving the area?' asked Swallow. Jerrik showed his contempt at the question by ignoring it but Pearson grinned, showing broken teeth.

'No saddlebags,' he said.

'Why don't we wait and hit him when he comes back?' asked Swallow.

'What if he comes back at night?' answered Jerrik.

Swallow lapsed into silence. Younger than the others, he felt a need to be heard with respect, yet every time he spoke he left himself open to mockery. Pearson slapped the blond youngster on the shoulder and grinned at him. He knew what the lad was thinking, as he knew also the cause of his problem. Swallow was too stupid to *know* that he was stupid. But Pearson liked him and they were well-matched in many ways. Both disliked the company of women, both enjoyed the power that came from a lack of conscience and the god-like joy of holding a life in their hands before snuffing it out. The only difference lay in the fact that Swallow enjoyed killing men, whereas Pearson found the torture of women to be an exquisite pleasure.

Jerrik was unlike them in that regard. He neither enjoyed nor abhorred killing. It was merely a task – like weeding, or felling trees, or skinning rabbits; something to be done swiftly. Watching Pearson and Swallow at their work only bored him, and the screams always kept him awake. Jerrik was approaching fifty and felt it was time to settle down and raise children; he had his eye on a farm in Rivervale, and the young widow who owned it. With the Barta coins he expected for the Jerusalem Man he would have some woollen clothes made, and pay court to the widow. She would have to treat him seriously, as a Committee man.

The trio followed Shannow's tracks high into the pine forest and it was coming to dusk when they spotted his camp-fire.

The three dismounted and hobbled their horses, creeping through the undergrowth towards the small blaze. Some fifty feet from the fire Jerrik saw the shadowy outline of the Jerusalem Man sitting with his back against a tree, his wide-brimmed hat tipped down over his eyes.

'You just sit there and think,' whispered Jerrik, hunkering down and priming his musket. He directed Pearson and Swallow to the left and right, ready to rush in once the mortal shot was fired. Then the two crept off into the trees.

Jerrik cocked the musket and sat back, resting his elbow on his knee. The gun was levelled on the seated figure . . .

Something cold touched Jerrik's temple.

And his head exploded.

At the sound of the shot Pearson loosed his crossbow bolt. It flashed across the clearing, slicing through Shannow's coat and the bush inside it. Swallow ran up, hurdling the camp-fire, and his knife followed Pearson's bolt. The coat fell from the bush, the hat toppling with it, and Swallow's mouth fell open. Something hit him a wicked blow in the back and a hole the size of a man's fist appeared in his chest. He was dead before he hit the ground.

Pearson backed away from the carnage and sprinted to his pony. Loosing the hobble, he leapt to the saddle and booted the animal into a run. The boom of Jerrik's musket came just as Pearson's pony had reached a gallop; the animal fell headlong and Pearson flew over its neck to land on his back against a tree. He rolled and came up with a knife in his hand.

'Show yourself!' he screamed.

The Jerusalem Man stepped from the screen of trees and moved into Pearson's view. In his hand was the ivory-handled percussion pistol.

'You don't have to kill me,' said Pearson, eyes locked on the pistol. 'I won't come back – I'll just ride away.'

'Who sent you?'

'Fletcher.'

'How many others has he sent?'

'None. We didn't think we'd need any more.'

'What is your name?'

'Why?'

'So that I can mark your grave. It would be unseemly otherwise.'

The knife fell from his fingers. 'My name is Pearson. Alan Pearson.'

'And the others?'

'Al Jerrik and Zephus Swallow.'

'Turn around, Mr Pearson.'

Pearson closed his eyes and began to turn.

He did not even hear the shot that killed him.

Jon Shannow rode into the yard as the moon broke clear of the screen of clouds. He was leading two ponies and he carried a long rifle across his saddle. Donna stood in the doorway wearing a white blouse of fine wool and a homespun skirt dyed red. Her hair was freshly brushed and glowed almost white in the moonlight. Shannow waved as he rode past and led the ponies into the pen. He unsaddled the gelding and brushed him down.

Donna walked across the yard and took Shannow's arm. He leaned down and kissed her lightly.

'Are you well, Jon?'

'Aye.'

'What are you thinking?'

'I was thinking that when I am with you, I understand something which has long escaped me.' He lifted her hand and kissed it gently, reverently.

'What? What do you understand?'

'It is a quotation from the Book.'

'Tell me.'

'*"Though I speak with the tongues of men and of angels, and have not love, I am become as sounding brass, or a tinkling cymbal.*

'*"And though I have the gift of prophecy, and understand all mysteries, and all knowledge, and though I have all faith, so that I could remove mountains, and have not love, I am nothing."* There is more, but I would need the Book to read it.'

'It is beautiful, Jon. Who wrote it?'

'A man named Paul.'

'Did he write it for a woman?'

'No, he wrote it for everyone. How is Eric?'

'He got upset when he heard the guns.'

'There was no danger, Donna,' he said softly. 'And we have several days together before anyone realizes they have failed.'

'You look tired, Jon. Come in and rest.'

'Each death lessens me, Lady. But still they come.'

She led him in to the house and trimmed down the wicks in the oil-lamp. He sat in the comfort chair and his head dropped back. Gently she removed his boots and covered him with a heavy blanket.

'Sleep well, Jon. Sweet dreams.' She kissed him and moved towards her room. Eric's door opened and he stood there rubbing sleep from his eyes. 'Is he back, Mother?' he whispered.

'Yes. He is all right.'

'Did he kill all the men?'

'I expect so, Eric. Go to bed.'

'Will you come in with me?'

She smiled and led him back to the narrow bed, where she lay beside him. Within minutes he was asleep. But Donna Taybard could not sleep. Outside was a man who in the space of a few days had killed five others – a man living on the edge of sanity, chasing the impossible. He was seeking a city that no longer existed in a land no one could find, in search of a god few believed in – a relic of a world which had passed into myth.

And he loved her – or thought that he did, which was the same thing to a man, Donna knew. And now he was trapped, forced to remain like a magnet drawing death to him, unable to run or hide. And he would lose. There would be no Jerusalem for Jon Shannow, and no home with Donna Taybard. The Committee would hunt him down and Donna would be Fletcher's woman – until he tired of her. Yet, even knowing this, Donna could not send Jon Shannow away. She closed her eyes and his face came unbidden to her mind, and she found herself staring at him as he slept in the comfort chair, his face so peaceful now and almost boyish in the lamplight.

Donna opened her eyes back in Eric's room and wished, not for the first time, that the Prester was alive. He always seemed to know what to do. And before advancing years sapped his judgement he could read men – and women. But he was gone and there was no one to turn to. She thought of Shannow's fierce god and, remembering Ash Burry's gentle loving Lord, found it incomprehensible that both men worshipped the same deity.

The two men were fleece and flint, and so was their God.

'Are you there, Shannow's God?' she whispered. 'Can you hear me? What are you doing to the man? Why do you drive him so hard? Help him. Please help him.'

Eric stirred and mumbled in his sleep and she kissed him,

lifting the blanket around his chin. His eyes opened dreamily.

'I love you, Mother. Truly.'

'And I love you, Eric. More than anything.'

'Daddy never loved me.'

'Of course he did,' whispered Donna, but Eric was asleep once more.

Shannow awoke in the hour before dawn and opened the door to Donna's room. The bed was still made and he smiled ruefully. He moved to the pump-room and found himself staring once more at his reflection.

'*Quo vadis*, Shannow?' he asked the grim grey man in the mirror.

The sound of horses in the yard made him stiffen and he checked his pistols and slipped out of the back door, keeping in the moon shadows until he reached the front of the house. Five long wagons drawn by oxen stretched in a line back to the meadow, and a tall man on a dark horse was dismounting by the water trough.

'Good morning,' said Shannow, sheathing his pistol.

'Do you mind if we water our animals?' asked the man. The sun was just clearing the eastern peaks and Shannow saw that he was in his thirties and strongly built. He wore a black leather riding jacket cut high at the waist and a hat sporting a single peacock feather.

'As long as you replenish it from the well yonder,' Shannow told him. 'Where are you journeying?'

'North-west, through the mountains.'

'The Plague Lands?' asked Shannow. 'No one goes there. I saw a man once who had come from there – his hair fell out and his body was a mass of weeping sores that would not mend.'

'We do not believe it is the land. All sicknesses pass,' said the man.

'The man I knew said that the rocks gleamed in the night and that no animals could be found there.'

'My friend, I have heard tales of giant lizards, flying

pillars and castles in clouds. I have yet to see any of them. Land is land, and I am sick of Brigands. Daniel Cade is raiding once more, and I have a yen for the far mountains where even brigands will not go. Now I myself have met a man who journeyed there – or said he did. He said that the grass grows green and the deer are plentiful, and much larger than elsewhere. He says he saw apples as big as melons, and in the distance a city the like of which he had never seen. Now I am a man who needs to travel, and I mean to see that city.'

Shannow's mouth was suddenly dry. 'I too would like to see that city,' he said.

'Then find yourself a wagon and travel with us, man! I take it those pistols are not mere ornaments?'

'I have no wagon, sir, nor enough Barta coin to raise one. And I have commitments here that must be fulfilled.'

The man nodded and then grinned. 'That's why I want you. I'd take no footloose rider straight from the Outlands and I won't import Brigands into Avalon. You are a sturdy soul, by the look of you. Do you have a family?'

'Yes.'

'Then sell your farm and follow after us. There'll be land waiting.'

Shannow left him watering the oxen and walked inside, where Donna was awake and standing by the open door.

'You heard that?' asked Shannow.

'Yes. The Plague Lands.'

'What do you feel?'

'I do not want you to go. But if you do, we will go with you if you'll have us.'

He opened his arms and drew her to him, too full of wild joy to speak. Behind him the tall man from the yard politely cleared his throat and Shannow turned.

'My name is Cornelius Griffin, and I may have a proposition for you.'

'Come in, Mr Griffin,' said Donna. 'I am Donna Taybard and this is my husband, Jon.'

'A pleasure, Fray Taybard.'

'You spoke of a proposition,' said Shannow.

'Indeed I did. We have a family with us who are not desirous of a risky journey and it could be that they will part with their wagon and goods in return for your farm. Of course there will be an extra amount in Barta coin, should the prospect interest you.'

Jon Shannow rode his steeldust gelding down the main street of Rivervale settlement, his long leather coat flapping against the horse's flanks, his wide-brimmed hat shading his eyes. The houses were mostly timber near the roadside, early dwellings of some three or perhaps four decades. On outlying hills above the shallow coal-mine rose the new homes of stone and polished wood. Shannow rode past the mill and across the hump-back bridge, ignoring the stares of workmen and loafers who peered at him from the shadows. Several children were playing in a dusty side street and a barking dog caused his horse to jump sideways. Shannow sat unmoving in the saddle and rode on, reining in his mount at the steps to the alehouse.

He dismounted and tied the reins to a hitching rail, mounted the steps and entered the drinking hall. There were some twenty men sitting or standing at the long bar – among them the giant, Bard, his head bandaged. Beside him was Fletcher and both men gaped as Shannow moved towards them.

A stillness settled on the room.

'I am come to tell you, Mr Fletcher, that Fray Taybard has sold her farm to a young family from Ferns Crossing, a settlement some two months' journey to the south. She has given them a bond of sale that should satisfy the Committee.'

'Why tell me?' said Fletcher, aware of the spectators, many of whom were known Landsmen of integrity.

'Because you are a murderous savage and a Brigand, sir, who would lief as not kill the family and pretend they were usurpers.'

'How dare you?'

'I dare because it is the truth, and that will always be a bitter enemy to you, sir. I do not know how long the people of Rivervale will put up with you, but if they have sense it will not be long.'

'You cannot think to leave here alive, Shannow?' said Fletcher. 'You are a named Brigand.'

'Named by you! Jerrik, Swallow and Pearson are dead, Mr Fletcher. Before he died, Pearson told me you had offered him a place on your Committee. Strange that you now have places for known woman-killers!'

'Kill him!' screamed Fletcher and Shannow dived to his right as a crossbow bolt flashed from the doorway. His pistol boomed and a man staggered back from sight to fall down the steps beyond.

A pistol flamed in Fletcher's hand and something tugged at the collar of Shannow's coat. The right-hand pistol flowered in flame and smoke and Fletcher pitched back, clutching his belly. A second shot tore through his heart. Bard was running for the rear door and Shannow let him go, but the man twisted and fired a small pistol which hammered a shell into the wood beside Shannow's face. Splinters tore into his cheek and he pumped two bullets into the big man's throat; Bard collapsed in a fountain of blood.

Shannow climbed slowly to his feet and scanned the room, and the men lying face down and motionless.

'I am Jon Shannow, and have never been a Brigand.'

Turning his back he walked into the street. A shell whistled past his head and he turned and fired. A man reared up from behind the water trough, clutching his shoulder – in his hand was a brass-mounted percussion pistol. Then Shannow shot him again and he fell without a sound. A musket boomed from a window across the street, snatching Shannow's hat from his head; he returned the fire, but hit nothing. Climbing into the saddle, he kicked the gelding into a run.

Several men raced to cut him off. One fired a pistol, but the gelding cannoned into the group and sent them sprawling to the dust – and Shannow was clear and over the hump-back bridge, heading west to join Donna and Eric . . .

. . . and the road to Jersualem.

Chapter Three

Con Griffin swung in the saddle and watched the oxen toiling up the steep slope. The first of the seventeen wagons had reached the lava ridge, and the others were strung out like vast wooden beads on the black slope.

Griffin was tired and the swirling lava dust burned his eyes. He swung his horse and studied the terrain ahead. As far as the eye could see, which from this height was a considerable distance, the black lava sand stretched from jagged peak to jagged peak.

They had been travelling now for five weeks, having linked with Jacob Madden's twelve wagons north of Rivervale. In that time they had seen no riders, nor any evidence of Brigands on the move. And yet Griffin was wary. He had in his saddlebags many maps of the area, sketched by men who claimed to have travelled the lands in their youth. It was rare for any of the maps to correspond, but one thing all agreed on was that beyond the lava stretch lived a Brigand band of the worst kind: eaters of human flesh.

Griffin had done his best to prepare his wagoners for the worst. No family had been allowed to join the convoy unless they owned at least one working rifle or handgun. As things now stood there were over twenty guns in the convoy, enough to deter all but the largest Brigand party.

Con Griffin was a careful man and, as he often said, a damned fine wagoner. This was his third convoy in eleven years and he had survived drought, plague, Brigand raids, vicious storms and even a flash flood. Men said Con Griffin was lucky and he accepted that without comment. Yet he knew that luck was merely the residue of hard thinking and harder work. Each of the twenty-two-foot wagons carried one spare wheel and axle suspended beneath the tailboards, plus sixty pounds of flour, three sacks of salt, eighty pounds of dried meat, thirty pounds of dried fruit and six barrels of water. His own two wagons were packed with trade goods and spares – hammers, nails, axes, knives, saw-blades, picks, blankets and woven garments. Griffin liked to believe he left nothing to luck.

The people who travelled under his command were tough and hardy and Griffin, for all his outward gruffness, loved them all. They reflected all that was good in people – strength, courage, loyalty and a stubborn willingness to risk all they had on the dream of a better tomorrow.

Griffin sat back in the saddle and watched the Taybard wagon begin the long haul up the lava slope. The woman, Donna, intrigued him. Leather-tough and satin-soft, she was a beautiful contradiction. The wagon-master rarely involved himself in matters of the heart, but had Donna Taybard been available he would have broken his rule. The boy, Eric, was running alongside the oxen, urging them on with a switch stick. He was a quiet boy, but Griffin liked him; he was quick and bright and learned fast. The man was another matter . . .

Griffin had always been a good judge of character, an attribute vital to a leader, yet he could make nothing of Jon Taybard . . . except that he was riding under an assumed name. The relationship between Taybard and Eric was strained, the boy avoiding the man at all but meal-times. Still, Taybard was a good man with a horse and he never complained or shirked the tasks Griffin set him.

The Taybard wagon reached the top of the rise and was followed by the elderly scholar Peacock. The man had no coordination and the wagon stopped half-way up the slope. Griffin cantered down and climbed up to the driving seat, allowing his horse to run free.

'Will you never learn, Ethan?' he said, taking reins and whip from the balding Peacock.

He cracked the thirty-foot whip above the ear of the leading ox and the animal lurched forward into the traces. Slowly the lumbering wagon moved up the hill.

'Are you sure you can't read, Con?' asked Peacock.

'Would I lie to you, scholar?'

'It is just that that fool Phelps can be tremendously annoying. I think he only reads sections that prove his case.'

'I have seen Taybard with a Bible – ask him,' said Griffin. The wagon moved on to the ridge and he stepped to the running board and whistled for his horse. The chestnut stallion came at once and Griffin climbed back into the saddle.

Maggie Ames' wagon was the next to be stopped on the slope, a rear wheel lodged against a lava rock. Griffin dismounted and manhandled it clear, to be rewarded with a dazzling smile. He tipped his hat and rode away. Maggie was a young widow, and that made her dangerous indeed.

Throughout the long hot afternoon, the wagon convoy moved on through the dusty ridge. The oxen were weary and Griffin rode ahead looking for a camp-site.

There was no water to be found and he ordered the wagons stopped on the high ground above the plain, in the lee of a soaring rock face. Griffin unsaddled the chestnut and rubbed him down, then filled his leather hat with water and allowed the horse to drink.

All around the camp people were looking to their animals, wiping the dust from the nostrils of their oxen and giving them precious water. Out here the animals were more than beasts of burden. They were life.

Griffin's driver, a taciturn oldster named Burke, had prepared a fire and was cooking a foul-smelling stew in a copper-bottomed pot. Griffin sat opposite the man. 'Another long day,' he remarked.

Burke grunted. 'Worse tomorrow.'

'I know.'

'You won't get much more out of these animals – they need a week at least and good grass.'

'You see any grass today, Jim?'

'I'm only saying what they *need*.'

'According to the map there should be good grass within the next three days,' said Griffin, removing his hat and wiping the sweat from his forehead.

'Which map is that?' asked Burke, smiling knowingly.

'Cardigan's. It seems about the best of them.'

'Yeah. Ain't he the one that saw the body-eaters at work? Didn't they roast his companions alive?'

'So he said, Jim. And keep your voice down.'

Burke pointed to the fat figure of Aaron Phelps, the arcanist, who was making his way to the wagon of Ethan Peacock. 'He'd make a good lunch for them Brigands.'

'Cardigan came through here twenty years ago. There's no reason to believe the same Brigands are still in the area. Most war-makers are movers,' said Griffin.

'Expect you're right, Mr Griffin,' agreed Burke with a wicked grin. 'Still, I should send Phelps out as our advance scout. He'd feed an entire tribe.'

'I ought to send you, Jimmy – you'd put them off human flesh for life. You haven't bathed in the five years I've known you!'

'Water gives you wrinkles,' said Burke. 'I remember that from when I was a yongen. It shrivels you up.'

Griffin accepted the bowl of stew Burke passed him and tasted it. If anything it was more foul than its smell – but he ate it, following it with flat bread and salt.

'I do not know how you come up with such appalling meals,' said Griffin at last, pushing his plate away.

Burke grinned. 'Nothing to work with. Now, if you gave me Phelps . . .'

Griffin shook his head and stood. He was a tall man, red-haired and looking older than his thirty-two years. His shoulders were broad and his belly pushed out over the top of his belt, despite Burke's culinary shortcomings.

He wandered along the wagon line chatting to the families as they gathered by their cook fires, and ignored the squabbling Phelps and Peacock. At the Taybard wagon he stopped.

'A word with you, Mr Taybard,' he said and Jon Shannow set aside his plate and rose smoothly, following Griffin out on to the trail ahead of the wagons. The wagon-master sat on a jutting rock and Shannow sat facing him.

'There could be difficult days ahead, Mr Taybard,' began

Griffin, breaking a silence which had become uncomfortable.

'In what way?'

'Some years ago there was a murderous Brigand band in these parts. Now when we come down from these mountains we should find water and grass, and we will need to rest for at least a week. During that time we could come under attack.'

'How may I help you?'

'You are not a farmer, Mr Taybard. I sense you are more of a hunter and I want you to scout for us – if you will?'

Shannow shrugged. 'Why not?'

Griffin nodded. The man had asked nothing of the Brigands, nor of their suspected armaments. 'You are a strange man, Mr Taybard.'

'My name is not Taybard; it is Shannow.'

'I have heard the name, Mr Shannow. But I shall call you Taybard as long as you ride with us.'

'As you please, Mr Griffin.'

'Why did you feel the need to tell me?'

'I do not like living a lie.'

'Most men find little difficulty in that respect,' said Griffin. 'But then you are not as most men. I heard of the work you did in Allion.'

'It came to nothing; the Brigands returned once I had gone.'

'That is hardly the point, Mr Shannow.'

'What is?'

'You can only show the way and it is for others to follow the path. In Allion they were stupid; when you have dusted a room, you do not throw away the broom.'

Shannow smiled and Griffin watched him relax. 'Are you a Bookman, Mr Griffin?'

The wagon-master returned the smile and shook his head. 'I tell people I cannot read, but yes, I have studied the Book and there is much sense in it. But I am not a believer, Mr Shannow, and I doubt that Jerusalem exists.'

'A man must look for something in life, even if it is only a non-existent city.'

'You should speak to Peacock,' said Griffin. 'He has a thousand scraps of Dark Age remnants. And now that his eyes are fading, he needs help to study them.'

Griffin rose to leave, but Shannow stopped him. 'I want to thank you, Mr Griffin, for making me welcome.'

'It is nothing. I am not a weak man, Mr Shannow. Shadows do not frighten me, nor reputations such as yours. I will leave you with this thought, though: What point is there in seeking Jerusalem? You have a fine wife and a growing son who will need your talents at home, wherever home may lie.'

Shannow said nothing and Griffin wandered back into the firelight. Shannow remained apart, sitting beneath the stars lost in thought. Donna found him there close to midnight and sat beside him, curling her arm around his waist.

'Are you troubled, Jon?'

'No. I was thinking of the past.'

'The Prester used to say, "The past is dead, the future unborn. What we have is the Now, and we abuse it."'

'I have done nothing to deserve you, Lady. But believe me I thank the Lord for you daily.'

'What did Mr Griffin want?' she asked, suddenly embarrassed by the intensity of his words.

'He wants me to scout for him tomorrow.'

'Why you? You do not know this land.'

'Why not me, Donna?'

'Will it be dangerous, do you think?'

'I don't know. Perhaps.'

'Damn you, Jon. I wish you would learn to lie a little!'

Shannow rode away from the wagons in the hour after dawn and once they were lost to sight behind him he removed the Bible from his saddlebag and allowed it to fall open in his hands. Glancing down, he read: *'Behold I create new heavens and a new earth, and the former shall not be remembered, nor come into mind.'*

He closed the book and returned it to his saddlebag.

Ahead of him stretched the black lava sand and he set the gelding off at a canter, angling towards the north.

For weeks now he had sat listening to the petty rows and squabbles of the two scholars, Phelps and Peacock, and though he had gleaned some food for thought the two men made him think of the words of Solomon: *'For in much wisdom is much grief, and he that increaseth wisdom increaseth sorrow.'*

Last night the two men had argued for more than an hour concerning the word 'train'. Phelps insisted it was a mechanized Dark Age means of conveyance, while Peacock maintained it was merely a generic term to cover a group of vehicles, or wagons in convoy. Phelps argued that he had once owned a book which explained the mechanics of trains. Peacock responded by showing him an ancient scrap of paper that talked of rabbits and cats dressing for dinner with a rat.

'What has that to do with it?' stormed Phelps, his fat face reddening.

'Many books of the Dark Age are not true. They obviously loved to lie – or do you believe in a village of dressed-up rabbits?'

'You old fool!' shouted Phelps. 'It is simple to tell which are fictions. This book on trains was sound.'

'How would you know? Because it was plausible? I saw a painting once of a man wearing a glass bowl on his head and waving a sword. He was said to be walking on the moon.'

'Another fiction, and it proves nothing,' said Phelps.

And so it went on. Shannow found the whole argument pointless.

Individually both men were persuasive. Phelps maintained that the Dark Age had lasted around a thousand years, in which time science produced many wonders, among them trains and flying craft, and also pistols and superior weapons of war. Peacock believed the Dark Age to be less than one hundred years, citing Christ's promise to his disciples that some of them would still be alive when the end came.

'If that promise was not true,' argued Peacock, 'then the

Bible would have to be dismissed as another Dark Age fiction.'

Shannow instinctively leaned towards Peacock's biblical view, but found Phelps to be more open-minded and genuinely inquisitive.

Shannow shook his mind clear of the foggy arguments and concentrated on the trail. Up ahead the lava sand was breaking and he found himself riding up a green slope shaded by trees. At the top he paused and looked down on a verdant valley with glistening streams.

For a long time he sat his horse, studying the land. There was no sign of life, no evidence of human habitation. He rode on warily, coming at last to a deer trail which he followed down to a wide pool of fresh water. The ground around the pool was studded with tracks of all kinds – goats, sheep, deer, buffalo and even the spoor of lions and bears. Near the pool was a tall pine and ten feet up from the ground were the claw-marks which signified the brown bear's territory. Bears were sensible animals; they did not fight each other for territory, they merely marked the trees. When a different bear arrived, he would rear up and try to match the scars. If he could outreach them he would make his mark, and the smaller bear would depart once he had seen his adversary was bigger and stronger. If he could not reach the scars he would amble on in search of new territory. The idea appealed to Shannow . . . but even here a little trickery could be used.

Back in Allion, a very small bear had staked out an enormous territory by coming out of hibernation in the middle of winter and scrambling up the snow banked against the trees, making his mark some three feet higher. Shannow had liked that bear.

He scouted the perimeter of the pool and then took a different route back towards the wagons. At the top of a rise he smelt woodsmoke and paused, searching the surrounding skyline. The wind was easterly and he angled his horse back through the trees, walking him slowly and carefully.

The smell was stronger now and Shannow dismounted and hobbled the gelding – making his way on foot through the thick bushes and shrubs. As he approached a circular clearing he heard the sound of voices and froze. The language was one he had never heard, though certain words seemed familiar. Dropping to his belly, he eased his way forward, waiting for the breeze to rustle the leaves above him and disguise the sound of his movements. After several minutes of soundless crawling he came to the edge of the clearing and squinted through a break in the leaves. Around a large fire sat seven men, near naked, their bodies stained with streaks of blue and yellow dye; by the side of one of the men was a severed human foot. Shannow blinked as sweat stung his eyes. Then a man stood and walked towards him, stopping some yards to his left where, pulling aside a deerskin loin-cloth, he urinated against a tree. Through the gap left by the man, Shannow could see the charred remains of a body spitted above the fire.

Shannow felt his stomach heave and averted his gaze. By the trees on the other side of the clearing two captives were tied together. Both were children of around Eric's age. They were dressed in buckskin tunics adorned with intricate patterns of shells and their hair was dark and braided. Both children seemed in a state of shock – their eyes wide, their faces blank and uncomprehending. Shannow forced himself to look at the corpse. It was short, and no doubt was another child. Shannow's fury rose and his eyes took on an almost feral gleam.

Desperately Shannow fought to hold the surging anger, but it engulfed him and he pushed himself to his feet, his hands curling around the butts of his pistols. He stepped into sight and the men scrambled to their feet, dragging knives and hatchets from their belts of rope and hide. Shannow's guns came up and then he spoke.

'*Thou shalt be visited by the Lord of Hosts with thunder and with earthquake and great noise . . .*'

He triggered the pistols and two men flew backwards. The other five screamed and charged. One went down with a bullet in the brain, a second fell clutching his belly. A third reached Shannow and the man's hatchet flashed for his head, but Shannow blocked the blow with his right arm and thrust the left-hand pistol under the attacker's chin. The top of his head flowered like a scarlet bloom. A club caught Shannow on the side of the head and he fell awkwardly; his pistol fired, shattering a man's knee. As a knife-blade rose above his face, Shannow rolled and shot the wielder in the chest. The man fell across him, but Shannow pushed the body clear and lurched to his feet. The man with the shattered knee was crawling backwards.

'. . . *and great noise, with storm and tempest and the flame of devouring fire.*'

The cannibal raised his arms against the pistols, covering his eyes. Shannow fired twice, the shells smashing through the outstretched hands and into the face beyond, and the man pitched back. Shannow staggered and fell to his knees; his head was pounding and his vision blurred and swam. He took a deep breath, pushing back the nausea that threatened to swamp him. A movement to his right! He pointed his pistol and a child screamed.

'It's all right,' said Shannow groggily. 'I'll not harm you. "Suffer little children to come unto me." Just give me a moment.'

He sat back and felt his head. The skin was split at the temple and blood was drenching his face and shirt. He sheathed his guns and crawled to the children, cutting them free.

The taller of the two sprinted away the moment the ropes were cut, but the other raised a hand and touched Shannow's face where the blood flowed. Shannow tried to smile, but the world spun madly before his eyes.

'Go, boy. You understand? *GO!*'

Shannow tried to stand, but fell heavily. He crawled for several yards and found himself lying next to a small clear pool of water. Watching his blood drip to the surface and flow away in red ribbons, Shannow chuckled.

'*He leadeth me beside the still waters. He restoreth my soul.*'

The child came to him, tugging at his arm. 'More come!'

he said. Shannow squeezed his eyes shut, trying to concentrate.

'More Carns come. You go!' shouted the child.

Shannow slipped his pistols into his hands and knocked out the barrel wedges, sliding the cylinders from the weapons and replacing them with two fully loaded cylinders from his coat pocket. He fumbled the wedges into place and sheathed the pistols.

'Let them come,' he said.

'No. Many Carns.' The boy's fingers flashed before Shannow's face. Ten, twenty, thirty, forty . . .

'I get the message, lad. Help me up.' The boy did his best, but Shannow was a tall man and the two made slow progress into the woods. Angry yells and cries pierced the stillness and he could hear the sounds of many men crashing through the undergrowth. He tried to move faster but fell, dragging the child with him. Forcing himself to his feet, he stumbled on. A blue- and yellow-smeared body lunged through the bushes and Shannow's right hand dropped and rose, the pistol bucking in his hand. The warrior vanished back into the undergrowth. The boy ran on ahead and unhobbled Shannow's horse, leaping into the saddle. Shannow staggered forward, caught hold of the pommel and managed to step into the saddle behind the child.

Three men burst into view and the horse swerved and took off at a run. Shannow swayed in the saddle, but the boy reached back and grabbed him; he managed to sheathe his pistol and then darkness overtook him. He fell forward against the boy as the horse raced on towards the west. The child risked a glance behind him. The Carns had given up the chase and were heading back into the trees. The boy slowed the gelding and hooked his fingers into Shannow's belt, holding him upright.

It was not easy, but Selah was strong and he owed this man his life.

Donna Taybard screamed once and sat up. Eric hauled on the reins and kicked the brake and the wagon stopped. The boy climbed over the back-rest and scrambled across the bulging food sacks to where his mother sat sobbing.

'What is it, Mother?' he cried.

Donna took a deep breath. 'Shannow,' she said. 'Oh my poor Jon.'

Con Griffin rode alongside and dismounted. He said nothing, but climbed into the wagon to kneel beside the weeping woman. Looking up into his powerful face, she saw the concern etched there.

'He is dead.'

'You were dreaming, Fray Taybard.'

'No. He rescued two children from the savages and now he is buried, deep in the ground.'

'A dream,' insisted Griffin, placing a huge hand on her shoulder.

'You don't understand, Mr Griffin. It is a Talent I have. We are going to a place where there are two lakes; it is surrounded by pine trees. There is a tribe who paint their bodies yellow and blue. Shannow killed many of them and escaped with a child. Now he is dead. Believe me!'

'You are an Esper, Donna?'

'Yes, . . . no. I can always see those close to me. Shannow is buried.'

Griffin patted her shoulder and stepped down from the wagon.

'What's happening, Con?' shouted Ethan Peacock. 'Why are we stopping?'

'Fray Taybard is unwell. We'll move on now,' he answered. Turning to Eric, he said, 'Leave her now, lad, and get the oxen moving.' He stepped into the saddle and rode back along the convoy to his own wagons.

'What was the hold-up?' Burke asked him.

'It's nothing, Jim. Pass me my pistols.'

Burke clambered back into the wagon and opened a brass-edged walnut box. Within were two engraved, double-barrelled flintlock pistols. Burke primed them both with powder from a bone horn and gathered the saddle holsters from a hook on the wagon wall.

Con Griffin slung the holsters across his pommel and

thrust the pistols home. Touching his heel to the chestnut, he cantered back to Madden's wagon.

'Trouble?' queried the bearded farmer and Griffin nodded.

'Leave your son to take the reins and join me at the head.'

Griffin swung his horse and rode back to the lead wagon. If Donna Taybard was right his convoy was in deep trouble. He cursed, for he knew without doubt that she would be proved correct.

Madden joined him within minutes, riding a slate-grey gelding of seventeen hands. A tall thin, angular man with a close-cropped black beard but no moustache, his mouth was a thin hard line and his eyes dark and deep-set. He carried a long rifle cradled in his left arm, and by his side was a bone-handled hunting knife.

Griffin told him of Donna's fear.

'You think she's right?'

'Has to be. Cardigan's diary spoke of the blue and yellow stripes.'

'What do we do?'

'We have no choice, Jacob. The animals need grass and rest – we must go in.'

The farmer nodded. 'Any idea how big a tribe?'

'No.'

'I don't like it, but I'm with you.'

'Alert all families – tell them to prime weapons.'

The wagons moved on and by late afternoon came to the end of the lava sand. The oxen, smelling water ahead, surged into the traces and the convoy picked up speed.

'Hold them back!' yelled Griffin, and drivers kicked hard on the brakes but to little avail. The wagons crested a green slope and spread out as they lurched and rumbled for the river below, and the wide lakes opening beside it. Griffin cantered alongside the leading wagon scanning the long grass for movement.

As the first wagon reached the water, a blue- and yellow-streaked body leapt to the driver's seat, plunging a flint dagger into Aaron Phelps' fleshy shoulder. The scholar lashed out and the attacker lost his balance and fell.

Suddenly warriors were all around them and Griffin pulled his pistols clear and cocked them. A man ran at him carrying a club. Griffin shot into his body and kicked his horse into a run. Madden's long rifle boomed and a tribesman fell with a broken spine. Then the other guns opened up and the warriors fled.

Griffin joined Madden at the rear of the convoy.

'What do you think, Jacob?'

'I think they'll be back. Let's fill the barrels and move on to open ground.'

Two wagoners were injured in the brief raid. Aaron Phelps had a deep wound in his right shoulder and Maggie Ames' young son, Mose, had been gashed in the leg by a spear. Four tribesmen were killed outright. Others had been wounded, but had reached the sanctuary of the trees.

Griffin dismounted next to one of the corpses.

'Look at those teeth,' said Jacob Madden. They were filed to sharp points.

Ethan Peacock came to stand beside Griffin and peered at the blue and yellow corpse.

'And idiots like Phelps expect us to agree with their theories of the Dark Age,' he said. 'Can you see that creature piloting a flying machine? It's barely human.'

'Damn you, Ethan, this is no time for debate. Get your barrels filled.'

Griffin moved on to Phelps' wagon, where Donna Taybard was battling to staunch the bleeding. 'It needs stitches, Donna,' said Griffin. 'I'll get a needle and thread.'

'I am going to die,' said Phelps. 'I know it.'

'Not from that, you won't,' Griffin told him. 'But, by God, it will make you wish you had.'

'Will they come back?' asked Donna.

'It depends on how big the tribe is,' answered Griffin. 'I would expect them to try once more. Is Eric gathering your water?'

'Yes.'

Griffin fetched needle and thread, passing them to Donna, then he checked his pistols. He had fired all four barrels, yet could remember only one. Strange, he thought, how instinct could overcome reason. He gave the pistols to Burke to load and prime. Madden had taken six men to watch the woods for any sign of the savages and Griffin supervised the water-gathering.

Towards dusk he ordered the wagons out and away from the trees to a flat meadow to the west. Here the oxen were unharnessed and a rope paddock set up to pen the beasts.

Madden organized guards at the perimeter of the camp and the travellers settled down to wait for the next attack.

Shannow's dreams were bathed in blood and fire. He rode a skeleton horse across a desert of graves, coming at last to a white marble city and a gate of gold that hurt his eyes as he gazed upon it.

'Let me in,' he called.

'No beasts may enter here,' a voice told him.

'I am not a beast.'

'Then what are you?'

Shannow looked down at his hands and saw they were mottled grey and black and scaled like a serpent. His head ached and he reached up to the wound.

'Let me in. I am hurt.'

'No beasts may enter here.'

Shannow screamed as his hand touched his brow, for horns grew there, long and sharp, and they leaked blood that hissed and boiled as it touched the ground.

'At least tell me if this is Jerusalem.'

'There are no Brigands for you to slay, Shannow. Ride on.'

'I have nowhere to go.'

'You chose the path, Shannow. Follow it.'

'But I need Jerusalem.'

'Come back again when the wolf sits down with the lamb, and the lion eats grass like the cattle do.'

Shannow awoke . . . he had been buried alive. He screamed once and a curtain to his left moved to show light in a room beyond. An elderly man crept in to sit beside him.

'You are well; you are in the Fever Hole. Do not concern yourself. You are free to leave when you feel well enough.' Shannow tried to sit, but his head ached abominably. His hand went to his brow, fearing that horns would touch his fingers, but he found only linen bandage. He glanced around the tiny room. Apart from his pallet bed there was a fire built beneath white stones, and the heat was searing.

'You had a fever,' said the man. 'I brought you out of it.'

Shannow lay back on the bed and fell asleep instantly.

When he awoke, the old man was still sitting beside him; he was dressed in a buckskin jacket, free of adornments, and leather trousers as soft as cloth. He was almost bald, but the white hair above his ears was thick and wavy and grew to his shoulders. The face, thought Shannow, was kindly, and his teeth were remarkably white and even.

'Who are you?' asked Shannow.

'I have long since put aside my name. Here they call me Karitas.'

'I am Shannow. What is wrong with me?'

'I think you have a cracked skull, Mr Shannow. You have been very ill – we have all been worried about you.'

'All?'

'Young Selah brought you to me. You saved his life in the eastern woods.'

'What of the other boy?'

'He did not come home, Mr Shannow. I fear he was recaptured.'

'My guns and saddlebags?'

'Safe. Interesting pistols, if I may say so. They are copies of the 1858 Colt; the original was a fine weapon, as cap and ball pistols go.'

'They are the best pistols in the world, Mr Karitas.'

'Just "Karitas", and yes, I expect you are right – at least until someone rediscovers the Smith and Wesson .44 Russian, or indeed the 1898 Luger. I myself have always held the Hi-power Browning in great esteem. How are you feeling?'

'Not good,' admitted Shannow.

'You almost died, my friend. The fever was most powerful and you were badly concussed. I am amazed that you remained conscious after being struck.'

'I don't remember being hit.'

'That is natural. Your horse is being well looked after. Our young men have never seen a horse, yet Selah rode him like a centaur to bring you home. It makes one inclined to believe in genetic memory.'

'You are speaking in riddles.'

'Yes. And I am tiring you. Rest now, and we will talk in the morning.'

Shannow drifted back into darkness and awoke to find a young woman by his bed. She helped him to eat some broth and bathed his body with water-cooled cloths. After she had gone, Karitas returned.

'I see you are feeling better – your colour is good, Mr Shannow.' The old man called out and two younger men ducked into the Fever Hole. 'Help Mr Shannow out into the sunlight. It will do him good.'

Together they lifted the naked man and carried him up out of the hole, laying him on a blanket under a wide shade made from interwoven leaves. Several children were playing nearby, and they stopped to watch the stranger. Shannow glanced around; there were more than thirty huts in view and to his right a shallow stream bubbled over pink and blue stones.

'Beautiful, isn't it?' said Karitas. 'I love this place. If it wasn't for the Carns, this would be paradise.'

'The Carns?'

'The cannibals, Mr Shannow.'

'Yes, I remember.'

'Sad, really. The Elders did it to them, polluted the land and the sea. The Carns should have died; they came here two hundred years ago when the plagues began. I wasn't in this area then, or I could have warned them to stay clear. The stones used to gleam at night and no animal could survive. We still suffer a high incidence of cancer, but the main effects seem to be on the brain and the glandular system. With some, they become atavistic. Others develop rare ESPer powers. While some of us just seem to live for ever.'

Shannow decided the man was mad and closed his eyes against the pain in his temple.

'My dear chap,' said Karitas, 'forgive me. Ella, fetch the coca.'

A young woman came forward bearing a wooden bowl in which dark liquid swirled. 'Drink that, Mr Shannow.' He did as he was bid. The drink was bitter and he almost choked, but within seconds the pain in his head dulled and disappeared.

'There, that's the ticket. I took the liberty, Mr Shannow, of going through your things and I see you are a Bible-reading man.'

'Yes. You?'

'I have been while you lay ill. It's a long time since I have seen a Bible. I'm not surprised it survived the Fall; it was a best-seller every day of every year. There were more Bibles than people, I shouldn't wonder.'

'You are not a believer, then?'

'On the contrary, Mr Shannow. Anyone who watches a world die is liable to be converted at rare speed.'

Shannow sat up. 'Every time you speak, I almost get a grip on what you are saying, and then you soar away somewhere. Lugers, Colts, tickets . . . I don't understand any of it.'

'And why should you, my boy? Does not the Bible say, *"For behold I shall create a new heaven and a new earth and the former shall not be remembered; nor come into mind"*?'

'That's the first thing you've said that I have understood. What happened to the wagons?'

'What wagons, Mr Shannow?'

'I was with a convoy.'

'I know nothing of them, but when you are well you can find them.'

'Your name is familiar to me,' said Shannow, 'but I cannot place it.'

'Karitas. Greek for love. Though I speak with the tongues of men and of angels, and have not Karitas – charity, love . . . You recall?'

'My father used to use it,' said Shannow, smiling. 'I remember. Faith, Hope and Karitas. Yes.'

'You should smile more often, Mr Shannow; it becomes you well. Tell me, sir, why did you risk your life for my little ones?'

Shannow shrugged. 'If that question needs an answer, then I cannot supply it. I had no choice.'

'I have decided that I like you, Mr Shannow. The children here call you the Thunder-maker and they think you may be a god. They know I am. They think you are the god of death.'

'I am a man, Karitas. You know that, tell them.'

'Divinity is not a light gift to throw away, Mr Shannow. You will feature in their legends until the end of time – hurling thunderbolts at the Carns, rescuing their princes. One day they will probably pray to you.'

'That would be blasphemy.'

'Only if you took it seriously. But then you are no Caligula. Are you hungry?'

'Your chatter makes my head spin. How long have you been here?'

'In this camp? Eleven years, more or less. And you must forgive my chatter, Mr Shannow. I am one of the last men of a lost race and sometimes my loneliness is colossal. I have discovered answers here to mysteries that have baffled men for a thousand years. And there is no one I would wish to tell. All I have is this small tribe who were once Eskimos and now are merely food for the Carns. It is all too galling, Mr Shannow.'

'Where are you from, Karitas?'

'London, Mr Shannow.'

'Is that north, south, what?'

'By my calculations, sir, it is north, and sits under a million tons of ice waiting to be discovered in another millennium.'

Shannow gave up and lay back on the blanket, allowing sleep to wash over him.

*

Mad though he undoubtedly was, Karitas organized the village with spectacular efficiency and was obviously revered by the villagers. Shannow lay on his blankets in the shade and watched the village life passing him by. The huts were all alike – rectangular and built of mud and logs with roofs slanting down and overhanging the main doors. The roofs themselves appeared to be constructed from interwoven leaves and dried grass. They were sturdy buildings, without ostentation. To the east of the village was a large log cabin, which Karitas explained held the winter stores, and beside it was the wood store – seven feet high and fifteen feet deep. The winter, Karitas told him, was particularly harsh here on the plain.

On outlying hills Shannow could see flocks of sheep and goats, and these he was told were communal property. Life seemed relaxed and without friction in Karitas' village.

The people themselves were friendly, and any that passed where Shannow lay would bow and smile. They were not like any people Shannow had come across so far in his wanderings; their skin was dull gold and their eyes wide-set and almost slanted. The women were mostly taller than the men, and beautifully formed; several were pregnant. There seemed few old people, until Shannow realized their huts were in the western sector, nearest the stream and protected from the harsh north winds by a rising slope at the rear of the dwellings.

The men were stocky and carried weapons of curious design, bows of horn and knives of dark flint. Day by day Shannow came to know individual villagers, especially the boy Selah and a young sloe-eyed maid named Curopet, who would sit by him and gaze at his face, saying nothing. Her presence unsettled the Jerusalem Man, but he could not find the words to send her away.

Shannow's recovery was painfully slow. The wound in his temple healed within days, but the left side of his face was numb and the strength of his left arm and leg had been halved. If he tried to walk, his foot dragged and he often stumbled. The fingers of his left hand tingled permanently and he was unable to hold any object for more than a few seconds before the hand would spasm and the fingers open.

Every day for a month Karitas would arrive at Shannow's hut an hour after dawn and massage his fingers and arm. Shannow was close to despair. All his life his strength had been with him, and without it he felt defenceless and – worse – useless.

Karitas broached the painful subject at the start of the fifth week. 'Mr Shannow, you are doing yourself no good. Your strength will not return until you find the courage to seek it.'

'I can hardly lift my arm and my leg drags like a rotting tree branch,' said Shannow. 'What do you expect me to do?'

'Fight it, as you fought the Carns. I am not a medical man, Mr Shannow, but I think you have had a mild stroke – a cerebral thrombosis, I believe it used to be called. A blood clot near the brain has affected your left side.'

'How sure are you of this?'

'Reasonably certain; it happened to my father.'

'And he recovered?'

'No, he died. He took to his bed like the weakling he was.'

'How do I fight it?'

'Bear with me, Mr Shannow, and I will show you.'

Each day Karitas sat for hours, pushing the Jerusalem Man through a gruelling series of exercises. At first it was merely forcing Shannow to raise his left arm and lower it ten times. Shannow managed six, and the arm rose a bare eight inches. Then Karitas produced a ball of tightly wound hide which he placed in Shannow's left hand. 'Squeeze this one hundred times in the morning, and another hundred times before you sleep.'

'It'll take me all day.'

'Then take all day. But do it!'

Each afternoon, Karitas forced Shannow to accompany him on a walk around the village, a distance of about four hundred paces.

The weeks drifted by and Shannow's improvement was barely perceptible; but Karitas – noting everything – would shout for joy over an extra quarter-inch on an arm raise, offering fulsome congratulations and calling in Selah or Curopet, insisting Shannow repeat the move. This was then greeted by much applause, especially from the maiden Curopet who had, in the words of Karitas, 'taken a shine' to the invalid.

Shannow, while recognizing Karitas' methods, was still lifted by the obvious joy the old man gained from his recovery, and tried harder with each passing day.

At night, as he lay on his blankets squeezing the leather ball and counting aloud, his mind would drift to Donna and the convoy. He felt her absence, but he knew that with her talent she could see him every day and would know how hard he was working to be beside her once more.

One morning, as Shannow and Karitas walked round the village, the Jerusalem Man stopped and gazed at the distant hills. The trees were still green, but at the centre was a golden shower that shimmered in the sunlight.

'That is wondrous beautiful,' said Shannow. 'It looks for all the world like a tree of gold coins, just waiting to make a man rich.'

'There are many beautiful things to see during Autumn here,' said Karitas softly.

'Autumn? Yes, I had not thought. I have been here so long.'

'Two months only.'

'I must get away before Winter, or there'll be no tracks to follow.'

'We'll do our best for you, Mr Shannow.'

'Do not misunderstand me, my friend. I am more than grateful to you, but my heart is elsewhere. Have you ever loved a woman?'

'More than one, I'm afraid. But not for thirty years now. Chines had a baby girl last night. That makes eleven babies this Summer for my little tribe – not bad, eh?'

'Which one is Chines?'

'The tall girl with the birthmark on her temple.'

'Ah yes. Is she all right?'

'Fine. Her husband is disappointed though, he wanted a boy.'

'Your tribe is doing well, Karitas. You are a good leader. How many people are there here?'

'Counting the babes, eighty-seven. No, eighty-eight; I forgot about Dual's boy.'

'A sizable family.'

'It would be bigger, but for the Carns.'

'Do they raid often?'

'No, they have never hit the village. They don't want to drive us away – we are a good source of amusement . . . and food. They usually attack our hunting parties.'

'You do not seem to hate them, Karitas. Whenever you mention the Carns, your face reflects regret.'

'They are not responsible for the way they are, Mr Shannow. It was the land. I know you think me a great liar, but when the Carns first came here they were a group of ordinary farming families. Maybe it was the water, or the rocks, or even something in the air – I don't know. But over the years it changed them. It was a gift from my generation; we were always good at lethal gifts.'

'After knowing you for these last months,' said Shannow, 'I cannot understand why you hold to your preposterous tales. I know you are an intelligent man, and you must know that I am not foolish. Why then do you maintain this charade?'

Karitas sat down on the grass and beckoned Shannow to join him. 'My dear boy, I hold to it because it is true. But let me say that the land may have affected me too – it could all be a dream, a fantasy. I think it is true – my memory tells me it is true – but I could merely be insane. What does it matter?'

'It matters to me, Karitas. I like you; I owe you a debt.'

'You owe me nothing. You saved Selah. One thing does concern me, however, and that is the direction your wagons are taking. You say you were heading north-west?'

'Yes.'

'But was there any intention of turning east?'

'Not that I know of. Why?'

'Probably it is of no matter. It is a strange land, and there are some who live there who would make the Carns seem hospitable.'

'That is as hard to swallow as some of your stories.'

The smile left Karitas' face. 'Mr Shannow, there was an old legend when I was a boy concerning a priestess called Cassandra. She was blessed with the gift of prophecy and always spoke the truth. But she was cursed also, to be believed by no one.'

'I am sorry, my friend. It was thoughtless and rude of me.'

'It is not important, Mr Shannow. Let us resume our walk.'

They continued in silence, which Shannow found uncomfortable.

The day was warm, a bright sun in a blue sky, with only occasional white scudding clouds bringing shade and relief. Shannow felt stronger than he had in weeks. Karitas stopped at a rock pile and hefted a fist-sized stone.

'Take that in your left hand,' he said.

Shannow obeyed.

'Now carry it for a second circuit.'

'I'll never make it all the way,' said Shannow.

'We won't know until we make the attempt,' snapped Karitas. They set off and within a few paces Shannow's left arm began to tremble. Sweat stood out on his forehead, and on the seventeenth step the rock tumbled from his twitching fingers. Karitas took a stick and thrust it into the ground. 'That is your first mark, Mr Shannow. Tomorrow you will go beyond it.'

Shannow rubbed at his arm. 'I have made you angry,' he said.

Karitas turned to him, his eyes gleaming. 'Mr Shannow, you are right. I have lived too long and seen too much, and you have no idea how galling it is to be disbelieved. I'll tell you something else that you will not be able to understand, nor comprehend: I was a computer expert, and I wrote books on programming. That makes me the world's greatest living author, and an expert on a subject that is so totally valueless here as to be obscene. I lived in a world of greed, violence, lust and terror. That world died, yet what do I see around me? Exactly the same thing, only on a mercifully smaller scale. Your disbelief hurts me harder than I can say.'

'Then let us start afresh, Karitas,' said Shannow, laying his hand on the old man's shoulder. 'You are my friend. I trust you, and no matter what you tell me I swear I will believe it.'

'That is a noble gesture, Mr Shannow. And it will suffice.'

'So tell me about the dangers in the east.'

'Tonight we will sit by the fire and talk, but for now I have things to do. Walk around the village twice more, Mr Shannow, and when you have your hut in sight, try to run.'

As the old man walked away Curopet approached Shannow, averting her eyes. 'Are you well, Thundermaker?'

'Better every day, Lady.'

'May I fetch you some water?'

'No. Karitas says I must walk and run.'

'May I walk with you?' Shannow gazed down at her and saw she was blushing.

'Of course; it would be my pleasure.' She was taller than most young women of the village, and her hair was dark and gleamed as if oiled. Her figure was coltish, and she moved with grace and innocent sensuality.

'How long have you known Karitas?' he asked, making conversation.

'He has always been with us. My grandfather told me that Karitas taught him to hunt when he was a boy.'

Shannow stopped. 'Your grandfather? But Karitas himself could not have been very old at that time.'

'Karitas has always been old. He is a god. My grandfather said that Karitas also trained *his* grandfather; it is a very special honour to be taught by Karitas.'

'Perhaps there has been more than one Karitas,' suggested Shannow.

'Perhaps,' agreed Curopet. 'Tell me, Lord Thundermaker, are you allowed to have women?'

'Allowed? No,' said Shannow, reddening. 'It is not permitted.'

66

'That is sad,' said Curopet.

'Yes.'

'Are you being punished for something?'

'No. I am married, you see. I have a wife.'

'Only one?'

'Yes.'

'But she is not here.'

'No.'

'I am here.'

'I am well aware of that. And I thank you for your . . . kindness,' said Shannow at last. 'Excuse me, I am very tired. I think I will sleep now.'

'But you have not run.'

'Another time.' Shannow stepped into the hut and sat down, feeling both foolish and pleased. He removed his pistols from the saddlebags and cleaned them, checking the caps and replacing them. The guns were the most reliable he had ever known, misfiring only once in twenty. They were well-balanced and reasonably true, if one compensated for the kick on the left-hand pistol. He checked his store of brass caps and counted them; one hundred and seventy remained. He had enough fulminates for twice that, and black powder to match. Karitas entered as he was replacing his weapons in the saddlebags.

'Black powder was a good propellant,' said the old man. 'But not enough of it burns, and that's why there is so much smoke.'

'I make my own,' said Shannow, 'but the saltpetre is the hardest to find. Sulphur and charcoal are plentiful.'

'How are you faring?'

'Better today. Tomorrow I will run.'

'Curopet told me of your conversation. Do you find it hard to talk to women?'

'Yes,' admitted Shannow.

'Then try to forget that they are women.'

'That is very hard. Curopet is breathtakingly attractive.'

'You should have accepted her offer.'

'Fornication is a sin, Karitas. I carry enough sins already.'

Karitas shrugged. 'I will not try to dissuade you. You asked about the east and the dangers there. Strangely, the Bible figures in the story.'

'A religious tribe, you mean?'

'Precisely – although they view matters somewhat differently from you, Mr Shannow. They call themselves the Hellborn. They maintain that since Armageddon is now a proved reality, and since there is no new Jerusalem, Lucifer must have overpowered Jehovah. Therefore they pay him homage as the Lord of this world.'

'That is vile,' whispered Shannow.

'They practise the worship of Molech, and give the firstborn child to the fire. Human sacrifice takes place in their temples and their rites are truly extraordinary. All strangers are considered enemies and either enslaved or burnt alive. They also have pistols and rifles, Mr Shannow – and they have rediscovered the rimless cartridge.'

'I do not understand.'

'Think of the difference between the percussion pistols you own and the flintlocks you have come across. Well, the cartridge is as far ahead of the percussion cap as that.'

'Explain it to me.'

'I can do better than that, Mr Shannow. I will show you.' Karitas opened his sheepskin jerkin and there, nestling in a black shoulder holster, was a pistol the like of which Shannow had never seen. It had a rectangular black grip and when Karitas pulled it clear he saw that the body of the gun was also a rectangle. Karitas passed it to Shannow.

'How does it load?'

'Press the button to the left of the butt.'

Shannow did so and a clip slid clear of the butt. Shannow placed the gun in his lap and examined the clip. He could see a glint of brass at the top and he slid the shell into his hand, holding it up against the light from the fire.

'That,' said Karitas, 'is a cartridge. The oval shape at the point is the lead bullet. The brass section replaces the percussion cap; it contains its own propellant and, when struck by the firing pin, explodes, propelling the shell from the barrel.'

'But how does the . . . bullet get from the clip to the breech?'

Karitas took up the automatic and pulled back the casing, exposing the breech. 'A spring in the clip forces the shell up, and releasing the block like so . . .' the casing snapped back into position '. . . pushes the shell into the breech. Now this is the beauty of the weapon, Mr Shannow: when the trigger is pulled the firing pin explodes the propellant and sends the shell on its way, but the blow-back from the explosion forces the casing backwards. A hook pulls clear the cartridge case, which is then struck from beneath by another cartridge and thrown from the pistol. As the casing springs back, it pushes the next shell into the breech. Simple and superb!'

'What is it called?'

'This, my dear fellow, is the Browning of 1911, with the single-link locking system. It is also the reason why the Carns will not raid where I am.'

'You mean it works?'

'Of course it works. It's not a patch on their later models, but it was considered a great weapon in its day.'

'I am still to be convinced,' said Shannow. 'It looks clumsy and altogether too complicated.'

'Tomorrow, Mr Shannow, I shall give you a demonstration.'

'Where did you come by these weapons?'

'I took them from the Ark, Mr Shannow. That is one of the surprises I have in store for you. Would you like to see Noah's Ark?'

Chapter Four

Shannow could not sleep; his mind was full of pictures of Donna Taybard. He recalled her as he had first seen her, standing before her farmhouse with a crossbow in her hand, looking both defiant and delicate. And then at the dinner-table, sad and wistful. And he remembered her in the wide bed – her face flushed, her eyes bright, her body soft.

Images of Curopet crept into his mind, blurring with Donna, and he groaned and rolled over.

Dawn found him irritable and tired and he dressed swiftly, having first exercised with the leather ball. His left hand was stronger now, yet still a shadow of what it had been.

The wind was chill and Shannow wished he had put on his leather top-coat, but he saw Karitas waiting for him by the rock pile.

'We will put this exhibition to good use,' said Karitas. 'Pick up a good-sized rock with your left hand and carry it to the flat ground yonder, about thirty paces.' Shannow did as he was bid, and his arm was aching as he returned.

'Now take another,' said Karitas. Six times he ordered Shannow to pick up rocks and then he told him to watch. The rocks were now in a line, each of them the size of a man's fist. Karitas drew the Browning and cocked it, his arm levelled and the gun fired with a sharp crack. There was little smoke and one of the rocks splintered. On the ground by Karitas' feet lay a brass shell, and the weapon in his hand was cocked and ready.

'Now you try, my dear fellow.' He reversed the gun and handed it to Shannow. The balance was good, the weight nestling back into his palm rather than forward like the percussion pistols.

He lined the weapon and squeezed the trigger and a spurt of dust leapt up a foot behind the rock. Shannow fired once more and the rock split apart. He was impressed, though he tried not to show it.

'My own pistols could duplicate the accuracy.'

'I don't doubt it, but the Browning can be loaded with nine shells in less than ten seconds.'

'And you say the Hellborn have these?'

'No, thank God. They have revolvers, copies of the Adams and some Remington replicas. But their craftsmen have evolved the weapons; their level of technology is fairly high.'

'Well, they are a problem for another day,' said Shannow. 'But tell me of Noah's Ark – or is that another joke?'

'Not at all. We will see it in the Spring, with the Guardians' permission.'

'I will not be here in the Spring, Karitas.'

The old man moved forward and retrieved his pistol. He uncocked it and slid it back into his shoulder holster. 'You are recovering well, but you are not yet strong enough to ride any distance. And there is something else you should know.' Karitas' voice was grave.

'What is it?'

'Let us go to your hut, and I will explain.'

Once inside beside a warm fire, Karitas opened the leather pouch at his hip and produced a round stone which he passed to Shannow. Warm to the touch and gleaming softly gold in the firelight, it was veined with black streaks and highlighted by tiny specks of silver.

'It is a pretty piece,' said Shannow. 'But what do you have to tell me?'

'You are holding your life in your hand, Mr Shannow, for that is a healing Stone and on you it has worked a miracle.'

'I have heard of such. The Daniel Stone?'

'Indeed it is. But its significance to you is very great. You see, Mr Shannow, you are in fact dead. When Selah brought you to me your skull was smashed. I don't know how you lived as long as you did. But the Stone held you . . .

as it still holds you. If you travel out of its influence, you will die.'

Shannow tossed the Stone to Karitas. 'Dead? Then why does my heart beat? Why can I still think and speak?'

'Tell me, Mr Shannow, when you lay in the Fever Hole and your heart stopped, what did you feel?'

'I felt nothing. I dreamed I sat outside the gates of Jerusalem, and they would not let me enter. It was but a dream. I do not believe that I am trapped in this village for ever.'

'Nor are you. But you must trust me, and my knowledge. I will know when you have broken the thread, when you can exist without the Stone. Have faith in me, Jon.'

'But my wife . . .'

'If she loves you she will wait. And you say she has power to see great distances. Build your strength.'

Day by dreary day Shannow worked – chopping wood, carrying water, scything grass for winter feed. And the Autumn passed before the freezing northerly winds piled snow against the huts. Night after night Shannow sat with Karitas, listening to his tales of the New World's birthing. He no longer knew nor cared if Karitas was telling the truth; the images were too many and too kaleidoscopic to contain. He listened much as he had when his father told stories, his disbelief suspended only for the telling time.

Yet though Karitas maintained he had lived long before the Fall of the world, he would not speak of his society, its laws or its history, refusing to answer any of Shannow's questions. Strangely, Shannow felt, this gave the old man credibility.

'I would like to tell you, Jon, for it is so long since I spoke of the old world. But I have a fear, you see, that one day Man will recreate the horrors of those days. I shall not be a willing party to it. We were so arrogant. We thought the world was ours, and then one day Nature put us in our place. The world toppled on its axis. Tidal waves consumed vast areas. Cities, countries, vanished beneath the water. Volcanoes erupted, earthquakes tore the world. It's a wonder anyone survived.

'And yet, now I look back, all the clues were there to see – to warn us of impending disaster. All we needed was to be humble enough to look at it without subjectivity. Our own legends told us that the earth had toppled before. The Bible talks of the sun rising in the west, and of the seas tipping from their bowls. And it did. My God, it did!'

The old man lapsed into silence. 'How did you survive?' asked Shannow.

Karitas blinked and grinned suddenly. 'I was in a magical metal bird, flying high above the waves.'

'It was a serious question.'

'I know. But I don't want to talk any more about those days.'

'Just one small question,' said Shannow. 'It is important to me.'

'Just the one,' agreed the old man.

'Would there have been a black road with diamonds at the centre, shining in the night?'

'Diamonds? Ah yes, all the roads had them. Why do you ask?'

'Would they have been at Jerusalem?'

'Yes. Why?'

'It is the city I am seeking. And if Noah's Ark is on a mountain near here, Jerusalem cannot be far away.'

'Are you mocking me, Shannow?'

'No. I seek the Holy City.'

Karitas held his hands out to the fire, staring thoughtfully into the flames. All men needed a dream, he knew. Shannow more than most.

'What will you do when you find it?'

'I will ask questions and receive answers.'

'And then what?'

'I shall die happy, Karitas.'

'You're a good man, Shannow. I hope you make it.'

'You doubt I will?'

'Not at all. If Jerusalem exists, you will find it. And if it doesn't you'll never know, for you'll look until you die. That's how it should be. I feel that way about Heaven; it's far more important that Heaven should exist than that I should ever see it.'

'In my dream, they would not let me enter. They told me to come back when the wolf sits down with the lamb, and the lion eats grass like the cattle do.'

'Get some sleep, Jon. Dream of it again. I went there once, you know. To Jerusalem. Long before the Fall.'

'Was it beautiful?'

Karitas remembered the chokingly narrow streets in the old quarter, the stink of bazaars . . . the tourist areas, the tall hotels, the pickpockets and the car bombs.

'Yes,' he said. 'It was beautiful. Good night, Jon.'

Karitas sat in his long cabin, his mood heavy and dark. He knew that Shannow would never believe the truth, but then why should he? Even in his own age of technological miracles there had still been those who believed that the earth was flat, or that Man was made by a benevolent bearded immortal out of a lump of clay. At least Shannow had a solid fact to back his theory of Armageddon. The world had come close to death.

There had been a lot of speculation in the last years about the possibility of a nuclear holocaust. But next to no one had considered Nature herself dwarfing the might of the superpowers. What was it that scientist had told him five years after the Fall?

The Chandler Theory? Karitas had a note somewhere from the days when he had studiously kept a diary. The old man moved into the back room and began to rummage through oak chests covered in beaver pelts. Underneath a rust-dark and brittle copy of the London *Times* he found the faded blue jackets of his diary collection, and below those the scraps of paper he had used for close to forty years. Useless, he thought, remembering the day when his last pencil had grown too small to sharpen. He pushed aside the scraps and searched through his diaries, coming at last to an entry for May 16. It was six years after the Fall. Strange how the memory fades after only a few centuries, he told himself with a grin. He read the entry and leaned back, remembering old Webster and his moth-eaten wig.

It was the ice at the poles, Webster had told him, increasing at the rate of 95,000 tons a day, slowly changing the shape of the earth from spheroid to ovoid. This made the spin unstable. Then came the day when mighty Jupiter and all the other major planets drew into a deadly line to exert their gravitational pull on the earth, along with that of the sun. The earth – already wobbling on its axis – toppled, bringing tidal waves and death and a new Ice Age for much of the hemisphere.

Armageddon? God the father moving from homilies to homicide?

Perhaps. But somehow Karitas preferred the wondrous anarchy of Nature.

That night Jon Shannow dreamed of war: strange riders wearing horned helms bore down on a village of tents. They carried swords and pistols and, as they stormed into the village in their hundreds, the noise of gunfire was deafening. The people of the tents fought back with bow and lance, but they were overpowered; the men brutally slain. Young women were dragged out on to the plain and repeatedly raped, and their throats were cut by saw-toothed daggers. Then they were hoisted into the air by their feet and their blood ran into jugs which were passed around amongst the riders, who drank and laughed, their faces stained red.

Shannow awoke in a cold sweat, his left hand twitching as if to curl around the butt of his pistol. The dream had sickened him and he cursed his mind for summoning such a vision. He prayed then, giving thanks for life and for love, and asking that the Lord of Hosts watch over Donna Taybard until Shannow could reach her.

The night was dark and snow swirled around the village. Shannow rose and wrapped himself in a blanket. Moving to the hearth he raked the coals until a tiny flame appeared, then added timber and fresh wood and blew the fire to life.

The dream had been so real, so brutally real.

Shannow's head ached and he wandered to the window where, in a pottery jug, were the coca leaves given him by Curopet. As ever, they dealt with the pain. He pushed open the window and leaned out, watching the snow. He could still see the riders – their curious helms adorned with curved horns of polished black, and their breastplates embossed with a goat's head. He shivered and shut the window.

'Where are you tonight, Donna, my love?' he whispered.

Con Griffin had been many things in his life, but no one had ever taken him for a fool. Yet the riders with the horned helms and the casually arrogant manner obviously thought him as green as the grass of the valley.

The convoy, having survived three Carn attacks and a heartstopping moment when an avalanche narrowly missed a wagon on the high trail, had come at last to a green valley flanked by great mountains whose snow-covered peaks reached up into the clouds.

At a full meeting the wagoners had voted to put their roots into the soil of the valley, and Con Griffin had ridden with Madden and Burke to stake out plots for all the families. With the land allocated and the first timber felled, the wagoners had woken on a chill Autumn day to find three strange riders approaching the settlement. Each wore a curious helm embossed in black and sporting goats' horns, and by their sides hung pistols the like of which Griffin had never seen.

Griffin strode to meet them while Madden sat on a nearby wagon, his long rifle cradled across his arm. Jimmy Burke knelt beside a felled log idly polishing a double-barrelled flintlock.

'Good morning to you,' said Griffin. The leader of the trio, a young man with dark eyes, forced a smile that was at best wintry.

'You are settling here?'

'Why not? It is virgin land.'

The man nodded. 'We are seeking a rider named Shannow.'

'He is dead,' said Griffin.

'He is alive,' stated the man, with a certainty Griffin could not ignore.

'If he is, then I am surprised. He was attacked by a cannibal tribe to the south and never rejoined his wagon.'

'How many of you are there?' asked the rider.

'Enough,' said Griffin.

'Yes,' agreed the man. 'We will be on our way – we are just passing through these lands.'

The riders turned their horses and galloped towards the east.

Madden joined Griffin.

'I didn't like the look of them,' volunteered Madden. 'You think we are in for trouble?'

'Could be,' admitted Griffin.

'They set my flesh crawling,' said Burke, coming up to join them. 'They reminded me of the cannibals, 'cepting they had proper teeth.'

'What do you advise, Griff?' asked Madden.

'If they are Brigands, they'll be back.'

'What did they talk about?' inquired Burke.

'They were asking about a man named Shannow.'

'Who's he?' asked Madden.

'He's the Jerusalem Man,' said Griffin, avoiding a direct lie. He had told none of his wagoners of Jon Taybard's true name.

'In that case,' said Burke, 'they'd better hope they don't find him. He's not a man to mess with, by God! He's the one that shot up the Brigands in Allion. And he gave Daniel Cade his limp – shot him in the knee.'

'Don't mention Shannow to the others,' said Griffin.

Madden caught Griffin's expression and his eyes narrowed. There was something here that remained unsaid, but he trusted Griffin and did not press the point.

That night, just after midnight, fifty riders thundered down on the settlement, riding at full gallop across the eastern pasture. The front line hit the tripwire in the long grass and the horses screamed as their legs were cut out from under them. Men pitched through the air. The second rank of riders dragged on their reins, stopping short of the wire. Shots exploded from twenty rifles, ripping into the raiders; twenty men went down, plus several horses. A second volley from fifteen pistols scythed through the milling riders, and the survivors galloped away. Several men who had been thrown from their mounts set off at a run. Individual riflemen picked them off in the bright moonlight.

As silence descended, Con Griffin reloaded his pistols and walked out into the pasture. Twenty-nine corpses lay on the grass, and eleven horses were dead or dying. Madden and the other wagoners joined him, collecting pistols from the fallen; they were revolvers and cartridge-fed.

'What will they come up with next?' asked Burke, thrusting a revolver into his belt.

'Look at this,' said Griffin, staring down at the corpses. 'They are all dressed alike – like an army in the old books. There's something very wrong here.' He turned to Madden. 'Mount up and follow them. Don't show yourself. And take no chances. I need to know where they are from – and how many there are.'

Donna Taybard moved alongside Griffin, slipping her arm through his.

'Who are they, Con?'

'I don't know. But they frighten me.'

'You think they will be back tonight?'

'No. But if they do come, Jacob will let us know.'

'Come home then. Eric will want to hear all about it; he'll be so proud of you.'

Griffin pulled her close and kissed her lightly on the brow. He wanted so desperately not to tell her about Shannow, wanted her to go on believing he was dead. They had become close after Shannow's disappearance and he had made a special fuss over Eric, which meant he was often invited to eat at the Taybard wagon. Then one night he had proposed to Donna, expecting a refusal and prepared to wait for her to change her mind. Instead she had accepted, kissed him and thanked him for his courtesy.

Few men could have been happier than Con Griffin at that moment. For days afterwards he had walked with her in the evenings, holding hands in the moonlight, until finally Donna herself precipitated the move he longed for. They had walked to a shallow stream and she turned to him and put her hands on his shoulders.

'I am not a fifteen-year-old maiden,' she said, loosening her dress.

And they had made love on the grass beside the water.

Since then Con Griffin had slept in Donna's wagon, much to the disgust of old Burke who did not hold with such flippant behaviour. Eric had adjusted well to his new father and seemed relaxed in Griffin's company. For his part Griffin taught him to rope, and to track, and to name the trees, and which of them grew near water. And they talked as man to man, which pleased Eric greatly.

'What should I call you?' asked Eric.

'Call me Griff.'

'I cannot call you Father. Not yet.'

'It would be nice if you could, but I will not worry about it.'

'Will you make my mother happy?'

'I hope so. I will try very hard.'

'My father couldn't.'

'It happens sometimes.'

'And I won't be cruel to you, Griff.'

'Cruel?'

'I was very cruel to Mr Shannow. And he saved my life. I wish I hadn't been; he told me he was very lonely and he wanted to be my friend.'

That conversation was in Griffin's mind now as he stood with Donna. He walked her away from the corpses to the canvas-covered wagon beside their home plot.

'Donna, there is something . . . The riders . . .'

'What? Come on, this is not like you.'

'Shannow is alive.'

'No!'

'I believe that he is. Use your talent – try to see him.'

'No, he's dead. I don't want to see him with maggots in his eyes.'

'Please, Donna. Otherwise I'll never be able to rest, wondering if the Jerusalem Man is hunting me.'

Her head sank down and she closed her eyes. Immediately she saw Shannow, limping through a village. Beside him was an old man, balding, who was smiling and chatting to Shannow.

Donna opened her eyes. 'Yes,' she whispered. 'He is alive. Oh, Con!'

'I will . . . of course, release you . . . from . . .'

'Don't say it. Don't ever say it! I'm pregnant, Con, and I love you.'

'But you and he . . .'

'He saved me, and Eric. And he was very lonely. I didn't love him. But I never would have done this to him – truly I wouldn't.'

'I know.' He took her in his arms.

'There's something else, Con. All the people with Jon are to die.'

'I don't understand.'

'I am not sure that I do. But they are all doomed. I saw skulls floating above all of them, and dark shadows in the distance with horned helmets like those riders there.'

'Today's drama has affected your talent,' he assured her. 'The important thing is that Jon Shannow is alive. And when he comes here he will be looking for you.'

'Con, he will never understand. I think he is a little insane.'

'I shall be ready.'

The following day Shannow rose early, refreshed despite his troubled night. He pulled on his woollen shirt and a thick pullover knitted for him by Curopet. Over this he added his ankle-length leather coat and a pair of woollen gloves. Then he belted on his guns and hefted his saddle over his right shoulder before making his way across the village to the makeshift paddock where the gelding stood. There he rubbed down the horse and saddled him.

The day was bright and clear as Shannow rode from the sleeping village. He steered the horse high into the hills to the north, picking his trail with care on the slippery ground. After an hour he found a different route and returned to the village, where he fed the gelding and removed his saddle. He was cold through, and bone-weary. By the time he dumped his saddle back in the hut, he was ready to drop. Shrugging out of his coat, he picked up the ball of hide and squeezed it two hundred times. Then tossing it aside, he stood. His hand dropped to his pistol and flashed up, the gun leaping to his hand, cocked and ready. He smiled; not so fast as he had been, but already fast enough. The rest would follow.

Curopet tapped at his door and he ushered her in. She had brought a wooden bowl of heated oats and goat's milk. He thanked her and she bowed.

'I thought you had left us,' she said softly, her eyes staring at the floor.

'Not yet, Lady. But soon I must.'

'To go to your wife?'

'Yes.'

She smiled and left him and he finished his breakfast and waited for Karitas. The old man was not long in arriving, his sheepskin jerkin covered in snow.

Karitas grinned and moved to the fire. 'Did you see anything on your ride?'

'Four or five deer to the north-east, and some beautiful country.'

'And how do you feel?'

'Tired, and yet strong.'

'Good. I think you are almost mended, Jon Shannow. I heard someone cry out in the night – I thought it was you.'

'It could have been,' said Shannow, moving to sit beside the fire. 'I had a bad dream. I saw men attacking a tent village . . . they were vile.'

'They had horned helms?' asked Karitas, staring intently at Shannow's face.

'Yes. How could you know?'

'I had the same dream. It is the land, Jon – as I told you, it grants rare powers. That was no dream, you saw the Hellborn in action.'

'Thank the Lord they are not near here!'

'Yes. My little village would be slain. We could not fight them, not even with the Ark weapons.'

'One pistol,' said Shannow, 'would not keep away a small Brigand band.'

'There is more than one pistol in the Ark, Jon. I will show you in the Spring.'

'The Hellborn have many riders. There must have been two to three hundred in the attack on the village.'

'Would that they only had three hundred. What we saw was one raiding column and there are more than twenty such. The sexual excesses among the Hellborn mean a plethora of babes and their tribe grows fast. It was always so throughout history: the migration of nations. Overpopulation causes people to move into the lands of their neighbours, bringing war and death. The Hellborn are moving and one day they will be here.'

'I find it hard to believe that the Lord of Hosts can permit such a people,' said Shannow.

'Read your Bible, Jon. Study the Assyrians, the Babylonians, the Egyptians and the Greeks. Even the Romans. And what of the Philistines, the Moabites and the Edomites? Without evil, there is no counterpoint to goodness.'

'Too deep for me, Karitas. I am a simple man.'

'I wish that I was,' said Karitas with feeling.

For much of the day Shannow chopped firewood, using a long axe with a six-pound head. His back ached, but by dusk he was satisfied that his strength was returning with speed.

That night he dreamt once more of the Hellborn. This time they raided the Carns and the slaughter was terrible to behold, the blue- and yellow-streaked savages caught in a murderous crossfire. Hundreds died and only a few escaped into the snow-covered woods.

At midnight Shannow was awakened by a light tapping at his door. He opened it and saw Curopet standing in the moonlight, a blanket around her slender form.

Shannow stepped aside to allow her in and pushed shut the door. She ran to the fire and added kindling to the coals.

'What is it, Curopet?'

'I am going to die,' she whispered.

Her face was strained and she was close to tears as Shannow moved to kneel beside her in the firelight.

'Everyone dies,' said Shannow, at a loss.

'Then you have seen it too, Thunder-maker?'

'Seen what?'

'The horned ones attacking our village.'

'No. The Carns have been attacked. Tonight.'

'Yes, the Carns,' she said dully. 'I dreamt of that two nights ago. I am to die. No children for Curopet. No man through the long winter nights. We are all to die.'

'Nonsense. The future is not set in stone; we make our own destinies,' said Shannow, pulling her to him. The blanket slid away from her shoulders as she moved towards him and he saw that she was naked, her body glowing in the dancing light of the blaze.

'Do you promise me that I will live?' she asked.

'I cannot promise, but I will defend you with my life.'

'You would do that for me?'

'Yes.'

'And I am not your wife?'

'No. But you are close to me, Curopet, and I do not desert my friends in their need.'

Curopet snuggled into him, her breasts pushing against the bare skin of his chest. Shannow closed his eyes and drew back.

'Let me stay?' she asked and he nodded and stood. She went with him to his blankets and together they lay entwined. Shannow did not touch her and she slept with her body pressed close to him and her head on his breast. Shannow slept not at all.

In the morning Shannow was summoned with all warriors to the long cabin where Karitas sat on a high chair, the only chair in the village. The warriors – thirty-seven in all, counting Shannow – sat before him.

Karitas looked tired and gaunt. When everyone was seated, he spoke.

'Five of our ESPer women have seen an attack on us by the Hellborn. We cannot run and we cannot hide. All our stores are here. Our lives are here. And we cannot fight, for they have thunder-guns and are many.' He fell silent and leaned forward, resting his arms on his knees, his head bent and eyes staring at the floor.

'Then we are to die?' asked a warrior. Shannow glanced at the man; he was stocky and powerful and his eyes glowed fiercely.

'It would appear that way, Shonal. I can think of nothing.'

'How many are they?' asked Shonal.

'Three hundred.'

'And all with thunder-guns?'

'Yes.'

'Why should they attack us?' questioned another man.

'It is their way.'

'Could we not send someone to them?' suggested a third man. 'Tell them we will be their friends – offer to share our food?'

'It will avail us nothing; they are killers and drinkers of blood. They have wiped out the Carns and we are next.'

'We must find their camp,' said Shannow, standing and turning to face the men. 'It is Winter and they must have tents and food stores. We will burn their tents, destroy their stores and kill many. Perhaps then they will be driven back to their homelands until the Spring.'

'And will you lead us, Thunder-maker?'

'Indeed I will,' promised the Jerusalem Man.

With sombre faces the men left the cabin to prepare their weapons and bid farewell to their wives and children. Shannow remained with Karitas.

'Thank you,' said the old man, his head still bowed.

'You owe me no thanks, Karitas.'

'I know you think me a little mad, but I am not stupid, Jon. There is no victory to be gained here. You have made a noble gesture, but my people will still die.'

'Nothing is certain,' Shannow told him. 'When I rode the hills I saw a number of shallow caves. Fetch the women and children, and as many stores as they can carry, and take them there. Cover your tracks where you can.'

Karitas looked up. 'You believe we have a chance?'

'It depends on whether this is an invasion or a raid.'

'That I can tell you. It is the ritual of the Blood Feast, where newly-ordained warriors gain their battle honours.'

'You know a great deal about them, old man.'

'Indeed I do. The man who leads them calls himself Abaddon and I used to know him well.'

'It is a name from the Book,' said Shannow sharply. 'An obscenity named in Revelation as the leader of the Devil's forces.'

'Yes. Well, in those days he was simply Lawrence Welby – a lawyer and a socialite. He organized curious parties, with nubile young women. He was witty, urbane and a Satanist. He followed the teachings of a man called Crowley, who preached, "Do what thou wilt is the whole of the law." Like me he survived the Fall, and like me he appears to be immortal. He believes he is the Anti-Christ.'

'Maybe he is,' said Shannow.

'He had a wife back then, a wonderful woman – like light and dark they were. I was a little in love with her myself; still am, for that matter.'

'What happened to her?'

'She became a goddess, Shannow.'

'Will Abaddon be with the raiders?'

'No, he will be in Babylon. They will be led by seasoned officers, though. I cannot see how my few people can oppose them – do you have a plan?'

'Yes. I shall prime my weapons and then I shall pray.'

'I think you have your priorities right, at least,' commented Karitas.

'They are only men, Karitas. They bleed, they die. And I

cannot believe the Lord of Hosts will allow them to succeed.'

As Shannow rose to leave, Karitas stopped him. He took the Stone from his pouch and offered it to the taller man.

'Without it you may die. Take it with you.'

'No, keep it here – you may need its powers.'

'It is almost used up, Shannow. You see, I refuse to feed it.'

'How do you feed a stone?'

'With blood and death.'

'Do not worry about me, Karitas. I will survive. Just get your people into the hills and keep that pistol primed.'

Shannow returned to his hut and loaded his three spare cylinders, stowing them in his greatcoat pockets. Then he took the Bible from his saddlebag and turned to Jeremiah:

'Thus, saith the Lord, Behold, a people cometh from the north country and a great nation shall be raised from the sides of the earth. They shall lay hold on bow and spear; they are cruel, and have no mercy; their voice roareth like the sea, and they ride upon horses, set in array as men for war against thee . . .'

Shannow set aside the Section and closed his eyes. In the distance thunder rolled across the heavens.

He rose and left the hut, his saddle on his right shoulder. In the open ground beyond, thirty of the warriors awaited him with set faces; their quivers full of arrows.

'I will ride out and scout the land. Follow my tracks and wait for me where you see this sign.' He made the sign of the cross with his arms and then walked past them to the paddock.

Shannow headed east and did not once look back to see the warriors in single file loping behind him.

The country was open and in places snow had drifted to a depth of more than ten feet. The gelding skirted the drifts and headed on towards the high ground and the distant timber line of the Carns' territory. Shannow had seen the attack on the Carns' village, and he guessed that the

Hellborn would camp there overnight. If he was right they now had two options: they could rest for the day at the site of their victory, or they could ride on immediately towards Karitas' village. If the former, Shannow's small band stood a chance. If the latter, then the two parties would meet on open ground and the villagers would be massacred.

The day was icy cool and a breeze was blowing from the north. Shannow shivered and gathered his coat at the collar. The gelding pushed on through the morning and the distant trees grew steadily closer.

The crack of a pistol echoed in the air and Shannow drew on the reins and scanned the trees. He could see nothing, and the distance was too great for the shot to have been aimed at him. Warily he rode on. Several more shots sounded from the woods – the Hellborn were hunting the last of the Carns. Shannow grinned. The first danger was past.

At the foot of the last rise before the woods, Shannow dismounted. He gathered two sticks and tied them in a cross which he thrust into a snowdrift; it would be many hours before fresh falls of snow would cover it. Then he guided the gelding up the rise and into the trees.

A blue- and yellow-streaked figure hurtled from the snow-covered bushes, saw Shannow, screamed and fell as he attempted to change the course of his flight. Then a horse leapt the bush. Shannow's pistol fired as the animal landed and the helmed rider catapulted from the saddle. Shannow cocked the pistol and waited, ignoring the cowering Carn who was gazing open-mouthed at the dead Hellborn. The rider was obviously alone and Shannow dismounted, tying the gelding's reins to a bush. He approached the corpse; the rider could not have been more than fifteen years of age – and a handsome boy, even with the round hole in his forehead. Shannow knelt beside him, lifting the boy's pistol. As Karitas had shown him, it was loaded with cartridges. Shannow opened the rider's hip pouch; there were more than twenty bullets there and he transferred them to his own pockets before thrusting the boy's pistol in his belt. Then he turned to the Carn.

'Can you understand me?' asked Shannow.

The man nodded.

'I have come to kill the Hellborn.'

The man edged close and spat into the dead rider's face.

'Where is your camp?' asked Shannow.

'By tall rocks,' answered the savage, pointing north-east.

Shannow tethered the rider's horse beside his own and moved forward on foot towards the north-east.

Three times riders came close to him, and twice he stumbled across the bodies of dead Carns. After an hour he found a steep path winding down into a sheltered glen. There he could see the huts of the Carns, a picket line and more than two hundred horses. The Hellborn were wandering freely around the camp, stopping at cooking fires or talking in groups around larger blazes.

Shannow studied the area for some time and then eased his way back into the trees. Every so often a pistol shot caused him to freeze and drop to the ground, but he made his way back to his horse unobserved. The Carn had gone – but not before ripping out the eyes of the dead Hellborn . . . The boy did not look handsome now. Shannow was cold and he sheltered behind the horses, huddled against a bush, waiting for the villagers. After an hour he moved to the edge of the trees and saw the group waiting stoically by the cross. One of them looked up and saw him, and he waved them to join him.

Shonal was the first to arrive. 'They are camped?' he asked.

'Yes.'

'When do we attack?'

'After midnight.' Shonal nodded.

Shannow spotted Selah in the group and summoned him. 'You should be back at the village.'

'I am a man, Thunder-maker.'

'So was he,' said Shannow, pointing to the corpse.

By dusk the pistol shots had ceased to sound and Shannow had begun to believe he was freezing to death. The villagers seemed not to notice the cold, and he cursed his ageing bones.

The moon rose in a clear sky and towards midnight the bushes by Shannow's head parted and a warrior stepped into sight. Shannow rolled, his right-hand pistol sweeping up. The man was a Carn and he squatted beside Shannow.

'I kill Hellborn also,' he said.

The villagers were alarmed. Many had weapons in their hands and several bows were bent and aimed at the newcomer. Shannow sheathed his pistol.

'You are welcome,' he said.

The Carn lifted his hands to his lips and blew a soft humming note. All around them Carn warriors appeared, armed with knives and hatchets. Shannow could not count them in the dim light, but guessed there to be twice as many Carns as villagers.

'Now we kill Hellborn, yes?'

'No,' replied Shannow. 'We wait.'

'Why wait?' asked the warrior.

'Many are still awake.'

'Good. We follow you.'

Shannow found the man's pointed teeth disconcerting. Shonal crept to his side.

'This is not right,' he whispered, 'to sit thus with Carns.'

The Carn leader hissed and spat, his hand curling round his knife-hilt.

'That's enough,' said Shannow. 'You may resume your war at a later time – one enemy is enough for today.'

'I will follow you, Thunder-maker. But this turns my stomach.'

'He probably feels the same, Shonal. Be patient.'

At midnight Shannow called the two leaders to him.

'They will have posted guards, and if they are disciplined they will change the guard some time soon. We must wait until the sentries are relieved and then kill those who remain. It must be silent – no screams, no shouts; no war-cries. Once the shooting starts you must flee. Bows and knives are no match for guns. You understand me?' Both leaders nodded.

'Also, we must steal as many of their horses as we can. Shonal, have Selah and several of the younger men assigned to that task. Tell them to head the horses west and wait for us about a mile away.'

'What do we do when we have killed the sentries?' asked Shonal.

'We walk into the camp and kill them as they sleep. As each man dies, take his pistol and keep it ready. You know how to fire a pistol?' Both men shook their heads and Shannow drew his own weapon and eased back the hammer. 'Like this; then you point it and pull the trigger, here.'

'I understand,' said Shonal.

'I also,' whispered the Carn.

'Good. Now take your best warriors and seek out the sentries. There should be four but there might be six, all around the camp perimeter. When you have killed them all, return here with their pistols.'

The Carn slid away and Shonal remained. 'It seems . . . unnatural,' he whispered.

'I know.' The villager vanished into the darkness.

Now began the long wait and Shannow's nerves were strained to the limits. Every minute that passed he expected to hear a pistol shot or a scream. After what seemed an age, the blue-yellow Carn leader appeared through the bushes.

'Eight men,' he said, holding up two pistols, both cocked.

'Be careful,' said Shannow, gently pushing the barrels away from his face.

He pushed himself to his feet and his left knee cracked with a sound he felt rivalled the earlier thunder.

'Old bones,' said the Carn, shaking his head. Shannow scowled at him and moved off, the warriors following silently. They arrived at the camp just as the moon vanished behind a cloud. Shannow squatted on the rise above the huts with Shonal and the Carn beside him.

'Split your men into groups of six. It is important that we enter as many huts as possible at the same time. All the men with guns will fade back to that point there, by the stream. Now at some point someone will wake, or scream, or shoot. When that happens, run into the woods. Then the men with guns will open fire. But remember that each pistol only fires six times. You understand?' Both men nodded, but Shannow ran through the strategy twice more to ram it home.

Then he drew his hunting knife and the warriors moved silently down the hill. Starting at the southern end of the village, they split into groups and entered the huts.

Shannow waited outside, eyes scanning the doorways and windows of the other dwellings. Gurgling cries came to him and some sounds of scuffling, but these were muted and the warriors emerged from the huts bathed in blood.

Dwelling by dwelling, the avengers moved on and the night breeze brought the stench of death to Shannow's nostrils. He sheathed his unblooded knife and drew his pistols; their luck could not hold out much longer.

By the sixteenth hut Shannow's nerves were at breaking point.

Then disaster struck. A warrior dragged back the hammer of a captured pistol while his finger was upon the trigger and the shot echoed around the camp. In an instant all was chaos as men surged into the night.

Shannow raised his pistols and rained shots into the milling crowd. Men fell screaming, and other pistols flared in the darkness. A shot from behind whistled past his ear and he turned to see a tribesman vainly seeking to re-cock his weapon. A bullet smashed the Carn from his feet. Shannow fired his left-hand pistol and a Hellborn warrior toppled to the ground, his head crashing into the coals of the dying fire. With a flash his hair caught light and blazed around his face.

'Back!' shouted Shannow, but his voice was lost in the thunder of shots. He emptied his pistols into the ranks of the Hellborn and then sheathed them, drawing the captured weapon from his belt. He ran back towards the stream, where at least a dozen warriors had remembered his commands. Elsewhere in the camp the Carns had charged the Hellborn and were in amongst them, shooting their pistols point-blank but hampering Shannow's force.

'Back into the trees,' Shannow ordered, but the men

continued to fire at the milling mob. 'Back, I say!' said Shannow, backhanding a man in the face. Hesitantly the warriors obeyed.

Shots screamed by Shannow as he ran, but none came close. At the top of the rise he stood with his back to a tree, breathing hard. Thrusting the captured revolver back in his belt, he took his own pistols and added fresh cylinders.

Shonal came alongside him. 'Most of our men are here, Thunder-maker.'

'What of the horses?'

'I could not see.'

'Without horses they will hunt us down before we are half-way home.'

'Selah will have done what he can; the boy is no coward.'

'All right,' said Shannow. 'Get your men out of the woods and head for home. If Selah has done his work well, there should be horses around a mile away. If there are, do not ride straight for the village but head north and then swing back when you reach firmer ground. Try to cover your tracks – and pray for snow.'

Shonal grinned suddenly. 'Many dead Hellborn,' he stated.

'Yes. But was it enough? Go now.'

Shannow reached his horse and mounted, wrenching free the reins. A Carn, whom he recognized as the leader, loomed out of the darkness. 'I am Nadab,' he said holding out his hand.

Shannow leaned forward and gripped the man's wrist.

'No more war with the Corn People,' said the Carn.

'That is good.'

'Shame,' corrected the man, grinning. 'They taste good!'

'Good luck,' said Shannow.

'We killed many, Thunder-maker. You think they run now?'

'No.'

'I also. It is the end of things for us.'

'All things must end,' said Shannow. 'Why not come west, away from here?'

'No. We will not run. We are of the blood of the Lion and

we will fight. We have many thunder-guns now.'

Shannow reached into his pocket, producing a cartridge.

'The thunder-guns fire these,' he said, 'and you must gather these from the bodies. Pass me your pistol.' Shannow took the weapon and flicked open the breech, emptying the spent shells one by one. Then he reloaded the weapon and handed it back.

Swinging the horse's head, Shannow rode to the west.

The Carn watched him go, then cocked the pistol and headed back towards his village.

Chapter Five

Shannow rode south for an hour before swinging his horse to the north-west. He did not know how many Hellborn had been killed in the night, and now he did not care; he was bone-tired and his muscles ached. He rubbed at his eyes and rode on. Once he could have gone for three days without sleep. But not now. After another hour Shannow began to doze in the saddle. Around him the snow was falling, the temperature dropping. Ahead was a grove of pine trees and he steered the gelding in amongst them.

Dismounting near a group of young saplings, he took a ball of twine from his saddlebag. Painstakingly he pulled the saplings together, tying them tightly and creating the skeleton of a tepee. Moving slowly so as not to sweat too heavily, he gathered branches and wove them between the saplings to create a round hut, open at the top. Then he led the gelding inside and packed snow over the branches until a solid wall surrounded him. Only then did he prepare a fire. His fingers were numb with cold and the snow fell faster, adding to the walls of his dwelling. Once the fire was under way, he left the shelter and gathered dead wood, piling it across the opening. By dusk he felt strong enough to allow himself to sleep; he added three large chunks of wood to the fire, wrapped himself in his blankets and lay down.

Far off the sound of gunfire echoed in the air and his eyes flickered open, but closed again almost immediately.

He slept without dreams for fourteen hours and awoke to a dead fire, but the snow had covered his shelter completely and he remained snug and warm in his blankets. He started a fresh fire and sat up. From his saddlebags he took some oatcakes, sharing them with the gelding.

By midday he was once more in the saddle and heading for the village. He arrived to see a smoking ruin and rode on towards the hills, his pistol in his hand.

By late afternoon he approached the caves and saw the bodies. His heart sank and he dismounted. Inside the women and children of the Corn People lay frozen in death. Shannow blinked hard and backed away. By the cave mouth he found Curopet, her eyes open, staring up at the sky. Shannow knelt beside her and closed her eyes.

'I am sorry, Lady,' he said. 'I am so sorry.'

He walked away from the corpses and remounted, steering the gelding down towards the plain.

Here, nailed to a tree with his arms spread, was Karitas. The old man was still alive, but Shannow could not free him for the nails were too deep. Karitas' eyes opened, and tears welled. Shannow looked away.

'They killed all my little ones,' whispered Karitas. 'All dead.'

'I'll try to find something to cut you loose.'

'No, I'm finished. They were looking for you, Shannow.'

'Why?'

'They had orders to seek you out. Abaddon fears you. Oh, Jon, they killed my little ones.'

Shannow drew his hunting knife and began to hack at the wood around Karitas' right hand, but it was tough and frozen and he could make no impression. Karitas began to weep and sob piteously. Shannow dropped his knife and put his hands on Karitas' face. He could not embrace him.

'Jon?'

'Yes, my friend.'

'Read me something from the Book.'

'What would you like to hear?'

'Psalm 22.'

Shannow fetched his Bible, found the passage and began to read: '*My God, My God, why hast thou forsaken me, why are thou so far from helping me, and from the words of my roaring . . .*' Shannow read on until he reached the verse: '*The assembly of the wicked have inclosed me: They pierced my hands and feet. I may tell all my bones: They look and stare upon me.*' Shannow stopped reading and the tears ran down his cheeks and dropped to the pages.

Karitas closed his eyes and his head fell forward. Shannow went to him and the old man rallied briefly, but Shannow watched the light of life go out of his bright eyes. He stumbled to his Bible and lifted it from the snow, brushing it clean. Returning to the old man, he read: '*The Lord is my Shepherd; I shall not want. He maketh me to lie down in green pastures: he leadeth me beside the still waters. He restoreth my soul. He leadeth me in the paths of righteousness for his name's sake. Yea, though I walk through the valley of the Shadow of Death I will fear no evil, for thou art with me . . .*' He could read no more.

Shannow screamed then in his anguish and his voice echoed in the hills. He fell to his knees in the snow and covered his face with his hands.

The boy Selah found him there at dusk, half-frozen and semi-coherent. He pulled him to his feet and took him to a small cave where he lit a fire. After a while Shannow slept. Selah led the horses into the cave and covered the Jerusalem Man with a blanket.

Shannow awoke in the night. Selah was sitting staring into the fire.

'Where are the men?'

'All dead,' Selah said.

'How?'

'I took the horses as you said and headed them west. Shonal and the others joined me there and we went north, as you ordered. There we ran into another group of Hellborn, they must have split up and attacked our women, even as we were attacking their camp. They caught us in the open ground and their guns cut into us, I was at the back, and I wheeled my horse and ran like a coward.'

'Dying is a poor way of proving your courage, Selah.'

'They have destroyed us, Thunder-maker. All my people are gone.'

'I know, boy. There are no words to ease the grief.'

'Why? Why would they just kill? There is no reason.

Even the Carns killed for food. Why should these Hellborn cause such pain?'

'There is no answer,' said Shannow. 'Get some sleep, lad. Tomorrow we will set out to find my people.'

'You will take me with you?'

'If you would like to come.'

'Will we hunt the Hellborn?'

'No, Selah. We will avoid them.'

'I want to kill them all.'

'I can understand that, but one man and a boy cannot change the face of the world. One day they will lose. God will not allow them to persevere and prosper.'

'Your God did not protect my people,' said Selah.

'No, but he kept you alive. And me.'

Shannow lay back, pillowing his head on his arms and staring at the fire shadows on the ceiling of the cave. He recalled Karitas' warning that the Hellborn were looking for him and puzzled at it. Why? What had he done to make them hunt him? Why should an army seek him?

He closed his eyes and drifted into sleep, dreaming that he floated above a great building of stone at the centre of a dark, drear city. Sounds like great hammers upon giant anvils boomed in the night and crowds milled around taverns and squares. Shannow floated down to the stone building and saw statues of horned and scaled demons beside a long stairway leading up to doors of oak. He moved up the stairway, passing through the closed doors and into a hall lined with carved shapes of dragons and lizards. A circular staircase led to an observatory where a long telescope pointed to the stars and several men in red robes were working with quill and parchment. Shannow floated by them. At another door two guards stood, holding rifles across their chests. Passing them, he entered a room lit with red candles.

Here sat a man studying maps. He was handsome, with dark hair greying at the temples. His nose was long and straight, his mouth full and sensual and his eyes grey and humorous.

He was wearing a white shirt, grey trousers and shoes of

snakeskin. He stiffened as Shannow floated behind him, and rose.

'Welcome, Mr Shannow,' he said, turning and staring directly up at him. His eyes were mocking now, and Shannow felt fear rising towards terror as a dark cloud coalesced around the man and rose towards him. The Jerusalem Man moved back and the cloud took form; a huge bloated head, horned and scaled, and a cavernous mouth rimmed with pointed teeth gaped before him. Arms grew from the cloud and taloned fingers reached out towards him . . . He fled to his body and awoke sweating, jerking up from his blankets and stifling a scream. His eyes swept around the cave past the sleeping Selah and the two horses. Fighting down his panic, Shannow drew his right-hand pistol from the scabbard beside his head. The gun was cold in his hand.

He lay back and closed his eyes and instantly the demon was upon him, its talons tearing at him. Again he awoke, shaking with terror. Calming himself, he prayed long and earnestly; then he sheathed his pistol, crossed his arms and slept.

Once more he was above the stone building with the demon racing towards him. He raised his hands and two shining swords appeared there. He sped towards the demon and the swords flashed into its bloated body. Talons ripped at him but he ignored them, slashing and cutting in a maniacal frenzy. The beast was forced back, and in its blood-red eyes Shannow saw the birth of fear. Rearing up, the Jerusalem Man plunged his swords into its face. Smoke writhed up from the wounds and the beast disappeared.

In its place floated the handsome man wearing a robe of purest white.

'I underestimated you, Mr Shannow,' he said.

'Who are you?'

'I am Abaddon. You should know the name.'

'The name is in the Book of Revelation,' said Shannow. 'The angel of the bottomless pit. You are not he – you are merely a man.'

'Who is to say, Mr Shannow? If a man does not die, then

he is divine. I have lived for three hundred and forty-six years, thanks to the Lord of this World.'

'You serve the Serpent,' stated Shannow.

'I serve the One who Conquered. How can you be such a fool, Mr Shannow? Armageddon is over, and where is the New Jerusalem? Where does the wolf sit down with the lamb? Where does the lion eat straw like the cattle? Nowhere, Mr Shannow. The world died and your God died with it. You and I are the opposite extremes of the new order. My land flourishes; my armies can conquer the world. And you? You are a lonely man wandering the world like a shadow, unwelcome and unwanted – just like your God.'

Shannow felt the weight of truth bear down on him like a rock, but he said nothing.

'Lost for words, Mr Shannow? You should have listened to old Karitas. He had the chance to join me over a century ago, but he preferred to live in the woods like some venerated hermit. Now he is dead, quite poetically so – and his grubby people died with him. You will be next, Mr Shannow, unless you would prefer to join the Hellborn?'

'There is no inducement under the stars which could tempt me to join you,' answered Shannow.

'Is there not? What about the life of Donna Taybard?'

Shannow blinked in shock and drew back. The handsome man laughed.

'Oh, Mr Shannow, you are truly not worth my enmity. You are the gnat in the ear of the elephant. Go away and die somewhere.' He lifted his hand and Shannow was catapulted away at dizzying speed.

He awoke and groaned. Reaching for his Bible, by the dawn light he searched in vain for a passage to lift the rock from his soul.

Shannow and Selah rode from the lands of the Corn People, heading north across a great plain. For weeks they rode, and camped in sheltered hollows, seeing no sign of man. Shannow remained silent and subdued and Selah respected his solitude. The young man would sit in the evenings watching Shannow pore over his Bible, seeking guidance and finding none.

One night Shannow put aside his Book and leaned back, staring at the stars. The horses were hobbled nearby and a small fire blazed brightly.

'The age of miracles is past,' said Shannow.

'I have never seen a miracle,' replied Selah.

Shannow sat up and rubbed his chin. Their diet had been meagre for over a week and the Jerusalem Man was gaunt and hollow-eyed.

'A long time ago the Lord of Hosts split a sea asunder so that his people could cross it as dry land. He brought water from rocks, and he sent his Angel of Death against the enemy. In those days his prophets could call upon him and he would grant them dazzling powers.'

'Maybe he is dead,' said Selah. 'Or sleeping,' he added swiftly, seeing the glare in Shannow's eyes.

'Sleeping? Yes, perhaps he is sleeping. Curopet came to me and said she would die. "No man for Curopet through the long winter nights." I wanted to save her, I wanted so much to be able to say, "There, Curopet, the nightmare has been proved false." I prayed so hard.' He fell silent and sat staring at his hands.

'We did what we could,' said Selah. 'We killed many Hellborn.'

'Rocks in the lake,' muttered Shannow. 'Perhaps she was right. Perhaps it is all predestined and we stalk through life like puppets.'

'What does it matter, Thunder-maker? As long as we do not know.'

'It matters to me; it matters desperately to me. Just once I would like to feel that I have done something for my God; something for which I can feel pride. But his face is turned from me and my prayers are like whispers in the wind.'

Shannow wrapped himself in his blankets and slept fitfully.

By mid-morning they spotted a small herd of antelope. Shannow kicked the gelding into a run and brought down a young doe with a shot to the heart. Dismounting, he cut the beast's throat, standing back as the blood drained into the soft earth. Then he skinned and quartered the doe and the two riders feasted well.

Two days later Shannow and Selah came out of the plain into an area of wooded hills.

To the north was a mountain range taller than any Shannow had ever seen, rearing up into the low scudding clouds. The mountains lifted Shannow's spirits, and he told Selah he would like to see them at close range.

The colour drained from the boy's face. 'We cannot go there,' he whispered. 'It is death, believe me.'

'What do you know of this place?'

'All the ghosts gather there. And monsters who can devour a herd of buffalo at a single sitting – the earth shakes when they move. My father came close to this place many years ago. No one travels there.'

'Believe me, Selah, I have travelled widely; I have seen few monsters and most of those were human in origin. I am going there.'

Shannow touched his heels to the gelding's sides and rode on without a backward glance, but Selah remained where he was – his eyes fearful, his heart pounding. Shannow had saved his life, and Selah regarded himself as a debtor; he needed to repay the Jerusalem Man in order to be freed from obligation. Yet every ounce of his being screamed against this venture, and the two opposing forces of his intellect and his emotions left him frozen in the saddle.

Without turning, Shannow lifted his hand and beckoned the boy to join him. It was all Selah needed to swing the balance and he kicked his horse into a run and rode alongside the Thunder-maker.

Shannow grinned and slapped him on the shoulder. It was the first time Selah had seen him smile in weeks. Was it a form of madness, Selah wondered? Did the prospect of danger and death somehow bring this man to life?

They rode along a deer trail that wound high into the hills where the air was fresh with the smell of pine and new grass. A lion roared in the near distance and Selah could picture it leaping upon its prey, for the roar had been the blood-freezing attack cry which paralysed the victim. Selah's horse shied and he calmed it with soft words. A shot followed, echoing in the hills. Shannow's Hellborn pistol appeared in his hand and he steered his gelding towards the sound. Selah tugged Shannow's percussion pistol from his own belt and followed but he did not cock the pistol, nor had he handled it since Shannow gave it to him on the morning they left Karitas' grave. The weapon terrified him and yet gave him strength, and he kept it in his belt more as a talisman than a death-dealing thunder-maker.

Selah followed Shannow over a steep rise and down a slope towards a narrow glen. Ahead the boy could see a man on the ground, a black-maned lion straddling him. The man's right hand was gripping the lion's mane, holding its jaws from ripping his throat, while his left hand plunged a knife time and again into the beast's side.

Shannow galloped alongside, dragged on the reins and, as the gelding reared, fired a shot into the lion's head. The animal slumped over the body of his intended victim and the man pulled himself clear. His black leather trousers were torn at the thigh and blood was seeping through; his face had been deeply cut and the flesh hung in a dripping fold over his right cheek. Pushing himself to his feet, he sheathed his knife. He was a powerful man with wide shoulders and a deep chest and he sported a forked black trident beard.

Ignoring his rescuers, he staggered to a spot some yards away and retrieved his revolver, which he placed in a leather scabbard at his side. He stumbled, but recovered and turned at last to Shannow.

'It was a fine shot,' he said, 'though had it been a fraction off it would have killed me rather than the lion.'

Shannow did not reply, and Selah saw his gun was still in his hand and trained on the wounded man. Then the boy saw why. To the man's right was his helm, and upon it were the goat's horns of the Hellborn.

Suddenly the man staggered and pitched to the ground. Selah sprang from his horse and ran to him. The wound in the thigh was gushing blood and Selah drew his knife and cut away the trouser-leg, exposing a deep rip almost a foot long.

'We must stop this bleeding,' he told Shannow, but the Jerusalem Man remained on his horse. 'Give me needle and thread,' said Selah. Shannow blinked, then reached into his saddlebag and passed a leather pouch to the boy.

For almost an hour Selah worked on the wounds, finally pushing back the folds of skin on the man's cheek and stitching them in place. Meanwhile Shannow had dismounted and unsaddled their horses. He said nothing, but prepared a fire within a circle of stones, having first ripped away the grass around it. Selah checked the wounded man's pulse; it was weak, but steady.

He joined Shannow by the fire, leaving the man wrapped in his blankets.

'Why?' asked Shannow.

'Why what?'

'Why did you save him?'

'I do not understand,' said Selah. 'You saved him by killing the lion.'

'I did not then know what he was . . . what he is.'

'He is a man,' stated Selah.

'He is your enemy, boy. He may even have been the man who killed Curopet, or nailed Karitas to the tree.'

'I shall ask him when he wakes.'

'And what will that tell you?'

'If he did attack my village, I shall tend him until he is well and then we will fight.'

'That is nonsense, boy.'

'Perhaps, but Karitas always taught us to follow our feelings, most especially compassion. I want to kill the Hellborn – I said that on the day we found our people. But this is different, this is one brave man who fought a lion with only a knife. Who knows, he might have won without you.'

Shannow shook his head. 'I don't understand. You went into the Hellborn camp and slew them while they slept. Where is the difference?'

'I did that to save my people. I failed. I have no regrets about the men I slew but I cannot slay this one – not yet.'

'Then step aside and I'll put a bullet in his ear.'

'No,' said the boy forcefully. 'His life is now mine, as mine is yours.'

'All right,' said Shannow. 'I will argue no more. Maybe he will die in the night. Did you at least take his gun?'

'No, he did not,' said a voice and Selah turned to see that the wounded man had raised himself on his elbow and his pistol was pointed at Shannow. The Jerusalem Man lifted his head, his eyes glittering in the firelight, and Selah saw that he was about to draw his own weapons.

'No!' he shouted, stepping between them. 'Put your pistol down,' he told the Hellborn.

Their eyes met and the man managed a weak smile. 'He's right, boy. You are a fool,' he said as slowly he uncocked the pistol and lay back. Selah swung towards Shannow, but the Jerusalem Man was walking away to sit on a rock some distance from the fire, his Bible in his hands. Selah, who normally left him alone at such times, approached him warily and Shannow looked up and smiled gently. Then, under the moon's silver light, he began to read. At first Selah had difficulty in understanding certain words, but overall the story fell into place. It seemed that a man was robbed and left for dead and that several people passed him by, offering no help. At last another man came and helped him, carrying him to a place of rest. This last man, Shannow explained, was from a people who were hated and despised.

'What does it mean, then?' Selah asked.

'I think it means that there is good in all men. Yet you have added a fresh twist to the parable, for you have rescued the Samaritan. I hope you do not come to regret it.'

'What is the Book?'

'It is the history of a people long dead, and it is the Word of God through the ages.'

'Does it give you peace, Shannow?'

'No, it torments me.'

'Does it give you power?'

'No, it weakens me.'

'Then why do you read it?'

'Because without it there is nothing but a meaningless existence of pain and sorrow, ending in death. For what would we strive?'

'To be happy, Shannow. To raise children and know joy.'

'There has been very little joy in my life, Selah. But one day soon I will taste it again.'

'Through your god?'

'No – through my woman.'

Batik lay back, feeling the pull of the stitches and the weakness he knew came from loss of blood. He had no idea why the boy wanted him saved, nor why the man had agreed to it. And yet he lived, and that was enough for now. His horse had reared when the lion roared and Batik had managed just one shot as it leapt. The shot had creased its side and then he had been catapulted from the saddle. He could not remember drawing his knife, but he recalled with brilliant clarity the arrival of the hard-eyed man on the steeldust gelding, and he had registered even as the gun was aimed that it was a Hellborn pistol.

Now, as he lay under the stars, it was no great work of the intellect to come up with the obvious answer: the man had been one of those who attacked Cabrik's Feasters some weeks back, killing over eighty young men in a single night . . . Which made his acquiescence in allowing Batik to live all the more curious.

While he was thinking, the boy Selah approached him. 'How are your wounds?'

'You did well. They will heal.'

'I am preparing some broth. It will help make more blood for you.'

'Why? Why do you do this for me?'

Selah shrugged, unwilling to enter debate.

'I was not in the attack on your village,' said Batik, 'though I easily could have been.'

'Then you tell me, Hellborn, why they wanted to kill my people?'

'Our priests could answer that better than I. We are the Chosen people. We are ordered to inhabit the lands and kill every man, woman and child we find. The priests say that this is to ensure the purity of our faith.'

'How can a babe in arms affect your faith?'

'I don't know. Truly. I never killed a babe or a child, though I saw it done. Ask our priests when you meet one.'

'It is a savagery beyond my understanding,' Selah said.

'My name is Batik,' said the man. 'And you?'

'Selah.'

'And your friend?'

'He is Shannow, the Thunder-maker.'

'Shannow. I have heard the name.'

'He is a great soul and a mighty warrior. He slew many of your people.'

'And now he is hunted in turn.'

'By you?'

'No,' said Batik. 'But the Lord Abaddon has declared him Unholy, and that means he must burn. Already the Zealots are riding – and they have great powers; they will find him.'

'When they do, Batik, he will slay them.'

Batik smiled. 'He is not a god, Selah. The Zealots will bring him down, even as they brought me down.'

'You are hunted?'

'I need some sleep. We will talk tomorrow.'

Batik awoke early, the pain from his wounds pulling him from a troubled sleep. Overhead the sky was clear and a black crow circled, banking and wheeling. He sat up, wincing as the stitches pulled at the wound to his face. Shannow was awake, sitting still in the dawn light and reading from a leather-covered book with gold-trimmed pages. Batik saw the tension in the man, and the way that his right hand rested barely inches from the pistol which lay beside him on the rock. Batik resisted the urge to smile; the stitches were too painful.

'You are awake early,' he said, lifting the blankets from his legs.

Shannow slowly closed the book and turned. His eyes met Batik's and the look was glacial. Batik's face hardened.

'I was hoping,' said Shannow tonelessly, 'that you would die in the night.'

Batik nodded. 'Before we enter into a prolonged debate on your views, perhaps you would care to know that we are being watched, and that within a short time we will be hunted.'

'There is no one watching us,' said Shannow. 'I scouted earlier.'

Batik smiled, in spite of the pain. 'You have no conception, Shannow, of the nature of the hunters. We are not talking about mere men. Those who hunt us are the Zealots and they ride under the name of the Hounds of Hell. If you look up, you will see a crow. It does not land, nor scavenge for food; it merely circles us, directing those that follow.

'The lion yesterday was possessed by a Zealot. It is a talent they have; it is why they are deadly.'

'Why would you warn me?' asked Shannow, flicking his eyes to take in the crow's flight.

'Because they are hunting me also.'

'Why should they?'

'I am not religious, Shannow, and I tried to ruin the midwinter offering. But all that is past. Just accept that I am – as you – an enemy to the Zealots.'

Selah groaned and sat up. On a rock, a reptilean creature with slavering jaws sat over the body of Shannow. Selah drew his pistol and cocked it. The monster's eyes turned on him, red as blood, as he pointed the pistol.

'What are you doing?' asked Shannow.

Selah blinked as the image shifted and blurred. His finger tightened on the trigger, but at the last second he twisted the barrel. The shot echoed in the hills and a shell whistled past Shannow's ear. Selah eared back the hammer for a second shot, but Batik had moved behind him. With a swift chop to the neck with the blade of his hand, Batik stunned the boy and retrieved the pistol.

Shannow had not moved. 'Is he all right?' he asked.

'Yes. The Zealots work well with the young, their minds are more malleable.'

Shannow drew his pistol and cocked it and Batik froze. The Jerusalem Man tipped back his head, his arm lifted and he fired. The crow exploded in a burst of flesh and feathers.

Shannow opened the pistol's breech, removed the spent casing and reloaded the weapon. Then he walked to Selah, kneeling by him and turning him over. The boy's eyelids fluttered and opened; he saw Shannow and jerked.

'You are dead!' he said, struggling to rise.

'Lie still, boy. I am fine.'

'I saw a monster over your body. I tried to scare it away.'

'There was no monster.' Shannow tried to explain, but the boy could not comprehend and Batik stepped in.

'It was magic, Selah. You were fooled by the hunters.'

'Magic?'

'Yes. They cast a spell that confused your eyes. It is unlikely they will try again through you – but they may. Be wary, and shoot at nothing.' He handed the pistol to the boy and then sagged back on the ground, his face gleaming with sweat.

Shannow watched him closely. 'You are a powerful man,' he said, 'but you lost a lot of blood. You need rest.'

'We cannot stay here,' said Batik.

'From which direction will they be coming?' asked Shannow.

'North-east,' said Batik. 'But do not go up against them, Shannow.'

'It is my way. How many are there?'

Batik shrugged. 'There could be six, or sixty. Whatever, they will travel in multiples of six; it is a mystic number.'

'Stay here and rest. I will return.'

Shannow walked to his saddle and hefted it, making his way towards the steeldust gelding which was hobbled some thirty feet from the camp. As Shannow approached he saw horse-flies settling on the gelding's hind quarters, yet the animal's tail was still. Shannow slowed his walk and the gelding dipped its head and watched him. Shannow approached the beast from the left and laid the saddle on its back, stooping to tighten the cinch. The gelding did not move and Shannow was sweating now. Gripping the bridle tightly in his right hand, he loosed the slip-knot hobbling the horse. As the rope fell away the gelding bunched its muscles to rear and Shannow grabbed the pommel and vaulted into the saddle. The gelding reared up and set off at a dead run, but Shannow manoeuvred his feet into the stirrups and held on. The gelding stopped and bucked furiously, but Shannow wrenched its head back towards the camp. Suddenly the horse rolled over; Shannow leapt from the saddle and, as the beast came upright, mounted swiftly.

At the camp Batik watched in admiration as the clash of wills continued. The horse bucked, jumped, twisted and rolled time and again, but always Shannow held on. As suddenly as it had started it was over and the gelding stopped, its head down and steam billowing from its nostrils. Shannow walked it back to the camp and dismounted, hobbling the animal once more. He unsaddled the beast and wiped it down, then stroked its neck and ears.

Hefting his saddle, he made his way to Selah's horse and without drama, saddled it and headed north-east.

Batik relaxed as Shannow crested the hill, and lay back on the grass.

'Whatever else, he is a fine rider.'

'He is the Thunder-maker,' said Selah with pride. 'He will return.'

'It would be pleasant to think so,' replied Batik, 'but he has never come up against the Zealots. I have seen their handiwork, and I am under no illusion as to their skill.'

Selah smiled and moved to the deer meat, hacking slices for the morning stew. Batik, he thought, was a clever man. But he had never seen Shannow in action.

Six miles to the north-east, a small group of riders drew rein and studied the hills ahead. The leader – a slender young man, hawk-nosed and dark-eyed – turned to his companion.

'Are you recovered?' he asked.

'Yes, Donai, but I am exhausted. How could he remain in the saddle? I all but killed the horse.'

'He rides well. I wish I knew more about him, and his connection with Batik.' Donai swivelled in the saddle, his gaze resting on the two corpses draped across their horses' backs. Xenon had possessed the lion, Cheros the crow. Both had been slain by the long-haired rider.

Donai dismounted. 'I will seek guidance,' he said. The other three riders sat in silence as their leader knelt on the grass with a round red-gold stone cupped in his hands. For some time he remained motionless. Then he rose.

'Achnazzar says that the man is Shannow, the Jerusalem Seeker. He is sending more men and we are to wait here.'

The men dismounted and removed their cloaks of black leather and their dark helms.

'Which six are they sending?' asked Parin, the youngest of the riders.

'They are sending six sections; I did not ask which,' replied Donai.

'Thirty-six men!' queried Parin. 'To tackle two men and a boy?'

'You wish to question Achnazzar's judgement?' asked Donai softly.

'No,' replied Parin swiftly.

'No,' agreed Donai, 'that is very wise. The man Shannow is a Great Evil and always there is strength in that. He is Unholy, and a servant of the old dark god. He must be destroyed. Achnazzar says he carries a Bible.'

'It is said that to touch a Bible burns the hand and scars the soul,' put in another rider.

'It could be, Karim. I don't know. Achnazzar says to kill the man and his horse, and to burn his saddlebags without opening them.'

'I have often wondered,' said Parin, 'how this Book survived Armageddon?'

'There is evil everywhere,' replied Donai. 'When the old dark god was destroyed, his body sundered and fell to the earth like rain, and where it touched it polluted the land.

Never be surprised at the places where evil dwells.'

'You can say that again,' said Karim, a lean middle-aged rider with a grey beard. 'I would have staked my life on Batik – there was no finer warrior among the Hellborn.'

'Your use of the word "fine" is questionable, Karim,' said Donai. 'The man was Unholy, but he hid the darkness within himself. But the Lord Satan has ways of illuminating the dark corners of the soul and I think it was no coincidence that Batik's sister was chosen for the midwinter sacrifice.'

'I believe that,' said Parin, 'but what did he hope to gain by asking Shalea to flee with him?'

'A good question, Parin. He underestimated the holiness of his sister. She was naturally proud to be chosen, and when his evil touched her she went straight to Achnazzar. A fine woman, who now serves the Lord!'

'But how could he underestimate her holiness?' persisted Parin.

'Evil is not logical. He thought she desired an earthly life and his blasphemy was his unbelief. He thought her doomed and sought to save her.'

'And now he is with the Jerusalem Man,' remarked Karim.

'Evil invites evil,' said Donai.

Towards noon, as the four riders ate an early meal, the sky darkened as heavy black-edged clouds masked the sun. Lightning forked in the east, and thunder cannoned deafeningly across the heavens.

'Mount up!' shouted Donai. 'We'll head for the trees.'

The men scrambled to their feet, moving towards their horses. Then Donai lifted his cloak and froze. Standing at the edge of their camp, his long coat flapping in the storm winds, was the long-haired rider. Donai dragged his pistol clear of its scabbard, but a white-hot hammer smashed into his chest and drove him back against his horse. Karim, hearing the shot, dived for the ground, but Parin and the other rider died where they stood as Shannow's pistols flowered in flame. Karim rolled and fired, his shot cutting Shannow's collar. The Jerusalem Man dropped to the grass and Karim fired twice more, but there was no return fire. Edging sideways, Karim hid behind Donai's body and closed his eyes. His spirit rose and entered the mind of his horse. From this high vantage point Karim scanned the area, but there was no sign of the attacker. He moved the horse's head and saw his own body lying behind Donai.

Shannow rose from the long grass behind Karim's body, his pistol pointed. Karim's spirit flew from the horse straight into Shannow's mind and the Jerusalem Man staggered as pain flooded his brain and bright lights exploded behind his eyes. Then darkness followed and Shannow found himself in a tunnel deep in the earth. Scuffling noises came to him and giant rats issued from gaping holes in the walls, their teeth as long as knives.

On the edge of panic Shannow closed his inner eyes, blocking the nightmare. He could feel the hot breath of the rats on his face, feel their teeth tearing at his skin. Slowly he opened his eyes, ignoring the huge rodents and looking beyond them. As if through a mist he could see horses and before them two bodies. Shannow lifted his hand and aimed his pistol.

The pistol became a snake that reared back, sinking its teeth into his wrist. Shannow ignored the snake and tightened his grip on the pistol butt he no longer felt. The gun bucked in his hand.

Karim fled for his body, arriving just as the second shell entered his skull. He twitched once and was still.

Shannow fell to his knees and looked around him. Four corpses littered the grass and two others were draped across two saddled horses. Shannow blinked.

'Do I not hate them, O Lord, that hate thee? And am I not grieved with those that rise up against thee? I hate them with a perfect hatred. I count them mine enemies.'

He gathered their weapons and ammunition and then searched the bodies. Each of the men carried a small stone, the size of a sparrow's egg, in a pouch around his neck. The stones were red-gold in colour and veined with black. Shannow pocketed them and then led the horses back to his own and returned to the camp-site.

Batik was huddled under his blankets as the rain doused the fire. Shannow called Selah to him.

'Let us get back to the trees and out of this weather,' he said, as the wind picked up and the sky darkened.

Batik did not move. 'What happened out there?' he called.

'I killed them. Now let's get out of the rain.'

'How many were there?'

'Four. Two others were already dead.'

'But how can I know that? How do I know you are still Shannow?' The blanket fell away and Shannow found himself staring down the muzzle of the Hellborn's pistol.

'How can I prove it to you?'

'Name your God.'

'Jehovah, Lord of Hosts.'

'And what of Satan?'

'The fallen star, the Prince of Lies.'

'I believe you, Shannow. No Hellborn could blaspheme like that!'

Beneath the spreading pine on the hillside, the strength of the rain lessened and Shannow struggled to light a fire. He gave up after some minutes and placed his back against a tree.

Batik sat nearby, his face grey, dark rings beneath his eyes. 'You are in pain?' asked Selah.

'A little. Tell me, Shannow, did you search the bodies?'

'Yes.'

'Did you find anything of interest?'

'What did you have in mind?'

'Small leather pouches, containing stones.'

'I took all six.'

'Let me have them, would you?'

'For what purpose, Batik?'

'My own was taken from me before I escaped and without it these wounds will take weeks to heal. It may be that I can use another.'

Shannow took the pouches from his greatcoat pocket and

dropped them into Batik's lap. One by one the Hellborn took the stones in his hand, closing his eyes in concentration. Nothing happened until he reached the fifth stone; it glowed briefly and Batik smiled.

'It was worth a try,' he said. 'But when you kill the man, you break the power. Still, it eased the pain before it faded.' He hurled the stones aside.

'Where do you get those things?' asked Shannow.

'They are birth gifts from Lord Abaddon; the size of the stone depends on your station. We call them Satanseeds.'

'Where are they from?'

'Who knows, Shannow? It is said that Satan delivers them to Abaddon at Walpurnacht, the Eve of Souls.'

'You believe that?'

'I disbelieve nothing – it's usually safer that way.'

Selah picked up a loose stone and twirled it in his hands.

'It's very pretty,' he said, 'and it feels warm to the touch – but I would prefer a fire.'

The wet kindling Shannow had set burst into flames and Selah leapt back, dropping the stone which glowed now like a lantern.

'Nicely done, boy,' said Batik. 'Now take the stone and hold it over my wounds.' Selah did as he was bid, but the glowing faded and the stone grew cold.

'Still we have a fire,' grunted Batik.

Shannow awoke with a start, his heart pounding. He sat up and looked around him. The cave was warm and snug and a fire blazed brightly against the far wall. He relaxed and settled back.

Cave?

He jerked upright and reached for his guns, but they were not with him. He had gone to sleep alongside Batik and Selah in a wood by a narrow stream. And he had awakened here, weaponless.

A shadow moved and a man approached the fire and sat down facing him.

It was the handsome, silver-templed Abaddon, Lord of the Hellborn.

'Do not be alarmed, Mr Shannow. I merely wished to talk.'

'We have nothing to talk about.'

'Surely not? With my hunters closing in?'

'Let them come.'

'Such arrogance, Mr Shannow. Think you to slay all my men with your pitiful pistols?'

Shannow said nothing and Abaddon warmed his hands at the fire. He was wearing a dazzling white robe which glistened gold in the firelight.

'A man, a boy and a traitor,' whispered Abaddon, 'set against a newborn nation of lusty warriors. It is almost comic.' His eyes met Shannow's. 'You know I have lived for almost as long as your friend, Karitas, and I have seen many things – both in my old world and in this new, squalling infant. There are no heroes, Mr Shannow. Ultimately we all compromise and secure for ourselves a little immortality, or a little wealth, or a little pleasure. There are no longer any Galahads; indeed, I wonder if there ever were.'

'I've never heard of a Galahad,' said Shannow.

'He was a Knight, Mr Shannow, a warrior who was said to fight for God. He never succumbed to women nor any pleasures of the flesh, and he was allowed to find the Holy Grail. It is a pleasant tale for children – though not Hellborn children.'

'What do you want from me?'

'I want you to die, Mr Shannow. To cease to be.'

'Why?'

'On a whim, perhaps. It has been said that you are a danger to me. I cannot see it, but I accept that the evidence suggests some truth to the fear.'

'You do not interest me,' said Shannow. 'You have nothing that I want. Where is the danger?'

'Who knows?' replied Abaddon, smiling smoothly. 'You are a thorn in my side and I need to pluck it out and throw it on the fire.'

'Then bring on your demons,' said Shannow, rising to his feet.

Abaddon chuckled and shook his head. 'I tried that, Mr Shannow, and you hurt me. Truly. But then what are my demons compared with yours?'

'I have no demons.'

'No? What drives you then to seek a buried city? Why do you cling to your superstitions? Why do you fight your lonely battles?'

'I will find Jerusalem,' said Shannow softly. 'Alive or dead, I will find my way home.'

'Home? What did you say to the delightful Fray Taybard? A rock in a lake? The ripples fade and all is as it was. Yes, you need to find a way home.' Abaddon lifted a stick and laid it gently on the fire. 'You know, Mr Shannow, many of my men are just like you – especially amongst the Zealots. They worship their god with a pure heart, and they would die gladly for him. Men like you are as leaves in the Autumn. You are a Bible-reading man – I am surprised you have not yet seen it.'

'There is nothing like the Hellborn in my Bible,' whispered Shannow.

'Mr Shannow! Is not lying a sin? I refer you to Joshua and the Israelite invasion of Canaan. Every man, woman and child in thirty-two cities was slain under the express orders of your god. How are the Hellborn different? Don't bother to answer; there is no difference. I founded the Hellborn two and a half centuries ago and I have built the nation along the same lines as Israel. I now have a fanatic army, and a people fired with a zeal you could not imagine. And they have had their miracles, their parting of the Red Sea, the healings and the unimaginable wonders of magic.

'In some ways your position is amusing. You are the man of god among a nation of devil worshippers. And yet you are the unholy one; you are the vampire in the night. Stories of you will one day be told to Hellborn children to keep them quiet in their beds.'

Shannow scowled. 'Everything you say is an obscenity.'

'Indeed it is – by your lights. By the way, did you know that Donna Taybard is now living on the edge of my lands?'

Shannow sat very still.

'She and her husband – a worthy man by the name of Griffin – have settled on the lands to the west. Good farmland. They could even prosper.'

'Why do you lie?' asked Shannon. 'Is it because your master is unable to face truth?'

'I do not need to lie, Mr Shannow. Donna Taybard, believing you dead, bedded down with Con Griffin. She is now pregnant, though she will not live to see her daughter born.'

'I do not believe you.'

'Of course you do, Mr Shannow. I gain no advantage by lying to you. Far from it. Had I left her as your white lady you would have raced to her side . . . and into my lands. Now you may decide to leave her be, and then I would have a merry job tracking you down.'

'Then why tell me?'

'To cause you pain.'

'I have been hurt before.'

'Of course you have, Mr Shannow. You are a loser and they always suffer. It is their lot in this world, as it was in mine. Your god does not bring you many gifts, does he? Have you not realized, Mr Shannow, that you follow a dead deity? That despite his propaganda and his awful book, he lost?'

Shannow raised his head and their eyes met. 'You are a fool, Abaddon, and I will not debate with you. You were right; Donna's betrayal hurts me. Deeply. Despite it I wish her only happiness, and if she has found it with Griffin then so be it.'

'Happiness?' sneered Abaddon. 'I am going to kill her, and her unborn child. She will be my sacrifice in two months. Her blood will flow on the Sipstrassi. How does that sit with you, Jerusalem Man?'

'As I said, you are a fool. Look into my eyes, Abaddon, and read the truth. As of this moment you are dead. Send your Zealots, send your demons, send your God – they will avail you nothing, for I will find you.'

'Just words,' said Abaddon, but the smile left his face. 'Come to me as soon as you can.'

'Count on it,' Shannow assured him.

Shannow awoke once more, and this time he was back at the camp-site by the stream. The fire had died to glowing ash and Batik and Selah were still asleep. Shannow rose and added sticks to the embers, blowing the fire to life. Then he sat, staring into the flames and seeing only Donna.

Vile as Abaddon undoubtedly was, there was no doubt in Shannow's mind that he had spoken the truth about Donna Taybard and Con Griffin. But he underestimated the Jerusalem Man's capacity for pain. His love for Donna had been too good; too joyful. Nothing in Shannow's life had ever been that easy. Other men mined pleasure as if it were an everlasting seam, their lives filled with smiles and easy happiness. Shannow panned in a pebble stream that yielded little and vanished swiftly.

And yet he was torn. A part of him wanted to ride swiftly to her, to kill Griffin and take her by force. An even darker thought was to ride, guns in hand, towards the Hellborn and die in a furious battle.

The sky lightened and the bird-song began in the trees. Batik stirred but did not wake. Shannow stood and wandered up a steep slope to scan the nearing northern mountains. Jagged they were and tall – piercing the clouds, like pillars supporting the sky.

Shannow could never have settled for farm life while the far mountains called him – while the lure of Jerusalem was hooked into his heart.

'I love you, Donna,' he whispered.

'It looks to be a fine day,' said Batik.

'I did not hear you approach.'

'It is a skill, Shannow. What are your plans?'

'I'm not sure. I saw Abaddon last night; he has threatened someone close to me.'

'Your woman?'

'No, not mine.'

'Then it is not your concern.'

'Not in the Hellborn philosophy,' said Shannow.

Batik sat down as Shannow outlined his conversation with the Hellborn king, and the background to it. He listened intently, seeing far more than Shannow intended.

'You cannot get to Abaddon, Shannow,' he said. 'I myself have rarely seen him. He is guarded by the Zealots and only occasionally ventures among the people. And anyway you say the caravan headed north-west, which puts the lands of the Hellborn between you and she. They are preparing for war, Shannow. The Hellborn army will not be turned aside by wagoners and farmers.'

'I cannot save her,' said Shannow, 'but I am pledged to destroy Abaddon.'

'It is not possible.'

'It may not be possible to succeed, it is certainly possible to try.'

'For what purpose? Are you the soul of the world?'

'I cannot explain it to you. Nor to any man. I cannot suffer evil, nor watch the wicked strong destroy the weak.'

'But the strong will always dominate the weak, Shannow. It is the nature of man and beast. You can be either the hunter or the hunted; there is no other choice, there is no neutrality. I doubt there ever was, even before the Fall.'

'I told you I could not explain it,' said Shannow, shrugging, but Batik was not to be diverted.

'Nonsense! At some time in your life you made a decision and weighed up the reasons for your actions. Be honest, man!'

'Honest? To a Hellborn? What do you know of honesty? Or love, or compassion? You were raised under Satan and you have drunk the blood of innocence. Reasons? Why does a farmer weed his land, or hunt wolves and lions? I hunt the wolves among men.'

'God's gardener?' sneered Batik. 'A sorry mess he must be in if you are all the force he can muster in this broken world.'

Shannow's hand flashed down and up and Batik found himself staring into the black, unwavering muzzle of a Hellborn revolver. He looked up into Shannow's eyes and saw the edge of madness lurking there.

'Insult me if you will,' hissed Shannow, 'but you will not denigrate my God. This is the only warning I give. Your next foulness will be your last.'

Batik grinned wolfishly. 'That's good, Shannow. That's very Hellborn – those who disagree with you die!'

Shannow blinked and uncocked the pistol. 'That is not the way I am,' he whispered, slumping down to sit beside Batik. 'I am not good in debate. My tongue stumbles into my teeth, and then I get angry. I am trapped, Batik, in a religion I can scarcely comprehend. In the Bible there are many passages I can follow, yet I am not a Christian. My Bible teaches me to smite the enemy hip and thigh, destroy him with fire and sword . . . it also teaches me to love my enemy and do good to him who hates me.'

'No wonder you are confused,' said Batik. 'But then I have long considered the possibility that Man is essentially insane. I believe in no god, and I am happier for it. I don't want eternal life. I want a little joy, a large amount of pleasure and a swift death once I lose the appetite for either.'

Shannow chuckled and his tension passed. 'I wish I could share that philosophy.'

'You can, Shannow; there is no charge.'

Shannow shook his head and looked towards the mountains.

'I shall go there,' he said, 'and then head west.'

'I'll stay with you as far as the mountains, then I head east.'

'You think that will take you out of reach of the Zealots?'

Before Batik could answer, the bushes to their left parted and a huge brown bear moved into the open. He saw the men sitting there and rose up on his hind legs, towering to almost eight feet. For some seconds he stood there, then he dropped to all fours and ambled away.

The two men sheathed their pistols.

'You are never out of reach of the Zealots, Shannow,' said Batik. Shannow let out a long juddering breath.

'I felt sure that they had possessed it.'

'Next time they probably will,' Batik assured him.

Chapter Six

Con Griffin was troubled. For most of the day he had worked hard on the new house, laying the foundation wall with care and measuring logs to interlace at the corners. Yet all the while he worked his eyes would flick to the skyline and the eternal watchers.

Since the first attack there had been no fresh violence – far from it, in fact. The following day six riders had approached the settlement. Once more Griffin had walked to meet them, covered by Madden and Burke, Mahler and five other men sporting rifles and guns taken from the dead raiders. The bodies had been removed to a field in the east and hastily buried.

The riders had entered the settlement without apparent fear and their leader, a slim young man with bright grey eyes, had approached Griffin smiling warmly.

'Good morning, my name is Zedeki.' He extended a hand. Griffin took it and engaged in a short perfunctory handshake.

'Griffin.'

'You are the leader here?'

Griffin shrugged. 'We don't think of ourselves as needing leaders. We are a group of farming men.'

Zedeki nodded and smiled. 'Yes, I understand. However, you do speak for the community, yes?'

'Yes.'

'Good. You were attacked last night by a group of renegades from our lands and this grieves us greatly. We apprehended the survivors, who were put to death immediately. We have come to offer our apologies for the incident.'

'No need for that,' Griffin told him. 'We dealt with it at

no loss to ourselves, and gained greatly by it.'

'You speak of the weapons,' said Zedeki. 'In fact they were stolen from our city and we would like them returned.'

'That is understandable,' said Griffin smoothly.

'Then you agree?'

'With the principle, yes. Stolen property should be returned to its owners.'

'Then we may take them?'

'Unfortunately there are other principles that must also be considered,' stated Griffin. 'But perhaps we could sit down and take refreshment?'

'Thank you.'

Griffin sat down on a felled tree and beckoned Zedeki to join him. The two men sat in silence for some minutes as Donna and two other women brought copper mugs filled with honey-sweetened herb tea. The other riders did not dismount, and looked to Zedeki before accepting refreshment.

'You mentioned other principles?' said Zedeki.

'Indeed I did, old lad. You see, where we come from there is a custom which says the spoils of war belong to the victor. Therefore most of the men here feel they have earned their new weapons. Secondly, there is the question of reparation. These raiders were your people – unless they also stole the clothes they were wearing. Therefore my people might feel entitled to some compensation for the terror inflicted on their wives and children, not to mention the cost of the operation in terms of spent ammunition and hard work preparing the tripwires and other devices which happily were not needed.'

'So, you are saying that our property will not be returned?'

'No, not at all, Zedeki. I am merely outlining possible objections to such a move. Not being the leader, I can make no prediction as to their individual reaction.'

'Then what *are* you saying?'

'I am saying that life is rarely simple. We like to be good neighbours, and we are hoping that we can trade with people living nearby. However, so far we have had few dealings with your people, so perhaps we should both sit back and study each other's customs for a while.'

'And then the weapons will be returned?'

'And then we will talk some more,' said Griffin, smiling.

'Mr Griffin, my people outnumber yours by perhaps a thousand to one. We are unaccustomed to being refused our desires.'

'But then I have not refused, Mr Zedeki. That would be presumptuous.'

Zedeki drained his tea and looked around the settlement. His soldier's eye took in the placements of some twenty felled trees which scattered the open ground. Each was positioned to provide cover for marksmen and planned in such a way that any raiding force, no matter from which direction they attacked, would come under a murderous cross-fire while their enemy would be firing from good cover.

'Did you organize these defensive positions?' asked Zedeki.

'No,' said Griffin. 'I'm just a humble wagon-master. We have several men here skilled in such matters, having dealt with all kinds of Brigands.'

'Well, let me thank you for your hospitality, Mr Griffin. I wonder if you would care to join me at my home? It is not a long ride, and perhaps we could discuss further the principles involved?'

Griffin's eyes narrowed, but he smiled with apparent warmth. 'That is indeed kind of you, and I am pleased to accept – but not at the moment. As you can see, we are currently building our own homes and it would be impolite of me to accept your hospitality without being able to respond in kind. You see, it is one of our customs – we always respond in kind.'

Zedeki nodded and stood. 'Very well. I will return when you are more . . . settled.'

'You will be welcome.'

Zedeki stepped into the saddle. 'When I return, I will be demanding our property.'

'New friends should not speak in terms of demands,'

replied Griffin. 'If you return peacefully, we can negotiate. If not, then some of your property will be returned to you at a speed you might not appreciate.'

'I think that we understand one another, Mr Griffin, but I do not believe you understand the strength of the Hellborn. We are not a few raiding Brigands, as you call them. We are a nation.'

As he rode away Madden, Burke and a score of the other men clustered around Griffin.

'What did you make of it, Griff?' asked Mahler, a short balding farmer whom Griffin had known for twenty years.

'It is trouble whichever way we look at it. I think we should move on to the west.'

'But this is good land,' argued Mahler. 'Just what we always wanted.'

'We wanted a home without Brigands,' said Griffin. 'What we have could be a hundred times worse. That man was right; we are outnumbered. You saw their armour – they are an army. They call themselves the Hellborn. Now I am not a religious man, but I don't like the name and I dread to think what it implies.'

'Well, I'm not running,' said Madden. 'I have put my roots here.'

'Nor I,' said Mahler. Griffin glanced around the faces of the other men to see all were nodding in agreement.

That night, as he sat with Donna Taybard under a bright moon, he felt despair settle on him like a cloak.

'I wanted Avalon to be a land of peace and plenty. I had a dream, Donna. And it is so close to being true. The Plague Lands – empty and open, rich and verdant. But now I'm beginning to see that the Plague Lands could earn their title.'

'You fought them off before, Griff.'

'I have a feeling they could return with a thousand men – should they choose.'

Donna moved closer and sat on his lap, draping her arm around his neck. Absently he rested his hand on her swollen belly and she kissed him lightly on the forehead.

'You'll think of something.'

He chuckled. 'You have great faith in . . .'

'. . . a humble wagon-master,' she finished for him.

'Exactly.'

But the attack he feared did not come to pass, and as the weeks drew by their homes neared completion. Yet every day the Hellborn riders crested the hills, sitting their dark mounts and watching the settlers. At first it was nerve-racking, but soon the families became used to the skylined riders.

A month had gone by before another incident alarmed the settlement. A young man named Carver had headed into the hills to hunt for fresh meat, but he did not return.

Madden found his body two days later. His eyes had been put out and his horse slain; all of his belongings were left untouched, but his Hellborn rifle was missing.

The following day Zedeki had returned, this time alone.

'I understand one of your men was killed,' he said.

'Yes.'

'There are some raiders in the hills and we are looking for them. It is best if your people stay in the valley for a time.'

'That will not be necessary,' stated Griffin.

'I should not like to see other deaths,' Zedeki said.

'Nor I.'

'I see your house is nearing completion. It is a fine dwelling.'

Griffin had built in the lee of a hill on a wall foundation of stone, topped by timbers snugly fitted under a steep roof.

'You are welcome to join us for our midday meal,' invited Griffin.

'Thank you, but no.'

He had left soon after, and Griffin was concerned that he had not repeated his request for the weapons.

Three days later Griffin himself rode from the settlement, a rifle across his saddle and a pistol in his belt. He made for the high ground to the west, where big-horn sheep had been sighted. As he rode, he examined the rifle loaned to him by Madden. It was a Hellborn weapon, short-barrelled and heavy; the stock was spring-stressed and Madden had explained that after each shot, when the stock was pulled back, a fresh shell would be slipped into the breech. Griffin disliked the feel and the look of the weapon, preferring the clean graceful lines of his flintlock. But he could not argue with the practical applications of a repeating rifle and had accepted the loan readily.

He headed north-west and dismounted in a clearing on a wide ledge that overlooked the valley. Left and right of him the undergrowth was thick around the base of tall pines, but here – out of the bright sunlight – Griffin looked out over the land and felt like a king. After a little while he heard horses approaching from the north. Picking up his rifle, he levered the stock, then placed the weapon against a rock and sat down.

Four Hellborn riders advanced into the clearing, pistols in their hands.

'Hunting raiders?' asked Griffin, pleasantly.

'Move away from the weapon,' said a rider. Griffin remained where he was and met the man's eyes; he was black-bearded and powerfully built, and there was nothing of warmth or friendship in his expression.

'I take it,' said Griffin, 'that you mean to kill me, as you killed young Carver?'

The man smiled grimly. 'He talked tough at the start, but he begged and pleaded at the end. So will you.'

'Possibly,' said Griffin. 'But, since I am to die anyway, would you mind telling me why?'

'Why what?'

'Why you are operating in this way. Zedeki told me you had an army. Could it be that my settlers frighten you?'

'I would like to tell you,' replied the man, 'because I'd like to know myself. But the answer is that we are ordered not to attack . . . not yet. But any one of you that strays is fair game. You strayed.'

'Ah well,' said Griffin, remaining seated. 'It looks like it's time to die.'

Shots exploded from the undergrowth and two riders pitched from their saddles. Griffin snatched up the rifle and pumped three shots into the bearded rider's chest. A shell ricocheted from the rock beside him and he swung the rifle to cover the fourth rider, but another shot from the undergrowth punched a hole in his temple. His horse reared and he toppled from the saddle. Griffin's ears rang in the silence that followed; then Madden, Burke and Mahler rose from the undergrowth and joined him.

'You were right, Griff, we're in a lot of trouble,' said Burke. 'Maybe it's time to leave?'

'I am not sure they would let us go,' said Griffin. 'We're caught between a rock and a hard place. The settlement is well-positioned and easier to defend than moving wagons. Yet, ultimately, we can't hold it.'

'Then what do you suggest?' asked Mahler.

'I'm sorry, old lad, but at the moment I'm bereft of ideas. Let us take one day at a time. Strip the ammunition and weapons from the bodies and hide them in the undergrowth. Lead the horses in and kill them too. I don't want the Hellborn knowing that we are aware of our danger.'

'We won't fool them for long, Griff,' said Burke.

'I know.'

It was after midnight when Griffin slipped silently into the cabin. The fire was dead, but the large room retained the memory of the flames and he removed his heavy woollen jacket. Moving across the timbered floor, he opened the door to Eric's room; the boy was sleeping peacefully. Griffin returned to the hearth and sat back in the old leather chair he had carried across half the continent. He was tired, and his back ached. He tugged off his boots and stared at the dead fire; it was not cold in the room, but he knelt, prepared kindling and lit the fire afresh.

You will think of something, Donna had told him.

But he couldn't. And it galled him.

Con Griffin, the humble wagon-master. He wore the title like a cloak, for it served many purposes. All his life he had seen leaders of men, and he had learned early to judge their strengths. Many relied on wit and charisma, which always seemed to link heavily with luck. He had never been blessed with charisma and had turned his considerable intellect to creating a different kind of leader. Men who did not know Griffin would see a ponderous, powerful, slow-moving man: a humble wagon-master. As the days passed they would, if observant, notice that few problems troubled the big man, seeming to disappear of their own volition as his plans progressed. They would see other men taking problems to Griffin, and watch their troubles shrink away like mist in a morning breeze. The truly intuitive watcher would then see that Griffin, unlike the dashing leaders of golden oratory, commanded respect by being the still centre, an oasis of calm amid the storms of the world. Rarely provocative, never loud, always authoritative. It was a creation of which Con Griffin was very proud.

Yet now, when he needed it most, he could think of nothing.

He added fuel to the fire and leaned back in the chair.

Donna Taybard awoke from a troubled sleep to hear the cracking of the unseasoned wood on the fire. Swinging her legs from the broad bed, she covered herself in a woollen gown and moved silently into the main room. Griffin did not hear her and she stopped for a moment, staring at him by the fire, his red hair highlighted by the flames.

'Con!'

'I am sorry, did I wake you?'

'No, I was dreaming. Such strange dreams. What happened out there?'

'The Hellborn killed young Carver – we found that out.'

'We heard shots.'

'Yes. None of us was hurt.'

Donna poured cold water into a large copper kettle and hung it over the fire.

'You are troubled?' she asked.

'I cannot see a way out of the danger. I feel like a rabbit in a snare, waiting for the hunter.'

Donna giggled suddenly and Griffin looked at her face in the firelight. She seemed younger and altogether too beautiful.

'Why do you laugh?'

'I never knew a man less like a rabbit. You remind me of a

bear – a great big, soft brown bear.'

He chuckled and they sat in silence for several minutes. Donna prepared some herb tea, and as they sipped it before the fire the problems of the Hellborn seemed far away.

'How many of them are there?' asked Donna suddenly.

'The Hellborn? I don't know. Jacob tried to track them on the first night, but they spotted him and he rode away.'

'Then how can you plan against them? You don't know the extent of the problem.'

'Damn!' said Griffin softly, and the weight lifted from his mind. 'Zedeki said there were thousands and I believed him. But that doesn't mean they are all here. You are right, Donna, and I have been a fool.' Griffin tugged on his boots, lifted her to her feet and kissed her.

'Where are you going?'

'We came back separately in case the watchers remain at night. Jacob should be home by now and I need to see him.'

Slipping on his dark jacket, he stepped out into the night and crossed the open ground to Madden's cabin. The windows were shuttered, but Griffin could see a gleam of golden light through the centre of the shutters and he tapped at the door.

The tall, bearded Madden opened it within seconds. 'Is everything all right?' he asked.

'Yes. Sorry to bother you so late,' said Griffin, once more adopting the slow, ponderous method of speech his people expected. 'But I think it's time to consider our plans.'

'Come in,' said Madden. The room was less spacious than Griffin's, but the layout was similar. A large table with bench seats was set in the centre of the room, and to the right was a stone hearth and two heavy chairs, ornately carved. The two men sat down and Griffin leaned forward. 'Jacob, I need to know how many Hellborn are close to us. It would also be a help to know something of the land and the situation of their camp and so on.'

'You want me to scout?'

Griffin hesitated. Both men knew the dangers involved in such an enterprise, and Griffin was acutely aware he was asking Jacob Madden to put his life at risk.

'Yes,' he said. 'It is important. Note everything they do, what kind of discipline they are under: everything.'

Madden nodded. 'Who will do the work on my fields?'

'I'll see that it's done.'

'And my family?'

Griffin understood the unspoken question. 'Like my own, Jacob. I'll look after them.'

'All right.'

'There's something else. How many guns did we take?'

Madden thought for a while. 'Thirty-three rifles, twenty-seven – no, twenty-eight – pistols.'

'I'll need to know how much ammunition we gathered, but I can check that tomorrow.'

'You won't find much more than twenty shells per weapon.'

'No. Take care, Jacob.'

'You can count on that. I'll leave tonight.'

'Good man.' Griffin stood and left the cabin. The moon was partially obscured by cloud and he tripped over one of the defensive logs, bruising his shin. He continued on, passing Ethan Peacock's ramshackle cabin; the little scholar was involved in a heated debate with Aaron Phelps. Griffin grinned; no matter what the perils, some things never changed.

Back at his own home he found Donna still sitting by the fire, staring vacantly into the flames.

'You should get some sleep,' he said, but she did not hear him. 'Donna?' He knelt beside her. Her eyes were wide open, the pupils huge, despite the bright firelight. He touched her shoulder, but she did not respond. Not knowing what to do he remained where he was, gently holding her. After a while she sighed and her head sagged forward. He caught her and lifted her to a chair; her eyes fluttered, then focused.

'Oh, hello Con,' she said sleepily.

'Were you dreaming?'

'I . . . I don't know. Strange.'

'Tell me.'

'Thirsty,' she said, leaning back her head and closing her

130

eyes. He poured her a mug of water, and she sipped it for several seconds. 'Ever since we came here,' she said, 'I have had the strangest dreams. They grow more powerful with every day that passes and now I don't know if they are dreams at all. I just drift into them.'

'Tell me,' he repeated.

She sat up and finished the water.

'Well, tonight I saw Jon Shannow sitting on a mountainside with a Hellborn. They were talking, but the words blurred. Then I saw Jon draw his gun – and there was a bear. But then I seemed to tumble away to a huge building of stone. There were many Hellborn there and at the centre was a man, tall and handsome. He saw me and smoke billowed from him and he became a monster, and he pursued me. Then I flew in terror, and someone came to me, and told me not to worry. It was a little man – the man I saw with Jon at the village when he was wounded. His name is Karitas. It is an ancient name which once meant Love, he told me, and the smoke monster could not find us. I drifted then and I saw a great golden ship, but there was no sea. The ship was upon a mountain, and Karitas laughed and said it was the Ark. Then all my dreams tumbled on themselves and I saw the Hellborn in their thousands riding south into Rivervale, and Ash Burry nailed to a tree. It was terrible.'

'Is that all you said?' asked Griffin.

'Almost. I saw Jacob creeping through bushes near some tents, but then I was inside the tent and there were six men seated in a circle – and they knew Jacob was coming, and they were waiting for him.'

'It couldn't have been Jacob – he has only just left.'

'Then you must stop him, Con. Those men, they were not like the other Hellborn. They were evil, so terribly evil!'

Griffin ran outside across the open ground, but there was no light from within Madden's cabin. Griffin circled the house to the paddock, but Madden's horse was gone.

He could feel panic rising in him, and quelled it savagely.

Returning to Donna, he sat beside her and took her hands in his. 'You told me you could always see those close to you, wherever they are. Can you see Jacob now?'

She closed her eyes.

Her mind misted, and Jon Shannow's face leapt to her.

He was riding the steeldust gelding along a mountain path which wound down towards a deep valley dotted with lakes. By the sides of the lakes hundreds of thousands of birds splashed in the water, or soared in their legions into the sky. Behind Shannow rode a Hellborn rider with a black forked beard, and behind him a dark-haired youngster of perhaps fifteen years.

Donna was about to return when she felt the chill of terror touch her soul. She rose above the scene, floating high above the trees, and then she saw them less than a quarter mile behind Shannow – some thirty men riding tall dark horses. The riders wore black cloaks and helms which covered their faces and they were closing fast. The sky darkened, and Donna found herself enveloped in cloud that thickened and solidified into leather wings which closed about her.

She screamed and tried to break free, but a soft, almost gentle voice whispered in her ear.

'You are mine, Donna Taybard, to take when I will.'

The wings opened and she fled like a frightened sparrow, jerking upright in the chair.

'Did you see Jacob?' asked Griffin.

'No,' she whispered. 'I saw the Devil and Jon Shannow.'

Selah cantered alongside Shannow and pointed down into the valley, where a cluster of buildings was ranged at the edge of a narrow river. Batik came alongside.

'I must have been dreaming,' said Shannow. 'I didn't notice them.'

Batik looked troubled. 'I am sure I scanned the valley. I could not have missed them.'

Shannow tugged the gelding and started down the slope, but they had not gone more than a hundred yards when they heard the sound of galloping hooves. Dismounting, Shannow led the gelding behind a screen of trees and thick bushes. Batik and Selah followed him. Above they watched the black-cloaked Hellborn riders thunder by them.

'They should have seen where we cut from the path,' mused Batik. 'Curious.'

'How many did you count?' asked Shannow.

'I did not need to count. There are six sections and that makes thirty-six enemies, skilled beyond our means to defeat them.'

Shannow did not reply, but swung himself into the saddle and headed the gelding down the slope. The buildings were of seasoned timber, bleached almost white, and beyond them was a field where dairy cattle grazed. Shannow rode into the central square and dismounted.

'Where are the people?' asked Batik, joining him.

Shannow removed his wide-brimmed hat and hung it on the pommel of his saddle. The sun was dipping behind the hills to the west, and he was tired. There were a dozen steps leading to a double door in the building facing them and Shannow walked towards them. As he approached, the door opened and an elderly woman in white stepped out and bowed low. Her hair was short and iron-grey, and her eyes were blue – so deep they were almost violet.

'Welcome,' she said.

At that moment the trio heard the sound of hoofbeats and swung to see the Hellborn riding down from the hills. Shannow's hands dropped to his guns, but the woman spoke, her voice ringing with authority.

'Leave your weapons where they are, and wait.'

Shannow froze. The riders swept past the buildings looking neither right nor left. The Jerusalem Man watched them until they were far away, heading north.

He swung to the woman, but before he could speak she said, 'Join us, Mr Shannow, for our evening meal.' She turned and vanished into the building.

Batik approached him. 'I have to tell you, Shannow, that I do not like this place.'

'It is beautiful here,' said Selah. 'Can you not feel it? The harmony. There is no fear here.'

'Yes, there is,' muttered Batik. 'It's all in here,' he said, tapping his chest. 'Why did they ride on?'

'They did not see us,' said Shannow.

'Nonsense, they couldn't have missed us.'

'Just as we couldn't have missed these buildings?'

'That makes it worse, Shannow, not better.'

Shannow walked up the stairs and into the building, Batik behind him. He found himself in a small room, softly lit by white candles. A tiny round table had been set with two places and at the table was the grey-haired woman. Shannow turned, but Batik was not with him. Nor Selah.

'Sit down, Mr Shannow, and eat.'

'Where are my friends?'

'Enjoying a meal. Be at ease; there is no danger here.'

Shannow's guns felt uncomfortable and he removed the belt and laid them on the floor beside him. He looked at his hands and noticed the dirt ingrained in them.

'You may refresh yourself in the next room,' said the woman. Shannow smiled his thanks and opened the oval door he had not noticed beyond the table. Inside was a metal bath, filled with warm water, delicately scented. He removed his clothes and climbed in. Clean at last, he rose from the bath to find his clothes gone and in their place a white woollen shirt and grey trousers. He felt no anxiety over the disappearance of his belongings and dressed in the garments he found, which fitted perfectly.

The woman sat where he had left her and he joined her. The food was plain, seasoned vegetables and fresh fruit, and the clear water tasted like wine.

They ate in silence until at last the woman rose and beckoned Shannow to join her in another room. Shannow followed into a windowless study where two deep leather chairs were drawn up against a round glass-topped table, upon which sat two cups of scented tea.

Shannow waited for the woman to seat herself, then sat back in a chair and stared at the walls of the room. They seemed to be of stone, yet were soft in appearance, like cloth. Upon the walls were paintings – mostly of animals, deer and horses, grazing beneath mountains topped with snow.

'You have journeyed far, Mr Shannow. And you are weary.'
'Indeed I am, Lady.'
'And do you ride towards Jerusalem, or away from her?'
'I do not know.'
'You did your best for Karitas. Feel no grief.'
'You knew him?'
'I did indeed. An obstinate man, but a kindly soul none the less.'
'He saved my life. I could not return the debt.'
'He would not have seen it as a debt, Mr Shannow. For him, as for us, life is not a question of balances earned and debited. How do you feel about Donna Taybard?'
'I am angry . . . was angry. It is hard to feel anger here.'
'It is not hard, Mr Shannow; it is impossible.'
'What is this place?'
'This is Sanctuary. There is no evil here.'
'How is this achieved?'
'By doing nothing, Mr Shannow.'
'But there is a power here . . . an awesome power.'
'Indeed, and there is a riddle in that for those with eyes to see and ears to hear.'
'Who are you? What are you?'
'I am Ruth.'
'Are you an angel?'
She smiled then. 'No, Mr Shannow, I am a woman.'
'I am sorry that I do not understand. I feel it is important.'
'You are right in that, but rest now. We will talk tomorrow.'
She rose and left him. He heard the door close and stood. A bed lay by the far wall and he lay upon it and slept without dreams.

Batik followed Shannow into the building and found himself in a round room, painted in soft shades of red. On the walls were weapons of every kind, artistically displayed – bows, spears, pistols and rifles, swords and daggers, each of exquisite workmanship.

The grey-haired woman sat at an oval table upon which was a joint of red meat, charred on the outside but raw at the centre. Batik moved to the table and picked up a silver carving knife.

'Where is Shannow?' he asked, carving thick slices of the succulent meat.

'He is close, Batik.'

'A pleasant room,' said the Hellborn, indicating the weapons.

'Do they relax you?'

He shrugged. 'It reminds me of my home.'

'The room bordering the garden of vines?'

'Yes. How did you know?'

'You entertained a friend of mine two years ago.'

'What was his name?'

'Ezra.'

'I know no one of that name.'

'He climbed the wall of your garden while being hunted. He hid among your vines, and when the searchers came you told them no one was there and sent them away.'

'I remember. A little man with frightened eyes.'

'Yes. A man of great courage, for he knew great fear.'

'What happened to him?'

'He was caught three months later and burned alive.'

'There has been a lot of that lately. He worshipped the old dark god, I take it?'

'Yes.'

'The Hellborn will stamp out the sect.'

'Perhaps, Batik. But why did you help him?'

'I am not a religious man.'

'What are you?'

'Just a man.'

'You know that if you stay with Shannow you could die.'

'We are parting company soon.'

'And yet without you he will fail.'

Batik lifted a goblet filled with red wine and drained it. 'What are you trying to tell me?'

'Do you feel you owe Shannow a debt?'

'For what?'

'For saving your life?'
'No.'
'Would you call yourself his friend?'
'Perhaps.'
'Then you like him?'
Batik did not reply. 'Who are you, woman?' he asked at last.
'I am Ruth.'
'Why did the riders not see us?'
'No evil may enter here.'
'*I* am here!'
'You saved Ezra.'
'Shannow is here.'
'He seeks Jerusalem.'
'What is this place?'
'For you, Batik, it is Alpha or Omega. A beginning or an end.'
'A beginning of what? An ending to what?'
'That is for you to decide. The choices are yours.'

Selah ran up the stairs after his friends and entered a small room. The grey-haired woman smiled and opened her arms.
'Welcome home, Selah.'
And joy flooded him.

The following morning Ruth led Shannow into a long hall, past trestle tables set for breakfast and on into a circular library with shelf upon shelf of books from floor to domed ceiling. At the centre of the room was a round table and the elderly woman sat, gesturing for Shannow to sit beside her.
'Everything you ever wanted to know is here, Mr Shannow, but you must decide what to look for.'
His eyes scanned the books and an edge of fear touched him, bringing a shiver.
'Are they all true books?' he asked.
'No. Some are fictions. Some are theories. Others are

partly true, or close to the truth. Most point a way to the truth for those with eyes to see.'

'I just want the truth.'

'Placed in your hand like a pearl, unblemished and perfect?'

'Yes.'

'No wonder you need Jerusalem.'

'Do you mock me, Lady?'

'No, Mr Shannow. Everything we do here is to instruct and to help. This room was made for you, created for you. It did not exist before you entered it, and will cease to exist when you leave it.'

'How long may I stay here?'

'One hour.'

'I cannot read all these books in an hour.'

'That is true.'

'Then why go to all this trouble? How can I use all this knowledge if I have no time?'

Ruth leaned towards him, taking his hand. 'We did not create this to torment you, Jon. Far too much effort went into it for that. Sit and think for a while. Be at ease.'

'Can you not tell me where to look?'

'No, for I do not know what you seek.'

'I want to find God.'

Ruth pressed his hand gently. 'Do you think he hides from you?'

'That's not what I meant. I have tried to live in a way that does his will. You understand? I have nothing, I want nothing. And yet . . . I am not content.'

'I will tell you something, Jon. Even were you to read all these books, and know all the secrets of the world, still you would not be content. For you see yourself as Batik saw you: God's gardener, weeding the land, but never fast enough, or fully enough, or completely enough.'

'Do you say it is wrong to defend the weak?'

'I am not a judge.'

'Then what are you? What is this place?'

'I told you last night. There are no angels here, Jon. We are people.'

'You keep saying "We", but I see no one else.'

'There are four hundred people here, but they do not wish to be seen. It is their choice.'

'Is this a dream?' he asked dully.

'No. Believe me.'

'I do believe you, Ruth. I believe everything you say – and it helps me not at all. Outside there are men hunting me, and the woman I love is in terrible danger. There is a man I am pledged to destroy – a man that I know I hate – yet here that hatred seems such a small thing.'

'You speak of the man who calls himself Abaddon?'

'Yes.'

'An empty man.'

'His warriors butchered Karitas and his people – women, children.'

'And now you will try to kill him?'

'Yes. As the Lord of Hosts told Joshua to kill the unholy.'

Ruth released his hand and leaned back. 'You speak of the destruction of Ai and the thirty-two cities. *"And so it was that all who fell that day, both of men and women, were twelve thousand, even all the men of Ai. For Joshua drew not his hand back . . . until he had utterly destroyed all the inhabitants of Ai."*'

'Yes, the very Book that Abaddon quoted to me. He said he had based all his methods on the atrocities of the people of Israel.'

'This hurt you, Jon – as it was intended to do.'

'How could it not hurt me? He was right. If I had lived in those days, and seen an invading army killing women and children, I would have fought against them with all my might. What was the difference between the children of Ai and the children of Karitas' village?'

'None,' said Ruth.

'Then Abaddon was right.'

'That is for you to decide.'

'I need to know what you think, Ruth. For I know there is no evil in you. Tell me.'

'I cannot walk your path, Jon, and I would not presume to tell you what was right five thousand years ago. I oppose

Abaddon in a different way. He serves the Prince of Lies, the Lord of Deceit. Here we answer that with the truth of Love – with Karitas, Jon.'

'Love does not turn aside bullets and knives.'

'No.'

'Then what good is it?'

'It turns hearts and minds.'

'Among the Hellborn?'

'We have more than two hundred converts among the Hellborn, despite the burnings and the killings. And the numbers grow daily.'

'How do you reach these converts?'

'My people go from here to live among the Hellborn.'

'By choice?'

'Yes.'

'And they are killed?'

'Many of them have died. Others will die.'

'But with all your power, you could destroy Abaddon and save their lives.'

'That is part of the truth, Jon. True power comes only when one learns not to use it. It is one of the Mysteries. But now the hour is past, and you must leave on your journey.'

'But I have learned nothing.'

'Time will tell. The boy, Selah, will remain here with us.'

'Does he desire this?'

'Yes. You may see him for your farewells.'

'Without him, Batik and I would have passed you by just like the Zealots?'

'Yes.'

'Because no evil may come here?'

'I am afraid so.'

'Then I have learned something.'

'Use your knowledge well.'

Shannow followed Ruth back to his room and there lay his clothes, fresh and clean. He dressed and made to leave, but the grey-haired woman stopped him.

'You have forgotten your guns, Jon Shannow.'

They lay on the floor where he had left them and he bent to lift the belt. As he touched it, his harmony vanished. He swung the belt around his waist and walked through the door. Batik waited by the horses, and Selah stood by him. The boy was dressed now in a robe of white and he smiled as Shannow approached.

'I must stay,' he said. 'Forgive me.'

'There is nothing to forgive, lad. You will be safe here.'

He mounted swiftly and rode from the buildings, Batik beside him. After a while he looked back, and the plain was empty.

'The world is a strange place,' said Batik.

'Where did you go?'

'I stayed with the woman Ruth.'

'What did she tell you?'

'Probably less than she told you. I tell you this, though – I wish we had never found the place.'

'Amen to that,' said Shannow.

The two men skirted a great lake edged with pine forests, and the ground beyond the water rose into a section of rock hills. Shannow drew rein and scanned the area.

'If they are there, you wouldn't see them,' Batik pointed out.

Shannow moved the gelding forward and they rode with care to the crest of the hill. Below them the last section of the plain stretched to the foothills of the mountain range. There was no sign of the Zealots.

'You know their methods,' said Shannow. 'What would they have done once they lost us?'

'They're not used to losing trails, Shannow. They would have possessed an eagle or a hawk and quartered the land looking for a sign. Since they couldn't see the buildings they would have then, perhaps, split up into their own sections and spread out for a search.'

'Then where are they?'

'Damned if I know.'

'I don't like the idea of heading out into open ground.'

'No. Let's just sit here on the skyline until they spot us!'

Shannow grinned and urged the gelding down the hill. They rode for an hour over the undulating plain, discovering deep gulleys that scored the ground as if giant trowels had scooped away the earth. In one of these gulleys they came across a huge, curved bone some fifteen feet in length. Shannow dismounted and left the gelding grazing. The bone was at least eight inches in diameter; Batik joined him and the two men lifted it.

'I wouldn't have wanted to meet the owner of this while he walked,' said the Hellborn. They dropped the bone and searched the ground. Jutting from the earth was a second bone and then Batik found a third, just showing in the tall grass ten paces to the right.

'It looks to be part of a rib-cage,' said Shannow. Thirty paces ahead Batik found an even larger section, with teeth attached. When the two men dug it clear, the bone was shaped like a colossal V.

'Have you ever seen anything with a mouth that big?' asked Batik. 'Or heard of such a thing?'

'Selah said there were monsters here; he said his father had seen them.'

Batik looked back. 'It must be thirty feet from head to rib-cage. Its legs must have been enormous.' They searched for some time, but found no evidence of such limbs.

'Maybe wolves took them,' suggested Batik.

Shannow shook his head. 'The leg bones would have been twice the thickness of the ribs; they must be here.'

'It's mostly buried – maybe the legs are way below ground.'

'No. Look at the curve of the bone jutting from the grass. The creature died on its back, otherwise we would find the vertebrae on the surface.'

'One of life's mysteries,' said Batik. 'Let's move on.'

Shannow dusted the dirt from his hands and mounted the gelding.

'I hate mysteries,' he said, staring down at the remains. 'There should be four legs. I wish I had time to examine it.'

'If wishes were fishes, poor men wouldn't starve,' said Batik. 'Let's go.'

They rode up out of the gulley, where Shannow dragged back on the reins and swung the gelding.

'What now?' asked Batik.

Shannow rode back to the edge and looked down. From here he could see the giant jaw and the ruined ribs of the creature. 'I think you have answered the mystery, Batik. It is a fish.'

'I am glad I didn't hook it. Don't be ridiculous, Shannow! First, it would be the great mother of all fishes – and second, how did it get into the middle of a plain?'

'The Bible talks about a great fish that swallowed one of the prophets – he sat in the belly of it and lived. Ten men could sit inside that rib-cage. And a fish has no legs.'

'Very well, it's a fish. Now you've solved it, we can go.'

'But, as you said, how did it get here?'

'I don't know, Shannow. And I don't care.'

'Karitas told me that in the Fall of the World the seas rose and drowned much of the lands and cities. This fish could have been brought here by a tidal wave.'

'Then where is the sea? Where did it go?'

'Yes, that's true. As you say, it is a mystery.'

'I'm delighted we've solved that – now can we go?'

'Do you have no curiosity, Batik?'

The Hellborn leaned forward on his saddle. 'Indeed I have, my friend. I am curious as to the whereabouts of thirty-six trained killers; you probably find it strange that I seem so preoccupied.'

Shannow lifted his hat and wiped the sweat from the brim. The sun was high overhead, just past noon, and the sky was cloudless. A speck caught his eye – it was an eagle, circling high above them.

'For much of my life, Batik,' he said, 'I have been hunted. It is a fact of my existence. Brigands soon became aware of me, and my description was well circulated. I have never known when a bullet or an arrow or a knife might come at me from the shadows. After a while I became fatalistic. I am unlikely to die in my bed at a grand old age, for my life depends on my reflexes, my keen eyesight and my strength. All will fade one day, but until that day I will retain an interest in things of this world – things that I do not understand, but which I sense have a bearing on what we have become.'

Batik shook his head. 'Well, thank you for sharing your philosophy. Speaking for myself I am still a young man, in my prime, and I have every desire to be the oldest man the world has ever seen. I am beginning to think that Ruth was right. If I stay in your company, I am sure to die. So I think this is the time to say farewell.'

Shannow smiled. 'You are probably right. But it seems a shame to part so swiftly. Up there looks to be a good camp-site. Let's share one last evening together?'

Batik's eyes followed Shannow's pointing finger to where, high up on a slope, was a circle of boulders. The Hellborn sighed and kicked his horse into a run. The ground within the circle was flat, and at the back of the ledge was a rock tank full of water. Batik dismounted and unsaddled his horse. Tomorrow, he decided, he would leave the Jerusalem Man to whatever fate his dark god intended.

Just before dusk Shannow lit a fire, despite Batik's protestations concerning the smoke, and brewed some tea. Thereafter he wrapped himself in his blankets against a rock wall and laid his head on his saddle.

'For this you wanted my company?' asked Batik.

'Go to sleep. You've a long ride tomorrow.'

Batik lifted his blanket around his shoulders and settled down beside the fire. A loose rock dug into his side and he pried it loose. After a while he dropped into a light sleep.

The moon rose over the hills and a solitary owl swooped down over the camp and back up into the night. An hour passed and six shadows moved slowly up the slope, pausing at the edge of the rocks. The leader stepped into the camp-site, pointing to the far rock face. Three men crept silently forward while the others stealthily approached Batik at the fire.

From his position twenty feet above the camp-site, wedged behind a jutting finger of rock, Shannow watched the men approach. His pistols levelled on the two men closest to Batik, he squeezed the triggers and flame blossomed, the guns bucking in his hands. The first of his targets was hurled from his feet, his lungs filling with blood;

the second was slammed sideways as a bullet lodged in his brain.

Batik rolled from his blankets, pistol in hand. The third attacker fired as he moved, the bullet kicking up dirt some inches to Batik's right. His own pistol thundered a reply and the man was lifted from his feet and thrown backwards.

Shannow, meanwhile, had turned his guns on the men by his own blanket. Two of them had fired into what they thought was his sleeping body, and a ricochet from one of the rocks hidden there had slashed a wound in a Zealot's thigh. Now the man was kneeling and trying to staunch the blood gushing from the wound. Batik ran forward, dived and rolled to come up on one knee, firing as he rose. Shannow killed one of the men, but the second sprinted for the slope. Batik fired twice, missing his target, then lunged to his feet and gave chase.

The Zealot was almost to the foot of the slope when he heard Batik closing on him. He whirled and fired, the shell whistling past Batik's ear. Batik took aim and pulled the trigger, but there was a dull click. He cocked the pistol and tried again. It was empty. The Zealot grinned and raised his own pistol . . .

A small hole appeared at the centre of his forehead, and the back of his head exploded.

As the Zealot tumbled to the ground, Batik spun round to see Shannow kneeling at the top of the slope, his pistol held two-handed. Batik cursed and ran back to the camp.

'You son of a slut,' he stormed. 'You left me like a sacrificial goat!'

'I thought you needed your sleep.'

'Don't give me that, Shannow; you planned this. When did you climb that damned rock?'

'About the time you started snoring.'

'Don't make jokes; they don't become you. I could have died tonight.'

Shannow moved forward, the moonlight glinting from his eyes, giving them a feral look.

'But you didn't, Batik. And if you want the lesson spelt

out for you, it is this: while you were berating me, you failed to notice an eagle circling above us for over an hour. You also missed the reflection of sunlight on metal west of us before we found the bones, which is one of the reasons I was happy to stay hidden in the gully. You are a strong man, Batik, and a brave warrior. But you have never been hunted. You talk too much and you see too little. Dead if you remain with me? You won't live a day *without* me!'

Batik's eyes blazed and he raised his pistol.

'Load it first, boy,' Shannow told him, moving towards his saddle and blankets.

Chapter Seven

Jacob Madden crouched on the hillside above the Hellborn camp and watched the men below gathering in line for the evening meal. There were almost two hundred men already in the camp, and over the last two days he had estimated that a further fifty were scattered over the surrounding countryside.

Griffin had asked him to study the discipline in the camp, and Madden had to accept that it was good. There were twenty-eight tents set in two rows on the banks of the river. A latrine trench had been dug downwind and earthworks had been thrown up around the camp to a height of around four feet, these were patrolled at night by six sentries working four-hour shifts. The horses were picketed in three lines north of the latrine trench, while the cooks' tents were set at the other end of the camp. Madden was impressed by the organization.

A skilled hunter himself, Madden had found no problems avoiding contact. His horse was well-hidden and the bearded farmer had never approached within sixty yards of the camp. His scouting had been conducted with patience and care.

But this morning six men had ridden into the camp, and from the moment of their arrival Madden had felt an increasing sense of disquiet. In appearance they seemed little different from the other Hellborn riders, dark armour emblazoned with a goat's head, black leather cloaks and high riding boots. But on their heads they wore dark helms which covered their faces, all but the eyes. For some reason that Madden could not pinpoint they had made his flesh crawl, and he was filled with an unreasonably burning desire to move to their tent and find out more about them.

With infinite patience Madden bellied down and dragged his long, lean frame into a tight circle of bushes to wait for nightfall. As he lay overlooking the camp, he worried at the problem of the riders. One of them had swung his head and seemed to be staring up at the hidden farmer. Madden had frozen in place, allowing not a flicker of movement, yet he was convinced the man had seen him. Common sense – a commodity Madden possessed in quantity – told him he must have been virtually invisible, but still . . .

He had waited for the inevitable pursuit, but nothing happened. The man could not have seen him. Yet the notion would not desert him.

He ignored the growing discomfort as the damp soil seeped into his clothing, and thought back to his farm near Allion. It had been a good site, and his wife Rachel had given birth to their first son there. But Brigands had driven them out, just as they had from his other four homes.

Jacob Madden was a tough man, but strength was not enough against the wandering bands of killers which moved across the lands like locusts. Two of his homes had been burnt out, and the third had been taken over by Daniel Cade and his men. Burning with shame, Madden had packed his belongings in an old wagon and headed north.

He would have taken to the hills for a guerrilla war, but he had Rachel and the boys to consider. So he had run, and tried not to notice the disappointment reflected in the eyes of his sons.

Now he would run no more. Griffin had sold him on the idea of Avalon, a land without Brigands; a land rich and verdant, with soil so fertile the seeds would spring to life as they touched the ground. His boys were older now, almost ready to stand alone against the savage world, and Madden felt it was time to be a man again.

The moon rose, bathing the hillside with silver light. Madden looked to his left where a rabbit was sitting staring at him. He grinned and snapped his fingers, but the rabbit did not move. Madden turned his attention back to the camp where the sentries were out now, patrolling the earthworks. He eased himself into a sitting position and stretched his back. The rabbit remained and Madden picked up a small stone and flicked it at the little creature. It jumped aside, blinked, saw him and scampered away into the bushes.

A rustling in the tree branches over his head caused him to look up. A brown owl was sitting on a branch above. No wonder the rabbit ran, thought Madden.

It was close to midnight and he eased himself from the bushes ready for the descent to the river camp. Suddenly a shimmering figure appeared before him. Madden leapt back. The figure became a small man dressed in white – his face round and kindly, his teeth almost too perfect.

Madden drew his pistol and cocked it. The figure pointed at Madden, looked at the camp, then shook its head.

'Who are you?' whispered the farmer. In response the figure pointed to the east of the camp; Madden followed his direction and saw a black-cloaked man creeping into the woods. The little old man then pointed west and Madden saw two other Hellborn warriors moving into the shadows.

They were surrounding him! He had been right all along – they *had* seen him.

The spectral figure vanished and Madden moved back and started to run towards the hollow where he had hidden his horse. He leapt boulders and fallen trees, panic rising with every step.

'Be calm!' said a voice, whispering in his mind. He almost fell, but righted himself and stopped by a thick oak tree, resting his hand on the bark. His breath came in great gulps. He could hear little above the beating of his heart and the roaring in his ears.

'Be calm,' said the voice once more. 'Panic will kill you.' He waited until his breathing steadied. His hat had fallen from his head and he bent to retrieve it.

A shot spattered wood splinters from the oak and Madden dived to the ground and rolled into the bushes. He moved forward on his elbows to a safer position, hidden in the undergrowth. A second shot sliced his ear.

'Kill the owl,' whispered the voice.

Madden rolled to his back to see above him the brown

owl perched on a tree branch. He pulled his pistol clear and aimed it and the bird leapt into the air. Madden blinked. The bird had known! Another shot came close. Madden crawled to a tree trunk, anger rising in place of his panic and fear.

He had been pushed around and threatened for years by Brigands of every sort. Now they thought they had him – just another farmer to torture and kill. Madden moved round the tree, then ducked low and sprinted from cover. Two shots came from his left and he hit the ground, rolled and fired left and right of the gun flashes. A man screamed. Madden was up and moving, even as other guns opened up. A wicked blow hit his thigh and he went down. A black figure leapt from the undergrowth, but Madden shot him in the face and his attacker disappeared. Pushing himself to his feet, Madden dived into the undergrowth. Above him the owl silently swooped to a thick branch, but Madden had been waiting for it. His shot blew it apart and feathers drifted down to where he lay.

'Get to your horse,' whispered the voice. 'You have less than a minute.'

With a groan Madden levered himself upright. His thigh was bleeding badly, but the bone was unbroken. He limped to the hollow and pulled himself into the saddle. Ripping the reins loose he swung the horse and thundered from the hollow. Then a bullet took him low in the back and pain seared him like hot irons. Leaning forward over the saddle, he urged the horse into a full gallop towards the west.

His eyes drifted closed.

'Stay awake,' came the voice. 'To sleep is to die.'

He could not sit upright for the pain in his back, and could feel the blood drenching his back and leg. Doggedly he hung on until he crested the last hill, seeing the settlement spread out below him.

The horse galloped on and Madden passed into darkness.

Shannow and Batik stripped the corpses of ammunition and supplies, but when the Jerusalem Man made to transfer the

Zealots' dried meat to his own saddlebags Batik stopped him.

'I do not think you would find it to your taste,' he said.

'Meat is meat.'

'Indeed, Shannow? Even if it is stripped from the bodies of young children?'

Shannow hurled the meat aside and swung on Batik. 'What kind of a society do you come from, Batik? How could this be allowed?'

'It is meat from the sacrificial offerings. According to Holy Law the flesh, when absorbed by the pure Zealots, brings harmony to the departed spirit of the victim.'

'The Carns were at least more honest,' said Shannow. Taking his knife, he cut hair from the tails of the Hellborn horses and began twisting it into twine. Batik ignored him and moved to the outer circle of rocks, staring out over the plain.

He felt humbled by Shannow's outburst following the attack; he felt young and stupid. The Jerusalem Man was right; he had no experience of being hunted, and would be an easy prey to the Zealots. And yet if Ruth was right – and he believed she was – then to stay with Shannow meant death anyway. Foolish and arrogant he might have been, but Batik was not without intellect.. At present his chances of survival rested with Shannow; the real trick would be timing the moment of their parting to give him a chance at life. Perhaps if he observed the Jerusalem Man for long enough, some of his innate skill would rub off on the young Hellborn.

He scanned the plain for sign of movement, but there was nothing suspicious. No birds flew, no deer moved out on the grass. As dawn lightened the sky Shannow and Batik rode from the rocks, veering east along the mountain's foothills. After an hour they came to a curling pass cutting through the peaks and Shannow urged the gelding up over the scree and into the narrow channel. Batik swung in the saddle to study the back trail. His eyes widened – just short of the far horizon twelve riders were galloping their horses.

'Shannow!'

'I know,' said the Jerusalem Man. 'Take the horses into the pass. I'll join you later.'

'What are you going to do?'

Without answering, Shannow slid from the saddle and clambered into the rocks high above the pass.

Batik rode on, leading Shannow's horse. The trail widened into a bowl-shaped valley, edged with forests of spruce and pine. Batik led the horses to a stream and dismounted; Shannow joined him almost an hour later.

'Let's move,' he said and the two men rode across the valley, scattering a herd of heavy-horned buffalo and crossing several small streams before Shannow called a halt. He glanced at the sun, then turned his horse to face the west. Batik joined him, saying nothing. It was obvious that Shannow was listening and concentrating. For some time nothing happened, then a gunshot split the silence. Two more followed. Shannow waited, his hand raised, three fingers extended. Another shot. Shannow seemed tense. A fifth shot.

'That's it,' said Shannow.

'What did you do?'

'I set up tripwires and wedged five Hellborn pistols into rocks overlooking the trail.'

Batik smiled. 'They'll rue the day they started hunting you, Shannow.'

'No, they'll just get more careful. They underestimated me. Now let's hope they overestimate my talents – it will give us more time.'

'I wonder if we hit any of them,' said Batik.

'Probably one. The other shots might have hit horses. But they'll proceed now with caution. We will ride through every narrow channel we can, whether it be between rocks or trees or bushes. They will have to stop and check every one for possible ambush and they won't catch us for days.'

'Aren't you overlooking something?'

'Like what?'

'Like we are heading west, back into Hellborn country. They'll have patrols ahead of us.'

'You are learning, Batik. Keep at it.'

152

Towards dusk Batik spotted some buildings to the north and they swung their horses and cantered down a gentle slope towards them. They were of white stone and spread over three acres. Some were more than single-storey, with outside staircases winding up to crenellated marble towers. Shannow eased his gun into his hand as they closed on the town. But there was no sign of life. The streets were cobbled and the iron horseshoes clattered on the stones.

The moon came out from behind dark clouds, bathing the scene in silver light, and suddenly the town took on a ghostly look. As the two men rode into a central square, Shannow drew rein alongside a statue of an armoured warrior wearing a plumed helmet; his left arm was missing, but in his right he held a short broad-bladed sword.

On the other side of the square was a broad avenue, lined with statues of young women in flowing robes, which led to a low palace with a high oval doorway.

'There is no wood anywhere,' said Batik, riding up to the doorway and running his hands over the stone.

Both men dismounted and tethered their horses and Shannow stepped inside the palace. Statues ringed the central hall and moving to each in turn, he studied them. Some were regal women, others young men of lofty bearing. Still more were older men, heavy-bearded and wise. On the far wall, past a raised dais, was a mosaic in bright-coloured stones showing a king in a golden chariot followed by an army of plumed warriors bearing long spears and bows.

'I have never seen clothes like these,' said Batik. 'The warriors appear to have worn skirts of wood or leather, studded with bronze.'

'They could be Israelites,' said Shannow. 'This might be one of the old cities. But why no wood?'

Batik wandered to another wall, then called Shannow to him. In an alcove, piled against a corner, were crushed goblets and plates of solid gold. Flowing script had been engraved on the goblets, but Shannow could not read it. Near a doorway he found a golden hilt, but with no dagger attached. He pressed his finger inside the hilt and withdrew it; the faintest red stained his skin.

'Rust,' said Shannow. 'No wood, no metal. Only stone.'

'I wonder why no one lives here,' said Batik. 'It wouldn't take much to restore this place.'

'Would you live here?' asked Shannow.

'Well . . . no. It is a little sinister.'

Shannow nodded. The bright moonlight shone through an upper window in a shaft of silver, illuminating a broad staircase. Climbing it, Shannow found himself in a round room open to the sky. The stars were bright and at the centre of the room, an equal distance apart, were four golden eagles, each flat on one side. Shannow lifted one and a golden screw fell from a small hole in a wing.

'I think it was a bed ornament,' said Shannow.

'The king's bedchamber,' said Batik. 'A little chilly.'

They returned to the main hall and Shannow noticed that Batik was sweating heavily. 'Are you all right?'

'No. My vision keeps blurring and I feel dizzy.'

'Sit down for a moment,' said Shannow. 'I'll get some water.'

Leaving Batik, he started to walk towards the horses but missed a step and staggered, his vision misting. Reaching out, he took the arm of a statue and held himself upright. When he looked up into the blank stone eyes, Shannow heard a roaring in his ears. Taking a deep breath he staggered to the doorway, nausea rising to choke him.

He fell heavily on the outer step. Bright sunlight bathed him and he looked up. People were moving in the square, the men clad in bronze armour and leather kilts, the women in flowing robes of silk or cotton.

Flower-sellers thronged the streets and here and there children gathered to play on the shiny stones. Suddenly the sky darkened, clouds racing across the heavens. The sun flashed away towards the east and in the distance a colossal black wall moved towards the city. Shannow screamed, but no one heard him. The wall advanced, blotting out the sky to thunder across the city. Water filled Shannow's lungs and he clung to the door-posts, choking and dying . . .

His eyes opened to the moon and the silent city. Shaking,

he rolled to his knees, took the canteen of water from his horse and returned to Batik.

'Did you see it?' asked Batik, his face grey, his eyes haunted.

'The tidal wave?'

'Yes, this whole city was under the sea. That's why there was no wood or metal. And your giant fish – you were right; it was dumped here.'

'Yes.'

'What the Hell is this place, Shannow?'

'I don't know. Karitas said the world was destroyed by the sea. But as you said, where did the sea go? This city must have been under water for centuries for all the wood and metal to disappear.'

'There is another thought, Shannow,' said Batik, sitting up. 'If all the world was destroyed by the sea, and yet this city is above the ocean, perhaps there have been two Armageddons?'

'I do not understand you.'

'The Fall of the World, Shannow. Perhaps it happened twice?'

'That could not be.'

'You told me yourself that Karitas talked about an Ark of Noah; you told me about a great flood which covered the earth. That was before Armageddon.'

Shannow turned away. ' *"The thing that hath been, it is that which shall be, and that which is done is that which shall be done, and there is no new thing under the sun."* '

'What is that?'

'The words of Solomon. And very soon after that he writes, *"There is no remembrance of former things, neither shall there be any remembrance of things that are to come with those that shall come after."* '

Batik chuckled and then laughed aloud, the sound echoing in the dead palace.

'What is amusing you?'

'If I am right, Shannow, it means we are now sitting on what was once the floor of the ocean.'

'I still do not see what is amusing.'

'It is you. If what was sea is now land, therefore what was land is now sea. So, Shannow, you will need gills to find Jerusalem!'

'Only if you are right, Batik.'

'True. I wonder what this city was. I mean, look at the statues; they must have been great men. And now no one will ever know of their greatness.'

Shannow studied the closest statue in the moonlight. It was of an old man with a tightly curled white beard and a high domed forehead. His right hand was held across his chest, and it carried a scroll. In the left, he had what looked like a tablet of stone.

'I don't think,' said Shannow at last, 'that he would have minded about immortality. He has a look of contentment. Of wisdom.'

'I wonder who he was.'

'A lawmaker. A prophet. A king.' Shannow shrugged. 'Whatever, he must have been a great man – his statue stands higher than all the others.'

'He was Paciades,' said a voice. Shannow rolled to his right and his pistol levelled at a tall figure standing in a doorway to the left. The man advanced into the hall, holding his hands out from his body. He was some six feet tall and his skin was black as ebony.

'I am sorry to startle you,' he said. 'I saw your horses.'

'What in Heaven's name are you?' asked Shannow, rising to his feet and keeping the gun trained on the man.

'I am a man.'

'But you are black. Are you of the Devil?'

'It is strange,' said the man without rancour, 'how the same prejudices can cling to the minds of men, no matter what the circumstances. No, Mr Shannow, I am not of the Devil.'

'How do you know my name?'

'Ruth contacted me and asked me to look out for you.'

'Are you armed?'

'No, not as you would understand it.'

'If you have come peacefully, I apologize,' said Shannow, 'but we are being hunted and I will take no risks. Batik, search him.' The Hellborn approached the man cautiously and ran his hands over the grey tunic and black leggings.

'No weapons,' he reported and Shannow sheathed his pistol.

'I'll check outside,' said Batik.

'If it's clear, gather some kindling for a fire,' asked Shannow, beckoning the stranger to sit. The black man stretched himself out and smiled.

'You are a careful man, Mr Shannow. I like to see that – it shows intelligence and that appears to be a rare commodity in this new world of ours.'

'Why would Ruth contact you?' asked Shannow, ignoring the statement.

'We have known each other for some years. We may disagree on points of theology, but in the main we seek the same ends.'

'Which are?'

'The re-establishment of a just society – a civilization, Mr Shannow, where men and women can live together in harmony and love without fear of Brigands or Hellborn.'

'Is such a thing possible?'

'Of course not, but we must strive for it.'

'What is your name?'

'Samuel Archer.'

Batik returned with an armful of dried wood, complaining that he had had to ride from the city to find it. As the fire crackled to life, Shannow asked the black man about the statue.

'I have studied this city for about eighteen years,' said Archer. 'There are some remarkable writings inscribed on gold foil; it took four years of effort to translate. It appears that old man was Paciades, the uncle of one of the kings. He was an astronomer – a student of the stars – and through his work people knew exactly when to plant for the best harvests. He also discovered the instability of the earth, though he didn't understand the awesome significance for his world.'

'Did he live to see the end?'

'I have no idea. His death is not recorded anywhere that I have found.'

'When was the city destroyed?' asked Batik.

'About eight thousand years ago.'

'Then for some seven and a half thousand years this *was* ocean?'

'True, Batik. The world is much changed.'

'What was this city?'

'My research shows it was called Balacris. It is one of supposedly thirty cities that made up the nation of Atlantis.'

Batik fell asleep long before midnight and Shannow and Archer walked together along the statue-lined avenues of Balacris.

'I often come here,' said Archer. 'There is a tremendous sense of peace to be found in a dead city. And often the ghosts of previous times join me on my walks.'

He glanced at Shannow and grinned. 'Do you think me mad?'

Shannow shrugged. 'I have never seen a ghost, Mr Archer, but I have no reason to doubt their existence. Do you speak with them?'

'I tried when I first saw them, but they do not see me. I do not believe they are spirits at all; they are images, much as the one you and Batik saw this afternoon. This is a magic land, Mr Shannow. Come, I will show you.'

Archer led the way up a winding hill and down into a bowl-shaped hollow where great stones had been raised in a circle around a flat altar. The stones were black, and towered over twenty feet high. Each was six feet square and polished like ebony.

'The sea smoothed them for thousands of years. Occasionally you can still see the hairline traces of carved inscriptions,' Archer told him, moving into the circle and stopping by the altar. 'Watch this,' he said, removing a Daniel Stone the size of a thumbnail from his pocket. Immediately, all around them Shannow saw swirling figures, translucent and shining; women in silken shifts twirled and danced, while men in tunics of many colours crowded between the stones to watch them. 'And this,' said Archer, covering the Stone. The dancers vanished. He moved the Stone a fraction of an inch and removed his hand; three children appeared, sitting by the altar and playing with knuckle bones. They were oblivious to the visitors. Shannow knelt beside them and reached out but his hand passed through them and they disappeared.

Archer returned the Stone to his pocket. 'Interesting, isn't it?'

'Fascinating,' said Shannow. 'Do you have an explanation?'

'A theory. I have now transcribed some two hundred thousand words of the Rolynd language – that is to say, Atlantean. They called themselves Rolynd – "the People of Heaven" would be a loose translation. I myself prefer "the People of Fable".' Archer sat down on the altar. 'Are you hungry, Mr Shannow?'

'A little.'

'If you could choose an impossible food, what would it be?'

'A rich honeycake. Why do you ask?'

'I ask because I am a showman.' Archer stood and moved out on to the grass by the altar, stooping to lift a fist-sized rock. He took the Daniel Stone from his pocket and touched it to the rock. Then he handed a honeycake to Shannow.

'Is it real?'

'Taste it.'

'There is trickery though, yes?'

'Taste it, Mr Shannow.' Shannow bit into the cake and it was soft and honey-filled.

'How? Tell me how?'

Archer returned to the altar. 'The People of Fable – they had a power source unlike any other. I don't know how they came upon it, or whether they created it, but the Stones were the secret of Atlantean culture and with them they could create anything the mind could conceive. When you were a child, Mr Shannow, did your mother tell you stories of magical swords, winged horses, sorcerers?'

'No, but I've heard them since.'

'Well, Atlantis is where all fables begin. I found an inventory at the palace which listed presents to the king on his one hundred and eighty-fifth birthday. Each of the gifts mentioned Sipstrassi – Stones. Swords had Sipstrassi set in the handle, a crown with a central Stone for wisdom, armour with a Stone above the heart for invincibility. Their entire society was founded on magic: on Stones that healed, fed and strengthened. One hundred and eighty-five and he still wore armour! Think of it, Shannow.'

'But they did not survive despite all their magic.'

'I am not sure about that either. But that's a story for another day. Let's get some sleep.'

'I am not tired. You go on. I need to think.'

'Of Jerusalem, Mr Shannow?'

'I see Ruth has indeed spoken of me.'

'Did you doubt me?'

'I still do, Mr Archer. But I am not a man of hasty judgement.'

'Because I am black?'

'I will admit that it makes me uneasy.'

'It is merely a pigment in the skin that separates us, Mr Shannow. But may I refer you to your own Bible and the song of Solomon. *"I am black but comely, o ye daughters of Jerusalem."* He was writing of the Queen of Sheba, which was a country in Africa where my ancestors were undoubtedly born.'

'I'll walk back with you,' said Shannow.

At the top of the hill he turned and stared back at the ring of black stones, remembering the words of Karitas. Blood and death fed them. The altar stood stark at the centre of the circle like the pupil of a dark eye.

'Ruth spoke well of you,' said Archer and Shannow swung his gaze from the altar.

'She is a remarkable woman. She showed me my life, though I did not recognize it.'

'How so?'

'She conjured a library all around me, and gave me but a single hour to find the Truth. It was impossible, just as my life is impossible. The truth is all around me, but I don't know where to look and there is so little time to seek it.'

'Surely that is a discovery in itself,' said Archer. 'Tell me, why did you first decide to seek Jerusalem?'

'It is an act of faith, Mr Archer – no more, no less. No high-blown philosophical reasons. I live by the Bible and to do that a man must believe. Implicitly believe. Seeking Jerusalem is my way of dealing with doubt.'

'Chasing the Grail,' said Archer softly.

'You are the second man to mention this Grail. I hope you are not friends.'

'Who was the first?'

'Abaddon.'

Archer stopped walking and turned towards Shannow. 'You have met the Satanlord?'

'In a dream. He taunted me with Galahad.'

'Do not let it concern you, Mr Shannow. There are worse things to be than a knight in search of the truth. I would imagine Abaddon envies you.'

'There is little to envy.'

'If that were really true, I would not have sought you out – nor would Ruth have asked me to.'

'I could not see the buildings of Sanctuary.'

'Nor I,' said Archer ruefully. 'There is great power there . . . awesome. Ruth can turn energy to matter – and without a Stone. I sometimes think she is on the verge of immortality.'

'How did she become so powerful?' asked Shannow.

'She claims, and I have no reason to doubt her, that the clue is in the Bible. Non-use of power makes you stronger.'

'In what way?'

'It's hard to explain, but it goes something like this: If a man strikes you on the right cheek, your desire is to strike back. Marshalling that desire and holding it in check makes you stronger.

'Think of it in these terms: You have an empty jug. Each time you get angry, or feel violent or emotional, the jug gains water. If you vent your anger, the water disappears. The more you control your feelings, the more full the jug.

When the jug is full you have power – all the power you did not use when first you felt the need to strike back. Ruth is very old and has been practising this art for many years. Her jug is now like a lake.'

'But you do not quite believe it?' said Shannow.

'Yes and no. I think she has a strong point, but these are the Plague Lands, Mr Shannow, and much happens here that defies rational explanation. This area was once a dumping ground for chemical weapons, weapons so deadly they were sealed in drums and dropped from the decks of ships to harbour their venom on the bottom of the ocean. Added to this, during the Fall there was a great deal of radiation – like a plague, Mr Shannow – which killed whomever it touched. The land was polluted beyond anything you could imagine. It still is. Where we now sit, the radiation level is a hundred times greater than that which would have killed a strong man before the Fall; this in itself has caused mutations in people and animals. There are more ESPers per head of the population than ever there were in the old days. Far to the east there are tribes of people with webbed hands and feet. To the north there is a people who are covered in hair; their heads are long and wolf-like. There are even tales of people with wings, but these I have never seen.

'I think Ruth has discovered part of the truth, but her talents have been vastly enhanced by the Plague Lands.

'You mentioned a library. She probably created it just for you – out of thick air, reassembling molecules to the shape of that which she desired.'

Shannow sat silent for a moment, then he said, 'God has very little place in your thinking, Mr Archer.'

'I have no idea what God is. The Bible says he created everything and that includes the Devil. A big mistake! Then he created Man – a bigger mistake. I can't follow someone who makes errors on such a colossal scale.'

'Yet Ruth, with all her power and knowledge, believes,' said Shannow.

'Ruth is almost on the verge of creating a God,' responded Archer.

'To me that is blasphemy.'

'Then forgive me, Mr Shannow, and put it down to ignorance.'

'You are not an ignorant man, Mr Archer, and I do not think you are an evil one. Good night to you.'

Archer watched the Jerusalem Man walk back to the palace, then he sat back and let his eyes roam the star-filled sky. Ruth had told him that Shannow was a haunted man, and Archer felt the truth of her diagnosis.

Less of a Galahad than a Lancelot, thought Archer. A flawed knight in a flawed world, unstable and yet unyielding.

'Good night, Shannow,' whispered Archer. 'I find no evil in you either.'

Ruth's image flickered in front of him, forming into flesh as she sat beside him.

'Stones into cakes, indeed! You are incorrigible, Samuel.'

He grinned. 'Did you divert the Zealots?'

'Yes. They are riding west, with Shannow and Batik just in sight.'

'You were right, Ruth. He is a good man.'

'He is strong in the broken places,' said Ruth. 'I like him. How is Amaziga?'

'Well, but she nags me constantly.'

'You're a man who needs a strong wife. And how is life at the Ark?'

'You should visit and see for yourself.'

'No, I do not like Sarento . . . no, don't tell me again what a good administrator he is. You like him because he shares your fascination for the dead cities.'

Archer spread his hands. 'Admit it, you would like to see the home of the Guardians?'

'Perhaps. Will you take Shannow to Sarento?'

'Probably. Why is he important to you?'

'I can't say, Sam – not won't, *can't*. The Hellborn are moving, death is in the air and the Jerusalem Man sits in the eye of the hurricane.'

'You think he plans to kill Abaddon?'

'Yes.'

'Not a bad thing for the world, surely?'

'Perhaps, but I sense there are wolves in the shadows, Sam. Keep Shannow safe for me.'

She smiled, touched his arm in farewell . . .

And vanished.

The Hellborn invasion of the southlands began on the first day of Spring when a thousand riders swept into Rivervale, killing and burning. Ash Burry was captured in his farm and crucified on an oak tree. Hundreds of other families were slain, and refugees took to the hills where the Hellborn riders hunted them down.

And the army continued ever south.

Forty miles from Rivervale, in the foothills of the Yeager mountains, a small band of men gathered in a sheltered hollow, listening to the tale of a refugee who had lost all his family. The listeners were tough brutal men, long used to the ways of Brigandry, but they listened in growing horror to the stories of butchery, rape and naked blood-lust.

Their leader – a thin almost skeletal man – sat on a rock, his grey eyes unblinking, his face emotionless.

'You say that they have rifles that fire many times?'

'Yes, and pistols too,' replied the refugee, an aging farmer.

'What should we do, Daniel?' asked a youth with sandy hair.

'I need to think, Peck. They're doing us out of our trade, and that's not right – not by a long haul. I thought we was doing all right, what with the three new muskets and the five pistols Gambion brought back. But repeating rifles . . .'

Peck pushed his hair from his eyes and scratched at a flea moving inside his stained buckskin shirt. 'We could get ourselves some of them guns, Daniel.'

'The boy's right,' put in Gambion, a huge misshapen bear of a man, heavily bearded and bald as a coot. He had been with Daniel Cade for seven years, and was a known man with knife or gun. 'We could hit them Hellborn damn hard, gather ourselves some weapons?'

'It may be true,' said Cade, 'but this problem is a little larger than just getting guns. We survive off the land, and we spend our Barta coin in towns that don't know us. These Hellborn are killing off the farmers and merchants and they're burning the towns. There will be nothing left for us.'

'We can't take on an army, Dan,' said Gambion. 'There ain't but seventy men among us.'

'You can count me in,' said the farmer. 'By God, you can count me in!'

Cade pushed himself to his feet. He was a tall man, and his left leg was permanently straight and heavily strapped at the knee with tight leather. He ran his hand through his thick black hair and then spat upon the grass.

'Gambion, take ten men and scour the countryside. Any survivors you come across, direct them to Yeager. If you find a group that don't know the mountains, escort them in.'

'Men and women?'

'Men, women, children – whatever.'

'Why, Daniel? There's not enough food for our own selves.'

Cade ignored him. 'Peck, you take a dozen men and round up any stray stock – horses, cattle, sheep, goats; there's bound to be plenty. Drive them back into the Sweetwater canyon and set a pen across the entrance. There's good grass there. And I don't want any of you tackling the Hellborn. First sign of the bastards and you run for it. Understand?'

Both men nodded and Gambion made to speak but Cade lifted his hand.

'No more questions. Move!'

Cade limped across the hollow to where Sebastian sat. He was a short, sallow-faced youth barely nineteen years old, but a scout more skilled than any Yeager mountain man.

'Take a good horse and get behind the Hellborn. They must have supplies coming in, ammunition and the like. Find me the route.'

Cade turned and twisted his knee. He bit back an angry oath and gritted his teeth against the blinding pain. Two years had passed since the incident, and there had not been a day during that time when the agony had been less than tolerable.

He could still recall with crystal clarity the morning when he, Gambion and five others rode into the market town of Allion to see a lone figure standing in the dusty main street.

'You are not wanted here, Cade,' the man had told him. Cade had blinked and leaned forward to study the speaker. He was tall, with shoulder-length greying hair and piercing eyes which looked right through a man.

'Jonathan? Is it you?'

'Hell, Daniel,' said Gambion, 'that's the Jerusalem Man.'

'Jonnie?'

'I have nothing to say to you, Daniel,' said Shannow. 'Ride from here. Go to Hell, where you belong.'

'Do not judge me, little brother. You have no right.'

Before Shannow could reply a youngster riding with Cade – a foolish boy named Rabbon – pulled a flintlock from his belt and cocked it. Shannow shot him from the saddle and the main street became a bedlam of rearing horses and gunshots, screaming men and the cries of the dying. A stray shot smashed Cade's knee and Gambion, wounded in the arm, had grabbed the reins of Cade's horse and galloped him clear. Behind them lay five dead or dying men.

Three weeks later the good people of Allion had sent Shannow packing and Cade had returned with all his men. By Heaven, they had paid for his knee!

He had not seen his brother since that painful day, but one day they would meet again, and meanwhile Cade dreamed of the sweetness of revenge.

Lisa, his woman, moved alongside him. She was a thin, hollow-eyed farm girl Cade had taken two years before. Normally he discarded his women within weeks, but there was something about Lisa which compelled him to keep her, some inner harmony which brought peace to Cade's bitter heart. She would cock her head to one side and smile at him, then all his aggression and violence would fade and he would take her hand and they would sit together, secure in each other's company. The single undeniable fact of Cade's nomadic life was that Lisa loved him. He didn't know why, and he cared less. The fact was enough.

'Why are you doing this, Daniel?' she asked, leading him to their cabin and sitting alongside him on the leather-covered bench he had made the previous autumn.

'Doing what?' he hedged.

'Bringing refugees into Yeager?'

'You think I shouldn't?'

'No, I think it is a good thing to save lives. But I wondered why.'

'Why a Brigand wolf should lead the lambs into his den?'

'Yes.'

'You rule out the milk of human kindness?'

She kissed his cheek and tilted her head and smiled.

'I know you have a kind side, Daniel, but I also know you are a cunning man! What do you see in this for you?'

'The Hellborn are destroying the land and they will leave no place for me. But if I oppose them alone, they will crush me. So, I need an army.'

'An army of lambs?' she asked, giggling.

'An army of lambs,' he conceded. 'But bear in mind that the reason the Brigands prosper is that the farmers can never link together to oppose us. There are brave men among them – skilful men, tough men. Together I can make them a force to be reckoned with.'

'But what do *you* get out of this?'

'If I lose . . . nothing. If I win? I get the world, Lisa. I will be the saviour. Ever thought of being a queen?'

'They'll never stand for it,' she said. 'As soon as the battle is over, they'll remember what you were and turn on you.'

'We shall see, but from now on there will be a new Daniel Cade – a caring, kind, understanding leader of men. The Hellborn have given me the chance, and damned if I'm not grateful to them.'

'But they'll come after you with all their terrible weapons.'

'True, little Lisa, but they have to come up the Franklin Pass and a child could hold that with a catapult.'

'Do you really think it will be that easy?'

'No, Lisa,' he said, suddenly serious. 'It will be the biggest gamble of my life. But then my men are always telling me they would follow me into Hell. Now's their chance to prove it!'

Shannow could not sleep. He lay back with his head on his saddle, his body warm in the blankets, but images flashed and swirled in his mind. Donna Taybard, Ruth and the library, Archer and his ghosts – but most of all, Abaddon.

It had been an easy threat to utter. But this was not some Brigand chief hiding in a mountain lair. This was a general, a king: a man who could command an army of thousands.

Donna had asked him once how he had the nerve to face a group of men, and he had told her the simple truth. Take out the leader and nullify the followers. But could that hold true in this case?

Babylon was some six weeks' ride to the south-west. Walpurnacht, according to Batik, was less than a month away. He could not save Donna, as he could not save Curopet.

All he could exact was vengeance. And for what?

His eyes burned with weariness and he closed them, but still sleep would not come. He felt burdened by the size of the task ahead. At last he fell into a fitful sleep.

He dreamt he walked upon a green hill, beneath a warm sun, where he could hear the sea lapping on an unseen shore and the sound of horses running over grass. He sat beneath a spreading oak and closed his eyes.

'Welcome, stranger,' said a voice.

Shannow opened his eyes to see a tall man sitting cross-legged in front of him. He was bearded and wore his shoulder-length hair in three braids; his eyes were sky-blue, his face strong.

'Who are you?'

'Pendarric. And you are Shannow the Questor.'

'How is it you know me?'

'Why should I not? I know all who dwell in my palace.'

The man was wearing a light blue tunic and a thick cloth belt braided with gold thread. By his side hung a short sword with an ornate hilt, and the pommel was a Daniel Stone the size of an apple.

'Are you a ghost?'

'An interesting point for discussion,' said Pendarric. 'I am as I always was, whereas you are not truly here. So who is the ghost?'

'This is a dream – Archer and his games.'

'Perhaps.' The man drew his sword and thrust it into the ground. 'Take a long look, Shannow. Be sure you will recognize it again.'

'Why?'

'Call it a game. But when you see it, in whatever form, reach out for it and it will be there.'

'I am no swordsman.'

'No, but you have a heart. And you are Rolynd.'

'No, I am not one of your people.'

Pendarric smiled. 'The Rolynd is not a race, Shannow, it is a state of being. Your friend Archer has it wrong. A man cannot be born Rolynd, nor even become Rolynd. It is what he is, or what he is not.

'It is an apartness, a loneliness, a talent. You have not survived this far on skill alone, that within you guides you. You have a sense for danger which you call instinct, but it is far more. Trust it . . . and remember the sword.'

'You think I can win?'

'No. What I am telling you is that you are not merely a lone warrior set against an impossible enemy. You are Rolynd and that is more important than winning.'

'Are you also Rolynd?'

'No, Shannow, though my father was. Had I been so lucky, my people would not have died so terribly. I killed them all. And that is why I brought you here. No one understands the power of the Sipstrassi. It can heal, it can kill. But in the main it enhances, transmutes dreams to reality. You wish to heal the sick? The Sipstrassi will do it, until its power is no more. You wish to kill, and the Stone will do that too. But here there is a terrible power, for the Stone will feed on death and grow in strength. It will gnaw the soul of the wielder, enhancing his evil. In the end . . . ? My people could tell you about the end, Shannow. The world almost died. We ripped apart the fabric of time and buried our world under an ocean. Tragic as that was, there was one great virtue; the Sipstrassi was buried too. But now it has returned and the terror waits.'

'Are you saying the world will fall again?'

'Within a year.'

'How can you be sure?'

'Have you not heard my words? I caused it once. I conquered the world; I built an empire across the centre of the lands, from Xechotl to Greece. I opened the gateways of the universe and gave your people the myths they carry to this day – dragons and trolls, demons and Gorgons. What man can imagine, the Sipstrassi will create. But there is a balance to Nature that must not be changed. I tore the thread that held the world.'

Shannow saw the anguish in Pendarric's face. 'I cannot stop the spread of evil. I can only kill Abaddon. He will be replaced and I cannot change the fate of the world.'

'Remember the sword, Shannow.'

The sun sank, and darkness covered Shannow like a blanket.

He opened his eyes and was once more within the ruined palace.

Batik was preparing a fire. 'You look well rested,' said the Hellborn.

Shannow rubbed his eyes and threw aside his blankets. 'I think I'll scout for sign of the Zealots.'

'Archer says they headed west.'

'I don't give a damn what Archer says!'

'You want company?'

'No.' Shannow tugged on his boots, then hefted his saddle to his shoulder and left the palace. Saddling the gelding, he rode from the city and for three hours scanned the lands bordering the mountains, but there was no trace of the hunters. Confused and uncertain, he returned to the city.

Batik had killed two rabbits, and was roasting them on a spit when Shannon entered the palace. Archer was asleep by the far wall.

'Find anything?'

'No.'

Archer stirred and sat up. 'Welcome back, Mr Shannow.'

'Tell me of Pendarric,' said the Jerusalem Man and Archer's eyes widened.

'You are a man full of surprises. How did you come by the name?'

'What does it matter? Tell me.'

'He was the last recorded King – or at least, the last I have found. It seems he was a warlord. He extended the Atlantean empire to the edges of South America in the west and up to England in the north; heaven knows how far south he went. Is there a reason for these questions?'

'I am becoming interested in history,' said Shannow, joining Batik at the fire. The Hellborn sliced some meat from the cindering carcass and placed it on a half-crushed gold plate.

'There you go, Shannow. Now you can eat like a king.'

Archer moved over and sat beside Shannow. 'Tell me, please, how did you learn of Pendarric?'

'I dreamt the name, and woke up with it on my mind.'

'That is a shame; he is my last great mystery. Ruth considers me obsessed.'

Outside the palace the sky darkened and thunder rumbled. The winds picked up and soon lashing rain scoured the dead city.

'Hardly worth travelling today,' observed Batik.

Shannow nodded and turned to Archer. 'Tell me more about the Sipstrassi.'

'There is very little of certainty. The name means "Stone from the sky" and the Rolynd took it to be a gift from God. I've discussed this with my leader, Sarento. He believes it could have been a meteor.'

'Meteor? What's he talking about, Shannow?' asked Batik.

Shannow shrugged. 'Archer has been studying the Stones, the ones you call Satanseeds. And I've never heard of a meteor either.'

'Put simply,' said Archer, 'it is a giant rock spinning in space, among the stars if you like. For whatever reason, it crashed into the earth. Now such a collision would cause an immense explosion, and the Rolynd legend says that the sky was dark as night for three days, and there was no sun or moon. Sarento suggests that the impact would have hurled thousands of tons of dust up into the atmosphere, blocking the sun. The meteor itself would have burst into millions of fragments, and these are the Sipstrassi.

'Apart from obvious myths, there is no valid record of the first use of the Stones. Even now, after much research, we understand little about them. With each use their power fades by a fraction, until at last they are merely small rocks. The black veins within the Stones swell, obliterating the gold; when the Stone becomes black, it is useless.'

'Unless you feed it blood,' put in Shannow.

'I'm not sure that's true, Mr Shannow. Blood-fed Stones become dull red and cannot be used for healing, or the creation of food. Sarento and I carried out experiments using small animals – rabbits, rats and the like. The Stones retain power, but they are altered. My own findings show that Blood Stones have a detrimental effect upon their users. Take the Hellborn, for example; their ruthlessness grows and their lust for blood cannot be sated. Tell me, Batik, when you lost your Stone?'

'How do you know I lost it?'

'Carrying a Satanseed, you would never have been allowed into Sanctuary. So, when you lost the Stone, how did you feel?'

'Angry, frightened. I could not sleep for almost a week.'

'How often did you feed the Stone?'

'Every month, with my own blood.'

'And were I to offer you a Stone now, would you take it?'

'I . . . yes.'

'And yet you hesitated.'

'I seem to feel more alive without one. But then again, the power . . .'

'Yes, the power. In another year, Batik, if you live that long, you will not hesitate. And that, Mr Shannow, is why I am fascinated by Pendarric. His laws were just in the early years, but he it was who discovered the obscene power of the Blood Stones. And within five years he was a merciless tyrant. But as yet I can find no end to his story. Did he succumb totally, or did he prevail? Or did the seas wash away all his deeds?'

Shannow was about to answer when he froze. An edge of fear touched him. 'Get away from the fire,' he hissed.

Batik was already moving, but Archer remained. 'What . . . ?'

The door burst open and two Zealots leapt inside, pistols blazing. Shannow dived to his right and rolled, shells shrieking around him.

Archer disappeared in a plume of red smoke. Another Zealot opened fire from the upper balcony and the shell exploded shards of mosaic from the floor by Shannow's head. His own pistol came up and fired and the Zealot spun from sight.

Batik wounded the nearest Zealot and pinned down the other behind a white statue. Shannow rolled to his back in an alcove and levelled both pistols at the door to the rear.

The door exploded inwards and three men raced into sight, only to be cut down in the rolling thunder of Shannow's guns. The one remaining Zealot made a run for the door, but was pitched from his feet as Batik's shell smashed a hole in his temple.

Batik reloaded his pistol and crept through the shadows towards the man he had wounded.

'Down!' yelled Shannow and Batik dived to the floor as the Zealot's pistol levelled. The Jerusalem Man fired twice and the would-be assassin slumped back. Shannow reloaded his pistols and waited, but only silence surrounded them.

'How the Devil do you do that, Shannow?' asked Batik,

moving across the mosaic floor. 'I heard nothing.'

'I used to think it was instinct but now I am not sure. Where is Archer?'

'Here,' said the black man. He was sitting by the fire, staring at a small black pebble in his palm. 'All used up. Shame! I was rather fond of that little Stone.'

'They were supposed to be far from here,' snapped Batik.

'Put not your faith in magic, boy,' Shannow told him, smiling. Together the two men searched the bodies, gathering ammunition while Archer added wood to the blaze. 'I don't think we should stay much longer,' said Shannow. 'I hate to sit here like a target.'

'I'll take you to the Ark,' said Archer. 'You'll be safe there.'

'I need to be heading south-west. To Babylon.'

'To kill the Satanlord?'

'Yes.'

'I don't think that's what Ruth has in mind for you.'

'Archer, it doesn't matter what she has in mind; I am not her servant. And despite her beliefs, surely she can see that the world would be a better place without him?'

'Perhaps. But then, in the case of Abaddon, there is a link between them that is stronger than blood.'

'What link?'

'Ruth is Abaddon's wife.'

Chapter Eight

Samuel Archer stood in the doorway as the two warriors dragged the corpses out into the open, dumping them by a low wall. There was no dignity in death, he realized, seeing that the dead had fouled themselves and the stench carried even through the rain.

There were some amongst the Guardians who were considered soldiers, men of action. Yet none that Archer could bring to mind could match that chilling quality possessed by the Jerusalem Man. How he had heard the approach of the assassins amid a storm baffled Archer. And without the Stone to mask him with invisibility, Archer himself would have died sitting at the fire. Neither Shannow nor Batik had mentioned the plume of red smoke, which Archer had been quite proud of – a distraction for the Zealots, giving the warriors time to react. He decided he would mention it himself when the opportunity arose.

The palace hall smelt of cordite and death and Archer wandered up the long steps to the balcony. There was a pool of blood by the rail, and the black man recalled how Batik had walked here earlier and heaved the body to the stones below where it had landed with a crunching thud.

Shannow came in out of the rain and removed his leather coat. He knelt for a few seconds at the fire, warming his hands, then took his Bible from his saddlebag.

'Clues as to the whereabouts of Jerusalem?' asked Archer, sitting beside him.

'No, I find reading eases my mind.' He shut the Bible. 'I saw Pendarric in a dream last night. He said he caused the world to drown by using Blood Stones and he warned me that it is about to happen again.'

'Through the Hellborn?'

'Yes, I believe so. Do you have anything in the Ark that could help me bring down Abaddon?'

'It's not my field, Mr Shannow. I am a researcher into things arcane. But there are weapons there.'

'And knowledge?'

'Indeed there is knowledge.'

'I will ride with you, Archer. Now leave me to read in peace.'

Archer wandered to the door and looked out into the rain. Batik joined him.

'You can't talk to him when the dark moods are upon him, and for a religious man he is in no hurry to share his God.'

'He has much on his mind, Batik.'

'I don't care about that, just so long as he hears the killers in the night. He's a remarkable man. All my life I have been taught to fear the Zealots as the greatest warriors in the world, but they are like children compared with him.'

'Will you stay with him?'

'For a little while, Archer. I have no intention of returning to Babylon and following Shannon as he charges the palace single-handed.'

'A strange attitude for a friend to take?'

'We are not friends, Archer. He has no friends – he does not need friends. Look at him, sitting there like a rock. I am a warrior, yet I am still shaking over the attack. I wonder how many other enemies are closing on us as we speak. Him? He reads his Bible.'

'But if he needed you, would you go?'

'No. What do I care if Abaddon conquers the world? I made one mistake, Archer, when I tried to save my sister. Otherwise I would probably now command a company and be invading the southlands myself.'

'You think he will succeed alone?'

'I don't know. But I tell you this – I would not want him hunting me, even if I sat in a fortress surrounded by guards. There is something inhuman about him; he is unable to recognize impossible odds. You should have seen him when the Zealots attacked just now – he turned and trained his guns on the rear door long before the other three came in. He knew they were coming, but all I could hear was gunfire and all I could see were the men before me. If I was Abaddon, I would not be sleeping well.'

'He does not know Shannow as you do.'

'No, but he will be counting the bodies.'

Archer glanced back. Shannow was no longer reading; his head was on his saddle, his blankets drawn around him, but his right arm was uncovered.

And in his hand was a pistol.

'Fine way to sleep,' said Batik. 'Whatever you do, don't make a sudden noise in the night!'

Shannow was awake and the words of the two men carried to him like whispers on the wind. How little Batik understood him. But then why should he? Shannow had long since learned that in loneliness there is strength. A man who needs to rely on others leaves a gap in his defences. A lonely man sits within walls.

A need for friends? No man could have it all, Shannow knew. It was all a question of balance and Nature was always miserly with gifts. A long time ago, Shannow had known a runner. To maintain his strength, the man forsook all the foods he desired and trained daily. It was so with Shannow the hunter. Alone he was a rock, relying on nothing and no one to defend his back.

For a while he had tasted the other life with Donna. And it was good . . .

Now he was back where he belonged.

And Jerusalem would have to wait.

He heard his companions settle in their blankets, then sat up.

'You think it advisable that we all sleep?' he asked Batik.

'You are suggesting that I stand watch?'

'Better than waking up dead.'

'I'll not argue with that.'

Shannow closed his eyes once more and fell into a dreamless sleep, waking as Batik crept towards him three hours later.

'I swear you could hear an ant break wind,' said Batik. 'It's all quiet out there.'

Shannow sat up and stretched, then took his place by the door. The night was still and the rain had passed. He walked from the palace, scanning deserted buildings which gleamed in the moonlight. In the distance he heard the coughing roar of a hunting lion and the far-off howl of a mountain wolf.

The whisper of leather on stone saw him swivel, his hand sweeping up and pistol cocked. Archer spread his hands in alarm.

'It is only me,' he whispered. 'I couldn't sleep.'

Shannow eased the hammer into place and shook his head. 'You are a fool, Archer. The difference between life and death for you just then was too small to be measured.'

'I apologize,' said Archer, 'though I don't know why. You were in no danger.'

'No, that is not true. I once killed someone who just happened to be behind me at the wrong moment. It is not something I wish to do again. But understand this – had you been a Zealot, that fraction of hesitation would have killed me. And the next time I hear a noise, I might just wonder if it is you being stupid or an enemy coming closer. Then I might die. You understand that?'

'No need to labour the point, Mr Shannow. I shall never again approach you without warning.'

Shannow sat back on a low wall and sheathed his pistol. He grinned suddenly, his face becoming boyish. 'Forgive me, Archer, that was terribly pompous. I am on edge but it will pass. How long will it take us to reach the Ark?'

'Two days. Three. You can relax there – and I'll show you a library that is not conjured from air.'

'Will it show me the way to Jerusalem?'

'Who knows?' replied Archer. 'I can certainly show you images of the Jerusalem that once was. Then at least you'll know it when you see it – that is, if God used the same architect.'

A flash of annoyance darkened Shannow's features, but he forced it to pass. 'I expect that he did, Mr Archer.' His eyes swept the buildings and the land to the south and east.

'You think there are more of them out there?' asked the Guardian.

'Of course. We have been lucky this far. Their arrogance has betrayed them, but I think they will be more careful now.'

'I wish I had not lectured Batik about his Stone. You have no idea how much I miss mine; I feel like a child in the dark.'

'There is a positive side to fear,' said Shannow. 'It sharpens the senses, keeps you alert.'

'I think you rather enjoy the danger.'

'Do not be taken in by appearances. I am not inhuman, as Batik thinks. I too shook after the attack. That's why I read my Bible – to take my mind from the fury and the fear. Now get some sleep, Mr Archer, and be assured that nothing will disturb your slumber. If you like, you can borrow one of my spare pistols.'

'No, thank you. I don't believe I could ever kill a man.'

'I wish more people felt like you. Good night.'

Soon after dawn the three men saddled their mounts and left the city, heading north-west. To the east of them a pride of lions was slumbering beneath a gnarled oak. Nearby the carcass of a buffalo was gathering flies. The lions were content and sleepy.

Suddenly the leader, a great beast with a red-gold mane, jerked as if stung. Then he stood and turned towards the west and five other young males rose with him.

In the distance three horsemen were riding slowly towards the mountains.

The six lions padded silently after them.

Abaddon stood on the tower ramparts above his palace and stared out over the city below him, listening to the steady rhythmic pounding of the weapons factory machines and watching the thick black smoke belching from the three mud brick-stacks above it.

Dressed in a black robe embroidered with a golden

dragon, Abaddon felt almost at peace here above the nation he had cultivated for so long.

Only one nagging doubt assailed his peace of mind.

The High Priest, Achnazzar, approached, bowing low.

'They have located Shannow, sire, and the renegade Batik. They are travelling with a Guardian,' said the hawknosed priest, his bald head shining with sweat.

'I know this,' said Abaddon.

'Do you wish them all dead?'

'It is necessary.'

'You have said, sire, that we should leave the Guardians be.'

'I know what I have said, Achnazzar.'

'Very well, sire. It will be as you command.'

'It was you, priest, who brought me the first word on Shannow; you said he was a danger. He was to have been killed in Rivervale, but instead he killed our man there. He was to have died at the camp of Karitas – but no, he led a raid which saw scores of our young men butchered as they slept. And how many Zealots has he slain? No, don't bother me with the arithmetic. But tell me this: if I cannot rely on you to kill one man, how can I rely on you to build me an empire?'

'Lord,' said Achnazzar, falling to his knees, 'you can rely on me to death and beyond. I am your slave.'

'I have many slaves, priest. What I need from you is results.'

'You shall have them, sire. I promise on my life.'

'Indeed you do,' whispered Abaddon.

Achnazzar blanched and backed away from the ferocious gleam in Abaddon's grey eyes. 'It will be done, sire.'

'And we need Donna Taybard on the High Altar on Walpurnacht Eve. Have you re-checked the star charts?'

'I have, sire.'

'And are the results the same?'

'Yes, sire. Even more promising, in fact.'

'There must be no error with her – she must not be harmed in any way until that night. The power contained in her must be harnessed for the Hellborn.'

'It will be, sire.'

'So far I have heard many promises.'

'The army is sweeping south and there is little resistance.'

'You hesitated on the word "little",' noted Abaddon.

'It seems that twenty of our men were ambushed near the Yeager mountains. But a punitive force has been despatched to deal with the attackers.'

'Who were they?'

'A Brigand named Daniel Cade. But he is not a problem, sire, I assure you.'

'Find out all you can about the man. He intrigues me.'

Daniel Cade looked down at the gathering of men and women on the mountainside below him. At the last count there were six hundred and seventy refugees, including eighty-four children. Cade had brushed back his hair and cleaned his black frock-coat with the wide leather lapels. Leaning on a handsomely carved stick, he cast his eyes over the crowd. He could see suspicion on many faces, blank open hatred on others.

He took a deep breath and cleared his throat.

'You all know me,' he said, his voice deep, clear and resonant in the mountain air. 'Daniel Cade. Cade the Brigand. Cade the Killer. Cade the Thief. Many of you have cause to hate me. And I don't blame you – I have been an evil man.'

'You still are, Cade,' shouted a voice from the crowd. 'So get on with it! What do you want from us?'

'Nothing. I want you to be safe.'

'What is it going to cost us?' asked another man.

'Nothing. Let me speak, and then I will answer all your questions. Ten days ago, something happened to change my life. I was on that mountain yonder, just short of the snow-line, when a voice came to me out of the sky and a bright light struck my eyes, blinding me. "Cade," it said, "you are an evil man, and you deserve death."'

'It was damned right about that!' came the shout.

'Indeed it was,' agreed Cade. 'I don't mind admitting that I lay there on that mountain begging for life. I knew it was God talking to me, and I knew I was done for. All the evil deeds came flooding back to me and I wept for the trouble I'd caused. But then he says to me, "Cade, the hour has come for your redemption. My people, whom you've sore beset, have come upon tribulation. And a people of the Devil have come to the borders like angry locusts."

'"I can't do nothing, God," I said. "I can't fight armies."

'Then he says, "I took the people of Israel from out of Egypt against the power of the Pharaoh. I took Joshua and gave him the Promised Land. I took David and gave him Goliath. To you I will give the Hellborn."

'"I can't do it," I said. "Take my life. End it here."

'But he refused. "Save my lambs," he told me. "Bring them here to the Yeager mountains. Suffer the little ones to come unto safety."

'And then the blindness lifted from my eyes, and I said to him, "But all these people hate me. They'll kill me."

'And he said, "They hate you with good reason. When I have led you to conquer the Hellborn, you will make amends to all the people you have made to suffer."

'I stood up then and I asked him how we could beat the Hellborn. And his voice came down – and I'll never forget it to my dying day – and said, "With their own weapons ye shall strike them down." And he told me that there was a convoy of wagons to the north, and I sent Gambion and forty men. And they captured that convoy and brought it here. And do you know what it contains? Rifles and pistols and bullets and powder. Two hundred weapons!

'And they are yours. For nothing. I ask nothing – only that you allow me to obey my God and lead you against the spawn of Satan.'

Cade waved Gambion forward and the huge man shuffled to the front of the crowd carrying several rifles. These he passed to the men in the front line.

A young farmer Cade recognized, but could not name, took a rifle and asked Gambion how to cock it. The bearded

Brigand showed him and the farmer swung the rifle on Cade, his eyes burning with anger.

'Give me one good reason, Cade, why I shouldn't kill you? And don't bother with talk of God, because I ain't a believer.'

'There's no reason, brother,' said Cade. 'I am a man who deserves death and I'll not complain.'

For several seconds Cade ceased to breathe, but he stood his ground. The man handed the rifle to Gambion. 'I don't know about you, Cade, but it seems to me that any man so unafraid of dying ought to be sincere. But if you ain't . . .'

'Trust in the Lord, brother. You'll have no reason to doubt my sincerity. And here's the proof: The Lord came to me yesterday and said: "Three hundred riders are bearing down on your mountains, Cade, but I will deliver them into your hands." How many of you will come with me to destroy the Devil's people?'

The air came alive with waving arms and a roaring cry echoed in the mountains.

Cade limped away to where Lisa sat with a canteen of water. She wiped his face with a towel and was surprised to see the sweat on his features.

'You look like you've been through Hell,' she said, kissing his cheek.

'You don't know the half of it. When that boy pointed the rifle, I thought it was all over. But I got them, Lisa. By God, I got them!'

'I wish you hadn't lied about God,' said Lisa. 'It frightens me.'

'There's nothing to be frightened of, girl. Who's to say? Maybe God *did* come to me. Maybe it was his idea that I should tackle the Hellborn. And even if it wasn't, I'm sure he won't mind me smiting the bastards hip and thigh. Where's the harm?'

'It mocks him, Daniel.'

'I didn't know you were a believer.'

'Well, I am, and don't you mock me.'

He took her hands and smiled. 'No mockery, I promise. But I was reading the Bible all last night, and I tell you there's power in it. Not miracles and suchlike, but the way one man can bind a people together merely by telling them he's God's mouthpiece. And it seems they'll fight like devils if they think God is with them.'

'But it wasn't God who told you about the convoy, it was Sebastian.'

'But who led Sebastian to the convoy?'

'Don't play with words, Daniel. I am afraid for you.'

He was about to reply when Lisa placed her fingers on her lips in warning and he turned to see Sebastian climbing the hill. The young man squatted down beside him.

'Was it true, Dan?'

'What, lad?'

'About God and the convoy?' His eyes were shining and Cade glanced at Lisa, suddenly ill at ease.

'Of course it was true, Sebastian.'

'Dammit, Daniel. Damn it all to Hell,' said Sebastian happily. He smiled at Lisa and then sprinted away over the mountainside.

'Would you believe that?' said Cade.

'No, but he did!'

'What does that mean?'

'Didn't you look at his face, Daniel? He was overjoyed. He looks up in the sky now and he sees God smiling down on him.'

'Is that so bad?'

'I don't think you realize the full power of such a deceit.'

'Power is what I want, Lisa. And it won't hurt Sebastian to think that God loves him.'

'I'm not sure that is true,' said Lisa, 'but let's wait and see. I am more worried about you. What will you tell them when things go wrong? How will you explain when God lies to you?'

Cade chuckled. 'That was all in the Bible too, Lisa. It's a smart book. When things go right, God did it. When they go wrong, it was because he was disobeyed, or the people were unholy, or it was a punishment. He never loses and neither will I. Me and God, we understand one another. Trust me.'

'I trust you, Daniel. I love you. You're all I have – all I want.'

'I'll give you the world, Lisa. Wait and see.'

Two days later Cade and Gambion sat their horses on the plain before the Yeager mountains, watching the column of Hellborn bearing down on them.

'Time to run, Daniel?'

'Not yet,' said Cade, pulling clear his long rifle and cocking it. Leaning forward, he sighted the weapon on the lead rider and gently tightened the trigger. The rifle bucked against his shoulder and the rider tumbled from the saddle.

Shells whistled round their ears.

'Now, Daniel?'

'Damn right!'

They wheeled their horses and thundered towards the pass.

Cade cursed, knowing he had left it a little late. A shot killed his horse and the animal pitched head-first to the ground, catapulting Cade from the saddle. He landed hard and screamed as his knee cracked against a rock. Gambion was almost clear and he dragged his mount back, drew his pistol and charged back towards Cade. By some miracle he was not hit and his hairy hand grasped Cade's collar, hauling him across the saddle.

Gambion's horse was hit twice but it gamely stuck to its run into the pass; then, with blood pumping from its nostrils, it sank to the ground. Gambion leapt clear, pulled Cade across his shoulders and ran for the rocks. Bullets screamed close and the Hellborn bore down on them.

Hidden in the rocks all around the pass, the riflemen of Yeager took careful aim. But they could not fire, for Gambion and Cade were virtually in the midst of the enemy.

Gambion shot two riders from their mounts before a bullet struck his shoulder, knocking him back. He fell heavily, pitching the stunned Cade to the ground.

Cade rolled and came up on his knees to find himself

staring into the black muzzles of the Hellborn rifles and pistols. His eyes raked the warriors with their shining black breastplates and curious helms.

'God damn you all!' he said.

A rifle shot broke the silence and Cade winced, but the shell came from the pass and smashed a Hellborn from the saddle. Suddenly the air was alive with a merciless hail of bullets that shrieked and screamed into the massed ranks of the enemy. The noise echoed in the mountains like the wrath of God, and when the smoke cleared the dozen or so Hellborn survivors were racing from the pass.

Cade limped back to Gambion. The big man was alive, the wound high in his chest cutting the muscle above his collar-bone.

He gripped Cade's arm. 'I never seen nothing like it, Daniel,' he whispered. 'Never! I thought you was lying to them farmers, but now I've seen it with my own eyes. Them Hellborn couldn't shoot you, and you on your knees and unarmed. And then you called on God . . .'

'Lie there, Ephram. Rest and I'll stop that bleeding.'

'Who would have believed it? Daniel Cade, chosen by God!'

'Yes,' said Cade sadly. 'Who could believe it?'

The spirit of Donna Taybard soared out of control in a blur of speed and light that caused her mind to spin. Her thoughts were incoherent and a thousand voices lashed at her like whips of roaring sound.

Stars sped by like comets and she hurtled through the hearts of many suns, feeling neither heat nor cold in her mad race to escape the voices in her mind.

A hand touched hers and she screamed, but the hand held on, pulling her, and the voices faded.

'Be calm, child, I am with you,' said Karitas.

'I can't endure this any more. What is happening to me?'

'It is the land, Donna. As your child grows within you, so too does the power.'

'I don't want it.'

'It is not a question of want; you must conquer it. You will never overcome fear by running away from it.'

Together they floated above a peaceful blue planet and watched the swirling clouds below.

'I cannot cope with it, Karitas. I am losing all sense of reality.'

'It is all real – both the life of the flesh and the power of the spirit. This is real. Con Griffin is real. Abaddon is real.'

'He covered me with black wings and talons. He told me he could take me whenever he chose.'

'He is a princely liar. Who knows where your power will lead you?'

'I can't control it, Karitas. I was sitting at home looking after Jacob, dressing his wounds, when he opened his eyes and could not see me. And I realized that my body was asleep in a chair before the fire and I had come to him as a spirit. And I did not even know!'

'But you *will*,' he said soothingly. 'I promise you. And I will help you.'

'What have I become, Karitas? What am I becoming?'

'You are a woman. And a very pretty woman. Were I a couple of hundred years younger, and not dead, I would pay court to you myself!'

She smiled then and some of the tension eased from her.

'What are the voices?'

'They are the souls of sleepers, dreamers. Imagine yourself in a river of souls; they are just random voices, not directed at you. You must learn to screen them out, as you screen out the noise of the wind in the trees.'

'And my pregnancy is the cause of this?'

'Yes and no. The babe and the land, working together.'

'And will she be harmed by what is happening to me? Will she be changed?'

'She?'

'It is a girl . . . she is a girl.'

'I do not know, Donna. We'll see.'

'Will you take me home?'

'No. You must find your own way.'

'I can't, I am lost.'

'Try. I will follow you.'

Donna flashed towards the blue planet, skimming mountains and crossing wide glistening lakes and rolling prairies. There was nothing she recognized. She saw settlements of tents, homes of stone – cabins, huts and even cave dwellings. She crossed an ocean and watched ships with triangular sails battling storms and reefs, until at last she came to a world of ice and glaciers, like palaces, tall and stately.

'I cannot find my way,' she said.

'Close your eyes and think yourself home.'

She tried, but when she opened them she was below the sea, watching sharks gliding around the spiked head of an enormous statue. She panicked and flew and Karitas caught her.

'Listen to me, Donna. Fear and panic are your enemies. Look on them with loathing as the servants of Abaddon and dismiss them from your mind. Your home is a warm cabin where your husband and your son wait for you. Be drawn by their love and their need; you can explore sunken cities at any time.'

She closed her eyes once more and thought of Con Griffin, but Jon Shannow's face came to her mind. She shut him out and saw the red-headed Griffin sitting beside her sleeping form. He had her hand in his and his face was troubled. She closed on the scene and opened the eyes of her body.

'Con,' she whispered.

'Are you well?'

'I am fine.' She lifted her hand to touch his face and he recoiled.

Both her hands were in her lap, and she had touched him with her spirit. Tears welled in her eyes.

'I cannot control it,' she said. 'There are no chains any more, holding me to my body.'

'I don't understand. Are you sick?'

'No.' She concentrated on standing and felt loose inside her body, as if her soul were liquid and her flesh a sponge that could not contain it. He helped her to her bed. In the other room Madden's wife, Rachel, sat by him as he slept.

Madden stirred. He had lost a great deal of blood, but his strength was returning. He opened his eyes to see Rachel's careworn face.

'Don't worry about me, lass. I'll be back on my feet in no time.'

'I know that,' she said, patting his hand.

He fell asleep once more and Rachel lifted the blankets to his chin and left him for a while, moving to sit beside Griffin at the wood-stove.

'What's happening to us, Con?' she asked. He looked at her lined, troubled face and pictured her as she must have been a decade before – a slim pretty woman with huge brown eyes that belied the strength hidden behind them. Now her hair was greying, her skin had the texture of worn leather and dark rings circled her eyes.

'These are not the best of times, Rachel. But we are still alive, and there's plenty of fight left in us.'

'But we didn't come here to fight, Con. You promised us Avalon.'

'I am sorry.'

'So am I.'

He poured her some tea. 'Are you hungry?'

'No.' she said. 'I'd best be going. How soon do you think we can move him home?'

'In a day or two.'

'How is Donna?'

'Sleeping.'

'Be careful with her, Con. Pregnancy often disturbs a woman's mind.'

'Often?'

She looked away. 'Well, no, not often, but I have heard of it before.'

'There is nothing wrong with her mind, Rachel. Had it not been for Donna's powers, Jacob would now be dead.'

'Had it not been for you, Jacob would not have been shot at all!'

'I cannot deny that, but I wish you wouldn't hate me for it.'

'I don't hate you, Con,' said Rachel, standing and smoothing her heavy skirt. 'I just see you as less of a friend.'

He saw her to the door and returned to the fire.

Events seemed to be moving out of control, leaving Griffin feeling like a leaf in a storm. Donna was caught in the grip of something Griffin could not begin to understand, and the Hellborn had sealed the valley tighter than sin.

But why did they not attack? What did they want?

Griffin rammed his fist down on the arm of the chair.

He had offered the people Avalon . . .

And he had brought them to Purgatory.

An hour out from the ruined city and a fresh storm broke over the riders. Driving rain lashed their faces and a howling wind raged before them like an invisible wall. Shannow dragged his long leather coat from behind his saddle and swung it over his shoulders; it billowed like a cape as he struggled to don it. The gelding ducked its head and pushed on into the fury of the storm. Shannow tied a long scarf over his hat as the winds continued to increase in power.

A tree nearby exploded with a tremendous crack as lightning ripped through it, and Shannow tried to ignore the weight of metal he carried in his pistols and knives. Batik turned in the saddle and shouted to him, but the words were torn away and lost in the wind.

The trail wound slowly upwards, narrowing to a rocky ledge. Riding at the rear, Shannow found his left stirrup grazing the cliff-face while his right hung over the edge. There was no going back now, for there was nowhere for a horse to turn.

Lightning flashed nearby, the gelding reared and Shannow fought to calm it. In the eerie light of the lightning's afterglow, the Jerusalem Man glanced down to the raging torrent some two hundred feet below where white water raced over jagged rocks. Lightning flashed again and some instinct made him turn in the saddle and look back down the trail.

Behind him, six lions were charging out of the storm like demons. His cold hand dropped to his pistol, but it was too late and the lead lion – a giant beast with a red-gold mane – leapt to land with terrible force on the gelding's back, its talons raking through flesh and muscle. Shannow's pistol pressed against the lion's head and the bullet entered its eye just as the gelding, in pain and terror, leapt from the ledge.

The pistol shot alerted Batik; he drew his own weapon and emptied it at the remaining beasts, who turned and ran. With no room to dismount, the Hellborn leaned in the saddle and stared down into the torrent far below.

There was no sign of the Jerusalem Man.

As Shannow's gelding leapt, the Jerusalem Man kicked himself from the saddle and spread his arms to steady his fall. Below him the rocks waited like spear-points and he tumbled through the air unable to control his movements. Down, down he fell, bringing his arms over his head, struggling to stop his dizzying spin. He hit the water at a deep section between rocks and the air was smashed from his lungs. He fought his way to the surface, sucked in a deep breath and was swept once more below the water. His heavy coat and pistol belt dragged him down; rocks cracked against his legs and arms as he battled the dreadful pull of the swollen river. Time and again, as he felt his lungs had reached bursting point, his head cleared the surface – only to be dragged below once more.

Grimly he fought for life until he was hurled out into the air over a waterfall some thirty feet high. This time he controlled his dive and entered the water cleanly. The river here swirled without violence and he struck out for the shore, dragging himself from the water with the last of his strength. He grasped a tree root and hung on, gasping for breath, his legs still under water. Then, having rested for some minutes, he eased his way up into thick undergrowth. Exhausted, he slept for over an hour and then awoke cold and shivering, his arms cramped and painful. Forcing himself to a sitting position, he checked his weapons. His left-hand pistol had been torn from his grasp after he killed the lion, but the other gun was still in his scabbard, the thong over the hammer saving it. His gelding lay dead some forty paces to his right, and he staggered to the body, pulling clear his saddlebags and looping them over his shoulder.

A dead lion floated by, half submerged, and Shannow smiled grimly, hoping that the Zealot who possessed it had died with the beast.

With the storm still venting its fury over the mountain Shannow had no idea in which direction to travel, so he found a limited shelter in the lee of a rock face and huddled out of the wind.

He could feel bruises beginning to swell on his arms and legs, and was grateful for the heat the throbbing caused in his limbs. Fumbling inside his saddlebags for his oilskin pouch, he removed six shells, then emptied his pistol and reloaded it. Looking round, he gathered some twigs from the ground close to the rocks. It was drier here and he carefully built a pyramid of tiny sticks. Breaking open the shells he had discarded, he emptied the black powder from the brass casings into the base of the pyramid and then reached into his shirt pocket to take out his tinder box; the tinder within was drenched and he threw it aside, but wiped the flint clean and worked the lever several times until white sparks flashed. Holding the box close to the base of the pyramid, he ignited the powder. Two sticks caught and he crouched down, blowing gently and coaxing the flame to life. Once the fragile blaze had taken, he gathered thicker branches and sat beside the fire, feeding it constantly until the heat drove him back. Then he pulled off his coat and laid it over a nearby rock to dry.

A shimmering light grew before him, coalescing into the form of Ruth. At first she was translucent, then her flesh became solid and she sat beside him.

'I have searched for you for hours,' she said. 'You are a tough man.'

'Are the others all right?'

'Yes, they are sheltering in a cave twelve miles from here.

The Zealots fled after you went over the ledge. I think their main purpose was to kill you; Batik is a much lesser prize.'

'Well, they failed, but not by much,' said Shannow, shivering as he added wood to the blaze. 'My horse is dead, poor beast. Best I ever had. He could run from yesterday into tomorrow. And he had heart – if he could have turned, he would have driven the lions away with his hooves.'

'What will you do now?'

'I'll find the Ark, and then Abaddon.'

'And you will try to kill him?'

'Yes, God willing.'

'How can you mention God in the same breath as murder?'

'Don't preach at me, woman,' he snapped. 'This is not Sanctuary, where your magic fills a man's mind with flowers and love. This is the world, the real world. Violent and uncertain. Abaddon is an obscenity to both God and Man. Murder? You cannot murder vermin, Ruth, he has forsaken all rights to mercy.'

'Vengeance is mine, saith the Lord?'

'An eye for an eye, a tooth for a tooth, a life for a life,' countered Shannow. 'Do not seek to debate with me. He has chosen to visit death and destruction upon the woman I loved. He taunted me with it. I cannot stop him, Ruth; a nation separates us. But, if the Lord is with me, I shall rid the world of him.'

'Who are you to judge when a man's life is forfeit?'

'What are you to judge when it is not? There is not this debate when a mad dog kills a child. You kill the dog. But when a man commits the blackest sins, why must we sermonize and rationalize? I am sick of it, Ruth. I've lost count of the number of towns and settlements that have called for me to rid them of Brigands. And when I do, what do I hear? "Did you have to kill them, Mr Shannow?" "Was there a need for so much violence, Mr Shannow?" It is a question of balance, Ruth. If a man throws his food on the fire, who will have pity on him when he runs around shouting, "I'm starving"? So it is with the Brigand. He deals in violence and death, theft and pillage. And I give them no pity. I don't blame you, woman; you're arguing for your husband. But I'm not listening.'

'Do not patronize me, Mr Shannow,' said Ruth, without anger. 'Your arguments are simplistic, but they carry weight. I am not, however, arguing for my husband. I have not seen him in two and a half centuries and he does not know I am alive, nor would he care greatly if he did. I am more concerned with you. I am not a prophet, yet I feel some terrible catastrophe looms and I sense you should not pursue this current course.'

Shannow leaned back. 'If I am not mad, Ruth, and it was not just a dream, then I can tell you the danger that waits. The world is about to fall again.'

He told of his dream of Pendarric, and the doom the Blood Stones carried. She listened in silence, her face set; when he had finished, she looked away and remained silent for some minutes.

'I am not omnipotent, Mr Shannow, but there is something missing. The catastrophe fits with my fears. But the Blood Stones of the Hellborn? Small fragments of minuscule power. To tear the fabric of the universe would require a mountain of Sipstrassi and a colossal evil.'

'Do not seek to fit the facts to your theories, Ruth. Examine the facts as they stand. Pendarric says blood and death unleashed the power of the Stones. Abaddon has sent his armies into the south. Where else can the evil lie?'

She shrugged. 'I don't know, I only know I feel very old. I was married eighteen years before the Fall, and I was not a young bride. I had such dreams, such romantic dreams. And Lawrence was not evil then.

'He was an occultist, but he was witty and urbane and very welcome at select parties. We had a daughter, Sarah. Oh Shannow, she was a lovely child.' She lapsed into a silence Shannow did not disturb. 'She was killed at the age of five in an accident and it broke Lawrence – cut him so deeply no one could see the scar. I just cried out my pain, and learned to live with it. He delved more deeply into occult matters, finding Satanism just before the Fall.

'When the earth toppled we survived with some three

hundred others and before long, in the sea of mud that was the new world, people started dying. It was Lawrence who bound the survivors together – he was wonderful, charismatic, understanding, strong and caring.

'For three years we were almost happy and then the dreams began – the visions of Satan talking to him, making him promises. He left us for a while to go into the wilderness. Then he returned with a Daniel Stone and the Hellborn age began.

'I stayed for another eight years, but one day when Lawrence was away on some blood-filled raid, I walked from the settlement with eight other women. We never looked back. From time to time I heard of the new nation, and the madman who called himself Abaddon. But the real disaster came eighty years ago when Abaddon met a man who gave him the key to conquest. He was another survivor from before the Fall, and though his early years had been spent in another career his abiding hobby had been weapons – pistols and rifles. Together he and Abaddon reconstructed the science of gun-making.'

'What happened to the gun-maker?'

'Sixty years ago he rivalled Abaddon in evil. But he repented, Mr Shannow, and fled the vileness he had helped to create. He became Karitas, and tried to build a new life among a peaceful people.'

'And you think I should spare Abaddon in case he suffers just such a repentance? I think not.'

'Why do you mock? You think God cannot change a man's heart? You think his power so limited?'

'I never question his power, or his actions,' said Shannow. 'It is not my place. I don't care that he wiped out men, women and children in Canaan, or that he caused Armageddon. It is his world and he is free to do as he likes without criticism from me. But I cannot see Abaddon walking the Damascus road, Ruth.'

'What about Daniel Cade?'

'What about him?'

'Can you see him walking the Damascus road?'

'Speak plainly, Ruth; this is no time for games.'

'The Brigand chief is now leading the people of the south against the Hellborn. He says he is being led by God, and he is performing miracles. People are flocking to him. What do you think of that?'

'Of all the things you could have told me, Lady, that gives me the most joy. But then you do not know, do you? Daniel Cade is my elder brother. And believe me, he will not be preaching forgiveness, he'll smite the Hellborn hip and thigh, as the Good Book says. By Heaven, Ruth, they'll find him harder to kill than me!'

'It seems I am preaching a lost cause,' said Ruth sadly. 'But then throughout history love has taken second place. We will talk again, Mr Shannow.'

Ruth turned away from him . . .

And vanished.

Daniel Cade received a number of shocks in that early Spring campaign, the first being that he became a man apart. People would approach him with disquieting deference, even men he had known for years. When he approached camp-fires, bawdy tales would die in an instant and the tellers would look away embarrassed. When men swore in his presence, an apology would be instantaneous. At first he had been amused, thinking that such displays would cease after a few days, or perhaps a week. But far from it.

The second shock was from Sebastian.

Cade was in his shack with Lisa when he heard the shouts and emerged into bright sunshine to see men streaming down the slope towards a small party of refugees. His knee was paining him and he used his cane to help him as he limped towards them. In the lead was a middle-aged woman, followed by four adolescent girls and some dozen children. They were leading a horse, across the saddle of which lay a body.

When the grey-haired woman saw him, she ran forward and threw herself to her knees. Around Cade the crowd drew back. Many were farmers who still retained some suspicion of the former Brigand and they fell silent as the woman wept at his feet. Cade stepped forward and self-consciously raised her and her eyes met his.

'You are free from trouble, sister,' Cade told her.

'But only through you and the Hand of God,' she answered, her voice trembling.

'What happened to you, Abigail?' asked a man, pushing forward.

'It is you, Andrew?'

'It is. We thought you were lost to us.'

The woman sank to the ground and the man knelt beside her. Cade felt lost and curiously alone standing at the centre of the circle, but Lisa joined him and took his arm.

'We had taken the children into the high hills for a picnic,' said Abigail, 'when the riders descended on the valley. We knew we could not return, so for days we hid in the caves on the north side, eating berries and roots and nettle soup. In the end, young Mary suggested trying for the Yeager mountains.

'For two days we moved only at night, but on the third we took a chance and struck out across the wide meadows. That's where the riders found us – evil men, cold-eyed and vile. Six of them there were, and I swear they were not human.' The woman lapsed into silence; by now, all the onlookers were seated round her in a wide circle, save for Cade whose stiff knee prevented him from stretching himself on the grass.

'Our terror was great, too great even for tears. One of the children passed out in a faint. The riders climbed down from their horses and removed their black helms, but instead of lessening the fear it increased it. For here were human faces so bestial they froze the blood.

'One of them struck me and I fell to the ground. I will not tell you what they then did to certain of us, but I do tell you there was no shame in it for those who suffered, for we were incapable of fighting back.

'Then one of them drew a long knife; he told me they were going to cut the throats of the children, and that if we wanted to live we must drink the blood and swear an oath to their demon god. I knew they lied, it was in their faces.

'I begged for the children's lives, and they laughed at me. Then we heard hoofbeats. The six of them swung round and we saw a rider thundering towards us. There were two loud explosions and – blessed be God – both shots hit home and two of our attackers collapsed to the grass. Then the other four opened fire, and the rider was hit in the chest and hurled from the saddle.

'You know, they did not even check their fallen comrades. The leader turned to me and said, "Your death will be very slow, you crone."

'But there was another shot and the young man, blood pouring from his body, came staggering forward. The Hellborn shot him again and again, but still he fired back and each shot claimed another victim. It was so swift and yet in my mind's eye I can see each second as if it was an hour – his young body pulled and torn, his teeth clenched against the pain, holding off death until we were safe. The Hellborn leader was the last to die, shot through the heart by the last bullet in the young man's pistol.

'I ran forward and had to close my eyes against the sight of the boy's wounds. His back was open, his ribs spread like broken wings and blood was gurgling in his throat, but his eyes were clear and he smiled at me, like he was happy to be lying there like a torn doll.

'It was hard to see through my tears as he spoke. "Daniel Cade sent me," he whispered.

'"How did he know we were here?" I asked him.

'"We're the Army of God," he said, and he died there. And his face was so peaceful and full of joy. I counted his wounds and saw there were fourteen, and there was no way a man could have lived through that save the Almighty had touched him.

'We lifted him to his horse, and he weighed no more than a child. We came here then, as we had always planned, and not a soul opposed our path. We saw the dark riders on their patrols, but they did not see us although we did not hide. We all knew we were protected by the spirit of that young man; he rode with us, to be buried here among his folk.

'But we don't even know his name.' She stopped and looked at Cade.

Cade cleared his throat. 'His name was Sebastian and he was nineteen.' He turned away and made as if to leave, but a farmer's voice stopped him.

'There's more to tell than that,' he said and Cade faced him, unable to speak. 'The boy was a killer,' said the man, 'a rapist and a thief. I knew his people and I can tell you he never did an honest deed in his life.'

'That cannot be so,' cried Abigail.

'By God I swear it,' said the farmer, 'but I'll help dig his grave, and be proud to lift the shovel.' He turned to the silent Cade. 'I cannot explain all this, Cade, and I've never believed in gods or devils, but if a boy like Sebastian can give his life there must be something in it. I'd be grateful if you'd have me at your next prayer meeting.'

Cade nodded and Lisa led him away to the cabin. He was shaking when they arrived and she was surprised to see tears streaking his face.

'Why?' he said, softly. 'Why did he do it?'

'You heard her, Daniel. He was a part of God's Army.'

'Don't you start that,' he snapped. 'I didn't tell him there was a woman and children. I just told him to scout for refugees.'

'What you said, Daniel, to impress him, was that God had told you to send him west to look for refugees.'

'What's the difference? I didn't tell him they were *there*.'

'For a man so sharp and quick-witted, you surprise me. You might send a man out on a half-chance, but for God there are no half-chances. In Sebastian's mind the refugees had to be there – and they were. And he was needed. And he came through, Daniel. Shot to pieces, he came through.'

'What's happening to me, Lisa? It's all going wrong.'

'I don't think so. What are you going to do about the prayer meeting?'

'What prayer meeting?'

'You didn't hear it, did you? The farmer asked if he could be present, and there must have been fifty other men who showed agreement. They want to hear you speak; they want to be there when God talks through you.'

'I can't do it – you know that.'

'I know it. But you have to. You began this charade and you must live it. You've given them hope, Daniel. Now you have to find a way to nourish it.'

Cade slammed his hand down on the chair-arm. 'I'm not a damned preacher. Christ! I don't even believe in it.'

'That hardly seems to matter now. You're Daniel Cade the Prophet, and you are about to bury your first martyr. There's not a man or a woman in Yeager who will miss your funeral oration.'

Lisa was right. That evening Gambion came to Cade and told him they would be burying Sebastian on a high hill overlooking the plain. He asked Cade to say a few words, and when the former Brigand walked out on to the hillside, with the sun beginning to die in fire beyond the western mountains, some six hundred people were gathered silently on the grass around the newly-dug grave. Cade carried his Bible to the graveside and took a deep breath.

'Way back,' he said, 'the Lord Jesus was asked about the last days when the sheep would be separated from the goats. And his reply was something that Sebastian would have liked to hear. For it don't say a damned word about being good all your life – which is just as well, for he was a hot-tempered boy, and there's some deeds behind him he'd just as soon have forgotten.

'But when the Lord came to the people chosen for fire and damnation, he said, "Be on your way from me, you who have been cursed, into the everlasting fire prepared for the Devil and his angels. For I became hungry, but you gave me nothing to eat, and I got thirsty but you gave me nothing to drink. I was a stranger, but you did not receive me hospitably; naked, but you did not clothe me; sick and in prison, but you did not look after me.

'"Then they answered with the words, 'Lord, when did we see you hungry or thirsty or a stranger, or naked or sick and in prison, and did not minister to you?' Then he answered them, 'Truly I say to you, to the extent that you did not do it to one of these little ones, you did not do it to me.'"

'You want to know what that means?' asked Cade. 'If you do, then ask it of your own hearts. Sebastian knew; he saw the little ones in danger and he rode into Hell to bring them back. He rode to the borders of death, and they couldn't stop him. And right now, as we speak and as the sun sets, he's riding on to glory.

'And when he gets there and someone says – as they surely will – that this man has been evil, he has killed and stolen and caused grief, the Lord will put his arm around Sebastian's shoulder and say, "This man is mine, for he took care of my little ones."' Cade stopped for a moment and wiped the sweat from his face. He had finished the speech he had so carefully rehearsed, but he was aware that the men were still waiting and knew there was something left unsaid. Raising his arms, he called out: 'Let us pray!'

The whole congregation sank to their knees and Cade swallowed hard.

'Tonight we bid farewell to our brother Sebastian, and ask the Lord Almighty to take him into his house for ever. And we ask that soon, when the dark days fall upon us, the memory of Sebastian's courage will lift the heart of every man and woman among us. When fear strikes in the night, think of Sebastian. When the Hellborn charge, think of Sebastian – and when the dawn seems so far away, think of a young man who gave his life so that others could live.

'Lord, we are your army, and we live to do your bidding. Be with us all, evermore. Amen.'

Three men lifted Sebastian's body on a blanket and laid him gently in the grave, covering his face with a linen towel. Cade stared down at the body, fighting back tears he could not understand. Gambion gripped his shoulder and smiled.

'Where to now, Daniel?'

'Nowhere.'

'I don't understand.'

'The enemy is coming to us. In their thousands.'

Chapter Nine

Shannow's irritation grew with the pain in his feet. Like most riding men he abhorred walking, and his knee-length boots with their thick wedged heels made his journey a personal nightmare. By the end of the first day his right foot was blistered and bleeding. By the third day, he felt as if both boots contained broken glass.

He was heading north and west, angling towards the mountains where he hoped to find Batik and Archer. His belly was empty, and the few roots and berries he had found did little more than increase his appetite. Despite switching his saddlebags from shoulder to shoulder, he was also finding the skin by his neck rubbed raw by the leather.

His mood darkened by the hour, but he strode on. Occasionally herds of wild horses came into sight, grazing on the hills. He ignored them. Without a rope, any pursuit would be doomed to failure.

The land was wide and empty, the surface creased and folded like a carelessly thrown blanket. Hidden gulleys crossed his path – some quite steep – forcing him to take a parallel route, often for some miles, before he could scramble down and up the other side.

An hour before dusk on the third day, Shannow came upon the tracks of shod horses. He scanned the land around him and then dropped to one knee to examine them more closely. The edges were frayed and cracked and the imprints criss-crossed with insect traces. Several days had passed since the horses rode this way. Slowly he examined all the imprints, until he was satisfied there were seven horses. This gave him some small relief; he had dreaded the thought that there might be six, and that the Zealots were once more on his trail.

He walked on and made a dry camp in a shallow arroyo out of the wind. He slept fitfully and set off again soon after dawn. By midday he had reached the foothills of the mountain range, but was forced to move north-east, looking for a pass.

Three riders approached him as he angled back down towards the flatlands.

They were young men dressed in homespun cloth, and they carried no guns that he could see.

'Lost your horse?' asked the first, a heavily built man with sandy hair.

'Yes. How far from your settlement am I?'

'Walking? I'd say about two hours.'

'Is there a welcome for strangers?'

'Sometimes.'

'What is this area called?'

'Castlemine. You'll see when you get there. Is that a gun?'

'Yes,' said Shannow, aware that all three were staring at his weapon intently.

'Best keep it hidden. Ridder allows no guns in Castlemine, save those he keeps for his men.'

'Thank you for the warning. Is he the leader there?'

'Yes, he owns the mine and was the first to settle the ruins. He's not a bad man, but he's run things for so long he kind of thinks he's a king – or a baron, or whatever they had in the old days.'

'I'll keep out of his way.'

'Be lucky if you do. Are you carrying coin?'

'Some,' said Shannow warily.

'Good. Keep most of that hidden too – but keep three silver coins handy for the inspection.'

'Inspection?'

'Ridder has a law about strangers. Anyone with less than three coins is a vagrant and subject to indenture – that is, ten days' work in the mine. But it ends up more like six months when they add on the transgressions.'

'I think I get the message,' said Shannow. 'Are you always so free with advice for strangers?'

'Mostly. My name is Barkett and I run a small meat farm north of here. If you are looking for work, I can use you.'

'Thank you, no.'

'Good luck to you.'

'And to you, Mr Barkett.'

'You're from way south, I see. Out here it is Meneer Barkett.'

'I'll remember that.'

Shannow watched them ride on and relaxed. Lifting his saddlebag to a rock, he removed his gun scabbards and hid them alongside his Bible. Then he removed his small sack of Barta coins, looped the thong over his head and swung the sack down behind his collar. He glanced back along the way Barkett and the other two had ridden, made one more adjustment and walked on with hands thrust deep into his coat pockets.

Hoofbeats made him turn once more to see Barkett was returning alone.

Shannow waited for him; the man was smiling as he approached.

'There was one other thing now that you've removed your guns,' said Barkett, producing a small, black single-shot pistol. 'I'll relieve you of the Barta coins.'

'Are you sure this is wise?' asked Shannow.

'Wise? They'll only strip it from you in Castlemine. You'll soon earn it back working in Ridder's mine – well, in a year or three.'

'I'd like you to reconsider,' said Shannow. 'I'd like you to put the gun away and ride on. I do not think you are an evil man, just a little greedy – and you deserve a chance to live.'

'I do?' said Barkett, grinning. 'And why is that?'

'Because you obviously intend only to rob me, otherwise you would have shot me down without a word.'

'True. Now hand me your money and let's make an end to this.'

'Do your friends know you are engaged in this venture?'

'I didn't come here to debate with you,' said Barkett, cocking the flintlock. 'Give me the saddlebag.'

'Listen to me, man, this is your last chance. I have a gun

in my pocket and it is trained on you. Do not proceed with this foolishness.'

'You expect me to believe that?'

'No,' said Shannow sadly, pulling the trigger. Barkett crumpled and pitched sideways, hitting the ground hard, his own flintlock firing a shot that ricocheted from the rocks. Shannow moved closer, hoping that the wound was not fatal – but Barket was dead, shot through the heart.

'Damn you!' said Shannow. 'I gave you more chances than you deserved. Why did you take none of them?'

Barkett's two companions came riding into view, both carrying hand weapons. Shannow drew the Hellborn pistol from his coat pocket and cocked it.

'One man is dead,' he called. 'Do you wish to join him?'

They drew on their reins and stared down at the fallen man, then they pocketed their weapons and rode forward.

'He was a damned fool,' said the first rider, a dark-eyed young man with a slender tanned face. 'We had no part in it.'

'Put him across the horse and take him home,' said Shannow.

'You are not going to take the horse?'

'I'll buy one in Castlemine.'

'Don't go there,' said the man. 'Most of what he told you was true – except the part about the three coins. It no longer matters what you are carrying; they'll take it as tax and make you work the mine anyway. It's Ridder's way.'

'How many men does he have?' asked Shannow.

'Twenty.'

'Then I'll take your advice. But I'll buy the horse – what is the going rate?'

'It's not my horse.'

'Then give the money to his family.'

'It's not that easy. Just take the beast and go,' said the young man, his face reddening. And Shannow understood. He nodded, slung his saddlebags across the horse's back and stepped into the saddle.

If the rider returned with cash, that would mean they had faced the killer of their friend without exacting revenge and it would brand them as cowards.

'I did not desire to kill him,' said Shannow.

'What's done is done. He has family and they'll hunt for you.'

'Best for them that they do not find me.'

'I don't doubt it.'

Shannow touched his heels to the horse and moved on. Turning in the saddle, he called back, 'Tell them to look for Jon Shannow.'

'The Jerusalem Man?'

He nodded and pushed the horse into a canter. Behind him the young men dismounted, lifted the dead body of their erstwhile friend and draped it across the back of one of the horses.

Shannow did not glance back. The incident, like so many in his life, was now filed and forgotten. Barkett had been given a chance at life, and had spurned it. Shannow did not regret the deed.

He carried only one burning regret . . .

And that was for a child who had been in the wrong place at the wrong time, and who had touched the orbit of death around the Jerusalem Man.

Shannow rode for an hour and his new horse showed no sign of fatigue. It was a chestnut stallion some two hands taller than his own gelding, and was built for strength and stamina. The horse had been well cared for and grain-fed. Shannow was tempted to run it hard to gauge the limits of its speed, but in hostile country the temptation had to be put aside.

It was coming to nightfall before Shannow saw the lights of Castlemine. There could be no doubt as to the identity of the settlement, for it sprawled against the mountains beneath a granite fortress with six crenellated towers. It was an immense structure, the largest building Shannow had ever seen, and below it the shacks and cabins of the mining community seemed puny, like beetles beside an elephant. Some larger dwellings were constructed on either side of a main street that ran to the castle's arched main gate, and a mill had been built across a stream to the left of the fortress.

Lights shone in many windows and the community seemed friendly under the gentle moonlight. Shannow was rarely deceived by appearances, however, and he sat his horse, quietly weighing the options. The young rider had advised him to avoid Castlemine, and in daylight he would have done so. But he was also short on supplies and from his high vantage point could see the town's store nestling beside a meeting hall, or tavern house.

He checked his pistols. The Hellborn revolver was fully loaded, as was his own ivory-handled percussion weapon. His mind made up, he rode down the hillside and tethered his horse behind the tavern house. There were few people on the streets, and those who were about ignored the tall man in the long coat. Keeping to the shadows, he moved to the front of the store, but it was bolted. Across the street was an eating-house and Shannow could see it sported around a dozen tables, only half of which were in use. Swiftly he crossed the street and entered the building. The eight diners glanced up and then resumed their meals. Shannow sat by the window facing the door and a middle-aged woman in a chequered apron brought him a jug of cooled water and a pottery mug.

'We have meat and sweet potatoes,' she told him. He looked up into her dull brown eyes and detected an edge of fear.

'That sounds fine,' he told her. 'What meat is it?' She seemed surprised.

'Rabbit and pigeon,' she said.

'I'll have it. Where can I find the storekeeper?'

'Baker spends most evenings in the tavern. There is a woman there who sings.'

'How will I know him?'

The woman glanced anxiously at the other diners and leaned close.

'You are not with Ridder's men?'

'No, I am a stranger.'

'I'll fetch you a meal, but then you must move on. Ridder

is short of workers since the lung fever massacred the Wolvers.'

'How will I know Baker?'

The woman sighed. 'He's a tall man who wears a moustache but no beard; it droops to his chin. His hair is grey and parted at the centre – you'll not miss him. I'll fetch your food.'

The meal was probably not as fine as Shannow's starved stomach told him it was, and he ate with gusto. The grey-haired woman came to sit beside him as he finished the last of the gravy, mopping it with fresh-baked bread.

'You look as though you needed that,' she said.

'I did indeed. It was very fine. How much do I owe?'

'Nothing – if you leave now.'

'That is kind, but I came to Castlemine for supplies. I shall leave when I have seen Baker.'

The woman shrugged and smiled. Years ago, thought Shannow, she must have been strikingly attractive. Now she was overweight and world-weary.

'Do you have a death wish?' she asked him.

'I don't think so.'

The other diners left and soon Shannow found himself alone. The woman locked the door and cleared away the plates and a thin man emerged from the kitchen, removing a stained apron. She thanked him and gave him two silver coins.

'Good night, Flora,' he said, and nodded in Shannow's direction. The woman let him out, then moved around the large room extinguishing the lamps before rejoining Shannow. 'Baker will be leaving the hall around midnight. You are welcome to sit here and wait.'

'I am grateful. But why do you do this for me?'

'Maybe I'm just getting old,' said Flora, 'but I'm sick of Ridder and his ways. He was a good man once, but too many deaths have hardened him.'

'He is a killer?'

'No – although he has killed. I meant the mine. Ridder produces silver for the Barta coin. There is a river sixty miles north that goes to the sea and he ships his silver to many settlements in exchange for grain, iron, salt and weapons – whatever he needs. But that mine eats people. Ridder used to pay for miners, but they died or left. Then he began trapping Wolvers and using them. But they can't live underground; they sicken and die.'

'What are these Wolvers?'

'You've never seen them? Then you must have travelled from a far place. They are a little people, covered in hair; their faces are stretched, their ears pointed. It is said that they once looked like us, but I do not believe it.'

'And there is a tribe of them?'

'There are scores – perhaps hundreds – of tribes. They tend to gather in small packs within the tribes and are pretty harmless. They live on rabbits, pigeons, turkeys – any small animal they can bring down with their bows or slings. Ridder says they make fine workers while they live. They're docile, you see, and do as they're told. But since the lung fever, Ridder has been desperate for workers. Now any stranger will end up in Castlemine. He even has men scouring the countryside. Sometimes we see wagons driven in to the castle with whole families doomed to the shafts and tunnels. It used to be that a man could work his way out in two or three months, but now we never see them.'

'Why is he allowed to do this?' asked Shannow. 'It is a big settlement – there must be three, maybe four hundred people here.'

'You don't know much about people, do you?' said Flora. 'Ridder is the main source of wealth. Those of us who live beneath the castle need have no fear of Brigands or raiders. We live comfortable lives; we have a school and a church. Life is good.'

'A church?'

'We are a God-fearing people here,' she said. 'The pastor sees to that.'

'And how does your pastor react to Ridder's methods?'

She chuckled. 'Ridder *is* the pastor!'

'You are right, Lady. I do not know much about people.'

'Ridder quotes the Bible with every other sentence. The

verse that always seems to surface is, "Slaves, obey your masters."'

'It would,' said Shannow. His eyes were fixed on the door of the hall, which opened as a tall grey-haired man stepped on to the porch.

'Is that Baker?' he asked.

'Yes.'

Shannow removed a shiny Barta coin from his pocket and placed it on the table. 'My thanks to you, Lady.'

'It is too much,' she protested.

'The labourer is worthy of the hire,' he told her. Flora let him out through the front door and he crossed the street swiftly, moving up behind the storekeeper. The man was a little unsteady on his feet.

'Good evening, Meneer Baker.' The man turned his watery blue eyes towards Shannow.

'Good evening.' He blinked and rubbed his eyes. 'Do I know you?'

'Only as a customer. Would you be so kind as to open your store?'

'At this time of night? No, sir. Come back when the sun is up.'

'I am afraid that will not be convenient, but I shall pay you well for the privilege.'

'I suppose you want hunting goods,' said Baker, fishing in his pocket for the key to the store.

'Yes.'

'I would have thought Ridder would have been well-pleased today.'

'How so?'

'With the pair Riggs brought back. I shouldn't have thought you would need to rush out in the dead of night.'

The storekeeper pushed open the door and Shannow followed him inside.

'Well, choose what you need. I'll put it on Ridder's bill.'

'That will not be necessary. I have coin.'

Baker seemed surprised but he said nothing, and Shannow took salt, dried oats, sugar, herb tea and a sack of grain. He also bought two new shirts and a quantity of dried meat.

'You are a friend of Riggs, I see,' said Baker, pointing to the Hellborn pistol at Shannow's side.

'He has one of these?'

'He took it from the man they captured today – not the black man, the other one with the forked beard.'

Ruth stared from her study window at the students taking their midday break on the wide lawns below. There were thirty-five young people at Sanctuary, all willing to learn and all yearning to change the world. Usually the sight of these young missionaries lifted Ruth's spirits, gave her renewed belief. But not today.

The evils of men like Abaddon she could withstand, for they could be countered by the love at Sanctuary. But the real dangers to the new world, she knew, were men like Jon Shannow and Daniel Cade – dark heroes, understanding the weapons of evil and turning them on their users, never realizing they were merely perpetuating the violence they sought to destroy.

'You are an arrogant woman, Ruth,' she told herself, turning from the window. The parable of Man was there to be seen within the Sipstrassi Stones – a gift from the Heavens that could heal, nurture and feed. But in the hands of men, that was never enough; it had to be turned to death and despair.

Ruth could feel herself slipping from harmony so she took a deep breath and prayed silently, drawing the peace of Sanctuary deep into her soul. The bay window disappeared as she closed the study to all intrusion. Pine-panelled walls surrounded her. The carved oak chair shimmered and became a bed. A stone hearth with a glowing log-fire appeared and Ruth lay back and watched the flames.

She felt the presence of another mind, and her defences snapped into place as she sat up and tentatively reached out her thoughts.

'May I enter?' came a voice. Power emanated from the source of the sound, but she could sense no evil there.

She lowered the defensive wall and a figure appeared

within the room. He was tall and bearded, with blue eyes and braided hair. Upon his brow was a circlet of silver, at the centre of which sat a golden stone.

'You are Pendarric?' she asked.

'I am, my Lady.'

'The Lord of the Blood Stones.'

'Sadly true.' A divan appeared beside him, with braid-edged cushions of down-filled satin. He lay on his side, resting on one elbow.

'Why are you here?'

'To make amends, Ruth.'

'You cannot undo the evil you sired.'

'I know that, you are not the world's only source of wisdom. You are still mortal, Lady. I was overwhelmed by the power of the Stones, and I would argue against judging me. At the end my own strength triumphed, and I saved many thousands of my people. Abaddon is not so strong.'

'What are you saying?'

'He is lost to the Sipstrassi. Nothing remains of the man you wed; he is not the father of the evil he sires, any more than I was. He has lost the balance, even as you have.'

'I am in harmony,' Ruth told him.

'No, you are mistaken. In obliterating the desires of self, you have lost in your struggle. Harmony is balance, it is understanding the evil we all carry, but holding it in stasis by the good we should desire. Harmony is achieved when we have the courage to accept that we are flawed. Everything you have achieved here is artificial. Yes, Sanctuary is pleasant. But even you, when you leave to travel the world, find that your doubts have grown. Then you fly back like a moth to the purifying candle. The truth should remain, even when Sanctuary is gone.'

'And you understand the truth?' she asked.

'I understand true harmony. You cannot eradicate evil, for without it how would we judge what is good? And if there is no greed, no lust, no baleful desires, what has a man achieved who becomes good? There would then be no mountains to climb.'

'What do you suggest that I do?'

'Take the swan's path, Ruth.'

'It is not time.'

'Are you sure?'

'I am needed. There is still Abaddon.'

'And the wolves in the shadows,' said Pendarric. 'If you need me, I will be with you.'

'Wait! Why did you appear to Jon Shannow?'

'He is Rolynd. And only he can destroy the wolf you fear.'

After he had gone Ruth sat alone, once more staring into the flames. For the first time in many years, she felt lost and uncertain and reached out, seeking Karitas and drawing him to her. His power was fading, his image drifting and unclear.

'I am sorry, Ruth, I will not be here to help you for much longer. The ties that hold me to this land are weakening by the hour.'

'How is Donna Taybard?'

'Her power is too great for her and it grows at a frightening pace. Abaddon plans to sacrifice her on Walpurnacht, and then her power will soak into the Blood Stone. You must stop it, Ruth.'

'I cannot.'

'You have the strength to destroy the entire Hellborn nation.'

'I know what power I have,' snapped Ruth. 'Do you believe the thought has not crossed my mind? Do you not think I was tempted when I saw the Hellborn bearing down on your village? I cannot help her in the way you desire.'

'I shall not argue with you, Ruth,' he said, reaching out a spectral hand which she took into her own. 'I have not the time. I love you, and I know that whatever you do will be for the best as you see it. You are a rare woman and without you I would probably still be Hellborn. But you saved me.'

'No, Karitas. You were strong enough to seek me out. It took great courage to see yourself as you were, and struggle to change.'

For one brief moment the image of Karitas glowed like fire, then it was gone. Ruth reached out, but nothing remained.

Loneliness settled on her and she wept for the first time in more than a century.

Con Griffin had trouble in controlling his temper. The Hellborn officer Zedeki had ridden in to the settlement alone and asked to speak to the community's leaders. Accordingly, Griffin had assembled Jacob Madden – still weak from his wounds – Jimmy Burke, Ethan Peacock and Aaron Phelps to listen to Zedeki's demands.

What Griffin heard made him tremble with fury:

'We will leave you in peace in return for one hostage who will accompany us to our city and meet our king. We want Donna Taybard.'

'Or else?' said Griffin.

'I now have a thousand men. My orders are to destroy you if you do not comply.'

'Why do you want my wife?'

'She will not be harmed.'

'She is pregnant and she cannot travel.'

'We know this and there is a comfortable wagon being prepared. Believe me, Mr Griffin, we wish to see no harm come to the child.'

'I will not do it,' declared Griffin.

'That is your choice. You have until tomorrow at noon.' With that he left them, and Griffin was dismayed to see that none of his friends would meet his eyes when he returned to the table.

'Well?' he asked them.

'They ain't left us many choices, Con,' said Burke.

'You don't mean you agree?'

'Hold on Griff,' put in Madden, 'and think it through. We can't survive against them in a war, and you've done us right proud so far. But we've all got families to care for . . . and they said no harm would come to her.'

'You believe that, Jacob? Look at me, damn you! You believe that?'

'I don't know,' he admitted.

'She's one of us,' said Peacock. 'We can't let them take her – it's not Christian.'

'What is Christian about starting a war where we all get wiped out?' asked Aaron Phelps, his fat face streaked with sweat.

'Let's sleep on it,' said Madden. 'We've got till noon.'

They agreed on that and left Griffin sitting by the cold wood-stove staring at the ceiling. As the last one left, the bedroom door opened and Eric walked across to Griffin.

'You won't let them take my mother, will you, Con?'

Griffin looked at the boy and tears fell suddenly, streaking his face. Eric ran forward, throwing his arms around Griffin's neck.

The following day dawned bright and clear, but in the west dark clouds gathered with the promise of storms. The committee met once more and Griffin forced a vote to include the whole community in the decision. Zedeki rode in to the settlement with a wagon and waited for the votes to be cast.

One by one, the settlers filed past the wooden box – even the children had been allowed to vote. Towards noon the Hellborn army came into sight, ringing the high ground at the valley's entrance and sitting their dark horses in chilling silence.

Madden and Peacock were detailed to count the votes and they carried the box into the scholar's small cabin. Ten minutes later, Madden called for Burke and the oldster joined them. Then he moved amongst the men and the crowd dispersed to their homes.

Griffin could barely contain himself.

Zedeki glanced up at the army and smiled. What a preposterous charade this was. He could see that Griffin knew the outcome as indeed did he, but the lengths to which ordinary people would go to preserve their pride remained a source of great amusement.

Madden emerged from the cabin and walked past Griffin, who half rose only to be waved back. The farmer made his way to the wagon.

'Might as well be on your way,' he said. 'We ain't giving her up.'

'Are you insane?' asked Zedeki, his arm sweeping up to

point to the armed riders. 'Do you think you can withstand them?'

'Only one way to find out,' said Madden. All around the settlement men and women were moving from their homes, weapons ready, to crouch behind the log screens.

Zedeki swallowed hard. 'You are condemning the settlement to death.'

'No,' said Madden. 'You're the man for that job. I don't trust you, Zedeki; I've seen your kind before. Your word ain't worth ant-spit. You want Donna, you ride in and take her.'

'We will,' said Zedeki, 'and you won't live long enough to regret your decision.'

Madden watched as Zedeki swung the wagon and toyed with the idea of killing him. Instead, he merely stood and waited as the wagon lumbered up the rise. He drew his pistol and cooked it as Griffin joined him.

'Thanks, Jacob.'

'Don't thank me. I voted for letting her go.'

'Thanks, anyway.'

As the wagon cleared the skyline, the Hellborn riders turned their mounts and disappeared. For an hour or more the settlers waited for the attack, but it never came. At last Madden and Griffin saddled their horses and rode up the rise. The Hellborn had gone.

'What's going on here, Con?'

'I don't know. They weren't frightened, that's for sure.'

'Then why?'

'It's got something to do with Donna. They want her badly, but I think they want her alive.'

'For what reason?'

'I don't know. I could be wrong, but it's the only thing that fits. I have a strong feeling that had we given her up to them they would have butchered the settlement. But they're frightened Donna might get hurt.'

'What do we do?'

'We've no choice, Jacob. We wait.'

*

Donna watched it all from the seeming sanctuary of the spirit sky. Her body lay in a virtual coma, but her spirit rose unchained to soar free between the gathering clouds and the green valley. She saw the settlers vote to fight for her, and was both gladdened and saddened, for she also saw the treachery in the heart of Zedeki.

The settlement was doomed.

Unable to face stark reality, Donna fled in a tumbling blur where colours swirled around her and stars grew large as lanterns. There was no time here, no feeling for the passing of seconds or hours or days. At last she stopped and floated above a blue sea, where gulls wheeled and dived around coral islands. It was peaceful here, and beautiful.

Calm came to her and peace filled her, like the coming of a dawn after the sleep of nightmare.

A woman appeared alongside her and Donna felt tranquillity flowing from the newcomer. She was middle-aged, with iron-grey hair and a face of ageless serenity.

'I am Ruth,' she said.

'They are going to kill my son,' said Donna. 'My boy!' There were no tears, but there was anguish and Ruth felt it.

'I am sorry, Donna. There are no words.'

'Why do they act in this way?'

'They have a dream, which has haunted men since the dawn of time. Conquest, victory, virility, power – it is evil's most potent weapon.'

'I'm going home,' said Donna. 'I want to be with my son.'

'They want you as a sacrifice,' said Ruth. 'They need to draw power from your death; they need you to feed their evil.'

'They won't have me.'

'Are you sure?'

'My strength has grown, Ruth. Abaddon cannot take me. I will take my soul and my strength far from him, and let my body die like a shell.'

'That will take great courage.'

'No,' said Donna, 'for then I will be with my son and my husband.'

Donna began the long journey home. This time she travelled without panic and the swirling colours became events, a kaleidoscopic history of a world touched with insanity. Caesars, princes, khans and kings, emperors, lords, dukes and thanes – all with a single purpose. She saw chariots and spears, bows and cannon, tanks and aircraft, and a light that shone over cities like a giant torch. It was all meaningless and insurmountably petty.

It was dark when she descended into the valley and Madden and Burke were standing guard, waiting with grim courage for the attack they knew was imminent. She floated above Eric's bed; his face was peaceful, his sleep soothing.

Karitas appeared beside her.

'How are you faring, Donna?' His voice was strangely cold, and she shivered.

'I cannot stand to see them die.'

'They do not have to die,' he said. 'We can save them.'

'How?'

'You must trust me. I need you to return to your body, then we will leave the valley. The settlers will be in no danger if you are not here, and I will take you to a place of safety.'

'My son will live? Truly?'

'Come with me, Donna.' She was unsure, and hesitated.

'I must tell Con.'

'No. Speak to no one. When it has all blown over, you may return. Trust me.'

Donna fled to her body and saw Con Griffin asleep in the chair beside her bed. He looked so tired. She settled back into herself and concentrated on rising, but once more she was liquid within a sponge.

'Picture your body as a thin sheet of copper,' Karitas advised. 'Believe it to be metallic.'

It was easier now and she half rose, then fell back.

'Concentrate, Donna,' urged Karitas. 'Their lives depend on you.'

She rose and dressed in silence. 'Dark clothes,' said Karitas. 'We must avoid the guards.' She could no longer see him now, but his voice came as a cold whisper in her mind.

She slipped out of the door and into the shadows. Madden and Burke had their eyes fixed on the surrounding hills and she moved away into the darkness unobserved. Moving from shrub to boulder to tree-shrouded hollows, she slowly climbed the rise. At the top she stopped.

'Over there,' said Karitas, 'by that circle of rocks, you will find something to help you. Come.'

She moved to the rocks and there, gleaming in the moonlight, lay five silver circlets.

'Place two over your ankles, two on your wrists and the last upon your brow. Quickly, now!'

She clipped them into place. 'Now try to leave your body.'

She relaxed and tried to soar. But there was nothing. No movement, no dizzying flight.

'Now what, Karitas?'

Six Zealots moved out of hiding and approached her. She tried to run, but they caught her easily. She fought to tear the circlets from her wrists, but they pinned her arms. Then another voice entered her mind.

'You are mine, Donna Taybard, as I promised,' hissed Abaddon.

Sanity spun away from her, and the world faded into blessed darkness.

Griffin stumbled from the cabin, pistol in hand.

'Jacob!' he screamed and Madden leapt to his feet.

'What is it, Con?'

'She's gone. Donna. Oh, my God!'

Suddenly Burke shouted and Madden's gaze followed his pointing finger. The Hellborn army sat once more on the crest of the rise. A single trumpet blast shrieked out into the dawn air, and the riders swept towards the settlement. Men and women ran from their cabins with weapons at the ready and took up positions behind the log screens.

Madden called for Rachel to bring him his rifle and she ducked into the house and came out cradling the Hellborn weapon. She ran towards him, but the first shot of the battle took her low in the chest. Madden saw her stumble and raced to her side, catching her as she fell.

'Something hit me, Jacob,' she whispered . . . and died. Madden snatched up the rifle, levering a shell into the breech just as the rolling thunder of hooves was upon him. He swivelled and fired twice, pitching two riders from their saddles. A third fired a pistol and dust mushroomed up by Madden's feet. His return shot all but tore the man's head from his shoulders.

Griffin threw a rifle to Eric and ran from the cabin. He saw Madden down and riders sweeping towards him. Coolly Griffin levelled his pistol, sending six shots into the mass.

Burke and some twenty men managed to get to the eastern log screen, sending volley after volley into the riders. But the Hellborn rode through the field of fire and leapt from their horses to engage the settlers in hand-to-hand combat.

Griffin rammed fresh shells into his pistol and ran from the cabin towards Madden. A rider bore down on him and he dived clear of the horse's hooves. His gun thundered, the bullet taking the horse in the head; the beast went down, hurling the rider head-first into the ground. Griffin was up and running when a bullet smashed into his back; he turned, but another shell caught him in the chest. Seeing Griffin's plight, Madden swung his rifle and emptied two saddles. A shell struck his temple and he fell face forward into the dust. As Griffin struggled to rise, he saw Eric move into the open with the rifle in his hands. He tried to wave the boy back. The rifle fired twice, then a score of guns turned on the boy and blasted him from sight.

Aaron Phelps sat trembling in the back room of his cabin, listening to the shots and the screams and the thunder of hooves. His pistol was pointed at the door. Someone's shoulder crashed against the wood and Phelps fired, then the door exploded inwards. He did not see the Hellborn crowded there, he pushed the barrel of his pistol into his mouth and blew out his brains.

Outside, the Hellborn had overcome all but one man. Jimmy Burke, blood seeping from a dozen wounds, had staggered into his cabin and slammed shut the door, dropping an oak bar in place. He reloaded his pistols and crawled to a chest by the rear wall from which he took an old blunderbuss. He charged it with a double load, then poured a measure of tack nails into the barrel.

The Hellborn began pounding against the door and an axe-blade crashed through. Burke switched his gaze to the wooden shutters of the window; a shadow blocked the sunlight at the centre and he sent a bullet punching through. A man screamed and Burke grinned. More axes swung against the door, smashing a head-sized hole above the bar. An arm reached through and Burke aimed the pistol and waited. As the man began to lift the bar, he exposed his neck; then Burke's pistol bucked in his hand and blood gushed to stain the wood of the door. Suddenly the window crashed inwards. A bullet took Burke in the chest and he winced as his lungs began to fill with blood. Taking up the blunderbuss, he swallowed hard and waited.

'Don't take too long, you bastards,' he muttered. Another arm reached through the hole in the door and Burke cocked his weapon. The bar slid clear, booted feet kicked open the door and the Hellborn surged inside.

'Suck on this!' screamed the old man. The blunderbuss exploded with a deafening roar and a half-pound of nails ripped into their ranks, scything them down. Burke dropped the weapon and reached for his pistol, but two more shots from the window ended his defiance.

Silence fell on the valley and the Hellborn collected their dead and rode from Avalon.

A westerly wind drove the storm clouds over the settlement and lightning speared across the valley. As the rain began, Griffin groaned and tried to move, but pain ripped through him and he rolled to his side. His weapons were gone and the ground below him was soaked with his blood.

'Come on, Griffin,' he told himself. 'Find your strength.'

Pushing his arms beneath him, he forced himself to a sitting position. Dizziness swept over him, but he fought it back. Madden was lying twenty yards to his right and he crawled through the rain to his friend's body. Madden's face was covered with blood and beyond him lay Rachel, her dead eyes staring up at the lowering sky.

'I'm sorry, Jacob,' said Griffin. When he placed his hand on his friend's shoulder, Madden moved and Griffin lifted his arm, feeling for a pulse. It was there, and beating strongly. Examining the head wound, he found that the bullet had glanced from Madden's temple, tearing the skin but not piercing the skull. He tried to lift the wounded man, but his own injuries had sapped him and he sat helpless in the rain.

The storm passed as he waited, the sun beaming down on the desolated settlement. Madden moaned and opened his eyes, seeing Griffin sitting beside him.

'Did we drive them off?' he whispered. Griffin shook his head.

'Rachel? The boys?'

'I think they killed everyone, Jacob.'

'Oh God!'

Madden sat up and saw Rachel. He crawled to her and shut her eyes, leaning forward to kiss her cold lips.

'You deserved better than this, my girl,' he said. Griffin swayed and fell as Madden stood and stared at the skyline.

Somewhere out there the Hellborn were riding and Madden sent his hatred out after them in one blood-curdling scream of frustrated rage and despair. He moved to Griffin and half-carried, half-dragged him into the nearest cabin, where the body of Burke lay beside an open chest. Madden managed to maneouvre Griffin to a bed and opened his shirt. There were two wounds, one high in the shoulder at the back, the second low on the left side of the chest, close to the heart. Neither showed an exit wound. Madden plugged the holes with linen and covered the unconscious man with a blanket.

Leaving the cabin, he found his boys together near the paddock behind his cabin. From the blood on the grass around them, they had made a fight of it. Pride and sorrow vied in Madden's mind as he turned away from the corpses and moved through the settlement, checking body after body. All were slain.

Back in his own cabin, Madden pulled the bed from the wall and lifted the sack he had hidden there. Inside were two Hellborn pistols and around thirty shells. He loaded the pistols and strapped them to his side.

All dead. All the dreams gone down to dust.

'Well, you didn't kill me, you sons of bitches! And I'll be coming after you. You want Hell? I'll give you Hell!'

Chapter Ten

Shannow stood outside the store with his supply sack over his shoulder, gazing up at the white marble fortress. There were six cylindrical towers, two of them flanking the high arched gate. There appeared to be no sentries. The storekeeper, Baker, had locked the door and wandered away into the shadows and Shannow stood alone, pondering his course of action.

Somewhere in or below that vast fortress Batik and Archer were prisoners. Yet was it any concern of his? What did he owe them? Would either of them come riding to his rescue? More to the point, *could* he rescue them?

Ridder had twenty men and Shannow did not know their dispositions or the layout inside the fortress. Riding inside would be a futile gesture achieving nothing. He returned to his horse and mounted, riding out into the main street and up towards the black-shadowed gateway.

The white towers loomed over him and he had the feeling that he was riding into a massive tomb, never to see the sun rise again. A man stepped into his path; he was carrying an old rifle.

'What's your business?' he asked.

'I've come to see Ridder.'

'He expecting you?'

'Can you think of another reason I should be here at this time of night?'

The man shrugged. 'I'm just told to watch for runaway Wolvers – nobody tells me anything else. Still, it's better than the mine, by God.'

Shannow nodded and touched his heels to the horse, riding on as if he knew where he was going. The gate arch led to a cobbled courtyard; straight ahead was a wide set of marble steps leading to a double door of oak, while to the right lay a narrow alleyway. Shannow chose the alley and soon found himself in a second yard housing a row of stables. A young lad moved out of the shadows scratching his head and Shannow dismounted and handed him the reins.

'Don't unsaddle him. I'm leaving shortly.'

'All right,' said the boy, yawning.

Shannow slipped him a silver coin. 'Give him some oats and a rub-down.'

'I will,' promised the lad, the brightness of the silver dispelling all thoughts of sleep.

'Where will I find Meneer Ridder?'

'In his rooms, this time of night.'

'How do I get there?'

'You new?'

'Yes.'

'Go back out into the courtyard, past the steps, and you'll see a staircase on the outside of the wall. Climb that, past the first two doors and go in through the third. The sentry there will take you the rest of the way.'

'Thank you.'

Shannow left the boy and returned to the main courtyard, waving to the sentry as he passed. He found the spiral stair and climbed to the third storey, pausing outside the timber door. Then he removed his coat and folded it across his arm before opening the door. Inside was a corridor hung with rugs and lit by oil-lamps. Stepping into the light, Shannow forced a smile for the sentry who was sitting with his feet on a small marble statue of a snarling dog. The man swung clear his legs and stood.

'What do you want?' he whispered. 'You ain't my relief.'

'True,' said Shannow, moving casually towards him. The coat slipped from his arm to reveal the black muzzle of the Hellborn pistol, he cocked it and the noise seemed to echo in the corridor like cracking bones. The man's eyes widened as Shannow moved closer, pushing the muzzle up under his chin.

'Which room is Ridder's?' he whispered.

The sentry pointed over Shannow's shoulder.

'Tell me,' said Shannow, without following the man's shaking finger.

'Two doors down on the left.'

'And where are the prisoners who were brought in today?'

'I've no idea, I've only just come on. I've been asleep all day.'

'Would they be kept in the mine?'

'Probably.'

'How do I get there?'

'Jesus, man, I couldn't tell you that. There's a score of staircases and corridors and a pulley lift. You could lose yourself in this place.'

'What's through the door behind you?'

'It's a store-room.'

'Be so kind as to open it.'

'Don't kill me – I've a wife . . . children.'

'Get inside.' The man turned and opened the door; Shannow followed him in and struck him savagely on the back of the neck and the sentry fell forward without a sound. Shannow searched the room for cord but found none, so he removed the man's belt and tied his hands behind his back. Then he gagged him with a linen kerchief which he stuffed into his mouth, binding it with a piece of torn curtain.

Stepping out into the corridor, he moved silently to Ridder's room, cursing softly when he saw a light showing under the door. He opened it and stepped inside, finding himself facing a small altar before which knelt a slim man with a shock of white hair. The man turned. He was around fifty years old, with round dark eyes and a hatchet face which bore no trace of humour.

'Who in God's name are you, sir?' exclaimed Ridder, surging to his feet, his thin face reddening.

'You can ask him yourself,' said Shannow, levelling the pistol.

All colour fled from Ridder's face. 'You can't mean to kill me?'

'Just so, Pastor.'

'But why?'

'On a whim,' snarled Shannow. 'I have no time for Brigands.'

'Nor I. I am a man of God.'

'I think not.' Shannow moved forward swiftly and, with his left hand, took hold of the lapels of Ridder's black jacket, pulling the man to him. 'Open your mouth.'

The terrified man did so and Shannow slid the muzzle of the pistol between his teeth.

'Now listen to me, Pastor, and note every word. You are going to take me to the two men you brought in here today and then we are going to leave together, all four of us. It is your only chance for life – you understand?'

Ridder nodded.

'Now, in case you think that once we are away from here your men will help you, bear this in mind: I am not a man who is afraid to die – and I will take you on the journey to Hell with me.'

Shannow withdrew the pistol and sheathed it. 'Wipe the sweat from your face, Pastor, and let us go.'

Together the two men walked into the corridor and down several flights of stairs. Shannow was soon lost within the maze of the building as they passed one shadow-haunted corridor after another. The air was musty and several times they passed sentries who stood to attention as Ridder went by. At last they emerged into a dimly lit hall where six men sat at a table dicing for copper coins. All were armed with handguns and knives.

'Prepare the lift,' said Ridder and the men moved swiftly to a series of pulleys and ropes beside an open shaft. A burly man with huge forearms cranked an iron handle and after a few seconds a large box rose into view. Ridder stepped inside and Shannow followed; within the box was a handbell on a rope. With a sickening lurch the box descended into darkness; Shannow blinked sweat from his eyes as the lift continued its descent.

After what seemed a lifetime, they reached another level and Ridder rang the handbell. The lift stopped and the two men emerged into a dimly lit tunnel filled with the stench of human excrement.

Shannow gagged and swallowed hard. Ridder stood gesturing to a series of bolted doors.

'I don't know which one they are in. But they'll be here somewhere.'

'Open every door.'

'Are you mad? We'll be torn limb from limb.'

'How many people are down here?'

'About fifty people. And maybe sixty Wolvers.'

Shannow's jaw tightened, for there were only six doors. 'You keep twenty people locked up in each of these? And you call yourself a man of God?' Shannow's rage exploded and he struck Ridder on the side of the head, hurtling the man from his feet. 'Get up and open the doors – every God-cursed one of them!'

Ridder crawled to the first, then turned. 'You don't understand. This whole community needs the mine. They're my responsibility – caring for my flock. I wouldn't have used people if I hadn't been forced to. I used Wolvers, but the lung fever killed scores of them.'

'Open the door, Pastor. Let's see your flock.'

Ridder pushed the bolt clear and swung the door open. Nothing moved in the darkness within.

'Now the others.'

'For God's sake . . .'

'You talk of God down here?' shouted Shannow. A dark shape moved into the half light and he stepped back in shock. The creature was maybe five feet in height and covered with fur; its face was long, caricaturing a wolf or dog, but its eyes were human. It was naked and covered in sores. More creatures came into sight, ignoring the two men. They limped to a chest by the far wall and stood apathetically, staring at nothing.

'What's in the chest?' asked Shannow.

'Their tools. They think it's work-time.'

'All the doors, Ridder!' The white-haired pastor stumbled from one dungeon to the next. From the last but one room the bloodied face of Batik could be seen above the smaller Wolvers.

'Shannow?'

'Over here, man. Quickly!'

Batik pushed his way through the milling slaves and Shannow handed him his percussion pistol.

'Stay down here with that creature,' he said, pointing at Ridder. 'I'll send the lift back. Try to get all of them to understand that they're free.'

'They'll only be rounded up again – let's get out while we can.'

'Do as I say, Batik, or I'll leave you here. Where's Archer?'

'Unconscious. They beat him badly and we'll have to carry him out.'

'Get something arranged,' said Shannow, stepping into the lift.

'Easy for you to say,' snapped Batik. 'I'll just stay down here with the wolf beasts and arrange a stretcher!'

'Fine,' said Shannow, ringing the handbell. The lift lurched upwards and once more the journey seemed interminable, but finally he came into the light where the six men laboured at the winch and stepped out.

'Where's Meneer Ridder?' asked the burly man with the huge arms.

'He'll be along,' said Shannow, producing his pistol. 'Lower the lift.'

'What the Hell is this?'

'This is death, my friend, unless you do exactly as you are told. Lower the lift.'

'You think you can take us all?'

Shannow's gun exploded and a man was smashed back into the far wall, a bullet through his heart.

'You think I can't?' he hissed.

The burly man turned the winch as if his life depended on it . . .

Which it did.

*

Within an hour most of the slaves had been lifted to the next level, but as Batik pointed out several of the Wolvers refused to leave, sitting silently staring at the tool-chest. Batik was not even sure they had understood his urgings.

Shannow went below and saw them, crouched in a half-circle around the chest. It was not locked and he opened it; inside were a dozen pick-handles and a stack of blades. He handed them to the waiting Wolvers, who stood and moved into a line facing the black tunnel that led to the mine. Shannow went to the hunched figure at the front of the line and gently took him by the shoulders, turning him to face the lift. When the Wolver moved obediently towards the shaft, the others followed.

Shannow rang the handbell and waited below as the box moved out of sight. Then he checked the six dungeons. In one he found seven bodies, small and emaciated; in another, two corpses had begun to rot and the stench was almost overwhelming. He forced himself to check the other rooms, and in the last he found Ridder crouching against the wall.

'It's not my fault,' said Ridder, staring down at the body of a child of around eleven.

'How long is it since you visited these cells?'

'Not for a year. It's not my fault. The mine had to work – you see that, don't you? Hundreds of people rely on it.'

'Get up, Pastor. It's time to go.'

'No, you can't take them away. People will see them and they'll blame me. They won't understand.'

'Stay here, then,' said Shannow and he left the man squatting in a corner and moved back into the tunnel. Batik had sent down the lift and he stepped inside and rang the bell.

On the upper level, Batik had disarmed the guards and had laid Archer's unconscious body across the table the men had used for their dice-game. Shannow examined the black man's swollen features; he had been beaten badly.

'Who did this?' he asked Batik.

'The man Riggs and a half-dozen others. I tried to help him, but he wouldn't help himself; he just stood there and took it. It seemed to make them more angry and when he fell, they started kicking him.'

'Why did they do it?'

'He simply told them he wouldn't work for them – that he would sooner just starve to death.'

Shannow moved to the guards. 'You,' he said, pointing to the burly man, 'lead us out of here. The rest of you can help carry my friend.'

'Are you going to let them live?' asked a man, pushing himself through the milling Wolvers. Shannow turned to see a wasted scarecrow of a figure, with a matted blond beard streaked with filth. He was naked but for a stained leather loin-cloth, and his upper body was a mass of sores.

'We need them, my friend,' said Shannow softly. 'Hold your anger.'

'My son is down there – and my wife. They died in that black hole.'

'But we're not free yet,' said Shannow. 'Trust me.'

He took the man by the arm and led him to Batik, collecting a double-barrelled flintlock pistol that the Hellborn had taken from one of the guards and pressing it into the man's hand.

'We may have to fight our way out. Take your revenge then.'

Shannow looked around the room and saw there were close to ninety people packing the chamber. He signalled the guards to lift Archer and then led the way into the tunnel beyond. Batik was at the rear. Shannow cocked his pistol and walked behind the guard he had chosen to lead. Slowly the column of slaves moved through the bowels of the castle, the air freshening as they climbed towards the light. Finally they came into a high-walled corridor where far above them the dawn light shone in majestic shafts through arched windows. A chittering noise broke from the Wolvers, who raised their skinny arms, hands stretching towards the golden glow.

Ahead was a double door of studded oak and the guard began to move more swiftly.

'Stop!' said Shannow, but the man merely dived for the

floor and the doors began to open.

'Down!' bellowed Shannow, dropping to his knees, his pistol coming up as the muzzles of several rifles appeared in the open doorway. Shannow fired, and the first rifleman pitched from sight. The corridor was filled with deafening explosions. Shells whistled past Shannow and his own gun boomed twice more, then there was silence. He flicked open the cylinder guard and reloaded his pistol, then ran forward, hugging the wall. A rifleman stepped into sight and Shannow put two shots in his chest.

Behind Shannow, the guard who had been leading them reached into his boot and produced a long-bladed knife. He rose silently and launched himself at the Jerusalem Man, but a shot rang out and he staggered. Shannow twisted and fired and the man slumped to the floor.

Batik sprinted along the other side of the corridor.

'Nice pistol,' he said. 'Pulls a little to the left.'

Shannow nodded and pointed to the right of the doorway and Batik sighed and cocked his pistol. Moving forward at a run, he dived through the doorway and rolled on his shoulder. Behind the door a crouching rifleman swung his weapon, but Batik shot him in the head before he could bring the barrel to bear. Shells ricocheted off the marble floor, shrieking past Batik's head. He glanced up and saw he was in a huge hall edged by a wide inner balcony where other marksmen were kneeling, covering the door. He scrambled to his feet and hurled himself back into the corridor.

'Any other ideas?' he asked Shannow.

'Not at the moment.'

'That's just as well!'

Behind them four of the Wolvers were down and dying, the others crouching around them keening softly.

'Can you climb?' asked Shannow. Batik glanced up at the high windows.

'I'll break my neck.'

'All right, we'll just sit here and wait for a miracle.'

'I thought your God was good at those.'

'He helps those who help themselves,' said Shannow dryly.

Batik exchanged pistols with Shannow and pushed the fully loaded Hellborn gun into his belt. The wall below the window was constructed of solid marble blocks about two feet square; between each block was a crack which allowed a tentative grip. Batik placed his foot on the first block and began to climb. He was a powerful man, but before he had climbed more than fifteen feet his fingers were aching with the effort; at thirty feet, he began to curse Shannow. At forty feet he slipped. His feet scrabbled for purchase and all of his weight hung on the three fingers of his right hand. Sweat dripped into his eyes and he fought down panic, moving his foot slowly into position to take his weight. His arms began to tremble, but he took a deep breath and pushed on, hooking his arm over the ledge of the arched window. Light blinded him and he blinked rapidly; he was overlooking the main courtyard and could see men running from the walls to the steps below, leading into the hall.

Swiftly he straddled the ledge and leaned out. As he had feared, there was no easy way to the windows above the hall balcony, and now the drop was even worse. With a whispered curse he lowered himself to the first foothold and started to traverse the outer wall. He had moved some ten feet when a musket ball hit the stone beside his head and screamed off above him. Glancing over his shoulder, he saw a man on the gate turret hastily reloading his weapon.

Batik moved on. How long would it take to reload? Thirty seconds? A minute? His heart was pounding furiously as he reached the window and clamped his hand on the secure ledge. He risked another glance and saw the man aiming the rifle. Batik swung out, hanging by his right arm as the shot hit the ledge, chipping stone fragments which stung his hand. He hauled himself over the ledge and tumbled on to the balcony. Two men were kneeling there watching the doorway below, and they both turned as Batik fell. The Hellborn threw himself at them, knocking aside a musket barrel. The weapon fired. Batik cracked his fist against the man's chin and kicked out at the second rifleman, catching him in the chest and knocking him flat. The first man drew a knife and leapt forward; Batik blocked the man's knife-arm with a chopping blow, grabbed his hair and, with a tremendous surge of power, hurled him over the balcony wall. The man's scream was cut off as he hit the marble floor.

Batik pulled his pistol clear and swung on the second man, who was sitting motionless with his hands above his head. He was a youngster, maybe sixteen, with wide blue eyes and an open face too pretty to be called handsome.

Batik shot him between the eyes.

Across the hallway other riflemen had seen the action and opened fire. Batik dived to the floor and scrambled towards a stone pillar at one corner of the hall. From this position he had two fields of fire and could also see the stairwell which led to the balcony. He glanced at the riflemen opposite; there were three of them, each armed with muskets.

'Shannow!' he called. 'There's only three. You want me to kill them?'

At the other end of the hall Shannow grinned. 'Give them a chance to surrender,' he shouted.

Batik waited for several seconds. 'They haven't surrendered,' he said.

'Wait!' came a cry from the balcony. 'We don't want any more killing.'

'Throw the muskets over the edge,' called Batik and three weapons clattered to the stone. 'And any pistols.' More weapons crashed to the floor. 'Now stand up where we can see you.'

The men did so. Batik would have killed them, but he only had five shots left and knew there were more enemies in the courtyard below. 'Bring them out, Shannow,' he yelled and then ran for the stairs, taking them two at a time and emerging into the shadowed doorway of the main entrance. Outside, several men were crouching behind hastily built barricades constructed of water-barrels and grain sacks.

'What now, general?' asked Batik as Shannow moved alongside him in the shadows.

'Now we talk,' said Shannow and moved forward. 'Hold your fire,' he called, descending the steps and moving slowly towards the crouching riflemen.

'That is far enough,' called a voice.

Shannow stopped. 'Inside there are seven dead men – some of them were probably friends of yours. Eight others surrendered and tonight they will be with their families enjoying supper. You decide what you want to do. Batik! Bring them out.'

The Jerusalem Man stood calmly before the riflemen as the first of the Wolvers stumbled into the daylight. One by one the guards put down their rifles and stood. Batik led the former slaves through the gates and out into the main street of the town, where the Wolvers huddled together behind the black-garbed Hellborn.

Back in the courtyard, a terrible scream tore through the air as the skeletal, bearded widower ran into the open clutching the flintlock pistol. He looked at Shannow and the guards and then ran out into the street behind the Wolvers, stopping only when he saw the crowds lining the buildings. He screamed again and fell to his knees, staring down at his filthy body and the pus-filled sores on his skin.

His wild eyes raked the crowd. 'You took it all!' he shouted, lifting the pistol under his chin and pulling the trigger. Blood gushed from his throat and he toppled forward.

Shannow rode from the castle, leading two horses. He paused by the body and then looked at the silent crowd. There were no words to convey his contempt and he rode on. The guards had carried Archer to the porch by the store; the black man was coming round, but he could not stand.

'Take him inside somewhere,' ordered Shannow. 'Find him a bed.'

'Bring him to my place,' said Flora. 'I'll see to him.'

Shannow nodded to the woman. The Wolvers were sitting in the centre of the street, some of them still holding their pick-axes. Shannow dismounted and moved to Batik. 'Get some food from the store for them. Clothes, suppplies . . . Jesus! I don't know. Get them anything they need.'

The storekeeper, Baker, walked out on to the street.

'Who is going to run the mine?' he asked.

Shannow hit him and the man fell to the dust.

'There was no need for that,' whimpered Baker.

Shannow took a deep breath. 'You are correct, Meneer Baker, and I cannot begin to explain it.' He left the man and walked to the Wolvers, moving in to kneel amongst them.

'Can any of you understand me?' he asked. They looked at him, but did not speak; their faces were cowed, their eyes dull. Flora approached, bringing with her the young boy who had stabled Shannow's horse.

'They do understand you,' she said. 'Robin here has lived with them.'

'We are going to get you some food,' Shannow told them. 'Then you are free to return to the plains, or the mountains, or wherever you call home.'

'Ree?' said a small dark figure to the right, his head tilting, his eyes fixed on Shannow's. The voice was piping and high, almost musical.

'Yes. Free.'

'Ree!' The creature blinked and touched one of its comrades on the shoulder. Shannow saw it was a female. It placed its arms around her shoulders and their faces touched. 'Ree,' the Wolver whispered.

'Archer wants to see you,' said Flora. Shannow stood and followed her through the eating-house and up a flight of rickety wooden steps to a bedroom above the kitchen.

Archer was dozing when Shannow entered, but he awoke when the Jerusalem Man sat on the bed beside him.

'Nicely done, Shannow,' he whispered.

'I was lucky,' said Shannow. 'How are you feeling?'

'Strange. Light-headed, but there's no pain. I'm so glad to see you, Shannow. When you went over that ledge I had a sinking feeling in my heart.' The black man leaned back and closed his swollen eyes; his face was badly cut and gashed and his words were slurring badly.

'Rest now,' advised Shannow, squeezing his shoulder. 'I'll come back later.'

'No,' said Archer, opening his eyes, 'I feel fine. I thought for a while that Riggs and his friends were going to kill me, and I knew Amaziga would be so angry. She's a fine woman and a wonderful wife, but nag? She's always telling me to take a weapon with me. But then how many enemies does a man meet in a dead city? You'll like her, Shannow; she made me wait eight years before agreeing to marry me – said I was too soft, that she wasn't going to risk falling in love with a man who would be killed during his first hostile encounter. She was nearly right. But my charm won her in the end. Tough lady, Shannow . . . Shannow?'

'What is it?'

'Why has it gone dark? Is it so late already?'

The sun was shining brightly through the open window.

'Light a lamp, Shannow. I can't see you.'

'There is no oil,' said Shannow desperately.

'Oh well, never mind. I like the dark. Do you mind sitting here with me?'

'Not at all.'

'I wish I had my Stone – then these bruises would be gone in seconds.'

'There'll be another at the Ark.'

Archer chuckled. 'How could you attack a fortress?'

'I don't know; it seemed like a good idea at the time.'

'Batik told me you are unable to comprehend impossible odds and I can quite believe him. Did you know that Ridder was a priest?'

'Yes.'

'Strange religion you have, Shannow.'

'No, Archer. Just that some very strange people are attracted to it.'

'Including you?'

'Including me.'

'Why are you sounding so sad? It's a fine day. I never thought to get out of there alive – they just kept kicking me. Batik tried to stop them, but they beat him down with staves. Staves . . . I'm very tired, Shannow. I think . . .'

'Archer . . . Archer!'

Flora moved forward and lifted the man's wrist. 'He's dead,' she whispered.

'He can't be,' protested Shannow.

'I'm sorry.'

'Where is Riggs?'

'He was in the meeting hall.'

Shannow strode from the room and down the stairs, emerging into the sunlight where Batik was passing food amongst the Wolvers. Batik saw the expression on his face and moved to join him.

'What's happened?'

'Archer is dead.'

'Where are you going?'

'Riggs,' said Shannow tersely, pushing past him.

'Wait!' called Batik, grabbing Shannow's arm. 'He's mine!'

Shannow turned. 'What gives you the right?'

'Poetry, Shannow. I'm going to beat him to death!'

Together the two men entered the meeting hall. There were two dozen tables and a long bar running the length of the room. At the back sat three men, all of them armed. As Shannow and Batik moved forward slowly, two of the men eased themselves to their feet and edged away from the third.

The man hurled the table away and stood. Riggs was over six feet tall and powerfully muscled, his face flat and brutal, his eyes small and cold.

'Well?' he said. 'What's it to be?'

Batik handed the pistol to Shannow and moved forward unarmed.

'You must be insane,' said Riggs. Batik hit him with a crashing right-hand blow and he staggered and spat blood from his mouth. The fight began. Riggs was the heavier, but Batik moved with speed and landed more blows, yet the punishment each man took was appalling to Shannow's eyes.

Grabbing Batik in a bear-hug, Riggs lifted him from his feet, but Batik hammered his open palms into Riggs' ears and broke free. Riggs kicked Batik's legs from under him and then leapt feet-first at his head. The Hellborn rolled and rose to his feet; then, as Riggs rushed at him he ducked under a left hook and hammered a combination of punches to Riggs' belly. The big man grunted and backed away and Batik followed, thundering blows to Riggs' chin. Both men were bloodied now and Batik's shirt was in tatters. Riggs tried to grapple, but Batik swung him round and tripped him. The bigger man landed on his face and Batik leapt on his back, grabbing his hair and his chin.

'Say goodbye, Riggs,' he hissed, then wrenched the chin up and to the right. The sound of the snapping neck made Shannow wince. Batik staggered to his feet, then moved to a nearby table where Shannow joined him.

'You smell awful,' said Shannow, 'and you look worse!'

'Always words of comfort from you just when they're needed.'

Shannow smiled. 'I'm glad you are alive, my friend.'

'You know, Shannow, after you went over that ledge and Archer and I raced clear of the lions, he talked about you. He said you were a man to move mountains.'

'Then he was wrong.'

'I don't think so. He said you would just walk up to a mountain and start lifting it a rock at a time, never seeing just how big it was.'

'Maybe.'

'I'm glad he lived long enough to see you attack a castle single-handed. He would have enjoyed that. Did he tell you about Sir Galahad?'

'Yes.'

'And his quest for the Grail?'

'Yes. What of it?'

'Are you still planning to kill Abaddon?'

'That is my intention.'

'Then I'll come with you.'

'Why?' asked Shannow, surprised.

'You might need a hand lifting all those rocks!'

Ruth floated above the fabled palaces of Atlantis, gazing in wonder at the broken spires and fractured terraces. From her position just below the clouds, she could even see the outlines of wide roads beneath the soil of the rolling prairies. Around the centre of the city was a flat uninspired wasteland which must once have housed the poorer quarters of Atlantis, where the homes were built of inferior stone long since eroded by the awesome might of the Atlantic Ocean. But now, once more, the gleaming marble of the palaces glistened beneath a silver moon.

She wondered what the city must have been like in the days of its glory, with its terraced gardens and vineyards, its wide statue-lined ways, its parks and colosseums. Part of the city to the north had been destroyed by a volcanic upheaval, and now a jagged mountain range reared above the ruins.

Wishing herself downwards, she floated gently to an open terrace before a gaunt and shadowed shell which had once been the palace of Pendarric. Wild grass and weeds grew everywhere, and a tree had taken root against a high wall – its roots questing like skeletal fingers for a hold in the cracked marble.

She stopped before a ten-foot statue of the king, recognizing him despite the artificially curled beard and the high, plumed helm. A strong man – too strong to see his weakness before it was too late.

A sparrow settled on the helm and then flew off between the marble pillars of a civilization which once had stretched from the shores of Peru to the gold mines of Cornwall. The land of fable!

But even the fable would fade. For Ruth knew that in centuries to come, her own age of technology and space travel would become embroiled in myth and legend to which few would give credence.

New York, London, Paris . . . all synonymous with the fiction of Atlantis.

Then one day the world would topple once more, and the survivors would stumble upon the statue of Liberty protruding from the mud, or Big Ben, or the Pyramids. And they would wonder, even as she did, what the future held now.

She turned her gaze to the mountains and the golden ship lodged in the black basaltic rock five hundred feet above the ruins.

The Ark. Rust-covered and immense, and strangely beautiful, she lay broken-backed on a wide ledge. Within her thousand-foot length the Guardians laboured, but Ruth would not go amongst them. She wanted no part of the old world, nor the knowledge so zealously guarded.

Ruth returned to Sanctuary and her room. As always when her mood was sombre, she created a study without doors or windows, lit only by candles that did not flicker.

For a while she sat and remembered Sam Archer, praying silently for the soul of the man. Then she called for Pendarric.

He came almost at once and stood by the far wall, which opened to become a window looking out on Atlantis in her glory. People thronged the winding streets and market-places. Chariots drawn by white horses clattered along the statue-lined main avenue.

Ruth joined him. 'As it was?' she asked.

'As it is,' he answered. 'There are many worlds which overlap our own, and many gateways to them. In the last days before the oceans drank my empire, I led my people through. But there are other gateways, Ruth, to darker worlds. These Abaddon has discovered – they must be closed.'

'I will close them, if I can.'

'Shannow will close them – if he lives.'

'And what can I do?'

'I told you, Lady. Take the swan's path.'

'I am not ready to die. I am afraid.'

'Donna Taybard has been taken. Her settlement is destroyed, her son is dead. Believe me, Ruth, if the woman is sacrificed the gateways will be ripped asunder. Worlds within worlds will be drawn together and the resulting catastrophe will be cosmic in scale.'

'How would my dying aid the world?'

'Think on it, Ruth. Find the answer.'

Madden prepared a grave for Rachel and the boys, laying them side by side and covering them with wild flowers of purple and yellow. For a long while he sat by the grave, not having the energy or the inclination to fill it. Robert's arm had flopped across his mother's breast and it seemed to Madden that he was hugging her. He had always been her favourite, and now they would lie together for eternity.

His eyes misted and he swung his gaze to the mountains, recalling the joy he had felt as he stood near this spot on their first day in Avalon. Rachel had been fussing about the size of cabin they would need and the boys had charged off into the woods above the valley. Everything had been peaceful then and the dream had seemed as solid as the rocks around them.

Madden's wounds still pained him and the right side of his face was heavily bruised, but he stood and lifted the shovel and slowly filled the grave. He had intended to cover it with more flowers, but he was too tired to gather them and returned to the cabin to check on Griffin.

The man was asleep and Madden fuelled the wood-stove and prepared some herb tea. He sat in a wide chair staring at the dusty floor, his mind drifting back to all the times when he had quarrelled with Rachel, or caused her to cry. She had deserved so much more than he could ever offer her, yet she had stuck by him through savage winters and dry summers, failed crops and Brigand raids. She it was who had convinced him they should follow Griffin's dream. Now the wagoner was probably dying and Madden would be alone in a strange land.

He sipped his tea and moved to the bedside. Griffin's pulse was erratic and weak; he was lying face down and Madden cut away the bandages to examine his wounds. About to turn him, he noticed a bulge near the swollen purple bruise on Griffin's side and touched it with his finger. It was hard, and it moved as he felt it. Removing his knife from its sheath, Madden pressed the razor-edge to the skin, which parted easily, spurting blood to his fingers as the misshapen shell popped into his hand. It must have hit one of Griffin's ribs and been redirected to his back, whereas Madden had feared the bullet was lodged in Griffin's stomach. Moving to the other side of the bed, he examined the second wound in Griffin's back; it was healing well, but there was no sign of the bullet. He stitched the knife-cut and returned to his chair.

The wagon-master would either live or die, and there was nothing more the bearded farmer could do for him. Madden ate some food – a little bacon and some stale bread – and left the cabin. Bodies littered the ground, but he ignored them and walked on towards the foothills of the mountains. Here he picked flowers until dusk, when he returned to the graveside where he sprinkled the blooms over the fresh-turned earth and dropped to his knees.

'I don't know if you're there, God, or what a man has to do to have the right to talk to you. I keep being told there's a paradise for them that believes, but I'm sort of hoping there's a paradise for them that don't know. She wasn't a bad girl, my Rachel; she never done evil to anybody, ever. And my boys didn't live long enough to learn what evil was, not until it killed them. So maybe you'll just overlook their disbelief and let 'em in anyway.

'I ain't asking nothing for myself, you understand. I ain't got much time for a God who allows this sort of thing to happen in his world. But I'm asking for them, because I don't want to think about my girl just being food for worms and suchlike.

'She deserves better than that, God. So do my boys.'

He pushed himself to his feet and turned. There at the edge of the paddock was Ethan Peacock's dapple-grey mare and Madden walked slowly over to her, speaking in a soft gentle voice. The mare's ears pricked up and she wandered towards him. He stroked her neck and led her into the paddock; she must have jumped the fence when the shooting started.

Back in the cabin, he found Griffin awake.

'How you feeling?' he asked.

'Weak as a day-old lamb.'

Madden made some fresh tea and helped Griffin to a sitting position.

'I'm sorry, Jacob. I brought you to this.'

'Too late for sorries, Con. And I don't blame you, so put

it from your mind. We got us a horse and guns. I figure to go after them bastards and at least get Donna back.'

'Give me a day, maybe two, and I'll ride with you.'

'I'll find you a horse,' said Madden. 'There must be more than one that the Hellborn didn't take. I'll scour the western valleys. You feel up to eating?'

Madden lit two oil-lamps and cooked bacon and the last three eggs on the griddle-iron of the stove. The smell of the frying bacon made Griffin acutely aware of his hunger.

'I reckon you might live,' said Madden, watching the wagon-master wolfing the food. 'No dying man would eat like that.'

'I've no intention of dying, Jacob. Not yet, anyhow.'

'Why did they do it, Con? Why did they hit us?'

'I don't know.'

'What did they gain? We must have killed a couple of hundred of them, and all they took was the guns. It don't make no sense. It's not as if they wanted the land – it was just killing for the sake of it.'

'I don't think there *are* answers for people like them,' said Griffin. 'It's like the Brigands. Why don't they farm? Why do Daniel Cade – and others like him – move around the land killing and burning? We can't understand them or their motives.'

'But it must be *for* something,' insisted Madden. 'Even Cade could argue that he gains by his evil . . . stores, coins, weapons.'

'There's no point in even wondering at it,' said Griffin. 'They are what they are. Plain evil. Sooner or later someone is going to give it back to them.'

'You ever hear of an army, Con? There ain't nobody to stop them.'

'There's always somebody, Jacob. Even if it starts with you and me.'

'Two wounded men, one horse and a couple of pistols? I don't think we'll put much of a scare into them.'

'We'll see,' said Griffin.

*

The grizzly had found the beehive in a rotting tree trunk and was busy tearing away the wood when the Zealot struck into its brain. The beast reared in anger and pain; settled down and ambled away to the south, towards the wooden homes of the Yeager men.

The bear was the undisputed monarch of the high country, weighing more than a thousand pounds, and even the lions crept from his path. Wisely he had avoided the haunts of Man, and even more wisely the hunters of Yeager had steered clear of the grizzly, for it was well-known that a large bear could soak up musket balls as if they were bee-stings – and no one wanted any part of a wounded grizzly.

It was an hour before dawn when the bear moved into the settlement, heading unerringly for the cabin of Daniel Cade. Mounting the porch, it reared up before the door; then its huge paw swept down, splintering the wood.

Cade awoke and scrambled from his bed. His captured Hellborn pistol hung in its scabbard from the bed-post and he whipped the gun clear. The bear moved into the room beyond, smashing a table. When it reached the bedroom door and crashed it inwards, Lisa screamed and Cade cocked the pistol, aiming it for the bear's head. The Zealot, his work all but done, fled the bear's mind and returned to his own body in the camp before the pass.

Back in the cabin, Cade shielded Lisa with his body and watched as the grizzly dropped to all fours, shaking its great head. Cade reached slowly for the jar on the shelf by the bed. Inside were flat sugar biscuits Lisa had made the day before and he tossed one to the floor. The bear growled and backed away, confused and uncertain. Then it sniffed at the biscuit, savouring the sweetness. Finally it licked out, lifting the biscuit to its mouth and noisily devouring it. Cade threw another – and another – and the grizzly settled down on its haunches.

'Climb out of the window,' Cade told Lisa. 'But move slow – and don't let any fool shoot the damned bear.'

Lisa opened the catch and stood on the bed. The bear ignored her, its eyes on Cade and the jar. She climbed over the ledge and ran to the front of the house where Gambion,

Peck and several others were waiting with rifles in their hands.

'Daniel says not to shoot the bear.'

'What the Hell is he doing in there?' asked Gambion.

'He's feeding it biscuits.'

'Why don't he climb out and let us kill it?' asked Peck. Lisa spread her hands and shrugged.

Inside, Cade was down to the last four biscuits. Slowly he stood and tossed one of them over the bear's head and into the room beyond. The grizzly sat looking at him.

Cade grinned. 'No more till you get that one,' he said. The bear growled, but Cade was beginning to enjoy himself. 'No use you losing your temper.' He tossed another over the shaggy head and the bear turned and ambled into the room. Cade followed and threw the third biscuit into the doorway. The bear lumbered after it and came face to face with the men beyond, who scattered in fear. Peck threw his rifle to his shoulder.

'Don't shoot it!' screamed Lisa.

The bear moved to the porch. It was frightened by the sudden noise and moved off at an ambling run towards the hills as Cade appeared in the doorway.

'What's the matter with you people?' he asked. 'Never seen a bear before?'

'It's no joke,' said Gambion.

'You're right about that. It only left me two biscuits!'

Gambion climbed the porch. 'I mean it, Daniel. A bear don't just come out of the hills and smash its way into a man's home. It's not natural. I don't know how, but the Hellborn are behind it; they were trying to kill you.'

'I know. Come inside.'

Cade sat down by the ruined table and Gambion pulled up a chair.

'They've tried frontal attacks on the pass and they know it's suicide,' said Cade. 'Now they'll be more cagey. They'll be scouting north and south and it won't be long before they find Sadler's Trail – and then they'll be behind us.'

'Did God tell you this?'

'He didn't need to; it's plain common sense. We need the

trail held. I've sent a rider south for help, but I don't know if there'll be any. I want you to take thirty men and hold Sadler's.'

'It's pretty open, Daniel. Any big attack will win through in the end.'

'You may be lucky. I only need ten days to get everyone back into the Sweetwater Valley. Now there's only one way in there and we can hold that for damn nigh a year.'

'If we had supplies,' put in Gambion.

'One day at a time. We've food enough for at least a couple of months, but we're running low on ammunition. I'll fix that. But you pick your men and hold Sadler's Trail.'

'Will God be with me, Daniel?'

'He'll be as much with you as he is with me,' promised Cade.

'That's good enough for me.'

'Take care, Ephram. And no heroics – I don't need another martyr. I just need ten days! With luck, you won't see any action at all.' The sound of distant gunfire came to them but neither man was unduly alarmed. Every day the Hellborn tried some action in the pass and always they were beaten back with losses.

'Better be going,' said Gambion.

'Evanson is already there, with Janus and Burgoyne – good men.'

'We're all good men now, Daniel.'

'Damned right about that!'

After Gambion had left, Cade dressed and rode to the rim of the pass, where down on the rocks were four Hellborn corpses. Cade dismounted and limped to the first defender, a youngster called Deluth.

'How we doing, boy?'

'Pretty good, Mr Cade. They tried just the once and we burned 'em good. Must have hit five or six more, but they rode out.'

'Where's Williams?'

Deluth pointed to a ledge some forty feet away.

'Go get him for me. I don't think I can make that climb.'
The boy left his rifle, bent double and ran along the rock-

line. Shots spattered close to him, but he moved too fast for the Hellborn snipers to catch him in their sights. Cade hefted the boy's rifle and sent a shot towards the tell-tale powder clouds on the far side of the pass. He hit nothing, but it kept their minds from the running Deluth.

Within minutes the manoeuvre was repeated with Williams running the gauntlet of shots; a short stocky man of forty-five, he was breathing hard as he slumped down beside Cade.

'What is it, Daniel?'

'I'm pulling everyone back to the Sweetwater.'

'Why? We can hold them here till the stars burn out.'

Williams was a farmer and his knowledge of the mountain range was limited. Most people believed the Yeagers were impenetrable but for the pass.

'There's another way in; it's called Sadler's Trail after a Brigand that rode these parts forty . . . fifty years ago – starts in a boxed canyon and unless you're real close you'll miss it. It cuts up through the range and on to the Sweetwater. Sooner or later the Hellborn will stumble on it and I can't take the risk. It would put them behind us, and we've not the numbers to hold on two fronts.'

Williams cursed and spat. 'How do we know they ain't found it already?'

'I've got people watching it. And anyway, I figure once they find it they'll stop these frontal assaults. That'll tell us they feel they're on to a better bet.'

'What do you want me to do?'

'Nothing. I just wanted you to know, in case you saw us moving and felt you've been left here.'

'Well, would you believe that?' said Williams, pointing over Cade's shoulder. He turned to see a small doe rabbit squatting several feet from the talking men. 'You surely do have a way with animals, Daniel.' The rabbit shook its head and darted away . . .

In the tents of the Hellborn a young warrior opened his eyes, a look of triumph on his face.

'There is another way in,' he told the hawk-faced young officer beside him. 'It's called Sadler's Trail and it starts in a boxed canyon – it must be one to the south. The entrance is hidden, but it backs on to an area called Sweetwater and Cade is trying to get his people there before we find a way behind them.'

'Fine work, Shadik. I will tell the general.'

'It is their first mistake,' said Shadik.

'May it also be the last. I shall have the attacks stopped at once.'

'No, sir. That's what Cade is waiting for.'

'He has a cunning mind, that one. Very well.'

The officer walked down the line of tents until he reached a dwelling of white silk and canvas. Before it were two guards; they saluted him and he ducked under the tent-flap.

Inside, working at a folding desk, was the general Abaal – said to be one of the great-grandsons of Abaddon. Many claimed this distinction, since it could not be proved, but in Abaal's case he could point to the special favour his family always received from the king.

'I take it, Alik, you have some good news for me?'

'Yes, Lord General.'

'The bear killed him?'

'No, Lord. The man lied. It seems he departed from the beast at the moment Cade pointed his pistol.'

'And what did the Brigand do? Pat it and send it on its way?'

'He fed it with sugar biscuits, Lord General.'

'Then your other news had better be good.'

'The man has been put to death – but another of my brothers has, I think, redeemed the situation. There is another way in to the valley.'

'Where is this place? The other pass?'

'In a boxed canyon; to the south, I believe. We scouted it last week, but the entrance is said to be hidden; this time we will find it.'

'Take three hundred men.'

'You are giving me the command? Thank you, Lord General.'

'Do not thank me, Alik. If you fail, you will die. How long will it take Cade to get his people back into this Sweetwater?'

'A week, ten days, I'm not sure.'

'You have six days to get behind him. If you have not breached the pass in that time, hand over the command to Terbac, and take your life.'

'Yes, Lord General. I shall not fail.'

Chapter Eleven

Gambion arrived two hours after dusk and advised his thirty men to make a cold camp while he scouted the entrance to Sadler's Trail. He took Janus and Evanson with him, leaving Burgoyne to point out the best camp-sites. Janus appeared to be in his early twenties, blond and lean, while Evanson was maybe ten years older and running to fat. The older man was soft-eyed and Gambion had no faith in him, but the younger had the look of eagles about him: sharp, sure and confident.

'They came about six days ago,' young Janus told them, 'but they missed the entrance to the pass. We were all set up and there were only ten of them; we could have stopped them. It's unlikely they'll be back.'

'If Cade asked me to come here, then they'll be back,' said Gambion. 'Count on it.'

'Was it a message from Heaven?' asked Evanson.

'Cade says no, but I'm not sure any more.' He told them about the bear that had smashed its way into Cade's cabin, only to leave with a few biscuits.

'And you saw it happen?' asked Janus.

'As true as I'm standing here,' answered Gambion. He wiped a piece of towelling across his shiny bald pate. 'Damn, but it gets hot here.'

'The sun reflects off the white rock, especially at dusk. It'll be mighty cool in a few minutes,' said Janus. 'The men can fix a fire – no one could see it from the pass.'

'Well, the three of you can go back into Yeager,' said Gambion. 'You'll be glad to see your folks, I don't doubt.'

'The other two can go,' declared Janus. 'I'll stay here. I know this land.'

'Pleased to have you.'

'If it's all right with you, I'll leave now,' said Evanson and Gambion nodded, dismissing the man from his mind.

Janus watched the big man, noting the cat-like movements and the sureness with which he carried himself.

'What are you staring at?' asked Gambion, sensing the other's hostility.

'I'm looking at a man who drove people from their farms,' said Janus evenly. 'And I was wondering why God would choose you.'

'Because I was there son,' said Gambion, grinning. 'You don't fight the Hellborn with a plough and this here's the work of men who know weapons.'

'Maybe,' said Janus doubtfully.

'You don't have to like me, boy. Just stand beside me.'

'Have no fear on that score,' said Janus. 'I'll stand as firm as any man.'

'I know that, Janus – I'm a good judge. Show me the killing ground.'

Together they strolled down the narrow slope which led to the cleft in the cliffs, opening on to the rich plain that flared from the mountains into the canyon. Once beyond the cleft, Gambion glanced back and the entrance had all but disappeared.

'The mountains are young,' said Janus, 'probably volcanic in origin and the cleft was made by lava flow.'

'But a few men could hold it for quite some time,' responded Gambion.

'Depends on how anxious the enemy were to take it.'

'What does that mean?'

'Well, if they charge they can ride through the gap in a couple of seconds. Sure we could catch them in a murderous cross-fire, but once they're through they can spread out and circle us.'

'Then we don't let them get through,' stated Gambion.

'Easy to say.'

'Son, we don't have no choice. Daniel needs ten days to get all the people back into Sweetwater. He says ten days to me, and I promised it. Ten days is what he'll get.'

'Then you better hope they don't find us,' said Janus.

'Whatever it is, it will be the way God planned it.'

'Yes? Well, I don't believe in God.'

'After all you've seen?' asked Gambion, amazed.

'What have I seen? A band of Brigands and a lot of death. If you don't mind, Gambion, I'll put my faith in this here rifle and God can keep the Hell out of my way.'

The young man strode back to the camp-site and ordered Burgoyne to watch the pass. Burgoyne refused, saying he was going back to Yeager, and Janus turned to Gambion.

'Any of your men who can be counted on not to fall asleep?'

'Peck!' called Gambion. 'Take the first watch, I'll relieve you in four hours.'

'Why me?'

'Because I told you to, you son of a bitch.'

'Nice line in discipline you have,' said Janus, sitting down and wrapping his blankets around him.

'Move yourself, Peck!'

'I'm going.'

'And don't go to sleep. Daniel is relying on us.'

'I hear you.'

'I mean it, Peck.'

'Have a little faith, Ephram.'

Gambion lay back in his own blankets for about two hours, but he could not sleep. Finally he got up and moved off towards the pass, where he found Peck curled up and fast asleep between two boulders. He grabbed the man by his shirt collar and hoisted him upright; then he hit him in the mouth, smashing two front teeth. Three more blows and Peck was unconscious, his face bloody and swollen. Gambion took away his rifle and pistol and sat until dawn watching the plain.

Janus joined him there as the sun was rising. He stopped to look down at the unmoving Peck.

'Heavy sleeper?' he asked.

'Shut it, Janus. I'm not in the mood.'

'Calm down, big man. Go and get some rest. I'll take it for a few hours.'

'I'm all right, I don't need much sleep.'

'Do it anyway. If they come, there'll not be much time for rest during your "necessary" ten days.'

Gambion had to admit that Janus was right and that he was beginning to feel bone-weary. He passed Peck's rifle and pistol to Janus and hoisted the unconscious Peck to his shoulder, walking off without a word.

Janus remained where he was, watching a distant herd of antelope grazing on the plain. It was so peaceful here, he thought, so hard to imagine a war with blazing guns and sudden death. He had been working on his father's farm when the Hellborn had struck and his father had gone down almost at once, his head blown away. His mother had followed as she ran from the house. Then Janus had picked up his father's gun – a single-shot musket – and downed the first rider. The man flew from the saddle. Janus had dropped the rifle and, as the horse swept past, grabbed the pommel and vaulted on to its back, galloping away across the fields with bullets shrieking past him. The horse had been hit twice, but by the time it died under him he was into the woods and away.

Alone now, he could not even consider the future. He had wanted to marry Susan McGraven, but she and all her family were dead, so he was told, killed by the same raiders who had struck his farm. Everything he knew was gone, everyone he had loved was dead.

He was nineteen years old, though he looked older, and he saw no future except to kill or be killed by the Hellborn. He had no faith in Daniel Cade and his visions. What little he knew of the Bible and its teachings negated any belief in Cade. Would God use a man like him, a killer and a thief? He doubted it. But then he doubted God. So what do you know, Janus, he asked himself?

Two hours later, a sullen young man relieved him and Janus moved off the ridge and down to the camp-site. On his way he passed a dozen men digging a broad trench across the trail and piling the earth in front of it. He saw Gambion directing operations and approached him.

'What's the idea?'

'If they get through the pass they'll be riding hard. This line ought to separate the men from the boys.'

'True, but there's nowhere to run to. If you don't stop them here, you'll be cut to pieces.'

'I wasn't sent here to run, Janus,' said Gambion, turning back to the trench.

'Why are you doing this?'

'Why do you think?'

'I haven't a clue, Gambion.'

'Then I can't explain it to you.'

'I mean, what do you get out of it?'

Gambion leaned on his shovel, his heavy face showing signs of strain. He scratched his thick black beard and thought for a moment. 'I joined Cade a lot of years ago, and I never thought too much about what we were. Then God spoke to Cade and I realized it's not too late to change. It's never too late. Now I'm part of God's Army and I'm not going back. Not for plunder, nor Barta coin, nor goddamned Hellborn. Daniel says to stand here, so here I'll stand. They can send men, beasts or demons, but they won't pass Ephram Gambion – not as long as there's life in this old body. That make it clear to you, farmer?'

'It's clear, Ephram, but would you mind a suggestion?'

'Not at all.'

'Dig a second trench up there, and put a few men in it. That way, if you are overrun they can give you covering fire while you withdraw.'

Gambion followed the direction and saw a natural screen of rocks and undergrowth rising some twenty feet above their present position.

'You've a good eye, son. We'll do it.'

'How's your man Peck?'

Gambion shrugged. 'He went and died on me. But that's life, isn't it?'

'It's not an easy life in God's Army, Ephram.'

'Not by a long haul. We've no time for shirkers.'

'You mind if I get some sleep?'

'You go right ahead.'

Janus left them and wandered on. He was hungry and ate

some dried fruit before settling back into his blankets.

The day passed without incident, but just before noon on the second day, three hundred Hellborn riders entered the canyon. The man on watch, a youngster named Gibson, ran to fetch Gambion. Janus came with him.

'They're not just scouting,' said Janus. 'They're looking for something.'

'I agree,' muttered Gambion. 'I'll get the men set.'

'How are you going to place them?'

'Fifteen in the two trenches, the rest with us here.'

'A suggestion?'

'Go ahead.'

'They won't be geared to charge straight away and they'll probably ride in slowly the first time. Put every man we have overlooking the entrance – that way we'll hit them hard. The next time we'll have men in the trenches for when they really put the spurs in.'

Gambion chewed his lip for a while, then he nodded. 'Sounds good.'

He spread the men evenly across the pass, telling them not to fire until he did, but then to pour it on like there was no tomorrow. Afterwards he returned to squat beside Janus as the Hellborn moved across the canyon.

Within the hour a scout had discovered the cleft and was riding through it while the main body of horsemen waited outside. The Yeager men kept their heads down as the dark-armoured rider mounted the first slope. If he rode much further he would come in sight of the trenches, but he stopped and removed his helm. He was young, about the same age as Janus, and from where Gambion lay he could see that his eyes were blue. The rider wheeled his horse and rode back to the canyon and the Hellborn began to move. Gambion pumped a shell into the breech and waited, his mouth dry. Beside him, Janus nestled the rifle stock into his shoulder and took a deep breath, willing himself to relax. With half the riders inside, Gambion sighted on the leader and took in the slack on the trigger.

'Not yet,' whispered Janus and Gambion froze. The Hellborn moved on, and Gambion could hear the laughter from some of the riders who were obviously sharing a joke.

'Now,' said Janus. Gambion's rifle thudded back against his shoulder and then he was up on his knees pumping shot after shot into the rearing, bucking ranks of the enemy. The pass was alive with gunfire as rider after rider was swept from the saddle. Horses went down screaming, and the Hellborn turned and galloped from the pass. Volleys swept through them and then there was silence. Gambion rose to charge down the slope, but Janus grabbed his arm. 'They're not all dead. Get the men to hold back.'

'Back to your positions!' yelled Gambion.

Most of the men obeyed him, but one youngster – oblivious to the commands – raced down the slope. A fallen Hellborn rolled and fired his pistol at point-blank range and the youngster stopped dead, gripping his belly. A second shot exploded his head. Janus lifted his rifle and killed the Hellborn.

Outside the pass Alik regrouped his men. He knew he should lead them straight back, but fear gnawed at him and he dithered. He did not want to risk such slaughter again so swiftly.

'How many lost?' he asked his deputy, Terbac.

The man cantered his horse along the line, returning some minutes later. 'Fifty-nine, sir.'

'We'll go in on foot.'

'With respect, a charge could carry us past them.'

'On foot, I said.'

'Yes, sir.'

The men dismounted and tethered their horses.

Back in the pass Janus watched them, his brow furrowed.

'They're coming in again,' he said, 'but without horses.'

'What are they playing at?' asked Gambion.

'They probably mean to secure the entrance and push forward slowly.'

'Can they do it?'

'It's possible, but unlikely. Move the men on the far side about thirty paces to the right.' Gambion shouted his orders and the men moved into position.

'What now?'

'Now we wait, and take as many as we can. If they've got sense, they'll wait till nightfall. But I don't think they will.'

The first Hellborn reached the cleft and ran for the rocks . . . He didn't make it.

But the third did, and that gave the enemy a chance to return fire. Gambion crept along the ridge and shot dead the marksman. The Hellborn retreated back to the canyon.

Gambion moved back alongside Janus, looking at him expectantly. The young man knew then that the command had passed to him and he grinned ruefully.

'Ask your God for a cloudless night,' he said.

'I'll do that. But what if it isn't?'

'A man will have to stay down there – someone with sharp ears.'

'I'll do it.'

'You're the leader, you can't do it.'

'You're the leader here, Janus. I'm not too pigheaded to see that.'

'But your men don't know that. Send someone else.'

'All right. You don't think they'll come again today?'

'Not with any serious intent. I think we struck lucky, Ephram. I think there is a coward leading them.'

'You call being outnumbered ten to one lucky?'

'It's only eight to one now – and, yes, I'd call that lucky. If they'd started with a charge they could have cut through us and been on their way into Yeager by now.'

'Well, you keep on out-thinking them, son, and I'll be for ever in your debt.'

'I'll do my best, big man.'

Two days out from Castlemine, having found a gap in the mountains that allowed them to move west, Shannow and Batik found themselves in a cool valley edged with spruce and pine.

They stopped at the shores of a lake that sheltered beneath tall peaks and watered their horses. Shannow had said little since they had buried Archer and Batik had left him to his solitude.

As the afternoon drew on, Batik saw a rider bearing down on them from the west. He stood and shaded his eyes against the falling sun and as the rider neared, Batik's eyes widened in shock.

'Shannow!'

'I see him.'

'It's Archer!'

'It can't be.'

The rider approached and slid from the saddle. He was a black man, over six feet tall and wearing the same style of grey shirt that Archer had sported.

'Good afternoon, gentlemen,' he said. 'I take it you are Shannow?'

'Yes. This is Batik.'

'I am pleased to see you. My name is Lewis, Jonathan Lewis. I have been sent to guide you in.'

'In to where?' asked Batik.

'Into the Ark,' he replied.

'You are one of the Guardians?' asked Batik unnecessarily.

'Indeed I am.'

'Archer is dead,' said Shannow, 'but then you knew that.'

'Yes, Mr Shannow. But you made his passing more easy and for that we are grateful. He was a fine man.'

'I see you are armed,' said Batik, pointing to the flapped scabbard at Lewis' waist.

'Yes. Samuel could never see the point . . .' He did not need to finish his sentence. 'Shall we go?'

They followed Lewis for more than two hours, turning into a wide canyon flanked by black basaltic rock.

Ahead of them lay another ruined city, larger than the first they had found before meeting Archer. But it was not the city which caused the breath to catch in Shannow's throat. Five hundred feet above the marble ruins lay a golden ship, glowing in the dying sunlight.

'Is it truly the Ark?' whispered Shannow.

'No, Mr Shannow,' said Lewis, 'though many have taken it to be so, and in the main we do not disenchant them.'

The trio rode into the ruins, along an overgrown cobbled street to the foot of the mountain. Here Lewis dismounted, beckoning the others to follow. He led his horse to the rock and stopped to turn a small handle set within it. A section of the rock face then moved sideways leaving a rectangular doorway seven feet high and twelve feet wide. Lewis entered, Shannow and Batik leading their horses behind. Two men waited within the tunnel; they took the horses and Lewis led Shannow and Batik to a steel doorway which slid open to reveal a small room, four feet square and seven feet high. With the three men inside, the door whispered shut.

'Level Twenty,' said Lewis and the room shuddered.

'What's happening here?' asked Batik, alarmed.

'Wait for a moment, Batik. All will be well.'

The door opened once more, this time to a bright hallway, and Shannow stepped out. It was lighter than day here, yet there were no windows. All along the walls were glowing tubes; when Shannow reached up and touched one, it was faintly warm.

'You must have many Stones to produce this much magic,' said Shannow.

'We do indeed, Mr Shannow. Follow me.'

Another door opened before them and the three men entered a round room at the centre of which was a white desk in the shape of a crescent moon. Behind it sat a white-haired man, who stood and smiled at their approach. More than six-feet-six tall, his skin was golden, his eyes slanted and dark. His hair was long, sweeping out from the scalp like a lion's mane.

Lewis bowed. 'My Lord Sarento, the men you wished to meet.'

Sarento moved around the table and approached Shannow.

'Welcome, my friends. For my sins I am the leader here and I am delighted to welcome you. Lewis, fetch chairs for my guests.'

With Batik and Shannow seated, and Lewis sent to bring refreshment, Sarento leaned back on the table and spoke.

'You are a remarkable man, Mr Shannow. I have followed your exploits for a number of years: the taming of Allion, the hunting down of the Brigand Gareth, the attack on the Hellborn and now the liberation of Castlemine. Is there nothing that can stop you, sir?'

'I have been fortunate.'

'Fortune favours the Rolynd, Mr Shannow. Have you come across the name?'

'Archer mentioned it, I believe.'

'Yes, dear Samuel . . . I cannot tell you how much his death depresses me. He more than anyone is responsible for the growth in Guardian wisdom. But I was speaking of the Rolynd. A wondrous race were the Atlanteans; they conquered mysteries which still baffled our elders eight thousand years later. They were the fathers of magic – and they understood the gifts men carried. Some could heal, others could grow plants. Still others could teach. But the Rolynd were special for they were lucky; they carried luck like a talisman – a personal god who would step in whenever needed. And with the Rolynd warriors it was needed often. Warriors like you, Mr Shannow, who could somehow hear a stealthy assassin creeping upon them in the mist of a storm. The Atlanteans believed the gift was linked to courage. Perhaps it is. But whatever the cause, you have the gift, sir.'

Lewis returned and served a goblet of white wine to each of the men, then laid the pitcher on the table and left the room.

'You have great power here,' said Shannow.

'Indeed we do, sir. With knowledge comes power, and we guard the secrets of the old world.'

'But you also have the Stones.'

'What is the point you are making?'

'With all this power, why do you not stop the Hellborn?'

'We are not meddlers, Mr Shannow, though we have tried to guide this world for more than three hundred years. Men like Prester John Taybard and the man you knew as Karitas have been sent from here to educate the people of this continent – to lead them towards an understanding of what they are, and from whence they come. I have no army and if I did, I have no God-given right to change the destiny of the Hellborn. On the other hand, since the battle is unequal, I am willing to help you.'

'In what way?'

'I can give you weapons to take to Daniel Cade.'

'How will that help me kill Abaddon?'

'It will help you to do more than that; it will help you to beat him.'

Shannow looked into Sarento's dark eyes and stayed silent.

'What sort of weapons?' asked Batik.

Sarento gave an order to one of his men, who opened a hidden door in the far wall to reveal a firing range. At the furthest end of the first line was a wooden statue, dressed in the armour of the Hellborn. Sarento stepped on to the range and lifted a bulky black weapon almost three feet long, which he handed to Batik. 'Pull back the bolt on the left, then aim it – but hold it steadily, it may surprise you.'

Batik sprang the bolt and pulled the trigger. The rolling explosion deafened them momentarily and the statue disappeared, its upper torso smashed beyond recognition. Batik laid the weapon gently to rest.

'Five hundred bullets a minute, moving at three thousand miles per hour,' said Sarento. 'Hit a man in the upper leg with just one and the hydraulic shock will drag his blood from his heart and kill him. You can destroy an army with ten of these and I'll give you fifty.'

'I'll think about it,' said Shannow.

'What is there to think about?' argued Batik. 'We could ride in and take Babylon itself with these.'

'Probably, but I'm tired. Is there somewhere I can rest?' Shannow asked Sarento.

'Of course,' was the reply, whereupon he opened a door which Lewis entered. 'Show our guests to suitable quarters. I will see you both in the morning.'

The Guardian took them to another level and into a T-shaped room containing two beds, a table, four chairs and a wide window looking out on a gleaming lake. Shannow moved to the window and tried to open it, but the lock would not shift.

'It does not open, Mr Shannow – it is not a window at all, but a light picture – what we call a mood-view.' He moved to a dial on the wall and turned it. The view mellowed into dusk, evening and finally moonlit night. 'Set it as it pleases you. I shall have food sent to you.'

Once the guardian had left Shannow lay back on the first bed, his head pillowed on his arms.

'What's bothering you, Shannow?' asked Batik.

'Nothing. I am just tired.'

'But those weapons . . . Even your God would be hard-pressed to come up with a better miracle.'

'You are easily pleased, Batik. Now leave me to think.'

Batik shrugged and wandered around the room until Lewis returned with food. For Batik he brought a huge rare steak and green vegetables. For Shannow, there was cheese and black bread. When they had consumed the food, Lewis rose to leave.

'Is there no water anywhere?' asked Shannow. 'I would like to clean the dust from my body.'

'How foolish of me,' said the guardian. 'Look over here.' As he spoke, he slid back the wall by the mood-view to reveal a cubicle of glass. Lewis reached inside and pressed a switch at which warm water jetted from a nozzle in the wall. 'Soap and towels are in here,' said Lewis, opening a wall cupboard.

'Thank you. This place is like a palace.'

'It was constructed from plans that existed before the Fall.'

'Did the Guardians build this place?'

'After a fashion, Mr Shannow. We used the Stones to recreate the magic of our forefathers.'

'Where are we now?'

'You are inside the shell of the Ark. Once we harnessed the Sipstrassi, we rearranged the interior to house our community. I think that was some three centuries ago; there have been some modifications since.'

Shannow sipped a glass of clear wine. He was bone-weary, but there was much he needed to know.

'I never really had a chance to talk to Archer about what you guard. Would you mind explaining?'

'Not at all. Our community exists to gather and hoard the secrets of Pre-Fall, in the hope of one day bringing it back. We have a library here with over thirty thousand books, most of them technical. But there are also four thousand classics in eleven languages.'

'How can you bring back what is past?' asked Batik.

'That is a question for Sarento, not a soldier.'

'And you believe you can help bring back civilization with guns that could kill five hundred men a minute?' said Shannow softly.

'Man is an inventive animal, Mr Shannow. Any weapon of death will be improved. Would you not sooner have the guns than the Hellborn? Sooner or later their gunsmiths will perfect them.'

'How many of you are there?'

'Eight hundred, including the women and children. We are a fairly stable community. Tomorrow I will show you around. Perhaps you would agree to meet Amaziga Archer – it will be painful, but I know she wants to hear of her husband's last hours.'

'He spoke of her at the end,' said Shannow.

'Perhaps you would be kind enough to tell her that.'

'Of course. Were you a friend of Archer's?'

'Very few people disliked Sam. Yes, we were friends.'

'His Stone turned black,' said Batik. 'It was very small.'

'He always over-used it; he treated it like a magic bauble. I shall miss him,' said Lewis with genuine regret.

'Was he the only guardian with a love of Atlantis?' asked Shannow.

'Very much so – he and Sarento, that is.'

'An interesting man. How old is he?'

'Just over two hundred and eighty, Mr Shannow. He is very gifted.'

'And you, Mr Lewis? How old are you?'

'Sixty-seven. Sam Archer was ninety-eight. The Stones are wondrous things.'

'Indeed they are. I think I will rest now. Thank you for answering my questions.'

'It was a pleasure. Sleep well.'

'One last question?'

'Ask it.'

'Do the Stones create your food for you?'

'They used to, Mr Shannow, but we needed the power for other and more important things. We now run a sizable herd of cattle and sheep, and we grow most of our vegetables.'

'Thank you again.'

'Not at all.'

Shannow lay awake long after Batik was asleep. The mood-view was set to moonlight and he watched as clouds drifted across the sky, the same clouds time and again in relentless regularity. He closed his eyes and saw once more the sundered statue, picturing a real man lying there with his entrails around him like torn ribbons.

Had Karitas possessed weapons such as these, the Hellborn would never have destroyed his village and young Curopet would still be alive.

Shannow rolled over and lay on his stomach, but sleep evaded him despite the softness of the bed. He was uneasy and tense. He swung his legs from the bed and moved to the water cubicle, stepping into the shallow basin and turning on the spray. In a tray to his right was a bar of scented soap and he scrubbed his skin, revelling in the heat of the shower. Towelling himself down, he returned to the mood-view and on impulse switched it to day and watched the sun hurtle into the sky.

He sat at the table and poured a glass of water. All his life he had been both hunter and hunted, and he trusted his instincts. There had to be a cause for his uneasiness, and he was determined to find it before his next meeting with Sarento.

Sarento. He did not like the man, but that was no reason to judge him harshly. Shannow liked few men . . . and the

265

Guardian leader had been pleasant enough. Despite his words he had not seemed unduly distressed by Archer's death, but then the man had merely been a follower, and Shannow knew that the emotions of men whom the world thought great rarely ran deep. Humanity invariably ran a poor second to ambition.

Shannow relaxed his mind. In hunting one used peripheral vision to spot movement and it was the same with a problem. Staring at it head on often blurred the perspective. He let his thoughts roam . . .

Karitas leapt from his subconscious – kind, gentle Karitas.

Hellborn Karitas, the father of guns.

Sent out by Sarento?

To serve Abaddon?

Shannow's jaw tightened. He knew little of Karitas' background, but had not Ruth told him that he gave Abaddon the secrets of firearms? And had not Sarento claimed he was a Guardian sent to instruct?

What game was being played here?

And why did the Guardians need cattle when their Stones could create such a palace of miracles within a ghost ship? Lewis said they needed the power for more important things. What was more important than feeding a colony?

Sarento had said that Shannow was Rolynd, which meant his knowledge of Atlantis was greater than Archer's. Why had he not shared it with the Guardian?

And lastly there was Cade: Cade the Brigand, Cade the killer, throwing his hat into the ring of war.

What right-thinking man would supply him with the weapons of empire?

Shannow had told Ruth that he was happy to hear of Daniel's actions, and that was true. Blood was thicker than water, but Shannow knew Cade better than any man alive. His brother was tough, and merciless. And if he had taken on the mantle of leadership, it would not be for altruistic reasons. Somewhere within the horror of war, Cade had seen the chance of profit.

He switched the mood-view to night and returned to his

bed, where with his thoughts more settled he fell into a deep sleep. When he awoke Batik was already dressed and sitting with Lewis at the table. Before the Hellborn was a plate stacked high with eggs and bacon. Shannow dressed and joined them.

'Would you like some food, Mr Shannow? I am afraid Batik ate your ration.'

'I am not hungry, thank you.'

Lewis glanced at a rectangular bracelet on his wrist. 'Sarento is ready to meet you.'

Batik belched and rose. 'How are we going to get those guns to Cade?' he asked.

Shannow smiled and ignored the question. 'Shall we go?' he said to Lewis.

Once more out into the glowing corridor, Shannow slipped the retaining thong from the hammer of his right-hand pistol. Batik noticed the surreptitious movement and silently freed his own pistol. He asked no more questions but dropped back a pace, keeping Lewis ahead of him.

Inside the meeting room, Sarento rose and greeted his guests with a warm smile.

'Did you sleep well?'

'We did indeed,' said Shannow. 'Thank you for your hospitality, but we must be leaving.'

'It will take time to prepare the guns for the journey.'

'We will not be taking the guns.'

The smile left Sarento's face. 'You are not serious?'

'Indeed I am. You misread me, sir. There is only one dream in my life: to find Jerusalem. Sadly, I must first kill Abaddon. It is a question of pride and revenge. I am not part of the Hellborn war. If you wish guns to go to Cade, send some of your men.'

'Is that not a little selfish, Mr Shannow?'

'Goodbye, Sarento.' Shannow turned his back on the Guardian leader and moved to the door. Behind him Batik spread his hands and backed out into the corridor. Shannow stood by the elevator, Lewis joined them, and the journey to the canyon floor was made in silence.

The horses were brought out and Lewis walked out into

the bright sunlight with the two men.

'Good luck in your quest, Mr Shannow.'

'Thank you, Mr Lewis.'

Shannow mounted and swung the stallion's head to the south. Batik cantered alongside him and the two rode in silence to the rim of the hills overlooking the ruined city and the golden Ark.

'What was that about, Shannow?' asked Batik as the men reined their mounts. 'I would have thought you would leap at the chance of using those guns?'

'Why? You think I am in love with killing?'

'For Cade – to beat the Hellborn.'

'I will not be used, Batik, in another man's game.' Shannow drew his pistol. 'With this gun I have slain many Hellborn. But is it mine? No, I took it from the body of an enemy. Tell me, Batik – how long before the Hellborn capture one of those disgusting rifles? How long before they dismantle one and learn to make their own? They are not an answer to the war, they merely enlarge it. I am not a child to be mesmerized by a pretty toy.'

'You think too much, Shannow.'

'All too true, my friend. I think the Guardians are playing their own game. I think they created the Hellborn weapons and took them to Abaddon. And I think we were lucky to leave there alive.'

'Why did they allow it?'

'Surprise. They did not expect us to refuse.'

'How many more enemies do you expect to make in this quest of yours?'

Shannow grinned and his expression softened as he leaned over and grasped Batik's shoulder. 'Let me tell you this: one friend is worth a thousand enemies.'

Above them the spirit of Ruth soared away, her joy golden.

She sped south and west, passing Babylon and searching for the wagon carrying Donna Taybard, which she located in the foothills some four days' journey from the city. Donna lay in the back of the wagon with silver bands around her brow, wrists and ankles, and she seemed in a deep enchanted sleep. The bands puzzled Ruth and she floated closer to the comatose body, but a sharp tug pulled at her and she soared away. Steeling herself, she approached the body once more and found that the bands acted like a magnet, exerting power against her. She drew closer still, and the pull became painful, but at last she could see the shards of Blood Stone within the bands. She tore herself clear and flew to Sanctuary, her knowledge complete.

Anger welled in her, and she understood at last the truth of the Blood Stones. It was not blood or life they drank, but ESPer power. The strength of the spirit.

Soulstones.

Donna Taybard's life was to flow on Abaddon's Sipstrassi, and her soul would enhance its power. Ruth's anger became fury.

A shimmering glow began in the corner of her study and she turned as the image of Karitas blossomed. She relaxed momentarily as he approached smiling, but suddenly his hands became talons, his face demonic.

He lunged . . . but Ruth's fury had not ebbed and in an instant her hands came up, white fire streaming from her fingertips. The demon screamed and burned. The form of Karitas became a mottled, scaled grey under the heat of Ruth's anger, and the beast within writhed and died.

The stench of decay filled the room and Ruth staggered back. Windows appeared all around her and a clean breeze swept the room. She sensed the presence of Pendarric and the king appeared, dressed in a black tunic with a single silver star at one shoulder.

'I see you have learnt how to kill, my Lady.'

Ruth sat down, staring at her hands. 'It was instinctive.'

'Like Shannow?'

'I need no lessons at this time.'

'The beast was not Karitas. It was summoned from a gateway by a great force and you had no choice but to kill it. That does not negate what you are, Ruth.'

She smiled and shook her head. 'Had I truly the courage of my belief, I would have let it kill me.'

'Perhaps. But then evil would have the victory.'

'Why are you here, Pendarric?'

'Only to help you, Lady. My powers in this world are limited to words – a punishment for wreaking havoc during my time here, maybe. But you have power, and you must use it.'

'I will not kill again. *Ever*.'

'That is your choice, but you can end the dream of Abaddon without taking life. The Sipstrassi works in two ways – it uses power and it receives power. It must be nullified.'

'How?'

'You can find the way, Ruth. It is important that you find it alone.'

'I do not need riddles.'

'It is time to know your enemy. Seek him out – then you will know.'

'Why can you not just tell me?'

'You know the answer to that, Lady. As with your students, you do not take a child and place the power of the world in his hands. You lead him, encourage him to grow, to seek his own answers – to develop his talents.'

'I am not a student.'

'Are you not, Ruth? Trust me.'

'If I destroy my enemies, then my life's work will have been for nothing. Everything I have believed and taught to others, will have proved to be empty, devoid of truth.'

'I accept that,' said Pendarric gently, 'but only if you kill your enemies. There is another way to restore harmony, Ruth, even if it is only the harmony of the jungle.'

'And I can do that by dying?'

'It depends what manner you choose.'

Ruth's head sank. 'Leave me, Pendarric. I have much to think on.'

Lewis returned to the tunnel, summoned the elevator and stepped inside. At Level Sixteen he stopped and moved out into a wide corridor. Passing the living quarters of the field men, he saw Amaziga Archer playing with her son, Luke. She saw him and waved and he responded and walked on. He could not yet find the words to tell her that Shannow had gone – and with him the last words of her husband.

He approached Control and stood outside the steel door; it opened after several seconds and Lewis walked inside.

'You wanted me, sir?' he asked Sarento. The tall man was staring at a set of architects' plans and he nodded absently, waving his hand at a chair. Lewis sat.

'You know what these are?' said Sarento, passing the blueprints to Lewis.

He scanned them swiftly. 'No, sir.'

'These are the original specifications for the Ark. In three days she will sail again.'

'I don't understand.'

'We are about to enjoy an influx of power, Lewis. With that power, to celebrate Rebirth, I shall transform the Ark for twelve hours to her original state.'

'The power needed will be colossal,' said Lewis.

'Indeed it will, but we now have two hundred per cent more energy than at this time last month and it grows daily. The ship will be the last test. After that we will begin to rebuild the world, Lewis. Think of it – London, Paris, Rome all rising from the ashes of the Fall. All the technology of the old world visited upon the new, with none of the errors.'

'That is fantastic, sir. But where is the power coming from?'

'Before I answer that, let me ask you this: What do you make of Shannow?'

'I liked him. He is a strong man, and it took nerve to rescue Archer from Castlemine.'

'Indeed it did,' said Sarento, leaning back in his chair, his golden skin glowing, his eyes bright. 'And I admire him for it, make no mistake. I had hoped to save his life – to use him – but he would have none of it.'

'He may still succeed,' said Lewis. 'I would not like him to be hunting me.'

'He will not succeed. I have alerted the Zealots and even now they are closing on him.'

'Why, sir?'

'Lewis, you are a fine soldier, a natural follower – a good man. But you are not involved in policy. You do not have the mantle of responsibility for ensuring the survival of a lost race. I do. When I became leader two hundred and sixty years ago, how much of this . . . wizardry around you existed? We lived in the caves below the Ark; we hunted for our food and we farmed, much like the other settlements to the south. But I brought Rebirth to the Guardians. I gave them purpose – and long life, let us not forget that.'

'I don't understand what this has to do with Shannow.'

'Patience, Lewis. Archer showed the way with his records of Atlantis. The Sipstrassi was power, pure magic. But the Stones soon exhausted themselves. So how did the Atlanteans build their fabled structures? Not on tiny stones, fragments and chips. No, they had the One Stone, the Mother Stone. I searched for twelve years in the mountains, burrowing deep through hidden caverns. And I found it, Lewis – eighty tons of pure Sipstrassi, in one piece. It was the great secret of the Atlantean kings and they built a circle of stones around it, below ground. It was their high altar. Pendarric, the last of their kings, hacked a section from it and used that one broken piece to carve an empire. We will go one better. We are using it all. And now to your question, Archer. What of Shannow?'

Sarento stood, towering over the seated Lewis. 'He plans, though unwittingly, to stop the power flowing to the Mother Stone.'

'Can he do it?'

Sarento shrugged. 'We will never know, for he will be dead within hours.'

'I asked you before where the power comes from,' repeated Lewis.

'Indeed you did, and I hope you are prepared by now for the answer. Every Hellborn soldier carries a Blood Stone and every time he kills – or even is killed – he transmits power back to the Mother Stone. When the Hellborn sacrifice their ESPers they use Sipstrassi knives, and much of the power returns to us.'

'Then the Mother Stone is no longer pure?'

'Pure? Don't be a fool, Lewis! It is merely stronger. Too strong to create food, which is a drawback, but it can now fulfil our dreams.'

'It can't be right to use the foulness of the Hellborn.'

'Lewis, Lewis!' said Sarento, laying his hand on the soldier's shoulder. 'We *are* the Hellborn. We created them from the dreams of the madman Welby. We gave him power, we gave him primitive guns and he is ours, though he does not know it.'

Lewis's mouth was suddenly dry. 'But what of the deaths?'

Sarento sat down on the edge of the desk. 'You think it doesn't grieve me? But our duty to the future is to keep alive the civilization of the past.

'You must try to understand that, Lewis. We can only keep our dreams alive for a short time in this vacuum of a colony. One natural disaster – or a plague – and it could all be wiped out. The past must be made to live again out there in the new world – cities, laws, books, hospitals, theatres. Culture, Lewis . . . and technology. And even the stars. For what science could not achieve, surely magic can.'

Lewis remained silent, his thoughts whirling. Sarento sat statue-still, his dark eyes locked on Lewis' face.

'One thing, sir,' said Lewis at last. 'As we build and grow, the Stone will need even more power. Yes? Do we fuel it with death for ever?'

'A good point, Lewis, and it proves that I was right about you. You have intellect. The answer is yes. But we do not have to be demonic. Man is a natural hunting, killing animal. He cannot survive without wars. Think back on your history – it is a kaleidoscope of cruelty and terror. But from each war man progressed. For war establishes unity. Take Rome – they conquered the world in blood and fire. But only then could civilization take root. After conquest there was unity. With unity came law. With law came culture. But not just the Romans, Lewis. The Macedonians, the British, the Spaniards, the French, the Americans. There will always be those who desire war. We will give that atavistic need a positive purpose.'

Lewis stood and saluted. 'Thank you, sir, for sharing this knowledge. Will that be all?'

'No. The reason I have taken you in to my confidence is a delicate one. I told you that Shannow must die. In all probability the Zealots will succeed. But Shannow is Rolynd. He may escape. He may return. I want you to find him and kill him, should the Zealots fail.'

Aware that Sarento was studying his reaction Lewis merely nodded, keeping his face blank.

'Can you do this thing?'

'I'll take one of the rifles,' replied Lewis.

Chapter Twelve

For five days the riders had tried tentative attacks, but now on the sixth their leader went berserk, and the Hellborn mounted their horses and thundered into the pass, through the cross-fire which decimated their ranks and on to the trench where Gambion waited with ten men.

Through the cloud of dust sent up by the pounding hooves of their horses the Hellborn bore down on the waiting men.

'Fire!' screamed Gambion and a ragged volley smashed into the first line of riders, bringing down men and horses. A second volley hammered into the horsemen; then Gambion's men broke and ran for the second trench.

Above them, with three riflemen, Janus cursed. He stood and emptied his rifle into the surging ranks of the enemy. Only Gambion remained in the first trench; his rifle empty, he tugged his pistols clear and shot a man from the saddle. Now the dust swirled above him. A horse leapt over him, then a second. He fired blindly into the dust. A hoof clipped the top of his skull and he fell as shots hammered into the dirt beside him.

Janus screamed at the running men to take up positions and they responded, dropping down beside the three men in the second trench. Shells tore once more into the Hellborn and they broke and ran.

'After them!' shouted Janus, sweeping up a rifle and leaping the earthworks. Some seven men followed him, the rest hunkered down behind the relative safety of the earthworks. Janus knew the next few moments would be crucial in the battle. If they did not push the Hellborn outside into the canyon, they would spread up on to the hillside and outflank the defenders. He ran to the first trench and waited for his men to join him.

'Together!' he shouted. 'Volley fire. But only at my signal.'

The men settled their rifles to their shoulders. 'Now!' A volley shrieked through the dust clouds.

'Again!' Three times more they fired into the fleeing Hellborn. Janus led his men further into the pass, aware that their position was perilous should the Hellborn turn, but in the billowing dust the enemy had no idea how many men pursued them. At last Janus stood in the mouth of the pass itself and watched the Hellborn galloping out of range.

'Take up positions,' he ordered the men around him.

'I'm out of bullets,' a man told him.

'I've only got two rounds left,' said another.

'Strip the dead,' said Janus. 'But be careful – some of them may only be wounded.'

They gathered what ammunition they could from the fallen riders and returned to their positions. Janus sprinted back to the first trench where Gambion was sitting up holding his head.

'You ought to be dead,' Janus told him and Gambion looked up at the blond youngster and grinned broadly.

'It'll take more than a kick from a horse.'

'We are almost out of ammunition – we can't hold much longer, Ephram.'

'We *have* to.'

'Be reasonable, man. When the bullets are gone, then so are we.'

'We've held this long, and we've made them pay. Just four more days.'

'What do you want us to do? Throw rocks at them?'

'Whatever it takes.'

'There are only twenty-two men left, Ephram.'

'But we've taken over a hundred of them bastards.'

Janus gave up and ran back to the pass, climbing high on to the ridge and shielding his eyes, trying to see the enemy. They had dismounted and were seated in a circle around two officers. Janus wished he had a long-glass to study the situation more closely. It seemed to him that one of the officers had a pistol in his hand and that the barrel was in his mouth. The crack of the pistol drifted to him and he watched the officer topple sideways.

Gambion joined him. 'What's happening out there?'

'One of their leaders has just killed himself.'

'Good for him!'

'What kind of people are they, Ephram?'

'They ain't like us, that's for sure. By the way, I done a count and we've roughly fifteen shells per man. Good enough for a couple more attacks.'

Janus chuckled. 'Your head's bleeding,' he said.

'It'll stop. You think they'll come in again today?'

'Yes. One more charge. I think we should take a chance on stopping it dead.'

'How?'

'Line everyone across the pass and hit them with ten volleys.'

'If they break through, there'll be nothing to back us.'

'It's up to you, Ephram.'

Gambion swore. 'I'll buy it. Damn, but I never thought to see the day when a boy would give me orders.'

'And a child shall lead them,' said Janus.

'What?'

'It's from the Bible, Ephram. Don't you ever read it?'

'I don't read – but I'll take your word for it.'

'Do it fast. I think they're coming in again.'

Gambion and Janus slid down the slope, calling the men to them. They came reluctantly for the most part and gathered in a ragged line.

'You'd better stand this time, by God!' yelled Gambion.

The riders came on at full gallop. The guns of the defenders bellowed, echoing up into the pass, and the rolling thunder of the volleys drowned the sound of galloping hooves.

The pass was black with cordite smoke and as it cleared Gambion watched the last of the Hellborn cantering away out of range. Fewer than fifty men remained of the three hundred who launched the attack on the first day, while seven defenders were dead and two wounded.

'We'd better gather some ammunition,' said Janus. 'Send ten men to strip the bodies.'

Gambion did so, while the other defenders kept a wary eye on the retreating riders.

'We did well today,' said Gambion. 'You believe in God now?'

Janus cursed. It was the first time Gambion had heard him swear.

'What is it?'

Janus pointed to where, on the far side of the valley, a column of riders could be seen.

'Shit!' hissed Gambion. 'How many?'

'I don't know. Five hundred maybe.'

The scavengers returned with sacks of bullets and some extra pistols. One of them moved alongside Gambion.

'They didn't have more than five shells apiece. Ain't enough to hold that bunch.'

'We'll see.'

'Well I ain't staying,' said the man. 'I done my share.'

'We've all done our share, Isaac. You want to run out on God?'

'Run out on him? He ain't doing us no favours here, is he? There must be four, five hundred more of them sons of bitches and we ain't even got enough shells for them all.'

'He's right, Ephram,' said Janus. 'Send a rider to Cade – tell him he's got less than a day and he'd better speed up.'

'I'll go,' said Isaac, 'and glad to be out of it.'

The two wounded men were carried back into the pass and Janus touched Gambion's arm. 'We ought to move back, Ephram. We can't do any good here.'

'We can thin them a little.'

'They can afford to lose more than we can.'

'You want to run, then *run*!' snarled Gambion. 'I'm staying.'

'Here they come!' yelled a defender, pumping a shell into the breech. Gambion wiped sweat from his eyes and peered out into the canyon. Then blinked and squinted into the sunlight.

'Hold your fire!' he shouted. The lead rider came closer

and Gambion waved, a broad smile breaking out on his face.

'Jesus,' whispered Isaac. 'They're Southerners!'

The troop cantered past the bodies of the Hellborn and the leader drew rein before Gambion. He was a short, stocky man with a red moustache.

'Well, Gambion, I swore to hang you and now I'm going to have to fight alongside you. There's no justice left in the world!'

'I never thought to be pleased to see you, Simmonds, but I could kiss your boots.'

The man stepped down from the saddle. 'We've had refugees streaming south for a while now, telling tales like a sane man couldn't believe. Do these bastards really worship the Devil and drink blood?'

'They do and more,' said Gambion.

'Where are they from?'

'The Plague Lands,' Gambion replied, as if that explained everything.

'Is it true that Cade's become a prophet?'

'As true as I'm standing here. You still carrying muskets?'

'It's all we've got.'

'Not any more. We didn't have a chance to collect all the weapons from them Hellborn. You help yourself. They carry repeating rifles – damn good weapons. Ten shot some of them. The others is eight.'

Simmonds sent some of his men to search the dead, while the rest rode back into the pass to make camp. He himself wandered up the ridge with Gambion and Janus.

'This your boy?' he asked.

'No, this is our general. And don't make jokes, Simmonds – he's done us proud the last six days.'

'You shaving yet, son?'

'No, sir, but I'm two inches taller than you so I guess that makes us even.'

Simmonds' eyebrows raised. 'You a Brigand?'

'No. My father was a farmer and the Hellborn killed him.'

'The world's changing too fast for my liking,' said Simmonds. 'Repeating rifles, boy generals, Brigand prophets and Devil worshippers from the Plague Lands! I'm too old for this.'

'Can we leave a hundred of your men here?' asked Gambion. 'Then I'll take you to Cade.'

'Sure. Is your general staying?'

'He is,' said Janus. 'For four more days. Then we make for Sweetwater.'

'All right. What happened to your head, Gambion?'

'Horse kicked it.'

'I expect you had to shoot the horse,' said Simmonds.

Shannow and Batik were camped in a shaded spot near a waterfall when Ruth appeared. Batik dropped his mug of water and leapt backwards, tripping over a rock and sprawling beside the fire. Shannow smiled.

'You must excuse my friend, Ruth. He is very nervous these days.'

'How are you, Batik?' she asked.

'Well, Lady. Yourself?'

She seemed older than when they had last seen her; dark rings circled her eyes and her cheeks were sunken. Her iron-grey hair had lost its sheen and the eyes themselves were listless.

'I am as you see me,' she said softly.

'Are you truly here with us?' asked Shannow.

'I am here and there,' she answered.

'Can you eat? Drink? If you can, you are welcome to share what we have.'

She shook her head and remained silent. Shannow was at a loss and moved to the fire. Wrapping his hand in a cloth he lifted the small copper pot from the flames and mixed some herbs into the water; then he stirred the tea with a stick before pouring it into a mug. Batik spread his blankets and removed his boots. Ruth remained statue-still, regarding them both.

'How goes your quest?' she asked and Shannow

shrugged, aware that her question was merely the precursor of heavier words. 'What did you make of the Guardians?'

'I liked Archer. Lewis seemed a good man.'

'Who leads them?' she asked.

'You do not know?'

'A long time ago Karitas urged me to respect their privacy.'

'It is a man called Sarento.'

'Did you like him?'

'An odd question, Ruth. What does it matter?'

'It matters, Mr Shannow. For you are a man of Talent. You are a Sensitive and you have not stayed alive this long merely by being skilful with weapons. You have a knack of being in the right place at the right time. You judge men too shrewdly. In a way, your powers in this respect are greater than mine. For mine have been cultivated over the centuries while yours are latent, unchannelled. Did you like him?'

'No.'

'Did you judge him to be . . . Ungodly?'

'He reminded me of Abaddon – the same arrogance.'

'And he offered you weapons?'

'Yes.'

'Why did you refuse?'

'War is a vile game, Ruth, and the innocent die along with the guilty. I want nothing to do with the war itself; my only interest is in avenging Donna.'

'Avenging? She is not dead yet.'

Shannow sat very still. 'Truly?'

'Would I lie?'

'No. Can I reach her before they kill her?'

'No, Mr Shannow, but I can.'

'Will you?'

'I am not sure. Something has been troubling me for some time now, and yesterday I made a discovery that frightened me – that rocked all my long-built security. The Hellborn are not the enemy. We are not dealing with an evil race; they are pawns in a game I cannot understand.'

'Are you saying that the Hellborn are not at war?' asked

Shannow. 'That they are not butchering their way across the continent?'

'Of course not. But why are they doing it?'

'To conquer,' answered Batik. 'Why else?'

'I thought that before yesterday – but believe me, my friends, I have been very stupid. You are a Bible-reading man, Mr Shannow, and you have read of possession. Demons? The Hellborn are possessed and the power emanates from Abaddon. He is the centre, but even he does not understand the source of his power; he is being used.'

'By the Devil?' said Shannow.

'No . . . or perhaps yes, in another form. There is a force that I have traced which focuses on Abaddon and is dispersed by him throughout the Hellborn lands, touching the Blood Stone of every man, woman and child. Quite simply it is hatred, lust, greed. It covers the land like an invisible fog and it travels with his armies, bloated like a great slug.'

'It will be gone then when I kill him,' said Shannow.

'That is not the point, Mr Shannow. The source is where the evil lies . . . and I have traced that source, and the power there is incredible.'

'You speak of the Guardians,' said Shannow.

'Indeed I do.'

'You say you traced the source?' asked Batik.

'It is a giant stone. It feeds, if that is the word, on soul power – ESPer talents, call them what you will.'

'Where is this Stone?' said Shannow.

'It is lodged beneath the mountain of the Ark and from there it draws power from every Blood Stone in the Hellborn empire. It must be destroyed, Mr Shannow; its power must be ended. Or else a new dark age will fall upon the world, if not the destruction of the world itself.'

'Why do you come to me? I cannot defeat magic with a pistol.'

'Nor can I approach the Stone. It registers my power. But there is a way. The Atlanteans found a method of harnessing the energies of their Stones, trapping the power. The secret is in the monolith circles around the altars. They built the standing Stones as conduits of power which transmit and receive the energy. The Mother Stone was so powerful that special monoliths were constructed. Inset into each structure is a spool of golden wire. If the conduits are linked by gold, no energy can pass to the Stone at the centre. It will become drained, and eventually useless.'

'Why should the gold still be there?' asked Shannow. 'Does Sarento not know its danger?'

'The spools are hidden within the monoliths. But, yes, he may have discovered their use and removed them. That you must find out.'

'I? This is not my war, Ruth.'

'Do you not care that the world may die?'

'I care that Donna Taybard lives.'

'Are you bargaining with me?'

'Call it what you will.'

'I cannot kill, and rescuing her may take just that.'

'Then you destroy the Mother Stone.'

'How could you ask this of me?'

'Let me understand you, Lady. You want me to risk my life against the Guardians? And yet you know they will try to stop me and that I will kill all who come against me. Apparently that sits all right with your principles. But to save a woman, and perhaps kill the Ungodly to do it – that is against your principles?'

'I will not argue, Mr Shannow. I have neither the strength nor the time. What I can do is to take Batik to Donna. Will that suffice?'

Shannow shook his head. 'I have no right to ask Batik to put himself in danger.'

'I wish I knew what you two were babbling about,' said Batik, 'and I'm fascinated to know at what point you bring me into this conversation.'

'It does not concern you,' said Shannow.

'What are you, my mother?' snapped Batik. 'You don't make decisions for me. Saving the world may be a horse I can't saddle, but pulling one wench from a dungeon in Babylon? Who knows, perhaps I can tackle that without falling over?'

'You know damned well it's more than that,' said Shannow. 'You owe Donna nothing – why should you put your life at risk?'

'If you're looking for selfish reasons, my friend, tell me this: Ruth says the world could perish if the Mother Stone is not destroyed. If that is the case, where would you suggest I hide?'

'Let me think on it,' said Shannow.

'What is to think about?' asked the Hellborn. 'You want to avenge Karitas? Sarento is the man responsible. Abaddon is a pawn in his game, and you don't win wars by killing pawns.'

'I will deal with Abaddon,' said Ruth. 'I promise you that.'

'And how will you get Batik to Babylon?'

'With my own magic.'

'I asked how.'

'I shall dismantle his molecular structure, absorb it into my own and reassemble him when I arrive.'

'Reassemble – what's she talking about, Shannow?'

'There is little danger to you, Batik,' declared Ruth. 'It is how I travel.'

'But you have done this before, with other people, yes?' asked the Hellborn.

'No,' she admitted.

'Why did you have to ask her, Shannow? I preferred it when she said by magic.'

'You still want to go?' asked the Jerusalem Man.

'I said so, didn't I?'

'Try not to get yourself killed,' said Shannow, offering his hand. Batik took it and shrugged.

'I'll do my best. Tell me, Ruth, can you reassemble me without scars and with a less prominent nose?'

'No. Shall we go?'

'I'm ready,' said Batik. 'Good luck, Shannow.'

'And to you. Tell Donna I wish her joy.'

'Don't give up on her, her new husband's probably dead.'

Before Shannow could answer, Batik and Ruth faded from sight.

And the Jerusalem Man was alone.

Batik felt no sensation of movement. One moment he was looking at Shannow, the next he was lying face down in the grass on a hillside west of Babylon. Ruth was nowhere in sight as he stood and took a deep breath.

He wandered to the hill-top and gazed at the city which lay squat and dark in the distance. Covered by a pall of black smoke, it had improved little since he had fled it and he realized in that moment that he had missed the place not at all.

Ruth appeared beside him, and this time he did not react.

'How are you feeling?' she asked.

'Well. But you look tired.'

'I am weary,' she admitted. 'You have no idea of the energy I expend holding this body image in place. And as for carrying you across eight hundred miles . . .'

'Sadly I recall nothing of the journey. Is Donna here yet?'

'No, the wagon is half a day due west. If you start now, you should sight their camp before dawn.'

'How many in the party?'

'Two hundred.'

'I'm only carrying eighteen shells, Ruth.'

'I am hoping you will use your brain, young man, and that there will be no need for killing.'

'I might be able to get to her and untie her. Together we could run, I suppose.'

'There is something else you should know, Batik.'

'I don't think I want to hear it.'

'She is pregnant, and in a coma.'

'I knew I didn't want to hear it.'

'I shall pray for you, Batik.'

'That will be nice, I'm sure. I suppose you couldn't conjure up one of Sarento's guns as well?'

'Goodbye, Batik.'

'Farewell, Ruth,' he said, and watched as she became ever more transparent.

As he set off towards the west with a jaunty stride he

pushed the problem of the rescue from his mind. The whole mission was palpably hopeless, and he decided to relax and enjoy the stroll. Wondering what Shannow would have done, he chuckled as he pictured the Jerusalem Man riding up to the army and demanding the release of his lady. And he'd probably get away with it, thought Batik. Clouds scudded across the moon and an old badger ran across his path, stopping to squint at the tall man with the broad shoulders. Then it was gone into the undergrowth.

He came across the camp-site an hour before dawn. They were camped in a hollow, having erected tents in a circle around the wagon. Batik knelt behind a screen of bushes and watched them for a while until he was sure he had placed all the sentries. Then, just as he was making ready to move, he saw a dark shadow creep across his line of vision. Pulling his pistol into his hand he crept out behind the watcher, moving slowly down until he was almost alongside. The man was lean and bearded and dressed in clothes of dark homespun wool. So intent was he on the camp-site that he failed to hear the approach of the Hellborn.

Batik cocked his pistol and the noise made the man freeze, but his body tensed and Batik knew he was about to do something rash.

'Don't be a fool,' he whispered. 'I only want to talk.'

'You've got the gun. Talk all you want,' hissed the man.

'You're obviously not Hellborn, so I wondered what you wanted from them.'

'None of your business. You finished now?'

'Probably. But I do have business here and I don't want you spoiling it.'

'Well, there's a shame, sonny.'

'Are you from Donna's settlement?'

The man rolled slowly to his side and gazed into Batik's eyes.

'What do you know of Donna?'

'I'm a friend of Jon Shannow. He asked me to help her.'

'Why isn't he here himself?'

'He would be if he could. Why are *you* here?'

'Why do you think?'

'You want to rescue her?'

'That's the general idea, but there's a sight too many of the bastards. There's no way to sneak in; they've got seven sentries and a man inside the wagon.'

'I only counted six sentries.'

'There's one in that tall oak. He's got a long rifle and I don't doubt he knows how to use it.'

Batik uncocked his pistol and slid it into its scabbard.

'My name is Batik,' he said, offering his hand.

'Jacob Madden,' responded the other, sitting up and uncocking his own pistol which had been concealed beneath his coat. The two men shook hands.

'We came very close to killing one another,' remarked Batik.

'You came very close to dying,' observed Madden. 'Let's pull back where we can talk more freely.' Together they eased their way into the undergrowth and back over the brow of the hill.

Here, hidden in a grove of trees, were two horses. On the ground nearby Batik saw a man lying on his side, a pistol in his hand. His face was waxen and haggard and blood was seeping through the front of his shirt.

Madden knelt beside him. 'Can't get to her, Griff. There's too many.'

Griffin struggled to rise, then fell back.

'Who is he?' asked Batik.

'Donna is his woman.'

Batik's eyebrows rose and he leaned over the injured man.

'Looks like he's dying,' he said conversationally.

Madden swore. 'Nobody asked for your opinion,' he snapped.

Griffin took a deep breath and forced himself to a sitting position. 'Well, I don't feel too great,' he remarked. 'Who's your friend?'

'His name's Batik and he's a friend of Shannow's. Says he's been sent to help Donna.'

'Do you trust him?'

'Hell, I don't know, Griff. He ain't killed no one yet and

he sure as Hades could have done for me.'

Griffin beckoned Batik to sit beside him and looked long and hard into the Hellborn's face. 'What do they plan for Donna?'

'They're going to sacrifice her, according to Shannow.'

'We must get to her.'

'Even if we did, how do we escape? Four people on two horses – and one of the escapers in a coma.'

Griffin fell back and closed his eyes.

Batik sat for a while, then he touched Madden's shoulder and the farmer turned. 'What is it?'

'There is a festival around this time of year. I have lost track of the date recently, but it must be close. It is called Walpurnacht and it is very holy; a great sacrifice is always made, there is dancing in the streets and wine, and all the pleasures of the flesh are sated. If it has not already passed, then that is the time when they will sacrifice her.'

'How does that help us?'

'They will not have hundreds of guards around her in the temple. We must hide in the city and then attempt a rescue before the festival.'

'We'll stand out like boils on a pig's backside.'

'I have several houses.'

'How do we know they're empty?'

'Are you always this gloomy, Jacob?'

'Yep.'

'With horses we should reach the outer city just after first light. At least your friend can rest for a while and gather his strength.'

Griffin reached up and gripped Madden's arm. 'He's right, Jacob. Help me to my horse.'

The journey took three hours and Madden rode warily down the narrow streets of Babylon – waiting for a challenge, or a shot, or a sign of treachery. But the people they passed seemed little different from the settlers of Avalon. Women walked with children, men chatted on street corners and few paid much attention to the riders, or to Batik walking at the head of Griffin's horse. The wagon-master was wearing a leather coat to shield his wounds, and he fought to stay upright in the saddle.

Batik stopped a young boy who was walking with a large grey wolfhound.

'What date is it, boy?'

'April 28th.'

Batik walked on, leading them into a maze of foul-smelling tenement buildings and filth-choked alleyways to emerge at last by a high wall and a locked gate. He lifted the narrow chain and hooked his fingers around it and Madden watched as the muscles in his forearms swelled. The central link stretched, then parted and Batik opened the gate and led them inside. The house beyond was of white stone with arched doors and windows. Around the second storey ran an open balcony beneath a slanted tile roof.

'My sister lived here,' said Batik.

At the back of the house was an empty stable and there Batik unsaddled the horses and helped Griffin into the building. Dust was everywhere, but the house was untouched by recent human occupancy.

The furniture was spartan and Griffin was half carried to a wide firm divan by the wall beneath a window.

'I will go out and get some food,' said Batik.

'Has the festival happened yet?' asked Griffin.

'No, we have two days.'

'What is this Holy Night?' said Madden.

'It is when the Devil walks amongst his children.'

Shannow rode into the canyon at midnight, thirty-seven hours after watching Batik and Ruth vanish into the night. As he came in sight of the ruined city, he reined in his mount and stared in awe at the ghost ship. No longer was it a rotting wreck — now it sat in colossal glory, four immense angled funnels and six rows of lights strung like pearls along her decks.

The night wind shifted and the sound of music echoed in the canyon.

An eerie blast reverberated around the mountains, causing Shannow's horse to rear. He calmed it and watched as a trail of light shot into the sky, exploding in a cloud of coloured stars which popped like distant gunshots. The sound of cheering came from the ship.

Shannow slipped the thongs from his pistols and drew a deep, slow breath. Touching his heels to the stallion's sides, he moved down towards the ruins.

A dark shadow moved into his path . . .

'It's about time you showed yourself, Lewis,' he said. 'Three times now you've had me in your sights.'

'I don't want to kill you, Shannow. Truly. Turn around and ride from here.'

'Into the Zealots, hidden in the woods?'

'You are a skilful man – you can avoid them.'

Shannow sat silently, staring into the muzzle of the black rifle and feeling the tension cast by the Guardian.

'Was I wrong about you, Lewis? I took you to be a good man in the Archer mould. I did not see you as a butcher of women and children, as a blood-sucking vampire.'

'I am a soldier. Don't make me kill you.'

'What happened to the Ark?'

Lewis licked his lips. 'Tonight we are celebrating Rebirth. Every year at this time we bring some aspect of the past to life, to show that what we guard is real and solid and not just a memory. Tonight the Ark sails once more in all her glory. Now leave, for God's sake!'

'God, Lewis? The Lords of the Hellborn speak of God? Tell it to the wind. Tell it to the farmers nailed to trees, and to the women spreadeagled and butchered. But don't tell it to me!'

'We did not create wars, Shannow. For centuries we have tried to steer mankind back to civilization but it hasn't worked. There was no unity. Sarento says that without unity there is no order, without order there is no law and without law no civilization. All great advances have come as a result of war. It will be different soon, Shannow. We are going to rebuild cities and we will make the world a garden. Please ride away.'

'I know nothing of your lost civilization, Lewis,' said Shannow softly. 'Karitas would never tell me. I don't know whether it was beautiful, but if that gun you are holding is an example of what they had then I doubt it. Did some version of the Hellborn exist even then, sweeping across the land to bring death to thousands? Or were there weapons even more terrible than that monstrosity? Perhaps whole cities were wiped out. And you want to bring this back? Some time ago I was wounded and I was taken to a small village. Peaceful people, Lewis; happy people. They were led by a man who was once a Guardian, but they're not alive now. The women were raped and then their throats were cut. And Karitas? He was crucified. I don't doubt that if their spirits were still here, they would applaud your dream. But then their souls aren't here, are they? They were sucked into your Blood Stone to fuel more death and despair.'

'That's enough! I was told to kill you and I've disobeyed that order. If you leave now, you'll live, Shannow. Doesn't that mean anything to you?'

'Of course it does, Lewis. No man wants to die and that's why I am talking to you. I don't want to kill you, but I must find the Stone.'

Lewis lifted the rifle to his shoulder. 'If you do not turn this instant, I will send you to Hell.'

'But that's where I want to go, Lewis. That's where it is,' answered Shannow, pointing to the Ark.

In the bright moonlight Shannow saw Lewis tense, the rifle butt being drawn more tightly into his shoulder. The Jerusalem Man hurled himself from the saddle just as the rifle exploded in a thundering roar of shells. He hit the ground hard and rolled behind a boulder as chips and fragments screamed around him. Then he came to his knees with his pistol in his hand. His horse was down, thrashing its legs in the air, and a coldness settled on Shannow as he cocked the pistol and dived to the left, rolling on his shoulder. Lewis spun, the rifle bucking in his hands, shells sending spurts of earth and stone to Shannow's right. The pistol levelled and a single shot punched Lewis from his feet. Shannow moved to the body: Lewis was dead. The Jerusalem Man walked to the dying horse and shot it through the head, then he reloaded his pistol and began the long walk to the ruins.

'No man wants to die, Lewis.' The words came back to him and he felt the truth of them. Shannow didn't want to die; he wanted to find Jerusalem and to know peace. He looked up at the Ark and the glowing lights, listening to the music. Then he glanced back at Lewis' body, merging with the moon shadows.

He walked on to the rock doorway and there, drawing his pistol, he stepped to the side. As the door opened, Shannow's pistol came up, but the steel tunnel beyond was empty. Keeping to the wall, he stepped inside and the door closed behind him. There were no stairs leading down, no doorways that he could see and he cursed softly.

The elevator door whispered open, beckoning him. Sheathing his pistol, he stepped inside.

The doors closed and the elevator lurched slightly; when they opened again he saw what he had expected to see: armed guards with pistols pointed at his chest. They were dressed strangely in flat dark blue peaked caps and doubled-breasted serge jackets. In their midst stood the giant Sarento in a similar suit, but white, with brass buttons and blue epaulettes each bearing three gold bars.

'You really are a disappointing man, Mr Shannow,' Sarento greeted him.

The guards moved in and disarmed the Jerusalem Man, who offered them no resistance. He was led out and found himself, not in the shining hallway he remembered, but in an enormous room filled with extravagantly carved furniture, luxurious carpets and stained glass windows.

'Magnificent, is it not?' said Sarento.

Shannow said nothing. He stared in silent wonder at the stained glass depicting sailing ships and Biblical saints, surrounded by gilded panels of exquisite carpentry.

'Why did you come back, Mr Shannow?'

'To destroy you.'

'Did you really believe you could work one of your Brigand-killing miracles amongst the Guardians? Surely not?'

People started to filter into the room – all were dressed in curious fashion. The women wore long elaborate dresses; the men had black coats and white shirts.

'Take him below,' said Sarento. 'I'll see him later.'

The four guards walked Shannow to a carpeted staircase and on to a door bearing a brass plaque: B-59. Inside was a four-poster bed with velvet curtains and a small writing table inlaid with gold.

'Sit down,' said one of the guards, a young man with short cropped blond hair. 'Make yourself comfortable.'

They waited in uneasy silence until Sarento joined them. He removed his white cap and dropped it to the table.

'Tell me about the ship,' said Shannow and Sarento chuckled.

'You are a cool man, Mr Shannow. I like you.'

The giant sat back on the bed and peeled off his white gloves. 'Are you impressed by Rebirth?'

'Of course,' admitted Shannow.

'And so you should be. This was one of the largest ships ever made. It was eight hundred and eighty-two feet long and weighed 46,000 tons. It was a miracle of engineering, and one of the wonders of the ancient world.'

Shannow suddenly laughed.

'What is amusing you, sir?'

'Do you like parables, Sarento? It seems to me that this ship mirrors your lunatic dreams – opulent and civilized, and buried by the sea.'

'Except that we have brought it back,' snapped Sarento.

'Yes, to sit on a mountain above the ruins of a civilization you did not know even existed. A ship on a mountain – huge and useless, like your ambition.'

'A ship on a mountain? Come with me, Mr Shannow. I would like to show you what real power is.'

With the guards around him, Sarento led Shannow to the upper promenade and out on to the boat deck. The sea stretched out to a distant horizon and the Ark glided majestically on a star-speckled ocean. Shannow could smell the salt in the air, while gulls wheeled and dived above the giant funnels.

'Stunning, is it not?' asked Sarento.

Shannow shivered. 'This is not possible.'

'All things are possible with the Mother Stone.'

'And we are truly at sea?'

'No. The Ark sits as always on her mountain. What you are seeing and feeling is an image projected by magic. However, were you to cut a hole in the ship's side water would pour in – salt water. For the Stone would carry on the charade. And if you were to jump over the side, you would hit the sea, ice-cold and deadly. But then you would pass through it and plummet to the ruins of Atlantis. This is power, Mr Shannow, just a fraction of the power the Stone can hold. Had I wished it, the Ark would sail on a real sea. One day it will and then I will sail it into the harbour of New York.'

'How many souls will that cost?' asked Shannow.

'You have a small mind, Shannow.' Sarento shook his head. 'What are a few lives compared with a golden future?'

'Can we go back inside?' said Shannow. 'It's a little cold out here.'

'We can, Shannow. You, I'm afraid, are leaving the ship here.'

'Just when I was beginning to enjoy it,' said Shannow. Then as Sarento signalled the guards forward, he crouched and whipped the double-edged hunting knife from his boot. The first guard died as the blade slashed across his throat; Shannow snatched the man's pistol from his hand and leapt at Sarento. As the big man dived to the deck, Shannow followed him, dropping the knife and hauling at Sarento's collar – the pistol cocked, the barrel pushing under Sarento's chin.

'Be so kind as to tell your guards to put up their weapons,' hissed Shannow, hauling Sarento to his feet.

The three remaining guards looked to their leader.

'Do it,' he said. 'I shall end this farce in my own way.'

'Take me to the Stone,' said Shannow.

'But of course. Your infantile heroics have earned you that, at the very least.'

'I congratulate you on your calm.'

Sarento's eyes met his. 'You may feel you have the upper hand, Mr Shannow, but the magic that raised the Ark from the sea floor will not be undone by a madman with a Hellborn revolver.'

Sarento led the way below.

And the *Titanic* sailed on through the ghostly sea . . .

Chapter Thirteen

Abaddon's dreams were troubled and he awoke clutching at the air. The black silk sheets were damp with sweat and he rolled to his feet. He had felt so good three hours before when Donna Taybard had been brought to Babylon. And tonight the reign of the Hellborn would begin in earnest; all the star charts had confirmed it. Donna was the sacrifice the Devil had been waiting for, and all the powers of Hell would flow through Abaddon the moment he devoured her.

Yet now the Hellborn king sat trembling on his bed, plagued by nameless fears which had haunted his dreams. He had seen Jon Shannow deep in Hell, battling Beelzebub with sword and pistol. And then the Jerusalem Man had turned his eyes on Abaddon, and in those eyes the king saw death.

The fear would not pass and Abaddon moved to the cabinet by the window and poured a goblet of wine, sipping it until his nerves settled. He thought of summoning Achnazzar, but dismissed it. The High Priest had become increasingly nervous in the king's presence these last few days.

'Daddy!' The child's cry jerked Abaddon from his reverie and he swung round, but the room was empty. He caught a glimpse of his reflection in a long rectangular mirror and stood, drawing in his belly to present a powerful profile.

Abaddon, Lord of the Pit!

'Daddy!' This time the sound came from the sitting room beyond. Abaddon ran through the open doorway only to be confronted by an empty desk and an open window. He blinked and wiped the sweat from his face.

In the streets beyond the palace walls he could hear the

chants of the mob: 'Satan! Satan! Satan!'

Walpurnacht was a night of beauty when the people could see their god walking amongst them, feel his presence in the air about them, see his image in the glow of their Blood Stones.

But this night was special. This night saw the dawning era of the Hellborn, for when Donna Taybard's powers flowed into the knives and her body was consumed by the Master, the magic of Hell would be unleashed upon the world.

The Lord of the Pit would become the King of the Earth.

'I'm frightened, Daddy.'

Abaddon whirled round to see a blonde child of seven, hugging a threadbare doll.

'Sarah?'

The child ran away into the bedroom and Abaddon followed, but the room was empty. He knew it was a hallucination, for Sarah had been dead for centuries. The wine was too strong.

But so were the memories . . . He poured another glass and returned to the mirror, staring at the bloodshot grey eyes and the flowing hair now silver at the temples. The face was as it had been for decades – a middle-aged man, strong and in his prime.

It was not Lawrence Welby who stared back at him. Welby was dead – as dead as his wife and daughter.

'I am the king,' he whispered. 'The Satanlord. Go away, Welby. Don't stare at me. Who are you to judge?'

'Read me a story, Daddy.'

'Leave me alone!' he screamed, squeezing shut his eyes and refusing to see the apparition he knew lay upon his bed.

'Read her a story, Lawrence. You know she won't sleep until you do.'

Welby opened his eyes and drank in the sight of the golden-haired woman by the door.

'Ruth?'

'Have you forgotten how to read a story?'

'This is a dream.'

'Don't forget us, Lawrence.'

'Are you truly here?' he asked, stumbling forward. But the golden-haired woman vanished and Welby sank to his knees.

The door opened. 'Ruth?'

'No, my Lord. Are you ill?'

Abaddon pushed himself to his feet. 'How dare you come here unannounced, Achnazzar!' said the king.

'The guards came for me, sire. They said you sounded . . . distraught.'

'I am well. What do the star charts show?'

'Magelin says it is a time of great change, as one would expect at the dawn of an empire.'

'And Cade?'

'He is bottled up in a nowhere pass where he can neither escape nor conquer.'

'That all sounds well, priest. Now tell me about Shannow. Tell me again how he died falling from a cliff.'

Achnazzar bowed low. 'It was an error, sire, but he is now a prisoner of the Guardians and they mean to kill him. The Jerusalem Man is a danger no longer. After tonight he will seem as the gnat in the ear of the dragon.'

'After tonight? The night is not yet over, priest.'

The morning of Walpurnacht dawned bright and clear and Batik awoke filled with a sense of burning anticipation. His skin had become hypersensitive to touch, and his body trembled with suppressed emotion.

Even the air in the room seemed to crackle with static, as if a lightning storm were hovering over the city.

Batik rose from his bed and drew in a deep, shuddering breath.

The joy of Walpurnacht was upon him. His memory flashed images of past festivals when he had been filled with a holy strength and had coupled with a dozen willing women, never seeming to tire.

Remembering Madden and Griffen, anger washed over him.

What link did he have with such farm-working peasants?

How had he allowed himself to become involved with their petty squabbles?

He would kill them both and enjoy the day, he decided.

He moved to his pistol and settled the butt in his palm. It felt good and he burned with a desire to kill, to destroy.

Jon Shannow leapt to his thoughts . . .

His friend.

'I have no friends. No need of friends,' hissed Batik.

But the image remained and again he saw Shannow standing in the dark of the dungeon hall.

His friend.

'Damn you, Shannow!' he screamed and fell to his knees, the gun clattering to the floor. His joy evaporated.

Downstairs Jacob Madden was battling with his own demons. For him it was almost worse than for Batik, for he had never experienced the surging emotions of Walpurnacht. There was no joy for Madden – only the pain of his memories, his defeats and his tragedies. He wanted to run from the building and kill every Hellborn he saw; wanted them to suffer as he suffered.

But Griffin needed him, Donna Taybard needed him and for Madden a duty like that was an iron chain on his emotions. It would not break for a selfish motive.

So he sat in his misery and waited for Batik.

The Hellborn dressed swiftly and cleaned his weapons. Then he moved down into the wide living area and checked on Griffin. The man's colour was good and he slept peacefully.

'How are you?' he asked Madden, laying his hand on the man's shoulder.

'Don't touch me, you bastard!' snapped Madden, knocking the arm away and surging to his feet.

'Be calm, Jacob,' urged Batik. 'It is Walpurnacht – it is in the air. Breathe deeply and relax.'

'Relax? Everything I loved is gone and my life is now a shell. When do we go after Donna?'

'Tonight.'

'Why not now?'

'In full light?'

Madden sank back into his chair. 'What is the matter with me?'

'I told you, it is Walpurnacht. Tonight the Devil walks and you will see him. But from now until he is gone, you will feel his presence in the air around you. During the next twenty-four hours there will be many fights, many deaths, many rapes and thousands of new lives begun.'

Madden moved to the table and poured himself a mug of water. His hands were trembling and sweat shone on his face.

'I can't take too much of this,' he whispered.

'I'll help you through it,' said Batik. Outside in the narrow alleys the sound of chanting came to them. From somewhere nearby a scream, piercing and shrill, rose above the chants.

'Someone just died,' said Madden.

'Yes, she won't be the last.'

The day wore on. Griffin awoke, and the pain from his wounds doubled. He screamed and cursed Madden, his language foul and his eyes full of malice.

'Take no notice,' said Batik softly.

Towards dusk, with Griffin asleep once more, Batik readied himself for the night, smearing his face with red dye. Madden refused to disguise himself and Batik shrugged.

'It is only paint, Jacob.'

'I don't want to look like a devil. If I am to die, I'll die like a man.'

Towards midnight the two men rechecked their guns and slipped out into the street, heading towards the centre of the city. In the main thoroughfare they came upon a huge crowd of dancing, chanting people. Scores of men and women writhed together in the nearby doorways and alleyways. Madden looked away.

A young girl, her scarlet dress spattered with blood, was slashing at herself with a curved knife. She saw Madden and ran to him, throwing her arms around his neck.

Madden hurled her from him, but another woman took her place, running her hands over his body and whispering promises of joy. He pulled himself clear and thrust his way into the crowd after Batik.

The crowd moved on towards the temple square and all the chants merged into a single word, repeated again and again.

'Satan . . . Satan . . . Satan . . .'

As they neared the long steps to the temple, the night sky blazed with red light and a shimmering figure appeared, hundreds of feet tall. Madden's mouth opened and he shrank back from the colossus. It had the legs of a goat and the body of a powerful man, but the head was bestial and double-horned.

A huge hand reached down towards the crowd and the young woman with the blood-drenched dress was lifted by the men around her and hurled into the taloned hand. It closed about her and lifted to the gaping mouth. The girl disappeared and the crowd cheered.

'This way,' shouted Batik, pulling Madden towards an alley beside the temple. 'We don't have long.'

'Acolytes' entrance,' said Batik as they reached an oval wooden door at the side of the temple. It was locked but he lifted his foot and sent the door crashing open. They stepped inside and Madden drew his pistol.

'We must get up to the temple – they will be bringing Donna out to him any moment now.'

'You mean he's going to eat her?' asked Madden incredulously.

Batik ignored him and set off at a run. Meanwhile a temple guard rounded the corner but Batik shot him down and hurdled the body, taking the stairs beyond two steps at a time.

They reached another corridor and two more guards appeared. A shell shrieked past Madden's ear and he dived for the floor, triggering his pistol twice. One guard pitched backwards, the other staggered but lifted his rifle once more. Batik fired twice and the man crumpled to the floor.

At the top of another winding stair, Batik paused before the door. He loaded his pistol and turned to Madden.

'This is it, my friend. Are you ready?'

'I've been ready all my life,' said Madden.
'I believe you,' replied Batik, with a grin.

Shannow pushed Sarento into the elevator and stepped in behind him. The doors closed and the giant smiled.

'Level G,' he said and the elevator shuddered. 'You have a number of surprises still in store, Mr Shannow. I hope you enjoy them.'

'Stand against the door, Sarento.'

'But of course, though your fears are groundless – there are no guards in the cavern. Tell me, what do you hope to achieve? You cannot destroy the Stone.'

The doors opened suddenly and Sarento spun and dived through. Shannow followed him and opened fire but the bullets ricocheted from a huge stalactite. The Jerusalem Man looked around him at the immense cavern with a spherical roof that glistened with gold threads and shining stones. Stalactites hung like pillars. He moved into the glowing light near the centre, where a small black lake surrounded an island on which stood a circle of standing stones, black and glistening.

'You stand at the heart of the empire, Shannow,' came Sarento's disembodied voice. 'Here every dream is a reality. Can you feel the power of the Blood Stone?'

Shannow scanned the cavern, but there was no sign of the giant. Walking to the edge of the lake, he saw a narrow bridge of seasoned wood on the other side of the stones. Traversing the lake, he mounted the bridge and crossed to the circle. At the first monolith he stopped to examine the sides. A deep indentation met his fingers. He pressed inside and heard a latch drop. A small section dropped away but when he thrust his hand inside it was empty.

'Did you think I would leave the gold there?' said Sarento.

Shannow spun to see the giant was standing at the altar. He was dressed now in the armour of Atlantis, a golden breastplate with a golden stone above the heart. Upon his head he wore a plumed helm and in his hands was a sword.

Shannow fired, but the bullet screamed away up into the cavern roof. Taking careful aim he fired once more, this time at the grinning face.

'Pendarric's armour of invincibility, Mr Shannow. Nothing can harm me now – whereas you are defenceless. It is fitting that we should meet like this: two Rolynd warriors within the great circle.'

'Where is the Mother Stone?' said Shannow, sheathing his pistol.

'You are standing on it, Shannow. Behold!'

The ground beneath his feet blurred, the covering of dank earth shimmering into nothing, becoming red-gold veined with slender black. All across the circle the ground glowed like a lantern.

'It is said that to kill a Rolynd brings great power,' said Sarento, moving forward with sword in hand. 'We shall see. How do you like the sword, Shannow? Beautiful, yes? It is a sword of power. Sipstrassi. In the old tongue they were called Pynral-ponas: swords from the Stone. What they cut, they kill. Come, Mr Shannow, let me cut you.'

Shannow backed away towards the bridge.

'Where can you run? Back to the *Titanic* and my guards? Face me, Rolynd. Meet your death with courage. Come, I do not have much time.'

'I'm in no hurry,' said Shannow.

Sarento leapt forward, the great sword flashing in the air, but Shannow dived under the blade and rolled to his feet.

'A nice maneouvre. It is always interesting to see an animal run for its life but what will it gain you? A few more seconds.' As Sarento ran at him Shannow vaulted to the altar and jumped down on the other side.

'Terean-Bezek,' hissed Sarento and two stone hands grabbed Shannow's ankles. He looked down and saw the bloodstone fingers trapping him, as Sarento laughed and moved slowly round the altar.

'How does it feel to lose, Jerusalem Man? Does your soul cry out in its anguish?'

'You'll never know,' hissed Shannow. As the sword came up, he looked away, down at the surface of the altar. There, engraved on the top, was the image of a sword with upswept hilt.

The sword of the dream!

Shannow reached out. Something cold touched his palm and his fingers clenched around the hilt. Then the sword flashed up and the ringing of steel upon steel filled the cavern.

Sarento stepped back. Gone was the perpetual smile. Shannow lowered the blade to the stone hands gripping his ankles and as the sword touched them, they disappeared.

'You were right, Sarento. This cavern holds many surprises.'

'That is Pendarric's sword. I never could find it, I could never understand why I was unable to find it, for it was said to be awaiting a Rolynd.'

'You are Rolynd no longer, Sarento. Your luck just ran out.'

The smile returned to the giant's face. 'We'll see. Unless of course you can find some armour?' As he moved in, his sword slashing towards Shannow's head, the Jerusalem Man blocked the blow and his riposte thundered against Sarento's neck. It did not even break the skin.

Now the giant took his blade two-handed and attacked ferociously. Shannow was forced back, blocking and parrying. Three times more Shannow's sword thrust or cut at Sarento's armour, but to no effect.

'It is as useless as your pistol.'

Sweat flowed on Shannow's face and his sword-arm was weary, while Sarento showed no sign of fatigue.

'You know, Shannow, I could almost regret killing you.'

Shannow took a deep breath and hefted his sword, his eyes drawn to the giant's breastplate as Sarento stepped forward. The golden stone set there was now almost black. Sarento's sword whistled down, Shannow blocked it and risked a cut to the head. The blade bounced away, but Sarento was shaken; his hand flew to his brow and came away stained by blood.

'It's not possible,' he whispered. He looked down at the stone and then screamed in fury, launching a berserk attack. Shannow was pushed back and back across the centre of the circle and Sarento's sword slashed through his shirt to score the skin. He fell. With a scream of triumph the giant slashed his blade downward, but Shannow rolled to his knees, blocking another cut and parrying a thrust.

The two men circled one another warily.

'You'll still die, Shannow.'

Shannow grinned. 'You're frightened, Sarento; I can feel it. You're not Rolynd – you never were. You're just another Brigand with large dreams. But they end here.'

Sarento backed away to the altar. 'Large dreams? What would you know of large dreams? All you want is some mythical city, but I want the world to be as it was. Can you understand that? Parks and gardens, and the joys of civilization. You've seen the *Titanic*. Everyone could enjoy its luxury. No more poverty, Shannow. No starvation. The Garden of Eden!'

'With you as the serpent? I think not.'

As Sarento's sword lunged towards him, Shannow moved in side-step and plunged his own blade under the breastplate and through Sarento's groin. The giant screamed and fell across the altar. Shannow wrenched the sword clear and as the cavern shuddered, almost lost his footing. A stalactite tore itself from the roof and plunged into the lake.

Sarento hauled himself on to the altar.

'Oh, my God,' he whispered, 'The *Titanic*!' His blood-covered hands scrabbled at the altar top. Shannow's sword touched his neck and he rolled slowly to his back. 'Listen to me. You *must* stop the power. The *Titanic* . . .'

'What about it?'

'It is sailing an identical course to that which destroyed it when it sank with the loss of 1,500 lives. The gold . . .'

'The ship is on a mountain. It cannot sink.'

'The iceberg will pierce the side – a 300-foot gash. The Stone will create . . . the . . . ocean.' Sarento's eyes lost their focus and his body slid to the stone. As his blood touched the glowing ground it hissed and bubbled, and a deep red stain was absorbed into the rock. Shannow dropped his sword and stepped to the altar. Sarento's fingers had been scrabbling near a raised relief and when he pulled at it the top moved. Crossing to the other side, the Jerusalem Man pushed the gap wider, then reached inside. There were four spools of wire.

He dragged them free and scanned the circle. There were thirteen standing Stones and he ran to the first and looped the gold around the base.

Far above him, the ghost ship sped through the eldritch sea, while people danced and sang in the great ballrooms. One young couple walked out on to the deck. The iceberg loomed in to the night like a gargantuan tombstone.

'Isn't that incredible?' said the man.

'Yes.' They were joined by other revellers, who leaned over the wooden rail to watch the ice loom ever closer.

The ship ploughed on, scraping the side of the ice mountain. The revellers shrieked with laughter and leapt back as chunks of ice fell to the promenade.

Deep below decks came a shuddering jolt, and the ship trembled as if sliding over shingle.

'You don't think Sarento has taken Rebirth too far?' asked the girl.

'There's no danger,' the man assured her.

And the ship tilted.

Shannow had attached the gold to six of the monoliths when a growling rumble set the ground vibrating. The vast roof trembled and a foot-wide crack opened. Stalactites began to fall like giant spears and water streamed from the fissure above him. Shannow grabbed the wire and pulled it tight. Below him the ground glowed ever brighter. Two more monoliths were connected when the far wall of the cavern exploded outwards, as millions of tons of icy water cascaded down from the stricken *Titanic*.

The lake swelled. Shannow ignored the chaos around him and struggled on; the spool he was carrying ran out, and he swiftly tied a second spool to the wire. Water swirled around his legs, making the stone surface slippery. Then four more monoliths were joined by the slender gold line, but now the lake had submerged the bridge and Shannow found himself wading through against the current. A stalactite splashed into the water beside him, cracking against his arm and tearing loose the spool. Cursing, he dived below the water, his arms fanning out to retrieve it. He was forced to swim back to the last monolith and follow the wire down, then with the spool once more in his hand he struck out. The water was rising faster now, but he ignored the peril until he had completed the golden circle.

He could no longer feel the stone beneath his feet, but the fading glow could still be seen. Water was now flooding the cavern and Shannow watched as the roof came steadily towards him.

He searched for a fissure through which he could climb, but there was no way out. Sarento's body bobbed alongside him, face down, and he pushed it away. As the roof loomed directly above him, he was forced to turn on his back to keep his mouth above water.

As Batik pushed opened the door, shells hammered into the frame and the Hellborn warrior dived through the doorway and rolled. Four guards turned their guns on him. Madden came through a fraction of a second later, his pistol blazing; one guard went down, another was stung by a bullet across the forearm. The other two opened fire on Batik and a bullet seared through his side, while another riocheted from the marble floor to tear the flesh under his thigh. Despite his wounds Batik coolly returned the fire – his first bullet taking a guard under the chin and hurling him from his feet, his second hammering home into the last man's shoulder, spinning him. Madden finished the man with a shot to the head.

All around them red-robed priests were scurrying for safety as Batik grabbed Madden's outstretched arm and hauled himself to his feet.

Outside the huge double doors, Achnazzar lifted his dagger over the unconscious Donna.

'No!' screamed Batik and he and Madden fired simultaneously. Punched from his feet, Achnazzar landed hard on the upper steps and rolled to his stomach. He could feel blood filling his lungs. Clutching the knife he crawled towards the comatose victim, but as he raised it a giant black shadow loomed over him.

Talons as long as sabres ripped through his back. The knife fell from nerveless fingers and Achnazzar could not even scream as the taloned hand carried him towards the dreadful maw.

Batik limped to Donna and tried to lift her.

'Christ Almighty!' shouted Madden. Batik looked up to see that the demon, having finished with Achnazzar, was now reaching down once more. He cocked his pistol and stood, straddling Donna.

The taloned fingers opened . . .

Batik fired and the hand jerked, but relentlessly came down once more. He threw his empty pistol aside and drew Griffin's weapon from his belt. As the fingers came within reach Batik leapt into the palm; his clothes burst into flame, but he ignored the agony as he held his gun two-handed and levelled it at the colossal face.

Eight hundred miles away, the created waters of the Atlantic ocean streamed across the Blood Stone, draining its power, blurring its energy.

Batik fell through the now transparent fingers and plunged into the crowd below. Madden ran to him, beating at the flames on his clothing with bare hands. Incredibly, once they were extinguished, he found that Batik was still conscious. He helped him to his feet, and together they staggered back to the temple steps.

Above them the demon was fading fast and a strange sense of calm settled on Madden.

'It's over,' he told Batik.

'Not yet,' replied the Hellborn, as the angry crowd surged towards them.

Soon after midnight Griffin awoke. The house was empty

and he knew that Madden and Batik had set out to save his wife. Shame burned in him, swamping the pain from his wounds. He should have been out there with them.

He struggled to sit, ignoring the pull at the stitches which Madden had expertly placed, and gazed from the window at the overgrown garden beyond. Never had Griffin felt so alone. He glanced down at his body and saw the wasted flesh; his shirt seemed voluminous now and his belt had needed an extra notch, which Madden had made with his hunting-knife. Anger surged, fuelled by frustration and helplessness. But he had nothing on which to vent his emotion and it turned inward as he saw again young Eric blasted from life in the doorway of their home. Tears brimmed and he blinked them away, swinging his head to focus his gaze on the garden. The trees should have been trimmed back, for their branches were spreading above the rose bushes and blocking the light needed for good blooms.

A shadow caught his eye – something had moved in the moonlight by the gate. Griffin scanned the area. Nothing. There were no lights in the house, and he knew he could not be seen. He waited, focusing his gaze on the gate and allowing his peripheral vision a chance to pick up movement. It was an old hunter's trick taught to him by Jimmy Burke many years before.

There! By the silver birch. A man was moving stealthily through the undergrowth. And there! Another crouched beside a holly tree.

Griffin's mouth was dry. He identified two other shapes as intruders and then cast his eyes about the darkened room for his pistol. But it was gone – Madden must have taken it. He lay back on the sofa and carefully eased himself to the floor, drawing his hunting-knife from its sheath. He was in no condition to fight *one* man – four might as well be four hundred!

'Think, man!' he told himself. His eyes flicked around the room – where would they come in?

The window was open and that seemed the best bet, so slowly he moved on all fours to sit beneath the ledge. The exertion weakened him and he felt dizzy. He took a deep breath and leaned his head against the cold stone. Minutes passed and his mind wandered. He had once hidden like this as a boy, when his father had been hunting him to deliver a thrashing. He couldn't remember what he had done, but he recalled vividly the sense of defeat within the excitement, knowing that he was only putting off the awful moment.

The window creaked. Griffin glanced up and saw a hand on the ledge.

With infinite care he eased himself into a crouch. A leg swung into sight, the booted foot almost grazing Griffin's shoulder, then the man was inside. Griffin rose to his feet, grabbing the long dark hair, and before the intruder could scream the hunting-knife sliced across his throat.

He began to struggle wildly and Griffin was thrown from him. The man fell to his knees, dropping his pistol. Griffin scooped it up and crawled back to the wall, waiting for the next man.

Across the room the first intruder had ceased to struggle. Griffin cocked the pistol and closed his eyes to aid his hearing. Nothing moved . . .

He awoke with a start. His mind had drifted him into a dream and he blinked hard, scanning the room. How long had he been asleep? Seconds? Minutes?

And what had awakened him?

The pistol butt was warm in his hand and slippery with sweat; he wiped his palm on his shirt and took up the gun once more. Outside he could hear the sound of distant chanting, and a red glow filled the room.

A man stepped inside from the door at the far wall and Griffin shot him twice. He stumbled and fell, then raised his pistol and a bullet smashed into the wall above Griffin's head. Holding his pistol two-handed, Griffin fired once more and the man fell dead. The room stank of cordite and smoke hung in the air. Griffin's ears rang, and he could hear nothing.

He pushed himself to his feet and risked a glance from the window. A man was running towards the house; Griffin's first shot missed him, but the second took him in the chest and he fell. The wagon-master wiped sweat from his eyes as he glanced up at the night sky.

. . . And saw the Devil looming above the house tops.

'My God!' he whispered.

'No, mine,' said a voice. Griffin did not turn.

'I wondered what had happened to you, Zedeki.'

'You are a hard man to kill, Mr Griffin.'

'I am surprised you did not just shoot me down?'

'I thought you might like to witness the last act in the drama. Watch his hand, Mr Griffin. The next person you see will be your wife being carried to his mouth . . . then I will kill you.'

The Devil disappeared and Zedeki screamed. Griffin swung and fired and the bullet punched Zedeki back against the wall; his knees buckled and he sank to the floor, still gazing at the star-filled night sky.

Griffin sat down and watched the young man die.

Abaddon stood on the black marble balcony overlooking the temple steps, revelling in the appearance of his god, feeling his doubts swirling away from him like mist in the morning. The sound of gunshots came from within the temple and the priests scattered. He saw Achnazzar hurled from his feet and devoured by the Devil. Then a dark-clad figure ran forward, the Devil's hand dropped and Abaddon screamed his triumph as the warrior was swept into his palm.

But the Devil disappeared and a pain clutched Abaddon's heart like fingers of fire. He screamed and fell back through the doorway, crawling to his bedside and the ivory-inlaid ebony box which lay there. He whispered the words of power, but the box did not open. Pulling himself to his knees, he struggled for calm and pressed the hidden button at the base. The lid sprang open and relief surged in him as his hands pulled clear the large oval Blood Stone. The pain in his chest eased slightly. He blinked and focused his eyes on the stone – the red was fading, the black veins growing as he watched.

'*No!*' he whispered. Brown liver spots blossomed on his hands, and the skin began to wrinkle. He managed to get to his feet and drew a silver embossed pistol from a leather scabbard hanging at the bedside.

'Guard!' he yelled and a young man ran into the room.

'What is it, sire?'

Abaddon shot him through the head, then carried the Stone to the twitching body and held it under the pumping jet of blood coming from the man's brow. Yet still the power ebbed, the black veins spreading and joining.

'There is nothing you can do, Lawrence,' said Ruth. Abaddon dropped the Stone and sank down beside the guard's body.

'Help me, Ruthie.'

'I cannot. You should have died a long time ago.'

His hair glistened white and his face took on the look of worn leather. He no longer had the strength to sit and his body slumped to the floor. Ruth sat beside him, cradling his head in her lap.

'Why did you go away?' he whispered. 'It could all have been so different.' The flesh melted from his face and his lips moved in a last ragged whisper. 'I did love you,' he said.

'I know.'

His body fell back in her arms and she could feel the bones beneath the skin, brittle and pointed. The skin peeled away and the bones crumbled to the floor.

On the steps of the temple, Batik swiftly reloaded his pistol and sat facing the crowd. The roar of rage died down and the mob fell back, staring at their painted hands and looking in confusion at their comrades. At the front of the crowd a man groaned and toppled forward and a friend knelt by him.

'He's dead,' said the man. Someone else in the crowd, feeling unwell, drew his Blood Stone from its pouch; it was blacker than sin. Another man died and the crowd backed away from the body. As other people checked their Stones, panic grew.

On the steps Madden helped Batik to his feet and they moved to Donna, ripping the silver bands from her body. She moaned and opened her eyes.

'Jacob?'

'It's all right. You're safe, girl.'

'Where is Con?'

'He's waiting for us. I'll take you to him.'

'And Eric?'

'We'll talk later. Take my hand.'

Below them the crowd was streaming away. Madden lifted Donna into his arms as a dark-haired young man approached him.

'God's greeting,' he said.

'Who are you?' asked Batik.

'Clophas. You do not know me, Batik, but I was at Sanctuary while you were there.'

'It seems a long time ago.'

'Yes, a lifetime. Can I help you with the lady?'

On the *Titanic*, people fought with one another to climb the choked stairways and escape the rising water. The Mother Stone, unleashing all its energy, played its role to the full, tilting the ship to imitate the original disaster. Scores of Guardians, their wives and children slid below the foaming torrent, thrashing and screaming for assistance. None was offered.

Whereas in the disaster of 1912 a number of brave men had manned the pumps until the last minute, not one Guardian now had the knowledge to do the same. Where the original tragedy had been enacted during three hours, this *Titanic* was sinking within minutes. Bulkheads collapsed and hundreds died, dragged to their deaths by the seething ocean.

There was no escape. Many threw themselves from the upper decks, splashing into the sea below only to find themselves piercing the edge of the Stone's field of energy, and dropping through the water to hurtle down the mountain on to the jagged marble ruins of Atlantis.

Amaziga Archer and her son, Luke, struggled through the Smoking Lounge and on to the A-deck foyer. The water here was waist-deep and rising. Lifting Luke to her shoulder, she climbed through a shattered window and out on to the steeply tilted deck. Luke clung to her as she fought her way up towards the stern, rearing like a tower above the swelling sea. Hooking her arm around a brass stanchion, she listened to the cries of the victims trapped below.

Slowly the dying ship slid under the waves. Cold water touched Amaziga's ankles . . . it shimmered and faded.

The Mother Stone was finished, choked by the thin thread of gold and exhausted by the disaster it had created. The ship shuddered and the sea disappeared. Amaziga sat up and touched her clothes. They were dry. Looking around her, she saw that she lay on a rusted deck and twenty feet from her a male survivor struggled to his feet.

'We made it!' he shouted, but the rotting deck parted beneath his feet and the dead ship swallowed him and his screams. Amaziga felt the deck move beneath her and crawled carefully to the stern where the ship touched the cliff-face. The deck gave way. Amaziga's hand flashed out to grip the rail and Luke screamed and hung from her neck. The muscles in her arm stretched and tore, but her fingers remained locked to the rail. She glanced down into the dark, empty bowels of the ghost ship.

'Hold on, Luke!' she shouted and the boy gripped her tunic. She took a deep breath, then dragged on her arm, hauling herself upwards and hooking her left arm to the rail. As her weight hit the rail it bent outwards, almost dislodging her. Swinging her feet up she scrambled on to the hull and inched her way to the cliff. Here the drop was even greater and the ruins of Atlantis gleamed like pointed teeth. She removed the leather belt from her tunic and looped it around Luke's back, tying him to her. Then she stepped to the rock face and began the long, hazardous climb.

Shannow found a concave bulge in the rocky roof where an

air pocket was trapped above the bubbling water. Death was close, and much as he tried to prepare himself for the end he knew he was not ready. Rage and despair tore at him. No Jerusalem! No end to the quest of his lifetime! The rising water lapped at his chin, spilling over into his mouth. He gagged and spat it out, his fingers scrabbling at the rocks as the weight of his coat and gun dragged him down.

'Calm yourself, Shannow!' came a voice in his mind. A glow began to his right and Pendarric's face appeared like a shimmering reflection on the stone roof. 'Follow me, if you wish to live.'

The glow sank below the water and Shannow cursed and took several deep breaths, filling his lungs with oxygen. Then he dived below the surface. Far below he could see the Mother Stone, its glow fading fast, but ahead of him floated the ghostly face. He swam towards it, ever deeper, his lungs beginning to burn as his weary arms pushed at the water. Pendarric glided further ahead to a black tunnel mouth near the cavern floor. Here Shannow felt the tug of the current and was swept into the tunnel. His chest was a growing agony and he released a little air. Panic began, but Pendarric's voice cut through his fear.

'Courage, Rolynd.'

His body was buffeted from rock to rock in the narrow tunnel, until he could hold his breath no longer, his lungs expelled the precious air and sucked in salt water. His head swam and he lost consciousness, just as his body tumbled free of the mountain. Pendarric's translucent form materialized beside Shannow, but the king was powerless to aid the dying man.

'Ruth!' he called, his plea roaring across the gulf of Spirit.

Shannow lay unmoving as Pendarric called again. And again.

She appeared and took in the scene in a moment. Kneeling, she rolled Shannow to his chest and straddled his back. Her hands pressed hard against the small of his back, forcing his lungs to expel the deadly liquid. But still the Jerusalem Man showed no sign of life. She jerked him to his back and lifted his head, pinching his nostrils closed. Her mouth covered his and her breath filled his lungs. The minutes passed and Shannow groaned, sucking in a long shuddering breath.

'He will live?' said Pendarric.

Ruth nodded.

'You are tired, Lady.'

'Yes, but I have found the way.'

'I hoped you would. Is the pain great?'

Ruth's eyes met his and she did not need to answer.

'You have great courage, Ruth. Hold to it. Do not let the power of the Blood Stones overpower you. They will make you dream great dreams – they will fill your heart with the desire to rule.'

'Do not fear for me, Pendarric – such thoughts of conquest are for men. But as I draw the power from the Stones I can feel my soul contaminated by the evil. I can feel the hatred and the lust swell within me. For the first time in my life, I understand the desire to kill.'

'And will you?' asked the king.

'No.'

'Can you stop the Hellborn in the south without killing?'

'I can try, Pendarric.'

'You are stronger than I, Ruth.'

'Wiser perhaps, and not as humble as I was. I do not want to die – and yet you were right. I cannot live with this seething force inside me.'

'Take the swan's path and know peace.'

'Yes. Peace. Would that I could carry all hatred from the world with my passing.'

Pendarric shrugged. 'You will destroy the Stones. It is enough.'

Shannow moaned and rolled.

'I will say farewell here, Ruth. It was a privilege to have known you.'

'I thank you for my lessons.'

'The pupil is greater than the teacher,' he said. And vanished.

*

Shannow awoke on the rocky ground a half-mile from the marble ruins and found himself gazing up at the *Titanic*. Once more it was the golden, rusting wreck he had first seen. Then a great tear ripped along the hull and the sea gushed from her like a giant waterfall, hurtling down on the ancient city below. The torrent continued for some minutes and Shannow could see tiny bodies carried in the foaming water.

He sat up to see Ruth beside him watching the second death of the legendary ship. Tears were falling and she looked away.

'Thank you for my life,' he said lamely.

'I bear the responsibility for theirs,' she replied, as bodies continued to rain down on Atlantis.

'They fashioned their own doom,' he told her. 'You cannot blame yourself.'

She sighed and turned from the ship. 'Donna is safe, and reunited with Con Griffin.'

'I wish them their happiness,' said Shannow.

'I know – it marks you as a special man.'

'What of Batik?'

'He was wounded, but he will survive. He is a tough man and he took on the Devil single-handed.'

'The Devil?'

'No,' said Ruth, smiling, 'but a close imitation.'

'And Abaddon?'

'He is dead, Jon.'

'Did Batik kill him?'

'No, you did, Jerusalem Man. Or perhaps the Guardians did, a very long time ago.'

'I don't understand.'

'Do you remember me telling you about Lawrence and how he was at peace and happy after the Fall? How he helped to rebuild?'

'Yes.'

'And, more importantly, how he came to have visions of the Devil speaking to him and guiding him?'

'Of course.'

'The Devil was here, Jon, in that accursed ship. It was

the Stone and those who used it; they were the wolves in the shadows all along, getting Lawrence to feed them souls. They found the weakness in him and caused Abaddon to blossom and grow. They fed him power and kept him alive through the centuries. When you sealed that power, Lawrence became himself – a man long dead.'

'Sarento was a man with a dream,' said Shannow. 'He wanted to rebuild the old world – bring back all the cities, restore civilization.'

'That wasn't a dream,' said Ruth. 'It was an obsession. Believe me, Jon, I lived in that old world and I can tell you that there is little I would recreate. For every blessing, there was a curse. For every joy, ten sorrows. Nine-tenths of the world went short of food and everywhere there were wars, plagues, famine and starvation. It was finished before the Fall, but it was taking a long time to die.'

'What will you do now?'

'I will return to Sanctuary.'

'Is Selah well?'

'He is fine. He has gone now, with all my people, out into the world. I sent him with Clophas; they get on well together.'

'You will be alone in Sanctuary?'

'For a little while.'

'Will I see you again?'

'I think not.' She turned back to the wreck and saw a tiny figure climbing down the mountain. 'One last favour, Jon?'

'Of course.'

'That is Sam Archer's wife and son. See them to safety.'

'I will. Farewell, Ruth.'

'God-speed. Seek your city and find your God.'

Shannow grinned. 'I'll find it.'

Back in Sanctuary, Ruth lay down on her beloved sofa and drew on all the power she had amassed through the centuries. Her body glowed and grew, absorbing not only all of Sanctuary but continuing to drain the power from every Blood Stone within her considerable reach. As her strength grew, so too did her pain and a war began within her as the might of the Blood Stones met the essence of Sanctuary. Rage welled in her soul and all the forgotten moments of anger, lust and greed flooded her being.

That which had been Ruth Welby pulsed out into the night like a glowing cloud, dispersing into the air, travelling on the currents of the night winds.

For a while Ruth fought to hold a sense of identity within the cloud, battling to subdue the dark power of the Stones, establishing harmony within her strength.

At last she came upon the Hellborn army massing for the final charge against the defenders of Sweetwater. Then she surrendered to infinity, and fell like a rain of golden light upon the valley.

The Hellborn general, Abaal, sat on the grass-covered crest of a hill staring sullenly towards the Sweetwater Pass while below him his army mustered for the charge. For two days now the ferocity of the defence had been weakening as Cade and his men ran short of shells. Yesterday the Hellborn had almost broken through, but Cade had rallied the defenders and Abaal's warriors had been pushed back after fierce hand-to-hand fighting.

Today, Abaal knew, would see an end to resistance. His eyes raked the entrance to the pass where the bodies of men and horses lay bloated in the sunshine – more than a thousand young men who would never return to their homes.

The warmth of the sun made him remove his heavy black top-coat and he lay back on the grass, fixing his gaze on the defenders. The enemy too had lost many men and by rights they should have run. They were hopelessly outnumbered, and victory was not an option they had. Yet they stayed.

Abaal searched for the comfort of his hatred. But it was gone.

How could he hate men and women prepared to die for their homelands?

His aide, Doreval, rode up the crest and dismounted. 'The men are ready, sir.'

'How do they feel about the loss of their Stones?'

'There is fear among them, but they are disciplined.'

Abaal gestured the young man to sit beside him. 'The day has a curious feel to it.'

'In what way, sir?'

'It's hard to explain. Do you hate them, Doreval? The defenders?'

'Of course; they are the enemy.'

'But is your hatred as strong today?'

The young man looked away, his gaze floating over the corpses on the plain. 'Yes,' he said at last.

Abaal caught the lie and ignored it. 'What are you thinking?'

'I was remembering my father, and our parting. As he lay dying, I just sat there thinking about the wealth I would have; how his concubines would be mine. I never thanked him. Such a strange feeling.'

'Tell me, Doreval, and with truth – do you want to fight today?'

'Yes, sir. It would be an honour to lead the men.'

Abaal looked deeply into the young man's eyes and knew once more that he lied. He could not blame him; the Abaal of yesterday would have killed him for the truth.

'Tell the men to stand down.'

'Yes, sir,' answered Doreval, unable to keep the relief from his face.

'And fetch me a jug of wine.'

At the entrance to the pass, Cade watched the enemy dismount.

'What they playing at, Daniel?' asked Gambion. Cade shrugged and opened the breech of his pistol; only two shells remained. He closed his eyes and Gambion thought he was praying and moved to one side, but Cade was merely trying to think, to concentrate. He opened his eyes and looked around at the defenders, swallowing hard. They had fought so well.

A long time ago – or so it seemed – Lisa had asked Cade

whether he would create an army from lambs. Well, he had – and brave they were! But courage could only carry a man so far. Now they were all to die and Cade realized he did not have the courage to see it. He sheathed his pistol and stood.

'Pass me my stick, Ephram.'

'Where are you going?'

'I'm going to talk to God,' said Cade. Gambion handed him the carved stick and Cade limped out into the entrance of Sweetwater, stopping to look at the Hellborn dead choking the grass. The stench turned his stomach and he walked on.

It was a beautiful day, and even his knee had ceased its throbbing.

'Well, God, seems like we ought to have one real chat before the end. I've got to be honest – I don't really believe in you – but I figure I've nothing to lose by this. If I'm talking to myself, it don't matter. But if you are there, then maybe you'll listen. These people are about to die. That's no big thing – people have been dying for thousands of years – but my lads are getting ready to die for *you*. And that should mean something. I may be a false prophet, but they're true believers and I hope they don't get short shrift from you merely because of me. I never was worth much – didn't have the guts to farm and spent my life stealing and the like. No excuses. But take Ephram and the rest and they're worth something more; they really have repented, or whatever the Hell you call it. I've brought them to their deaths and I don't want to think about them lining up, expectant-like outside the gates, only to be told they ain't getting in. That's all I got to say, God.'

As Cade walked on towards the distant Hellborn, he pulled his pistol from his belt and hurled it out on to the grass.

Hearing the sound of movement behind him, he turned and saw Ephram Gambion lumbering towards him, his bald head shining with sweat.

'What did he say, Daniel?'

Cade smiled and patted the giant on the shoulder. 'He let me do the talking this time, Ephram. You fancy a walk?'

'Where we going?'

'To the Hellborn.'

'Why?'

Cade ignored the question and limped away. Gambion joined him.

'You still with me, Ephram?'

'Did you ever doubt it?'

'I guess not. Look at that sky. Mackerel-back and streaked with clouds. Hell of a good day to die, I'd say.'

'Is that where we're going? To die?'

'You don't have to come with me; I can do it alone.'

'I know that, Daniel. But we've come this far together so I guess I'll stay awhile yet. You know, we done pretty good against that damned army – not bad for a bunch of Brigands and farmers.'

'The best days of my life,' admitted Cade, 'but I should have said goodbye to Lisa.'

The two men walked on in silence through the ranks of the dead and on to the plain before the Hellborn. There they were spotted by a scout, who took the news to Doreval; he rode to Abaal and the general ordered his horse saddled. Gambion watched as a score of Hellborn soldiers galloped towards them and drew his pistol.

'Throw it away, Ephram.'

'I ain't dying without a fight.'

'Throw it away.'

Gambion swore . . . and hurled the pistol out over the grass.

The Hellborn slowed their mounts and ringed the two men. Cade ignored the rifles and pistols pointed at him, watching as the steel-haired general dismounted.

'You would be Cade?'

'I am.'

'I am Abaal, Lord of the Sixth. Why are you here?'

'Thought it was time we met. Face to face – man to man.'

'To what purpose?'

'Thought you might like to bury your dead.'

'This is a strange day,' said Abaal. 'Like a dream. Is it magic of yours?'

'No, maybe it's just something that happens when a lot of men have to die for nothing. Maybe it's just weariness.'

'What are you saying, Cade? Speak openly.'

Cade laughed. 'Openly? Why not? What are we doing here, killing each other? What are we fighting for? A field of grass? A few empty meadows? Why don't you just go home?'

'There is an enchantment working here,' said Abaal. 'I do not understand it, but I feel the truth of what you say. You will allow us to bury our dead?'

Cade nodded.

'Then I agree. The war is over!'

Abaal extended his hand and Cade stared down at it, unable to move. This man had led the massacres, causing untold grief and horror. Looking into Abaal's eyes, he forced himself to accept the grip and as he did so the last vestiges of bitterness fled from him and he fought back the tears welling inside.

'You are a great man, Cade,' said Abaal. 'And I shall be killed for listening to you. Perhaps we will meet in Hell.'

'I don't doubt it for a second,' said Cade.

Abaal smiled, then mounted his horse and led his men back to their tents.

'Jesus Christ!' said Gambion. 'Did we win, Daniel?'

'Take me home, Ephram.'

As they neared Sweetwater the defenders and their wives and children streamed out to meet them. Cade could not speak, but Gambion swiftly told them of the peace and Cade was swept shoulder-high and carried back into the pass.

Lisa was standing in a grove of elm, tears in her eyes, when Cade finally came to her. The sound of singing echoed through the mountains.

'Is it truly over, Daniel?'

'It is.'

'And you won. Now you'll want to be a king?'

He pulled her to him and kissed her gently. 'That was another man in another place. All I want now is for us to marry and start a home and a family. I want nothing more to do with war, or guns, or death. I'll grow corn and raise cattle and sheep. I just want to be with you – and I don't give a damn about being a king.'

Lisa lifted his chin and smiled. 'Well,' she said, 'now that you don't want it, you're bound to get it!'

Epilogue

In the year following the Hellborn war, Daniel Cade was elected Prester of Rivervale. He married Lisa in the biggest wedding ceremony seen in the area for thirty years. The whole community attended and the gifts were brought in several wagons.

Con Griffin, Donna and their daughter Tanya returned to Rivervale and the farm built by Tomas the carpenter. Once clear of the Plague Lands Donna's powers faded, though often she would be seen in the far meadow, sitting silently with her daughter. At those times, Con Griffin left them alone with their faraway dreams.

Jacob Madden married a young widow and took possession of the farm adjoining Griffin's land; the two remained close friends until Madden's death eighteen years later.

Batik spent two years hunting for sign of Jon Shannow and finally tracked down Amaziga Archer, who directed him north.

As winter was approaching, he rode into a wide valley and came to a farmhouse of white stone. Near the trees were three bodies covered with a tarpaulin. The farm was run by two women, a mother and daughter, and they told him that the dead men had been robbers.

'What happened?' Batik asked the mother.

'A stranger rode in as they were attacking the house and he killed them all. But he was wounded. I asked him to stay, but he refused; he rode on towards the High Lonely,' she said, pointing to the distant snow-covered peaks.

'What did he look like?' asked Batik.

'He was a tall man, with long hair and burning eyes.'

As Batik turned his horse to the north and rode from the yard the daughter, a blonde girl of around fifteen, ran after him and caught at his stirrup.

'She didn't tell the whole truth,' she whispered. 'She didn't ask him to stay. She was frightened of him and told him to ride on. I gave him some bread and cheese and he told me not to worry. There was a shining city just over the farthest mountain, he said, and his wound would be tended there. But there isn't a city, it's just a wilderness. And the blood was streaming down his saddle.'

Batik had tried to follow, but a blinding blizzard blew up and he was forced to give up the search.

That same night Daniel Cade had a strange dream. He was walking through a mountain wood, through thick snow, yet he felt no cold. He came to a frozen stream, and a small camp-fire which gave no heat. Beside it, his back against a tree, sat the Jerusalem Man.

'Hello, Daniel,' he said and Cade moved close.

'You are hurt.'

'There is no pain.'

'Let me help you, Jonnie.'

'I hear you're a great man now, in Rivervale?'

'Yes,' said Cade.

'Dad would have been proud of you. *I* am proud of you.' Shannow smiled, and the ice in his beard cracked and fell away.

'Let me build up the fire.'

'No. Are you happy, Daniel?'

'Yes. Very.'

'Do you have children?'

'Two. A boy and a girl.'

'That's good. So, the wolf sits down with the lambs. I'm glad. Help me to my horse, Daniel.'

Cade lifted him and saw the blood on the ice. He half-carried him to the black stallion and heaved him up into the saddle. Shannow swayed and then took up the reins.

'Where are you going?' asked Cade.

'There,' said Shannow, pointing to the peaks piercing the clouds. 'Can you see the spires, Daniel?'

'No,' whispered Cade.

'I'm going home.'

The Last Guardian

This novel is dedicated with love to my children Kathryn and Luke who, thankfully, are still too young to know what fine people they are.

Foreword

There was no doubt in my mind about what happened to Jon Shannow when he rode into the mountains, wounded and alone. He was dying. And Jerusalem beckoned.

Yet once the novel was published reader reaction was immediate. How long to the next Shannow story? In those days reader's letters did not arrive in bulging post bags and I was able to answer all of them. The answer was simple: Thank you for your letter, and I am glad you enjoyed Jon Shannow's tale, but he is dead. There will be no more adventures.

I sent just such a response to a fan in Liverpool. He knew better and wrote back immediately. 'No he's not! No way!'

It was a real shock – as if he knew something I didn't. I showed the letter to one of my test readers. Her amused response was 'Hey, maybe he's right. You don't know everything, Dave. You're only the author.'

From that moment I started wondering about Shannow. Could there have been some miracle on the mountain?

At around the same time I received a number of reviews for *Wolf in Shadow*. Some were very good, some were indifferent, but one was downright vile. One of the lines in it struck me particularly. *I dread to think of people who look up to men like Jon Shannow*. The writer was named Broome.

Twenty years of journalism had taught me not to over-react to criticism. A writer's work is not his child. It is just work. A work of love and passion, but a work nonetheless. Even so I wanted to react in some way. All the characters in my novels are based on real people, and I thought it would be a neat response to use a character named Broome, a man passionately opposed to violence who would loathe the hero, but be drawn into his world. It was in my mind that he would be a cannon fodder character, of little consequence, who would die early. But, as with so much in the magical world of creative writing, events did not – as you will see – turn out anything like I had planned.

It took only one more little nudge to push me into a second Shannow novel. I was driving home one night, listening to the radio, when the haunting lyric of a new song struck home like an arrow.

The singer was a brilliant new American artiste named Tracy Chapman, and the song spoke of racism and riots, and the appalling violence that has sadly become commonplace in the impoverished inner cities of America. One line had immense power for me...

Across the lines who would dare to go...

I knew who would dare.

I got home around 2 am and immediately switched on the word processor. I had no idea how to get round the obvious death of my hero in the first book, and did not wish to write a prequel. In the end I used the simplest device there is. I began with the words:

But he did not die.

David A. Gemmell   Hastings, 1995

1

SOUTH OF THE PLAGUE LANDS – 2341 AD

But he did not die. The flesh around the bullet wound over his hip froze as the temperature dropped to thirty below zero, and the distant spires of Jerusalem blurred and changed, becoming snow-shrouded pine. Ice had formed on his beard and his heavy black, double-shouldered topcoat glistened white in the moonlight. Shannow swayed in the saddle, trying to focus on the city he had sought for so long. But it was gone. As his horse stumbled, Shannow's right hand gripped the saddle pommel and the wound in his side flared with fresh pain.

He turned the black stallion's head, steering the beast downhill towards the valley.

Images rushed through his mind: Karitas, Ruth, Donna; the hazardous journey across the Plague Lands and the battles with the Hellborn, the monstrous ghost ship wrecked on a mountain. Guns and gunfire, war and death.

The blizzard found new life and the wind whipped freezing snow into Shannow's face. He could not see where he was heading, and his mind wandered. He knew that life was ebbing from his body with each passing second, but he had neither the strength nor the will to fight on.

He remembered the farm and his first sight of Donna, standing in the doorway with an ancient crossbow in her hands. She had mistaken Shannow for a brigand, and feared for her life and that of her son, Eric. Shannow had never blamed her for that mistake. He knew what people saw when the Jerusalem Man came riding – a tall, gaunt figure in a flat-crowned leather hat, a man with cold, cold eyes that had seen too much of death and despair. Always it was the same. People would stand and stare, first at his expressionless face and then their eyes would be drawn down to his guns, the terrible weapons of the Thunder Maker.

Yet Donna Taybard had been different. She had taken Shannow to her hearth and her home and, for the first time in two weary decades, the Jerusalem Man had known happiness.

But then had come the brigands and the war-makers and finally the Hellborn. Shannow had gone against them all for the woman he loved, only to see her wed another.

Now he was alone again, dying on a frozen mountain in an uncharted wilderness. And, strangely, he did not care. The wind howled about horse and man and Shannow fell forward across the stallion's neck, lost in the siren song of the blizzard. The horse was mountain bred; he did not like the howling wind, nor the biting snow. Now he angled his way through the trees into the lee of a rock-face and followed a deer trail down to the mouth of a high lava tunnel that stretched through the ancient volcanic range. It was warmer here and the stallion plodded on, aware of the dead weight across his back. This disturbed him, for his rider was always in balance and could signal his commands with the slightest pressure or flick of the reins.

The stallion's wide nostrils flared as the smell of smoke came to him. He halted and backed up, his iron hooves clattering on the rocky floor. A dark shadow moved in front of him . . . in panic he reared and Shannow tumbled from the saddle. A huge taloned hand caught the reins and the smell of lion filled the tunnel. The stallion tried to rear again, to lash out with iron-shod hooves, but he was held tight and a soft, deep voice whispered to him, a gentle hand stroking his neck. Calmed by the voice, he allowed himself to be led into a deep cave, where a camp-fire had been set within a circle of round flat stones. He waited calmly as he was tethered to a jutting stone at the far wall; then the figure was gone.

Outside the cave Shannow groaned and tried to roll to his belly, but he was stricken by pain and deep cold. He opened his eyes to see a hideous face looming over him. Dark hair framed the head and face and a pair of tawny eyes gazed down at him; the nose was wide and flat, the mouth a deep slash, rimmed with sharp fangs. Shannow, unable to move, could only glare at the creature.

Taloned hands moved under his body, lifting him easily, and he was carried like a child into a cave and laid gently by a fire. The creature fumbled at the ties on Shannow's coat, but the thick paw-like hands could not cope with the frozen knots. Talons hissed out to sever the leather thongs and Shannow felt his coat eased from him. Slowly, but with great care, the creature removed his frozen clothing and covered him with a warm blanket. The Jerusalem Man faded into sleep – and his dreams were pain-filled.

Once more he fought the Guardian Lord, Sarento, while the *Titanic* sailed on a ghostly sea and the Devil walked in Babylon. But this time Shannow could not win, and he struggled to survive as the sea poured into the stricken ship, engulfing him. He could hear the cries of drowning men, women and children, but he could not save them. He awoke sweating and tried to sit. Pain ripped at his wounded side and he groaned and sank back into his fever dreams.

*

He was riding towards the mountains when he heard a shot; he rode to the crest of a hill and gazed down on a farmyard where three men were dragging two women from their home. Drawing a pistol, Shannow kicked his stallion into a run and thundered towards the scene. When the men saw him they flung the women aside and two of them drew flintlocks from their belts; the third ran at him with a knife. He dragged on the reins and the stallion reared. Shannow timed his first shot well and a brigand was punched from his feet. The knife-man leapt, but Shannow swung in the saddle and fired point-blank, the bullet entering the man's forehead and exiting from the neck in a bloody spray. The third man loosed a shot that ricocheted from the pommel of Shannow's saddle to tear into his hip. Ignoring the sudden pain, the Jerusa-

lem Man fired twice. The first shell took the brigand high in the shoulder, spinning him; the second hammered into his skull.

In the sudden silence, Shannow sat his stallion gazing at the women. The elder of the two approached him and he could see the fear in her eyes. Blood was seeping from his wound and dripping to the saddle, but he sat upright as she neared.

'What do you want of us?' she asked.

'Nothing, Lady, save to help you.'

'Well,' she said, her eyes hard, 'you have done that, and we thank you.' She backed away, still staring at him. He knew she could see the blood, but he could not – would not – beg for aid.

'Good day to you,' he said, swinging the stallion and heading away.

The younger girl ran after him; blonde and pretty, her face was leathered by the sunlight and the hardship of wilderness farming. She gazed up at him with large blue eyes.

'I am sorry,' she told him. 'My mother distrusts all men. I am so sorry.'

'Get away from him, girl!' shouted the older woman, and she fell back.

Shannow nodded. 'She probably has good reason,' he said. 'I am sorry I cannot stay and help you bury these vermin.'

'You are wounded. Let me help you.'

'No. There is a city near here, I am sure. It has white spires and gates of burnished gold. There they will tend me.'

'There are no cities,' she said.

'I will find it.' He touched his heels to the stallion's flanks and rode from the farmyard.

*

A hand touched him and he awoke. The bestial face was leaning over him.

'How are you feeling?' The voice was deep and slow and slurred, and the question had to be repeated twice before Shannow could understand it.

'I am alive – thanks to you. Who are you?'

The creature's great head tilted. 'Good. Usually the question is *what* are you. My name is Shir-ran. You are a strong man to live so long with such a wound.'

'The ball passed through me,' said Shannow. 'Can you help me to sit?'

'No. Lie there. I have stitched the wounds, front and back, but my fingers are not what they were. Lie still and rest tonight. We will talk in the morning.'

'My horse?'

'Safe. He was a little frightened of me, but we understand each other now. I fed him the grain you carried in your saddlebags. Sleep, Man.'

Shannow relaxed and moved his hand under the blankets to rest on the wound over his right hip. He could feel the tightness of the stitches and the clumsy knots. There was no bleeding, but he was worried about the fibres from his coat which had been driven into his flesh. It was these that killed more often than ball or shell, aiding gangrene and poisoning the blood.

'It is a good wound,' said Shir-ran softly, as if reading his mind. 'The issue of blood cleansed it, I think. But here in the mountains wounds heal well. The air is clean. Bacteria find it hard to survive at thirty below.'

'Bacteria?' whispered Shannow, his eyes closing.

'Germs . . . the filth that causes wounds to fester.'

'I see. Thank you, Shir-ran.'

And Shannow slept without dreams.

*

Shannow awoke hungry and eased himself to a sitting position. The fire was burning brightly and he could see a large store of wood stacked against the far wall. Gazing around the cave, he saw it was some fifty feet across at the widest point and the high domed ceiling was pitted with fissures, through which the smoke from the fire drifted lazily. Beside Shannow's blankets were his water canteen, his leatherbound Bible and his guns, still sheathed in their oiled leather scabbards. Taking the canteen, he pulled clear the brass-topped cork and drank deeply. Then in the bright firelight he examined the bullet wound in his hip; the flesh around it was angry, bruised and inflamed, but it looked clean and there was no bleeding. Slowly and carefully he stood, scanning the cave for his clothes. They were dry and casually folded atop a boulder on the other side of the fire. Dried blood still caked the white woollen shirt, but he slipped it on and climbed into his black woollen trousers. He could not buckle his belt on the usual notch, for the leather bit into his wound, bringing a grunt of pain. Still, he felt more human now he was clothed. He pulled on socks and high riding boots and walked to where his stallion was tethered at the far wall. Shannow stroked his neck and the horse dropped his head and nuzzled him in the chest. 'Careful, boy, I'm still tender.' He half-filled the feed-bag with grain and settled it over the stallion's head. Of Shirran there was no sign.

Near the wood-store was a bank of rough-hewn shelves. Some carried books, others small sacks of salt, sugar, dried fruit and meat. Shannow ate some of the fruit and returned to the fire. The cave was warm and he lay back in his blankets and took up his guns, cleaning them with care. Both were Hellborn pistols, single or double action, side-feed weapons. He opened his saddlebag and checked his shells. He still had forty-seven, but when these were gone the beautifully balanced pistols would be useless. Delving deep into the saddlebag he found his own guns, cap and ball percussion pistols that had served him well for twenty years. For these he could make his own powder and mould ammunition. Having cleaned them, he wrapped them in oilskin and returned them to the depths of the saddlebag. Only then did he take up his Bible.

It was a well-thumbed book, the pages thin and gold edged, the leather cover as supple as silk. He banked up the fire and opened the pages at The Book of Habakkuk. He read the section aloud, his voice deep and resonant.

'*How long, O Lord, must I call for help, but you do not listen? Or cry out to you, "Violence," but you do not save? Why do you make me look at injustice? Why do you tolerate wrong? Destruc-*

tion and violence are before me, there is strife, and conflict abounds. Therefore the law is paralysed and justice never prevails. The wicked hem in the righteous so that justice is perverted.'

'And how does your God answer, Jon Shannow?' asked Shir-ran.

'In his own way,' Shannow answered. 'How is it you know my name?'

The huge creature ambled forward, his great shoulders bowed under the weight of the enormous head. He sank to the floor by the fire and Shannow noticed that his breathing was ragged. A thin trickle of blood could be seen coming from his right ear, matting the dark hair of his mane. 'Are you hurt?' asked Shannow.

'No. It is the Change, that is all. You found food?'

'Yes. Some dried fruit in crystallised honey. It was good.'

'Take it all. I can no longer stomach it. How is your wound?'

'Healing well – as you promised. You seem in pain, Shir-ran. Is there anything I can do?'

'Nothing, Shannow. Save, perhaps, to offer me a little company?'

'That will be a pleasure. It is too long since I sat by a fire, secure and at peace. Tell me how you know me?'

'Of you, Shannow. The Dark Lady speaks of you – and your deeds against the Hellborn. You are a strong man. A brave friend, I think.'

'Who is this Dark Lady?' countered Shannow, uncomfortable with the compliments.

'She is who she is, dark and beautiful. She labours among the Dianae – my people – and the Wolvers. The Bears will not receive her, for their humanity is all gone. They are beasts – now and for ever. I am tired, Shannow. I will rest ... sleep.' He settled down on his belly, taloned hands supporting his head. His tawny eyes closed – then opened. 'If ... when ... you can no longer understand me, then saddle your stallion and ride on. You understand?'

'No,' replied Shannow.

'You will,' said Shir-ran.

Shannow ate some more fruit and returned to his Bible; Habakkuk had long been a favourite. Short and bitter-sweet were his words, but they echoed the doubts and the fears in Shannow's heart and, reflecting them, calmed them.

For three days Shannow sat with Shir-ran, but although they talked often the Jerusalem Man learned little of the Dianae. What meagre information the creature did impart told Shannow of a land where men were slowly changing into beasts. There were the People of the Lion, the Wolf and the Bear. The Bears were finished, their culture gone. The Wolvers were dying out. Only the Lion people remained. Shir-ran spoke of the beauty of life, of its pains and its glories, and Shannow began to realise that the great creature was dying. They did not speak of it, but day by day Shir-ran's body changed, swelling, twisting, until he could not stand upright. Blood flowed from both ears now and his speech was ever more slurred. At night in his sleep he would growl.

On the fourth morning Shannow awoke to hear his stallion whinnying in terror. He rolled from his bed, his hand sweeping out and gathering a pistol. Shir-ran was crouched before the horse, his head swaying.

'What is wrong?' called Shannow. Shir-ran swung – and Shannow found himself staring into the tawny eyes of a huge lion. It advanced on him in a rush and leapt, but Shannow hurled himself to his right, hitting the ground hard. Pain lanced his side, but he swivelled as the lion surged at him, its roaring filling the cave.

'Shir-ran!' bellowed Shannow. The lion twisted its head and for a moment Shannow saw the light of understanding in its eyes ... then it was gone. Again the beast leapt. A pistol shot thundered in the cave.

The creature that had been Shir-ran sank to the floor and rolled to its side, eyes locked to Shannow's own. The Jerusalem Man moved forward and knelt by the body, laying his hand upon the black mane.

'I am sorry,' he said. The eyes closed and all breathing ceased.

Shannow laid aside his pistol and took up his Bible. 'You saved my life, Shir-ran, and I took yours. That is not just, yet I had no choice. I do not know how to pray for you, for I do not know if you were man or beast. But you were kind to me, and for that I commend your soul to the All-High.' He opened his Bible.

Laying his left hand on Shir-ran's body, he read, *'The Earth is the Lord's, and everything in it, the world, all who live in it, for he founded it upon the seas and established it upon the waters. Who may ascend the Hill of the Lord? Who may stand in his Holy place? He who has clean hands and a pure heart, who does not lift up his soul to an idol, or swear by what is false.'*

He walked to the trembling stallion and saddled him. Then he gathered what remained of the food, stepped into the saddle and rode from the cave.

Behind him the fire flickered ... and died.

2

THE CITY OF AD – 9364 BC

The Temple was a place of great beauty still, with its white spires and golden domes, but the once tranquil courtyards were now thronged with people baying for the blood sacrifice. The white tent at the entrance to the Holy Circle had been removed and in its place stood a marble statue of the King, regal and mighty, arms outstretched.

Nu-Khasisatra stood in the crowd, his limbs trembling. Three times had the vision come to him and three times had he pushed it aside.

'I cannot do this, Lord,' he whispered. 'I do not have the strength.'

He turned away from the spectacle as the victim was brought out, and eased his way through the crowds. He heard the new High Priest chant the opening lines of the ritual, but he did not look back. Tears stung his eyes as he stumbled along the corridors of white marble, emerging at last at the Pool of Silence. He sat at the Pool's edge; the roar of the crowd was muted here, yet still he heard the savage joy which heralded the death of another innocent.

'Forgive me,' he said. Gazing down into the Pool, he looked at the fish swimming there and above them his own reflection. The face was strong and square, the eyes deep-set, the beard full. He had never considered it the face of a weak man. His hand snaked out, disturbing the water. The sleek silver and black fish scattered, carrying his reflection with them.

'What can one man do, Lord? You can see them. The King has brought them wealth, and peace; prosperity and long life. They would tear me to pieces.' A sense of defeat settled upon him. In the past three months he had organised secret meetings, preaching against the excesses of the King. He had helped the outlawed Priests of Chronos to escape the Daggers, smuggling them from the city. But now he shrank from the last commitment; he was ashamed that love of life was stronger than love of God.

His vision swam, the sky darkened and Nu-Khasisatra felt himself torn from his body. He soared into the sky and hovered over the gleaming city below. In the distance a deeper darkness gathered, then a bright light shone beyond the darkness. A great wind blew and Nu trembled as the sea roared up to meet the sky. The mighty city was like a toy now as the ocean thundered across the land. Huge trees disappeared under the waves, like grass beneath a river flood. Mountains were swallowed whole. The stars flew across the sky and the sun rose majestically in the West.

Looking down upon the city of his birth, Nu-Khasisatra saw only the deep blue-grey of an angry sea. His spirit sank below the waves, deeper and deeper into the darkness. The Pool of Silence was truly silent now, and the black fish were gone. Bodies floated by him ... men, women, tiny babes. Unencumbered by the water, Nu walked back to the central square. The statue of the King still stood with arms outstretched, but a huge black shark brushed against it. Slowly, the statue toppled striking a pillar. The head sheared off and the body bounced against the mosaic tiles.

'No!' screamed Nu. 'No!'

His body jerked, and once more he was sitting by the Pool. Bright sunlight streamed above the temple and doves circled the wooden parapets of the Wailing Tower. He stood, swept his sky-blue cloak over his shoulder and marched back to the Courtyard of the Holy Circle. The crowd was milling now and the priests were lifting the victim's body from the flat grey sacrifice stone. Blood stained the surface, and had run down the carved channels to disappear through the golden vents.

Nu-Khasisatra strode to the steps and walked slowly towards the sacrifice stone. At first no one made a move to stop him, but as he drew nearer to the stone a red-robed priest intercepted him. 'You cannot approach the Holy Place,' said the priest.

'What holy place?' countered Nu. 'You have corrupted it.' He thrust the man aside and walked to the stone. Some people in the crowd had watched the altercation, and now began to whisper.

'What is he doing?'

'Did you see him strike the priest?'

'Is he a madman?'

All eyes turned to the broad-shouldered man at the stone as he removed his blue cloak; beneath it he wore the white robes of a Priest of Chronos. Temple guards gathered at the foot of the steps, but it was forbidden to carry a weapon to the Holy Place and they stood their ground, uncertain.

Three priests approached the man at the sacrifice stone. 'What madness is this?' asked one. 'Why do you desecrate this Temple?'

'How dare you speak of desecration?' countered Nu-Khasisatra. 'This Temple was dedicated to Chronos, Lord of Light, Lord of Life. No blood sacrifice was ever made here.'

'The King is the living image of Chronos,' the priest argued. 'The conqueror of worlds, the Lord of Heaven. All who deny this are traitors and heretics.'

'Then count me among them!' roared Nu and his huge hands took hold of the sacrifice stone and wrenched it clear of its supports. Forcing his fingers under the stone, he lifted it high above his head and hurled it out over the steps, where it shattered. An angry roar rose from the crowd.

Nu-Khasisatra leapt to stand upon the altar base. 'Faithless people!' he shouted. 'The end of all days is upon you. You have mocked the Lord of Creation, and your doom will be terrible. The seas will rise against you and not one stone will be left upon another. Your bodies will be dashed to the deep and your dreams will be forgotten, even as you are forgotten. You have heard that the King is the living god. Blasphemy! Who brought the Rolynd Stones from the vault of Heaven? Who led the chosen people to this bountiful land? Who dashed the hopes of the wicked in the Year of Dragons? It was Chronos, through his prophets. And where was the King? Unborn and unmade. He is a man, and his evil is colossal. He will destroy the world. You have wives and sons; you have loved ones. All will die. Not one of you listening to these words will be alive at year's end.'

'Drag him down!' shouted someone in the crowd.

'Kill him!' yelled another, and the cry was taken up by the mob.

The Temple guards drew their swords and ran up the steps. Lightning seared amongst them, leaping from sword to sword, and the guards, their flesh blackened, toppled to the stone. A great silence settled on the crowd.

Smoke drifted up from the bodies of the guards as Nu-Khasisatra raised his hands to the heavens.

'There is no turning back now,' he said. 'All will be as I have told it. The sun will rise in the West, and the oceans will thunder across the land. You will see the Sword of God in the heavens – and despair!'

He stepped down from the altar and walked slowly past the dead guards. The crowd parted before him as he marched from the Temple.

'I recognise him,' said a man, as he passed by. 'That was Nu-Khasisatra, the shipbuilder. He lives in the south quarter.'

The name was whispered amongst the mob and carried from the Temple, coming at last to the woman Sharazad.

And the hunt began.

3

For three days Shannow travelled south, the trails winding ever down into a long valley of half-frozen streams and tall stands of pine, wide meadows and rolling hills. He saw little game, but came across tracks of deer and elk. Each day, around mid-morning he would halt in a spot shielded from the wind and clear the snow from the grass, allowing the stallion to eat, while Shannow himself sat by a small fire reading his Bible or thinking about the journey ahead.

His wounds were healing fast; Shir-ran had done a fine job on them. He thought of the strange Man-beast often, and came to the conclusion that Shir-ran had wanted his company for just the purpose it had served. The Man-beast had stitched his wounds, then left his guns by his side. Yet within the sanctuary of the cave he had no need of weapons. The doomed creature had spoken of the Change and it had been awesome to witness – the move from humanity to bestiality. What could cause such a transformation Shannow had no idea, but in the strange world after Armageddon there were many mysteries.

Two years before, in a bid to rescue Samuel Archer and the reformed Hellborn, Batik, Shannow had seen at first hand a new race of people called Wolvers, part man and part animal. Archer himself had spoken of other such creatures, though Shannow had yet to see them.

It was warmer here in the valley and as he moved further south the snow thinned, great patches of verdant grass shimmering on the hillsides. Every day Shannow scanned the skies, looking for the signs of wonder. But ever the heavens remained blue and clear.

On the fourth day, as dusk gathered, Shannow guided the stallion into a wood, seeking a camp-site. Ahead, through the tall trees, he glimpsed a glittering fire.

'Hello, the camp!' he yelled. At first there was no answer, then a gruff voice called out, beckoning him in. Shannow waited for a moment and then delved into his pack, bringing out the short-nosed percussion pistol and tucking it into his belt just inside the flap of his long coat. Then he rode forward.

There were four men sitting around the fire and five horses tethered to a picket line. Shannow stepped from the saddle and tied his stallion's reins to a jutting root. On the fire a large black pot was hanging from a tripod, and within it Shannow could smell a simmering broth. Casually he moved to the fire and squatted down, his eyes sweeping the group. They were hard men, for the most part lean and wolf-like; Shannow had known men like these all his life. His gaze halted on a burly, round-shouldered man with a short-cropped salt-and-pepper beard and eyes that were merely slits under heavy lids.

There was a tension in the air, but it did not affect the Jerusalem Man though he acknowledged it. His eyes locked to the burly man and he waited.

'Eat,' said the man at last, his voice low.

'After you,' said Shannow. 'I would not wish to be impolite.'

The man smiled, showing stained teeth. 'The wilderness is no place for manners.' He reached out and ladled some broth into a metal dish and the others followed suit. As the tension grew, Shannow took a dish with his left hand and placed it before the fire. Then, still with his left hand, he lifted the ladle and filled the bowl, drawing it to him. Slowly he finished the meal and pushed the plate from him.

'Thank you,' he said into the silence. 'It was most welcome.'

'Help yourself to more,' offered the leader.

'No, thank you. There will not be enough left for your scout.'

The leader swung round. 'Come in, Zak, supper's waitin'!' he called. Across from the fire a young man rose from the bushes, a long rifle in his hands. He walked slowly to the fire, avoiding Shannow's gaze, and sat beside the leader with the rifle by his side.

Shannow rose and moved to his stallion, untying his blanket roll and spreading his bed beside the horse. Loosening the cinch, he lifted the saddle and dropped it to the ground; then, taking a brush from his saddlebag, he ducked under the stallion's neck and, with smooth even strokes, groomed the horse. He did not look at the men around the fire, but the silence grew. The Jerusalem Man had been tempted to finish his meal and ride on, to be clear of the immediate danger – but such a move would be foolishness, he knew. These men were brigands and killers and to ride on would display weakness like the scent of blood to a wolfpack. He patted the stallion's neck and returned to his bed. Without a word to the men he removed his hat and lay down, pulling a blanket over him and closing his eyes.

At the fire the young man reached for his rifle, but the leader gripped his arm and shook his head.

The youth pulled his arm clear. 'What the Devil's wrong with you?' he whispered. 'Let's take him now. That there is one Hell of a horse, and his guns . . . you see them guns?'

'I saw,' answered the leader, 'and I saw the man who wears 'em. You see how he rode in? Careful. He spotted you rightaways, and hunkered down where you couldn't get no shot. And all through the meal he only used his left hand. And where was his right? I'll tell you where. It was inside that long coat, and it weren't scratching his belly. Now you leave it be, boy. I'll think on it.'

Towards midnight, with all the men asleep in their blankets, the youth rose silently, a double-edged knife in one hand. He crept forward towards where Shannow slept. A dark figure loomed behind him and a pistol clubbed across the youth's neck; he fell without a sound. The leader holstered his pistol and dragged the boy back to his blankets.

Twenty feet away Shannow smiled and returned his own gun to its scabbard.

The leader walked across to him. 'I know you ain't asleep,' he said. 'Who the Hell are you?'

Shannow sat up. 'That boy will have a sore head. I hope he has sense enough to thank you for it.'

'The name's Lee Patterson,' the man answered, thrusting out his right hand. Shannow smiled at him, but ignored the offer.

'Jon Shannow.'

'Jesus God Almighty! You hunting us?'

'No. I'm riding south.'

Lee grinned. 'You wanna see them statues in the sky, eh? The Sword of God, Shannow?'

'You have seen them?'

'Not me, man. They call that the Wild Lands. There's no settlements there, no way for a man to make a living. But I seen a man once who swore he'd stood under 'em; he said it gave him religion. Me, I don't need no religion. You sure you're not huntin' us?'

'You have my word. Why did you save the boy?'

'A man don't have too many sons, Shannow. I had three. One got killed when I lost my farm. Another was shot down after we . . . took to the road. He was hit in the leg; it went bad and I had to cut it from him. Can you image that, Shannow, cutting the leg from your son? And he died anyway, 'cause I left it too long. It's a hard life, and no mistake.'

'What happened to your wife?'

'She died. This is no land for women, it burns them out. You got a woman, Shannow?'

'No. I have no one.'

'I guess that's what makes you dangerous.'

'I guess it does,' Shannow agreed.

Lee stood and stretched. He looked down. 'You ever find Jerusalem, Shannow?'

'Not yet.'

'When you do, ask *Him* a question, will you? Ask Him what the Hell is the point of it all.'

*

4

Nu-Khasisatra ran from the Temple, out on to the broad steps and down into the teeming multitudes who thronged the city thoroughfares. His courage was exhausted and reaction had set in; his limbs were trembling as he pushed his way through the crowds, trying to lose himself among the thousands who packed the market streets.

'Are you a priest?' a man asked him, clutching his sleeve.

'No,' snapped Nu. 'Leave me alone!'

'But you wear the robes,' the man persisted.

'Leave me!' roared Nu, wrenching the man's hand from him. Once more swallowed by the throng, he cut left into an alleyway and walked swiftly through to the Street of Merchants. Here he bought a heavy cloak; it had a deep hood, which he pulled over his dark hair.

He stopped at an eating house on the Crossroads corner, taking a table by the east window where he sat staring out on to the street, overwhelmed by the enormity of his deed. He was a traitor and a heretic. There was nowhere in the Empire to hide from the wrath of the King. Even now the Daggers would be hunting him.

'Why you?' Pashad had demanded the previous night. 'Why can your God not use someone else? Why must you throw away your life?'

'I do not know, Pashad. What can I say?'

'You can give up this foolishness. We will move to Balacris – put this nonsense behind us.'

'It is not nonsense. Without God I am nothing. And the King's evil must be opposed.'

'If your Lord Chronos is so powerful, why does he not strike the King dead with a thunderbolt? Why does he need a shipbuilder?'

Nu shrugged. 'It is not for me to question Him. All I

have is His. All the world is His. I have been a Temple student all my life – never good enough to be a priest. And I have broken many of His laws. But I cannot refuse when He calls upon me. What kind of a man would I be? Answer me that?'

'You would be a live man,' she said.

'Away from God there is no life.' He saw the defeat in her dark eyes, saw it born in the bright tears that welled and fell to her cheeks.

'What of me and the children? A traitor's wife suffers his fate – have you thought of that? Do you wish to see your own children burning in the fires?'

'No!' The word was torn from him in a cry of anguish.

'You must get away from here, beloved. You must! I spoke to Bali this afternoon and he says you can go to him tomorrow night; he has something for you.'

They had talked for more than two hours, making plans, then Nu had gone to his tiny prayer room where he knelt until the dawn. He begged his God to release him, but as the dawn streaked the sky he knew what he must do . . .

Go to the Temple and speak against the King.

Now he had – and death awaited him.

'Are you eating or drinking, Highness?' asked the House-keeper.

'What? Oh. Wine. The best you have.'

'Indeed, Highness.' The man bowed and moved away. Nu did not notice his return, nor the jug and goblet he placed upon the table. The House-keeper cleared his throat and Nu jerked, then delved into his purse and dropped a large silver coin into the man's hand. The House-keeper counted out Nu's change and placed it on the table. Nu ignored the money and absently poured the wine; it was from the south-west, rich and heady. He drained the goblet and refilled it.

Two Daggers moved into sight beyond the window and the crowd parted for them, people jostling and pushing to avoid contact with the reptiles.

Nu averted his eyes and drank more of the wine.

A figure moved into the seat opposite. 'To know the future is to be assured of fortune,' he said, as he spread out a series of stones on the table.

'I do not need my future read,' replied Nu. But the seer swept up two small silver pieces from the change on the table. Then he scattered the stones.

'Pick three,' he said.

Nu was about to order the man away when the two Daggers entered the room. He swallowed hard. 'What did you say?' he asked, turning to face the newcomer. 'Pick three stones,' the seer repeated and Nu did so, leaning forward so that his hood fell further over his face. 'Now give me your hand,' ordered the seer.

The man's fingers were long and slender, cold as knife-blades as he studied Nu's palm for several seconds.

'You are a strong man, but then I need no special skill to see that,' he said, grinning. He was young, hawk-faced, with deep-set brown eyes. 'And you are worried.'

'Not at all,' whispered Nu.

'Curious,' said the man suddenly. 'I see a journey, but not over water, nor yet over land. I see a man with lightning in his hands and death in his dark fingers. I see water ... rising ...'

Nu wrenched his hand away. 'Keep the money,' he hissed. He looked into the seer's eyes and saw the fear there. 'How does a man travel, and yet not move over land or water?' he asked, forcing a smile. 'What kind of seer are you?'

'A good one,' said the man softly. 'And you can relax, for they have gone.'

'Who?' Nu asked, not daring to look up.

'The reptiles. You are in great danger, my friend. Death stalks you.'

'Death stalks us all,' Nu replied. 'No man avoids him for ever.'

'There is truth in that. I do not know where you are going – nor do I want to know. But I see a strange land and a grey rider. His hands hold great power. He is the man of thunder. He is the doom of worlds. I do not know if he is a friend or an enemy, but you are linked to him. Walk warily.'

'Too late for that,' said Nu. 'Will you join me in a drink?'

'Your company is – I think – too perilous for me. Go with God.'

5

Beth McAdam climbed down from the wagon, gave the broken wheel a hard kick and cursed long and fluently. Her two children sat in amused silence on the tailboard. 'Wouldn't you just know it?' said Beth. The wooden rim had split and torn free the metal edge; she kicked it again. Samuel tried to stifle the giggle with his fist, but it exploded from him in a high peal. Beth stormed round to the rear of the wagon, but the boy squirmed up over the piled furniture where she could not reach him.

'You little snapper-gut!' she yelled. Then Mary began to laugh and Beth swung on her.

'You think it's funny to be trapped out here with the wolves . . . and the enormous lions?'

Mary's face fell and Beth was instantly contrite. 'I'm sorry, honey. There ain't no lions. I was only joking.'

'You promise?' said Mary, gazing out over the plain.

'I do. And even if there was, he'd know better than to come anywhere near your Ma when she's angry. And you come down from there, Samuel, or I'll rip out your arms and feed 'em to the wolves.'

His blond head peeped over the chest of drawers. 'You ain't gonna whack me, Ma?'

'I ain't gonna whack you, snapper-gut. Help Mary get the pots unloaded. We're going to have to camp here and figure a way to mend the wagon.'

While the children busied themselves preparing a campfire, Beth sat on a boulder and stared hard at the wheel. They would need to unload everything, then try to lever up the empty wagon while she manhandled the spare wheel into place. She was sure she could do it, but could the children handle the lever? Samuel was big for a seven-year-old, but he lacked the concentration necessary for such a task, and Mary, at eight, was wand-thin and would never muster the power needed. But there had to be a way... there always was.

Ten years ago, when her mother was beaten to death by a drunken father, the twelve-year-old Beth Newson had taken a carving-knife and cut his throat in his sleep. Then, with seven silver Barta coin, she had walked seventy miles to Seeka Settlement and spun a terrible tale of brigands and killers raiding the farm. For three years the Committee made her live with Seth Reid and his wife, and she was treated like a slave. At fifteen she had set her cap at the powerful logger, Sean McAdam. The poor man had no chance against her wide blue eyes, long blonde hair and hip-swinging walk. Beth Newson was no beauty, with her heavy brows and large nose, but by Heaven she knew what to do with what God had given her. Sean McAdam fell like a poleaxed bull and they were wed three months later. Seven months after that Mary had been born, and a year later Samuel. Last Fall, Sean had decided to move his family south and they had purchased a wagon from Meneer Grimm and set off with high hopes. But the first town they reached had been hit by the Red Death. They had left swiftly, but within days Sean's huge body had been covered with red weeping sores; the glands under his arms swelled and all movement brought pain. They had camped in a high meadow and Beth tended him day and night, but despite his awesome strength Sean McAdam lost the fight for life, and Beth buried him on the hillside. Before they could move on, Samuel was struck down by the illness. Exhausted, Beth continued to nurse the boy, going without sleep and sitting by his bedside dabbing at the sores with a damp cloth. The child had pulled through, and within two weeks the sores had vanished.

Without the strength of Sean McAdam the family had pushed on, through snow and ice, through spring floods, and once across a narrow cliff trail under threat of avalanche. Beth had twice driven wolves from the six oxen, shooting one great beast dead with a single shot from Sean's double-barrelled flintlock. Samuel's pride in his mother's achievement was colossal.

Five days ago he found another source for pride when two brigands had accosted them on the road – sour-looking men, bearded and eagle-eyed. Beth laid down the reins and took up the flintlock pistol.

'Now, you scum-tars don't look too bright to me, so I'll speak slow. Give me the road or, by God, I'll send your pitiful souls straight to Hell!'

And they had. One even swept his hat from his head in an elaborate bow as she passed.

Beth smiled at the memory now, then returned her gaze to the wheel. Two problems faced her: one, finding a length of wood to use as a lever; and two, figuring out how to do both jobs – levering and fitting the wheel – herself.

Mary brought her some soup; it was thin but nourishing. Samuel made her a cup of herb tea; there was too much sugar in it, but she thanked him with a bright smile and ruffled his hair. 'You're a pair of good kids,' she said. 'For a pair of snapper-guts, that is!'

'Ma! Riders comin'!' cried Mary and Beth stood and drew the flintlock from her wide belt. She eared back the hammers and hid the weapon in the fold of her long woollen skirt. Her blue eyes narrowed as she took in the six men and she swallowed hard, determined to show no fear.

'Wait in the wagon,' she told the children. 'Do it now!' They scrambled up the tailboard and hid behind the chest.

Beth walked forward, her eyes moving from man to man, seeking the leader. He rode at the centre of the group, a tall, thin-faced rider with short-cropped grey hair and a red scar running from brow to chin. Beth smiled up at him. 'Will you not step down, sir?' she asked. The men chuckled but she ignored them, keeping her eyes fixed to Scar-face.

'Oh, we'll step down right enough,' he said. 'I'd step down into Hell for a woman with a body like yours.' Lifting his leg over the saddle pommel, he slid to the ground and advanced on her. Taking a swift step forward, she curled her left arm up over his shoulder, drawing him down to a passionate kiss. At the same time her right hand slid up between them and the cold barrels of the flintlock pressed into his groin. Beth moved her head so that her mouth was close to his ear.

'What you are feeling, pig-breath, is a gun,' she whispered. 'Now tell your men to change the wheel on the wagon. And touch nothing in it.'

'Ain't ya gonna share her, Harry?' called one rider.

For a moment Scar-face toyed with the idea of making a grab for the pistol, but he glanced down into Beth's steely blue eyes and changed his mind.

'We'll talk about it later, Quint,' he said. 'First, you boys change that wheel.'

'Change . . . we didn't ride in here to change no damned wheel!' roared Quint.

'Do it!' hissed Scar-face. 'Or I'll rip your guts out.'

The men swung down from their mounts and set to work – four of them taking the weight of the wagon and the fifth, Quint, hammering loose the wheel-pin and manhandling the broken wheel free. Beth walked Scar-face to the edge of the camp, where she ordered him to sit on a round boulder. She sat to the right of him, leaving his body between her and the working men; out of sight, the flintlock remained pressed now to his ribs.

'You're a smart bitch,' said Scar-face, 'and – except for that big nose – a pretty one. Would you really shoot me?'

'Sooner than spit,' she assured him. 'Now, when those men have finished their chore you'll send them back to wherever your camp is. Am I making myself clear, dung-brain?'

'It's done, Harry. Now do we get down to it?' called Quint.

'Ride back to camp. I'll see you there in a couple of hours.'

'Now wait a goddamned minute! You ain't keepin' the whore to yourself. No ways!' Quint turned to look to the others for support, but the men shifted nervously. Then two of them mounted their horses and the others followed.

'Dammit, Harry. It ain't fair!' protested Quint, but he backed to his mount and stepped into the saddle nevertheless.

As they rode from the camp, Beth lifted the heavy pistol from the scabbard at Scar-face's hip. Then she stood and moved away from him. The children climbed out of the wagon.

'What you going to do now, Ma?' asked Samuel. 'You gonna kill him?'

Beth passed the brigand's gun to Mary; it was a cap and ball percussion revolver. 'Get the pliers and pull off the brass caps, girl,' she said. Mary carried the gun to the wagon and opened the tool box; one by one she stripped the caps from the weapon, then returned it to her mother. Beth threw it to Scar-face and he caught it deftly and slid it home in its scabbard.

'Now what?' he asked.

'Now we wait for a while, and then you go back to your men.'

'You think I won't come back?'

'You'll think about it,' she admitted. 'Then you'll realise just how they'll laugh when you tell them I held a gun to your instrument and forced you to mend my wagon. No, you'll tell them I was one Hell of a lay and you let me ride on.'

'They'll be fightin' mad,' he said. Then he grinned. 'Sweet Jesus, but you're a woman worth fightin' over! Where you headed?'

'Pilgrim's Valley,' she told him. There was no point in lying; the wagon tracks would be easy to follow.

'See those peaks yonder? Cut to the right of them. There's a trail there – it's high and narrow, but it will save you four days. You can't miss it. A long time ago someone placed out a stone arrow, and cut signs into the trees. Follow it through and you'll find Pilgrim's Valley is around two days beyond.'

'I may just take your advice, Harry,' she said. 'Mary,

prepare some herb tea for our guest. But don't get too close to him; I'd like a clear shot if necessary.'

Mary stoked up the fire and boiled a kettle of water. She asked Harry if he took sugar, added three measures and then carried a steaming mug to within six feet of him. 'Put it on the ground,' ordered Beth. Mary did so and Harry moved to it cautiously.

He sipped the tea slowly. 'If I'm ever in Pilgrim's Valley, would you object if I called on you?' Harry asked.

'Ask me when you see me in Pilgrim's Valley,' she told him.

'Who would I ask for?'

'Beth McAdam.'

'Greatly pleased to meet you, ma'am. Harry Cooper is my name. Late of Allion and points north.'

He went to his horse and mounted. Beth watched as he rode east, then uncocked the flintlock.

Harry rode the four miles to the camp, his mind aflame with thoughts of the spirited woman. He saw the camp-fire and cantered in, ready with his tale of satisfied lust. Tying his horse to the picket line, he walked to the fire . . .

Something struck him in the back and he heard the thunder of a shot. He swung, dragging his pistol clear and cocking it. Quint rose from behind a bush and shot him a second time in the chest. Harry levelled his own gun, but the hammer clicked down on the empty nipple. Two more shots punched him from his feet and he fell back into the fire which blazed around his hair.

'Now,' said Quint. '*Now* we all share.'

6

Nu-Khasisatra eased his huge frame into the shadows of a doorway, pulling his dark cloak over his head and holding his breath. His fear rose, and he could feel his heart beating in his chest. A cloud obscured the moon and the burly shipbuilder welcomed the darkness. The Daggers were patrolling the streets and if he was caught he would be dragged to the prison buildings at the centre of the city and tortured. He would be dead by the dawn, his head impaled on a spike above the gates. Nu shivered. The sound of distant thunder rumbled above the City of Ad, and a jagged spear of lightning threw momentary shadows across the cobbled street.

Nu waited for several seconds, calming himself. His faith had carried him this far, but his courage was near exhausted.

'Be with me, Lord Chronos,' he prayed. 'Strengthen my failing limbs.'

He stepped out on to the street, ears straining for any sound that might warn him of the approach of the Daggers. He swallowed hard; the night was silent, the curfew complete. He moved on as silently as he could until he reached Bali's high-towered home. The gate was locked and he waited in the shadows, watching the moon rise. At the prearranged hour he heard the bolt slide open. Stepping into the courtyard beyond, he sank to a seat as his friend shut the gate, locking it tight.

Bali touched a finger to his lips and led the dark-cloaked Nu into the house. The shutters were closed and curtains had been hung over the windows. Bali lit a lantern and placed it on an oval table.

'Peace be upon this house,' said Nu. The smaller Bali nodded his bald head and smiled.

'And the Lord bless my guest and friend,' he answered.

The two men sat at the table and drank a little wine; then Bali leaned back and gazed at his friend of twenty years. Nu-Khasisatra had not changed in that time. His beard was still rich and black, his eyes bright blue and ageless beneath thick jutting brows. Both men had managed to purchase Sipstrassi fragments at least twice to restore youth and health. But Bali had fallen on hard times, his wealth disappearing with the loss in storms at sea of three of his prize ships, and now he was beginning to show the signs of age. He appeared to be in his sixties, though he was in fact eighty years older than Nu, who was one hundred and ten. Nu had tried to acquire more Sipstrassi, but the King had gathered almost all the Stones to himself and even a fragment would now cost all of Nu's wealth.

'You must leave the city,' Bali said, breaking the silence. 'The King has signed a warrant for your immediate arrest.'

'I know. I was foolish to speak against him in the temple, but I have prayed hard and I know the Great One was speaking through me.'

'The Law of One is no more, my friend. The Sons of Belial have the ears of the King. How is Pashad?'

'I ordered her to denounce me this morning, and seek the severing of the Knot. She at least will be safe, as will my sons.'

'No one is safe, Nu. No one. The King is insane, the slaughter has begun . . . even as you prophesied it. There is madness in the streets – and these Daggers fill me with terror.'

'There is worse to come,' Nu told him sadly. 'In my prayer dreams I have seen terrible sights: three suns in the sky at one time, the heavens tearing, and the seas rising to swamp the clouds. I know it is close, Bali, and I am powerless to prevent it.'

'Many men have dreams that do not presage evil days,' said Bali.

Nu shook his head. 'I know this. But my dreams have all come true so far. The Lord of All Things is sending these visions. I know he has ordered me to warn the people, and

I know also that they will ignore me. But it is not for me to question His purpose.'

Bali poured another goblet of wine and said nothing. Nu-Khasisatra had always been a man of iron principles and faith, devout and honest. Bali liked and respected him. He did not share his principles, but he had come to know his God – and for that gift alone, he would give his life for the shipbuilder.

Opening a hidden drawer below the table, he removed a small purse of embroidered deerskin. For a moment he held it, reluctant to part with it, then he smiled and pushed it across the table.

'For you, my friend,' he said. Nu picked it up and felt the warmth emanating from within the purse. Then he opened it with trembling fingers and tipped out the Stone within. It was not a fragment but a whole Stone, round as if polished, golden with thin black veins. He closed his hand around it, feeling the power surging in him. Gently he placed it on the table top and gazed at the bald, elderly man before him.

'With this you could be young again, Bali. You could live for a thousand years. Why? Why would you give it to me?'

'Because you need it, Nu. And because I never had a friend before.'

'But it is worth perhaps ten times as much money as is contained in the entire city. I could not possibly accept it.'

'You must. It is life. The Daggers are seeking you and you know what that means. Torture and death. They have closed the city and you cannot escape, save by the Journey. There is a gateway within the stone circle the princes used to use, to the north of the seventh square. You know it? By the crystal lake? Good. Go there. Use these words and hold the Stone high.' He passed Nu a small square of parchment.

'The Enchantment will take you to Balacris. From there you will be on your own.'

'I have funds in Balacris,' said Nu, 'but the Lord wants me to stay and continue to warn the people.'

'You gave me the secret of the Great One,' Bali told him,

'and I accept His will overrides any wishes of our own. But similarly you have done as He commanded. You gave your warnings, but their ears were closed to you. Added to this, Nu my friend, I prayed for a way in which I might help you, and now this Stone has come into my possession. And yes, I wanted to keep it, but the Great One touched me and let me know it was for you.'

'How did you come by it?'

'An Achean trader brought it to my shop. He thought it was a gold nugget and wished to sell it to me in return for the money to buy a new sail.'

'A sail? With this you could buy a thousand sails, perhaps more.'

'I told him it was worth half the price of a sail, and he sold it to me for sixty pieces of silver.' Bali shrugged. 'It was with such dealings that I first became rich. You must go now. The Daggers surely know we are friends.'

'Come with me, Bali,' Nu urged. 'With this Stone we could reach my new ship. We could sail far from the reach of the King and his Daggers.'

'No. My place is here. My life is here. My death will be here.' Bali rose and led the way to the gate. 'One thing more,' he told his friend as they stood in the moonlight. 'Last night, as I held the Stone I had a strange dream. I saw a man in golden armour. He came to me and sat beside me. He gave me a message for you; he said you must seek the Sword of God. Does it mean anything to you?'

'Nothing. Did you recognise him?'

'No. His face shone like the sun, and I could not look at him.'

'The Great One will make it plain to me,' said Nu as he reached out to embrace the smaller man. 'May He watch over you, Bali.'

'And you, my friend.'

Bali silently opened the gate and peered out into the shadows. 'It is clear,' he whispered. 'Go quickly.'

Nu embraced him once more, then stepped into the shadows and was gone. Bali re-bolted the gate and returned to his room, where he sank into his chair and tried to repress his regrets. With the Stone he could have rebuilt his empire and enjoyed eternal youth. Without it? Penury and death.

He moved back into the main house, stepping over the body of the Achean sailor who had brought him the Stone. Bali had not even possessed the sixty silver pieces the man had requested, but he still owned a knife with a sharp blade.

The sound of crashing timber caused him to spin and run back towards the garden. He arrived to see the gate on its hinges and three dark-armoured Daggers moving towards him, their reptilian eyes gleaming in the moonlight, their scaled skin glistening.

'What . . . what do you want?' asked Bali, trembling.

'Where iss hee?'

'Who?'

Two of the Daggers moved around the garden, sucking the air through their slitted nostrils.

'He wass here,' hissed one of them and Bali backed away. One of the Daggers lifted a strangely shaped club from a scabbard at his side, pointing it at the little trader.

'Lasst chance. Where iss he?'

'Where you will never find him,' said Bali, and drawing his knife he leapt at the Dagger. A sound like thunder came from the small club in the reptile's hand, and a hammer smote Bali in the chest. The little man was hurled on his back to the path where he lay sprawled, staring sightlessly up at the stars.

A second shot sounded and the Dagger pitched to the ground, a black hole in his wedge-shaped head. The other creatures spun to see the golden-haired woman, Sharazad.

'I wanted Bali alive,' she said softly. 'And my orders will be obeyed.'

Behind her a dozen more Daggers crowded into the garden.

'Search the house,' she ordered. 'Rip it apart. If Nu-Khasisatra escapes, I will see you all flayed alive.'

7

Of all the seasons God had granted it was the Spring that Shannow loved above others, with its heady music of life and growth, its chorus of bird-song and richly coloured flowers pushing back the snow. The air too was clean and a man could drink it in like wine, filling his lungs with the essence of life itself.

Shannow dismounted before the crest of a hill and walked to the summit, gazing out over the rippling grass of the plain. Then he squatted on the ground and scanned the rolling lands before him. In the far distance he could see a wandering herd of cattle, and to the west several mountain sheep grazing on a hillside. He moved back from the skyline and studied the back-trail through the mountain valley, memorising the jagged peaks and the narrow ways he had passed. He did not expect to return this way, but if he did he needed to be sure of his bearings. He unbuckled the thick belt which carried his gun scabbards and removed his heavy topcoat, then swung the guns around his hips once more and buckled the belt in place before rolling his coat and tying it behind his saddle. The stallion was contentedly cropping grass and Shannow loosened the saddle cinch.

Taking his Bible he sat with his back to a boulder, slowly reading the story of King Saul. He always found it hard to avoid sympathising with the first King of Israel. The man had fought hard and well to make the nation strong, only to have a usurper preparing to steal his crown. Even at the end, when God deserted him, Saul still fought gallantly against the enemy and died alongside his sons in a great battle.

Shannow closed the book and took a long cool drink from his canteen. His wounds were almost healed now, and last night he had cut the stitches with the blade of his hunting-knife. Although he could not yet move his right arm with customary speed, his strength was returning.

He tightened the saddle and rode out on to the plain. Here and there were the tracks of horses, cattle and deer. He rode warily, watching the horizon, constantly hitching himself in the saddle to study the trail behind.

The plain stretched on endlessly and the far blue mountains to the south seemed small and insubstantial. A bird suddenly flew up to Shannow's left. His eyes fastened to it and he realised that he was following its flight with the barrel of his pistol; the weapon was cocked and ready. He eased the hammer back into place and sheathed the gun.

A long time ago he would have been delighted with the speed at which he reacted to possible danger, but bitter experience had long since corroded his pride. He had been attacked outside Allion by several men and had killed them all; then a sound from behind had caused him to swivel and fire ... and he had killed a child who happened to be in the wrong place at the wrong time.

That child would have been a grown man by now, with children of his own. A farmer, a builder, a preacher? No one would ever know. Shannow tried to push the memory from his mind, but it clung to him with talons of fire.

Who would want to be you, Shannow? he asked himself. *Who would want to be the Jerusalem Man?*

The children of Allion had followed him during his nightly tours, copying the smooth straight-backed walk. They carried wooden guns thrust in their belts and they worshipped him; they thought it wonderful to be so respected and feared, to have a name that travelled the land ahead of you.

Is it wonderful, Shannow?

The people of Allion had been grateful when Jon Shannow put the brigands to flight – or buried them. But when the town was clean they had paid him and asked him to move on. And the brigands returned, as they always did. And perhaps the children followed *them* around, copying their walks and fighting pretend battles with their wooden guns.

How far to Jerusalem, Shannow?

'Over the next mountain,' he answered aloud. The stallion's ears pricked up and he snorted. Shannow chuckled as he patted the beast's neck and urged him into a run over the level ground. It was not a sensible move, he knew; a rabbit-hole or a loose rock could cause the horse to stumble and break a leg, or throw a shoe. But the wind in his face felt good and life was never without perils.

He let the horse have his head for about a half mile, then drew back on the reins as he saw wagon tracks. They were fresh, maybe two days old; Shannow dismounted and examined them. The wheels had bit deep into the dry earth – a family moving south with all their possessions. Silently he wished them good fortune and remounted.

By mid-afternoon he came upon the broken wheel. By now he knew a little of the family: there were two children and a woman. The children had gathered sticks and dried cattle droppings for fuel, probably depositing them in a net slung under the tailboard. The woman had walked beside the lead oxen; her feet were small, but her stride long. There was no sign of a man but then, thought Shannow, perhaps he is lazy and rides in the wagon. The broken wheel, though, was a mystery.

Shannow studied the tracks of the horsemen. They had ridden to the camp and changed the wheel, then returned the way they had come. The woman had stood close to one of the riders, and they had walked together to a boulder. By the wagon tracks Shannow found six brass caps, still with their fulminates intact. At some time during the encounter someone had unloaded a pistol. Why?

He built a fire on the ashes of the old one and sat pondering the problem. Perhaps the caps were old and the woman – for he knew now there was no man with them – had doubted their effectiveness. But if the caps were old, then so would be the wads and charges and these had not been stripped clear. He read the track signs once more, but could make no more of them – save that one of the horsemen had ridden to the right of the main group, or had left at a different time. Shannow walked out along the trail and a hundred paces from the camp he saw a hoofprint from the lone horse which had overstamped a previous print. So then, the lone rider had left *after* the main group. He had obviously sat talking with the woman. Why did they not all stay?

He prepared himself some tea, and ate the last of the fruit from Shir-ran's store. As he delved at the bottom of the sack his fingers touched something cold and metallic and he drew it out. It was like a coin, but made of gold, and upon the surface was a raised motif that Shannow could not make out in the gathering dusk. He tucked the coin into his pocket and settled down beside the fire. But the tracks had disturbed him and sleep would not come; the moon was bright and he rose, saddled the stallion and rode off after the horsemen.

When he came to their camp-site they were gone, but a man lay with his head in the ashes of a dead fire, his face burned. He had been shot several times and his boots and gun were missing, though the belt and scabbard remained. Shannow was about to return to his horse when he heard a groan. He could hardly believe life still survived in that ruined body. Unhooking his canteen from the saddle, he knelt by the man, lifting the burnt head.

The man's eyes opened. 'They gone after the woman,' he whispered. Shannow held the canteen to his lips, but he choked and could not swallow. He said no more and Shannow waited for the inevitable. The man died within minutes.

Something glinted to Shannow's right. Under a bush, where it must have fallen, lay the man's gun. Shannow retrieved it. The caps had been removed; he had no chance to defend himself against the attack. Shannow pondered the evidence. The men were obviously brigands who had shot down one of their own. Why? Over the woman? But they had all been at the camp. Why leave?

A group of men had come across a woman and two

children by a wagon with a broken wheel. They had mended the wheel and left – save one, who followed after. His pistol had been tampered with. But then surely he would have known that? When he arrived his . . . friends? . . . had shot him. Then they had headed back to the woman. There was no sense in it . . . unless he had stopped them from taking the woman in the first place. But then, why would he unload his gun before returning?

There was only one way to find out.

Shannow stepped into the saddle and searched for the tracks.

*

'Why did God kill my Dad?' asked Samuel, as he dipped his flat baked bread in the last of his broth. Beth put aside her own plate and looked across the camp-fire at the boy, his face white in the moonlight, his blond hair shining like silver threads.

'God didn't kill him, Sam. The Red Fever done that.'

'But the Preacher used to say that nobody died unless God wanted them to. Then they went to Heaven or Hell.'

'That's what the Preacher believes,' she said slowly, 'but it don't necessarily mean it's true. The Preacher used to say that Holy Jesus died less than four hundred years ago, and then the world toppled. But your Dad didn't believe that, did he? He said there were thousands of years between then and now. You remember?'

'Maybe that's why God killed him,' said Samuel, ''cos he didn't believe the Preacher.'

'Ain't nothin' in life that easy,' Beth told him. 'There's wicked men that God don't kill, and there's good men – like your Pa – who die out of their time. That's just life, Samuel; it don't come with no promises.'

Mary, who had said nothing throughout, cleared away the dishes, carrying them beyond the camp-site and scrubbing them with grass. Beth stood and stretched her back. 'You've a lot still to learn, Samuel,' she said. 'You want something, then you have to fight for it. You don't give ground, and you don't whinge and whine. You take your knocks and you get on with living. Now help your sister clear up, and put that fire out.'

'But it's cold, Ma,' Samuel protested. 'Couldn't we just sleep out here with the fire?'

'The fire can be seen for miles. You want them raiders coming back?'

'But they helped us with the wheel?'

'Put out the fire, snapper-gut!' she stormed and the boy leapt to his feet and began to kick earth over the blaze. Beth walked away to the wagon and stood staring out over the plain. She didn't know if there was a God, and she didn't care. God had not helped her mother against the brutality of the man she married – and, sure as sin, God had never helped her. Such a shame, she thought. It would have been nice to feel her children were safe under the security of a benign deity, with the faith that all their troubles could be safely left to a supreme being.

She remembered the terrible beating her mother had suffered the day she died; could still hear the awful sounds of fists on flesh. She had watched as he dragged her body out to the waste ground behind the house, and listened as the spade bit into the earth for an unmarked grave. He had staggered back into the house and stared at her, his hands filthy and his eyes red-streaked. Then he had drunk himself into a stupor and fallen asleep in the heavy chair. 'Jus' you an' me now,' he mumbled. The carving-knife had slid across his throat and he had died without waking.

Beth shook her head and stared up at the stars, her eyes misting with unaccustomed tears. She glanced back at the children, as they spread their blankets on the warm ground beside the dead fire. Sean McAdam had not been a bad man, but she did not miss him as they did. He had learned early on that his wife did not love him, but he had doted on his children, played with them, taught them, helped them. So devoted had he been that he had not noticed his wife's affection growing, not until close to the end when he had lain, almost paralysed, in the wagon.

'Sorry, Beth,' he whispered.

'Nothin' to be sorry for. Rest and get well.'

For an hour or more he had slept, then his eyes opened and his hand trembled and lifted from the blanket. She took hold of it, squeezing it firmly. 'I love you,' he said. 'God's truth.'

She stared at him hard. 'I know. Sleep. Go to sleep.'

'I . . . didn't do too bad . . . by you and the kids, did I?'

'Stop talkin' like that,' she ordered. 'You'll feel better in the morning.'

He shook his head. 'It's over, Beth. I'm hanging by a thread. Tell me? Please?'

'Tell you what?'

'Just tell me . . .' His eyes closed and his breathing became shallow.

She held his hand to her breast and leaned in close. 'I love you, Sean. I do. God knows I do. Now please get well.'

He had slipped away in the night while the children were sleeping. Beth sat with him for some time, but then considered the effect on the children of seeing their father's corpse. So she had dragged the body from the wagon and dug a grave on the hillside while they slept.

Lost in her memories now she did not hear Mary approach. The child laid her hand on her mother's shoulder and Beth turned and instinctively took her in her arms.

'Don't fret, Mary love. Nothing's going to happen.'

'I miss my Pa. I wish we were still back home.'

'I know,' said Beth, stroking the child's long auburn hair. 'But if wishes were horses then beggars would ride. We just got to move on.' She pushed the girl from her. 'Now, it's important you remember what I showed you today, and do it. There's no tellin' how many bad men there are 'twixt here and Pilgrim's Valley. And I need you, Mary. Can I trust you?'

'Sure you can, Ma.'

'Good girl. Now get to bed.'

Beth stayed awake for several hours, listening to the wind over the grass of the plain, watching the stars gliding by.

Two hours before dawn she woke Mary. 'Don't fall asleep, girl. You watch for any riders and wake me if you see them.'

Then she lay down and fell into a dreamless sleep. It seemed to last for only a few moments before Mary was shaking her, but the sun was clearing the eastern horizon as Beth blinked and pushed one hand through her blonde hair.

'Riders, Ma. I think it's the same men.'

'Get in the wagon. And remember what I told you.'

Beth lifted the flintlock pistol and cocked both barrels; then she hid the gun once more in the folds of her skirt and scanned the group for sign of Harry. He wasn't with them. She took a deep breath and steadied herself as the horsemen thundered into the camp and the man she remembered as Quint leapt from the saddle.

'Now, Missy,' he said. 'We'll have a little of what old Harry enjoyed.'

Beth raised the flintlock. Quint stopped in his tracks. She loosed the first barrel and the ball took Quint just above his nose, ploughing through his skull. He fell back into the dust with blood pumping from a fatal wound in his head as Beth stepped forward.

The sudden explosion had alarmed the horses and the four remaining riders fought to settle them as Quint's mount galloped out over the plain. In the silence that followed, the men glanced at one another. Beth's voice cut into them.

'You whoresons have two choices: ride, or die. And make the choice fast. I start shooting when I stop speaking.' The gun rose and pointed at the nearest man.

'Whoa there, lady!' the rider shouted. 'I'm leaving.'

'You can't take all of us, bitch!' shouted another, spurring his horse. But a tremendous explosion came from the wagon and the brigand was whipped from the saddle, half his head blown away.

'Any other doubters?' asked Beth. 'Move!'

The three survivors dragged on the reins and galloped away. Beth ran to the wagon, took her powder horn and reloaded the flintlock. Mary climbed down from the tailboard with the shortened rifle in her arms.

'You did well, Mary,' said Beth, ramming home the wad over the ball and charge. 'I'm proud of you.'

She took the rifle and leaned it against the wagon, then cradled the trembling child in her arms. 'There, there. It's all right. Go and sit at the front; don't look at them.' Beth guided Mary to the driving platform and helped her up, then walked back to the bodies. Unbuckling Quint's pistol belt, she strapped it to her own waist and then searched the body for powder and ammunition. She found a small hide sack of caps and transferred them to the wagon, then took a second pistol from the other body and hid it behind the driver's seat. Sean McAdam had never been able to afford a revolving pistol; now they had two. Beth gathered the oxen, hitched them to the wagon and then walked to the brigand's horse, a bay mare, and pulled herself into the saddle. Awkwardly she rode alongside where Mary sat.

'Take up the reins, child. And let's move.'

Samuel clambered up beside Mary and grinned at his mother. 'You look just like a brigand, Ma.'

Beth smiled back at him, then transferred her gaze to Mary who was sitting white-faced, staring ahead.

'Take the reins, Mary, goddammit!' The girl flinched and unhooked them from the brake. 'Now let's go!' Mary flicked the reins and Beth rode up alongside the lead ox and whacked her palm across its rump.

High above, the carrion birds had begun to circle.

8

Nu-Khasisatra reached the old stone circle an hour before dawn. He waited, hidden in the trees, searching for any guards who might be patrolling here, but there were none that he could see. Under the bright moonlight he studied the words on the parchment, memorising them. Then, Stone in hand, he ran from the trees on to the open ground before the circle.

At once there was a thin, piercing whistle. Shadows darted for him and a woman's voice cried out: 'Alive! Take him alive!'

Nu sprinted for the stone circle, its tall grey slabs promising sanctuary. A reptilean figure in black armour ran into his path but Nu swung his huge fist into the creature's face, dashing him to the grass. Hurdling the falling body, he made it to the shadows of the stones. Once there, he swung to see more Daggers closing on him.

He lifted his hand. *'Barak naizi tor lemmes!'* he shouted. Lightning flashed across his eyes, blinding him, and his mind was filled with whirling colours. All sense of weight and strength left him, and he tumbled like a wind-blown feather into a storm. With a sickening lurch he felt the ground under his feet, stumbled and fell. His eyes opened, but at first he could see nothing save flickering lights. Then his vision cleared and he found himself in a small clearing. Close by was a dead man, his face hideously burnt. Nu got to his feet and moved to the body. The man was wearing strange apparel and he studied it; the clothing was unlike anything he had encountered. He walked out of the clearing and stared at the surrounding landscape. There was no city of Balacris, no view of a distant ocean. Grasslands drifted to a blurred horizon where jagged mountains soared to meet the sky.

Returning to the clearing, Nu sat and examined his Stone. The black veins in the gold had swelled. He had no way of knowing how much power the journey had sucked from the Sipstrassi.

Moving to his knees, Nu-Khasisatra began to pray. For some time he gave thanks for his deliverance from the hands of Sharazad and her Daggers; then he asked for his family to be protected. Finally he sought the silence in which the voice of God could be heard.

The wind whispered about him, but he heard no words within it. Sunlight bathed his face, but no visions came. At last he stood. It would be safer, he knew, if his clothing matched that of the people of this land. The Stone glowed warm in his hand, and his robes and cloak shimmered and changed. Now he was wearing trousers and boots, shirt and long jacket identical to those of the dead man.

'Be careful, Nu,' he warned himself. 'Do not waste the power.'

He recalled the words of Bali: 'Seek the Sword of God.' He had no idea in which direction to travel, but looking down at the ground he saw the tracks of a horse, heading towards the mountains. With no other omen to guide him, Nu-Khasisatra followed them.

*

Sharazad sat at an ornate table, her ice-blue eyes locked to the face of Pashad, wife of the traitor Nu-Khasisatra.

'You denounced your husband yesterday. Why?'

'I discovered he was plotting against the King,' she answered, averting her eyes and gazing at the surface of the desk on which lay a curious white-handled ornament of silver.

'With whom was he plotting?'

'The merchant, Bali, Highness. He was the only one I knew.'

'You know that the family of a traitor shares his sentence?' whispered the golden-haired inquisitor and Pashad nodded.

'Yet he had not been declared a traitor when I denounced

him, Highness. Also, I am no longer of his family, for after denouncing him I divorced him.'

'So you did. Where is he hiding?'

'I do not know, Highness. The list of our property was taken this morning. There are only five houses, and three store buildings by the dock. Other than that, I cannot help you.'

Sharazad smiled. Then reaching into the pocket of her pearl-embroidered tunic, she drew out a red-gold stone and placed it upon the desk. Three words of power she uttered. 'Place your hand over the stone,' she told the slim, dark-haired girl before her. Pashad did so.

'Now I will ask you some more questions, but I want you to be aware that if you lie the stone will kill you instantly. Do you understand this?'

Pashad nodded, but her eyes showed her fear.

'Do you know the whereabouts of the man, Nu-Khasisatra?'

'I do not.'

'Do you know the names of any of his friends who may have been involved in the plot?'

'That is difficult to answer,' said Pashad, sweat glistening on her brow. 'I know some of his ... friends, but I would have no way of knowing whether they shared his treason.'

'Do you share his treason?'

'No. I do not understand any of it. How can I tell if the King is a god? My life has been spent in making my husband happy and raising his children. What should it matter to us whether the King is a god or not?'

'If you did know the whereabouts of the man, Nu-Khasisatra, would you tell me?'

'Yes,' answered Pashad. 'Instantly.'

Sharazad's surprise was genuine. Lifting Pashad's hand, she took the stone and replaced it in her pocket.

'You are free to go,' she said. 'If you hear any news of the traitor, then make sure I know of it.'

'I will, Highness.'

Sharazad watched the woman leave and then leaned back

in her chair. A curtain by the left wall parted and a young man stepped through – tall and wide-shouldered, yet slim of hip. He grinned and sat down in a nearby chair, lifting his booted foot to rest on the table.

'You owe me,' he said. 'I told you she would know nothing.'

'Always so smug, Rhodaeul?' she snapped. 'But I am somewhat taken aback. From all I have heard of this shipbuilder, he adored his wife. I would have expected him to have taken her into his confidence.'

'He's a careful man. Have you any idea where he has gone?'

'Yes,' she said, smiling, 'as a matter of fact, I have. You see, the Circle has been linked to the world we discovered two months ago. Nu-Khasisatra thought he was escaping, but instead he has travelled to our latest field of conquest. It is the land that has brought us these strange weapons.' She lifted the pistol from the desk-top and tossed it to Rhodaeul; it was silver-plated, with grips of carved white bone. 'The King wishes you to become proficient with these . . . these guns.'

'Will he equip the army with them?'

'No. The King believes them to be vulgar. But my Daggers will prove their potency in war.'

Rhodaeul nodded. 'And Nu-Khasisatra?'

'He is stranded in that strange land. He does not speak the language, nor does he know a way back. I will find him.'

'So sure of yourself, Sharazad? Beware!'

'Do not mock me, Rhodaeul. If I am arrogant, it is with good cause. The King knows my talents.'

'We all know your talents, dear Sharazad. Some of us have even enjoyed them. But the King is right. These weapons are vulgar beyond description; there is no honour in despatching an enemy with such a monstrosity.'

'You fool! You think there is more honour in an arrow, or a lance? They are merely weapons of death.'

'A clever man can dodge an arrow, Sharazad, or sidestep a lance. But with these, death strikes a man unawares. And their mastery takes no skill.' He walked to the window and stepped out into the courtyard beyond. Two prisoners were tied to stakes; wood had been piled around their feet and legs.

'Where is the skill?' asked Rhodaeul, cocking the pistol smoothly. Two shots rang out and the victims at the stakes sagged against their ropes. 'All a man needs is a good eye and a swift hand. But with the sword, there are over forty different variations on the classic block and riposte, sixty if you count the sabre. But – if it is the King's wish – I will learn how to handle the thing.'

'It is the King's wish, Rhodaeul. Perhaps you will be able to polish your skills in my new world. There are men there who are legends because of their skill with such weapons. I will hunt them down for you, and have them brought back for your . . . education.'

'How sweet of you, Sharazad. I will look forward to it. Can you give me a name to disturb my dreams?'

'There are several. Johnson is one, Crowe another. Then there is Daniel Cade. But above them all, there is a man called Jon Shannow. They say he seeks a mythical city and they call him the Jerusalem Man.'

'Bring them all, Sharazad. Since our conquests in the north, we have been sadly lacking in good sport.'

9

Shannow knew from the moment he set off in pursuit that he would be too late to help the woman and her family, and anger burned in him. Even so he rode with care, for in the light of the moon he could not clearly see the ground ahead. It was dawn before he came upon the bodies; they had been disturbed by carrion-eaters, the faces and hands stripped of flesh. Shannow sat his horse and stared down at them.

His respect for the unknown woman soared. Dismounting he examined the ground, finding the spot from which Beth McAdam had fired. Judging by the angle at which the other corpse lay, the second shot must have come from the wagon. Shannow remounted and headed towards the mountains.

The land rose sharply, becoming thickly wooded with towering pine. The stallion was tired and stumbled twice; Shannow stepped down and led the horse up and into the trees. They came to a crest on the mountainside and Shannow gazed down on a sprawling camp with six fires and a dozen tents. Men were working under torchlight in an immense pit from which jutted a towering structure of metal, almost triangular but with one side slightly curved. There was a wide stream to the south of the camp and, beside it, a wagon. The Jerusalem Man led his mount down into the camp-site, tethering him at a picket line and removing the saddle. A man approached him.

'You got word from Scayse?' the man asked, and Shannow turned.

'No. I've just come in from the north.' The man swore and walked away.

Shannow made his way to the largest tent and stepped into the lantern-lit interior. There were a dozen or so men inside, eating and drinking, while a large-boned, well-fleshed woman in a leather apron was ladling food into round wooden bowls. He joined the queue and took a bowl of thick broth and a chunk of black bread, carrying it to a bench table near the tent opening. Two men made room for him and he ate in silence.

'Looking for work?' asked a man across the table and Shannow looked up. The speaker was around thirty years of age, slender and fair-haired.

'No . . . thank you. I am heading south,' Shannow replied. 'Can I purchase supplies here?'

'You could see Deiker, he may have some spare. He's on site at the moment; he should be in any time now.'

'What are you working on?'

'It's an old metal building from before the Fall. We've found some interesting artefacts. Nothing of great value yet, but we're hopeful. It has given us a great insight into the Dark Times; they must have been living in fear to build such a great iron fortress here.'

'Why in fear?' Shannow asked.

'Oh, you can only see a section of the building from here. It goes on and on. There are no windows or doors for over a hundred feet from the foundation base, and then when you do find them they are too small to allow anyone to climb through. They must have had terrible wars in those days. By the way, my name is Klaus Monet.' The young man thrust out his hand and Shannow accepted the grip.

'Jon Shannow,' he said, watching for any response. There was none.

'And another thing,' Monet went on. 'It is all built of iron, and yet there are no significant iron ore deposits in these mountains, nor trace of any mines – save the silver mines at Pilgrim's Valley. So, the inhabitants must have carted ore right across the Big Wide. Incredible, isn't it?'

'Incredible,' agreed Shannow, finishing his meal and rising.

Outside the tent he walked to the edge of the pit and watched the men below; they were finishing their work and packing their tools away. He waited until they reached the upper level.

'Meneer Deiker!' Shannow called.

'Who wants him?' asked a thickset man with a black and silver beard.

'I do. I am looking to buy some supplies – grain, dried fruit and meat. And some oats if you have them.'

'For how many?'

'Just myself.'

The man nodded. 'I think I can accommodate you, but Pilgrim's Valley is only two days away. You'd get better prices there.'

'Always take food where you can find it,' Shannow said.

'There's wisdom in that,' Deiker agreed. He led Shannow to the store tents and filled several small sacks. 'You want sugar and salt?'

'If you can spare it. How long have you been working on this site?'

'About a month; it's one of the best. There will be a lot of answers here, mark my words.'

'And you think it is a building?'

'What else can it be?' asked Deiker, with a broad grin.

'It is a ship,' Shannow told him.

'I like a man with a sense of humour, Meneer. I estimate that it is over three hundred feet long – most of it still buried. And it is made of iron. Did you ever see anyone float a piece of iron?'

'No, but I have seen an iron ship before – and considerably bigger than this one.'

Deiker shook his head. 'I am an Arcanist, Meneer. I know my business. I also know you do not get ships at the centre of a land mass. That will be three full Silvers.'

Shannow said no more but paid for the food with Barta coin and carried it back to his saddle, stowing it in his cavernous bags. Then he walked back through the camp towards the wagon by the stream. He saw a woman sitting by a blazing fire with her two children asleep in blankets by her feet.

She looked up as he approached and he watched her hand slide towards the pistol scabbard on her belt.

*

Beth McAdam looked long at the tall newcomer. His hair was shoulder-length and dark, with silver streaks at the temples, and a white fork at the chin showed in the close-trimmed beard he wore. His face was angular and strong, his blue eyes cold. By his side were two pistols in oiled leather scabbards.

He sat down opposite her. 'You coped well with a perilous journey. I congratulate you. Very few people would have dared to cross the Big Wide without the protection of a wagon convoy.'

'You get straight to it, don't you?' she said.

'I do not understand you?'

'Well, I do not need a guide, or a helper, or a man around me. Thank you for your offer. And good night.'

'Have I offended you?' Shannow asked softly, his blue eyes locked to her own.

'I don't offend easily. Neither do you, it seems.'

He scratched at his beard and smiled; in that moment his face lost some of its harshness. 'No, I do not. If you would prefer me to leave, I will do so.'

'Help yourself to some tea,' she said. 'After that, I would like some privacy.'

'That is kind of you.' As he leaned forward to lift the kettle he froze, then stood, turning to face the darkness. Two men walked into the firelight; Beth eased her hand around the butt of her pistol.

'Meneer Shannow, do you have a moment?' asked Klaus Monet. 'There is someone I would like you to meet.' He gestured to his companion, a small, balding figure with a sparse white beard. 'This is Boris Haimut; he is a leading Arcanist.' The man dropped his head in a short bow and offered his hand. Shannow took it.

'Meneer Deiker told me of your conversation,' said Haimut. 'I was fascinated. I have thought for some time that we were studying a vessel of some kind, but it seemed so improbable. We have only excavated some one-fifth of the ... the ship. Do you have an explanation as to how it got here?'

'Yes,' replied Shannow. 'But I fear we are intruding on the lady's privacy.'

'But of course,' agreed Haimut. 'My apologies, Frey ...'

'McAdam. And Meneer Shannow is correct; I do not wish the sleep of my children disturbed.'

The three men bowed and silently left the camp-site. Beth watched them vanish into the shadows and then reappear on the torch-lit slopes of the site.

She poured herself some tea and sipped it, Shannow's face hovering in her mind. Was he brigand or Landsman? She shook her thoughts clear of him. What difference did it make? She would not see him again. Throwing the remains of her tea to the ground, she settled down under her blankets.

But sleep did not come easily.

*

'You have to understand, Meneer Shannow,' said Boris Haimut with an apologetic smile, 'that Meneer Deiker is Oldview. He is a Biblical man and believes the world is currently enduring the Last Days. To him Armageddon was a reality that began – to the best of our knowledge – three hundred and seventeen years ago. For myself, I am a Longview scholar. It is my belief that we have seen at least a thousand years of civilisation following the death of the man, Jesus; that civilisation knew wonders that are now lost to us. This find has already cast great doubts on the Oldview. If it is a ship ... the doubts could become certainties.'

Shannow sat silently, uncomfortable within the small tent and acutely aware that the bright lantern was casting shadows on the canvas. He knew he should be in little danger here, but years of being both hunter and hunted left him uneasy when sitting in exposed places.

'I can tell you little, Meneer,' he said. 'More than a

thousand miles from here is a tall mountain. High on a ledge there is a rotting vessel of iron, around a thousand feet long. It was a ship – I learned this from people who lived close by it and knew its history. It seems this land mass was once at the bottom of an ocean, and many ships sank during storms.'

'But the ancient cities we have found?' questioned Haimut. 'There are even ruins less than two miles from here. How is it they were built at the bottom of an ocean?'

'I too wondered this. Then I met a man named Samuel Archer – a scholar like yourself. He proved to me that the world had toppled not once, but twice. The cities themselves are indeed ancient – from an empire called Atlantis that sank below the oceans before the time of Christ.'

'Revolutionary words, Meneer. In some areas you could be stoned to death for saying them.'

'I am aware of that,' said Shannow. 'However, when you excavate more of the ship you will find the great engines that powered it, and a wheelhouse from where it was steered. Now, if you will excuse me, I need to rest.'

'A moment, sir,' put in Klaus Monet, who had been sitting in silence as the two older men spoke. 'Would you stay with us – become part of the team?'

'I do not think so,' answered Shannow, rising.

'It is just that . . .' Monet looked to the elderly Haimut for support, but the scholar shook his head and Monet lapsed into embarrassed silence.

Shannow stepped from the tent and made his way to his horse. He fed the beast some grain, then spread his blankets on the ground beside it. He could have told them more: the glowing lights that burned without flame, the navigational devices – all the knowledge he had gained from the Guardians during the Hellborn War. But what would it serve? Shannow was caught in the no-man's land of the Arcane debate.

Instinctively he longed for the Oldview to be correct, but events had forced a different understanding on him. The old world was gone. Shannow had no wish to see it rise from the ashes.

Just as he was drifting to sleep, he heard a gentle footfall on the earth. He drew a pistol and waited.

The slender figure of Klaus Monet crouched beside him. 'I am sorry to intrude on you, Meneer Shannow. But... you seem a man of action, sir. And we sorely need someone like you.'

Shannow sat up. 'Explain yourself.'

Monet leaned in close. 'This expedition was led by Boris; we won the finance from a group of Longviewers in the east. But since we have been here, a man named Scayse has become involved in the project. He has put his own men – led by Deiker – in charge, and now some of the finds are being sent to him in Pilgrim's Valley.'

'What kind of finds?'

'Gold bars, gems from steel boxes in one of the deep rooms. It is theft, Meneer Shannow.'

'Then put a stop to it,' Shannow advised.

'I am a scholar, sir.'

'Then study – and do not interfere with matters beyond your strength.'

'You would condone such thievery?'

Shannow chuckled. 'Thievery? Who owns this ship? No one. Therefore there is no theft. Two groups of men desire what is here. The strongest will take what he wills. That is the way of life, Meneer Monet; strength always decides.'

'But with you, we would be stronger.'

'Perhaps... but you will never know. I leave in the morning.'

'Are you afraid, Meneer Shannow, or do you just desire more coin? We can pay.'

'You could not afford me, sir. Now leave me to sleep.'

The morning sky was grey and rain on his face woke Shannow soon after dawn. He rose from his blankets and rolled them into a tight bundle, tying them with strips of oiled hide. Then he put on his heavy, double-shouldered topcoat and saddled the stallion. Two men came walking towards him through the misty rain and Shannow turned and waited.

'Looks like you beat us to it,' said the first, a broad-shouldered man with a gaping gap where his front teeth should have been. His comrade was shorter and more lean; both were wearing pistols. 'Well, don't let us stop you,' continued the big man. 'Be on your way.'

Shannow remained silent.

'Are you deficient in the hearing?' the second man asked. 'You are not wanted here.'

A small crowd had gathered in the background and Shannow caught sight of Haimut and Klaus Monet. Of Deiker there was no sign.

'That's it, let's help him on his way,' said the big man, stepping in; but Shannow's hand shot up with fingers extended, and hammered into his throat. He fell back choking, then sank to his knees. Shannow's eyes fixed on the second man.

'Be so kind as to tie my blanket roll to my saddle,' he said softly.

The man swallowed hard and licked his lips, his hand hovering over the pistol butt.

'Today,' stated Shannow, 'is not a good day to die. A man should at least see the sun in the heavens.'

For several seconds the man stood tense; then he cast a nervous glance at his comrade who was kneeling and holding his throat, his breathing hoarse and ragged. He knew he should grab for his pistol, but could not make his hand obey him. His eyes flicked up to meet Shannow's.

'Damn you!' he whispered. His hand fell away from the gun and he moved to the blanket roll, swinging it over the back of the saddle and tying it into place.

'Thank you,' said Shannow. 'And now see to your friend.' He stepped into the saddle and swung the stallion towards the north. The crowd parted and he resisted the urge to glance back. Now was the moment of greatest danger. But there was no shot. He angled the stallion down to where Frey McAdam's wagon had been camped; it was gone.

Shannow was angry with himself. There was no need to have shamed the men Deiker had obviously sent to see him on his way. He should have mounted and left as they had asked him. Only pride had prevented him from doing just that, and pride was a sin in the eyes of the Almighty.

That is why you cannot find Jerusalem, Shannow, he told himself. Your sins burden you down.

There is no Jerusalem!

The thought leapt unbidden to his mind and he shivered. He had seen so much in these last few years and his doubts were many. But what choice do I have, he wondered. If there is no Jerusalem, then all is in vain. And so the search must go on. *For what purpose?* For me! For as long as I search, then Jerusalem exists – if only in my mind. And that is enough. I need no more. *You lie, Shannow!* Yes, yes, I lie. But what does that prove? I must search. I must know. *Where next will you search?* Beyond the Great Wall. *And if not there?* To the ends of the earth and the borders of Hell!

Coming to the top of the rise, he turned west seeking the pass through the mountains. He rode the deer trails for more than two hours before joining the main track, which was scarred by the rims of wagon wheels and the hooves of many horses. The rain had ceased and the sun broke clear of the clouds. He rode more warily now, halting often and studying his surroundings. With the sun at its height he stopped and rested in the shadow of a looming natural pillar of stone. It was cool here and he read his Bible for an hour, enjoying the Song of Solomon. By mid-afternoon the Jerusalem Man had passed the mountains and was following a narrow track down into the valley beyond.

To the west he could see the McAdam wagon, following the wider trail which led into the town. To the north, beyond the buildings, the valley stretched for miles, ending in a huge wall that vanished into the distance. Shannow drew a long glass from his bags and through it he scanned the Wall. It was massive and even at this distance he could make out the flowers and lichens sprouting between its great blocks. He transferred his gaze to the sky, seeking the wonders beyond the Wall, but only huge white clouds could be seen gently rolling across the vault of Heaven. Hitching himself round in the saddle, he focused on the McAdam wagon. The woman was at the reins; he could see her honey-blonde hair and the flesh of her right leg as it rested against the brake. The children were walking behind, leading the horse. They would be in the town long before Shannow. He studied the buildings below. Most were wood structures – some timber, some log – but there were stone dwellings of several storeys, mostly at the eastern end. There appeared to be one main thoroughfare stretching for around four hundred paces and then, in the shape of a 'T', buildings branched north and south of it. It was a thriving community and many more dwellings were in the process of completion. Beyond the town was a meadow packed with tents, large and small, and Shannow could see more than a dozen cook-fires. Families were moving in to settle the land and soon Pilgrim's Valley would house a city.

Shannow considered avoiding the town and riding on to the Wall, and beyond. But the stallion needed rest and grain feeding and the Jerusalem Man had not slept in a bed in what seemed an age. He rubbed at his chin and imagined a long, hot bath and the feel of a razor on his face. His clothes too were way overdue for a cleaning, and his boots were leaf-thin. Flicking a glance at the wagon, he could no longer see the driver nor the flesh of her leg at the brake.

10

Oshere eased his swollen, misshapen frame into the room and tried to sit down in a wide chair. The discomfort was supreme; the muscles of his back no longer stretched as they should. He rose and squatted on his haunches, watching the Dark Lady as she sat, statue still, at the huge desk. Her eyes were closed, her spirit absent from her body. Oshere knew where she flew. She was deep down inside the drying smear of his blood that stained the crystal on her desk. Oshere sat silently until Chreena stretched her back and opened her eyes. She cursed softly.

'You must not be impatient,' said Oshere.

The black woman turned and smiled. 'Time races away from me,' she replied. 'How are you feeling?'

'Not good, Chreena. Now I know how Shir-ran felt . . . and why he left. Perhaps I should go too.'

'No! I will not hear such talk. I am close, Oshere; I know I am. All I need to find out is *why* the daughter molecules depart from the norm. They should not; it is against nature.'

Oshere chuckled. 'Are we not against nature, my dear? Did God ever intend a lion to walk like a man?'

'I am not worthy to discuss God's aims, Oshere. But your genetic structure was altered hundreds of years ago and now it is reverting. There must be a way to halt it.'

'But that is what I am saying, Chreena. Perhaps God wants us back the way he created us.'

'I should never have told you the truth,' Chreena whispered.

His tawny eyes locked on her dark face. 'We have left the others in the joy of their myths, but it is better for me to know the truth. Dear Lord, Chreena, I am a lion. I should be padding the forests and the mountains. And I will be.'

'You were born as a human,' she told him, 'and you grew into a man. A fine man, Oshere. You were not intended to prowl the wilds – I know it.'

'And Shir-ran was? No, Chreena. You are a fine scientist, and you have cared for the People of the Dianae. But I think your emotions are ruling your intellect. We always thought that we were the Chosen People. We saw the statues in the cities and believed that Man was once subservient to us. The truth may not be as palatable, but I can live with it. It will not change the Law of the One that Oshere becomes a lion.'

'Nor if he does not,' said Chreena. 'Someone, a long time ago, began an experiment on chromosome engineering. The reasons I can only guess at. But the chain of life was altered in several species and this was successful – until now. What could be done then, can be done now. And I will find a way to reverse the process.'

'The Bears have all reverted,' he pointed out. 'The Wolvers are dying. And did you not make the same promise to Shir-ran?'

'Yes, damn you, I did. And I'll say it to the next unfortunate. I'll keep saying it until I make it true.'

Oshere looked away. 'Forgive me, Chreena. Do not be angry.'

'Dear God, I'm not angry with you, my dear. It is me. I have the Books inside my head, and the knowledge. But the answer eludes me.'

'Take your mind from it for a while. Walk with me.'

'I can't. I have no time.'

Oshere pushed himself painfully to his feet, his great head lolling to one side. 'We both know that a tired mind will find no answers. Come. Walk with me on the hillside.'

He put out his hand, sheathing the talons that leapt unbidden from the new sockets at the ends of his swollen fingers. She put her fingers into the black mane on his cheek and kissed him gently. 'Just for a little while, then.'

Together they walked along the statue-lined hall and out into the bright sunlight blazing down on the terraced gardens. He stopped at a long marble bench and stretched himself along it. She sat beside him with his head resting on her lap.

'Tell me again of the Fall,' he said.

'Which one?'

'The disaster that destroyed Atlantis – the one with the Ark.'

'Which Ark?' she asked him. 'During the Between Times there were more than five hundred legends involving Great Floods. The Hopi indians, the Arabs, the Assyrians, the Turks, the Norse, the Irish – all had their own racial memories of the day the world toppled. And each had their Ark. For some it was gopherwood, for others reeds. Some were giant vessels, others huge rafts.'

'But the Between Times people did not believe the legends, did they?'

'No,' she admitted. 'It was part arrogance. They knew the earth had changed, that the axis was no longer what it was, but they believed it was a gradual happening. However, the evidence was there. High water marks on the sides of mountains, seashells found in deserts; huge bone graveyards of animals found in mountain caves, where they must have gathered to escape the floods.'

'And why did the earth topple, Chreena, that first time?'

She smiled down at him. 'Your desire for knowledge is insatiable. And you know I will not tell you the secrets of the Second Fall. You are too guileless to attempt cunning, Oshere.'

'Tell of the First Fall. Tell me.'

'I do not have all the answers. There was tremendous seismic activity. Tidal waves rolled across the lands – thousands of feet of rushing water. There are indications in legends I have read of the sun and the moon reversing their motions, the sun rising in the West. That phenomenon could only have been caused by the earth suddenly rolling. One of my teachers believed it was the result of a meteor striking the earth; another claimed it was the increasing weight of ice at the poles. Perhaps it was both. Many legends talk of the Atlanteans finding a source of great power and disturbing the balance of the world. They did indeed find such a power source. Who knows the truth? Whatever the answer, the roaring seas destroyed much of the world. And most of the continent that had been Atlantis sank beneath the new oceans.'

'Did no Atlanteans escape?'

'Some who lived in the far north survived. Another group lived on a large island which had once been a mountain range; it used to be called the Canaries. They lived there undisturbed until the middle 1300s AD; then they were discovered by a seafaring nation called the Spanish. The Spanish butchered them all, and the language and the culture were destroyed for all time.'

'The Between Times people were unusually harsh,' said Oshere. 'Most of your stories concerning them deal with death and destruction.'

'They were harsher than you could possibly imagine,' Chreena responded.

'And the Second Fall was worse than the first?'

'A thousand times worse. By then the world's population had multiplied many times, and almost eighty per cent of them lived in lands that were at best no more than 100 feet above sea level. Some were below it, and relied on sea walls or dykes. When the earth toppled, they were destroyed utterly.'

'And yet Man survived, as did the People of the Dianae.'

'We are tough, Oshere – and incredibly resourceful. And God did not want us all to die.'

'But is Human Man still evil and harsh? Does he still slaughter his fellows Beyond the Wall?'

'He does. But not all men are evil. There are still those who resist the Spell of the Land.'

'When they breach the Wall, will they come peacefully?'

'I don't know, Oshere. Now I must return to my work.'

*

Oshere watched the woman walk to her laboratory. Her

skin was ebony dark and glistened as if oiled, and the undulating sway of her hips was a joy to behold. He realised he was now appreciating her beauty on a more aesthetic plane – yet another sign of the impending change. He raised himself from the bench and ambled down the terraces until he came to the main street. Everywhere there were people moving about their business. They saw him and bowed low – as befitted a man soon to be a god. A god?

The humour of it touched him fleetingly. Soon his mind would lose its intelligence, his voice would become a roar and he would spend the rest of his days driven not by a lust for knowledge, but by the desire to fill a swaying belly.

He remembered the first day when the woman known as Chreena had arrived at the city. Crowds had gathered to gaze on the blackness of her skin. Priests had bowed down before her and Oshere's older brother, the Prince Shir-ran, had been smitten by her unearthly beauty. She had a child with her then, a sickly boy with wide sorrowful eyes, but he had died within the first two months of her stay. The physicians had been powerless; his blood, they said, was weak and diseased. Chreena had mourned him for a long time. Shir-ran, tall and handsome, and the finest athlete among the Dianae, had spent his days walking with her, telling her of the legends of the Dianae; showing her statues and holy buildings. At last – when they had become lovers – he had taken her on the long walk to the mountains of the Sword. She had returned dazed from the experience.

Then the Change had begun in Shir-ran. The priests gave thanks and blessed him, and a great celebration was ordered for the dwellers of the city. But Oshere had noticed that Chreena did not join in the festivities.

One night he found her in the ancient medi-chamber of the palace, poring over Scrolls of the Lost Ones. And he remembered her words:

'Damn you, you bastards! Was there no end to your arrogance?'

Oshere had walked forward. In those days he too had been tall and well formed, his eyes wide-set and tawny, his hair dark and gleaming, held in place by a band of gold. 'What troubles you, Chreena?'

'Your whole stupid civilisation!' she stormed. 'You know, once upon a time a people called the Incas believed that they could make people gods by cutting out their hearts.'

'Stupidity,' Oshere agreed.

'You are no different. Shir-ran is being mutated into some kind of beast and you all drink to it. I have never mocked your legends, nor sought to fill you with the arcane knowledge I possess. But this?'

'What are you saying, Chreena?'

'How can I explain this to you? You have seen that dust and water combine to make clay. Yes? Well, all living organisms are the same. We are all a combination of parts.'

'I know all this, Chreena. Heart, lungs, liver. Every child knows it.'

'Wait,' she commanded. 'I don't mean just the organs, or the bones or the blood. Oh, this is impossible . . .'

Oshere sat down facing her desk. 'I am not slow-witted. Explain it to me.'

Slowly she began to talk of the genetic material that was vital to all living organisms. She did not use its Between Times name – *deoxyribonucleic acid* – nor the initials by which it became better known. But she did try to explain its importance in terms of controlling hereditary characteristics. For an hour she spoke, accompanying her words with sketches.

'So,' said Oshere at last, 'you are saying that these magic chains divide themselves into exact replicas? For what purpose?'

With extraordinary patience Chreena moved on to talk of genes and chromosomes. At last the light of understanding dawned in Oshere.

'I begin to see. How fascinating! But how does this make us stupid? Until we are told – or discover – new knowledge, we cannot be accused of foolishness. Can we?'

'I guess not,' said Chreena, 'but that is not what I meant. What I am saying is that Shir-ran's genetic structure is changing, mutating. The daughter chains are no longer identical to the parent – and now I know why.'

'Tell me.'

'Because you are not people. You are...' she stopped suddenly and looked away and Oshere's tawny eyes narrowed.

'Finish what you were saying.'

'Someone – some group – in the Between Times inserted a different gene into your ancestors – into your basic genetic code, if you like. Now – once in maybe five generations – the structure breaks down and reverts. Shir-ran is not becoming a god – he's becoming what his ancestor was. A lion.'

Oshere rose. 'There are statues in the old cities which show lion-headed gods. They were worshipped. I have been educated to believe in the religion of my ancestors and I will not throw it aside. But I will speak to you again; I will learn which is correct.'

Chreena rose and took his arm. 'I'm sorry, Oshere. I should never have told you. You must not mention it to anyone else – especially Shir-ran.'

'It is rather too late for that,' said Shir-ran as he ambled into the room, his huge leonine head tilted. 'I am sorry, Chreena. It was rude to listen, but I could not help myself. I don't know about you, Oshere, but I do know I never felt less like a god.'

Oshere had seen tears in the great tawny eyes and had backed away from the former lovers.

Shir-ran had fled the city three months later, passing from the land without comment. Oshere had spent the time since then with Chreena, learning in secret all the dark lore of the Between Times – save how it fell. Then – a month ago – Oshere himself had woken in the dawn to find his muscles racked with pain and his face strangely distended.

Chreena had worked ceaselessly to help him. But to no avail.

Now all he wanted was to learn as much as he could

about the land, the stars and the Lord of All Things. And he had one dream he held in his heart like a jewel.

He wanted to see the Ocean. Just once.

*

Her dreams were troubled. She was sitting at a feast, the only woman present. Around her the men were handsome and tall, their smiles easy, full of warmth and friendliness. She reached out to touch her companion and her hand rested on his arm, felt the fur. Then she recoiled and looked up into tawny eyes that chilled her, saw the long fangs that could rend her flesh. She sat frozen as, one by one, the men became lions, their eyes no longer friendly.

She awoke in a cold sweat and swung her long legs from the bed. The night was cool and the breeze from the balcony window caressed her naked body as she walked to the balcony and gazed over the moonlit city.

The People of the Dianae slept now in blissful ignorance of the real doom that awaited them. She shivered and returned to the bedroom. Sleep would not come again, but she was too tired to work. Wrapping herself in a warm woollen blanket, she pulled a chair to the balcony and sat beneath the stars.

'I miss you, Samuel,' she said, picturing the kindly face of the husband she had lost, the father of the son she had lost. 'If all men had been like you, the world would have remained Eden.'

But all men were not as Samuel Archer had been. They were driven by greed, or lust, hate or fear. She shook her head. The People of the Dianae had never known war. They were gentle and conciliatory, kind and understanding. Now, like a perverse cosmic jest, they were beginning a reversion to savagery.

The Bear-people had long since lost their humanity. Chreena had journeyed with Shir-ran to one of their settlements close to the Pool of the Sword and what she had seen there was terrifying. Only one human was left among them, and he had begun to revert.

'Go away from us,' he had said. 'We are cursed.'

Now their settlement was deserted, the tribe moving to the high timberlands away from prying eyes; far from pity or loathing.

A hunting roar sounded in the distance from the pride that roamed the plain before the city and Chreena shivered. Some thirty lions were living there, preying upon the deer and antelope. Yet once they had been men and women who talked and laughed, and sang.

Her eyes scanned the ancient buildings. Just four hundred of the Dianae remained – not enough to survive and grow.

'Why do you see the lions as gods?' Chreena had asked the old Priest, Men-chor. 'They lose the power of speech and become mindless.'

'The tale of Elder days,' he replied, smiling as he closed his eyes and began to recite the opening of the Book. 'First there was the goddess Marik-sen, who walked under the sun and knew no words, nor ancient stories, nor even the name of her father, nor even that her father had a name. The Law of the One touched her and her name was born. And she knew. Yet in knowing she also realised that she had lost a great gift – something wonderful – and it grieved her. Her son was born, but was no god. He was a man. He spoke like a man, and walked like a man. He knew his name and the name of his mother, and many more names. But he too sensed a loss: an empty place in the depths of his soul. And he was the father of the Dianae, and the people grew. And they lived in the Great Garden, with the walls of crystal. But one day the Law of the One was assailed by many enemies. The land was in turmoil, the walls split asunder and great waters destroyed the garden. The Dianae themselves were almost destroyed. Then the waters subsided and the people gazed upon a different world. The Law of the One visited his presence upon Pen-ran, and he became the Prophet. He told us what was lost and what was gained. We had lost the Road to Heaven, we had gained the Path to Knowing. He was the first to lead us here, and the first to leave the Path and find the Road.'

The old man opened his eyes. 'There is far more, Chreena, but only the Dianae could understand.'

'You believe that knowledge prevents you from seeing Heaven?'

'It is the great barrier. The soul can exist only in purity. Knowledge corrupts, it fills us with dreams and desires. Such ambition keeps our eyes from the Law of the One.'

'Yet a savage lion knows only hunger and lust.'

'Perhaps. But he does not slay wantonly, and if his belly is full a young antelope can walk to a pool beside him and drink in safety.'

'You will forgive me for not sharing your . . . faith?'

'Even as you have forgiven me for not sharing yours. Perhaps we are both correct,' said Men-chor. 'For do we not have similar origins? Did you not also originate in a Garden, and were you not also cast from it? And did you not also, with the sin of Adam and the crime of Cain, lose the Road to Heaven?'

Chreena had laughed then, and politely conceded the argument. She liked the old man. But she had one last question.

'What happens when, like the Bears, all the Dianae are lions?'

'We will all be close to God,' he told her simply.

'But there will be no more songs.'

'Who knows what songs are heard in the heart of a lion? But can they be more discordant than the songs of death we hear from Beyond the Wall?'

11

Shannow left the stallion at the stock paddocks, paid the hostler to grain-feed and groom the beast, then hitched his saddlebags over his left shoulder and made his way to the Traveller's Rest, a three-storey building to the west of the town. They had one room vacant but the owner – a thin, sallow-faced individual called Mason – asked Shannow if he could wait for an hour while they 'cleaned it up'.

Shannow agreed and paid for a three-day stay. He left his saddlebags behind the counter and walked into the next room where a long bar stretched some fifty feet. The barman smiled as he entered.

'Name it, son,' he said.

'Beer,' ordered Shannow. He paid for the drink and took the brimming jug to a corner table where he sat with his back to the wall. He was tired and curiously on edge; his thoughts kept drifting to the woman with the wagon. Slowly the bar began to fill with working men – some straight from the mine, their clothes black, their faces streaked with grime and sweat. Shannow cast his eyes swiftly over each newcomer. Few wore pistols, but many carried knives or hatchets. He was ready to move to his room when a young man entered. He was wearing a white cotton shirt, dark trousers and a fitted jacket of tanned leather; and he wore a pistol with a smooth white grip. Watching him move, Shannow felt his anger rise. He pulled his eyes from the newcomer and finished his beer. They always looked the same, bright-eyed and smooth as cats: the mark of the hunter, the killer, the warrior.

Shannow left the bar, collected his belongings and climbed the two flights to his room. It was larger than he had expected, with a brass-fitted double bed, two easy chairs and a table on which sat an oil light. He dumped his bags behind the door and checked the window. Below it was a drop of around forty feet. Stripping off his clothes, he lay back on the bed and slept for twelve hours. He awoke ravenous, dressed swiftly, strapped on his guns and returned to the ground floor. The owner, Mason, nodded to him as Shannow approached.

'I could do with a hot bath,' he said.

'Outside and turn to your left. About thirty paces. You can't miss it.'

The bath-house was a dingy shed in which five metal tubs were separated by curtains hung on brass rings. Shannow moved to the end and waited while two men filled the bath with steaming water, then he stripped and climbed in. There was a bar of used soap and a hard brush. He lathered himself clean and stepped from the tub; the towel was coarse and gritty, but it served its purpose. He dressed, paid the attendants and wandered across the main street, following the aroma of frying bacon.

The eating house was situated in a long cabin under the sign of The Jolly Pilgrim. Shannow entered and found a table against the wall, where he sat facing the door.

'What will you have?' asked Beth McAdam.

Shannow glanced up and reddened. Then he stood and swept his hat from his head. 'Good morning, Frey McAdam.'

'The name's Beth. And I asked what you wanted?'

'Eggs, bacon . . . whatever there is.'

'They've got a hot drink here made from nuts and tree bark; it's good with sugar.'

'Fine. I'll try some. It did not take you long to find work.'

'Needs must,' she said and walked away. Shannow's hunger had evaporated, but he waited for his meal and forced his way through it. The drink was bitter, even with the sugar, and black as the pit, but the after-taste was good. He paid from his dwindling store of Barta coins and walked out into the sunshine. A crowd had gathered, and he saw the young man from the night before standing in the centre of the street.

'Hell man, it's easy,' he said. 'You just stand there and drop the jug any time you're ready.'

'I don't want to do this, Clem,' said the man he was addressing, a portly miner. 'You might kill me, goddammit!'

'Never killed no one yet with this trick,' said the pistoleer. 'Still, there's always a first time.' The crowd hooted with laughter. Shannow stood against the wall of the eating house and watched the crowd melt away before the two men, forming a line on either side of them. The fat miner was standing some ten feet from the pistoleer, holding a clay jug out from his body at arm's length.

'Come on, Gary. Drop it!' someone shouted.

The miner did so as Shannow's eyes flicked to the pistoleer. His hand swept down and up and the crack of the shot echoed in the street. The jug exploded into shards and the crowd cheered wildly. Shannow eased himself from the wall and walked around them towards the hotel.

'You don't seem too impressed,' said the young man, as Shannow passed.

'Oh, I was impressed,' Shannow assured him, walking on, but the man caught up with him.

'The name's Clem Steiner,' he said, falling into step.

'That was exceptionally skilful,' commented Shannow. 'You have fast hands and a good eye.'

'Could you have done it?'

'Never in a million years,' Shannow replied, mounting the steps to the hotel. Returning to his room, he took the Bible from his saddlebag and flicked through the pages until he came to the words that echoed in his heart.

'And he carried me away in the spirit to a mountain great and high and showed me the Holy City, Jerusalem, coming down out of Heaven from God. It shone with the glory of God, and its brilliance was like that of a very precious jewel, like a jasper, clear as crystal. It had a great high wall with twelve gates and with twelve angels at the gates... The city does not need the sun or the moon to shine on it for the glory of God gives it light, and the Lamb is its lamp... Nothing impure will ever enter it, nor will anyone who does what is shameful or deceitful...'

Shannow closed the book. *A great high wall.* Just like the one at the end of the valley.

He hoped so. By God, he hoped so...

*

Awoken by the sound of gunshots, Shannow rolled from the bed and moved to the side of the window, glancing down into the moonlit street below. Two men lay sprawled in the dust; still standing was Clem Steiner, a pistol in his hand. Men were running from the drinking houses and the sidewalks. Shannow shook his head and returned to his bed.

In the morning he took his breakfast in the Long Bar, a simple bowl of hot oats and a large jug of the black drink, called Baker's after the man who had introduced it to the area some eight years before.

Boris Haimut approached his table. 'Do you mind if I join you, sir?' he asked diffidently. Shannow shrugged and the small, balding Arcanist pulled up a chair and sat. The barman brought him a Baker's and Haimut sat in silence for a while sipping it.

'An interesting mixture, Meneer Shannow. Do you know it also cures headaches and rheumatic pain? It is also mildly addictive.' Shannow put down his jug. 'No, no,' said Haimut, smiling. 'I mean that one acquires a taste for it. There are no harmful effects. Are you staying long in Pilgrim's Valley?'

'Two more days. Maybe three.'

'It could be a beautiful place, but I fear they will have more trouble here.'

'You have finished work on the ship?' Shannow asked.

'We... Klaus and I... were ordered to leave the site. Meneer Scayse has taken over.'

'I am sorry.'

Haimut spread his hands. 'There was not much more to see. We dug further and found the ship was only a piece – it must have broken up as it sank. But any theory of it being a building was destroyed.'

'What will you do now?'

'I will wait here for a wagon convoy and then journey back to the east. There is always an expedition to somewhere. It is my life. Did you hear the shootings last night?'

'Yes,' said Shannow.

'Fourteen people have died violently here in the last month. It is worse than the Big Wide.'

'There is wealth here,' said Shannow. 'It draws men of violence, weak men, evil men. I have seen it in other areas. Once the wealth is gone, the boil bursts.'

'But there are some men, Meneer Shannow, who have a talent for lancing such boils, are there not?'

Shannow looked into the man's pale blue eyes. 'Indeed there are, Meneer Haimut. But it seems there are none such in Pilgrim's Valley.'

'Oh, I think there is one, sir. But he is disinterested. Do you still seek Jerusalem, Jon Shannow?'

'I do. And I no longer lance boils.'

Haimut looked away – and changed the subject. 'I met a travelling man two years ago who said he had been south of the Great Wall. He talked of astonishing wonders in the sky – a great sword that hung below the clouds, a crown of crosses above its silver hilt. Less than a hundred miles from it there was a ruined city of incredible size. I would sell my soul to see such a city.'

Shannow's eyes narrowed. 'Do not say that – even lightly. You might be taken up on it.'

Haimut smiled. 'My apologies, sir. I forgot – momentarily – that you are a man of religion. Do you intend to venture past the Wall?'

'I do.'

'It is a land of strange beasts and great danger.'

'There is danger everywhere, Meneer. Two men died on the street last night. There is no safe place in all the world.'

'That is increasingly true. Since the last full moon there have been – in Pilgrim's Valley alone – six rapes, eight murders, six fatal shootings and innumerable injuries from knife fights and other brawls.'

'Why do you retain such figures?' asked Shannow, finishing his Baker's.

'Habit, sir.' He produced a wad of paper and a pencil from the bulging pocket of his coat. 'Would you do me the kindness, sir, of telling me the whereabouts of the giant ship you saw in your travels?'

For almost half an hour Haimut questioned the Jerusalem Man about the ghost ship and the ruined cities of Atlantis. Finally Shannow rose, paid for his breakfast and strolled on to the street. For most of the morning he toured the town. It was quiet at the western end, where most of the houses betrayed the wealth of the inhabitants, but towards the east where the buildings were more mediocre and flimsy he saw several scuffles outside taverns and drinking-houses. At the end of the town was a vast meadow, filled by tents of various sizes. Even here there were drinking areas, and he saw drunkards sitting or lying on the grass in various stages of stupor.

The town had sprung up around a silver mine and this had attracted vagrants like ants to a picnic. And with the vagrants came the brigands and the thieves, the dice rollers and the Carnat players. He left the Tent Town and moved back along the main thoroughfare. The sound of children singing came from a long, timber-built hall. He stopped for a while and listened to the tune, trying to place it. It was a pleasant sound, full of youth and hope and innocent joy; at first it lifted him, but this was followed by a sense of melancholy and loss and he walked on.

Outside the Traveller's Rest a large crowd had gathered and a man's voice could be heard, deep and stirring. Shannow joined the crowd and looked up at the speaker who was standing on a barrel. The man was tall and broad-shouldered, with thick red hair tightly curled. He wore a black robe belted at the waist with grey rope, and a wooden cross hung from a cord around his neck.

'And I say to you, brothers, that the Lord is waiting for you. All he wants is a sign from you. To see your eyes lifted from the mud at your feet, lifted towards the glories of

Heaven. To hear your voices say, "Lord, I believe." And then, my friends, the joys of the Spirit will flow in your souls.'

A man stepped forward. 'And then he'll make us wear pretty black dresses like that one? Tell me, Parson, do you have to squat to piss?'

'Such is the voice of ignorance, my brothers,' began the Parson, but the man shouted him down.

'Ignorance? You puking son of a bitch! You can take your puking Jesus and tell him go . . .'

The Parson's booted foot flashed out, catching the man under the chin and catapulting him from his feet. 'As I was saying, dear friends,' he continued, 'the Lord waits with love in His heart for any sinner who repents. But those who persist in evil ways will fall to the Sword of God, to burn in lakes of Hellfire. Put aside evil and lust and greed. Love your neighbour as yourself. Only then will the Lord smile on you and yours and your rewards will be all the greater.'

'Do you love *him*, Parson?' shouted another man in the crowd, pointing down at the unconscious heckler.

'Like my own son,' replied the Parson, grinning. 'But children must first learn discipline. I will stand bad language, for that is the way of sinful man. But I will not stand for blasphemy, or any insult to the Lord. Faced with such, I will smite the offender hip and thigh as Samson among the Philistines.'

'How do you feel about drinking, Parson?' called a man at the back.

'Nice of you to ask, my son. I'll have a strong beer.' As the laughter began, the Parson raised his arms for silence.

'Tomorrow is the Sabbath, and I will be holding a service beyond the Town of Tents. There will be singing and praise, followed by food and drink. Come with your wives, your sweethearts and your children. We'll make a day of it in the meadow. Now where's that beer I was promised?' He stepped down from the barrel and moved to the fallen man. Hoisting him to his feet, the Parson lifted the man to his shoulder and marched up the steps into the Traveller's Rest.

Shannow remained in the sunlight.

'Impressive, is he not?' asked Clem Steiner. When Shannow turned, the young man's eyes were bright and challenging.

'Yes,' Shannow agreed.

'I hope the little fracas didn't trouble you in the night?'

'No, it did not. Excuse me,' replied Shannow, moving away.

Steiner's voice floated after him. 'You bother me, friend. I hope we will not fall out.'

Shannow ignored him. He returned to his room and checked his remaining Barta coin, finding he had seven full silvers, three halves and five quarters. He searched his pockets and came up with the gold coin he had found in Shir-ran's food store. It was just over an inch in diameter and upon the surface was stamped the image of a sword surrounded by stars; the reverse of the coin was blank. Shannow took it to the window to examine it more closely. The sword was of an unusual design, long and tapering, and the stars were more like crosses in the sky.

The thunder of hooves sounded from the street and a large group of riders came hurtling into sight. Shannow opened the window to see the body of a beast being dragged in the dust behind two of the riders, and a large crowd gathering. The horsemen pulled up their mounts and Shannow was amazed to see the bloodied beast rise up on all fours, and then lurch to its hind legs.

It ran – but a rope pulled it up. Two shots exploded and gaping wounds appeared on the creature's back. Several more of the onlookers produced guns and the beast was smashed from its feet. Shannow left his room and moved swiftly down the stairs. On the street beside the Traveller's Rest was a store, outside which stood several barrels and a stack of long wooden axe- or pick-handles. Lifting one of them, Shannow walked down into the milling group of riders and stopped before a bearded man on a black horse.

The pick-handle slashed through the air to hammer into the man's face; his body flew back over the saddle and hit the ground, raising a cloud of dust. Shannow dropped the club on the rider's body and, taking hold of the pommel of the saddle, vaulted to the stallion's back.

There was silence now as Shannow eased the horse past the stunned riders. He tugged on the reins, turning the stallion to face the group.

'When he awakes, point out to him the perils of stealing a man's horse,' Shannow told them. 'Make it clear to him. I will leave his saddle with the hostler.'

'He'll kill you for this, friend,' said a young man close to him.

'I am no friend of yours, child. Nor ever will be.'

Shannow rode on, pausing only to glance down at the dead beast. It looked almost exactly as Shir-ran had in those last days – the spreading lion's mane, the hideously muscled shoulders. Shannow touched his heels to the stallion's flanks and cantered down to the stables, where the hostler came out to meet him.

'I'm sorry, Meneer, but I couldn't stop them. There were eight . . . ten of them. They took three other horses that weren't theirs.'

'Who were they? The thieves?'

'They ride for Scayse,' replied the man, as if that answered everything.

Shannow dismounted and led the stallion into the stable. He stripped the saddle from him and flung it in a corner; then he groomed the horse, rubbing the lather from him and brushing the gleaming back.

'It's a fine horse,' said the hostler, limping forward. 'Must be seventeen hands. I'll bet he runs like the wind.'

'He does. What happened to your leg?'

'Timber cracked in the mine, years ago. Busted my knee. Still, it's a damn sight better living above ground than below. Not so much coin, but I breathe a lot easier. What was all the shooting?'

'They killed the lion they captured,' Shannow told him.

'Hell, I'd like to have seen that. Was it one of them Mandemons?'

'I do not know. It ran on its hind legs.'

'Lord, what a thing to miss! There ain't so many as there was, you know. Not since the gates vanished on the Wall. We used to see them often in the Spring. They killed a family near Silver Stream. Ate them all, would you believe it? Was it male or female?'

'Male,' said Shannow.

'Yep. Never seen no females. Must be Beyond the Wall, I reckon.'

'Does anyone ever go there?'

'Beyond the Wall?' queried the hostler. 'No way. Not ever. Believe me, there's beings there to frizzle a man's soul.'

'If no one goes there – how can you know?'

The hostler grinned. 'No one goes there *now*. But five years ago there was an expedition. Only one man – of forty-two who started out – got back alive. It was him that told about the sword in the sky. And he only lived a month, what with the wounds and the gashes in his body. Then, two years ago, the gateways vanished. There were three of them, twenty feet high and as broad. Then one morning they were gone.'

'Filled in, you mean?'

'I mean *gone*! Not a trace of them. And no mark of any breaks in the Wall. Lichens and plants growing over old stones, like there never was no gates at all.'

*

She knew the problem and could see the results. Yet she was powerless to change the process... just as she had been powerless to save her son. The woman known as Chreena prowled the medi-chamber, her dark eyes angry, her fists clenched.

One small Sipstrassi Stone could change everything; one fragment with its gold veins intact could save Oshere and others like him. Little Luke would have been alive, and

Shir-ran would still have been standing beside her, tall and proud.

She had searched the mountains and the valleys, had questioned the Dianae. But no one had ever seen such a Stone, black as coal and yet streaked with gold, warm to the touch and soothing to the soul.

She blamed herself, for she had carried her own Stone to this distant land and had used it to seal the Wall – one great surge of Sipstrassi power to wipe out the gates which would have allowed Man to corrupt the lands of the Dianae. And then she had made the great discovery – Man had already corrupted them ... back before the Second Fall.

The People of the Dianae. The People of the DNA. The Cat-people. There had been mutants and freaks in the world for hundreds of years. Chreena had been educated to believe they were the result of the poisons and toxic wastes which littered the land, but now she was beginning to see the true wickedness that was the legacy of Between. Genetic engineering gone rogue in a hostile environment. New races birthed; others, like the Dianae, slowly dying.

The priests here believed that the Changes were gifts from Heaven. But they were happening more frequently, whole families showing signs of reversion.

Chreena's anger rose. She had seen the books and the records back at Home Base. Many diseases of the Between Times had been treated by producing bacterial DNA and using it in commercial production. Insulin for diabetics was one such. Food production had been boosted by inserting genes for growth into pigs and cattle – promoter genes, these had been called. But the Betweeners had gone much further.

May you rot in Hell! she thought. Suddenly she smiled. Because, of course they *were* rotting in Hell. Their disgusting world had been swept away by the power of nature, like blood washing the pus from a boil.

And yet it had not affected the core of the infection – Man himself: the ultimate carnivore, the complete killer.

Even now they warred amongst themselves, butchering and plundering.

The Spell of the Land was at work. Colossal radiation levels, toxic wastes in the air they breathed – all coming together to create abnormally high levels of aggression and violence.

The circle of history spun on. Already Man had rediscovered guns and had risen to the level the world had known in the middle 1800s. It would not be long before they took to the skies, before nations were formed and wars spread.

Slowly she climbed the stairs to the observatory platform. From here she could see the streets of the city and watch the people moving about their business. Further out she could see the farmlands, and the herds of cattle. And away into the distance, like a shimmering thread, the Wall between Worlds. She could almost hear Man beating upon it, venting his rage upon the ancient stones.

Chreena transferred her gaze to the south, where heavy clouds drifted over the new mountains and the Sword of God was hidden. She shivered.

A sudden storm broke in the east and she swung to watch the lightning fork up from the ground, the dark thunderclouds swirling furiously. A cold wind screamed across the plain and she shivered again and stepped inside.

The city would withstand the storm, as it had withstood the First Fall and the terrible fury of the risen ocean.

As she turned away, she failed to see a glimmer of blue within the storm, as if a curtain had flickered in the wind, showing clear skies amid the lowering black clouds. At the centre of the blue shone the golden disc of a second sun so that, for no more than a heartbeat, two shadows were cast on the streets of the city.

12

The riders dismounted and gathered around the fallen man. His nose was crushed and both eyes were swelling fast; his upper lip was split and bleeding profusely. Two men lifted him, carrying him from the street to the sidewalk outside the Jolly Pilgrim.

The owner, Josiah Broome, took a bowl of fresh water and a towel and moved to join them, kneeling beside the injured man. He immersed the towel in the cool water and then folded it, placing it gently over the man's blackened eyes.

'It was a disgrace,' he said. 'I saw it. Unwarranted violence. Despicable!'

'Damn right about that,' someone agreed.

'People like him will ruin this valley, even before we get a chance to build something lasting here,' said Broome.

'He stole a horse, goddammit!' exclaimed Beth McAdam, before she could stop the words. Broome looked up.

'These men were hunting a beast that could have devoured your children and they took the first mounts they could find. All he had to do was to ask the man for his horse. But no. Men like him are always the same. Violence. Death. Destruction. It follows them like a plague.'

Beth held her tongue and walked back into the eating-house. She needed this job to swell the funds she had hidden in her wagon, and to pay for the children to remain at the Cabin School. But men like Broome annoyed her. Sanctimonious and blinkered, they saw only what they wished to see. Beth had been in Pilgrim's Valley for only two days, but already she knew the political structure of the settlement. These riders worked for Edric Scayse, and he was one of the three most powerful men in Pilgrim's Valley. He owned the largest mine, two of the stores and, with the man Mason, the Traveller's Rest and several of the gambling-houses on the east quarter. His men patrolled the Tent City, extorting payment for their vigilance. Any who did not pay could guarantee to see their wagons or their belongings lost through theft or fire. In the main, Scayse's men were bullies or former brigands.

Beth had watched the beast dragged in and shot down, and had seen Shannow recover his horse. The man who stole it was bruised but alive. Shannow could have asked for its return, but Beth knew the chances were the man would have refused and almost certainly that would have led to a gun battle. Broome was a dung-brain of the first order. But he was also her boss and, in his own way, a nice man. He believed in the nobility of Man, that all disputes could be settled by reason and debate. She stood in the doorway and watched him tend the injured victim. Broome was tall and thin, with long, straight, sandy hair and a slender face dominated by large protruding blue eyes. He was not an unhandsome man, and his manner towards her had been courteous. He was a widower with no children, and as such Beth had scrutinised him carefully; she knew it would be wise to find a good man with a solid base so that she could ensure security for her children. But Broome could never fill her requirements.

The injured man regained consciousness and was helped to a table. Beth brought him a cup of Baker's and he sipped it.

'I'll kill the whoreson,' he mumbled. 'So help me God, I'll kill him!'

'Don't even think like that, Meneer Thomas,' Broome urged. 'What he did was appalling, but further violence will not eradicate it.'

The man pushed himself to his feet. 'Who's with me?' he asked. Two men joined him, but the others hung back. Thomas pulled his pistol from his belt and checked the loads. 'Where'd he go?'

'He took the stallion back to the stable,' said a short lean man.

'Thanks, Jack. Well, let's find him.'

'Please, Meneer . . .' began Broome, but Thomas pushed him aside. Beth eased her way back through the kitchen and out into the yard, then she hitched up her long skirt and ran behind the buildings, cutting through an alleyway and on to the main street ahead of the three men. At the end of the street she saw Shannow talking to the hostler in the doorway of the stable. Quickly she crossed to him.

'They are coming for you, Shannow,' she said. 'Three of them.'

He turned to her and smiled softly. 'It was kind of you to think of me.'

'Never mind kindness. Saddle up and move.'

'My belongings are still in my room. I would suggest that you wait here.'

'I said, there are three of them.'

'Is the man I struck among them?'

'Yes,' she told him. Shannow nodded, removed his coat and laid it across the stall beam. Then he moved out into the sunlight. Beth crossed to the doorway and watched him make his way to the centre of the street. There he stood and waited with arms hanging by his sides. The sun was high now, shining in the faces of the three pistoleers. They came closer, the two on the outside angling themselves away from Thomas in the centre. Beth felt the tension rise.

'Now how do you feel, you whoreson?' shouted Thomas. Shannow said nothing. 'Cat got your tongue?' Closer now they came until only about ten paces separated them. Then Shannow's voice sounded, low and clear.

'Have you come here to die?' he asked. Beth saw the man on the right rub sweat from his face and glance at his friend. Thomas grabbed for his pistol, but a single shot punched him from his feet. His legs twitched in the dust, and a slow stain spread on the front of his trousers.

The other two men stood statue-still. 'I would suggest,' said Shannow quietly, 'that you carry him off the street.' They hurried to obey as he walked back to Beth and the hostler.

'I thank you again, Frey McAdam. I am sorry that you needed to witness such an act.'

'I've seen dead men before, Meneer Shannow. But he has a lot of friends and I don't think it will be safe for you here. Tell me, how did you know those others would not fight?'

'I did not,' he told her. 'But he was the man carrying the anger. Will you be going to the Parson's gathering tomorrow?'

'Might be.'

'I would be privileged if you and your children would accompany me.'

'I am sorry, Meneer,' said Beth. 'I think you are now in some peril, and I will not allow my children to be in your dangerous company.'

'I understand. You are correct, of course.'

'Were I without children . . . the answer might have been different.'

He bowed and walked out into the sunshine.

'Damn, but he's cool,' said the hostler. 'Well, Thomas ain't gonna be missed, not by a long shot.'

Beth did not reply.

*

The Jerusalem Man paused on the street where only a dark patch of blood showed where a life had been taken. He felt no regret. The dead man had made his own decision and Shannow recalled the words of Solomon: *Such is the end of all who go after ill-gotten gain; it takes away the lives of those who get it.*

It was a long walk back to his rooms and Shannow could feel the eyes of many upon him as he strode along the dusty street. The former riders were now grouped around the eating-house, but they did not speak as he passed. Clem Steiner was waiting inside the Traveller's Rest; the young man rose as he entered.

'I knew,' he said. 'Something told me you were a fighter

when I first seen you sitting in the Long Bar. What is your name, friend?'

'Shannow.'

'I should have guessed it: the Jerusalem Man. You're a long way from home, Shannow. Who sent for you? Brisley? Fenner?'

'No one sent for me, Steiner. I ride where I please.'

'You realise we may have to go up against one another?'

Shannow stared at the young man for several seconds. 'That would not be advisable,' he said softly.

'Damn right there. You'd better remember that. Meneer Scayse would like a few words with you, Shannow. He's in the Long Bar.'

Shannow turned away and made for the stairs.

'You hear what I said?' Steiner called, but Shannow ignored him and climbed to his room. He poured himself a cup of water from a stone jug and sat down to wait in a chair by the window.

*

Edric Scayse stepped from the Long Bar. 'He's gone, Mr Scayse,' said Steiner. 'Want me to fetch him back?'

'No. Wait here for me.'

He was a tall man, broad-shouldered, his raven-black hair cut short and swept back over his head without a parting. Clean-shaven, his face was strong and angular, the dark eyes deep-set, and he moved with smooth assurance. Reaching the door of Shannow's room he knocked once.

'Come in. It is open,' came a voice from within.

Scayse stepped inside. His eyes fastened on the man sitting in the chair by the window, and he re-evaluated his plan. He had intended to offer Shannow employment, but this was now an option that would serve only to make the man before him more of an enemy.

'May I sit, Mr Shannow?'

'I thought the term was Meneer in this part of the country.'

'I am not from this part of the country.' He walked to

the chair opposite the Jerusalem Man and lowered himself into it.

'What is it that you want, Mr Scayse?'

'Merely to apologise, sir. The man who stole your horse worked for me. He was a hot-headed youngster. I wished to assure you that there will be no revenge attacks – I have made that clear to all my riders.'

Shannow shrugged, but his expression did not change. 'And?'

Scayse felt a flicker of anger but suppressed it, forcing a smile instead. 'There is no "and". It is merely a call of courtesy, sir. Do you intend staying long in Pilgrim's Valley?'

'No. It is my intention to ride further south.'

'To seek the wonders in the sky, no doubt. I envy you that. It will be at least three months before I have assembled a force to cross the Wall.'

'A force? For what purpose?' asked Shannow.

'*Out of his mouth comes a sharp sword with which to strike down the nations,*' quoted Scayse. '*He will rule them with an iron sceptre.*'

He watched Shannow's expression change from open hostility to wariness.

'So you read your Scripture, sir. But what does it mean to you?'

Scayse leaned forward, pressing home his advantage. 'I have gathered information about the land Beyond the Wall, and the wonders there. There are great signs in the sky. Of this there is no doubt. There is a shining sword, surrounded by stars and crosses, and upon the sword is a name that no one can read. Exactly as the Scripture says. What is more, the land is peopled by beasts who walk like men and worship a dark goddess – a witch who performs obscene rites among them. Or as the Scripture has it, Mr Shannow: "*There I saw a woman sitting on a scarlet beast that was covered with blasphemous names.*" Or there again: "*The Beast I saw resembled a leopard, but had feet like those of a bear and a mouth like that of a lion.*" All these things are Beyond the Wall,

Mr Shannow. I intend to go there and find the Sword of God.'

'And for this you gather brigands and pistoleers?'

'You would have me take farmers and teachers?'

Shannow stood and moved to the window. 'I am no debater, sir. Nor am I a judge.' Behind him Scayse masked a smile of triumph and remained silent. Shannow turned, his pale eyes fixing on Scayse. 'But neither am I a fool, Mr Scayse. You are a man who seeks power – domination over your fellows. You are not a seeker after truth. Down there your men are feared. But that is no business of mine.'

'You are correct, Mr Shannow, when you talk of the pursuit of power. But that is not an evil thing in itself, surely? Was not David the son of a farmer, and did he not rise to be King over Israel? Was not Moses the child of a slave? God gives a man talents and therefore it is right that he should use them. I am no wilful murderer, nor brigand. My men may be . . . boisterous and rough, but they pay for their wares and treat the folk of this community with respect. Not one of them has been found guilty of murder or rape, and those who have been caught stealing have been dealt with by me. There will always be rulers, Mr Shannow. It is not a sin to become one.'

Shannow returned to his chair and poured a mug of water which he offered to Scayse, who refused it with a smile. 'As I said, I am no judge. I will not be in this community for long. But I have seen other such communities. The violence will grow, and there will be many more deaths unless order is established. Why is it, sir, that with your quest for power you have not established such order?'

'Because I am not a tyrant, Mr Shannow. The gambling places in the eastern sector are not under my jurisdiction. I have a large farm and several herds of dairy and beef cattle – and I own the largest silver mine. My lands are patrolled by my men, but the town itself – though I have interests here – is not my concern.'

Shannow nodded. 'Did you find anything of interest in the wreck of the ship?'

Scayse chuckled. 'I heard about your ... altercation. Yes, I did, Mr Shannow. There were some gold bars and several interesting pieces of silver plate. But nothing as grand as you saw on the *Titanic*.'

Shannow betrayed no surprise, he merely nodded and Scayse went on: 'Yes, I have seen the *Titanic*. I know of the Sipstrassi Demon Stone that resurrected it, and of your battle with Sarento. I also am no fool, sir. I know that the world of the past contained wonders beyond our imaginings, and that they are lost to us, perhaps for ever. But this new world has power also. And I will find it Beyond the Wall.'

'The Demon Stone was destroyed,' said Shannow. 'If you know of Sarento, you know of his evil and of the Hellborn War he caused. Such power is not suited to men.'

Scayse rose. 'I have been honest with you, Mr Shannow, because I respect you. I do not seek a confrontation with you. Do not misunderstand me; I do not speak from fear. But I want no unnecessary enemies. Sipstrassi is merely a power source, not unlike the guns you wear. In evil hands, it will create evil. But I am not an evil man. Good day to you.'

Scayse moved back into the hallway and continued down the stairs to where Steiner waited.

'You want me to take him out, Mr Scayse?'

'Stay away from him, Clem. That man would kill you.'

'Is that a joke, Mr Scayse? There's no one could take me with a pistol.'

'I didn't say he could beat you, Clem. I said he would kill you.'

13

For two long, hot days Nu-Khasisatra walked across the Great Wide. The mountains seemed no closer, but his strength was ebbing. As a shipbuilder and a craftsman, he had long been proud of the enormous strength he could bring to bear, lifting great weights of wood or stone. But this seemingly endless walk called not for strength but for stamina, and on this count Nu realised he was lacking. He sat down in the shade of a shallow gully and took the Sipstrassi Stone from the deep pocket of his coat. He was loath to use its power, not knowing how much was left, nor how much was needed to allow him to return home to Pashad and his children. Unlike many from the City of Ad, Nu had taken only one wife, the daughter of Axin the sailmaker. He had loved her from the first moment their hands had touched, and he loved her still. There was little strength in Pashad, fragile as a spring flower, but there was a well of giving in her without which Nu felt lost.

The last time Nu had been in possession of Sipstrassi it had been a fragment, a sliver no bigger than a torn fingernail. Its power had been used up in a day – fuelling his strength; forcing back the awesome power of time, turning his greying hair black and filling his muscles with the strength of youth. But what he held now was twenty times larger, the gold veins thick and pulsing with power.

Nu had escaped the Daggers, but he had not journeyed to Balacris. He had come to some foreign land far across the sea, where men wore strange raiment. *Use your mind, you fool!* he told himself. *How can you return home unless you first know from where you are starting?* According to legend, the Elder Priests had used Sipstrassi to free their spirits to fly the universe. If they could do it, so could Nu-Khasisatra. He moved to his knees and prayed to the Great One, using ten of the thousand names known to Man, then he gripped the stone tightly and pictured himself rising through the gathering clouds above. His mind swam and he felt suddenly free, like a ship whose anchor falls away. Opening his eyes, he found himself staring down at a white wilderness of mountains and valleys with not a trace of life. Above him the sky was blue and clear, but the landscape below was ghostly and silent. Fear swept through him. Where had he flown? He dropped towards the snow-covered world ... and passed into the clouds.

For a time he was blind, then he broke through the grey-white mist and saw the land far below, green and lush, sectioned by snow-topped mountains and ribbon rivers, great valleys and dales, forests and plains. He scanned the horizon for signs of life, for cities or towns, but there was nothing save the vastness of nature. Nu's spirit swooped closer to the plain. Now he could see his own tiny figure in the gully below and, some miles to the west, a camp of wagons with white canvas covers and oxen feeding on the hillside.

He ventured further, over the mountains, and saw an ugly township with squat wooden buildings and a large gathering of people in a meadow. Passing over them, he continued south. A great wall, similar in structure to the sea wall at Ad, met his eyes and he dropped towards it. The stones were hewn in the same way, but they were far older than Pendarric's Wall. He moved on, wondering how a nation which could erect such a wall could have regressed to creating such hideous buildings as he had seen in the small town. Then he saw the city – and his heart sank.

There was the domed palace, the marble terraces, the long statue-lined Road of Kings – and to the south the curving line of the dock. But beyond it there was no glittering ocean, only fields and meadows. Nu hovered, scanning the people strolling the streets. Everything was as he remembered, yet nothing was the same. He sped to the temple and halted by the statue of Derarch the Prophet.

The prophet's face was worn away, the holy scrolls in his hands reduced to no more than white sticks.

Shaken beyond endurance, Nu fled back to the sky.

What he had seen was like a vision from the Fires of Belial.

And he knew the truth. This was not some strange, distant land; this was home, this was the City of Ad. He recalled his vision of the sea roaring up, and the three suns in the sky. This was the world of the future.

He returned to his body and wept for all that had been lost: for Pashad and his sons, for Bali and his friends, and for all the people of a world soon to die ... of a world that had already died.

Nu-Khasisatra wept for Atlantis.

*

At last his tears dried and he lay back against a rock, his body aching, his heart heavy. What point was there in his warnings to the people? Why had the Lord Chronos used him, if there was no hope?

No hope? You of all men should know the folly of that thought.

His first ship had been caught in a terrible storm. All his money had been tied into the venture, and more. He had borrowed heavily, pushing himself and his family into awesome debt. As the voyage was nearing completion with the cargo secure in the hold and his fortune assured, the winds had turned foul, the sea had roared; great waves pummelled the vessel, hurling it towards the black cliffs poised like a hammer above them.

Most of his crew had panicked, flinging themselves over the side and risking almost certain death in the raging sea. Not so Nu-Khasisatra. Holding to the tiller, straining with all the power in his formidable frame, he locked his gaze to the black monstrosity looming over him. At first there had been no response, but then the sleek craft began to turn. Nu's muscles had been stretched to tearing point, but his ship missed the cliff and raced on towards the peril of a hidden reef.

Only three out of thirty crew members remained with him, and these clung to the timbers, unable to aid their master for fear of being washed overboard.

'The anchor!' yelled Nu into the teeth of the storm. Salt spray lashed his face, hurling the words back at him. Lifting one arm from the tiller, he pointed at the rope brake by the iron anchor and one of his crewmen began to haul himself back to the stern. A huge wave hit him and he lost hold; his body slid down the deck. Nu released the tiller and dived for the man, catching his tunic just as he was about to topple over the side. Clamping his right hand to a stay, Nu hauled the seaman to safety. The ship sped towards the reefs, hidden like the fangs of a monster below the foaming waves. Nu staggered upright and forced a path to the tiller. The seaman struggled with the anchor brake... suddenly it gave and the iron weight hissed over the side.

The ship shuddered and Nu let out a cry of despair, for he believed they had struck the reef. But it was only the anchor biting hard into the coral below them. The ship bobbed and the cliff which had been such a threat now became a shelter from the ferocity of the storm.

The wind died down in the bay. 'We're still shipping water,' shouted the crewman Nu had rescued.

'Start the pump, and see where the problem lies,' Nu ordered, and the man raced below. The two other crewmen followed him and Nu sank to the wet deck. The moon broke clear of the storm clouds as he glanced to port. Rows of jagged rocks, black and gleaming, could be seen above the swell. Had the ship struck any of them, it would have been ripped open from prow to stern. Nu hauled himself upright and moved to the starboard side. Here too the reef could be seen. Somehow – by some miracle – he had steered the vessel through a narrow channel between the reefs.

The crewman returned. 'The level is dropping. The ship is sound, master.'

'You have earned a good bonus, Acrylla. I'll see you get it.'

The man grinned, showing broken front teeth. 'I thought we were finished. It looked so hopeless.'

Nu-Khasisatra's fortune had been built on that first adventure, and his reply to Acrylla was now carved on the tiller of each of his ships:

'Nothing is ever hopeless – as long as courage endures.'

The memory of that night came flooding back to him and he pushed himself to his feet. Despair, he realised, was as great an enemy as Sharazad or the King's Daggers. His world was doomed, but that did not mean Pashad must die. He had a Sipstrassi Stone and he was alive.

'I will come for you, my love,' he said. 'Through the vaults of time or the Valleys of the Damned.' He glanced up at the sky. 'Thank you for reminding me, Lord.'

*

Beth sat on the hillside under a spreading pine and watched the children playing on the makeshift swing-boards and see-saw planks down by the stream. The high meadow was seething with townspeople, farmers and miners, enjoying the bright sunshine and the food at the stalls. Elsewhere there were games of strength or skill, knife and hatchet hurling, rifle shooting, wrestling and boxing. The miners held a jousting tourney, where one man sat upon the shoulders of another gripping a mock lance with a wooden ball at either end. A similar team would rush at them, and there was much shouting of encouragement as the riders proceeded to hammer their opponents to the ground. The barbecue fires were lit and the smell of roasting beef – compliments of Edric Scayse – filled the air. Beth leaned her back to the tree and relaxed for the first time in days. Her small hoard of coin was swelling, and soon she would move the family out to the rich southland north of the Wall, and there build a farm of her own on land leased from Scayse. It would be a hard life, but she would make it work.

A shadow fell across her and she looked up to see Jon Shannow standing hat in hand.

'Good morning... Beth. Your children are far from us, and in little danger. May I join you?'

'Please do,' she said and he swung round and sat with his back to the tree. She moved out to sit in front of him. 'I know who you are,' she told him. 'The whole town knows.'

'Yes,' he said wearily. 'I expect they do. It is a fine gathering and people are enjoying themselves. That is good to see.'

'Why did you come here?' she pressed.

'It is only a stopping place, Beth. I shall not be staying. I was not summoned here; I have not come to deal death to all and sundry.'

'I did not think for one moment that you had. Is it true that you seek Jerusalem?'

'Not, perhaps, with the same fervour as once I had. But, yes, I seek the Holy City.'

'Why?'

'Why not? There are worse ways for a man to live. When I was a child I lived with my parents and my brother. Raiders came and slaughtered my family. My brother and I escaped and were taken in by another family, but the raiders hit them too. I was older then and I killed them. For a long time I was angry, filled with hate for all brigands. Then I found my God and I wanted to see Him, to ask Him many things. I am a direct man. So, I look for Him. Does that answer your question?'

'It would have, were you younger. How old are you? Forty? Fifty?'

'I am forty-four years old, and, yes, I have been searching since before you were born. Does that make a difference?'

'Of course it does,' she told him. 'Young men – like Clem Steiner – see themselves as adventurers. But surely with maturity a man would come to see that such a life is wasted?'

'Wasted? Yes, I suppose it has been. I have no wife, no children, no home. But for all people, Beth McAdam, life is like a river. One man steps into it and finds it is cool and sweet and gentle. Another enters and finds it shallow and cold and unwelcoming. Still another finds it a rushing torrent that bears him on to many perils; this last man cannot easily change his course.'

'Just words, Mr Shannow – and well you know it. A strong man can do anything he pleases, live any life he chooses.'

'Then perhaps I am not strong,' he conceded. 'I had a wife once. I put aside my dreams of the Holy City and I rode with her seeking a new life. She had a son, Eric, a shy boy who was frightened of me. And we rode, unknowingly, into the heart of the Hellborn War . . . and I lost her.'

'Did you look for her? Or did she die?' Beth asked.

'She was taken by the Hellborn. I fought to save her. And – with the help of a fine friend – I did. She married another man – a good man. I am what I am, Beth. I cannot change. The world we live in will not allow me to change.'

'You could marry. Start a farm. Raise children.'

'And how long before someone recognises me? How long before the brigands gather? How long before an old enemy hunts me or my children? How long? No, I will find Jerusalem.'

'I think you are a sad man, Jon Shannow.' She opened the basket by her side and produced two apples, offering one to the Jerusalem Man. He took it and smiled.

'Less sad in your company, Lady. For which I thank you.'

Angry words instantly gathered in her mind, but she saw the expression on his face and swallowed them back. This was no clumsy attempt to bed her, nor the opening shots in a campaign to woo her. It was merely a moment of genuine honesty from a lonely fellow traveller.

'Why me?' she whispered. 'I sense you do not allow yourself many friends?'

He shrugged. 'I came to know you when I rode in your tracks. You are strong and caring; you do not panic. In some ways we are very alike. When I found the dying brigand, I knew I would be too late to help you. I expected to find you and your children murdered and my joy was great when I found your courage had saved you.'

'They murdered Harry,' she said. 'That is a shame. He asked if he could call on me in Pilgrim's Valley.' Beth lay down, resting on her elbow, and told Shannow the story of the brigands. He listened in silence until she had finished.

'Some women have that effect on a man,' he said. 'Harry respected your courage, and hung on to life long enough to send me to help you. For that I think the Almighty will look kindly on him.'

'You and I have different thoughts on that subject.' She looked down the hill and saw Samuel and Mary making their way up towards them. 'My children are returning,' she said softly.

'And I will leave you,' he replied.

'Will you take part in the pistol contest?' she asked. 'It is being held after the Parson gives his sermon. There is a prize of 100 Bartas.'

He shrugged. 'I do not think so.' He bowed and she watched him walk away.

'Damn you, Beth,' she whispered. 'Don't let him get to you.'

*

The Parson knelt deep in prayer on the hillside as the crowd gathered. He opened his eyes and looked out over the throng, and a deep warmth flowed within him. He had walked for two months to reach Pilgrim's Valley, crossing desert and plain, mountain and valley. He had preached at farms and settlements, performed marriages, christenings and funerals at isolated homes. He had prayed for the sick, and been welcomed wherever he walked. Once he had delivered a sermon at a brigand camp, and they had fed him and given him supplies of food and water to enable him to continue his journey. Now he was here, looking out over two thousand eager faces. He ran his hand through his thick red hair and stood.

He was home.

Lifting his borrowed pistols, he cocked them and fired two shots in the air. Into the silence that followed, his voice rang out.

'Brothers and sisters, welcome to God's Holy Day! Look at the sun shining in the clear blue heavens. Feel the warmth on your faces. That is but a poor reflection of the Love of God, when it flows into your hearts and your minds.

'We spend our days, brethren, grubbing in the dirt for wealth. Yet true wealth is here. Right here! I want each one of you to turn to the person beside you and take their hand in friendship. Do it now! Touch. Feel. Welcome. For the person beside you is your brother today, or your sister. Or your son. Or your daughter. Do it now! Do it now in love.'

A ripple ran through the crowd as people turned, mostly in embarrassment, to grasp and swiftly release the hands of the strangers beside them.

'Not good enough, brethren,' shouted the Parson. 'Is this how you would greet a long-lost brother or sister? I will show you.' He strode down amongst them and took an elderly woman in a deep hug, kissing both her cheeks. 'God's love upon you, mother,' he said. He seized a man's arm and swung him to face a young woman. 'Embrace her,' he ordered. 'And say the words with meaning. With belief. With love.'

Slowly he moved through the crowd, forcing people together. Some of the miners began to follow him, taking women in their arms and kissing them soundly on the cheeks. 'That is it, brethren!' shouted the Parson. 'Today is God's Day. Today is love!' He moved back to the hillside.

'Not that much love!' he shouted at a miner who had lifted a struggling woman from her feet. The crowd bellowed with laughter, and the tension eased.

'Look at us, Lord!' The Parson raised his arms and his face to the heavens. 'Look down on your people. Today there is no killing. No violence. No greed. Today we are a family in your sight.'

Then he launched into a powerful sermon about the sins of the many and the joys of the few. He had them then, as his powerful voice rolled over them. He talked of greed and of cruelty, the mindless pursuit of wealth and the loss of joy it created.

'For what does it profit a man if he gain the world, and yet lose his soul? What is wealth without love? Three hundred years ago the Lord brought Armageddon to the world of sin, toppling the earth, destroying Babylon the Great. For in those days evil had spread across the earth like a deadly plague, and the Lord washed away their sins even as Isaiah had prophesied. The sun rose in the West, the seas tipped from their bowls and not one stone was left upon another. But what did we learn, brethren? Did we come to love one another? Did we turn to the Almighty? No. We threw our noses into the mud and we scrabbled for gold and silver. We lusted and we fought, we hated and we slew.

'And why? Why?' he roared. 'Because we are men. Sinful, lustful men. But not today, brethren. We stand here in God's sunshine, and we know peace. We know love. And tomorrow I will build me a church on this meadow, where the love and peace of today will be sanctified; where it will be planted like a seed. And those of you who wish to see God's love remain in this community will come to me here, bringing wood and hammers and nails and saws, and we will build a church of love. And now, let us pray.'

The crowd knelt and he blessed them. He allowed the silence to grow for more than a minute, then, 'Up, my brethren. The fatted calf is waiting, the fun and the joy are here for all. Up and be happy. Up and laugh!'

People surged away to the tents and stalls, the children racing down the hill to the swing-boards and the mud around the stream. The Parson walked down into the throng, accepting a jug of water from a woman selling cakes. He drank deeply.

'That was well spoken,' said a voice and the Parson turned to see a tall man with silver-streaked shoulder-length hair and a greying beard. The man was wearing a flat-brimmed hat and a black coat and two pistols hung from scabbards at his hips.

'Thank you, brother. Did you feel moved to repent?'

'You made me think deeply. That, I hope, is a beginning.'

'Indeed it is. Do you have a farm here?'

'No, I am a travelling man. Good luck with your church.' He moved away into the crowd.

'That was the Jerusalem Man,' said the woman selling cakes. 'He killed a man yesterday. They say he's come to destroy the wicked.'

'Vengeance is mine, says the Lord. But let us not talk of violence and death, sister. Cut me a slice of your cake.'

14

Shannow watched the pistol-shooting contest with interest. The competitors, twenty-two of them, lined up facing open ground and loosed shots at targets thirty paces away. Gradually the field was whittled down to three men, one of them Clem Steiner. Each was obliged to fire at plates which were hurled in the air by children standing to the right of the range. Steiner won the competition and collected his prize of 100 Bartas from Edric Scayse. As the crowd was beginning to disperse, Scayse's voice rang out.

'We have with us today a legendary figure, possibly one of the greatest pistol shots on the continent. Ladies and gentlemen – Jon Shannow, the Jerusalem Man!' A ripple of applause ran through the spectators and Shannow stood silently, crushing the anger welling up in him. 'Come forward Meneer Shannow,' called Scayse and Shannow stepped up to the line. 'The winner of our competition, Clement Steiner, feels that his prize cannot be truly won unless he defeats the finest competitors. Therefore he has returned his prize until he has matched skills with the Jerusalem Man.'

The crowd roared approval. 'Do you accept the challenge, Jon Shannow?'

Shannow nodded and removed his coat and hat, laying them on the wooden rail that bordered the range. He drew his guns and checked his loads. Steiner stepped alongside him.

'Now they'll see some real shooting,' said the young man, grinning. He drew his pistol. 'Would you like to go first?' he asked. Shannow shook his head. 'Okay. Throw, boy!' called Steiner and a large clay plate sailed into the air. The crack of the pistol shot was followed by the shattering of the plate at the apex of its flight. Shannow then cocked his pistol and nodded to the boy. Another plate flew up and disintegrated as Shannow fired. Plate after plate was blown to pieces until finally the Jerusalem Man called a halt.

'This could go on all day, boy,' he said. 'Try two.' Steiner's eyes narrowed.

Another boy was sent to join the first and two plates were hurled high. Steiner hit the first but the second fell to the ground, shattering on impact.

Shannow took his place and both plates were exploded. 'Four!' he called, and the crowd stood stock-still as two more boys joined the throwers. Shannow cocked both pistols and took a deep breath. Then he nodded to the boys and as the plates soared into the air his guns swept up. The shots rolled out like thunder, smashing three of the spinning plates before they had reached the top of their flight. The fourth was falling like a stone when the bullet smashed through it. The applause was thunderous as Shannow bowed to the crowd, reloaded his pistols and sheathed them. He put on his coat and hat and collected the prize from Scayse.

The man smiled. 'You did not enjoy that, Mr Shannow. I am sorry. But the people will not forget it.'

'The coin will come in useful,' said Shannow. He turned to Steiner. 'I think it would be right for us to share this prize,' he suggested. 'For you had to work much harder for it.'

'Keep it!' snapped Steiner. 'You won it. But it doesn't make you a better man. We've still to decide that.'

'There is nothing to decide, Meneer Steiner. I can hit more plates, but you can draw and shoot accurately with far greater speed.'

'You know what I mean, Shannow. I'm talking about man to man.'

'Do not even think about it,' advised the Jerusalem Man.

*

It was almost midnight before Broome allowed Beth to leave the Jolly Pilgrim. The morning's entertainment had spilled over into the evening and Broome wanted to stay open to cater for the late-night revellers. Beth was not concerned about the children for Mary would have taken Samuel back to the wagon and prepared him some supper, but she was sorry to have missed an evening with them. They were growing so fast. She moved along the darkened sidewalk and down the three short steps to the street. A man stepped out in front of her from the shadows at the side of the building; two others joined him.

'Well, well,' he said, his face shadowed from the moonlight by the brim of his hat. 'If it ain't the whore who killed poor Thomas.'

'His stupidity killed him,' she said.

'Yeah? But you warned the Jerusalem Man, didn't you? You went running to him. Are you his whore, bitch?'

Beth's fist cracked against his chin and he staggered; she followed in crashing a second blow with her left that spun him from his feet. As he tried to rise she lashed out with her foot, catching him under the chin. 'Any other questions?' she asked. She walked on but a man leapt at her, grabbing her arms; she struggled to turn and kick out, but another man grabbed her legs and she was hoisted from her feet.

They carried her towards the alley. 'We'll see what makes you so special,' grunted one of her attackers.

'I don't think so,' said a man's voice and the attackers dropped Beth to the ground. She scrambled to her feet and looked up to see the Parson was standing in the street.

'You keep your puking nose out of this,' said one of the men, while the other drew a pistol.

'I do not like to see any among the brethren behaving in such a manner towards a lady,' said the Parson. 'And I do not like guns pointed at me. It is not polite. Go on about your business.'

'You think I won't kill you?' the gunman asked. 'Just because you wear a black dress and spout on about God? You're nothing, man. Nothing!'

'What I am is a man. And men do not behave as you do.

Only the basest animals act in such a manner. You are filth! Vermin! You do not belong in the company of civilised people.'

'That's it!' shouted the man, his pistol coming up and his thumb on the hammer. The Parson's hand swept out from behind his cassock and his gun roared. The man was hurled backwards by the force of the shell as it hit his chest, then a second bullet smashed through his skull.

'Jesus Christ!' whispered the survivor.

'A little late for prayers,' the Parson told him. 'Step forward and let me see your face.' The man stumbled towards him and the Parson lifted his hand and removed the man's hat, allowing the moonlight to illuminate his features.

'Tomorrow morning you will report to the meadow where you will help me build my church. Is that not so, brother?' The gun pushed up under the man's chin.

'Whatever you say, Parson.'

'Good. Now see to the body. It is not fitting that it should lie there to be seen by children in the morning.'

The Parson moved to Beth. 'How are you feeling, sister?'

'I've had better days,' Beth told him.

'I shall walk you to your home.'

'That will not be necessary.'

'Indeed no. But it will be a pleasure.' He took her arm and they walked off in the direction of Tent Town.

'I thought your God looked unkindly on killing,' said Beth.

'Indeed he does, sister. But the distinction he makes concerns murder. The Bible is full of killing and slaughter, and the Lord understands that among sinful men there will always be violence. There is an apt section in Ecclesiastes: *There is a time for everything, and a season for every activity. A time to be born, and a time to die, a time to plant and a time to uproot, a time to kill, and a time to heal . . .* There is more, and it is very beautiful.'

'You speak well, Parson. But I'm glad you also shoot well.'

'I've had a lot of practice, sister.'

'Call me Beth. I never had no brothers. Do you have a name?'

'Parson is fine. And I like the sound of Beth; it is a good name. Are you married?'

'I was. Sean died on the journey. But my children are with me. I expect they're sleeping now – or they damn well better be.'

They made their way through the tents and wagons until they reached the McAdam camp-site. The fire was low and the children asleep in their blankets beside the wheels. The oxen had been led to a second meadow where they grazed with other cattle. Beth stoked up the fire.

'Will you join me for tea, Parson? I always drink a cup before sleeping.'

'Thank you,' he answered, sitting cross-legged by the fire. She boiled some water, added herbs and sugar and poured the mixture into two pottery mugs.

'You come far?' she asked, as they drank.

'Very far. I heard God calling me, and I answered. But what of you? Where are you bound?'

'I'll be staying in the valley. I am going to lease some land from Meneer Scayse – start a farm. I have some seed corn and other such.'

'Hard work for a woman alone.'

'I won't be alone long, Parson. It's not my way.'

'No, I can see that,' he answered without embarrassment. 'By the way, where did such a charming young mother learn the rudiments of the left hook? It was a splendid blow with all your weight behind it.'

'My husband Sean was a fist-fighter. He taught me that – and much more.'

'He was a lucky man, Beth.'

'He's dead, Parson.'

'Many men live a long lifetime and never meet a woman like you. They, I think, are the unlucky ones. And now I must bid you good night.' He rose and bowed.

'You come again, Parson. You're always welcome.'

'That is nice to know. I hope we will see you in our new church.'

'Only if you have songs. I like to sing.'

'We will have songs just for you,' he told her, and walked away into the shadows.

For a while Beth sat quietly by the dying fire. The Parson was a strong man, and extraordinarily handsome with that fine red hair and easy smile. But there was something about him that disturbed her and she thought about it, trying to pin down her unease. Physically she found him attractive, but there was about him a tightness, a tension that left her wary. Her thoughts strayed to Jon Shannow. Similar men, and yet not so. Like thunder and lightning. Both were companion to inner storms. But Shannow was aware of his own dark side. She was not sure about the Parson.

Beth stripped off her long woollen skirt and her white blouse and washed in cold water. Then she slipped into a full-length bed-gown and settled down into her blankets. Her hand moved under the pillow, curling round the walnut butt of her pistol.

And she slept.

*

During the night there were two killings and a woman was raped behind a gambling-house in the east section. Shannow sat silently in the corner of the Long Bar drinking a Baker's and listening to the tales. It seemed the Parson had killed one man who was attacking a woman but the other shooting was a mystery, save for the fact that the dead man had won a large amount of coin playing Carnat at a gambling house run by a man named Webber.

Shannow had seen it all before: crooked gamblers, thieves and robbers congregating in a community that had no law. When would the upright citizens ever learn, he wondered? There were around two thousand people in Pilgrim's Valley, and no more than a hundred villains. Yet the brigands swaggered around the town and the good people stepped aside for them. He stared sourly into the dark depths of the drink before him, and knew that he was tempted to cut away the disease afflicting the community; to storm the bastions of the Ungodly and root out the evil. Yet he would not.

I no longer lance boils – that's what he had told Boris Haimut. And it was true. A man could take only so much of rejection and the contempt of his fellows. It always began with fine words and promises. 'Help us, Mr Shannow.' 'We need you, Mr Shannow.' 'Good work, Mr Shannow.' 'That will show them, sir.' And then . . . 'But do you have to be so violent, Mr Shannow?' 'Is the bloodshed necessary?' 'When will you be moving on?'

But no more. If the town was diseased it was a problem for those who lived here, who wanted to work here, raise children in the valley. It was for them now to put their house in order.

He had said as much to the merchants Brisley and Fenner who had waited for him that morning. Brisley, fat and gregarious, had extolled the virtues of the community, blaming its ills on men like Scayse and Webber.

'No better than brigands, sir, I assure you. Scayse's men are arrogant and ill-mannered. And as for Webber, the man is a thief and a killer. Four times in the last month, men who have won large amounts of money have been slain close to his establishment. And he killed two others in gun battles over alleged cheating. It is insufferable, sir.'

'Then do something about it,' advised Shannow.

'That's what we are doing,' put in Fenner, a dark-eyed young man of slender build. 'We have come to you.'

'You do not need me. Get together twenty men. Go to Webber. Close him down. Order him from the community.'

'His men are thugs and villains,' said Brisley, wiping the sweat from his face. 'They thrive on violence. We are merchants.'

'You have guns,' said Shannon simply. 'Even a merchant can pull a trigger.'

'With respect, sir,' Fenner interposed, 'it takes a certain kind of man to be able to kill a human being in cold blood.

Now I don't know if killing will be necessary. I hope not. But surely a man with your reputation would find it more easy to stamp his authority on the villains?'

'In cold blood, Meneer?' responded Shannow. 'I do not consider it in those terms. I am not a wanton slayer, nor am I a kind of respectable brigand. Mostly the men I have killed have died in the act of trying to kill me. The rest have been in the process of wilfully attacking others. However, such points are meaningless in the current circumstances. I have no wish to give birth again to seven devils.'

'You have me at a loss, sir,' said Fenner.

'Read your Bible, Meneer. Now leave me in peace.'

Shannow finished his drink and returned to his room. For a while he sat thinking about the problems posed by the Wall, but Beth McAdam's face kept appearing before his mind's eye.

'You are a fool, Shannow,' he told himself. Loving Donna Taybard had been a mistake, and one he had come to regret. But it was folly of the worst kind to allow another woman to enter his heart.

He forced her from his mind and took up his Bible, leafing through to the Gospel of Matthew.

'When an evil spirit goes out of a man, it goes through arid places seeking rest and does not find it. Then it says, "I will return to the house I left." When it arrives it finds the house unoccupied, swept clean and put in order. Then it goes and takes with it seven other spirits more wicked than itself and they go in and live there. And the final condition of that man is worse than the first.'

How often had the Jerusalem Man seen the truth of that? In Allion, Cantastay, Berkalin, and a score of other settlements. The brigands had fled before him – or been buried because of him. Then he had ridden on and the evil had returned. Daniel Cade had visited Allion two weeks after Shannow left, and the town had been ruined by his attack.

It would not happen here, he decided.

In Pilgrim's Valley the Jerusalem Man was merely an observer.

15

The pistol competition had left Shannow short of shells for his Hellborn pistols. There were twenty-three left, including the ten in the cylinders of his guns. Pilgrim's Valley boasted one gunsmith and Shannow made his way to the man's small shop in the eastern section. It was a narrow building, lit by lanterns, the wall behind the service area filled with weapons of every kind from flintlock pistols to percussion rifles, flared-barrelled blunderbusses alongside sleek gravity-fed weapons with walnut stocks. But there were no pistols like Shannow's.

The shop-owner was a short, bald elderly man who identified himself as Groves. Shannow drew one of his guns and laid it on the double plank unit that served as a long table between the gunsmith and his customers. Groves sniffed and lifted the weapon, flicking open the gate and ejecting a shell. 'Hellborn,' he said. 'There are a lot of these in the north now. We're hoping to get some – but they're mighty expensive.'

'I need bullets for it,' said Shannow. 'Can you make them?'

'I'd have no trouble with the moulds, or the fulminates. But these brass cases? It will not be easy, Mr Shannow. Nor cheap.'

'But you can do it?'

'Leave me five shells with which to experiment. I will do what I can. When are you leaving?'

'I was due to ride on today.'

Groves chuckled. 'I need at least a week, sir. How many do you require?'

'One hundred would suffice.'

'That will cost fifty Bartas. I would appreciate half now.'

'Your price is very high.'

'So is the level of my craftsmanship.'

Shannow paid the man and returned to the hotel where he found Mason sitting in a comfort chair by an open window, dozing in the sun.

'I need the room for another week,' he said.

Mason blinked and stood. 'I thought you were moving on, Meneer Shannow.'

'I am, sir, but not for a week.'

'I see. Very well. A week, then.'

Shannow walked to the stable and saddled the stallion. The hostler grinned at him as he rode out and Shannow waved as he steered the horse to the south, heading for the Wall. He rode for two hours, crossing rich grassland and cutting high into the timberline of the hills. He saw cattle grazing, and a herd of antelope moving along the line of a stream. The Wall grew ever nearer. From the high ground where he rode, Shannow could see over the colossal structure and the rolling hills beyond it. There was no sign of life; no cattle, sheep, goats or deer. Yet the land looked rich and verdant. Angling the stallion downwards, he halted on the hillside, drawing his long glass from the saddlebag. He followed the line of the Wall first to the east where it disappeared in the blue haze of the mountains; then he swung the glass west. As far as he could see the Wall went on for miles, unbroken and unbreachable; he focused the glass on a section of it some half a mile away, and saw a group of men camped nearby. Then he continued his descent and rode on. The Wall now reared above him and he estimated its height at more than sixty feet. It was constructed of giant rectangular blocks each approximately ten feet wide and more than six feet high.

Shannow dismounted and approached the edifice. He drew his hunting-knife and tried to push the blade between two stones, but the fit was too tight and there was no sign of mortar. From the hill above he had judged the Wall to be at least ten feet thick. He sheathed his knife and ran his fingers over the blocks, seeking handholds that might permit him to climb. But apart from lichens and curious shells imbedded in the surface, there was no purchase.

He stepped into the saddle and followed the line of the Wall west until he reached the camp-site where Boris Haimut was chipping away at one of the blocks with a hammer and chisel. The scholar put down his tools and waved.

'Fascinating, is it not?' said Haimut, grinning cheerfully. Shannow dismounted, his eyes scanning the small group of men who continued with their work. To the far right he could see the two men who had tried to force him to leave the site of the shipwreck; they avoided his gaze, and continued to chip away at the blocks.

Shannow followed Haimut to the camp-site where a large pot of Baker's was brewing. Haimut wrapped a cloth around the handle and lifted the pot, filling two mugs. He passed one to Shannow.

'Have you ever seen anything like it?' asked Haimut and Shannow shook his head. 'Neither have I. There are no windows, no towers and no gates. It could not have been built for defence; any invading army would simply throw grappling lines over the top and climb it. There are no parapets. Nothing. Just a colossal Wall. Take a look at this.' He fished in his pocket and produced a shining shell, slightly larger than a Barta coin. Shannow took it, turning it over and holding it to the light. There were many colours glistening within the grooves – purple, yellow, blue and white.

'It is very pretty,' Shannow said.

'Indeed it is. But it is also from the sea, Mr Shannow. This towering structure was once below the ocean.'

'This whole land was once under water,' Shannow told him. 'There was a civilisation here – a great civilisation. But the seas rose up and devoured them.'

'So then, you are saying this is an Oldworld site?'

'No. The Oldworld sites are now mostly beneath the seas. I learned several years ago that the earth had toppled not once, but twice. The people who lived beyond this Wall were destroyed thousands of years ago. I have no way of knowing, but I would guess it happened about the time of the Flood described in the Book.'

'How do you know all this?' asked Haimut.

Shannow considered telling him the whole truth, but dismissed the thought. What credibility he had would disappear if he explained how the long-dead King of Atlantis had come to his rescue in the battle against the Guardians during the Hellborn War.

'Two years ago, with a friend, I rode into the ruins of a great city. There were statues everywhere. Beautifully carved. While there, I met a scholar named Samuel Archer. He was a fine man: strong, yet gentle. He had studied the ruins and others like them for many years and had even managed to decipher the language of the ancients. The city was called Balacris, the land was known as Atlantis. I learned much from him before he died.'

'I'm sorry that he is dead. I would like to have met him,' said Haimut. 'I too have seen the inscriptions on gold foil. But to meet a man who could read them... How did he die?'

'He was beaten to death because he would not work as a slave in a silver mine.'

Haimut looked away and sipped his Baker's. 'This is not a contented world, Meneer Shannow. We live in strange circumstances, fighting over scraps of knowledge. Everywhere there are isolated communities, and no central focus. In the wildlands the brigands rule, and in settled communities there are wars with rivals. There is no peace. It is most galling. Far to the east there is a land where women are not allowed to show their faces in public and men who deny the Book are burned alive. To the north there are communities where child sacrifice has become the norm. Last year I visited an area where women are not allowed to marry; they are owned by the men and used as breed cows for the community. But wherever you go there is violence and death, and the rule of the powerful. Have you been to Rivervale?'

'I have,' replied Shannow. 'I lived there once.'

'Now that is an oasis. It is ruled by a man named Daniel Cade. They have laws there, good laws; and families can raise their children in peace and prosperity. If only we could all find such a way. You say you lived there? Do you know Daniel Cade?'

'I know him,' said Shannow. 'He is my brother.'

'Good Lord! I never knew that. I have heard of you, of course. But no one ever spoke of a brother.'

'We were parted as children. Tell me, what do you hope to achieve here?'

'Meneer Scayse is looking for a way to breach the Wall. He has asked me to examine it. And I need the coin, in order to be able to return home.'

'I thought you disapproved of him?'

'I do. He is – like all men who seek power – eminently selfish. But I cannot afford too many scruples. And I harm no one by examining this edifice.'

Shannow finished his drink and rose.

'Will you stay the night, Meneer?' Haimut asked. 'It would be good to have some intelligent conversation.'

'Thank you, no. Another time perhaps. Tell me, what do you know of Scayse?'

Haimut shrugged. 'Very little. He came here a year ago with a great deal of coin and a large herd of cattle. He is said to be from the far north. He is a clever man.'

'I don't doubt that,' said Shannow.

*

Shannow returned to the settlement just before dusk. He left the stallion at the stable, paid the hostler to groom and feed him and then walked to the Jolly Pilgrim. Beth McAdam smiled as he entered and moved across to greet him.

'Haven't seen much of you, Shannow,' she said. 'Food not good enough?'

'The food is fine. How are you faring?'

'Can't complain. You?'

'Well enough,' Shannow replied, aware of a rising tension. 'Would you bring me some food? Anything hot that you have.'

'Sure,' she told him. He sat quietly facing the door and glanced around the room. There were eight other diners – they studiously avoided looking at him. Beth brought him a bowl of thick broth and some dark bread and cheese. He ate it slowly and considered ordering a Baker's, but then he remembered Haimut's warning about the drink being habit-forming and decided against. Instead he asked for a glass of water.

'Are you all right, Shannow?' asked Beth, as she brought it to his table. 'You seem a little . . . preoccupied.'

'I have been studying the Wall,' he told her, 'looking for a way through. It looks as if I will have to climb it and proceed on foot. I do not like travelling that way.'

'Then ride around it. It cannot stretch across the world, for goodness' sake.'

'That could take weeks.'

'And you, of course, are a man with no time on his hands.'

He grinned at her. 'Will you join me?'

'I can't; I'm working. But tomorrow morning I get a free hour at noon. You could come then.'

'Perhaps I will,' he said.

'Maybe, if you do, you should consider getting that coat brushed and cleaning your other clothes. You smell of dust and horses. And that silver-forked beard makes you look like Methuselah.'

Shannow scratched his chin and smiled. 'We will see.' Just then Alain Fenner entered. He spotted Shannow and approached.

'May I sit down, Meneer?' he asked.

'I thought we had concluded our conversation,' said Shannow, annoyed that the interruption caused Beth to leave.

'It is only advice I am seeking.'

Shannow gestured to the chair opposite. 'How can I help you?'

Fenner leaned forward, lowering his voice. 'We are going to close down Webber tonight. As you suggested there will be a group of us – Brisley, Broome and a few others. But we are none of us men used to sudden violence. I would appreciate your thoughts.'

Shannow looked into the man's open, honest face and realised that he liked him. Fenner had courage, and he cared. 'Who will be your spokesman?' he asked.

'I will.'

'Then it is you the ungodly will look to for action. Do not allow Webber or anyone else to take the lead. Do not enter into any discussion. Say what you want and make it happen. Do you understand me?'

'I think so.'

'Keep all talk to a minimum. Move in, get Webber out and close the place. If there is the least suggestion of opposition, shoot someone. Keep the mob off balance. But it is Webber you must control. He is the head of the snake – cut him off and the others will stand and wonder what to do and while they are wondering, you will have won. Can you trust the men with you?'

'Trust them? What do you mean?'

'Are they close-mouthed? Will Webber know of your plan before you arrive?'

'I do not think so.'

'I hope you are right. Your life depends on it. Are you married?'

'I have a wife and four sons.'

'Think of them, Fenner, when you walk in. If you make a mistake, it is they who will pay for it.'

'Can it be done without shooting anyone?'

'Perhaps. I did not say you should walk in with guns blazing. I am trying to tell you how to stay alive. If Webber starts to talk and you respond his men will begin to gather themselves – and your men will start to waver. Be strong, be swift and be direct. No shades of grey, Meneer Fenner. Black and white. Win or lose. Live or die.'

Fenner took a deep breath. 'I will try to follow your advice. Thank you for your time.'

'It cost me nothing. If trouble starts – or even looks like starting – kill Webber.' But Shannow knew he would not, for even as he said it the young man's eyes wavered from his direct gaze. 'Do your best, Meneer.'

When the young man had left, Beth returned to the table. 'He's a good man,' she said.

'He may not live very long,' Shannow told her.

*

There were eight armed men in the group that entered Webber's gambling-house. It was crowded with more than twenty tables and a long bar packed with customers. Webber himself sat at a Carnat table to the rear and Fenner led the group through to him.

'You will come with us, Meneer Webber,' he said, drawing his pistol and pointing it at the gambler. As the revellers realised what was happening a silence fell on the room. Webber stood and folded his arms. He was a tall man, running to fat but powerfully built; his eyes were black and deep-set and he smiled at Fenner. Gleaming gold flashed in his grin and Fenner saw that the teeth on either side of his incisors were moulded from precious metal.

'Why in the Devil's name should I?' Webber asked.

Fenner cocked the pistol. 'Because you'll be dead if you don't,' he told him.

'Is this fair?' Webber thundered. 'What have I done? I run a gambling-house. I have killed no one – save in fair battle.'

'You are a thief and a scoundrel,' said Josiah Broome, pushing forward, 'and we are closing you down.'

'Who says I am a thief? Let him stand forward,' Webber shouted.

Fenner waved Broome back, but the man pushed on.

'People who win from you are killed. Do you deny any responsibility?'

'Why is that my fault, Meneer? A man who wins a great deal of coin is seen by many other – unluckier – gamblers.'

Fenner glanced around. The crowd had fallen back now and Webber's men ringed the group. Brisley was sweating heavily and two of the others were shifting uneasily. Fenner's pistol levelled at Webber's chest.

'You will move now, Meneer. Or suffer the consequences.'

'You would shoot me down? Murder me, Meneer? What sort of law is this you are proposing?'

'He ... he's right, Alain,' whispered Broome. 'We didn't come here to kill anyone. But let this be a lesson to you, Webber! We'll not stand for any more violence.'

'I stand and quake in my shoes, Meneer Bacon-server. Now all of you put down your weapons, or my men will blow you into tiny pieces.' Brisley's gun clattered to the floor and the others followed ... all save Alain Fenner. His eyes locked to Webber's and understanding flowed between them.

But Fenner was no killer. He uncocked the pistol and thrust it deep into the scabbard at his hip, but as he did so Webber drew his own pistol and shot Fenner twice in the chest. The young man scrabbled for his gun and fell to his knees, but a third shot struck his breastbone and spun him back to the floor.

'Emily ...' he whispered. Blood bubbled from his lips and his body twitched.

'Get the fool out of here,' ordered Webber. 'There's a game in progress.'

Brisley and the others hauled Fenner out into the street and back past the Traveller's Rest. Shannow was sitting on the porch; a great sadness weighed down on him as he stood and walked to the group.

'He just shot him down,' said Broome. 'Alain was putting away his gun, and Webber just shot him down.'

Shannow leaned over and touched his hand to Fenner's neck. 'He's dead. Put him down.'

'Not in the street,' Broome protested.

'Put him down!' stormed Shannow. 'And wait here.' He took off his coat and left it by the body, then walked swiftly to Webber's establishment. He entered and stalked across the room where the gambler was drinking and joking with his men. Then he drew his pistol, cocked it and slid it against Webber's lips.

'Open your mouth!' said Shannow. Webber blinked twice and saw the light of fury in Shannow's eyes. He opened his mouth and the barrel slid between his teeth. 'Now stand!' Webber eased himself to his feet. Shannow walked him slowly back through the throng and out of the door into the street. He did not need to look back to know that everyone in the gambling-house had followed. Word spread to other establishments and the crowd grew. Webber backed away, the gun almost making him choke. His own pistol was still in its holster, but he kept his hands well away from it. Shannow halted by the body of Alain Fenner, and turned slightly to look at the crowd.

'This young man risked his life for many of you. And now he lies dead, and his wife is a widow, and his sons have been robbed of a father. And why? Because you have no courage. Because you allow the vermin to walk among you. This man died as a result of sin.' His eyes swept the crowd. 'And as the Book says, "The Wages of Sin is death"!'

Shannow pulled the trigger. Webber's brains mushroomed from his skull and the body fell back to the earth with dark powder-smoke streaming from the blackened mouth.

'Now you listen to me!' Shannow roared into the stunned silence that followed. 'I know many of you brigands. If you are in Pilgrim's Valley come morning, I will hunt you down and kill you on sight. You may be sitting breaking your fast, or sleeping snug in a warm bed, or quietly playing Carnat with friends. But I will fall upon you with the wrath of God.

Those with ears to hear, let them understand. Tomorrow you die.'

A stocky man stepped from the crowd, wearing two guns thrust into his belt. 'You think you can tackle all of us?' he challenged.

Shannow's pistol boomed and the man flew from his feet, his skull smashed.

'There will be no questions,' declared the Jerusalem Man. 'Tomorrow I will hunt you down.'

16

The long night had begun. Shannow sat in his room with his Hellborn pistols on the table beside him, his trusted cap and ball weapons in the scabbards at his side. He had cleaned the old guns and reloaded them; he had only sixteen shells for the Hellborn revolvers, and if the night turned sour he would need more than that. He had moved his chair away from the window and now sat in the darkness of his room. The pillows of his bed had been rolled tight and placed under the blankets to imitate a sleeping form, and now the Jerusalem Man had nothing to do but wait for the inevitable.

As the first hour crept by he heard the sound of horsemen leaving the town. He did not look from the window to check the numbers. At least two-thirds of the brigands would be leaving before dawn, but it was not the runners who worried Shannow.

He sat in the darkness, his fury gone, blaming himself for Fenner's death; he had known deep in his soul that the young man could not survive, and yet he had let him walk into the Valley of the Shadow.

Am I my brother's keeper? The answer should have been yes. He recalled the shocked looks on the faces of the mob as he had blown Webber to Hell, and he knew what they had seen: the crazed fanatic the world knew as the Jerusalem Man taking one more helpless victim. They would forget that Webber had mercilessly murdered poor Alain Fenner, but they would remember the tormented Webber, standing in the moonlight with a pistol barrel in his mouth.

And so would Shannow. It was not a good deed. He could convince himself of its necessity, but not of its virtue. There was a time when Jon Shannow would have fought Webber man to man, upright and fearless. But not now.

His powers and his speed were waning. He had seen that well enough when he watched Clem Steiner shoot the jug. Once, maybe, the Jerusalem Man could have duplicated such a feat. Not any more. Not even close.

A floorboard creaked in the corridor outside. Shannow hefted a pistol, then heard a door open and close and the sound of a man sitting down on a mattress. He relaxed, but left the pistol cocked.

Rivervale. That was where his life had changed. He had ridden through the wild lands and found himself in a predominantly peaceful community. There he had met Donna Taybard. Her husband, Tomas the carpenter, had been murdered, and she herself was under threat. Shannow had helped her and had grown to love her. Together they had journeyed with Con Griffin to a hoped-for new life in a world without brigands and killers. Griffin had called it Avalon.

Yet what had they found? Shannow had been wounded by the Carns, a strange race of cannibals, and rescued by the saintly Karitas, a survivor of the Fall of the world. Donna had believed Shannow dead and had married Griffin.

And something in Jon Shannow had given up the ghost and died. He remembered his father once saying: 'Better to have loved and lost than never to have loved at all.' But it was not true.

He had been more content before he met Donna. Perhaps not happy, but he knew who he was and what he was . . .

The soft scuff of a boot sounded on the roof above his head.

Come then, my would-be killers. I am here. I am waiting. He heard the stretching groan of a rope and saw a booted foot in a loop easing down outside the window.

Lower and lower it came until a man's body appeared. He was holding the rope with his left hand while in his right was a long-barrelled pistol. As his torso came level with the window he sighted on the bed and fired twice. At the same time, the door to Shannow's room was smashed open and two men rushed in.

The Jerusalem Man shot them both with his left-hand pistol, then twisted his right and fired point-blank into the belly of the man on the rope, who screamed and pitched back out of sight. Shannow lifted his pistols high and blasted three shots through the ceiling. He heard a man yell; the rope sailed past the window and he heard the thumping crash of the body splitting the planks of the sidewalk.

Silence fell. The room stank of gunfire and a fine mist of powder and cordite hung in the air.

Outside in the corridor Shannow could hear whispered commands, but there was no movement.

Swiftly he reloaded his pistols with the last of his shells.

Two shots came from the corridor. A man screamed and a body thudded against the wooden landing.

'Hey, Shannow,' called Steiner. 'It's clear out here. Can I come in?'

'Your hands better be empty,' Shannow replied.

Steiner stepped across the bodies and entered the room. 'There were only two of them,' he said, smiling. 'Damn, but you do make life interesting. You know, at least thirty men have already left the settlement. What I wouldn't give for a reputation like yours!'

'Why did you help me?'

'Hell, Shannow, I couldn't take the risk of someone else killing you. Where in the world would I find an opponent like you?'

Steiner eased his way to the side of the window and pulled the thick curtain across it, then he struck a match and lit the lantern on the table. 'Mind if I move these bodies into the hall – they're starting to stink up the place?' Without waiting for a response he moved over to the corpses. 'Both shot through the head. Pretty good. Pretty damn good!' He grabbed the collar of the first man and dragged him out into the hall. Shannow sat and watched as he pulled the second corpse after it. 'Hey, Mason!' Steiner shouted. 'Can you get some men up here to move this dead meat?'

Stepping back inside, he wedged the broken door shut and returned to his seat. 'Well, Shannow, you going to thank me, or what?'

'Why should I thank you?'

'For taking out the two on the stairs. What would you have done without me? They had you trapped in here like snared game.'

'Thank you,' said Shannow. 'And now you should leave. I'm going to get some sleep.'

'You want me to walk with you tomorrow, when the hunting starts?'

'That will not be necessary.'

'Man, you are crazy. There're still twenty, maybe thirty men who won't be run out. You can't take them all.'

'Good night, Meneer Steiner.'

*

The following morning, after three hours' sleep, Jon Shannow made his way down to the lobby and called Mason to him. 'Send someone out to find me six children who can read. Have them brought here.'

Then the Jerusalem Man sat down at a table with six large sheets of paper and a charcoal stub. Slowly and carefully he spelled out a simple message on each sheet.

Shannow made the children read aloud the message and then sent them to the gambling and drinking houses in the east section with instructions to hand a notice to each of the owners, or barmen. The message was simple:

WARNING
ANYONE CARRYING A GUN WITHIN THE TOWNSHIP OF PILGRIM'S VALLEY WILL BE CONSIDERED A BRIGAND AND A WARMAKER AND WILL BE DEALT WITH AS SUCH.
SHANNOW

When the children had left, Shannow sat back and waited patiently, emptying his mind of fear and tension. Mason brought him a cup of Baker's and sat down opposite.

'For what it's worth, Shannow, the room is free – and any food or drink you consume.'

'That is kind of you, Meneer.'

Mason shrugged. 'You are a good man. This will make you no friends, however.'

'I am aware of that.' He looked into the man's cadaverous face. 'I do not think you were always a room-keeper?'

Mason gave a thin smile. 'You chased me out of Allion – put a bullet in my shoulder. When it rains, it hurts like the Devil.'

Shannow nodded. 'I remember you; you rode with Cade. I am glad you found something more productive.'

'A man gets older,' said Mason. 'Most of us took to the road because we were forced from our farms, either by raiders, or drought, or men with more power. But it's no life. Here I have a wife, two daughters and a roof over my head. My meals are regular, and in the winter I have a large log fire to keep out the cold. What more can a man rightly ask for?'

'Amen to that,' Shannow agreed.

'What will you do now?'

'I'll wait until noon and then root out whoever is left.'

'This isn't Allion, Shannow. There you had townspeople who backed you. There was a Committee, I recall – all good with rifles – and they protected your back. Here it is suicidal. They will wait for you in alleys, or shoot you as you appear on the street.'

'I have spoken the words, Meneer, and they are iron.'

'I guess so,' agreed Mason, rising. 'God's luck be with you.'

'It generally is,' said the Jerusalem Man.

From where he sat, he could see the sun slowly ascending the heavens. It looked to be a beautiful day; a man could not choose a more beautiful day to die. One by one the children returned and Shannow gave them each a coin, asked them where they had taken the notices and what had been the response. In most cases the recipients had read them aloud to the gathering, but in one instance a man had read out the notice and then torn it to pieces. The crowd had laughed, the boy told Shannow.

'Describe the place.' The boy did so. 'And did you see men with guns there?'

'Yes. One was sitting by a window with a long rifle aimed at the street. There were two others on a balcony above and to the right of the door. And I think there was another man hidden by some barrels at the far wall by the bar.'

'You are an observant boy. What is your name?'

'Matthew Fenner, sir.' Shannow looked into the boy's dark eyes and wondered why he had not seen the resemblance to the martyred farmer.

'How is your mother?'

'She's been crying a lot.'

Shannow opened the hide pouch in which he kept his coin and counted out twenty pieces. 'Give these to your mother. Tell her I am sorry.'

'We are not poor, sir. But thank you for the thought,' said Matthew. The boy turned and walked from the room.

It was almost noon. Shannow returned the coin to his pouch and stood.

He left the Traveller's Rest by the back door and stepped swiftly into the alley, moving to his right with gun poised. The alley was deserted. He walked along behind the buildings until he came to the side of the gambling-house the boy had described. It was run by a man named Zeb Maddox and Mason had told him Maddox was a fast man with a pistol: 'Damn near as sudden as Steiner. Don't give him no second chances, Shannow.'

The Jerusalem Man paused outside a tiny service door to the rear, took a deep breath and then eased open the latch. Stepping inside, he saw the back of a man who was kneeling behind some barrels. Beyond him everyone's eyes were on the front door. Shannow moved forward and cracked his pistol against the back of the kneeling man's neck. As he grunted and slid sideways, Shannow caught him by the collar and eased him to the floor.

Just then someone shouted, 'There's a crowd gathering, Zeb.'

Shannow watched as a tall, thin man in a black shirt and leather trousers emerged from behind the bar and moved to the door. He was wearing a pistol scabbard of polished leather which housed a short-barrelled gun with a bone handle.

From outside came a voice.

'You men inside, listen to me; this is the Parson speaking. We know you are armed, and we are ready to give battle to you. But think on this: There are forty men out here, and when we rush the place the carnage will be terrible. Those we do not kill will be taken to a place of execution and hanged by the neck until dead. I suggest you put down your weapons and walk – in peace – to your horses. We will wait for a few minutes, but if we are forced to storm in you all will die.'

'We got to get out of here, Zeb,' shouted a man Shannow could not see.

'I'll not run from a pack of Townies,' hissed Zeb Maddox.

'Then run from me,' said Shannow, moving forward with pistol raised.

Maddox turned slowly. 'You going to try to put that pistol in my mouth, Shannow, or will you be a man and face me?'

'Oh, I'll face you,' said Shannow as he strode forward and pushed his pistol into Maddox's belly. 'Draw your gun and cock it.'

'What the Hell is this?'

'Do it. Now put it against my stomach.' Maddox did so. 'Fine. There's your chance. I'll count to three and we'll both pull the triggers,' whispered Shannow coldly.

'You're crazy. We'll both die, for sure.'

'One,' said Shannow.

'This is mad, Shannow!' Maddox's eyes were wide with terror.

'Two!'

'No!' screamed Maddox, hurling away his pistol and throwing himself backwards, his hands over his face.

The Jerusalem Man looked around at the waiting gunmen. 'Live or die,' he told them. 'Choose now.'

Guns clattered to the floor. Shannow walked to the doorway and nodded to the Parson and the men gathered with him. Broome was there. And Brisley... and Mason... and Steiner. Beth McAdam was standing beside them, her pistol in her hand.

'I killed no one,' said Shannow. 'They are ready to go. Let them ride.' He walked away, his gun hanging at his side.

'Shannow!' screamed Beth and the Jerusalem Man spun as Zeb Maddox fired from the doorway. The shell punched Shannow from his feet; his vision misting, he returned the fire. Maddox doubled over, then staggered upright, but a volley of shots from the crowd lifted him and hurled him back through the doorway.

Shannow struggled to his feet and staggered. Blood was dripping to his cheek. He bent to retrieve his hat...

And darkness swallowed him.

*

Bright colours were everywhere, hurting his eyes. And blood flowed upon his face. Flames flickered at the edge of his vision and he saw a terrible beast stalking towards him, holding a rope with which to throttle him. His pistol blazed and the creature staggered, but came on, blood pouring from its wound. He fired again. And again. Still the beast advanced until finally it slumped to its knees before him, its taloned claws opening.

'Why?' the beast whispered.

Shannow looked down and saw that the creature was carrying not a rope but a bandage. 'Why did you kill me, when I was trying to help you?'

'I'm sorry,' whispered Shannow. The beast vanished and he rose and walked to the cave-mouth. Hanging in the sky, awesome in its scale, was the Sword of God, with around it crosses of many colours – green and white and blue. Below it was a city, teeming with life: a huge, circular city, ringed with walls of white

stone and a massive moat which boasted a harbour where wooden ships with banks of oars were anchored.

A beautiful woman with flame-red hair approached Shannow. 'I will help you,' she said... but in her hand was a knife. Shannow backed away.

'Leave me alone,' he told her. But she advanced and the knife came up to sink in his chest. Darkness engulfed him. Then there was the noise of a great roaring and he awoke.

He was sitting in a small seat, surrounded by crystal set in steel. Upon his head was a tight-fitting helmet of leather. Voices whispered in his ear.

'Calling Tower. This is an emergency. We seem to be off course. We cannot see land... Repeat... We cannot see land.'

Shannow leaned over and looked through the crystal window. Far below he could see the ocean. He glanced back. He was sitting in a metal cross, suspended in the air below the clouds which flashed by above him with dizzying speed.

'What is your position, Flight Leader?' came a second voice.

'We are not sure of our position, Tower. We cannot be sure just where we are... We seem to be lost...'

'Assume bearing due west.'

'We don't know which way is west. Everything is wrong... strange... we can't be sure of any direction – even the ocean doesn't look as it should...'

The cross began to tremble violently and Shannow scrabbled at the window. Ahead, the heavens and the sea appeared to merge. All around the window the sky disappeared, and blackness swamped the cross. Shannow screamed...

'It's all right, Shannow. Calm. Stay calm.'

His eyes opened to see Beth McAdam leaning over him. He tried to move his head, but sickening pain thundered in his temple and he groaned.

Beth laid a cool towel on his brow. 'You're all right, Shannow. You were turning as the bullet struck you. It did not pierce the skull, but it gave you a powerful blow. Rest now.'

'Maddox?' he whispered.

'Dead. We shot him down; the others we hanged. There

is a Committee now, patrolling the town. The brigands have gone.'

'They will return,' he said. 'They always return.'

'Sufficient unto the day is the evil thereof,' came another voice.

'That you, Parson?'

'Yes,' answered the man, leaning over him. 'Take it easy, Shannow. All is peaceful.'

Shannow slept without dreams.

17

'I see you have two Bibles,' said the Parson, sitting by Shannow's bedside and holding the leather-covered books. 'Surely one is enough?'

Shannow, his head bandaged, his left eye swollen and blue, reached out and took the first. 'I carried this with me for many years. But last year a woman gave me the second; the language is more simple. It lacks the majesty, but it makes many passages easier to understand.'

'I have no trouble in understanding it,' said the Parson. 'Throughout it makes one point – God's law is absolute. Live by it and you prosper, both here and in the Afterlife. Defy it and you die.'

Shannow eased himself back into the pillows. He was always wary of men who claimed to understand the Almighty, yet the Parson was good company, by turns witty and philosophical; he had an active mind and was strong on debate.

His presence made Shannow's enforced rest less galling.

'How goes the church building?' Shannow asked.

'My son,' said the Parson, grinning, 'it is no less than a miracle. Every day scores of the brethren hurl themselves into work with gusto. You have never seen such spirit.'

'Could it have anything to do with the Committee, Parson? Beth tells me that miscreants are now sentenced to work on the church or hang.'

The Parson chuckled. 'Faith without works is dead. These lucky... miscreants... are finding God through their labours. And only three were offered the ultimate choice. One proved to be a fine carpenter and the others are developing like skills, but most of the workers are towns-people. When you are well enough you must come along and hear one of my sermons. Though I say it myself, the Spirit moves me powerfully at such times.'

Shannow smiled. 'Humility, Parson?'

'I am exceptionally proud of my humility, Shannow,' the Parson replied.

Shannow chuckled. 'I do not know what to make of you, but I am glad of your company.'

'I do not understand your confusion,' said the Parson seriously. 'I am as you see me, a servant of the Almighty. I wish to see His plan fulfilled.'

'His plan? Which one?'

'The new Jerusalem, Shannow, coming down from Heaven in glory. And the secret is here, in the southlands. Look at the world we see. It is still beautiful, but there is no cohesion. We search for God in a hundred different ways in a thousand different places. We must gather together, work together, build together. We must have laws that hold like iron from ocean to ocean. But first we must see Revelation fulfilled.'

Shannow's unease grew. 'I thought it had been. Does it not speak of terrible catastrophes, cataclysms that will destroy most of Mankind?'

'I am talking of the Sword of God, Shannow. The Lord sent it to scythe the land like a sickle – yet it has not. And why? Because it is over an unholy place, peopled by the beasts of Satan and the Whore of Babylon.'

'I think I am ahead of you, Parson,' said Shannow wearily. 'You seek to destroy the beasts, bring down the Whore? Yes?'

'What else should a God-fearing man do, Shannow? Do you not wish to see the work of the Lord fulfilled?'

'I do not believe it to be fulfilled by slaughter.'

The Parson shook his head, eyes wide with disbelief. 'How can you, of all men, say that? Your guns are legendary, and corpses mark the road of your life. I thought you were well read, Shannow. Recall you not the Cities of Ai, and the curse of God upon the heathen? Not one man or woman or child was to be left alive among the worshippers of Molech.'

'I have heard this argument before,' said Shannow, 'from a Hellborn king who worshipped Satan. Where is the talk of love, Parson?'

'Love is for those of the Chosen People, created in the image of Almighty God. He made Men and he made the beasts of the earth. Only Lucifer would have the brazen gall to mould beasts into men.'

'You are swift to judge. Perhaps you are swift to misjudge.'

The Parson rose. 'You may be right, for I appear to have misjudged you. I thought you a warrior for God – but there is a weakness in you, Shannow, a doubt.'

The door opened and Beth entered, carrying a tray on which was some sliced dark bread and cheese and a jug of water. The Parson eased his way past her with a friendly smile, but left without farewells. Beth set the tray down and sat at the bedside.

'Do I sense angry words?' she asked.

Shannow shrugged. 'He is a man touched by a dream I do not share.' He reached out and took her hand. 'You have been kind to me, Beth McAdam, and I am grateful. I understand it was you who went to the Parson and got him to form the Committee which came to my aid.'

'It was nothing, Shannow. The town needed cleaning, and men like Broome would have spent a year debating the ethics of direct action.'

'Yet he was there, I recall.'

'The man doesn't lack courage – just common sense. How's your head?'

'Better. There is little pain. Would you do something for me? Would you fetch me razor and soap?'

'I'll do better than that, Jerusalem Man. I'll shave you myself. I'm longing to see what kind of a face you have hidden under that beard.'

She returned with a stiff badger-fur brush and a razor, borrowed from Mason, plus a cake of soap and a bowl of hot water. Shannow lay back with his eyes closed as she softened his beard with lather. The razor was cool on his cheek as she expertly scraped away the bristle and hair. At last she wiped his face clean of soap and handed him a towel. He smiled at her.

'What do you see?'

'You are not unhandsome, Shannow, but you'll win no prizes. Now eat your lunch. I'll see you this evening.'

'Don't go, Beth. Not just yet.' His hand reached up and took her arm.

'I have to work, Shannow.'

'Yes. Yes, of course. Forgive me.'

She stood and backed away, forced a smile and left. Outside in the corridor she stopped and pictured again the look in his eyes as he asked her to stay.

'Don't be a fool, Beth,' she told herself.

Why not? There's an hour before you are expected back. Swinging on her heel, she opened the door once more and stepped inside. Her hand moved to the buttons of her blouse.

'Don't you read too much into this, Shannow,' she whispered as she dropped her skirt to the floor and slid into bed beside him.

*

For Beth McAdam it was a revelation. Afterwards she lay beside the sleeping Shannow, her body warm and wonderfully relaxed. Yet the surprise of his love-making had been in the inexperience he showed; in the passive, grateful manner in which he had received her. Beth was no stranger to the ways of men and she had enjoyed lovers long before she met and seduced Sean McAdam. She had learned that there was a great similarity about the actions of the aroused male. He fumbled, he groped, and then he drove himself into a rhythmic frenzy. Not so with Shannow . . .

He had opened his arms to her and stroked her shoulders and back. It was she who had made all the moves. For all his awesome powers in dealing with situations of peril, the

Jerusalem Man was untutored and surprisingly gentle in the arms of a woman.

Beth slid from the bed and Shannow awoke instantly.

'You are going?' he asked.

'Yes. Did you sleep well?'

'Wonderfully. Will you come back this evening?'

'No,' she said firmly. 'I must see to my children.'

'Thank you, Beth.'

'Don't thank me,' she snapped. She dressed swiftly and pushed her fingers through her blonde hair, roughly combing it. At the door she paused. 'How many women have you slept with, Shannow?'

'Two,' he answered, without trace of embarrassment.

She walked across the street to the Jolly Pilgrim where Broome was waiting, his face red with anger.

'You said an hour, Frey McAdam, and it has been two. I have lost customers – and you will lose coin.'

'Whatever you decide, Meneer,' she said, moving past him to where the dishes waited for cleaning. There were only two customers and both were finishing their meals. Beth carried the plates to the rear of the eating-house and scrubbed them clean with water from the deep well. When she returned the Pilgrim was empty.

Broome approached her. 'I am sorry for losing my temper,' he said. 'I know he is wounded and needs attention. You will keep the coin. I was wondering . . . if you would join me at my house this evening?'

'For what purpose, Meneer?'

'To talk . . . have a little meal . . . get to know one another. It is important for people who work together to understand each other.'

She looked into his thin face and saw arousal in his eyes. 'I am afraid not, Meneer. I am seeing Meneer Scayse this evening to discuss a business matter.'

'A lease of land, I know,' he said and her eyes darkened. 'Do not misunderstand, Frey McAdam. Meneer Scayse spoke to me because I know you. He wishes to be sure of your . . . integrity. I told him I felt you were honest and hard-working. But do you really want the lonely life of a farm widow?'

'I want a home, Meneer.'

'Yes, yes.' She could see him building towards a proposal and headed him off. 'I must get on with my work,' she told him, easing past him to the rear of the building.

That evening she was welcomed to Scayse's permanent rooms at the Traveller's Rest by a servant, who led her through to a long room where a log fire blazed in a wide hearth. Scayse rose from a deep, comfortable chair and took her hand, lifting it to his lips.

'Welcome, madam. Might I offer you some wine?'

A handsome man, he was even more striking in the light from the fire – his swept-back hair gleaming, his sharp powerful features almost savage. 'No, thank you,' she said. He led her to a chair, waited as she sat and then returned to his own.

'The land you wish to lease is of little use to me. But tell me, Frey McAdam, why you approached me? You will know that no one has title to land. A man takes what he can hold. You could merely have driven your wagon to a spot of your choosing and built a home.'

'Were I rich, Meneer, with fifty riders, I would have done just that. But I am not. It remains your land – and if I am troubled I will come to you for assistance. You have men riding the high pastures, and it is known that brigands rarely trouble you. I hope the same will be true of me.'

'You have learned a great deal in your short time here. You are obviously a woman of great intelligence. I find it rare that a woman should combine beauty with wit.'

'How curious, I find exactly the same thing with men.'

He chuckled. 'Will you dine with me?'

'I don't think so. Is the price agreed?'

'I will waive the price – in return for dinner.'

'Let us be clear, sir. This is a business arrangement.' She opened the small bag she carried and counted out thirty silver coins. 'That is for the first year. And now I must be leaving.'

'I am disappointed,' he said, rising with her. 'I had great hopes.'

'Hold on to them, Meneer. They are all any of us have.'

*

After Beth had gone, Shannow sat up. He could still smell the perfume of her body on the sheets, and feel the after-warmth of her presence. Never before had he experienced a phenomenon like her. Donna Taybard had been soft, gentle and passive, deeply loving and wonderfully comforting. But Beth . . . there had been with her a power, an almost primordial hunger that had both drained him physically and elevated him emotionally.

He eased himself from the bed and stood. For a moment he swayed, and the room spun; but he held on, breathing deeply until it passed. He had wanted to dress and walk out into the air, but he knew he was too weak. A child with a short stick could lay him low in this condition. Reluctantly he returned to his bed. The bread and cheese were still on the tray nearby and he ate them, discovering to his surprise that he was ravenous. He slept for several hours and awoke refreshed.

A light knock came at the door. He hoped it was Beth. 'Come in!' he called.

Clem Steiner stepped into view.

'Now there's a sight,' said Steiner, grinning. 'The Jerusalem Man laid up and shaved. You don't look half as formidable without that silver-forked beard, Shannow.' The young man reversed a chair and sat facing the Jerusalem Man. Shannow looked into the other's eyes.

'What is it you want, Steiner?'

'I want something you can't give me. It's something I shall have to take from you – and that's a shame, because I like you, Shannow.'

'You make more noise than a pig with wind. And you are too damned young to understand it. What I have – whatever it is – is beyond you, boy. It always will be. You only get it when you don't want it. Never when you do.'

'Easy for you to say, Shannow. Look at you, the most famous man I've ever seen. And who's heard of me?'

'You want to see the price of fame, Steiner? Look in my saddlebags. Two worn-out shirts, two Bibles and four pistols. You see a wife anywhere, Steiner? A family? A home? Fame? I wasn't looking for fame. And I wouldn't care a jot if it all left me – and it will, Steiner. Because I'll keep travelling, and I'll find a place where they've never heard of the Jerusalem Man.'

'You could have been rich,' said Steiner. 'You could have been like some king of olden times. But you threw it away, Shannow. On you fame has been wasted. But I know what to do with it.'

'You know nothing, boy.'

'I haven't been called "boy" in a long time. And I don't like it.'

'I don't like the rain, boy, but there's not much I can do about it.'

Steiner pushed himself to his feet. 'You really know how to push a man, don't you, Shannow? You really know how to goad?'

'Hungry to kill me, Steiner? Your fame would be sky-high. Meet the man who shot Shannow in his bed.'

Steiner relaxed and returned to his seat. 'I'm learning. I won't shoot you down in the dark, Shannow, or in the back. I'll give it to you straight. Out on the street.'

'Where everyone can see?'

'Exactly.'

'And then what will you do?'

'I'll see you get a great funeral, with tall black horses and a fine stone to mark your grave. Then I'll travel, and maybe I'll become a king. Tell me, why did you pull that stunt with Maddox? You could have blown each other apart.'

'But we didn't, did we?'

'No. He almost killed you. Bad misjudgement, Shannow. It's not like what I've heard of you. Has the speed gone? Are you getting old?'

'Yes to both questions,' answered Shannow. Easing himself up on the pillow he turned his gaze to the window, ignoring the young man. But Steiner chuckled and reached out to pat Shannow's arm.

'Time to retire, Shannow – if only they'd let you.'

'The thought has occurred to me.'

'But not for long, I'll bet. What would you do? Grub around on the land, waiting for someone who recognises you? Waiting for the bullet, or the knife? Always staring at the distant hills, wondering if Jerusalem was just beyond the horizon? No. You'll go out with guns blazing on some street, or plain, or valley.'

'Like they all do?' put in Shannow softly.

'Like we all do,' Steiner agreed. 'But the names live on. History remembers.'

'Sometimes. You ever hear of Pendarric?'

'No. Was he a shootist?'

'He was one of the greatest kings who ever lived. He changed the world, Steiner; he conquered it, and he destroyed it. He brought about the First Fall.'

'What of it?'

'You'd never heard of him. That's how well history remembers. Tell me a name you do remember.'

'Cory Tyler.'

'The brigand who built himself a small empire in the north – shot through the head by a woman he'd spurned. Describe him, Steiner. Tell what he dreamed of. Tell me where he came from.'

'I never saw him.'

'Then what difference does his name make? It is just a sound, whispered into the air. In years to come, some other foolish boy may wish to be like Clement Steiner. He will not know either whether you were tall or short, fat or thin, young or old, but he will chant the name like a talisman.'

Steiner smiled and rose. 'Maybe so. But I will kill you, Shannow. I'll make my own tracks.'

18

Nu-Khasisatra could see something was seriously wrong with the wagon convoy long before he reached it. The sun was up and yet there was little movement from amongst the twenty-six wagons. A dead body lay close to the convoy, and Nu could see other corpses laid side by side some thirty paces away.

He stopped and decided to pass them by, but a voice called out to him from the long grass beside the track and Nu turned to see a young woman lying in a gulley; she was cradling a babe in her arms. Her words were unintelligible, the language coarse and unknown to Nu. Her face was pinched and drawn, and red, open sores scarred her cheeks and throat. For a moment Nu drew back in horror, then he looked into her eyes and saw the fear and the pain. He took his Stone and moved to her side. She was terribly thin and as Nu laid his hand on her shoulder he could feel the sharpness of her bones beneath the grey woollen dress she wore. As he touched her, the whispered words she spoke became instantly clear to him. 'Help me. For the sake of God, help me!' He touched the Stone to her brow and the sores vanished instantly, as did the hollow dark rings below her large blue eyes. 'My babe,' she said, lifting the tiny bundle towards Nu.

'I can do nothing,' he told her sadly, staring at the corpse. A terrible moaning cry came from the woman and she hugged the child to her. Nu stood and helped her to her feet, leading her back to the wagons. Some twenty paces ahead on the road a man was lying on his back, dead eyes staring up at the sky. They passed him by. As they entered the camp, an elderly woman with iron-grey hair ran towards him. 'Get back!' she shouted. 'There is plague here.'

'I know,' he told her. 'I . . . I am a healer.'

'There's nothing more to be done,' said the woman. Then she noticed the girl. 'Ella? Dear God, Ella. You are well?'

'He couldn't save my baby,' whispered Ella. 'He was too late for my little Mary.'

'What is your name, friend?' asked the woman, taking his arm.

'Nu-Khasisatra.'

'Well, Meneer New, there are more than seventy people bad sick here, and only four of us that are holding the plague at bay. I pray to God you *are* a healer.'

Nu looked around him. Death was everywhere. Some bodies lay uncovered, flies settling on the still weeping sores, while others had blankets casually tossed over them. Several paces to his right he saw a child's arm protruding from a large section of sackcloth. Moans and cries came from the wagons and here and there helpers – themselves stricken – staggered from victim to victim, giving aid where they could, helping the sick to drink a little water. Nu swallowed hard as the elderly woman touched his arm. 'Come,' she said. He looked down at her hand and saw the ugly red blotches that stained her lower arm. Taking his Stone, he reached out and stroked her hair. 'God's Love,' he told her. The sores disappeared.

She stared down at her arms, feeling the rush of strength as if she had just awoken from a deep refreshing sleep. 'Thank you,' she whispered. 'God's blessing on you. But come quickly, for there are others in sore need.'

She led him to a wagon where a woman and four children lay under sweat-soaked blankets. Nu laid the Stone on each of them, and the fever passed. From wagon to wagon he moved, healing the sick and watching as the black veins in the Stone swelled. As dusk came, he had healed more than thirty of the company. The elderly woman, whose name was Martha, busied herself preparing food for the survivors and Nu was left to himself. Under the moonlight he studied the Stone. There was more black than gold now and, under cover of darkness, he slipped away into the night.

He had no choice, he told himself. If ever he was to see Pashad and the children again, he had to leave some power in the Stone. But with each step he took, his heart became heavier.

At last he sat down under the bright moonlight and prayed. 'What would you have me do?' he asked. 'What are these people to me? You are the giver of life, the bringer of death. It was you who brought this plague to them. Why can you not take it away?' There was no answer, but he recalled his boyhood days in the temple under the great teacher Rizzhak.

He could see the old man's hooded eyes and his hawk nose, the white straggly beard. And he remembered the story Rizzhak had told of Heaven and Hell:

'I prayed to the Lord of All Things to let me see both Paradise and the Torment of Belial. And in my vision I saw a door. I opened it and there, in a great room, was a sumptuous feast placed on a great table. But all the guests were wailing, for the spoons in their hands had long, long handles and, though they could reach the food the spoons were too long for them to place it in their mouths. And they were cursing God and starving. I closed the door and asked to see Paradise. Yet it was the same door that stayed before me. I opened it and inside was an identical feast, and all the guests had the same long-handled spoons. But they were feeding each other and praising God in the thousand names known only to the angels.'

Nu stared up at the moon and thought of Pashad. He sighed and stood.

Back at the wagons he moved amongst the sick, healing them all. He laboured long into the night, and at the dawn he stared down at the Stone in his hand. It was black now, with not a trace of gold.

Martha came and sat beside him, giving him a cup in which was a dark, bitter drink.

'I've heard of them,' she said, 'but I never saw one before. It was a Daniel Stone. Is it used up?'

'Yes,' said Nu, dropping it to the ground in front of the fire.

'It saved many lives, Meneer New. And I thank you for it.'

Nu said nothing.

He was thinking of Pashad...

*

Beth McAdam was thoughtful and silent as she steered the wagon south over the rolling grasslands towards the Wall. The children were sitting on the tailboard squabbling, but the noise passed her by. Shannow was making good progress, but still confined to his room at the Traveller's Rest, and the Parson had been a frequent caller at their campsite in Tent Town. Now there was Edric Scayse, tall and confident, courteous and gallant. He had taken her to dinner twice, and amused her with stories of his upbringing in the far north.

'They have cities there now, and elected leaders,' he had told her. 'Some of the areas have formed treaties with neighbouring groups and there was talk last year of a Confederation.'

'They won't get together,' said Beth. 'People don't. They'll row over everything and fight over nothing.'

'Don't be too sure, Beth. Mankind cannot grow without organisation. Take the Barta coin – that's universally accepted now, no matter which community you enter. Old Jacob Barta, who first stamped the coins, had a dream of one nation. Now it looks as if it has a chance. Just imagine what it would be like if laws were as readily accepted as Barta coin?'

'Wars will just get bigger,' she said with certainty. 'It's the way of things.'

'We need leaders, Beth – strong men to draw us all together. There's so much we don't know about the past, that could help us with the future... so much.'

The lead oxen stumbled, jerking Beth back to the present and she hauled on the reins, giving the beast time to recover its footing. She was attracted to Scayse, drawn by his strength, but there was something about him that left her with a vague sense of unease. Like the Parson, he had a dangerous, uncertain quality. With Shannow, the danger was all on the surface – what you saw was what you got. How much easier life would have been had she found Josiah Broome attractive. But the man was such a blinkered fool.

'I dread to think of people who look up to men like Jon Shannow,' he had told her one morning, as they waited for the first customers of the day. 'Loathsome man! A killer and a war-maker of the worst kind. People like him wreck communities, destroy any sense of civilised behaviour. He is a cancer in our midst and should be ordered to leave.'

'When has he stolen anything?' she countered, holding the anger from her voice. 'When has he been disrespectful? When? When has he killed a man without first being threatened with death himself?'

'How can you ask such a thing? Did you not see on the night poor Fenner died? When he stood before the crowd, and that man asked him if he thought he could take on all of them? Shannow shot him down without warning; the man did not even have a gun in his hand.'

'You'll never understand, Meneer Broome. I am surprised you have lived this long. If Shannow had let the moment pass, they would all have turned on him and he would have been shot to pieces. As it was, he held them, he took the initiative... unlike poor Fenner. I spoke to Shannow about him. Did you know Fenner went to Shannow for advice? The Jerusalem Man told him to give Webber an order and not engage in any conversation; he said that as soon as Webber is allowed to debate you will lose the moment. Fenner understood this, Meneer Broome. But he was betrayed, by you and all those with you. Now he is dead.'

'How dare you accuse me of betrayal? I went there with Fenner; I did my part.'

'Your part?' she hissed. 'You got him killed and crawled away like a gutless snake.'

'There was nothing we could do. Nothing anyone could do.'

'Shannow did it. Alone. So don't criticise him to my face. The man's worth ten of you.'

'Get out! You don't work here any more. Out, I say!'

With her job lost, Beth saw Scayse who agreed to let her move on to the land immediately. He even offered men to help her with building her home, but she refused him.

Now she was almost there. The oxen were tired as they laboured up the last rise before the land she had leased, and she was ready to allow them a breather at the top of the hill. But when they reached it, Beth looked down into the vale and saw five men shaping felled trees into logs. Close by was a roped-off area which had been stamped out to form the dirt floor of a cabin. Beth's fury rose and she drew her pistol and stepped down from the wagon, walking back to where her horse was tethered at the rear. Telling the children to stay where they were, she rode down where the men were working. As she approached, one of them put down his hatchet and strolled across to her, doffing his leather hat and grinning.

'Mornin', Frey. Nice day for it, what with the sun and the breeze.'

The pistol came up and the man's smile vanished. 'What the Hell are you doing on my land?' she asked him, cocking the pistol.

'Hold up, lady,' he said, lifting his hands. 'Meneer Scayse asked us to give you a hand with the footings – felling the trees and suchlike. We've also taken water bearings to see how the land lies.'

'I asked for no help,' she told him, the pistol steady in her hands.

'I don't know nothin' about that. We ride for Meneer Scayse. He says jump, we don't say why – we just jump.'

Beth uncocked the pistol and returned it to her scabbard. 'Why did you choose this spot for the cabin?'

'Well,' he said, the smile returning, 'it's got a good range of open ground to front and rear, there's water close by and the front windows will catch the evening sun.'

'You chose well. What is your name?'

'They call me Bull, though my name is rightly Ishmael Kovac.'

'Bull it is,' she told him. 'You carry on. I'll fetch the wagon.'

19

The first tremor hit the city just after dawn. It was no more than an insistent vibration that rattled plates upon shelves and many slept through it; others awakened and rose, rubbing sleep from their eyes and wondering if a storm was due. The second tremor came at noon and Chreena was working in the laboratory when it struck. The vibration was stronger now. Books fell from shelves and she ran to the balcony to see people milling in the streets. A twelve-foot statue toppled near the main square, but no one was hurt. The tremor passed.

Oshere limped in to the laboratory. 'A little excitement,' he said, his words more slurred than usual.

'Yes,' said Chreena. 'Have there been quakes before?'

'Once, twelve years ago,' he told her. 'It was not serious, though some farmers lost cattle and there were many stillborn calves. How is your work progressing?'

'I'll get there,' she replied, looking away.

He squatted on the mosaic floor and looked up at her. 'I wonder if we are tackling the problem in the right way,' he said.

'What other way is there? If I can find out what causes the genetic structure to regress, I might be able to stop it.'

'That's what I mean, Chreena. You are staring into the heart of the problem and you cannot see the whole. I have been looking at the records of the others who have gone through the Change before me. All were male, and all under twenty-five years of age.'

'I know that. It is not a great help,' she snapped.

'Bear with me. Almost all the Changelings were about to be married. You did not know that, did you?'

'No,' she admitted. 'But how is that important?'

He smiled, but she did not recognise the expression in

his swollen, leonine face. 'Our custom is for the groom to take his lady to the southern mountains, there to pledge his love beneath the Sword of the One. Everyone does it.'

'But the women go too, and they are not affected.'

'Yes,' he said. 'I have given great thought to this. I do not understand your science, Chreena, but I understand how to solve a problem. First look for the deviation and then ask – not where is the problem, but where is *not* the problem. If all the Changelings journey to the Sword, but the women are unaffected, then what do the men do that is different? What did Shir-ran do while you were there?'

'Nothing that I did not,' she replied. 'We ate, we drank, we slept, we made love. We came home.'

'Did he not climb to the Chaos Peak and dive to the waters two hundred feet below?'

'Yes. The custom, as I understand it, is for the men to purify themselves in the water of the Golden Pool before they pledge themselves. But all men do this – and not all are affected.'

'This is true,' he agreed, 'but some men merely bathe in an easily accessible part of the Pool. Others dive from low rocks. But only the most foolhardy climb to the Chaos Peak and dive.'

'I still do not understand what you are trying to say.'

'Five of the last six changelings climbed that Peak. Eleven others who were unaffected only bathed in the Pool. That is the deviation: the greatest percentage of Changelings come from those who climb the Peak.'

'But what of you? You are not in love. You took no one to the Sword.'

'No, Chreena. I went alone. I climbed the Peak, and I dived. Oshere flew and pledged himself.'

'To what?'

'To love. I was going to ask . . . a woman to accompany me, but I did not know if I would have the courage to dive. So I went alone. Two weeks later, the Change began.'

Chreena sat down and stared at the Man-beast. 'I have

been a fool,' she whispered. 'Can you come with me, back to the Sword?'

'I may not survive the journey as a man,' he said. 'Do you still have the Thunder-maker you brought with you?'

'Yes,' she answered, opening the drawer of her desk and removing the Hellborn pistol.

'Best to bring it with you, Chreena.'

'I could never kill you, Oshere. *Never*.'

'And I believe I could never harm you. But neither of us knows, do we?'

*

Shannow pulled on his boots and settled his gun scabbards in place at his hips. He was still weaker than he liked, but his strength had almost returned. Beth McAdam had filled his thoughts ever since the afternoon when she had shared his bed; she had not returned to him since then. Shannow sat by the window and recalled the joy of the day. He did not blame her for avoiding him. What did he have to offer? How many women would want to be tied to a man of his reputation? The days of his convalescence had given him a great deal of time for thought. Had his life been a waste? What had he done that would live after him? Yes, he had killed evil men, and it could be argued that in so doing he had saved other innocent lives. Yet he had no sons or daughters to continue his line, and nowhere in this untamed world was he welcome for long.

The Jerusalem Man. The Killer. The Destroyer.

'Where is love, Shannow?' he asked himself.

He wandered down the stairs, acknowledged Mason's wave and stepped out into the daylight. The sun was shining in a clear sky and the breeze was lifting dust from the dried mud of the roadway.

Shannow crossed the street and made his way to the gunsmith's shop. Groves was not behind his counter and he walked through the shop and found the man crouching over a work bench.

Groves looked up and smiled. 'You set me a fair task, Meneer Jerusalem Man. These aren't rim-fire cartridges.'

'No. Centre-fire.'

'They have heavy loads. A man needs to shoot straight with such ammunition. A stray bullet would pass through a house wall and kill an occupant sitting quietly in his chair.'

'I tend to shoot straight,' said Shannow. 'Have you completed my order?'

'Is the sky blue? Of course I have. I also made some five hundred shells for Meneer Scayse to the same requirements. It seems his Hellborn pistols arrived – without ammunition.'

Shannow paid the man and left his store. A sharp pebble under his foot made him remember how thin were his boots. The town store was across the street and he bought a new pair of soft leather boots, two white woollen shirts and a quantity of black powder.

As the man was preparing his order, an earth tremor struck the town and from outside came the sound of screaming. Shannow gripped the counter to stop from falling, while all around him the store's wares – pots, pans, knives, sacks of flour – began to tumble from the shelves.

As quickly as it had come the tremor passed. Shannow moved back into the bright sunlight.

'Will you look at that!' yelled a man, pointing to the sky. The sun was directly overhead, but way to the south a second sun shone brightly for several seconds before suddenly disappearing.

'You ever seen the like, Shannow?' asked Clem Steiner, approaching him.

'Never.'

'What does it mean, do you think?'

Shannow shrugged. 'Maybe it was a mirage. I've heard of such things.'

'It fair makes your skin crawl. I never heard of a mirage that could cast a shadow.'

The storekeeper came out carrying Shannow's order.

The Jerusalem Man thanked him and tucked it under his arm, along with the package he had taken from Groves.

'Fixing to leave us?' Steiner asked.

'Yes. Tomorrow.'

'Then maybe we should complete our business,' said the young pistoleer.

'Steiner, you are a foolish boy. And yet I like you – I have no wish to bury you. You understand what I am saying? Stay clear of me, boy. Build your reputation another way.'

Before the young man could answer Shannow had walked away, climbing the steps of the Traveller's Rest. A young woman stood in the doorway with her eyes fixed on something across the street. Easing past her, Shannow glanced back to see that she was staring at a black-bearded man sitting on the sidewalk outside the Jolly Pilgrim. He looked up and saw her; his face lost all colour and he stood and ran back towards Tent Town. Puzzled, Shannow studied the woman. She was tall, and beautifully dressed in a shimmering skirt of golden yellow. A green shirt was loosely tucked into a wide leather belt and she wore riding boots of the softest doeskin. Her hair was blonde, streaked with gold, and her eyes sea green.

She turned and saw him looking at her and for a moment he felt like recoiling under the icy glare she gave him. Instead he smiled and bowed. Ignoring him, she swept past and approached Mason.

'Is Scayse here?' she asked, her voice low, almost husky.

Mason cleared his throat. 'Not yet, Frey Sharazad. Would you like to wait in his rooms?'

'No. Tell him we will meet in the usual place. Tonight.' She swung on her heel and stalked from the building.

'A beautiful woman,' Shannow commented.

'She makes my hair stand on end,' said Mason, grinning. 'Beats me where she comes from. She rode in yesterday on a stallion that must have been all of eighteen hands. And those clothes . . . that skirt is a wonder. How do they make it shine so?'

'Beats me,' said Shannow. 'I'll be leaving tomorrow. What do I owe you?'

'I told you once, Shannow, there's no charge. And it'll be that way if ever you return.'

'I doubt I'll come back – but thanks for the offer.'

'You hear about the Healer? Came in with the wagons this afternoon?'

'No.'

'Seems like the Red Plague hit the convoy and this man walked out of the wilderness with a Daniel Stone. He healed everybody. I'd like to have seen that. I've heard of Daniels before, but I never touched one. You?'

'I've seen them,' said Shannow. 'What did he look like, this Healer?'

'Big man with the blackest beard you ever saw. Big hands too. Like a fighter.'

Shannow returned to his room and sat once more at the chair by the window. The golden-haired woman had been staring with naked hatred at just such a man. He shook his head.

Nothing to do with you, Shannow.

Tomorrow you put Pilgrim's Valley far behind you.

20

Sharazad sat, seemingly alone, on a flat rock under the moonlight. The day had brought an unexpected pleasure: Nu-Khasisatra was here in this cursed land of barbarians. It had been a source of constant fury that he had escaped from Ad, and the King had been most displeased. Seven of her Daggers had been flayed and impaled, and she herself had lost ground in the King's affections. But now – Great be the Glory of Belial – the shipbuilder was within her reach once more. Her mind wandered back to the man she had seen staring at her in the hovel that passed for a resting place. Something about him disturbed her. He was not handsome, nor yet ugly, but his eyes were striking. A long time ago she had enjoyed a lover with just such eyes. The man had been a gladiator, a superb killer of men. Was that it? Was the barbarian a danger?

She heard the rumble of the wagon coming through the trees and wandered to the crest of the hill, gazing down at the two men who drove it. One was young and handsome, the other older and balding. She waited until they came closer, then stepped out on to the path.

The older man heaved on the reins and applied the clumsy brake. 'Good evening, Frey,' he said climbing down and stretching his back. 'You sure you want to unload here?'

'Yes,' she said. 'Just here. Where is Scayse?'

'He couldn't come,' said the younger man. 'I represent him. The name's Steiner.'

What do I care what your name is, thought Sharazad. 'Unload the wagon and open the first box,' she said aloud. Steiner loosened the reins of a saddled horse that was tied to the rear of the wagon and led the beast back a few paces. Then both men struggled with the heavy boxes, manhandling them to the ground. The older man drew a hunting-knife and prised open a lid. Sharazad stepped closer and leaned forward, pulling back the greased paper and lifting a short-barrelled rifle clear of the box.

'Show me how it works,' she ordered.

The older man opened a packet of shells and slid two into the side gate. 'They slide in here – up to ten shells; there's a spring keeps the pressure on. You take hold here,' he said, gripping a moulded section under the barrel, 'and pump once. Now there's a shell in the breech and the rifle is cocked. Pull the trigger and pump the action, and the spent shell is ejected and a fresh one slides home.'

'Ingenious,' admitted Sharazad. 'But, sadly, after this load we will need no more. We will make our own.'

'Ain't sad to me,' said the man. 'Don't make no difference to me.'

'Ah, but it does,' she said, smiling and she raised her hand. From the bushes all around them rose a score of Daggers, pistols in their hands.

'Sweet Jesus, what the Hell are they?' whispered the man, as the reptiles moved forward. At the back of the wagon Clem stood horror-struck as the demonic creatures appeared, then backed away towards his horse.

'Kill them,' ordered Sharazad. Clem dived for the ground, rolled and came up firing. Two of the reptiles were hurled from their feet. More gunfire shattered the night, spurts of dust spitting up around Clem's prone body. His horse panicked and ran but Clem dived for the saddle, grabbing the pommel as it passed. He was half-carried, half-dragged into the trees, shells whistling about him.

'Find him,' ordered Sharazad and six of the reptiles loped away into the darkness. She turned on the older man, who had stood stock-still throughout the battle. Her hand dipped into the pocket of her golden skirt and she lifted out a small stone, dark red and veined with black.

'Do you know what this is?' she asked. He shook his head. 'This is a Bloodstone. It can do amazing things, but it needs to be fed. Will you feed my Bloodstone?'

'Oh, my God,' he whispered, backing away as Sharazad drew a silver pistol and stared down at it.

'I am surprised that the greatest minds of Atlantis never discovered such a sweet toy. It is so clean, so lethal, so final.'

'Please, Frey. I have a wife . . . children. I never harmed you.'

'You offend me, barbarian, merely by being.' The pistol came up and the shell hammered through his heart; he fell to his knees, then toppled to his face. She turned him over with the toe of her boot and laid the Bloodstone on his chest. The black veins dwindled to nothing.

She sat by the corpse and closed her eyes, concentrating on her victory. An image formed in her mind and she saw Nu-Khasisatra waiting unarmed and ready to be taken. But a dark shadow stood between her and the revenge she desired. The face was blurred, but she focused her concentration and the shadow became recognisable. It was the man from the Traveller's Rest – only now his eyes were flames and in his hands were serpents, sharp-fanged and deadly. Holding the image, she called out to her mentor and his face appeared in her mind.

'What troubles you, Sharazad?'

'Look, Lord, at the image. What does it mean?'

'The eyes of fire mean he is an implacable enemy, the serpents show that in his hands he has power. Is that the renegade prophet behind him?'

'Yes, Lord. He is here, in this strange world.'

'Take him. I want him here before me. You understand, Sharazad?'

'I do, Lord. But tell me, why are we no longer dealing with Scayse? I thought their guns would be of more use.'

'I have opened other gates to worlds with infinitely more power. Your barbaric kingdom offers little. You may take ten companies of Daggers if you wish, and blood them on the barbarians. Yes, do it, Sharazad, if it would bring you pleasure.'

His face disappeared. Ten companies of Daggers! Never

had she commanded so many. And, yes, it would be good to plan a battle; to hear the thunder of gunfire, the screams of the dying. Perhaps if she did well she would be given a command of humans and not these disgusting, scaled creatures from beyond the gates. Lost in her dreams, she ignored the sounds of distant gunfire.

*

Clem Steiner had been hit twice. Blood seeped from the wound in his chest, and his left leg burned as sweat mixed with the blood at the outer edges of the jagged wound. His horse had been shot from under him, but he had managed to hit at least one of the creatures giving pursuit.

What in the Devil's name were they?

Clem hauled himself behind a rock and scrabbled further up the wooded hillside. At first he had thought them men wearing masks, but now he was not so sure. And they were so fast . . . they moved across his line of vision with a speed no human could match. Licking his lips, he held his breath, listening hard. He could hear the wind sighing in the leaves above him, and the rushing of a mountain stream to his left. A dark shadow moved to his right and he rolled and fired. The bullet took the reptile under the chin, exiting from the top of its skull, and it fell alongside Clem, its legs twitching. He stared, horror-struck, at the grey, scaled skin and the black leather body armour. The creature's hand had a treble-jointed thumb and three thick fingers.

Jesus God, they're demons! he thought. *I am being hunted by demons!*

He fought for calm and reloaded his pistol with the last of his shells. Then he gathered up the reptile's weapon and sank back against the rock. The wound in his chest was high and he hoped it had missed his lung. *Of course it has, you fool! You're not coughing blood, are you?*

But he felt so weak. His eyes closed but he jerked himself awake. *Got to move! Get safe!* He started to crawl, but loss of blood had weakened him terribly and he made only a few yards before his strength was spent. A rustling movement came from behind him and he tried to roll, but a booted foot lashed into his side. His gun came up, but was kicked from his hand. Then he felt himself being dragged from the hillside, but all pain passed and he slid into unconsciousness.

The pain awoke him and he found he had been stripped naked and tied to a tree. Four of the reptiles were sitting together in a close circle around the body of the creature he had killed on the hillside. As he watched, one of the others took a serrated knife and cut into the chest of the corpse, ripping open the dead flesh and pulling clear the heart. Clem felt nausea overwhelming him, but he could not tear his eyes from the scene. The reptiles began to chant, their sibilant hissing echoing in the trees; then the first cut the heart into four pieces, and the others all accepted a portion which they ate.

Then they knelt around the corpse and each touched his forehead to the body. Finally they rose and turned to face the bound man. Clem looked into their golden, slitted eyes, then down at the serrated knives they all held.

No glittering reputation for Clem Steiner, no admiring glances. No treasure would be his, no adoring women. Anger flooded him and he struggled at the ropes that bit into his flesh as the reptiles advanced.

'Behold,' said a voice and Clem glanced to his right to see Jon Shannow standing with the sun behind him, his face in silhouette. The voice was low and compelling, and the reptiles stood and stared at the newcomer. *'Behold, the whirlwind of the Lord goeth forth in fury, a continuing whirlwind: it shall fall with pain upon the heads of the wicked.'*

Then there was silence as Shannow stood calmly, the morning breeze flapping at his long coat.

One of the reptiles lowered his knife. He stepped forward, his voice a sibilant hiss.

'You sspirit or man?'

Shannow said nothing and the reptiles gathered together, whispering. Then the leader moved away from them, approaching the Jerusalem Man.

'I can ssmell your blood,' hissed the Dagger. 'You are Man.'

'I am death,' Shannow replied.

'You are a Truthsspeaker,' said the reptile at last. 'We have no fear, but we underssstand much that men do not. You are what you ssay you are, and your power iss felt by uss. Thiss day is yourss. But other dayss will dawn. Walk warily, Man of Death.'

The leader gestured to the other Daggers, then turned on his heel and loped away.

Time stood still for Clem and it seemed that Shannow had become a statue. 'Help me,' called the wounded man and the Jerusalem Man walked slowly to the tree and squatted down. Clem looked into his eyes. 'I owe you my life,' he said.

'You owe me nothing,' said Shannow. He cut Clem's bonds and plugged the wounds in his chest and leg; then he helped him dress and led him to the black stallion.

'There're more of them, Shannow. I don't know where they are.'

'*Sufficient unto the day is the evil thereof,*' said the Jerusalem Man, lifting Steiner into the saddle. He mounted behind him and rode from the hills.

*

Sharazad watched as Szshark and his three companions loped into the clearing. She lifted a hand and waved the tall reptile to her; he approached and gave a short bow.

'You found the man?'

'Yess.'

'And killed him?'

'No. Another claimed him.'

Sharazad swallowed her anger. Szshark was the leader of these creatures, had been the first of the reptiles to pledge allegiance to the King. 'Explain yourself,' she said.

'We took him – alive, as you ssaid. Then sshadow came. Tall warrior. Ssun at his back. He sspoke power wordss.'

'But he was human, yes?'

'U-man, yess,' Szshark agreed. 'I go now?'

'Did he fight? What? What happened?'

'No fight. He wass Death, Goldenhair. He wass power. We felt it.'

'So you just left him? That is cowardice, Szshark!'

His wedge-shaped head tilted, and his huge golden eyes bored into her own. 'That word for U-manss. We have no fearss, Goldenhair. But it would be wrong to die for nothing.'

'How could you know you would die? You did not try to fight him. You have guns, do you not?'

'Gunss!' spat Szshark. 'Loud noisses. Kill very far. No honour! We are Daggerss. Thiss man. Thiss power. He carry gunss. But not hold them. You ssee?'

'I see everything. Gather twenty warriors and hunt him down. I want him. Take him. Do you understand that?'

Szshark nodded and moved away from her. She did not understand, she would never understand. The Death man could have opened fire on them at any time, but instead he spoke words of power. He gave them a choice: life or death. As starkly simple as that. What creature of intelligence would have chosen anything but life? Szshark gazed around at the camp-site. His warriors were waiting for his word.

He chose twenty and watched them run from the camp. Sharazad summoned him again.

'Why are you not with them?' she asked.

'I gave him thiss day,' he said, and walked away. He could feel her anger washing over him, sense her longing to put a bullet in his back. He walked to the stream and squatted down, dipping his head under the surface and revelling in the cool quiet of Below.

When the King of Atlantis led his legions into the jungles, the *Ruazsh* had fought them to a standstill. But Szshark had seen the inevitable outcome. The *Ruazsh* were too few to withstand the might of Atlantis. He had journeyed alone to seek out the King.

'Why have you come?' the King asked him, sitting before his battle tent.

'Kill you or sserve you,' Szshark answered.

'How will you determine which course of action?' the King enquired.

'Iss already done.'

The King nodded, his face stretching, baring his teeth. 'Then show me,' he said.

Szshark knelt and offered the King his curved dagger. The monarch took it and held the point to Szshark's throat.

'Now it seems I have two choices.'

'No,' said Szshark, 'only one.'

The King's mouth opened and a series of barking sounds disturbed the reptile. In the months that followed he would learn that this sound was laughter, and that it denoted good humour among humans. He rarely heard that sound now from Sharazad – unless something had died.

Now as he lifted his head from the water, a rippling of faint music echoed inside his mind. He answered the Calling.

'Speak, my brother, my son,' his mind answered.

A Dagger moved from the bushes and crouched low to the ground, his eyes averted from Szshark's face.

The music in Szshark's mind hardened and the language of the *Ruazsh* flowed in the corridors of his mind. 'Golden-hair wishes to attack the homes of the land humans. Her mind is easy to read. But there are few warriors there, Szshark. Why are we here? Have we offended the King?'

'The King is a Great Power, my son. But his people fear us. We are now . . . merely playthings for his bed-mate. She longs for blood. But we are pledged to the King and we must obey. The land humans are to die.'

'It is not good, Szshark.' The music changed again. 'Why did the Truthspeaker not kill us? Were we beneath his talents?'

'You read his thoughts. He did not need to kill us.'

'I do not like this world, Szshark. I wish we could go home.'

'We will never go home, my son. But the King has

promised never to re-open the gate. The Seed is safe, but we are the hostages to that promise.'

'Goldenhair hates us. She will see us all dead. There will be no one to eat our hearts and give us life. And I can no longer feel the souls of my brothers beyond the gates.'

'Nor I. But they are there, and they carry our souls. We cannot die.'

'Goldenhair comes!' The reptile climbed to his feet and vanished into the undergrowth.

Szshark stood, observing the woman. Her ugliness was nauseating, but he closed his mind to it, concentrating instead on the grossness of the language of Man.

'What you wissh?' he asked.

'There is a community close by. I wish to see it destroyed.'

'As you command,' he replied.

21

Shannow rode with care, holding the wounded man in place but stopping often to study his back-trail. There was no sign of pursuit as yet and the Jerusalem Man headed higher into the hills, riding across rocky scree that would leave little evidence of his passing. Steiner's chest wound had ceased to bleed, but his trouser-leg was drenched with blood and he had fallen into a feverish sleep, his head on Shannow's shoulder.

'Didn't mean it, Pa,' he whispered. 'Didn't mean to do it! Don't hit me, Pa!' Steiner began to weep – low moans, rhythmic and intense.

Shannow halted the stallion in a rough circle of boulders high on the hillside overlooking the great Wall. Holding on to Steiner, he dismounted, then lowered the unconscious man to the ground. The stallion moved off a few paces and began cropping grass as Shannow made up a bed and covered Steiner's upper body with a blanket. Taking needle and thread, he sewed the wounds in the pistoleer's leg. The gaping hole at the rear of the thigh caused him concern, for the shell had obviously ricocheted from the bone and broken up, causing a large exit wound. Shannow sealed this as best he could, then left Steiner to rest. He walked to the ridge and stared down over the countryside. Far in the distance he could see dark shadows moving, seeking a trail. He knew he and Steiner had a three-hour start, but loaded down with a wounded man that would mean nothing.

He considered riding back to Pilgrim's Valley, but dismissed the idea. It would mean setting a course that would take him across the line of the reptiles, and he didn't feel he could be as lucky a second time.

Shannow had left the settlement at dawn, but had been drawn to the east by the sound of gunshots. He had seen the black-clad reptiles dragging Steiner to the tree and stripping his clothes, and he had watched them eat the heart of their dead comrade. He had never seen the like of them, nor heard of any such creatures. It seemed strange that they should appear in Pilgrim's Valley unheralded.

According to local legend, there were beasts Beyond the Wall that walked like men, but never had he heard them described as scaled. Nor had he heard of any Man-beasts who sported weapons – especially the remarkable Hellborn pieces.

He put the problem from his mind. It did not matter where they came from – they were here now, and had to be faced.

Steiner began to weep again in his sleep and Shannow moved across to him, taking his hand. 'It's all right, boy. You're safe. Sleep easy.' But the words did not penetrate and the weeping continued.

'Oh please, Pa. Please? I'm begging you!' Sweat coursed on Steiner's face and his colour was not good. Shannow added a second blanket and felt the man's pulse; it was erratic and weak.

'You've two chances, boy,' said Shannow. 'Live or die. It's up to you.'

He eased back up to the ridge, careful not to skyline himself. To the east the dark shadows were closer now and Shannow counted more than twenty figures moving slowly across the landscape. Far to the west he could see a thin spiral of smoke that could be coming from a camp-fire.

Steiner was in no shape to ride, and Shannow did not have the firepower to stop twenty enemies. He scratched at the stubble on his cheek and tried to think the problem through. Steiner's mumbling had faded away and he went to him. The man was sleeping now, his pulse a little stronger. Shannow returned to the ridge and waited.

How many times had he waited thus, he wondered, while enemies crept upon him? Brigands, war-makers, hunters, Hellborn Zealots – all had sought to kill the Jerusalem Man.

He recalled the Zealots, frenzied killers whose Bloodstones had given them bizarre powers, enabling their spirits to soar and take over the bodies of animals and direct them to their purpose. Once Shannow had been attacked by a lion possessed by a Zealot; he had fallen from a high cliff and almost drowned in a torrent.

Then there were the Guardians, with their terrible weapons recreated from the Between Days, guns that fired hundreds of times per minute, screaming shells that could rip a man to pieces.

But none had mastered the Jerusalem Man.

Pendarric, the ghost King of Atlantis, had told Shannow he was Rolynd, a special kind of warrior with a God-given sixth sense that warned him of danger. But even with Pendarric's aid, Shannow had almost died fighting the Guardian leader, Sarento.

How much longer could his luck hold?

Luck, Shannow? He glanced at the sky in mute apology. A long time ago, when he was a child, a holy man had told him a story. It was about a man who came to the end of his days and, looking back, he saw his footprints in the sands of his life. And beside them was a second set, which he knew to be God's. But when the man looked closely he saw that in the times of his greatest trouble there was only a single set. The man looked at God and asked, 'Why is it that you left me when my need was greatest?' And God replied, 'I never left you, my son.' And when the man asked, 'Why then was there only one set of footprints?' God smiled and replied, 'Because those were the times when I carried you.'

Shannow grinned, recalling the days in the old schoolhouse with his brother Daniel. Many were the stories told by Mr Hillel, and always they were uplifting.

The figures out on the plain were closer now. Shannow could make out the black armour on their chests, and the grey scaled skin of their wedge-shaped faces. He eased himself back from the ridge and tethered the stallion to a rock, then took his spare pistols from the saddlebag and thrust them into his belt. Returning to the ridge he studied the slope before him, estimating distances between cover and choosing the best fields of fire.

He wished Batik was here. The giant Hellborn was a warrior born, fearless and deadly. Together they had fought their way through a vast stone fortress to free a friend. Batik had journeyed into the city of New Babylon to rescue Donna Taybard, and fought the Devil himself. Shannow needed him now.

The leading Dagger had found the scent and was waving the others forward. They gathered in a tight bunch some two hundred yards away, then loped towards the ridge. Shannow drew his Hellborn pistols and cocked them.

Just then a group of four horsemen appeared, coming from the west. They saw the reptiles and reined in, more curious than afraid. One of the reptiles fired and a man lurched in the saddle. As the other three returned the fire, Shannow took the opportunity to roll over the ridge and run to a large boulder half-way down the slope. The shooting continued for several seconds and he saw a horse go down, the rider lying flat, shielded by the body; the man had a rifle and was coolly sending shot after shot into the reptiles. Five of them were down and the rest began to run for cover. Shannow stepped out into their path with his pistols blazing – two were swept from their feet, a third fell clutching his throat. The shock of his sudden attack was too much for them and the survivors turned and ran back over the plain, their speed incredible. Shannow waited for several seconds, watching the bodies. One of the downed reptiles suddenly rolled, bringing up a pistol . . . Shannow shot him in the head. Then he walked out to the riders. Two men were dead, a third wounded; the fourth man stood cradling his rifle in his arms. He was sandy-haired, with a wide friendly face and narrow eyes. Shannow recognised him as one of the riders who had been present when he repossessed his horse.

'Very grateful for your assistance, Shannow,' said the man, holding out his hand. 'My friends call me Bull.'

'Glad to meet you, Bull,' said Shannow, ignoring the hand. 'You arrived at the right time.'

'That's a matter of opinion,' the rider answered, looking down at his dead comrades. The wounded man was sitting up, clutching his shoulder and cursing.

'There's another wounded man up on the ridge,' said Shannow. 'I suggest you ride into Pilgrim's Valley and have a wagon sent.'

'I'll do that. But looks like there's a storm brewing. I should get him to Frey McAdam's cabin – we finished it yesterday and at least he'll be under cover and in a bed.'

Bull gave Shannow directions, then he and the wounded man rode off towards the north. Shannow stripped the guns and ammunition from the dead men and walked back to the bodies of the reptiles, crouching to examine them. The eyes were large and protruding, golden in colour, the pupils long and oval like those of cats. Their faces were elongated, the mouths lipless and rimmed with pointed teeth. But what made Shannow most uneasy was that they all wore identical body armour, and that reminded him of the Hellborn. These creatures were not individual killers, they were part of an army... and that did not bode well. He gathered their guns and hid them behind a rock. Then returning to the ridge, he dragged the unconscious Steiner upright and pushed him across the saddle of the stallion. Gathering his blankets, he mounted behind Steiner and rode for Beth McAdam's cabin.

*

When Samuel McAdam walked from the new cabin and saw the man sitting on the ground in the shade of the building, his fear rose and he stepped back a pace, staring at the newcomer. The man was very large, with the blackest beard Samuel had ever seen; he was gazing intently at the distant wall.

'It is a hot day,' the man observed, without turning round.

Samuel said nothing.

'I am not a man to fear, child. I carry no weapon and I

am merely sitting here, enjoying the breeze before moving on.' The voice was low, deep and reassuring, but Beth McAdam's son had been warned many times about trusting strangers.

'Some,' Beth had told him, 'look fair, but feel foul. Others look foul and are foul. Treat them all the same. Keep away from them.' But this was difficult, for the man was sitting virtually in the doorway of their house. He had not come in, though, thought Samuel, which at least showed he had good manners. Beth was in the meadow with Mary, the oxen hitched to the plough, the long, arduous work of preparing the soil under way. Samuel wondered if he should just run back through the house and fetch his mother.

'I would appreciate a drink of water,' said the man, pointing to the well dug out by Bull and the others. 'Would it be permissible?'

'Sure,' Samuel replied, happy to be able to grant a favour to an adult, and enjoying the unaccustomed power that came with bestowing a gift. The man stood and walked over to the well and Samuel saw that his hands were huge and his arms long. He had a swaying walk, like a man unused to solid ground who feared it might pitch beneath him. He dropped the bucket into the well and hauled it up with ease, dipping the long-handled ladle into it and drinking deeply. Then he walked back slowly and sat watching Samuel.

'I have a son of your age,' he said. 'His name is Japheth. He has golden hair, and he too is forbidden to talk with strangers. Is your father home?'

'He died and went to Heaven,' Samuel told him. 'God wanted him.'

'Then he must be happy. My name is Nu. Is your mother here?'

'She's working and she won't want to be disturbed, especially not by no man. She can get awful angry, Meneer Nu.'

'I understand that. In my short time here I have discovered this to be a violent world. It is pleasant, however, to meet so many people who know of God and his works.'

'Are you a preacher?' asked Samuel, squatting down with his back to the wall.

'I am – after a fashion. I am a shipbuilder, but I am also an Elder of the Law of One and I preach in the Temple. Or rather I did.'

'Do you know about Heaven?' Samuel asked, his blue eyes wide.

'I know a little. Though, thankfully, I have not yet been called there.'

'How do you know my Dad is happy? Maybe he doesn't like it there. Maybe he misses us?'

'He can see you,' said Nu. 'And he knows the Great One . . . God . . . is looking after you.'

'He always wanted a fine house,' said the boy. 'Do they have fine houses there?'

Nu settled back and did not notice the blonde woman who moved slowly through the house with a large pistol in her hand. She halted in the shadow of the doorway listening. 'When I was a child I wondered that and I went to the Temple Teacher. He told me that the houses of Heaven are very special. He said there was a rich woman once who had been very devout, but not very loving to her neighbours; she prayed a lot, but never thought of being kind to others. She died and went to Paradise; when she arrived there she was met by an angel who said he would take her to her new home. They walked near great palaces of marble and gold. "Will I live here?" she asked. "No," the angel replied. They went further to a street of fine houses of stone and cedarwood. But they passed these by too. At last they came to a street of small houses. "Will I live here?" she asked. "No," replied the angel. They walked on until they came to an ugly piece of ground by a river. Here there were several rotting planks loosely nailed to form two walls and a roof, and a moth-eaten blanket for a bed. "Here is your home," said the angel. "But this is terrible," the rich woman said. "I cannot live here." The angel smiled and said, "I am sorry. It was all we were able to build with the materials you sent up."' Nu grinned at the perplexed boy. 'If your father was a kind man, then he has a wonderful house,' he said.

Samuel smiled. 'He was kind. He really was.'

'Now you should tell your mother I am here,' said Nu, 'lest she be frightened when she sees me.'

'She's seen you,' said Beth McAdam. 'And the man ain't been born who could frighten me. What's your business here?'

Nu rose and bowed. 'I am seeking a way through the Wall, and I paused here to drink of your water. I will not stay.'

'Where's your gun?'

'I do not carry weapons.'

'That's a little foolish,' said Beth, 'but it's up to you. You're welcome to stay for a meal. I liked the story about Heaven; it may be nonsense, but I liked the sound of it.'

An earth tremor rippled across the valley and Beth pitched sideways into the door-frame, dropping her pistol. Samuel screamed and Nu staggered. Then it passed. He bent and picked up the pistol and Beth's eyes hardened, but he merely handed it to her.

'Look at that, Ma!' Samuel shouted.

Two suns were blazing in the sky, and twin shadows forked from the trees around the cabin. For several seconds the brightness remained, then the second sun faded and was gone.

'Wasn't that wonderful?' said Samuel. 'It was so hot, and so bright.'

'It wasn't wonderful,' said Nu softly. 'Not wonderful at all.'

Mary came running round the cabin. 'Did you see it?' she yelled, then pulled to a halt as she saw the stranger.

'We saw it,' replied Beth. 'You and Samuel go into the house and prepare the meal. One extra portion for our guest.'

'His name's Meneer Nu,' said Samuel, disappearing into the house. Beth gestured to Nu and the two of them walked out into the sunshine.

'What is happening?' she asked. 'I sense you know more about the weird signs than I do.'

'There are things that should not be,' he told her. 'There are powers Man should never use. Gateways that should not be opened. These are times of great danger, and greater folly.'

'You're the man with the Daniel Stone, aren't you? The one who cured the plague?'

'Yes.'

'They say the Stone was all used up.'

'It was. But it served a fine purpose – God's purpose.'

'I heard talk of them, but I never believed it. How can a Stone do magic?'

'I do not know. The Sipstrassi was a gift from Heaven; it fell from the sky hundreds of years ago. I spoke to a scholar once who said that the Stone was merely an enhancer, that through it the dreams of men could be made real. He claimed that all men have a power of magic, but it is submerged deep in our minds. The Sipstrassi releases that power. I have no idea if that is true, but I know the magic is real. We just saw it in the sky.'

'That is strong magic,' said Beth, 'if it can make another sun.'

'It is not another sun,' Nu told her, 'and that is why it is dangerous.'

22

'Your weapons are terrible indeed,' said Nu, as he looked down at the wound in Clem Steiner's chest. 'Swords can kill, but at least a man must needs face his enemy at close range, risking his own life. But these thunder-makers are barbaric.'

'We are a barbaric people,' answered Shannow, laying his hand on Steiner's brow. The man was sleeping now, his pulse still weak.

'You said something about reptiles, Shannow,' remarked Beth as the three of them walked back into the large living room. 'What did you mean?'

'I've not seen anything like them. They wear dark armour and carry Hellborn pistols. From what Steiner says, they are led by a woman.' He glanced at Nu. 'I think you know of her, Healer.'

'I am no healer. I had ... magic. But it is gone. And, yes, I know of her. She is Sharazad; she was one of the King's concubines. But she has a lust for blood and he fulfils her desires. The reptiles are known as Daggers. They first came to the realm four years ago, from beyond a gateway to a world of steaming jungles. They are swift and deadly and the King has used them in several wars. With sword and knife they are without equal. But these weapons of yours...'

'What is all this about kings?' snapped Beth. 'There are no kings here that I have heard of. You mean Beyond the Wall?'

Nu shook his head, then he smiled. 'In a way, yes. But also, no. There is a city Beyond the Wall. I grew to manhood there, yet it is not my city. It is hard for me to explain, dear Lady, since I do not understand it all myself. The city is called ... was called ... Ad. It is one of the seven great cities of Atlantis. I was being hunted by the Daggers and I used my... Daniel Stone?... to escape. It was supposed to bring me to Balacris, another city by the coast. Instead it brought me here, into the future.'

'What do you mean, the future?' Beth asked. 'You are making no sense.'

'I am aware of that,' said Nu. 'But when I left Ad, the city was bordered by the sea and great triremes sailed on the bays. Yet here the city is landlocked, the statues worn away.'

'That happened,' Shannow told him softly, 'when the seas swallowed Atlantis twelve thousand years ago.'

Nu nodded. 'I guessed that. The Lord has granted me a vision of just such an upheaval. I am glad, however, that some understanding of our world survived. How did you hear of it?'

'I have seen Balacris,' said Shannow. 'It is a ruined shell, but the buildings survived. And once I met a man called Samuel Archer who told me of the first Fall of the World. But tell me, how many of the Daggers are there?'

'I do not know exactly, but there are several legions. Perhaps five thousand, perhaps less.'

Shannow wandered to a window, looking out over the night. 'I don't know how many are here,' he said, 'but I have a bad feeling. I shall stay outside and keep watch. I am sorry to bring trouble to your home, Beth, but I think you will be safer with me here.'

'You are welcome here... Jon. You do what you have to do and I'll see to Steiner. If he lasts the night, he has a chance.'

Shannow took some dried meat and fruit and walked out on to the hillside beyond the cabin, where he sat beneath a spreading pine and scanned the dark horizon. Somewhere out there the demons were gathering, and a golden-haired woman was dreaming of blood. He shivered and pulled his coat tight around him.

Nu joined him at midnight and the two men sat in comfortable silence beneath the stars.

'Why were they hunting you?' asked Shannow at last.

'I preached against the King. I warned the people ... or I tried to ... that a great doom was about to befall. They did not listen. The King's conquests have led to a great swelling of the treasuries. People are richer now than ever before.'

'So they wanted to kill you? That's always the way with prophets, my friend. Tell me about your god.'

'Not my god, Shannow. Just God. The Lord Chronos, creator of Heaven and Earth. One God. And you, what do you believe?'

For an hour or more the two men discussed their faiths, and were delighted to find great similarities between the two religions. Shannow liked the big shipbuilder and listened as he talked of his family, his gentle wife Pashad, and his sons; of the ships he had built and the voyages he had sailed. But when Nu asked about Shannow and his life the Jerusalem Man merely smiled, and returned to questions about Atlantis and the distant past.

'I would like to read your Bible,' said Nu. 'Would that be permissible?'

'Of course. I am surprised that the ancients of Atlantis speak our language.'

'I'm not sure that we do, Shannow. When first I came here, I could not understand a word of it. But when I touched the Stone to the brow of a woman in need of healing all the words became clear inside my head.' He chuckled. 'Perhaps when I return I will not be able to speak the language of my fathers.'

'Return? You say your world is about to fall. Why would you go back?'

'Pashad is there. I cannot leave her.'

'But you might go back merely to die with her.'

'What would you do, Shannow?'

'I would go back,' he replied without hesitation. 'But then I have always been considered less than sane.'

Nu clapped his hand on Shannow's shoulder. 'Not

insanity, Shannow. Love – the greatest gift God can bestow. Where will you go from here?'

'South, across the Wall. There are signs there in the sky. I'd like to see them.'

'What sort of signs?'

'The Sword of God is there, floating in the clouds. Perhaps Jerusalem is close by.'

Nu fell silent for a while. Then: 'I will travel with you. I too must see these signs.'

'It is said to be a land of great peril. How will it help you to return home?'

'I have no idea, my friend. But the Lord has commanded me to find the Sword and I do not question His will.'

'I can lend you a gun or two.'

'I do not need one. If the Lord has me marked for death, I will die. Your thunder-makers will not alter the situation.'

'That is too fatalistic for me, Nu,' Shannow told him. 'Trust in God, but keep your pistols cocked. I have found He likes a man who stays ready.'

'Does He talk to you, Shannow? Do you hear His voice?'

'No, but I see Him in the prairies and on the mountains. I feel His presence in the night breezes. I see His glory in the dawn.'

'We are lucky men, you and I. I spent fifty years learning the thousand names of God known to Man, and another thirty absorbing the nine hundred and ninety-nine names known to the Prophets. One day I will know the thousand that are sung only by angels. But all this knowledge is as nothing compared with the sense of knowing you describe. Few men experience it; I pity those who do not.'

A shadow flickered out in the valley and Shannow held up his hand for silence. He watched for several minutes, but saw nothing further.

'I think you should go inside, Nu. I need to be alone.'

'Have I offended you?'

'Not at all. But I need to concentrate – to feel the presence of my enemies. I need all my strength, Nu. And that only happens when I am alone. If you cannot sleep, take one of my Bibles from the saddlebag by the door. I will see you come the dawn.'

When the man had gone Shannow stood and moved silently into the trees. The shadow could have been a wolf or a dog, a fox or a badger.

But equally it could be a Dagger...

Shannow loosened the guns in their scabbards and waited.

*

Shannow remained alert until an hour before sunrise. Then his feeling of unease drifted away, his muscles relaxing; he put his back to a broad pine and slept.

Beth McAdam walked out into the early morning light and gazed at the sky. Dawn was always special to her – those few precious minutes when the sky was blue and yet the stars still shone. She glanced up to the wooded hillside and walked towards where Shannow slept. He did not hear her approach and for some minutes she sat down beside him, staring intently at his weatherbeaten face. His beard was growing again, silver at the chin, yet his features seemed strangely youthful in sleep.

After a while, he awoke and saw her. He did not jump or start, he merely smiled lazily.

'They were out there,' he said, 'but they passed us by.'

She nodded. 'You look rested. How long did you sleep?'

He glanced at the sky. 'Less than an hour. I do not need much. I have been having curious dreams. I see myself trapped within a crystal dome in a huge cross that hangs in the sky; I am wearing a leather helmet and there is a voice in my ear; it is someone called Tower giving me directions. But I cannot escape or move.' He took a deep breath and stretched. 'Are the children still asleep?'

'Yes. In each other's arms.'

'And Steiner?'

'His pulse is stronger, but he is not yet awake. Do you believe Nu? That he came from the past?'

'I believe him, Beth. The Daniel Stones are incredibly

powerful. I once stood on the wreck of a ship beached on a mountain, but by the power of a great Stone it sailed again. They can give a man immortality, cure any disease. Once I ate a honeycake that had been a rock; a Daniel Stone reshaped it. I think there is nothing such power cannot achieve.'

'Tell me about it.'

Shannow told her about the Hellborn and their crazed leader, Abaddon; then about the Guardians of the Past and the rebirth of the *Titanic*. And finally he spoke of the Motherstone, the colossal Sipstrassi meteorite that had been corrupted by blood and sacrifice.

'So there are two kinds of Stones?' she said.

'No, just one. Sipstrassi is the pure power; but the more it is used, the sooner it fades. If fed with blood, it swells again, but it can no longer heal or make food. Also it affects the mind of the user, bringing with it a lust for pain and violence. The Hellborn all had Bloodstones, but their power was drained during the War.'

'How did you survive, Jon Shannow, against such odds?'

He smiled and pointed to the sky. 'Who knows? I ask myself that question often – not just about the Hellborn Zealots, but about all the perils I have faced. Much is timing, more is luck or the will of God. But I have seen strong men cut down by enemies, or disease, or accident. When I was young I had another name; I was Jon Cade. I met a town tamer called Varey Shannow, who taught me about people and the ways of evil men. He could stand alone against a mob and they would turn away from his eyes. But one day a young man – no more than a boy – walked up to him as he was having breakfast. "Pleased to meet you," he said, holding out his hand. Varey took it. At the same time the boy produced a pistol in his left hand and shot Varey through the head. When they asked him later why he had done it, he said he wanted to be remembered. Varey was a man to walk the mountains with; he helped people to settle this wild land of ours. The boy? Well, he was remembered. They hanged him and put a marker on his grave that said, "Here lies the killer of Varey Shannow".'

'So you took his name? Why?'

Shannow shrugged. 'I didn't want to see it die. And also my brother, Daniel, had become a brigand and a killer. I was ashamed.'

'But did not Daniel become a prophet? Did he not fight the Hellborn?'

'Yes. That pleased me.'

'So a man can change, Jon Shannow? He can make a new life for himself?'

'I guess that he can – if he has the strength. But I do not.'

Beth sat silently for a moment, then she reached out and touched his arm. He did not pull away. 'You know why I never came back to you?'

'I think so.'

'But if you made the decision to change your life, my hearth *would* be open to you.'

He looked away at the far Wall and the lands rolling out beyond it. 'I know,' he said sadly. 'I have always been lonely, Beth. There is an emptiness in my life which has been there ever since my parents were murdered. But look at Steiner. Until yesterday the boy wanted nothing more than to kill me – to be the man who beat Jon Shannow. How long before some boy comes to me at breakfast and says, "Pleased to meet you"? How long? And could I sit at night at your table, wondering if your children will intercept a bullet meant for me? I do not have that kind of strength, Beth.'

'Change your name,' she said. 'Shave your head. Whatever it takes. I'd travel with you and we could build a home somewhere where no one has ever heard of you.' He said nothing, but she looked into his eyes and saw the answer. 'I'm sorry for you, Shannow,' she whispered. 'You don't know what you're missing. But I hope you are not fooling yourself. I hope you are not in love with what you are: the Jerusalem Man, proud and alone, bane of the wicked. Is there something to that? Do you fear putting aside your reputation and your name? Do you fear anonymity?'

'You are a very astute woman, Beth McAdam. Yes, I fear it.'

'Then you are a weaker man than you know,' she said. 'Most men fear dying. You just fear living.' She rose and walked back to the cabin.

23

Josiah Broome closed the front door of his small house and wandered along the street towards the Jolly Pilgrim. The sun was shining brightly, but Broome did not notice it. For days now he had been seething over the departure of Beth McAdam, and the hurtful untrue words she had hurled at him like knives.

How could she not see? Men like Jon Shannow were no help to civilisation. Violence and despair followed him, giving birth to yet more of the same. Only men of reason could change the world. But how the words stung! She had called him a fool and a coward; she had blamed him for Fenner's death.

Could you blame a man for a summer storm, or a winter flood? It was so unfair. Yes, Fenner would still be alive if they had walked into Webber's establishment and shot him down. But what would that have achieved? What would it have taught the youngsters of this community? That in certain situations murder was acceptable?

He remembered Shannow shooting down the man in the street, just after he had executed Webber. The man's name had been Lomax. He was a tough, arrogant man, but he had helped the Parson build his church and he had worked hard for Meneer Scayse to support a wife and two children. Those children were now orphans who would grow up knowing their father had been gunned down in the street to make a point. Who would blame them if they turned bad? But Beth McAdam did not see that.

Broome crossed the street and heard the sounds of gunfire coming from the west. More trouble-makers he thought, swinging to see the cause of the disturbance. His jaw dropped open to see hundreds of black-armoured warriors advancing with their guns blazing. Men and women were running and screaming. A shell whistled past Broome and he ducked instinctively and ran to an alley between two buildings. A man sprinted past ... his chest exploded and he fell face forward in the dirt.

Broome turned and cut down the alley, arms pumping. He scaled a fence and ran out over the fields towards the newly-built church in the meadow.

At the Traveller's Rest Mason glanced out of his window to see the reptiles advancing down the main street killing all in their sights. He swore and took down his Hellborn rifle from its rack on the wall. Swiftly he fed shells into the side gate, then pumped one into the breech. He heard sounds of booted feet on the stairs and as the door exploded inwards he swivelled and fired. One reptile hurtled back into the hallway, but several more ran in. Mason's gun jumped in his hands as he pumped shell after shell into them, then a bullet took him high in the chest, spinning him against the window. Two more shells ripped into his belly and he plunged out of the window, toppling to the street below.

At the gunsmith's shop Groves grabbed two pistols, but he was shot to death before he could loose a single round.

Hundreds of reptiles surged through the town. Here and there men returned their fire, but the attack was so sudden there was no organised defence.

At the church the Parson had been delivering an impassioned sermon about the Whore of Babylon and the beasts Beyond the Wall. When the sounds of the battle reached them, men and women had streamed from the building. The Parson pushed his way through them and stared in horror at the flames beginning to spring from the town buildings. Josiah Broome staggered towards the milling crowd.

'Beasts from Hell!' he shouted. 'There are thousands of them!'

Men began to run but the Parson's voice stopped them cold. 'Brethren! To run is to die.' He looked around at the gathering. More than two hundred people were present, two-thirds of them women and children. The men had left their guns in the front porch. 'Gather your weapons,' he ordered. 'Broome, you and Hendricks lead the women and children to the south. There are woods there. Find hiding places and we will join you later. Go now!' He swung to the men who had gathered rifles and pistols. 'Follow me,' he said, striding off towards the town. For a moment they hesitated, then one by one they joined him. He stopped at the edge of the meadow where a shallow ditch had been built for drainage. 'Line up here,' he said, 'and do not open fire until I give the word.'

The fifty-six men who had joined him settled down in the dirt, their weapons held before them. The Parson stood, listening to the screams from the town; he would like to have charged in, bringing the vengeance of God on the killers, but he fought down the impulse and waited.

A large group of Daggers came into sight. Seeing the Parson they lifted their rifles, but just before they fired he jumped down into the ditch and the shots whistled harmlessly overhead. Twenty of the reptiles ran across the open ground.

'Now!' yelled the Parson. A ragged volley swept through them and only one was left standing; the Parson took up a pistol and shot the creature in the head. Scores more of the reptiles came surging through the alleyways. Glancing back, the Parson could see Broome and Hendricks leading the women and children to safety, but they were not sufficiently clear to allow the defenders to withdraw. The reptiles charged. There were no screams from them, no terrible battle cries; they ran forward with incredible speed, firing as they came. Three volleys smashed into their ranks and the charge broke.

'I'm out of ammunition,' shouted one of the men in the ditch. Someone else passed him a handful of shells. The Parson glanced to his right and saw more than a hundred reptiles running to outflank them.

Just then Edric Scayse and thirty riders came thundering from the east. The reptiles opened fire and horses and men fell. Scayse, two pistols in his hand, galloped in amongst the enemy, firing coolly. The surviving riders followed. The carnage was awful, but Scayse and seventeen men made it through to leap from their horses and clamber into the ditch.

'You're a welcome sight, man,' said the Parson, thumping Scayse's shoulder.

'Where the Hell are they from?' shouted Scayse.

'Beyond the Wall... sent by the Great Whore,' the Parson replied.

'I think we'd best get out of here,' Scayse urged.

'No, we must protect the women and children. I have sent more than a hundred of them to the south. We must hold these beasts for a while.'

'We can't do it here, Parson; it's too easy for them to go round us. I suggest we back off to the church and hold them there.'

The reptiles charged again. Bullets shredded their ranks, but four got through to leap in among the defenders. Scayse hammered his pistol into a grey scaled head, then fired at point-blank range into the beast's body. The others were despatched with knives, but not before they had killed three of the defenders.

'Fall back in two lines,' shouted the Parson. 'Every second man get back thirty paces, then cover the second group.'

The ground began to tremble violently. Men were pitched from their feet as a great, jagged crack opened in the meadow, snaking across the front of the ditch like the jaws of a giant beast. In the town buildings buckled and a second quake scored the earth. The Daggers fled towards open ground, the battle forgotten.

'Now's the time, Parson,' said Scayse and the defenders rose and sprinted back across the meadow. Clouds of dust obscured their passing, but the earth opened and two men fell into the depths of a vast pit. The rest managed to reach the church, which was sagging in the centre. The Parson stood and watched as the building slowly tore itself apart.

'Back to the woods,' he said. 'The Wrath of God is upon us.'

*

Josiah Broome sat and watched as the Parson organised the digging of a trench across the north side of the woods. Earth was being thrown up to form a rampart, the labour carried out in grim silence. Without tools the workers dug into the soft clay with their bare hands, casting nervous eyes to the north for the expected attack. Broome was in a state of shock; he sat grey-faced as people bustled around him.

It was all gone. The town was ruined, the community decimated, the survivors trapped in the woods with no food, no shelter and precious little ammunition for the few guns they carried. All that remained was to wait for death at the hands of the beasts. Broome blinked back tears.

Edric Scayse had rounded up three horses and had ridden to his own lands, where extra rifles were stored. Two men had been sent to outlying farms to warn other settlers of the invasion. Broome cared nothing for any of it.

A child approached him and stood with head tilted, staring at him. He looked down at her.

'What do you want?'

'Are you crying?' she asked.

'Yes,' he admitted.

'Why?'

The question was so ludicrous that Broome began to giggle. The child laughed with him, but when his eyes filled with tears and racking sobs shook his spare frame, she backed away and ran to the Parson. His face streaked with mud, the red-headed preacher moved to Broome's side.

'It does not look good, Meneer,' he said. 'You are frightening the children. Now stand like a man and do some work, there's a good fellow.'

'We are all going to die,' whispered Broome through his tears. 'I don't want to die.'

'Death comes to all men – and then they face the Almighty. Do not be afraid, Meneer Broome. It is unlikely that a maker of breakfasts has done much to offend Him.' The Parson put his arm around Broome's shoulder. 'We are not dead yet, Josiah. Come now, help the men with the ditch.' Broome allowed himself to be led to the ramparts; he stared out over the valley.

'When will they come, do you think?'

'When they are ready,' said the Parson grimly.

Work ceased as the sound of a walking horse was heard in the woods behind them, then they heard the lowing of cattle. Three milk cows were herded into the clearing, their calves beside them. Jon Shannow rode his stallion up to the ditch and stepped down from the saddle.

'I thought these might be of use,' he said. 'If you slaughter the calves for meat, you'll be able to milk the cows to feed the children.'

'Where did you find them?' the Parson asked.

'I heard the shooting this morning, and watched your flight. I rode to a farm and cut these from the herd there. The owner was dead – with his whole family.'

'We are grateful, Shannow,' said the Parson. 'Now if you could come up with around a thousand shells and a couple of hundred rifles, I would kiss your feet.'

Shannow grinned and reached into his saddlebag. 'These are all the shells I have – they're for Hellborn rifles or pistols. But I'll fetch some weapons for you; I hid them yesterday about four miles from here.'

'Walk with me aways,' said the Parson, leading him through the camp. They stopped by a stream and sat. 'How many of them are there?' he asked.

'As near as I could see, more than a thousand. They are led by a woman.'

'The black whore,' the Parson hissed.

'She's not black; she has golden hair and she looks like an angel,' Shannow told him. 'And they are not from Beyond the Wall.'

'How do you know that?'

'I just know it. Speaking of the Wall, the last earthquake ripped a hole in it. I would think we would have more chance of survival if we can get there and go through it. A few men would then be able to hold the gap, allowing the rest of the community to find a safe camping place.'

'We have around three hundred people here, Shannow. Everything they had has been taken from them. We have no food, no spare clothing, no canvas for tents, no shovels, axes or hammers. Where can we go that is safe?'

'Then what is your plan?'

'Wait here, hit them hard and pray for success.'

'I agree with the praying,' said Shannow. 'Look, Parson, I don't know much about warfare on this scale, but I do know that we're not going to beat these reptiles by sitting and waiting for them. You say we need supplies – axes, hammers and the like. Then let's get them. And at the same time, let's pick up a few guns.'

'Where?'

'Back in the town. There are still wagons, and there are oxen and horses aplenty wandering the meadows. Not all of the buildings were destroyed, Parson. I studied the town through a long glass. Groves' shop still stands; he had powder there, and lead for ammunition. Then there's the smithy – and the whole of Tent Town is untouched.'

'But what of the reptiles?'

'They're camped just south of the town. I think they're afraid of another quake.'

'How many men will you need?'

'Let's say a dozen. We'll swing round to the west and come in by night.'

'And you expect to load up wagons and drive them away under the noses of the enemy?'

'I don't know, Parson. But it's surely better than sitting here and starving to death.'

The Parson was silent for a while, then he chuckled and shook his head. 'Do you ever think of defeat, Shannow?'

'Not while I breathe,' said the Jerusalem Man. 'You get these people to the hole in the Wall. I'll fetch the tools you need, and some supplies. Can I choose my own men?'

'If they'll go with you.'

Shannow followed the Parson back to the camp and waited as the preacher gathered the men together. When he outlined Shannow's plan and called for volunteers, twenty men stepped forward. Shannow summoned them all and led them from the gathering to a small clearing where he addressed them.

'I need only twelve,' he said. 'How many have wives here?' Fifteen raised their hands. 'How many with children?' he asked the fifteen. Nine hands went up. 'Then you men get back; the rest gather round and I'll tell you what we need to do.' For over an hour Shannow listed the kinds of supplies they would require and ways to obtain them. Some men offered good advice, others remained silent, taking it all in. Finally Shannow gave them a warning.

'No futile heroics. The most important thing is to get the supplies back. If you are attacked and you see friends in trouble, do not under any circumstances ride back to help. Now you will not see me, but I will be close. You will hear a commotion in the enemy camp – that is when you will move.'

'What you going to do, Shannow?' asked Bull.

'I'm going to read to them from the Book,' said the Jerusalem Man.

24

For two days Chreena had studied the Pledging Pool, analysing the crystal-clear water that flowed away beneath the cliffs to underground streams and rivers. She sat now in the shade of the Chaos Peak, a tall, spear-straight tower of jagged rocks and natural platforms from which the more reckless of the Dianae men would dive.

Shir-ran had climbed almost to a point just below the crest of the Peak. He would have gone further had the crown of the rock not jutted from the column, creating an overhang no man could negotiate. His dive had been flawless and Chreena remembered him rising from the water with his dark hair gleaming, the light of triumph in his golden eyes.

She pushed back the memory. There had to be something in the Pool that had affected Shir-ran's genetic structure. To dive from such a height meant that he would have plunged deep into the water . . . perhaps the problem was there. Chreena closed her eyes and let her spirit flow over the rocks of the Pool and down, down into the darker depths. She knew what she was seeking – some toxic legacy from the Between Times. Drums of chemical waste, nerve gases, plague germs. The Betweeners had rarely given any thought to the future, dumping their hideous war-refined poisons into the depths of the ocean. One theory back at Home Base had been that the Betweeners must have known their time was short. Why else would they poison their rivers and streams, strip away the forests that gave them air and pollute their own bodies with toxins and carcinogens? But the theory was offered more as a debating point for children than a serious topic for study.

Now Chreena blanked such thoughts from her mind and drew from her memories everything she had been taught concerning water: the essence of life. In the Between Days it had covered 70.8 per cent of the earth's surface, but now the figure was 71.3. Water made up two-thirds of total body weight. Man could survive months without food, but only days without water. *Think! Think!* Two parts hydrogen to one part oxygen. She honed her concentration, adjusting her focus, shrinking, ever shrinking deeper into the Search-trance, analysing the trace elements at the bottom of the Pool. One by one she dismissed them – reactive silica, magnesium, sodium, potassium, iron, copper, zinc. There were minute traces of lead, but these could not have been harmful unless a person drank around sixty gallons a day for who knew what number of years.

She returned to her body and leaned back exhausted. The sun had moved past the Chaos Peak and her naked skin was burning. Moving several yards to her left, she looked around for Oshere. He was lying asleep in the shade; there was little of humanity left in him, and his voice was almost gone.

Not the water. What then? She glanced up at the sky and the awesome Sword of God pointing to the heavens. She shivered. Not that!

Her eyes flicked to the Peak. Was it something there? Chreena stood and stretched, then dressed swiftly and made her way to the base. There were many handholds in the heavily barnacled rock and she began to climb slowly. Her mind fled back to the last time she had clung to a rock face, almost three years before, when the *Titanic* had been breached and she had carried her son Luke from the doomed ghost ship and down the sheer face of the mountain above the ruins of Balacris.

Then she had been Amaziga Archer, widow of Samuel and a teacher to the children of the Guardians. Guardians? All the knowledge of the Betweeners had been held by them for future generations, yet the work had been ruined, corrupted by one man: Sarento. He had longed to see Rebirth, the world back as it was. His patience had worn thin and he had begun, through the Motherstone, to manipulate events. He had given Bloodstones to a growing nation that became the Hellborn; he had encouraged their warlike tendencies, giving them the secrets of automatic weapons. 'In war,' he said, 'man is at his most inventive. All great historical advances have come through the battlefield.'

With the power of the Motherstone he had reassembled the wreck of the *Titanic* as it lay broken upon the mountainside over Atlantis. He had made it Home Base for the Guardians. But his doom had been sealed when the Hellborn took Donna Taybard as a blood sacrifice, for that alone had led the Jerusalem Man to Balacris and the *Titanic*.

Amaziga remembered that awful night when Sarento used the Motherstone to duplicate the first voyage. Though the ship remained on the mountain, those on board – under its glittering lights and beautiful saloons – could gaze out on a star-filled sky over a black and shining ocean.

But Shannow had fought Sarento in the subterranean cavern of the Motherstone, killing him and sealing off the power of the Stone. The *Titanic* had once more struck the iceberg and a sorcerous sea filled the ship, destroying the Guardians and obliterating the knowledge of eons.

And Amaziga had climbed down from the wreck and walked away without a backward glance.

The Jerusalem Man had come to her.

'I am sorry,' he said. 'I do not know if my actions were right – but they were just. I will lead you to a safe place.'

They had parted at a small town hundreds of miles to the north, and Amaziga had journeyed with her son to the lands of the Wall.

She climbed higher and glanced down at the shimmering Pool below. Her fingers were tired and she hauled herself on to a ledge to rest. There was nothing harmful here that she could feel. 'You are getting old,' she told herself. She had lived more than a century, her youth guaranteed by the Sipstrassi carried by the Guardians. But that was gone now and silver flecks highlighted her tightly curled hair. How old are you in real terms, Amaziga? she asked herself. Thirty-five? Forty?

Taking a deep breath, she rose and climbed on. It took her an hour to reach the ledge beneath the Peak and as she scrambled over it, her hand gripped a sharp stone which split the skin of her palm. She cursed and sat with her back to the rock-face, heart hammering. She could detect nothing baleful in the rock of the Peak. The climb had been a waste of time, and had served only to bring her bitter memories and a painful wound. Settling herself down, preparing her body for the return journey, she thought of jumping to the Pool far below, but dismissed the idea; she had never been comfortable in the water. The sun bathed her and she felt warm and curiously refreshed. Her pulse slowed. When she lifted her injured hand, ready to apply pressure to stop the bleeding, the cut had disappeared. She rubbed her fingers at the skin but there was no mark. Reaching out, she picked up the stone with the serrated edge. Blood had stained it. Carefully she rose to her knees on the narrow ledge and turned to the rock-face. Above her the overhang jutted from the Peak, and above that the Sword of God and the tiny crosses that surrounded it. She closed her eyes, her spirit flowing into the barnacled stone. Deeper she moved, coming at last to shaped marble and beyond that to a network of golden wire and crystals. She followed the network up to a silver bowl, six feet in diameter. At the centre of this lay a huge Sipstrassi Stone with golden threads inches wide.

Her eyes snapped open. 'Oh God!' she whispered. 'Oh God!'

The Chaos Peak was not a natural formation. It had become encrusted as it lay beneath the ocean. It was a tower, and the Sipstrassi Stone was still pulsing its power after 12,000 years. Amaziga gazed down at the sleeping Oshere – and understood.

The healing powers of Sipstrassi!

There had been no intention of harming the Dianae. The almost mechanical magic of the Stone had bathed Shir-ran and the others – it had repaired them, eliminating the promoter genes and the carefully wrought genetic engineering. It had returned them to a state of perfection. 'Dear God!'

Amaziga rose and pushed her back to the face, then stared down at Oshere. Normally a wielder would need to touch a Stone to direct its powers... but with something of this size? Her concentration grew and far below Oshere stirred in his sleep. Pain lanced him and he roared, his great head snapping at unseen enemies. His body twisted and he sank back, his new fur shrinking, his limbs straightening. Amaziga pictured him as she remembered him, holding the vision before her eyes. Finally she relaxed and gazed down at the naked young man lying asleep in the sunshine.

Without a moment's hesitation she stepped forward and dived, her lithe ebony frame falling like a spear to cleave the water below. She surfaced and swam to the edge, heaving herself up on to the rocks beside Oshere. Removing her wet clothes, she let the sun dry her skin.

Oshere stirred and opened his golden eyes. 'Is this a dream?' he asked.

'No. This is the reality dreams are shaped of.'

'You look so... young and beautiful.'

'So do you,' she told him, smiling. He sat up and gazed in wonder at his bronzed body.

'Truly this is no dream? I am returned?'

'Yes.'

'Tell me. Tell me everything.'

'Not yet,' she whispered, stroking his face. 'Not now, Oshere. Not when I have just dived for you.'

*

Clutching her Bloodstone to her breast, Sharazad stepped through the gateway. Her mind swam, her vision blurred with colours more vivid than any she had seen in life. She held herself steady until the whirling movement before her eyes ceased; she had moved from a star-filled night to a bright dawn and for a moment or two she felt disorientated.

The King was sitting by a window, staring out at his

armies engaged in their training manoeuvres on the far fields.

'Welcome,' he said softly, without turning.

She dropped to her knees with head bent, golden hair falling over her face.

'I cannot tell you how wondrous it is to be once more in your presence, Lord.'

The King swung round and smiled broadly. 'Your flattery is well timed,' he said, 'for I am not best pleased with you.' She looked up into his handsome face, seeing the sunlight glisten on his freshly curled golden beard and the warm, humorous – almost gentle – look in his eyes. Fear rose. She was not fooled by his easy manner, nor the apparent lightness of his mood.

'In what way have I earned your displeasure, Great One?' she whispered, averting her eyes and staring at the ornate rug on which she knelt.

'Your attack on the barbarian village – it was badly timed, and appallingly led. I took you for a woman with a mind, Sharazad. Yet you only attacked from one direction, allowing the enemy room to flee. Where you should have delivered a crushing blow, you merely drove them into the woods to the south, there to plan and prepare a defence.'

'But they cannot defend against us, Great One. They are merely barbarians; they have no organisation, few weapons and little skill.'

'That may be so,' he agreed. 'But if you are so bereft of ideas, strategies and skills, why should I allow you to command?'

'I am not bereft of ideas, Lord, but it was my first engagement. All generals must learn. I will learn; I will do anything to please you.'

He chuckled and stood. He was tall and well-built, his movements easy and graceful as he raised her to her feet. 'I know that you will. You always have. That is why I allow you your ... small pleasures. Before I make love to you, Sharazad, I want you to see something. It may help you to understand.'

He lifted a Sipstrassi Stone from a gold-embroidered pouch at his belt and held it in the air. The far wall vanished and she found herself gazing down on the Dagger encampment; their low, flat leather tents were bunched together on a rocky slope by a stream. There were guards posted all around the camp, and two sentries on the rocky escarpment above.

'I see nothing amiss,' she said.

'I know. Watch... and listen.' The wind sighed across the hillside and the whisper of bats' wings could be heard. Then she caught the sound of lowing cattle; there was nothing else. 'You still cannot sense it, can you?' said the King, laying his hand on her shoulder and unbuckling the straps of her golden breastplate.

'No. They are natural sounds of the night, are they not?'

'They are not,' he said, lifting her breastplate clear and removing the belted dagger at her waist. 'One of them is out of place.'

'The cattle?'

'Yes. They rarely move at night, Sharazad, therefore they are being driven. And they are moving towards the Daggers. A gift, do you think? A peace offering?'

She could see the herd now – a dark, shifting mass moving slowly across the plain towards the camp. Several of the sentries stopped their pacing to watch them approach. Suddenly a shot sounded from behind the herd and a series of hair-raising screams followed. The cattle broke into a run, thundering towards the camp. Sharazad watched with growing horror as the sentries opened fire on the lead beasts; she saw the bulls fall, but the herd ploughed on. Daggers slithered from their tents and ran, diving into the stream or sprinting up the scree-covered slope. Then the stampeding cattle swept through the camp and were gone. As the dust settled, Sharazad gazed down on the ruins where some thirty bodies lay crushed and torn.

The King's hands moved to her silk tunic, untying the laces and sliding the garment down over her shoulders, but she could not tear her eyes from the carnage.

'Look and learn, Sharazad,' he whispered, his fingers sliding over the skin of her hips. The scene shifted to a gulley some three hundred paces from the camp where a man was sitting on a tall, black horse. The rider leaned back in the saddle and removed his hat. Under the moonlight she could see his features clearly, and remembered the man who had bowed to her in the Traveller's Rest.

'One man, Sharazad, one special man. His name is Shannow. He is respected and feared among these barbarians; they call him the Jerusalem Man, for he seeks a mythical city. *One man.*'

'The camp is nothing,' she said. 'And thirty Daggers can be replaced.'

'Still you do not see. Why did he stampede those cattle? Petty revenge? That man is above that.'

'What other reason could there be?'

'You have patrols out?'

'Of course.'

'Where are they now?'

She scanned the plain. The three patrols, each with twenty warriors, were hurrying back towards the ruined camp. Once more the scene shimmered and she found herself looking at the town.

'Of course you searched the town and destroyed anything that might be of use to the enemy?'

'No. I . . . did not . . .'

'You did not think, Sharazad – that is your great crime.' She saw the men at work, loading wagons with food, tools, spare rifles from the gunsmith's store and other weapons still lying beside the dead Daggers. The King moved away from her, but she did not notice, for she saw the man Shannow riding slowly along the main street, watched him dismount before the gunsmith's store. Hatred surged through her blood like a fever.

'Can I have the Hunters?' she asked. 'I want that man.'

'You can have anything you want,' said the King, 'for I love you.'

His whip snaked out, lashing across her buttocks. She screamed once, but did not move.

And the long day of pain began.

*

The King gazed down on Sharazad's sleeping form as she lay face down on the white silken sheets with her long legs drawn up to her body. She looked like a babe, all innocence and purity, thought the King. He had whipped her until she had collapsed, the blood flowing to stain the rug beneath her feet. Then he had healed her.

'Foolish, foolish woman,' he said. A tremor shook the city, but the power of the Sipstrassi Motherstone beneath the temple cut in, repairing cracks in the masonry and shielding the inhabitants from the quakes that rippled across the surrounding countryside.

The King wandered to the window. Below the palace, beyond the tall marble walls the people of Ad were moving about their business. Six hundred thousand souls born in the greatest nation the earth had ever seen – or ever would see, he thought. Through the power of the Stone from Heaven the King had conquered all the civilised world and opened gates to wonders beyond imagination.

Fresh conquests meant little to him now. All that mattered was that his name would ring like a clashing shield down through the ages of history. He smiled. Why should it not? With Sipstrassi he was immortal and therefore would be ever present when his continuing story was sung by the bards.

A second tremor struck. They were beginning to worry him, they had increased so much of late. Clutching his Stone, he closed his eyes.

And disappeared . . .

He opened them to find himself standing in the same room overlooking an identical view. There were the marble walls, beyond them the city, and the docks silent and waiting. It was perhaps his greatest artistic achievement: he had created an exact replica of Ad in a world unpeopled by

Man. Here there were no earthquakes, only an abundance of deer, elk and all the other wondrous creatures of nature.

Soon he would transfer the inhabitants here and build a new Atlantis where no enemies could ever conquer them, for there would be no other nations.

He returned to his room and considered waking Sharazad for an hour of love-making, then dismissed the thought, still angry at her stupidity. He did not mind the deaths of the Daggers; the reptiles were merely tools and, as Sharazad so rightly pointed out, could be replaced with ease. But he hated undisciplined thought, he loathed those who could not see or understand the simplest strategies. Many of his generals dismayed him. They could not comprehend that the object of war was to win, not merely to engage in huge and costly battles with a plethora of heroics on either side. Defeat the enemy from within. First convince him of the hopelessness of his cause and then strike him down while he sits demoralised. But in victory, be magnanimous, for a defeated and humiliated enemy will live only for the day when he can be revenged. Blame the war on the defeated leaders and court the people. But did the generals understand?

Now a new dawn was beginning for Atlantis. The King had seen a world of flying machines and great wonders. So far the links had been tentative, but soon he would open the gateway wider and send out scouts to learn of the new enemy.

His thoughts returned to Sharazad. The world she had discovered was not worthy of their attention – save for the weapons known as guns. But now they had seen them, they could duplicate them – improve on them. There was nothing there of interest. Yet he would allow Sharazad to play out her game to the end; there was the faintest glimmer of hope that she would learn something of value. And if she did not, there was always the whip and her deliciously satisfying screams.

The man Shannow, at least, was of transient interest. The Hunters would kill him, of course, but not before he had provided great sport. How many to send? Five would ensure success. One would give Shannow a chance. Then let it be three, thought the King. But which three?

Magellas must be one; haughty and proud, he needed a tough task. Lindian? Cold, that one, and lethal – not a man to allow into your presence with a weapon of any kind. Yes, Lindian. And to complete the mixture, Rhodaeul. He and Magellas hated one another, constantly vying for supremacy. It should be a fascinating mission for them. They had mastered the new guns with rare brilliance.

Now it was time to see if they could use them to good purpose against an enemy of great skill.

The King lifted his Stone and concentrated on Shannow's face. The air rippled before him and he saw the Jerusalem Man heaving a sack across the back of his saddle.

'You are in great danger, Jon Shannow,' said the King. 'Best to be on your guard!'

Shannow swung as the eerie voice filled his mind. His gun swept up, but there was no target in sight.

The sound of mocking laughter drifted away into echoes.

25

The withdrawal took place just after dawn. The Parson and twenty of the men moved out to flank the straggling column as it headed across the valley towards the great gash the quake had ripped into the ancient Wall. The Parson carried a short-barrelled rifle, his pistols jutting from the belt of his black cassock. The rescued wagons carried some of the children, but most of the three hundred survivors of the raid – reinforced by farmers and settlers from outlying regions – walked in silence, casting nervous glances around them. Everyone expected the reptiles to attack, and the Parson had been hard pressed to convince the refugees of the need to move from the seeming sanctuary of the woods.

Edric Scayse had returned in the night with two wagons loaded with food and spare guns. He had volunteered with thirty others to man the defensive trench in the woods.

'This is partly my fault,' he had told the Parson before the column moved out. 'Those demons are carrying guns I supplied, may God forgive me.'

'He has a habit of forgiving people,' the Parson assured him.

As he walked, the Parson prayed earnestly. 'Lord, as you saw your chosen people from the clutches of the Egyptians, so be with us now as we walk across the valley of the shadow. And be with us when we enter the realm of the Great Whore, who, with your blessing, I will cut down and destroy, with all the beasts of Hell over whom she reigns.'

The wagons were raising dust and the Parson ran back to the column, organising children to scatter water around the wheels. In the distance the Wall loomed, but if they were found here there would be no defence. He loped back to the flanking men.

'You see anything?' he asked Bull.

'Not a movement, Parson. But I feel like I'm sitting on the anvil with the hammer over me – know what I mean? If it ain't the reptiles, we've still got to walk into the land of the Lion-men.'

'God will be with us,' said the Parson, forcing sincerity into his voice.

'Hope so,' muttered the man. 'Surely do need some edge. Look there! More survivors.'

The Parson followed his gaze and saw a wagon moving down to join them. He recognised Beth McAdam at the reins, a black-bearded man beside her. Waving them into the column, he strode across.

'I am pleased to see you are well, Beth,' he said.

'This ain't well, Parson. I just built my god-damned house, and now I'm being run out by a bunch of lizards. What's worse, I got a sick man in the back and this bumping around is doing him no good at all.'

'Within a couple of hours, God willing, we should be behind the Wall. Then we can defend ourselves.'

'Yeah, against the reptiles. What about the other beasts?'

The Parson shrugged. 'As God wishes. Will you introduce me to your friend?'

'This is Nu, Parson. He healed the convoy; he's another man of God – getting to be so I feel hip-deep in them.'

Nu climbed down from the wagon and stretched. The Parson offered his hand, which Nu shook, and the two men strolled together.

'Are you new to this country, Meneer?' the Parson asked.

'Yes and no,' replied Nu. 'I was here . . . a long time ago. Much has changed.'

'Do you know of the lands Beyond the Wall?'

'Not much, I am afraid. There is a city there – a very old city. It used to be called Ad. There are temples and palaces.'

'It is inhabited now by beasts of the Devil,' said the Parson. 'Their evil keeps the Sword of God trapped in the sky. It is my dream to destroy their evil and release the Sword.'

Nu said nothing. He had seen the city in his spirit-search, but there were no signs of beasts or demons. The two men walked together with the flanking gunmen and soon the Parson, tiring of the silence, moved away. Nu strode on, lost in thought. How, he wondered, could a man who professed to believe in the supreme power of God be so convinced that such an awesome power would need his help? Trapped in the sky? What kind of petty creature did this man believe God to be?

The convoy moved slowly across the landscape.

A horseman came galloping across the valley. The Parson and his flankers ran to intercept him; the man was one of Scayse's riders.

'Better move fast, Parson,' he said, leaning over the saddle of his lathered mount. 'There's two groups of the creatures. One is moving on Meneer Scayse in the woods, the second and largest is coming to intercept you. They're not far behind.'

The Parson swung to gauge the distance to the Wall – it was over a mile. 'Ride in and get the wagons moving at speed. Tell everyone to run.' The horseman dug his heels into the flanks of his weary horse and cantered down to the leading wagons. Whips cracked and the oxen strained into the traces.

The Parson gathered his men. 'We can't hold them,' he said, 'but we'll keep together at the rear of the convoy. When we see them, we can at least slow their advance. Let's go.'

The morning sun blazed down on them as they ran into the dust-cloud left by the fleeing convoy.

*

As the mocking laughter faded, Shannow stepped into the saddle. He cast his eyes around the silent street. There in the dust by the Traveller's Rest lay Mason, his body riddled with bullet holes. Some yards to the left was Boris Haimut, who would now never find the answers to his questions. The crippled hostler lay in the street by the livery stable with an old shotgun in his hands. Elsewhere were the bodies of men, women and children Shannow had never known in life. Yet all must have nurtured their own dreams and ambitions. He turned the stallion's head and rode out into the valley.

He had been lucky at the gunsmith's store. As he had hoped, Groves had made more of the Hellborn shells, obviously planning on larger orders from Scayse. Shannow now had more than a hundred bullets. He had also gathered a short rifle, three sacks of black powder and sundry other items from the debris of the general store.

As he rode, he thought back to the voice that had whispered in his mind: *Be on your guard?* When in the last two decades had he not been on his guard, or in peril? Neither the voice nor the implied threat worried him unduly. A man lived, a man died. What could frighten a man who understood these truths?

For some time Shannow rode in sight of the wagons, but there was no pursuit and he cut his trail at right-angles and rode for the hills to the east. If the Parson took his advice and moved his people, then the valley would become the place of greatest danger.

Shannow rode warily, altering direction often, allowing no hidden observer to plot his path. The ground rose and he guided the stallion up into the boulder-strewn hills, dismounting and tethering him. Then he lifted the sack and opened it, spreading the contents on the ground before him. There were seven clay pots with narrow necks stopped with corks, six packets of small nails and a coil of fuse wire. He filled each pot with black powder mixed with nails, tamping them down firmly. With a long nail he pierced each of the corks and fed lengths of fuse wire into them. Satisfied with his handiwork, he returned the pots to the sack and sat down to wait. With his long glass he studied the valley below; in the far distance he saw the wagons reach the woods and, later, watched as the convoy began its slow progress towards the Wall.

For an hour he sat and then the first of the Daggers came

into view, running towards the woods. Shannow focused the glass and watched the enemy closing in on the makeshift fortifications. Another movement caught his eye – several hundred of the reptiles were running towards the south. A horseman cut across them and thundered away. Shannow stood and heaved the sack over the back of his saddle. Taking the reins, he mounted and steered the stallion through the trees towards the eastern slopes. Shielded by the hills he rode at speed, ignoring the danger of pot-holes or rocks. The stallion was sure-footed and strong, and he loved to run. Twice Shannow was forced to duck under overhanging branches that would have swept him from the saddle, and once the stallion surged over a fallen tree. As the hills levelled out, Shannow swung his mount to the west, into a shallow gulley that led out on to the plain. Shots whistled by him and he could see the reptiles closing fast as he leapt from the saddle, dragging the sack with him and pulling one of the pots clear. He struck a match and applied it to the fuse, which crackled and spat. Shannow heaved it over the gulley edge and then lit another. The explosion was deafening and red-hot nails screamed overhead. Three more pots sailed into the advancing ranks of the Daggers before Shannow grabbed the pommel of his saddle and vaulted to the stallion's back.

Kicking the beast into a run he headed him west, glancing back once to see the Daggers regrouping. There were many bodies lying on the long grass, but many more were still standing.

Shells came close, but the speed of the stallion soon carried the Jerusalem Man out of range.

*

Edric Scayse reloaded his rifle. The reptiles had charged the slope just once, but the withering volley fire from the defenders had scythed through their ranks. Now they were more cautious, creeping forward and waiting until the defenders skylined themselves. Eleven men were down and Scayse knew the position was hopeless.

He was angry with himself. All of his dreams were ashes now – and all because of the gold supplied by the woman, Sharazad. She had first come to him three months before, claiming to be from a community far to the east. Could he get her weapons? Of course he could if the price was right. And the gold was of spectacular quality. Now he was pinned down in a wood – his silver mine deserted, his town destroyed, the people who would have made him their leader decimated and scattered. He reared up and pumped three shots down the hill before dropping back behind the earthworks.

A man to his left screamed and fell, a ghastly wound in his temple. 'We'd best be thinking about leaving,' said another man beside him.

'Seems like a good time,' Scayse agreed. Word was passed along the line and the eighteen survivors moved back from the ditch into the woods. Shots screamed into them from the trees and Scayse dived for cover, his wide hat ripped from his head. He rolled into the bushes and sprinted off to the right as shells ricocheted from the trees around him. One struck the butt of his rifle, spinning it from his numbed hand, but he drew his pistol and ran on. A reptile reared up before him, with a serrated dagger in its hand, but Scayse triggered the pistol point-blank and the creature fell. Hurdling the body, he ran on. Behind him came the screams of the dying. He looked back once to see the dark, scaled forms of the reptiles were giving chase. He loosed two shots in their direction, but hit nothing. Ducking behind a tree, Scayse fed shells into the cylinder of his pistol and waited.

'Get down, Scayse,' came a voice, 'and cover your ears.' A clay pot soared overhead and exploded in the path of the hunters. A second followed it. Scayse dived for the ground as the explosion ripped into the woods, then he was up and running.

Shannow rode into his path, offering his hand. Scayse swung up behind him and the stallion cantered away through the woods.

They rode for two miles before Shannow halted to allow the stallion to rest; its breathing was laboured, its flanks covered with lather. Scayse climbed down and patted the beast. 'Some horse, Shannow. If ever you feel like selling, I'll buy.'

'With what?' asked Shannow, stepping down. 'All you own is what you're wearing.'

'I'll get it back. Somehow I'll find a way to beat those creatures – and that damned woman.'

'You should be grateful to her,' said Shannow. 'She's surely not a general. With a hundred well-armed, well-mounted men we could destroy them in a day.'

'Maybe,' Scayse agreed. 'But I'd say she has the upper hand around now. Wouldn't you?'

Shannow did not answer and the two men walked on for some time. Finally, Shannow turned the horse on to a narrow side trail leading up to a cave. The opening was less than four feet wide, but inside the cave itself was huge and almost circular. Shannow unsaddled the stallion and rubbed him down. 'We'll stay here for an hour or two, then I guess we should find a way to get over the Wall.'

'Easier said, Shannow. By now those reptiles will be swarming over it like bees on honey. By the way, thanks for the timely rescue. I'll pay you back one day.'

'That's an interesting thought,' answered Shannow, taking his blankets and spreading them for a bed. 'Wake me in an hour.'

'We could be trapped in here. Shouldn't we move on?'

'It's unlikely they'll hunt for long. Having removed your force, they'll congregate at the Wall.'

'And if you're wrong?'

'Then we'll both be dead. Wake me in an hour.'

*

The great Wall had been torn asunder by the quake, a huge gash appearing more than twenty feet across. On either side massive stone blocks hung precariously, looking as if a breath of wind would tumble them down on the rumbling wagons.

The Parson watched the column inch its perilous way along the stone-strewn pathway. Behind them the explosions had stopped – as had the headlong advance of the enemy.

'Shannow?' asked Bull and the Parson nodded. 'He don't give up, do he?'

With the last wagon through the gap, the Parson sent a group of men to scale the Wall and lever down the hanging blocks. They crashed to the ground, sending up clouds of dust.

'We should be able to hold them here for a while,' said Bull. 'Mind you, I think them beasts could climb over anywheres they chose.'

'We'll head south,' said the Parson. 'But I'd like you and a dozen others to hold this breach for a day ... if you're willing?'

Bull chuckled and ran his fingers through his long, sandy hair. 'Given the choice between this and having boils lanced, I'd surely plump for the knife, Parson. But I reckon it needs doing. Anyways, I think it would be neighbourly to wait for Meneer Scayse and the others.'

'You're a good man, Bull.'

'I know it, Parson. And don't you forget to tell the Almighty!'

Bull sauntered among the men, choosing those he felt he could trust in a tight spot. They unloaded extra ammunition, filled their water canteens from the barrels on the wagons and took up positions on the Wall or behind fallen blocks to await the enemy.

From the north came the sound of gunfire and two more muted explosions.

'He surely does get around,' observed Bull to a young rider named Faird.

'Who?'

'The Jerusalem Man. Hope to God he makes it.'

'I hope to God *we* make it,' said Faird with feeling.

'Goddammit, there's that second sun again.' The brilliance was overpowering and Bull shielded his eyes. He felt the rumble beneath his feet.

'Get back from the Wall!' he bellowed. Men started to run, then the tremor struck and they were hurled from their feet. Jagged lines scored the surface of the Wall, blocks shifting and falling. A chasm opened across the valley and a great roaring filled the air, as flames spewed from the pit.

'Son of a bitch!' whispered Bull as the smell of sulphur blew across him. He pushed himself to his knees. Another massive section of the Wall had collapsed and from out of the dust-storm walked a tall reptile, his right hand held before him. Faird levelled his rifle. 'Hold it,' said Bull, and he rose and walked out to meet the beast, halting some three paces short.

The creature snorted dust from its slitted nostrils, then fixed Bull with its golden eyes.

'Speak your mind,' said Bull, his hand resting on the pistol butt at his side.

'Yess. Sspeak. Thiss war no good, U-man. Much death. No point.'

'You began it.'

'Yess. Great sstupidity. We only soldierss. You undersstand? No choicess. Now Goldenhair ssays talk. We talk.'

'Who is this Goldenhair?'

'Sharassad. Leader. She ssays to give uss the man Nu and we will leave you in peace.'

'Why should we believe her?'

'I don't believe her,' said the reptile. 'Treacherouss woman. But she ssays sspeak so I sspeak.'

'You're telling me not to trust your own leader?' asked Bull, amazed. 'Then why the Hell come here in the first place?'

'We are *Ruazsh*-Pa. Warriors. We fight good. We lie bad. She ssay come, talk, tell you words. I tell you words. What answer you?'

'What answer would you give?'

The reptile waved his hand. 'Not for me to ssay.' He snorted once more, then began to cough.

'You want some water?' asked Bull. He called Faird over.

'Yess.' Faird brought a canteen and handed it gingerly to the creature, who lifted it high and poured the cool liquid over his face. Immediately the dry scaled skin took on a healthy glow. The reptile handed back the canteen, ignoring Faird.

'Very much bad, thiss war,' he told Bull. 'And these,' he added, patting the pistol at his hip, 'no good. Battle sshould be fought close, daggerss and swordss. No win souls from sso far. I, Szshark, kill twenty-six enemies with dagger, face close, touch their eyess with my tongue. Now . . . bang . . . enemy fall. Very much very bad.'

'You seem like a decent sort,' said Bull, aware that the others had gathered close. 'I . . . we . . . never seen nothing like you before. Shame we got to go on killing one another.'

'Nothing wrong with killing,' hissed the creature, 'but it musst be according to cusstom. What answer you give treacherouss woman?'

'Tell her we need time to think about it.'

'Why?'

'To discuss it amongst ourselves.'

'You have no leader? What of the red-headed one in black? Or the Deathrider?'

'It's hard to explain. Our leaders need time to discuss it. Then maybe they'll say yes, maybe no.'

'It sshould be no,' said Szshark. 'It would lack honour. Better to die than betray a friend. Yet I will take your words to Goldenhair. Water wass good. For that gift I will kill you the right way, with dagger.'

'Thanks,' said Bull, grinning. 'That's nice to know.'

Szshark bowed stiffly and loped back to the Wall. With one leap he cleared a ten-foot block and was gone.

'What the Hell do you make of that?' Faird asked.

'Damned if I know,' answered Bull. 'Seemed a reasonable . . . thing, didn't he?'

'You could almost like him,' agreed Faird. 'We'd better get back to the Parson – tell him about the offer.'

'I don't like the feel of it,' said Bull. 'No way.'

'Me neither. But my wife and children are with that convoy, and if it comes to a choice between a stranger and them, I know where my vote goes.'

'He saved you and your wife on the trail, Faird. You surely don't go too long on gratitude in your family.'

'That was then, this is now,' snapped Faird, swinging away.

535

26

The bodies of the three sacrificial victims were carried from the altars. The High Priest lifted the three gleaming Bloodstones and placed them in a golden bowl.

'By the Spirit of Belial, by the blood of the innocent, by the law of the King,' he chanted. 'Let these tokens carry you to victory.'

The three men remained kneeling as the High Priest brought the bowl to them. From his jewel-encrusted throne the King watched the ceremony with little interest. He could see the giant Magellas and feel the warrior's discomfort as he knelt. The King smiled. Beside Magellas, the slender Lindian showed no expression; his grey eyes were hooded, his face a taut mask. On the extreme right Rhodaeul waited with eyes closed, mind locked in prayer. All three looked like brothers with their snow-white hair and pale faces. The High Priest gave them their Stones, then blessed them with the Horns of Belial. They rose smoothly and bowed to the King.

He acknowledged their obeisance, gestured them to follow him and strode to his rooms. Once there, he stood by the window and waited as the three warriors entered. Magellas was by far the largest, his black and silver tunic stretched by the enormous muscles of his shoulders and arms. Lindian looked almost boylike beside him. Rhodaeul moved some paces to the right.

'Come,' invited the King. 'Meet your enemy.' He lifted his Sipstrassi, the wall shimmered and disappeared and they saw a man standing beside a tall, black horse. Another man was sitting close by. 'That is the victim you seek,' said the King. 'His name is Shannow.'

'He is old, sire,' said Magellas. 'Why are the Hunters needed?'

'Find him and see,' the King told him. 'But I do not want him killed from ambush, or destroyed from distance. You will face him.'

'It is a test then, Father?' asked Rhodaeul.

'It is a test,' the King agreed. 'The man is a warrior and I suspect he is – as you are – Rolynd. His disadvantage is that he was not fed with Sipstrassi strength while he was in the womb, nor tutored as you have been by the finest assassins in the Empire. Yet still he is a warrior.'

'Why three of us, Lord?' asked Lindian. 'Would not one suffice?'

'Most probably. But your enemy is a master of the new weapons – perhaps you will acquire something from him. To that end my reward will be great. The Hunter who kills him will become Satrap of the Northern Province of Akkady; his companions will receive six talents of silver.'

The three warriors said nothing, but the King could see their minds working. No unity of purpose now. No combined plan. Each of them was plotting to defeat not only Shannow but each other.

'Are there no questions, my children?'

'None, Father,' volunteered Magellas. 'It will be as you say.'

'I will watch your progress with interest.'

The three having bowed and left the room, the King sealed the chamber with his Stone and settled back on a silk-covered divan. The wall shimmered once more and he gazed down on the land of the Wall. At last Sharazad had begun to think; she had laid the seed of division within the enemy and was moving her troops to encircle them. He looked further, into the heavily wooded hills to the west of the refugees. Then he chuckled.

'Oh, Sharazad, if only I could tire of your beauty. Yet again you conspire to snatch defeat from the jaws of victory.' He touched the Stone and viewed the lands to the south. His body arched upright as he saw the distant city. As he stood, his pale eyes widening, his mouth was dry and for the first time in decades a lance of fear smote him.

'What demonic trickery is this?' he whispered aloud. Leaving the image shimmering, he summoned his astrologers. There were four men, all appearing to be in their middle twenties.

'Look, and tell me what you see,' ordered the King.

'It is the City of Ad,' said the leader, Araksis. 'Bring it closer, Majesty. Yes, it is Ad. But see the way the statues are worn and the roadways buckle. Move further south, Lord. Find the tower.' But there was no tower, only a barnacle-encrusted peak. For some time the Atlanteans stared at the Sword of God. 'It is baffling, my Lord,' said Araksis. 'Unless someone copied the city, or . . .'

'Speak!' ordered the King.

'We could be looking at the city as it will one day be.'

'Where is the sea? Where are the ships?'

The astrologers looked at one another. 'Show us nightfall, sire, on this world.' The King touched his Stone and the astrologers grouped together to study the star-filled sky.

'We will return to the tower, Lord,' said Araksis. 'We will study more closely and report back to you.'

'By midday, Araksis. Meanwhile, send Serpiat to me.'

The King sat lost in thought, staring at the vision before him. He did not notice the arrival of the general, Serpiat. The man was squat and powerfully built, wearing golden armour and a jet-black cloak.

'Not good, sire,' he observed, his voice rough and grating, 'to allow an armed man easy access to your chambers.'

'What? Yes, you are right, my friend. I did not secure the chamber. But my mind was occupied with that,' said the King, pointing to the distant city. Serpiat removed his black-plumed helm and approached the vision. He rubbed at his beard.

'Is it real?'

'All too real. Araksis is returning here at midday, but when he left his face was white, his eyes frightened. It frightens me also. With the Towerstone we have opened gates to other worlds – and conquered them. But this . . . this is no other world, Serpiat. What have we done?'

'I do not understand, sire. What is it you fear?'

'I fear that!' shouted the King. 'My city. I built it. But where is the ocean – and where am I?'

'You? You are here. You are the King.'

'Yes, yes. Forgive me, Serpiat. Gather ten legions. I want that city surrounded and taken – all its records. *Everything*. Capture its people. Question them.'

'But this was to be Sharazad's realm, was it not? Do I serve under her?'

'Sharazad is finished. The game is over. Do as I ask and prepare your men. I will open a wide gateway three days from now.'

*

The Parson listened to the reports of his scouts. The southland was wide and open; there was evidence of past cultivation, and an incredible number of lion tracks on the plain before the city. Several prides had been seen moving in the distance. To the east, he was told, there were other tracks, bigger, showing talon marks of prodigious size.

'Did you see any beasts?' he asked the rider.

'No, sir. Nothing unnatural, like. But I seen some big bears – biggest I ever saw. High up in the timber country. I didn't get too close.'

They had camped by a lake where the Parson ordered trees to be felled and dragged to the lakeside, forming three perimeter walls. Within this rough stockade he allowed tents to be erected and cook-fires lit. The people moved through their chores like sleepwalkers. Many of the women had lost husbands in the attack on the town. Other men, who had chosen to go to church on that fateful morning, knew their wives and children had been butchered. All had lost. For some it was only a building, or a tent or a wagon. For others it was loved ones. Now the survivors were in shock.

The Parson gathered them together and prayed for the souls of the departed. Then he allocated tasks for the survivors – gathering wood for the fires, helping to erect tents, preparing food, scouting the woods for root crops, tubers, wild onions.

In the distance he could see the glistening towers of the Whore's city, and wondered how long it would be before her satanic legions fell upon them.

Bull's arrival with Faird was a surprise – yet even more surprising was his news of the meeting with Szshark.

'You spoke with one of the Devil's minions?' he said, aghast. 'I hope your soul was not burned.'

'He seemed...' Bull shrugged. '...honest, at least, Parson. He warned us to beware of the woman.'

'Don't be a fool, Bull. He is a creature of darkness and he knows nothing of the truth. His ways are the ways of deceit. If the woman has made us an offer, we must regard it as honest – if only because the demon says otherwise.'

'Hold on there, Parson. You didn't speak to him. I did. I kinda trust what he says.'

'Then the Devil has touched you, Bull, and you are not to be trusted.'

'That's kinda harsh, Parson. Does that mean you'd consider giving up the Healer to them creatures?'

'What do we know of him – or his connection with them? He could be a killer. He could have brought this doom upon us all. I will pray on it and then the men will vote. You ride back and keep an eye on the enemy.'

'Don't I get a vote, Parson?'

'I will make it for you, Bull. I take it you are against any... trade?'

'You couldn't be more damn right!'

'I hear what you say. Go now.'

The Parson summoned Nu to him and the two walked together on the shores of the lake.

'Why are these creatures hunting you, Meneer?' he asked.

'I spoke against the King in the temple. I warned the people of coming disasters.'

'So then they consider you a traitor? It is not surprising, Meneer Nu. Are we not told in the Bible to respect the power of Kings, as they are ordained by God himself?'

'I am not versed in the lore of your Bible, Parson. I follow the Law of the One. God spoke to me and He told me to prophesy.'

'If He was truly with you, Meneer, He would have kept you safe from harm. As it is, you fled before the law of your King. No true prophet fears the way of kings. Elijah stood against Ahab, Moses against the Pharoahs, Jesus against the Romans.'

'I do not know of Jesus, but I read Shannow's Bible concerning Moses, and did he not run away to the desert before returning to save his people?'

'I will not bandy words with you, sir. Tonight the people will decide your fate.'

'My fate is in God's hands, Parson. Not yours.'

'Indeed? But which God? You know nothing of Jesus, the Son of God. You do not know the Bible. How can you be a man of God? Your deceit is colossal – but it does not fool me for the Lord has given me the gift of discernment. You will not leave this camp-site. I will give orders to see that if you attempt it you will be confined in chains. Do you understand?'

'I understand only too well,' Nu replied.

As the sun set the Parson called the men together and began to address them. But Beth McAdam strode into the circle.

'What do you want here, Beth?' the Parson asked.

'I want to hear the arguments, Parson. So do all the women here. Or did you think to exclude us from this meeting of yours?'

'It is written that women should be silent at religious meetings, and it is not fitting that you should question holy law.'

'I don't question holy law – whatever the Hell it might be. But two-thirds of the people here are women and we've got a point to make. Nobody lives my life or makes decisions for me. And I've sent the souls of men who've tried to Hell. Now you're deciding on the fate of a friend of mine and, by God, I'll have a say in it. *We'll* have a say in it.'

Beyond the circle the women crowded in and Martha stepped forward, her hair silver in the gathering dusk.

'You weren't there on the trail, Parson,' she said, 'when Meneer Nu healed all the people. He had him a Daniel Stone – and we all know what one of them is worth. It could have made him rich, given him a life of ease. But he used it up for people he didn't know. I don't think it a Christian deed to hand him to a bunch of killers.'

'Enough!' stormed the Parson, surging to his feet. 'I call upon the men here to vote on this matter. It is obvious that the Devil, Satan, has once more reached into the hearts of Woman – as he did on that dreadful day when Man was cast from the joys of Eden. Vote, I say!'

'No, Parson,' said Josiah Broome, pushing himself to his feet and clearing his throat. 'I don't think we should vote. I think it demeans us. I am not a man of violence, and I fear for all of us, but the facts are simple. Meneer Nu, you say, is not a true man of God. Yet the Bible says, "By their works shall ye judge them." Well, by his works I judge him. He healed our people; he carries no weapons; he speaks no evil. The woman, Sharazad, whom you urge us to believe, bought guns from Meneer Scayse and then loosed the demons upon our community. By her works I judge her. To vote on such a trade would be a shame I will not carry.'

'Spoken like the coward you are!' shouted the Parson. 'Do not vote then, Broome. Walk away. Turn your back on responsibility. Look around you! See the children and the women who will die. And for what? So that one man – whom we do not know – can escape the penalties of his treason.'

'How dare you call the man a coward?' stormed Beth. 'If you are right, he just accepted death rather than shame. I've got two kids and I'd give my life to see them happy and healthy. But I'll be damned before I give someone else's.'

'Very well,' said the Parson, fighting to control his anger. 'Then let the vote take in all the people. And let the Lord God move in your hearts when you do so. Let all who wish the man Nu to be returned to his people walk over here and stand behind me.'

Slowly some of the men began to shift and Faird rose.

'You go with him, Ezra Faird, and you don't come back to me,' shouted a woman. Faird shifted uneasily, then sat down. In all, twenty-seven men and three women moved to stand behind the Parson.

'Looks like that settles it,' said Beth. 'Now let's see to the cook-fires.' She turned to leave, then stopped. Slowly she approached Josiah Broome.

'We don't always see eye to eye, Meneer, but for what it's worth I am sorry for the things I said to you. And I'm right proud to have heard you speak tonight.'

He bowed and gave a nervous smile. 'I am not a man of decisive action, Beth. But I too am proud of what the people did here tonight. It's probably meaningless in the long run, but it shows what greatness Mankind is capable of.'

'Will you join my family and me for a meal?'

'I would be glad to.'

27

Shannow and Scayse walked to the crest of the last hill and found themselves looking down on a lake of dark beauty. The moon hung in the sky between two distant peaks, and the surface of the water shone like silver. By the shoreline the camp-site was lit by fires, the wagons spread like a necklace of pearls to reinforce the perimeter walls. From where they stood, all seemed peaceful.

'This is a beautiful country,' said Scayse. 'God-forsaken, but beautiful.'

Shannow said nothing. He was scanning the horizon, seeking any sign of the reptiles. He and Scayse had passed through the gap in the Wall and come across many tracks, but of the enemy there was no sign. Shannow was disturbed. As long as he knew where his enemy was, he could plan to defeat or avoid him. But the Daggers had vanished, the tracks seeming to indicate they had headed for the woods to the west of the camp-site.

'Not much of a talker, are you, Shannow?'

'When I have something to say, Scayse. There seems to be a meeting going on down there,' said Shannow, pointing to the centre of the camp-site.

'Well, let's get down there. I don't want decisions taken without me.'

Shannow walked ahead, leading the stallion. A sentry spotted them, recognising Scayse, and the two men were ushered through a break in the perimeter wall. As the Parson strode to meet them, Shannow saw that his face was flushed and his eyes angry.

'Trouble, Parson?' he asked.

'A prophet is not without honour – save in his own land,' snapped the Parson. 'Where are the other men?'

'All dead,' replied Scayse. 'What's going on?' Swiftly the

Parson told them of the meeting and what he described as its satanic outcome.

'It might have been different had you been here,' he told Shannow, but the Jerusalem Man did not reply; he led his horse to the picket line by the lake, stripped the saddle and brushed the stallion down for several minutes. Then he fed him grain, allowed him to drink at the lakeside and tethered him to the line.

Shannow wandered through the camp-site seeking Beth McAdam. He found her by her wagon, sitting at a fire with Josiah Broome and Nu, her children lying asleep beside her wrapped in blankets. 'May I join you?' asked the Jerusalem Man.

Beth made a space for him beside her, but Broome stood. 'Thank you, Beth, for your company. I will leave you now.'

'There's no need to rush, Josiah. Where is there to go?'

'I think I'll get some sleep.' He nodded to Shannow and walked away.

'The man does not like me,' said Shannow as Beth passed him a cup of Baker's.

'No, he doesn't. You heard what happened?'

'Yes. How are you faring, Nu?'

The shipbuilder shrugged. 'I am well, Shannow. But your Parson is unhappy; he feels I am a devil's disciple. I am sorry for him. He is under great strain, yet has performed wonders holding the people together. He is a good leader, but like all leaders he has a belief that only he is right.'

A burst of gunfire came from the western woods, more than a mile away. Shannow stood and gazed across the open ground, but he could see nothing and the sound faded.

Returning to his seat, he finished his drink. 'I think I know how I might get home,' said Nu. 'The Temple at Ad had an inner sanctuary, where once a year the Elders would heal supplicants. They had Sipstrassi. If the end came suddenly, perhaps the Stones are still hidden there.'

'A good thought,' said Shannow. 'I am riding there myself. Come with me.'

'What do you plan there?' asked Beth.

'It is said – by the Parson and others – to be a city of beasts ruled by a dark queen. I shall go to her, tell her of the reptiles and the attack.'

'But she is evil,' protested Beth. 'You'll be killed.'

'Who is to say she is evil?' answered Shannow. 'The Parson has never seen her. No one has come Beyond the Wall in years. I trust my own eyes, Beth McAdam.'

'But the beast back in the town, the lion-creature. You saw it. It was terrifying.'

'I also met such a creature when I was in need, Beth. He healed my wounds and tended me. He told me of the Dark Lady; he said she was a teacher who worked among the people of the Lion, the Bear and the Wolf. I will not trust to rumour. I will make no judgements.'

'But if you are wrong . . .'

'So be it.'

'I will come with you, Shannow,' Nu said. 'I need a Stone. I need to return home. My world is about to die and I must be there.'

Shannow nodded. 'Let us walk a while. There are matters we must speak of.' The two men strolled to the lake and sat by the waters. 'When we spoke on the hillside,' said Shannow, 'you told me of the King and his evil. But you did not say his name. Tell me, is it Pendarric?'

'Yes. The King of Kings. Is it important?'

'I owe the man my life. He saved me twice. He came to me in a dream three years ago and showed me his sword – saying that if ever I saw it in life and had need of it, I should reach for it and it would come to me. When I fought Sarento in the cavern of the Motherstone, I saw the image of the sword carved on an altar. I stretched out my hand and the blade appeared. Later, when the cavern flooded and I was dying, Pendarric's face appeared beside me, leading me to safety.'

'I do not understand all this, Shannow. What are you trying to tell me?'

'I owe him. I cannot go against him.'

Nu picked up a flat stone and skimmed it across the

water. 'There was a time when Pendarric was a good King – even a great one. But the Sons of Belial came to him and showed him the power of Sipstrassi when fed by blood. He changed, Shannow. Evil swamped him. I have seen children hauled up by their ankles over the altars of Molech-Belial, their throats cut. I have seen young women slaughtered in their hundreds.'

'But I have not. Though I know you speak the truth, because Pendarric told me he was the King who had destroyed the world. He will fall whatever I do, or do not do.'

Nu skimmed a second stone. 'I build ships, Shannow. I shape the keels, I work the wood. Everything in its place and its rightful order. You cannot start with the deck and build around it. It is the same with Pendarric. You and I are servants of the Creator and He also believes in order. He created the universe, the suns and moons and stars. Then the world. Then the creatures of the sea. Lastly He placed man upon the earth. All in order.'

'What has this to do with Pendarric?'

'Everything. He has changed the order of the universe. Atlantis is dead, Shannow; it died twelve thousand years ago. Yet it is here, its sun shining alongside our own. The spirit Pendarric who saved you is yet to be. The King beyond is not yet him. You understand? The evil ruler who is trying to conquer worlds beyond imagination has not yet met you. Only *after* the doom of Atlantis will he come into your life. Therefore you owe him nothing. There is another thought too, Shannow. You have already gone against him and perhaps he now knows of you. Perhaps that is why he came to you three years ago. He already knew you, though you had no knowledge of him.'

'My mind feels like a kitten chasing its tail,' said Shannow, smiling, 'but I think I understand. Even so, I will not go against him directly.'

'You may be forced to,' Nu told him. 'If two ships are lashed together in a storm and one is holed, what happens to the other?'

'I do not know. They both sink?'

'Indeed they do. Then think on this, my friend. Pendarric has joined our two worlds together. There is a gateway to the past. What happens when the oceans rise?'

Shannow shivered and gazed at the stars. 'In Balacris,' he said, 'I had a vision. I saw the tidal wave sweeping towards the city – higher than mountains, and black as the pit. I watched it roar. It was a terrible sight. You think it would pour through the gateway?'

'What would stop it?'

Both men were silent for a while, then Shannow reached into his pocket and removed the golden coin he had found in Shir-ran's cave. He stared down at the engraving.

'What is it?' asked Nu.

'The Sword of God,' Shannow whispered.

*

Bull reined in his horse and listened to the sudden flurry of gunshots. He had followed the Daggers at a discreet distance, watching them climb into the timberline, guessing their objective was to circle the camp-site and attack under cover of darkness. He had been just about to ride back and warn the Parson when the shots shattered the silence. He glanced back at the distant camp with its twinkling fires. If he returned now, he would have little to report. He drew his gun and checked the loads, then with pistol in hand he steered his horse into the trees. He rode slowly, following a deer trail, stopping often to listen. The wind was picking up and the branches above him whispered and crackled, but every now and then the wind would drop and then Bull thought he heard the sounds of roaring beasts. Sweat beaded his brow.

He pulled his hat from his head and wiped his face with the sleeve of his shirt. 'You gotta be crazy, boy,' he told himself, touching his heels to the mare's side. She was a good cattle pony, mountain-bred for stamina and speed over short distances, but her ears were pressed flat against her skull and she moved skittishly, as if a scent on the night breeze frightened her. The wind died and Bull heard a terrible growling from ahead. He pulled on the reins and considered riding back; instead he dismounted, looped the pony's reins around a branch and crept forward.

Pushing aside a thick bush, he gazed on a scene of carnage. The bodies of reptiles littered the clearing beyond, and giant bears were ripping at their flesh. At the centre of the clearing he saw a flash of golden hair as the body of the woman Sharazad was dragged away into the night. Swiftly he did a count. There were some forty huge creatures here, and he could hear growling from all around him. He backed away, his pistol cocked.

Suddenly a colossal beast reared up alongside. Bull rolled and put a shot into the gaping jaws that towered over him, but a massive taloned arm swept out, hammering him to the ground. He landed heavily, but managed another shot as the beast moved in, its mouth spewing blood.

Szshark leapt from the undergrowth with a serrated dagger in his hand. He landed on the bear's back and the knife plunged into the beast's right eye. It fell with a great crash. Bull scrambled to his feet and ran back for the pony, the reptile moving alongside. Reaching his mount, Bull scrambled into the saddle, dragging the reins clear. From all around him came the sounds of huge bodies crashing through the undergrowth. Szshark hissed and waited, his bloody dagger raised. Instinctively Bull stretched out a hand.

'We'd best get out of here,' he shouted. Szshark reached up, took the hand and vaulted up behind Bull. The little pony took off down the deer trail as if its tail was on fire. They emerged on to open ground and galloped clear of the trees.

'Much good fighting,' said Szshark. 'Many soulss.'

Bull dragged on the reins and glanced back. The bears had halted by the tree-line and were gazing after them. He allowed the pony a short breather and then headed in a walk towards the camp-site.

'I ain't sure as how you'll be too welcome, Szshark,' he said. 'The Parson's likely to boil you in oil.' The reptile said nothing, its wedge-shaped head resting on Bull's shoulder. 'You hear me?'

There was no movement and Bull cursed and rode on. The sentries allowed him through, then saw his passenger. Word swept the camp-site faster than a fire through dry grass. Bull climbed down, twisting to catch Szshark's falling body. He laid him on the grass, then saw the awful talon cuts on his shoulders and back. Blood seeped to the ground as Szshark's golden eyes opened.

'Many soulss,' he hissed. He blinked and looked up at the faces gazing down. His eyes misted, his scaled hand reached up and took Bull's arm. 'Cut out my heart,' he said. 'You . . .' The golden eyes closed.

'Why did you bring this demon here?' asked the Parson.

Bull stood. 'They're all dead, Parson, God be praised. This one was Szshark; he rescued me back in the woods. There's creatures there, damn big – ten, twelve feet tall. Look like bears. They wiped out the reptiles. The woman's dead too.'

'Then we can return to Pilgrim's Valley,' said Beth McAdam. 'Now that's what I call a miracle.'

'No,' said the Parson. 'Don't you understand? We were led here, like the children of Israel. But our work is only beginning. There is the Great Whore to be destroyed, and the Sword of God to be loosed over the land. Then, in truth, God will bless us, the wolf will lie down with the lamb and the lion eat grass like the cattle. Don't you see?'

'I don't want no more fighting,' declared Beth. 'I'm going home tomorrow.' Murmurs of agreement came from the listeners. 'Listen, Parson, you've done right proud by all of us. If it weren't for you, we'd all be dead. I'm grateful – and I mean that. You're always welcome in my home. But that's where I'm going – home. I don't know anything about this whore of yours, and I don't care a damn about some sword.'

'Then I will go on alone,' said the Parson. 'I will follow God's path.'

He walked away from the group and saddled a horse.

Shannow moved across to him. 'Be sure of God's path, Parson, before you attempt to ride it,' he said.

'I have the Gift, Shannow. No harm will befall me. Won't you ride with me? You are a man of God.'

'I have other plans, Parson. Take care.'

'My destiny lies with the Sword, Shannow. I know it. It fills my mind, it swells my heart.'

'God be with you, Parson.'

'As He wills,' replied the other, stepping into the saddle.

28

Araksis pushed the computations from him and stared at the midday sun. He was a frightened man. He had been four hundred and twenty-seven years old, sick and dying, when Pendarric first had him summoned to the winter palace at Balacris. But the Sipstrassi had changed his life. The King had healed him, given him back his lost youth. Yet since that time there had been many astrologers, and seventeen had been put to death for causing the King displeasure. It was not that Pendarric did not wish to hear bad omens, rather that he expected the astrologers to be exact in their predictions. However, as all initiates knew, the study of the Fates was an art, not a science. Now Araksis faced the same predicament as many of his erstwhile colleagues. He sighed and rose, gathering his parchments.

A doorway appeared in the wall and he stepped through, holding his head high, pulling his slender shoulders back.

'Well?' said the King.

Araksis spread the parchments on the table before Pendarric. 'The stars have moved, sire – or rather, the world has shifted. There is great difficulty in deciding how this occurred. Some of my colleagues believe that the world – which as we know, spins around the sun – gradually changed its position. I myself tend towards the theory of a cataclysm that tipped the earth on its axis. We exhausted two Stones in an effort to discover the truth. All we could determine for certain is that the land you showed us was once below the ocean.'

'You are aware of the prophecies of the man Nu-Khasisatra?' asked the King.

'I am, sire. And I thought greatly before bringing this theory to you.'

'He says the earth will topple because of my evil. Are you telling me you concur with his blasphemy?'

'Majesty, I am not a leader, nor a philosopher; I am a student of the Star-magic. All I can say on the question you raised is that all the evidence points to Atlantis resting for thousands of years on the sea bed. How this will occur I cannot determine. Or when. But if Nu-Khasisatra is right, it will happen soon. He said the year's end would see the doom of Atlantis – that is six days from now.'

'Has there ever been a king with more power than I, Araksis?'

'No, sire. Not in all recorded history.'

'And yet this cataclysm is beyond my control?'

'It would appear so, sire. We have seen the future City of Ad, and our own Star-tower encrusted with seashells and the muck of oceans.'

'Serpiat will be leading his legions through into that world in three days. Then we will see. Is it possible that we can learn from the future and alter the present?'

'There are many questions hidden in the one, sire. The future will tell us what *happened*. But can we change it? In the future the cataclysm has already taken place. If we avert it, then we change the future, and therefore what we have seen cannot exist. Yet we have seen it.'

'What would you advise?'

'Close all the gateways, and hold all the City Mother-stones in readiness for any shift in the earth. Focus all the power of Sipstrassi on holding the world in balance.'

'All the world? That would take all the power we have. And what are we without Sipstrassi? Merely men . . . men who will decay and die. There must be another way. I will wait for Serpiat's report.'

'And Sharazad, sire?'

'She is dead . . . killed by stupidity. Let us hope it is not an omen. What do my stars show?'

Araksis cleared his throat. 'There is nothing I can tell you that is not already obvious, sire. This is a time of great stress, and greater peril. A journey is indicated, from which there is no return.'

'Are you speaking of my death?' stormed the King, drawing a gold-adorned dagger and holding it to the astrologer's throat.

'I always swore to be truthful, majesty. I have remained so,' whispered Araksis, staring into the gleaming eyes of the monarch. 'I do not know.'

Pendarric hurled the astrologer from him.

'I will not die,' he hissed. 'I will survive – and so will my nation. There is no other law in the world than mine. There is no other God but Pendarric!'

*

Clem Steiner hauled himself up from the bed in the wagon and pulled on his shirt. His chest wound dragged on the stitches and his leg felt numb, but he was healing well. He dressed slowly and climbed over into the driver's seat. Beth was fixing the traces to the oxen but she stopped as she saw him.

'Damn if you ain't as stupid as you look,' she stormed. 'Get back and lie down. You break those stitches and I won't put them back.'

Samuel giggled, and Steiner smiled down at the blond boy. 'Don't she get fired up easy?' Samuel nodded, his eyes flicking to his mother.

'Suit yourself,' said Beth. 'If you're so anxious to be up and moving, climb down and help Mary with the breakfast. We're leaving in an hour.'

Shannow arrived as the injured man was negotiating the painful climb down. Clem was out of breath by the time he made it to the ground and clung to the brake, his face chalk-white. Shannow took his arm and helped him to the cook-fire. 'Always there to rescue me, Shannow. I'm starting to look on you as a mother.'

'I'm surprised you're alive, Steiner. You must be tougher than I gave you credit for.'

Clem managed a weak grin, then lay back as Shannow

sat beside him. 'I hope you have purged yourself of the wish to kill me?'

'I have that,' Steiner answered. 'It would be downright bad manners. What was all the commotion during the night?'

'The reptiles were wiped out. Your friend Bull can give you the details.'

A sentry gave out a shout of warning and Shannow left Steiner and ran to the perimeter. More than a hundred of the bears were moving slowly across the open ground. One man levelled a rifle, but Shannow shouted, 'Don't shoot!' and reluctantly he laid down the weapon. The beasts were of prodigious size, with massive shoulders and hairless snouts. Their arms were out of proportion to their bodies, and hung low to the ground before them. Mostly they walked on their hind legs, but occasionally they dropped to all fours. Shannow climbed over the perimeter log and walked out to meet the animals.

'You a crazy man?' shouted Scayse, but Shannow waved him to silence. He walked slowly forward and then stood, his hands hooked in his belt.

Close up, the creatures reminded him of Shir-ran. Though their bodies were bestial and twisted, their eyes were round and humanoid, their faces showing glimpses of past humanity.

'I am Shannow,' he said. The beasts stopped and squatted down, staring at him. One, larger than the rest, dropped to all fours and moved in. Shannow found his hands itching to grasp the pistol butts ... yet he did not. The beast came closer still, then reared up before him, its taloned arms flashing past his face and coming to rest on his shoulders. The creature's face was almost touching his own.

'Sha-nnow?' it said.

'Yes. That is my name. You have killed our enemies and we are grateful.'

A talon touched Shannow's cheek; the great head shook. 'Not enemies, Sha-nnow. Rider brought one to your camp.'

'He is dead,' Shannow said.

'What do you want in the land of the Dianae?'

'We were driven here – by the reptiles. Now the wagons will return to the valley Beyond the Wall. We mean no harm to you – or your people.'

'People, Sha-nnow? Not people. Things. Beasts.' He growled, lifted his talons from Shannow's shoulders and squatted on the grass. Shannow sat beside him.

'My name is Kerril – and I can smell their fear,' said the creature, angling his head towards the camp.

'Yes, they are afraid. But then so am I. Fear is a gift, Kerril. It keeps a man alive.'

'Once I knew fear,' said Kerril. 'I knew the fear of becoming a beast; it terrified me. Now I am strong and I fear nothing... save mirrors, or the still water of pools and lakes. But I can drink with my eyes closed. I still dream as a man, Sha-nnow.'

'Why did you come here, Kerril?'

'To kill you all.'

'And will you?'

'I have not decided yet. You have weapons of great power. Many of my people would be struck down – perhaps all. Would that not be wonderful? Would that not be an answer to prayer?'

'If you want to die, Kerril, just say the word. I will oblige you.'

The beast rolled to its back, scratching its shoulders on the grass. Then it reared up, its talons once more touching Shannow's cheek, but this time it felt the cold metal of his pistol resting under its chin.

A sound close to laughter came from Kerril's fanged mouth. 'I like you, Sha-nnow. Take your wagons and leave our lands. We do not like to be seen. We do not like grubbing in the ground for insects. We wish to be alone.'

Kerril stood, turned and ambled away towards the distant woods, his people following him.

*

Magellas lay on his stomach, watching the scene, enhancing

his vision and hearing through the power of the Bloodstone. Beside him Lindian's cold gaze also rested on the Jerusalem Man.

'He handled that well,' said Magellas. 'And did you note the speed with which his pistol came into action?'

'Yes,' answered Lindian. 'But how did he know the beast would not kill him? Can he read minds? Is he a seer?'

Magellas elbowed himself back from the skyline and stood. 'I don't know – but I would doubt it. The Lord, our Father, would have warned us of such talent.'

'Would he?' Lindian queried. 'He admitted it was a test.'

Magellas shrugged. 'We will see during the next three days. Why have you remained with me, Lindian? Why did you not ride off, like Rhodaeul?'

The slender warrior smiled. 'Perhaps I like your company, brother.' He walked off towards his horse, leaving Magellas staring after him.

Curiously, he realised, his words had been true: he did like Magellas. The giant had helped him many times when they were growing in the War-pens, when Lindian had been small and weak. And Magellas was easy company – unlike the arrogant Rhodaeul, always so sure of victory.

He vaulted into the saddle and grinned at Magellas.

It will be no pleasure to kill you, thought Lindian.

But that was the real secret of the test. Smaller and weaker than the other hunters, Lindian had developed skills of the mind. He had watched and studied, learning the secrets of men. Pendarric loathed Rhodaeul and disliked Magellas. Yet each of them, in their own way, had the talent to succeed the Atlantean King. And that was the doom they carried. For, with Sipstrassi, a king needed no heirs, and the last talent a man should develop in Pendarric's presence was that of charismatic leadership.

No, better to be like me, thought Lindian – efficient, careful, and undeniably loyal. I will make a good satrap of Akkady, he thought.

The two Hunters rode together for most of the morning. In the distance they saw lions, and they passed a small deserted settlement of tiny huts that aroused Magellas' interest. He dismounted and ducked to his knees to enter a doorway. Moments later he emerged. 'They must have seen us coming and scampered off to the trees. Fascinating.'

They rode on, guiding their mounts up a steep slope and halting on the crest. The city lay before them.

Lindian disguised the shock he felt, but the breath hissed from Magellas' throat, turning into a foul obscenity. He studied the Wall, the line of the docks, the distant spires of the temple.

'Where is the sea?' he whispered.

Lindian swung in the saddle, his eyes scanning the mountains and valleys. 'It is all different. Everything!'

'Then this is not Atlantis, and that . . . monstrosity . . . is merely a replica of Ad. But why would anyone build it? Look at the docks. Why?'

'I have no idea, brother,' said Lindian. 'I suggest we complete our mission and return home. We must have passed a score of places where we could waylay Shannow.'

Magellas could not tear his eyes from the city. 'Why?' he asked again.

'I am not a seer,' snapped Lindian. 'Perhaps the King created it to disturb us. Perhaps this is all some dark game. I do not care, Magellas. I merely want to kill Shannow and return home – that is if Rhodaeul does not beat us to the quarry.'

At the sound of his enemy's name Magellas jerked his gaze from the white-marbled city. 'Yes, yes, you are right, my brother. But Rhodaeul's arrogance is, I think, misplaced this time. You recall the teachings of Locratis? First study your enemy, come to know him, learn of his strengths and in them you will find his weaknesses. Rhodaeul has come to expect victory.'

'Only because he is skilful,' Lindian pointed out.

'Even so, he is becoming careless. It is the fault of these new weapons. A man can at least see an arrow in flight, or hear the hissing of the air it cuts. Not so with these,' he said, drawing the pistol. 'I do not like them.'

'Rhodaeul does.'

'Indeed he does. Though when has he faced an enemy as skilled in their use as the man Shannow?'

'You are taking a great risk in allowing Rhodaeul to make the first move. How will you feel if he rides in and kills the Jerusalem Man?'

Magellas chuckled. 'I will bid him a fond farewell on his journey to Akkady. However, it is wise when hunting a lion to consider the kill – not where one will place the trophy. There is a stream yonder. I think it is time to locate our brother and watch his progress.'

29

Nu-Khasisatra felt awkward on the horse he had borrowed from Scayse. He had never enjoyed riding and on every slope he closed his eyes and prayed as he swayed in the saddle, his stomach churning.

'I would sooner ride a storm at sea than this ... this creature.'

Shannow chuckled. 'I have seen sacks of carrots ride with more style,' he said. 'Do not grip with your calves, just the thighs, letting the lower leg hang loose. And when going downhill, keep her head up.'

'My spine is being crushed,' grumbled Nu.

'Relax, settle down in the saddle. By Heaven, I've never seen a worse rider. You're unsettling the mare.'

'The feeling is mutual,' said Nu. They rode on through a wide valley, leaving the wagons far behind. The sun was obscured by clouds and the threat of rain hung in the air.

Towards noon Shannow spotted a rider approaching them; he reined in and took out his long glass. At first he thought the man was elderly, for his hair was bone-white, but as he focused the glass he saw that he was mistaken. The rider was young and wearing a black and silver tunic with dark leggings and high riding boots. He passed the glass to Nu and the shipbuilder cursed.

'It is one of Pendarric's killers. They are the Hunters. He is searching for me, Shannow – best you ride away.'

'It is only one man, Nu.'

'Maybe so – but such men you would not want to meet. They are reared in War-pens; they fight and kill each other from their earliest days; they are bred for strength, speed and stamina, and there are no fighting men to equal them. Believe me, Shannow, ride away – while there is still time! Please – I do not want to see you come to any harm.'

'We share that wish, my friend,' Shannow agreed, watching as the rider moved ever closer.

Rhodaeul smiled as he saw the men waiting for him. Truly his rewards would be great, for the second rider was the traitor Nu-Khasisatra – a prophet of the One God, and a man opposed to violence. He could not decide whether to kill him here, or take him back to face Pendarric's justice.

He halted some twenty paces from the pair. 'Jon Shannow, the King of Kings has spoken the words of your death. I am Rhodaeul the Hunter. Do you have anything to say before you die?'

'No,' said Shannow, palming his gun and blasting Rhodaeul from the saddle. The Atlantean hit the ground hard, a hammering pain in his chest; he tried to draw his pistol, but Shannow rode forward and fired a second shot that smashed his skull.

'Sweet Chronos!' exclaimed Nu. 'I cannot believe it.'

'Neither could he,' said Shannow. 'Let us move on.'

'But . . . what of the body?'

'That's why God made vultures,' answered Shannow, touching heels to his stallion.

Two miles away, Magellas opened his eyes and gave a deep, throaty chuckle. 'Oh joy,' he said. Lindian returned his Stone to its pouch and shook his head but Magellas laughed again, the sound rich with humour. 'What I would have paid to see that scene! The satrapy of Akkady? That and ten more like it. Did you see the look on Rhodaeul's face as Shannow fired? Was it not wonderful? Shannow, I am in your debt. I will light candles to your soul for a thousand years. Oh, Belial, how I wish I could see it again.'

'Your grief for your brother is deeply touching,' said Lindian, 'but I still do not understand what happened.'

'That is because your eyes were on Rhodaeul. For myself I cannot – could not – stomach the man. Therefore I watched Shannow. He drew his gun as he spoke; there was no sharp movement, and the weapon was almost clear before Rhodaeul realised he was in peril.'

'But surely Rhodaeul must have known Shannow would attempt to fight?'

'Of course – but that is where timing is all-important. He asked Shannow a question and was waiting for a response. How many times have we both done exactly that? It has never mattered, because we dealt with sword and knife. But these guns... they are sudden. Rhodaeul expected conversation, fear, nervousness... even pleading or flight. Shannow merely killed him.'

Lindian nodded. 'You guessed, didn't you? You expected this?'

'I did – but the outcome was beyond my greatest hopes. It is the guns, Lindian. We can master their uses with ease, but not the great changes they create in man-to-man battles. It's what I tried to say earlier. With the sword, the lance or the mace, battle becomes ritualised. Opponents must circle one another, seeking openings, risking their lives. It all takes time. But the gun? A fraction of a heartbeat separates man from corpse. Shannow understands this, he has lived all his life with such weapons. There is no need for ritual or concepts of honour. An enemy is there to be shot down and forgotten. He will light no candles for Rhodaeul.'

'Then how do we tackle him? We cannot kill him from ambush; we must face him.'

'He will show us his weakness, Lindian. Tonight we will enter his dreams and they will give us the key.'

*

Shannow and Nu made their camp in the lee of a hill. The Jerusalem Man said little and moved away to sit alone, staring at the city they would visit in the morning. His mood was dark and sombre. A long time ago he had told Donna Taybard, 'Each death lessens me, Lady.' But was it still true? The execution of Webber had been a first: an unarmed man made to stand, humiliated, in front of his peers and then gunned down. The other man in the crowd had done nothing but speak – for that he too was dead.

'What separates you from the brigand now, Shannow?'

There was no answer. He was older, slower, more reliant on skill than speed. And worse, he had cocooned himself within his reputation, allowing the legend to awe lesser men into bending to his will.

'For what?' he whispered. 'Is the world a better place? Is Jerusalem any closer?'

He thought back to the white-haired young man who had accosted them on the trail. Was that a duel, he asked himself? 'No, it was a murder.' The young warrior had no chance. You could have waited and met him on equal terms. Why? Honour? Fair play?

Why not? You used to believe in such virtues. He rubbed at his tired eyes as Nu strode over to him.

'Do you wish to remain alone?'

'I will be alone whether you join me or not. But sit anyway.'

'Talk of it, Shannow. Let the words bring out the bile inside.'

'There is no bile. I was thinking about the Hunter.'

'Yes. He was Rhodaeul, and he had killed many. I was surprised at the ease with which you sent him to the grave.'

'Yes, it was easy. They are all easy.'

'Yet it troubles you?'

'Sometimes, in the dark of the night. I killed a child once, ended his life by mistake. He troubles me, he haunts my dreams. I have killed so many men, and it is all becoming so easy.'

'God did not make Man to be alone, Shannow. Think on it.'

'You think I have not? I tried once to settle down, but I knew before I lost her that it was not for me. I am not a man made for happiness. I carry such guilt over that child, Nu.'

'Not guilt, my friend. Grief. There is a difference. Yours is a skill I would not wish to acquire – yet it is necessary. In my own time there were wild tribes bordering our lands; they would raid and kill. Pendarric destroyed them, and we all slept easier in our beds. As long as Man remains the hunter-killer, there will be a need for warriors like you. I can wear my white robes and pray in peace. The evil can dress in black. But there must always be the grey riders to patrol the border between good and evil.'

'We are playing with words, Nu. Grey is only a lighter shade of black.'

'Or a darker shade of white? You are not evil, Shannow; you are plagued by self-doubt. That is what saves you. That is where the Parson is in peril. He has no doubts – and therefore is capable of enormous evil. It was the downfall of Pendarric. No, you are safe, Grey Rider.'

'Safe?' repeated Shannow. 'Who is safe?'

'He who walks with God. How long since you sought His word in your Bible?'

'Too long.'

Nu stretched out his hand, holding Shannow's leather-covered Bible. 'No man of God should be lonely.'

Shannow took the book. 'Maybe I should have devoted myself to a life of prayer.'

'You have followed the path set for you. God uses both warrior and priest and it is not for us to judge His purposes. Read a little, then sleep. I will pray for you, Shannow.'

'Pray for the dead, my friend.'

*

As the horse reared and died, Shannow leapt from the saddle. He hit the ground hard, rolled and came to his knees with guns in hand. The roaring of the pistols and the screams of his attackers faded. A sound from behind! Shannow swivelled and fired. The boy was hurled from his feet. A small dog began yapping; it ran to the boy, licking his dead face.

'What a vile man you are,' came a voice and Shannow blinked and turned. Two young men stood close by – their hair white, their eyes cold.

'It was an accident,' said Shannow. 'I was being attacked ... I didn't realise.'

'A child-killer, Lindian. What should we do with him?'

'He deserves to die,' said the smaller of the two. 'There is no question of that.'

'I never meant to kill the child,' Shannow repeated.

The tall man in the black and silver tunic stepped forward, his hand hovering over the gun butt. 'The King of Kings has spoken the words of your death, Jon Shannow. Do you have anything to say before you die?'

'No,' said Shannow, palming his pistol smoothly. A bullet smashed into Shannow's chest, the pain incredible as his own gun dropped from his twitching fingers and he sank to his knees.

'You should not try the same trick twice, old man,' whispered his killer.

Shannow died...

And awoke beside the fire on the hillside. Nu was sleeping soundly beside him, the night breeze was cool. Shannow built up the fire and returned to his blankets.

He was standing at the centre of an arena. Seated all around him were men he had killed: Sarento, Webber, Thomas, Lomax, and so many others whose names he could not remember. The child was leaning back on a golden throne, blood dripping steadily to stain the breast of the white tunic he wore.

'These are your judges, Jon Shannow,' said a voice and the tall white-haired warrior stepped forward. 'These are the souls of the slain.'

'They are evil men,' stated Shannow. 'Why should they have the right to judge me?'

'What gave you the right to judge them?'

'By their deeds,' answered the Jerusalem Man.

'And what was his crime?' stormed his accuser, pointing to the blood-drenched child.

'It was a mistake. An error!'

'And what price have you paid for that error, Jon Shannow?'

'Every day I have paid a price with the fire in my soul!'

'And what price for these?' shouted the warrior as down the central aisle came a score of children – some black, some white, toddlers and infants, young boys and girls.

'I do not know them. This is trickery!' said Shannow.

'They were the children of the Guardians, drowned when you destroyed the Titanic. What price for these, Shannow?'

'I am not an evil man!' shouted the Jerusalem Man.

'By your deeds we judge you.' Shannow saw the warrior reach for his pistol.

His own gun flashed up, but at the moment he fired the man disappeared and the bullet smashed into the chest of the boy on the throne. 'Oh dear God, not again!' screamed the Jerusalem Man.

His body jerked and he came awake instantly. Beyond the fire sat a lioness and her cubs. As he sat up, the lioness growled and moved back, the cubs scampering after her. Shannow banked up the fire and Nu awoke and stretched.

'Did you sleep well?' he asked.

'Let's pack up and move on,' Shannow answered.

*

As always when the Parson needed to pray in solitude he headed for the high country, bordering the clouds. His route took him through the woods of the Bear-people, but he cared nothing for danger; a man on his way to speak with his Maker, he knew that nothing would keep him from that appointment.

His soul was heavy, for the people had rejected him. He should have expected that, he knew, for it was always the way with prophets. Did they not reject Elijah, Elisha, Samuel? Did they not spurn the Son of God himself?

The people were weak, thinking only of their bellies or their small needs. Just like the monastery, with their constant prayers and works of little good.

'The world is evil,' the Abbot had told him. 'We must turn our faces from it, and seek the greater glory of God through worship.'

'But God made the world, Abbot, and Jesus himself asked us to go among the people as yeast to dough.'

'No, He did not,' the Abbot answered. 'He asked His disciples to do that. But this is Armageddon, these are the

End days. The people are not for saving; they have made their choices.'

He had left the monastery and taken a meagre living in a mining town, preaching in a bell-shaped tent. But the Devil had come to him there and found him wanting. Lucifer had led the girl to his sermon, and Lucifer had put the carnal thoughts in her mind. Oh, he had fought the desires of the flesh. But how weak is man!

His people – not understanding his temptations, nor the inner battles that went with them – had driven him from the town. It was not his fault! It was God's judgement when the girl hanged herself.

The Parson shook his head and looked around him, realising he had come deep into the woods. He saw the dismembered body of a reptile, then another. Drawing the horse to a halt he looked around. Bodies lay everywhere. He dismounted and saw that by a bush, her corpse wedged beneath the jutting roots of an old oak, lay Sharazad. There were terrible rips and tears on her body, but her face was remarkably untouched.

'Shannow was right,' said the Parson. 'You do look like an angel.' By her hand lay a red-veined Stone and he lifted it; it was warm and soothing to the touch. He dropped it into the pocket of his black cassock and mounted his horse, but his hand seemed to miss the warmth of the Stone, and he drew it out once more. He rode on, ever rising, until he came out on to a clearing at the crest of the range. It was cold here, but the air was fresh and clean, the sky unbearably blue. Dismounting once more, he knelt in prayer.

'Dear Father,' he began, 'lead me to the paths of righteousness. Take my body and soul. Show me the road I must walk to do your work, fulfil your word.' The Stone grew hot in his hand and his mind blurred.

A golden face appeared before him, bearded and stern, pale-eyed and regal. The Parson's heart began to hammer.

'Who calls on me?' came a voice in the Parson's mind.

'I, Lord, the humblest of your servants,' the Parson whispered, falling forward and pressing his face to the ground.

Miraculously the image remained before him, as if his eyes were still open.

'Open your mind to me,' said the voice.

'I do not know how.'

'Hold the Stone to your breast.' The Parson did so. Warmth enveloped him, and for a while there was peace and serenity; then the glow faded and he felt alone once more.

'You have sinned greatly, my son,' said Pendarric. 'How will you cleanse yourself?'

'I will do anything, Lord.'

'Mount your horse and ride a little way to the east. There you will find the survivors of the . . . reptiles. You will lift the Stone and say to them: "Pendarric". They will follow you and do your bidding.'

'But they are creatures of the Devil, Lord.'

'Yes, but I will give them the opportunity to redeem their souls. Go to the city, enter the Temple, then call for me again and I will guide you.'

'But what of the Great Whore? She must be destroyed.'

'Do not seek to contradict me!' thundered Pendarric. 'In my own time will I bring her down. Go to the Temple, Nicodemus. Seek out the Scrolls of Gold hidden beneath the altar.'

'But if the Whore tries to prevent me?'

'Then kill her and any who stand with her.'

'Yes, Lord. As you bid. And the Sword?'

'We will speak again when you have accomplished your mission.' The face faded . . . the Parson rose.

All his anguish left him.

At last he had found his God.

30

Back at her cabin Beth was happily surprised to find no damage from the earthquakes. In the fields below there were still pits and chasms, and several trees had fallen; but on the flat ledge of the hillside where Bull had chosen to place the McAdam home, there was no evidence of movement at all.

The sandy-haired rider grinned at Beth. 'If you say "I told you so", Bull, I'll crack your skull,' Beth said to him.

'Me? The thought never crossed my mind.' He tethered his horse and helped Beth carry the wounded Steiner into the house.

'I can walk, dammit,' Steiner grumbled.

'I ain't having those stitches opening again,' Beth told him. 'Now keep quiet.'

Bull and the children manhandled the furniture from the wagon, while Beth fuelled the iron stove and set a pot of Baker's to simmer. As dusk stained the sky, Bull rose.

'Best be getting back to Meneer Scayse,' he said. 'I reckon there'll be enough to do there. You want me to bring you anything tomorrow?'

'If there's anything left in the town, I wouldn't mind some salt.'

'I'll fetch it – and some dried beef. You're looking mighty low on stores.'

'I'm short on Barta coin, Bull. I'll have to owe you.'

'You do that,' he said. She watched him ride off and shook her head, allowing a smile to show. Now he wouldn't make a bad husband, she thought. He's caring, strong, and he likes the kids. But the face of Jon Shannow cut across the smiling image of Bull. 'Damn you for a fool, Shannow!' whispered Beth.

Samuel and Mary were sitting by the stove, Samuel's

head resting against the wall, his eyes closed. Beth walked to him, lifting him from his feet. His eyes opened and his head dropped to her shoulder. 'It's bed for you, snapper-gut,' she said, carrying him into the back room and laying him down. She didn't bother to strip his clothes, but removing his shoes she covered him with a blanket.

Mary came in behind her. 'I'm not tired, Ma. Can I sit up for a while?'

Beth looked into the child's puffy eyes. 'You can snuggle in next to your brother, and if you're still awake in an hour you can sit with me.' Mary grinned sheepishly and climbed under the blanket; she was asleep within minutes.

Beth returned to the main room and lit the fire, then walked out on to the porch where Bull had erected a bench seat made from a split log, planed and polished. She sat back and stared over the moonlit valley. The Wall was down everywhere, although some sections still reared like broken teeth. She shivered.

'Nice night,' observed Steiner, limping out to sit beside her. His face was pale, dark rings staining the skin beneath his eyes.

'You're a damn fool,' said Beth.

'And you're as pretty as a picture under moonlight,' he told her.

'Except for the nose,' she replied. 'And it's no good making up to me, Clem Steiner. Even if I let you, it would kill you for certain.'

'There's truth in that,' he admitted. Beth continued to stare at the horizon. 'What are you thinking?' he asked.

'I was thinking about Shannow – not that it's any of your business.'

'You in love with him?'

'You're a prying sort of fella, Steiner.'

'You are then. You could do worse, I guess – except I don't see you travelling the world looking for some city that don't exist.'

'You're right. Maybe I should marry you.'

'That's not a bad thought, Frey McAdam,' he responded, smiling. 'I can be right good company.'

'You've been hiding that light under a bushel,' she said sharply.

He chuckled. 'Come to think of it, that *is* a pretty big nose.' She laughed and her tension eased. Clem stretched his wounded leg out in front of him and rubbed at it. 'Does Shannow know how you feel?' he asked, his voice low and serious.

Beth cut off a sharp retort. 'I told him – in a way. But he won't change. He's like you.'

'I've changed,' he said. 'I don't want to be a pistoleer; I couldn't give a damn about reputations. I had a father who beat the Hell out of me. He said I'd never make anything of my life and I guess I've been trying to prove him wrong. Now I don't care about that no more.'

'What will you do?'

'I'll find a nice woman. I'll raise kids and corn.'

'There's some hope for you yet, Clem Steiner.' He was about to answer when he spotted two riders angling up towards the house.

'Strange-looking pair,' said Beth. 'Look how the moonlight makes their hair seem white.'

*

Shannow was ill at ease as they rode. The dreams had unnerved him, but worse than that he had the constant feeling he was being watched. Time and again he would turn in the saddle and study the skyline, or alter the direction in which they travelled, dismounting before the crest of every hill.

But now the city was ahead of them, and still the feeling would not pass.

'What is troubling you?' Nu asked. 'We should have been at the city hours ago.'

'I don't know,' admitted Shannow. 'I feel uncomfortable.'

'No more than I feel, perched on this horse,' responded Nu.

A rabbit darted across their path and Shannow's guns swept up. He cursed softly, then flicked the stallion's flanks with his heels.

The city was protected by a great Wall, but the recent earthquakes had scored it with cracks. There were no gates, but as they entered the city Shannow could see deep holes in the stones where hinges had once been placed.

'The gates,' Nu told him, 'were of wood and bronze, emblazoned with the head of a lion. And this entrance would take you through the Street of Silversmiths, and on to the Sculptors' Quarter. My home was close by.'

People in the streets stopped and stared at the riders. There was no animosity here, only curious gazes. There were more women than men, Shannow noticed, and they were tall and well-formed – their clothes mainly hide, beautifully embroidered.

He halted his horse. 'I seek the Dark Lady,' he said, removing his hat and bowing. The nearest woman smiled and pointed to the east.

'She is in the High Tower with Oshere,' she answered.

'God's peace upon you,' Shannow told her.

'The Law of the One be with you,' she replied.

The horses' hooves clattered on the cobbled street. 'In my time, no beasts were allowed into this quarter,' said Nu. 'The residents found the smell of manure less than appealing.'

A bent and crippled shape loomed before them, and Shannow's mind was hurled back to Shir-ran. His stallion reared, but he calmed it with soft words. The Man-beast ambled past, not able to lift his huge, misshapen head.

'Poor soul,' said Nu, as they walked their horses on.

The street widened into a statue-lined road that stretched, arrow-straight, towards a tall palace of white marble. 'Pendarric's summer home,' explained Nu. 'It also houses the temple.' The road ended at a colossal stairway more than a hundred paces wide, slowly rising to an enormous archway.

'The Steps of the King,' said Nu. Like the road the steps

were lined with statues, each one carved from marble and each bearing a sword and a sceptre. Shannow urged on the stallion and rode the steps; Nu dismounted and led the mare after him. As the Jerusalem Man reached the archway a slender black woman moved from the shadows to greet him. Shannow recalled the moment he had first seen her, carrying her son from the wreck of the resurrected *Titanic*. 'Amaziga? You are the Dark Lady?' he said as he climbed down from the saddle.

'The same, Shannow. What are you doing here?' He noted the tension in her voice, the lack of warmth in her eyes.

'Am I such an unwelcome visitor?'

'There are no evils here for you to slay, I promise you that.'

'I am not here to kill. Do you think me such a villain?'

'Then tell me why you are here.'

Shannow saw a movement behind her, deep in the shadows of the archway. A young man appeared; once he must have been strikingly handsome, but now his face was distended and his shoulders bowed. Guiltily Shannow averted his eyes from the man's deformities. 'I asked you a question, Shannow,' said Amaziga Archer.

'I came to warn you of impending perils – and also to see the Sword of God. But it would be pleasant if we could talk inside somewhere.' Nu reached the archway, saw Amaziga and bowed low. 'This is my companion, Nu-Khasisatra. He is from Atlantis, Amaziga, and I think you should hear what he has to say.'

'Follow me,' she said, turning on her heel and striding back through the archway. The deformed man followed her silently, Nu and Shannow bringing up the rear. They found themselves in a wide, square courtyard; Amaziga crossed it, passed a circular fountain and continued on through a huge hallway. Shannow tethered his stallion and Nu's mare in the courtyard and entered the building. It was ghostly quiet within, and their footsteps created eerie echoes.

They mounted a long circular staircase and emerged into

a room where Amaziga had already seated herself behind a mahogany desk on which were scattered papers, scrolls and books. She looked younger than Shannow remembered, but her eyes seemed full of sorrow.

'Say what you want to say, Jerusalem Man. Then leave us in whatever peace remains.'

Shannow took a deep breath, stilling the rise of anger he felt. Slowly he told her of the attack on the township of Pilgrim's Valley, and their flight beyond the fractured Wall. He spoke of the woman, Sharazad, and the Parson, and the fears that she was some evil goddess. And he told her of Pendarric. She listened without comment, but her interest grew when Nu began his tale; she questioned him sharply, but his soft-spoken answers seemed to satisfy her. At last, when both men had finished, she asked the deformed man to fetch some drink. Neither Shannow nor Nu had stared at him, and after he had gone Amaziga fixed her eyes on the Jerusalem Man.

'Do you know what is happening to him?' she asked.

'He is turning into a lion,' Shannow answered, holding her gaze.

'How did you know?'

'I met a man, named Shir-ran, who suffered the same horror. He rescued me, gave me aid when I needed it, healed my wounds.'

'What happened to him?'

'He died.'

'I said what happened to him?' Amaziga snapped.

'I killed him,' said Shannow.

Her eyes grew cold, and her smile chilled Nu. 'Now *that* has a familiar ring, Shannow. After all, how many stories are there concerning the Jerusalem Man when he doesn't kill something – or someone? Have you destroyed any communities lately?'

'I did not destroy your Home Base; Sarento did that when he sailed the *Titanic*. I merely blocked the power of the Motherstone. But I will not argue with you, Lady, nor debate my deeds. I will leave now and seek the Sword.'

'You must not, Shannow! You must not go near it.' The words hissed from her. 'You do not understand.'

'I understand that the gateway between past and present must be closed. Perhaps the Sword of God will close it. If not, when the disaster befalls Atlantis we could be dragged down with it.'

'The Sword of God is not the answer you seek. Believe me.'

'I will not know until I have seen it,' Shannow told her.

Amaziga's hand came up from below the desk and in it was held a Hellborn pistol. She cocked it and pointed the barrel at Shannow. 'You will promise me to stay away from the Sword – or you will die here,' she said.

'Chreena!' came a voice from the doorway. 'Stop it! Put the pistol away.'

'You don't understand, Oshere. Stay out of this!'

'I understand enough,' said the Man-beast, moving clumsily forward and placing the silver tray on the desk. His deformed hand closed over the pistol, gently removing it from her grasp. 'Nothing you have told me about this man suggests he is evil. Why would you wish to harm him?'

'Death follows wherever he rides. Destruction! I can feel it, Oshere.'

She stood and ran from the room and Oshere laid the pistol on the desk. Shannow leaned forward and uncocked it. Oshere eased himself into the chair Amaziga had used, his dark eyes fixed on the Jerusalem Man.

'She is under great strain, Shannow,' he said. 'She thought she had found a way to cure me, but it was only a temporary respite. Now she must suffer again. She loved my brother, Shir-ran, and he became a beast. Now...' He shrugged. 'Now it is my turn. Your arrival made her distraught. But she will gather her strength and consider what you have said. Now, have some wine, and rest. I will see your horses are taken to a field nearby where there is good grass. Through that door you will find beds and blankets.'

'There is no time to rest,' said Nu. 'The end is near, I can feel it.'

Shannow pushed himself wearily to his feet. 'I had hoped for aid. I thought the Dark Lady would be a person of power.'

'She is, Shannow,' Oshere assured him. 'She has great knowledge. Give her time.'

'You heard Nu. There *is* no time. We will ride on to the Sword – but first Nu needs to search the Temple sanctuary.'

'Why?' Oshere asked.

'There could be something there that will help me to return home,' Nu told him.

The sound of gunshots came from close by, followed by screams of terror.

'You see!' shouted Amaziga Archer from the doorway, pointing at Shannow. 'Where he rides, death always follows.'

31

The Parson rode boldly into the clearing where twenty-three survivors of the Daggers' force had gathered. Several were wounded, their scaled limbs bound. Others were keeping watch, rifles poised, for any attack from the Bears. Holding the Bloodstone high, the Parson guided his mount in amongst his enemies and voiced the single word that his God had commanded him.

'Pendarric,' he said, as rifles were aimed at his chest; the guns were lowered instantly. 'Follow me,' ordered the Parson, riding from the clearing. The reptiles took up their weapons, formed two lines and marched out behind his horse. The Parson was exultant.

'How mysterious are the ways of the Lord,' he told the morning air. 'And how great are His wonders.' On the plain before the city lions gathered in great numbers, padding forward to stand in the Parson's path. He lifted his Stone. 'Give way!' he bellowed. A black-maned beast reared up in pain, then ran to the left. The others followed it, leaving a path through which the Parson heeled his mount.

He led the reptiles to the northern gateway and then turned in the saddle. 'All who resist the Will of God must die,' he declared. Confident that the awesome power of the Creator was with him, he entered the gateway. Beyond it he saw many people. None stood in his way; they gazed with frank, open curiosity as the marching reptiles and the Parson rode on through white-walled streets.

A young woman with a child stood close by, holding the toddler's hand. 'The Temple,' enquired the Parson. 'How shall I reach it?' The woman pointed to a high domed building and he approached it. The Temple pillars were massive, and close-set. He dismounted and walked up the long stairway with the reptiles behind him.

An old man moved out to stand before him. 'Who seeks the wisdom of the Law of One?' he asked.

'Step aside for the Warrior of God,' the Parson told him.

'You cannot enter,' replied the old man pleasantly. 'The priests are at prayer. When the sun touches the western wall, then may your entreaties be heard.'

'Out of my way, old man,' the Parson ordered, drawing his pistol.

'Do you not understand?' asked the High Priest. 'It is not allowed.'

A shot echoed in the Temple corridors and the High Priest fell back without a sound, blood pumping from a hole in his brow. The Parson ran into the Temple, the reptiles swarming after him. Taking their new master's lead, they began firing on the priests inside who ran for shelter. Ignoring the carnage, the Parson scanned the building, seeking the Inner Sanctum. There was a narrow doorway at the end of the long hall and he ran to it, kicking it open. Within was an altar and another old man was hastily gathering scrolls of gold foil. He looked up and struggled to rise, but the pistol bucked in the Parson's hand and he fell. The Parson knelt by the scrolls and lifted his Stone.

'Hear me, Lord. I have done your bidding.'

Pendarric's face shimmered before him. 'The scrolls,' he said. 'Read them.'

The Parson lifted a section of gold foil and unrolled it. 'I cannot make out the symbols,' he said.

'I can. Discard that one. Take another.'

One by one the Parson opened the foils, his eyes scanning the curious stick-like symbols. At last, when he had finished, he looked into the eyes of God and saw they were troubled.

'What must I do, Lord?' he whispered.

'Bring the Sword of God to the earth,' Pendarric told him. 'Today. There is a peak to the south. Climb it – but first lay your Stone upon the body of the priest beside you. Place it on his blood. There it will gather strength. When you have climbed the peak, lift the Stone and call upon the Sword. Bring it to you. You understand?'

'Yes,' answered the Parson. 'Oh, yes. My dreams fulfilled. Thank you, Lord. What then must I do?'

'We will speak again when you have obeyed me.' The face disappeared.

The Parson laid his Stone on the bleeding chest of the priest, watching as the blood seemed to flow into it, swelling its veins. Then he took it once more and rose.

From outside came the sound of more gunshots. He ran through the hallway, down the steps, and leapt to his horse. Ignoring the reptiles, he galloped back to the main gateway, and on to fulfil God's wishes.

*

Shannow ran from the room when the first shots sounded, pushing past Amaziga and taking the steps two at a time. The courtyard was deserted, save for the two horses tethered there. More shots came from the Temple building and Shannow drew his pistols and advanced across the courtyard. A reptile ran into view with a rifle in his hands. As Shannow's pistol came up, the reptile spotted him and swung his weapon to bear. Shannow's gun fired, the creature spun back into the wall and fell to his face on the stones.

The Jerusalem Man waited for several seconds, watching the entrances, but no other reptiles came in sight. He ducked past the fountain and ran across the open space to the rear of the Temple, where a wooden door blocked his access. Lifting his foot, he crashed it against the lock and the door burst inwards. A shot splintered the wood of the frame as he dived through and rolled to his left. Bullets hissed and whined around him, ricocheting from the mosaic floor. As he came to his knees behind a pillar, he heard the sound of running feet from his right. Twisting, he levelled his pistols . . . three reptiles died. He watched the Parson run from a doorway to the left; two Daggers moved aside to let him pass and Shannow killed them both. A shell tore through the collar of his coat and he returned the fire, but missed. Then he was up and running for a second pillar as bullets hissed by him. A Dagger ran into his path with knife raised. Shannow shot twice into the beast's body. All around, the reptiles were running for the great doorway.

Silence fell within the Temple as Shannow reloaded his pistols and stood. Amaziga appeared in the doorway, Nu and Oshere with her, and ran to the room Shannow had seen the Parson emerge from. The Jerusalem Man returned his guns to their scabbards and followed them. Within the small chamber, Nu was kneeling with Amaziga beside a dying priest. He was old, white-bearded, and his chest was stained with blood.

'I am the leaf,' whispered the priest as Nu lifted his head and cradled him.

'God is the tree,' Nu responded softly.

'The circle is complete,' said the man. 'Now I will know the Law of the One, the Circle of God.'

'Now you will know,' said Nu. 'The streams flow into the rivers, the rivers into the sea, the sea into the clouds, the clouds into the streams. The rich earth into the tree, the tree to the leaf, the leaf to the earth. All life forms the Circle of God.'

The dying priest smiled. 'You are a Believer. I am glad. Your circle goes on.'

'What did they want? What did they take?' asked Amaziga.

'Nothing,' answered the priest. 'He read the sacred scrolls, and summoned a demon. The demon told him to bring the Sword of God to the earth.'

'No!' Amaziga whispered.

'It is of no matter, Chreena,' said the priest, his voice fading. His head fell back in Nu's arms; the shipbuilder gently lowered the body to the floor and rose.

'They were fine words,' Shannow told him.

'They are part of the writings of the One. There is perfection only in the circle, Shannow: to understand that is to understand God.' Nu smiled and began to walk around the chamber, searching the carved walls, studying each projection. Shannow joined him.

'What do you seek?'

'I'm not sure. The Stones would have been kept in this room but I have no idea where – only the High Priest knew, and he passed the knowledge to his successor.'

The room was small and square, though the altar was circular. The limestone walls were splendidly sculpted, graceful figures with painted eyes and long, tapering hands that reached for the sky. Shannow walked to the altar and stood gazing down on the flat, polished surface. Engraved there, and filled with gold leaf, was a wondrous tree with golden leaves. He ran his fingers lightly over the surface, tracing the branches. The design was beautiful and restful to the eye. Around the rim of the altar birds were carved – some in flight, some nesting, others feeding their young. Again the principle was the circle from the egg to the sky. His fingers traced over the carvings, resting at last on the nest and the single egg. It moved under his fingers and taking a firm grip, he lifted the egg clear. It was small and perfectly white; but once in his hand it became warm, the colour growing from white to cream, to yellow and finally to gold.

'I have what you seek,' he said and Nu came to him and took the golden egg from his palm.

'Yes,' Nu agreed, his voice low. 'You have indeed.'

'The Stone from Heaven,' said Oshere. 'Wondrous. What will you do now?'

'It is not mine to take,' replied Nu. 'But if it were, I would return to my land and try to save my wife and children from the coming cataclysm.'

'Then take it,' Oshere told him.

'No!' cried Amaziga. 'I need it. You need it. I cannot watch you change again.'

Oshere turned away from her. 'I . . . wish you to have the Stone, Nu-Khasisatra. I am a prince of the Dianae. The High Priest is dead and I have the right to bestow the Stone. Take it. Use it well.'

'Let me have it just for a moment,' pleaded Amaziga. 'Let me make Oshere well again.'

'No!' Oshere shouted. 'The Sipstrassi will not work

against itself, you have seen that. It made me what I am. The power is too great to waste on a man like me. Can you not understand that, Chreena? I am a lion who walks like a man. Even magic cannot change what I am ... what I will become. It does not matter, Chreena. You and I, we will see the ocean and that is all I want.'

'What about what I want?' she asked him. 'I love you, Oshere.'

'And I love you, Dark Lady ... more than life. I always will. But nothing is for ever, not even love.' He turned to Nu. 'How will you find your way home?'

'There is a circle of stones beyond what was once the Royal Gardens. I shall go there.'

'I will walk with you,' said Oshere and the three men left the chamber. Amaziga stayed beside the dead priest, staring at the golden scrolls.

The circle of stones had been largely untouched by the centuries, though one had cracked and fallen. Nu walked to the centre of the circle and offered his hand to Shannow.

'I learned much, my friend,' he said. 'Yet I did not discover the Sword of God as I was commanded.'

'I'll find it, Nu ... and do what needs to be done. You find your family.'

'Farewell, Shannow. God's love be with you.'

Shannow and Oshere walked out of the circle and Nu lifted the Stone and cried out in a language Shannow could not understand. There was no flash of light, no drama. One moment he was there ... the next he had gone.

Shannow felt a sense of loss as he turned to Oshere. 'You are a man of courage,' he said.

'No, Shannow, I wish that I were. But Sipstrassi has made me what I am. Chreena used the magic of the Stones to reshape me, but almost immediately I began to revert. She is a stubborn woman and she would use all the Stones in the world to hold me. Such a gift from God should not be wasted in that way.'

The two men walked slowly back to the Temple. Crowds had now gathered and the bodies of the slain priests were being carried from the building. 'Why did they not fight?' asked Shannow. 'There were so few of the enemy.'

'We are not warriors, Shannow. We do not believe in murder.'

Inside the Temple Amaziga joined them, her face set and hard.

'We must talk, Shannow. Excuse us, Oshere.' She led the Jerusalem Man back into the Inner Sanctum; the priest's body was gone, but blood still stained the floor. Amaziga swung on him. 'You must follow the killer, and stop him. It is vital.'

'Why? What harm can he do?'

'The Sword must be left as it is.'

'I still do not see why. If it serves God's purposes...'

'God, Shannow? God has nothing to do with the Sword. Sword? What am I saying? It is not a sword, Shannow; it is a missile – a nuclear missile. A flying bomb.'

'Then the Parson will blow himself to Hell. Why concern yourself?'

'He will blow us *all* to Hell. You have no conception of the power of that missile, Shannow. It will destroy everything that you could see from the tower. For two hundred miles the earth will be scorched and laid bare. Can you comprehend that?'

'Explain it to me.' Amaziga took a deep breath, trying to marshal her words. As a Guardian and a teacher, her memory had been enhanced by Sipstrassi and she could summon all the facts concerning the missile, yet none of them would serve to help her explain it to Shannow. It was an MX (Missile eXperimental). Length: 34.3 metres. Diameter: 225 centimetres at first stage. Speed: 18,000 miles per hour at burn-out. Range: 14,000 kilometres. Yield: 10 X 350 kilotons. Ten warheads, each with the capacity to destroy a city. How could she explain that to an Armageddon savage?

'In the Between Times, Shannow, there was great fear and hatred. Men built awesome weapons and one was used on a city during a terrible war. It destroyed the city utterly;

hundreds of thousands of people were killed by that single blast. But soon the bombs were made even more powerful, and great rockets were constructed that could carry the bombs from one continent to another.'

'How did the nations survive?'

'They didn't, Shannow,' she said simply.

'And these bombs caused the earth to topple?'

'Not exactly. But that is not important. The... Parson?... must not be allowed to interfere with the missile.'

'Why does it stand in the sky? Why is it surrounded by crosses, if not from God?' he asked.

'Come back to my rooms and I will tell you as best I can. I do not have all the answers. But promise me, Shannow, that when I have explained it to you, you will ride to stop him.'

'I will decide that *when* you have explained it all.'

He followed her to her chambers and sat down opposite her desk. 'You know,' she said, 'that this land was once below the oceans? Where we are now was once an area of sea known as the Devil's Triangle. It acquired that name because of the unexplained disappearances of ships and planes. You understand about planes?'

'No.'

'Men used to... It was discovered that it was possible for machines to take to the skies. They were called planes; they had wide wings, and engines that propelled them at great speeds through the air. What you will see clustered in the sky around the... Sword, are not crucifixes or crosses, but planes. They are trapped in some sort of stasis field.... Dear God, Shannow, this is impossible!' She poured a goblet of wine from the pitcher on her desk and drank deeply, then she leaned forward. 'The Atlanteans used the power of a great Sipstrassi Stone and aimed it at the sky. Why, I do not know, but they did it. When Atlantis sank beneath the oceans, the power of the Stone continued. It trapped more than a hundred planes and ships. It would have been more, but the field is very narrow; the power has been decreasing over the years, and the ships fell to earth. You can still find their ruined hulks out on the desert beyond the Chaos Peak. How it trapped the missile, I can only guess. When the earth toppled for the second time, there were massive earthquakes. By then the weapons centres were run by computers and they probably registered the enormous earthquakes as nuclear strikes, and responded. That's why the levels of radiation are still so high over most of the world. The earth toppled, missiles were released and any opportunity of salvaging some remnants of civilisation was gone. This missile was probably fired from somewhere in a country called America. It crossed the stasis field and has remained there for three hundred years.'

'But surely the Between Timers would have seen – as we do – the planes hanging in the air? If they had such great weapons, why did they not destroy the Stone?'

'I don't think they *could* see the planes. I think the Sipstrassi was originally programmed to hold the objects in another dimension, invisible to us. Only when the power began to drain did they become visible.'

Shannow shook his head. 'I do not understand any of this, Amaziga; it is beyond me. Planes? Stasis fields? Computers? But I have been having strange dreams lately. I am sitting in a crystal bubble inside a giant cross high in the sky. There is a voice whispering in my ear; it is someone called Tower and he is telling me to assume a bearing due west. My voice – and yet not my voice – tells him we do not know which way is west. Everything is wrong... strange. Even the ocean does not look as it should.'

'The crystal bubble, Shannow, is the cockpit of a plane. And the voice you heard was not from someone called Tower, but the Control Tower in a place called Fort Lauderdale. And the voice that was yours – and yet not yours – was that of Lieutenant Charles Taylor, flying one of five Navy Avenger torpedo-bombers on a training run. You can still see them in formation close to the missile. Trust me, Shannow. Stop the Parson.'

He rose. 'I don't know that I can. But I will try,' he told her.

32

Beth McAdam awoke with her head pounding, her body sore. She sat up – and saw the two men who had dragged her from her cabin. Grabbing a rock, she pushed herself to her feet. 'You slimy sons of bitches!' she hissed. The taller of the men rose smoothly to his feet and moved towards her. Her hand flew up, with the rock poised to smash his temple, but he blocked the blow with ease and backhanded her to the ground.

'Do not seek to annoy me,' he said. His hair was chalk-white, his face young and unlined. He knelt beside her. 'You will come to no harm, you have the promise of Magellas. We merely need you to help us to complete a mission.'

'My children?'

'They are unharmed. And the man Lindian struck was only unconscious – there was no lasting damage.'

'What is this mission?' she asked, tensing herself for a second attack.

'Do not be foolish,' he advised her. 'If you choose to be troublesome, I will break both your arms.' Beth let the rock fall from her fingers. 'You ask about our mission,' he continued, smiling. 'We are sent to despatch Jon Shannow. He holds you in some esteem and he will give himself up to us in return for your safety.'

'In a pig's eye!' she retorted. 'He'll kill you both.'

'I do not think so. I have come to know Jon Shannow; to respect him – even to like him. He will surrender himself.'

'If you like him, how can you think of killing him?'

'What has emotion to do with duty? The King, my Father, says Shannow must die. Then he *will* die.'

'Why don't you just face him – like men?'

Magellas chuckled. 'We are executioners – not duellists. Had I been instructed to face him on equal terms, then I would have done so – as would my brother Lindian. But it is not necessary and therefore would constitute a foolish risk. Now we will proceed with – or without – your willing help. But I do not wish to break your arms. Will you help us? Your children need you, Beth McAdam.'

'What do you want me to say?'

'That you will stay with us – and not try any more foolishness with rocks.'

'I don't have a lot of choices, do I?'

'Say the words anyway. It will make me feel more relaxed.'

'I'll do as you say. That good enough for you?'

'It will suffice. We have prepared some food and it would be our pleasure if you joined us for a meal.'

'Where are we?' Beth asked.

'We are sitting in one of your holy places, I believe,' answered Magellas, pointing to the star-filled sky. Several hundred feet above them, glistening silver in the moonlight, hung the Sword of God.

*

Amaziga Archer sat alone after Shannow had gone. On her desk now were the Sacred Scrolls guarded by the Dianae. Her husband Samuel had spent four years teaching her the meaning of the symbols, which resembled the cuneiform writings of ancient Mesopotamia. For the main part the gold foils were covered with astrological notes, and charts of star systems. But the last three – including one missed by the Parson – contained the thoughts of the astrologer Araksis.

Amaziga read the words of the first two and shivered.

There was much here that was beyond her, but it tallied with ancient legends concerning the doom of Atlantis. They had found a great power source, but had misused it, and the oceans had risen up, the continent been buried beneath the waves. Now Amaziga understood. In opening the Gates of Time, they had altered the delicate balance of gravity. Instead of spinning contentedly around the sun, the earth was exposed to the gravitational pull of a second sun, and perhaps more. The earthquakes and volcanic eruptions outlined in Araksis' scrolls were merely indications of a tortured world, pulled in opposing directions and teetering on its axis. The earthquakes now were exactly the same; with two colossal suns in the sky, the gravitation drag was causing the planet to tremble.

Shannow was right: the imminent fall of Atlantis represented a deadly danger to the new world. One of the great mysteries the Guardians had never been able to solve was the eye-witness accounts of the Second Fall, when ten thousand years of civilisation were ripped from the surface of the planet. Those eye-witnesses had spoken of two suns in the sky. Amaziga had been educated in the theory that what had been seen was, in fact, a nuclear explosion. Now she was not so sure. The gold scrolls spoke of a gateway to a world of flying machines and great weapons. The circle of history? When Atlantis fell, did it drag the twenty-first century with it? And what of the twenty-fourth... What of now? Dear God, was the earth to fall again?

The dusk breeze was cold against her skin. Rising, she drew the heavy curtains and lit the lanterns on the wall. What is it about our race, she wondered, that leads us always along the road of destruction?

Returning to her desk, she picked up the last scroll and traced the words under the dim, golden light of the lanterns. Her eyes widened.

'Sweet Jesus!' she whispered and taking her pistol, she ran from the room and down the stairs to the courtyard. Nu's mare was still tethered there and she climbed into the saddle and raced through the city. Beyond the main gate the lions were feasting on the bodies of the reptiles; they ignored her and she lashed the mare into a gallop.

*

Shannow did not follow the Parson at speed. The stallion was weary and in need of rest; also, the light was failing and he knew he would be too late if any mishap should befall the horse. The Jerusalem Man swayed in the saddle. He also was tired; his mind reeled with all that Amaziga had told him. Once upon a time the world had been a simple place where there were good men and evil men and the hope of Jerusalem. Now all had changed.

The Sword of God was just a weapon created by men to destroy other men. The crown of crosses was planes from out of the past. So where was God? Shannow lifted his water canteen and drank deeply. Far ahead he could see the outline of the Chaos Peak. As the clouds parted he saw the Sword, glittering like silver in the night sky.

'Where are you, Lord?' said Shannow. 'Where do you walk?'

There was no answer. Shannow thought of Nu, and hoped the shipbuilder had returned home safely. The stallion plodded on and dawn was breaking as Shannow angled his mount up the rocky slope leading to the Chaos Peak and the Pledging Pool. Glancing back, he could see in the distance a rider coming towards the Peak. Taking his long glass, he focused it and recognised Amaziga. The mare was all but finished, lather-covered and scarcely moving. Returning the glass to his saddlebag, Shannow crested the last rise. His eyes were burning with fatigue as he headed the stallion down to the Pool, then dismounted and gazed about him. The Peak reared like a jagged finger, and he could see the Parson almost at the last ledge. It was a long shot for a pistol.

'Welcome, Shannow,' came a voice and the Jerusalem Man spun, his pistols levelling at the speaker. Then he saw Beth McAdam. A slender, white-haired man had his arm about her throat, a pistol pointed to her head. The speaker – the man from his dreams – stood several paces to the left. 'I have to say, Shannow, that I am grateful to you,' Magellas told him. 'You killed that arrogant swine, Rhodaeul, and that did me a great service. However, the King of Kings has spoken the words of your death.'

'What has she to do with this?' asked Shannow.

'She will be released the moment you lay down your weapons.'

'And that is the moment I die?'

'Exactly. But it will be swift.' Magellas drew his pistol. 'I promise you.'

Shannon's guns were still trained on the young man, hammers cocked, fingers on the triggers. 'Don't listen to him, Shannow. Blow him away!' cried Beth McAdam.

'You will let her go?' Shannow asked.

'I am a man of my word,' said Magellas and Shannow nodded.

'Then it is done,' he agreed.

At that moment Beth McAdam lifted her booted foot and slammed it down on Lindian's instep. Ramming her head back into his face, she tore loose from his grip. As Lindian cursed and raised his pistol, Clem Steiner reared up from behind a rock. Lindian saw him and swung, but he was too late. Steiner's pistol boomed and the slender warrior was hurled to the ground with a bullet in his heart.

As Beth made her move, Magellas fired and the shell swept Shannow's hat from his head. The Jerusalem Man triggered his pistols. Magellas staggered, but did not go down. Again Shannow fired and Magellas sank to his knees, still struggling to lift his gun. The pistol dropped from his fingers and he raised his head. 'I like you, Shannow,' he said, with a weak smile. Then his eyes closed and he toppled forward.

Shannow ran to Steiner. The wound in his chest had opened, and his face was ghostly as he sat back on a rock.

'Paid you back, Shannow,' he whispered.

Beth approached him. 'You're crazy, Clem... but thanks. How the Hell did you get here?'

'I wasn't out for long. Bull came by to see me and I left the kids with him and followed the tracks. Looks like we should be safe now.'

'Not yet,' said Shannow.

The Parson had reached the ledge and was now out of range. They watched him lift his hand.

The Sword of God trembled in the sky.

*

Shannow ran to the base of the Peak and stripped off his black coat, dropping it to the ground. Then he reached up, took hold of a jutting rock and hauled himself up. The Peak loomed above him. His fingers reached for other holds and the slow climb began.

Beth and Steiner sat down to watch his progress. High above, on the ledge, the Parson began to chant broken verses from the Old Testament.

'A sword, a sword, drawn for the slaughter, polished to consume, and to flash like lightning ... For thus saith the Lord God: When I shall make thee a desolate city ... when I shall bring up the deep upon thee, and great waters shall cover thee ... I shall make thee a terror, and thou shalt be no more; though thou be sought for, yet shall thou never be found again, saith the Lord God.' His voice echoed on the wind.

Amaziga stumbled over the crest of the hill, the mare dead on the slope. She ran down to the poolside and saw Shannow inching his way up the rock-face.

'No,' she shouted. 'Let him be, Shannow. Let him be!' But the Jerusalem Man did not respond. As Amaziga drew her pistol and aimed it at him, Beth ran across the stones and hurled herself at the other woman. The pistol fired, splintering the rock by Shannow's left hand; he flinched instinctively and almost fell. Beth tore the gun from Amaziga's hand and threw the woman from her.

'We have to stop him!' said Amaziga. 'We have to!'

A rumbling roar came from the sky ... the base of the Sword was becoming flame and smoke. Shannow climbed on. Minutes fled by. On the rock-face Shannow was tiring, his arms trembling with the effort of dragging himself upwards. But he was close now. Sweat bathed his face as he forced his weary limbs to respond.

He could hear the Parson's voice above him: 'I will breathe out my wrath upon you, and breathe out my fiery anger against you ... Wail and say Alas for that day ... a time of doom for the nations.'

As the missile trembled, several planes on the edge of the stasis field broke clear, the sound of their engines roaring over the desert beyond the Peak. Shannow reached the ledge and hauled himself over it. For several seconds, exhausted, he could do nothing.

The Parson saw him. 'Welcome, brother. Welcome! Today you will hear a sermon unlike any other, for the Sword of God is coming home.'

'No,' Shannow told him. 'It is no sword, Parson.' But the man did not hear him.

'This is a blessed day. This is my destiny.' With a terrifying roar, the missile burst clear of the field and began to rise. 'NO!' screamed the Parson. 'No! Come back!' He held up his hand. The missile slowed its rise and began to turn in the air. The tower rumbled. A great flash of lightning seared the sky to the south, the air parting like a curtain, and a second sun shone in the sky. Shannow pushed himself to his knees. From the ledge he could see the immense gateway opened by Pendarric and the massed ranks of his legions beyond it. The light was unbearable. In the sky, the missile had almost completed its turn. Shannow drew his pistol. The earthquake hit just as he was about to fire on the Parson. A huge crack snaked across the desert ... the Pool disappeared ... the tower buckled, great slabs of stone peeling from the walls. Shannow dropped his pistol and grasped a jutting rock. The Parson, concentrating on the missile, lost his footing and tumbled from the ledge, his body shattering on impact with the rocks below where once the Pool had been.

Clem Steiner, Beth and Amaziga ran from the edge of the new chasm, taking shelter higher on the slopes. Shannow pushed himself upright. The missile was coming back towards him.

He stared sullenly at the weapon of his own destruction, wishing he could hurl the monster through the gaping gateway. In response to his thoughts, the missile wavered and twisted in the air. Shannow did not understand the miracle, for he did not know of the Sipstrassi Stone pulsing its power beyond the rock, but his heart leapt with the realisation that the Sword of God was responding to *his* wishes. He concentrated with all the strength he could muster. Like a spear, the silver missile sped through the Gate of Time. Pendarric's legions watched it pass ... on it flew, one section breaking away. For some moments Shannow experienced a sense of bitter disappointment, for nothing had happened. Then came the light of a thousand suns and a sound like the end of worlds.

The gateway disappeared.

33

Nu-Khasisatra opened his eyes to find he was standing within the circle of stones beyond the Royal Gardens, two hundred paces from the Temple of Ad. Stars shone brightly in the sky and the city slept. He ran from the circle, down the tree-lined Avenue of Kings and on through the Gates of Pearl and Silver. An old beggar awoke as he passed, stretching out his hand.

'Help me, Highness,' he said drowsily, but Nu ran by him. The man sent a whispered curse after him and settled down to sleep beneath his thin blankets.

Nu was breathing heavily by the time he reached the Street of Merchants. He slowed to a walk, then ran again, coming at last to the bolted gate by his own gardens. Glancing left and right, he grasped the iron grille and began to climb. Once over the top, he dropped to the earth and loped towards the house. A huge hound bore down on him, but when Nu knelt and held out his hand the hound stopped short, sniffing at him.

'Come on, Nimrod. It hasn't been that long,' said Nu. The black hound's tail began to wag and Nu rubbed at the beast's long ears. 'Let's find your mistress.'

The house doors were also bolted, but Nu pounded on the wood. A light flickered in an upper window and a servant stepped out to the balcony.

'Who is it?' came a voice.

'Open the door. The master of the house is home,' called Nu.

'Sweet Chronos!' exclaimed the servant, Purat. Moments later the bolts were drawn back and Nu stepped into the house. Purat, an elderly retainer, blinked as he saw the strange garb worn by his master, but Nu allowed no time for questions. 'Rouse the servants,' he said, 'and pack all your belongings – and food for a journey.'

'Where are we going, Lord?' Purat asked.

'To safety, God willing.' Nu ran up the winding staircase and opened the door to his bedroom where Pashad was asleep. He sat on the wide silk-covered bed and stroked her dark hair and her eyes opened.

'Is this another dream?' she whispered.

'It is no dream, beloved. I am here.' She sat up and threw her arms around her husband's neck.

'I knew you would come. I prayed so hard.'

'We have no time, Pashad. The world we know is about to end, even as the Lord Chronos told me. We must get away to the docks. Which of my ships is in harbour?'

'*Arcanau* alone stands ready. She will carry a shipment of livestock to the eastern colony.'

'Then *Arcanau* it is. Fetch the children, pack warm clothes. We will go to the dock and seek out Conalis the Master; he must be prepared to sail at dusk tomorrow.'

'But the manifest has not been cleared, beloved. They will not allow us to sail; they will close the harbour mouth.'

'I do not think so – not on this coming Day of Days. Now dress swiftly and do as I bid you.'

Pashad pushed aside the silk sheet and rose from the bed. 'Much has happened since you left us,' she told him, slipping from her nightgown and pulling a warm woollen dress from the chest by the window. 'Half the merchants and artisans from the east quarter have vanished; it is said that the King has taken them to another world. There is great excitement in the city. You know my second cousin, Karia? She is married to the court astrologer, Araksis. She says that a huge Sipstrassi Stone has been taken to the Star Tower; it is set to catch a great weapon our enemies are sending against us.'

'What? The Star Tower?'

'Yes. Karia says Araksis is very concerned. The King told him that enemies in another world will be seeking to destroy the Empire.'

'And they have set up a Stone to prevent it? Listen to me, Pashad. Take the children and find Conalis; tell him to prepare for a dusk sailing. I will join you at the dock. Where is *Arcanau* berthed?'

'The twelfth jetty. Why are you not coming with us?'

He strode to her, taking her in a powerful embrace. 'I cannot. There is something I must do. But trust me, Pashad. I love you.'

He kissed her swiftly and then ran from the room. Two of the retainers were waiting in the courtyard; beside them were hastily packed chests, while Purat was leading a horse and wagon along the pathway from the gate. The dawn was bright in the sky now.

'Purat! Harness the chariot. I need it now.'

'Yes, Lord. But the white pair have been loaned to Bonantae. There is only the bay mare and a gelding and they are not a team.'

'Do it.'

'At once, Lord.'

Within minutes Nu-Khasisatra was lashing the team back along the Avenue of Kings towards the distant Star Tower. The gelding was stronger than the mare, and it was hard to control the wooden chariot, but Nu drove recklessly, relying on his strength to keep the beasts under control. The chariot bounced on a jutting stone, lifting Nu from his feet, but he steadied himself and raced on through the doomed city.

The Lord had commanded him to find the Sword of God . . . he had failed. But Shannow had promised to find it and do what needed to be done. At last Nu understood what that meant. Shannow would send the Sword through the gateway and this was how the world would end. The Sword of God was the bright light of Nu's vision, and Araksis was using Sipstrassi power to stop it.

The sky was bright now, the morning upon him as Nu swung the chariot into the courtyard below the Star Tower. Two sentries ran to him, seizing the bridles of the sweating horses.

Nu leapt to the ground. 'Is Araksis here?' he asked.

The men eyed his strange clothing and exchanged glances.

'I have to see him on a matter of great urgency,' stated Nu.

'I think you should come with us, sir,' said one of the sentries, moving towards him. 'The captain of the guard will want to question you.'

'No time,' said Nu, his huge fist clubbing into the man's jaw. The sentry dropped like a stone. The other man was struggling to draw his sword when Nu leapt at him; Nu's fist rose and fell and the second sentry fell alongside his companion.

The door to the Tower stairs was bolted from the inside. When Nu slammed his shoulder against it, the wood buckled but did not give. He stepped back and hammered his foot against the lock; the door exploded inwards.

Taking the steps two at a time, Nu climbed to the Tower. A second door was not locked and he stepped inside. A dark, handsome man wearing a golden circlet on his brow was leaning over a desk, working on a large chart. He glanced up as Nu entered.

'Who are you?' he demanded.

'Nu-Khasisatra.'

The man's eyes widened. 'You have been named as a traitor and a heretic. What do you want here?'

'I have come to stop you, Araksis . . . in the name of the Most Holy.'

'You don't know what you are saying. The world is at risk.'

'The world is dead. You know that I speak the truth; you have seen the future, Astrologer. The King's evil has destroyed the balance of harmony in the world. The Lord Chronos has decreed his evil should end.'

'But there are thousands – hundreds of thousands – of innocents. We have a thousand years of civilisation to protect. You must be wrong.'

'Wrong? I have seen the fall of worlds. I have walked in

the ruins of Ad. I have seen the statue of Pendarric toppled by a shark in the depths below the oceans. I am not wrong.'

'I can stop it. I *can*, Nu. This Sword of God is only a mighty machine. I can hold it with the Sipstrassi... send it where it can cause no killing.'

'I cannot allow you to make the attempt,' said Nu softly, glancing at the clear blue sky.

'You cannot stop it, traitor. The power is spread across the gateway like a shield. It also covers the city. Any metallic object in the sky around Ad will be trapped – nothing can get through. You can kill me, Nu-Khasisatra, but that will not change the magic. And you cannot approach the Stone and live, for there are mighty spells protecting it.'

Nu swung to look at the giant Sipstrassi Stone. Golden wires were welded to its surface and these led to six crystal spheres supported on a framework of silver. 'Get out while you can,' said Araksis. 'Since we are linked by marriage, I will give you an hour before I notify the King of your return.'

Nu ignored him. Striding to the desk, he swept the parchment from it and pushed his hands under the oak top. The heavy desk lifted.

'No!' screamed Araksis, hurling himself at the larger man. Nu released the desk and turned just as the astrologer's body struck him. As both men fell, Nu sent a back-hand blow into Araksis' face; stunned, yet still he clung to Nu. The shipbuilder surged upright, hurling Araksis against the far wall; then he turned again to the desk, hoisted it high above his head and, with a grunt, threw it into the silver framework. Lightning lanced around the room, shattering a long window and setting fire to the velvet curtains that hung there. The silver framework melted. One of the crystals had been smashed by the desk, three others had fallen to the floor; Nu seized a stool and hammered them to shards.

'You don't know what you've done,' whispered Araksis, blood seeping from a cut on his temple.

A shout went up from the courtyard. Nu cursed and ran

to the window. Three more guards had appeared and were kneeling by the bodies of the sentries.

Nu raced down the stairs. Two of the guards were entering the doorway as he came into sight and he dived at them, his weight sending them sprawling to the ground. Running into the sunlight, he ducked a sweeping sword-cut and back-handed the wielder from his feet. Then leaping into the chariot, he took up the whip and cracked it over the heads of the two horses. They surged into the traces and hurtled out through the gateway.

In the high Star Tower Araksis struggled to his feet. Four of the crystals were ruined and he had no time now to repair the damage. Two still hung in place – enough to send a beam of power over the City of Ad. If the Sword was directed towards Ad, the Stone could still catch it in the sky and nullify its awesome power. If it missed the city, then it could explode harmlessly in the wide ocean beyond. Araksis moved to the great Stone and began to whisper words of power.

As the racing chariot sped towards the city, Nu hoped he had done enough to wreck Araksis' plans. If he had not, then Shannow's world would face the agony of Pendarric's evil.

The horses were tired and it was two hours before Nu guided the chariot into the docks. The *Arcanau* was berthed at the twelfth jetty as Pashad had told him. He left the chariot and ran up the gangplank. Conalis saw him and moved from the tiller to usher him below deck.

'This is madness, Highness,' said the burly master. 'The tides are against us, we have no manifest and the livestock are still being loaded.'

'This is a day of madness. Is my wife here?'

'Yes, and your sons and your servants; they are all below decks. But there is an inspection planned. What will I tell the Port Master?'

'Tell him what you please. Do you have a family, Conalis?'

'A wife and two daughters.'

'Get them on board now.'

'Why?'

'I wish to give them a great present... you also. That should suffice. Now I am going to sleep for a couple of hours. Wake me at dusk. Now tell any of the crew who have wives or sweethearts to bring them aboard also. I have presents for all.'

'Whatever you say, Highness. But it would be best for me to say the Lady Pashad has presents; you are still named as a traitor.'

'Wake me at dusk – and put off the inspection until tomorrow.'

'Yes, Highness.'

Nu spread himself out on the narrow bunk, too tired even to seek Pashad. His eyes closed and sleep overcame him within seconds...

He awoke with a start to find Pashad sitting beside him. His eyes were heavy with sleep, and it seemed only moments before that he had lowered himself to the bunk.

'It is dusk, my lord,' said Pashad and he rose.

'Are the children well?'

'Yes. All are safe, but the ship is crowded now with the wives and children of the crew.'

'Get them all below. I will speak to Conalis. Send him to the tiller.'

'What is happening, Nu? This is all beyond me.'

'You will not have long to wait, beloved. Believe me.'

Conalis met him at the tiller. 'I do not understand this, Highness. You said you wanted to sail at dusk, but now we are full of women and children who must be put ashore.'

'No one is going ashore,' Nu told him, scanning the sky.

Conalis muttered a curse – at the far end of the dock a squad of soldiers was marching towards them. 'Word must be out that you are here,' said the Master. 'Now we are all doomed.'

Nu shook his head. 'Look there!' he shouted, his arm lancing up, finger pointing to the sky where a long silver arrow was arcing across the heavens. 'Cut the ropes,' bellowed Nu. 'Do it now if you value your life!'

Conalis lifted an axe from a hook near the stern and hammered it through the docking rope. Running forward, he did the same at the prow. The *Arcanau* drifted away from the jetty and Nu pushed the tiller hard left. Feeling the ship move, many of the women and children surged up to the deck. On the dock the soldiers ran to the quayside, but the gap was too great to jump. Across the mouth of the bay a long trireme waited, its bronze ramming horn glinting in the light of the dying sun.

'It'll sink us,' shouted Conalis.

'No, it will not,' Nu told him. In the distance a colossal burst of white light was followed by an explosion that rocked the earth. A terrible tremor ran through the city and the *Arcanau* trembled.

'Shall I loose the sail?' Conalis shouted.

'No, a sail would destroy us. Get everyone below.'

The sky darkened. Then the sun swept majestically back into the sky and a hurricane wind roared across the city. Nu took his Sipstrassi Stone from the pocket of his jacket and whispered a prayer. The tidal wave, more than a thousand feet high, thundered across the city and Nu could see giant trees whirling in the torrent. If any were to strike the *Arcanau*, the vessel would be smashed to tinder. Their prow slowly swung until it pointed straight at the gigantic wall of water. Clutching the Sipstrassi, Nu felt the shock of the wave. The ship was lifted as if by a giant hand and carried high into the roaring swell, yet not one drop of water splashed the decks. Up and up soared the vessel until it crested the wave and bobbed on the surface. Far below them, the trireme was lifted like a cork and hammered against the cliffs on the outer curve of the bay; the ship exploded on impact and disappeared beneath the torrent. To the east, the plume of the wave raced on.

In the sudden silence Conalis moved alongside Nu, his face ashen.

'It's all gone,' he whispered. 'The world is destroyed.'

'No,' said Nu. 'Not the world. Only Atlantis. Raise the sail. When the waters subside, we must find a new home.'

The lowing of the livestock brought a wry smile from Nu. 'At least we'll have cattle and sheep,' he said.

Pashad came on to the deck, leading her sons, Shem, Ham and Japheth. Nu strode to meet her.

'What will we do now?' she asked. 'Where shall we go?'

'Wherever it is, we will be together,' he promised.

34

Shannow sank back on his haunches. Suddenly he felt good – better than he had in years. It was a most curious sensation. Despite his lack of rest, he felt such strength in his limbs. A crack opened on the ledge and he felt the Tower move. Swiftly he levered himself over the side and began to climb down. The Tower shivered, the top section breaking away and crashing down. Shannow hugged himself to the wall as the rocks and stones plunged past him, then slowly he completed his descent.

Beth ran to him. 'My God, Shannow. Look at you! What the Hell happened up there?'

'What's wrong?' he asked.

'You look young,' she said. 'Your hair is dark, your skin . . . It's incredible.'

A low groan came from the left and Shannow and Beth walked to where the Parson lay, his body broken, blood seeping from his right ear, his left leg bent under him. Shannow knelt by the man.

'The Sword . . . ?' whispered the Parson.

Shannow cradled the man's head. 'It went where God intended.'

'I'm dying, Shannow. And He won't appear to me. I failed Him . . .'

'Rest easy, Parson. You earned the right to make mistakes.'

'I failed Him.'

'We all fail Him,' said Shannow softly. 'But He doesn't seem to mind much. You did your best and you worked hard. You saved the town. You did a lot of good. He saw that, Parson. He knows.'

'I wanted . . . Him . . . to love me. Wanted . . . to earn . . .' his voice faded.

'I know. Rest easy. You're going home, Parson. You'll see the glory.'

'No. I've... been evil, Shannow. I've done such bad things.' Tears welled in the Parson's eyes. 'I'll be in Hell.'

'I don't think so,' Shannow assured him. 'If you hadn't come to this Peak, then maybe the world would have toppled again. None of us is perfect, Parson. At least you tried to walk the road.'

'Pray for... me... Shannow...'

'I'll do that.'

'It wasn't God... was it?'

'No. Rest easy.' The Parson's eyes closed and the last breath rattled from his throat. Shannow stood.

'Did you mean that?' Beth asked. 'You think he won't roast in Hell?'

The Jerusalem Man shrugged. 'I hope not. He was a tortured soul and I like to think God looks kindly on such men.'

Amaziga Archer approached. 'Why did you shoot at me?' asked Shannow.

'To try to change the past, Shannow. I read the gold scrolls.' Suddenly she laughed. 'The circle of history, Jerusalem Man. Pendarric took over the mind of the Parson – or Godspeaker, as he was named in the scrolls of Araksis. Through him Pendarric learned that a great weapon would be hurled at Atlantis, that through this weapon the world would topple. Do you know what Pendarric did? He had Sipstrassi transferred to this tower, and ordered Araksis to set the power to trap the Sword when it came over Ad. Do you understand what I am saying? Twelve thousand years ago, Pendarric set this stasis field in operation in order to catch a missile. And it caught it – twelve thousand years later. Can you see?'

'No,' said Shannow.

'It's so disgustingly perfect. If Pendarric had not learned of the missile and had made no effort to catch it – then it would not have been here at all. You can't change the past, Shannow. You can't.'

'But why did you try to kill me?'

'Because you just destroyed two worlds. If you had not sent that bomb into the past, our old world could not have been destroyed. You see, Pendarric was also responsible for the Second Fall. I thought I could change history . . . but no.' She looked at Shannow and he saw the anguish and hatred in her eyes. 'You're not the Jerusalem Man any more, Shannow. Oh, no. Now you are the Armageddon Man: the destroyer of worlds.'

Shannow did not reply and Amaziga turned from him and strode to the ruins of the Tower. The encrusted rocks had been dashed away, the white marble showing through. There was a broken doorway and Amaziga pushed her way inside. A dust-covered skeleton lay close to the Sipstrassi, which had fallen from its bowl; there were rings on the skeletal fingers and a gold band still circled the brow. Then Shannow, Beth and Steiner entered the chamber. Shannow led Steiner to the Sipstrassi and touched the pistoleer's hand to it; the veins of gold were thin now but still the power surged through him, healing his wounds.

Outside they could hear the roaring of engines as the once trapped planes continued to circle, seeking places to land.

Amaziga knelt and lifted a scroll of golden foil. 'The Sword,' she read, 'did not pass near Ad. But then a noise came, and a pillar of smoke. A strange phenomenon has just occurred. The sun, which was setting, has just risen again. And I can see dark storm-clouds racing towards us. Dark, blacker than any storm of memory. No, not a storm. The traitor was right. It is the sea!' Amaziga dropped the foil and stood. 'The missile was the final touch to a world straining on its axis.' She turned to the skeleton. 'I would guess this was Araksis. Even the Sipstrassi could not save him from the tidal wave he saw. God, Shannow, how I hate you!'

'Stop your whingeing!' snarled Beth McAdam. 'It wasn't Shannow who destroyed the worlds – it was Pendarric. He opened the gates; he set up whatever it was you called it, to trap the Sword of God. And it destroyed him. What right have you to condemn a man who only fought to save his friends?'

'Leave her alone,' said Shannow softly.

'No,' answered Beth, her cold blue eyes locked to Amaziga. 'She knows the truth. When a gun kills a man, it is not the weapon that goes on trial, but the man whose finger is on the trigger. She knows that!'

'He is a bringer of death,' Amaziga hissed. 'He destroyed my community. My husband died because of him, my son is dead. Now two worlds have toppled because of him.'

'Tell me, Shannow,' asked Beth, 'why you came to the Sword?'

'It does not matter,' answered the Jerusalem Man. 'Let it rest, Beth.'

'No,' she said again. 'While Magellas and Lindian held me captive, they used their Power Stones to observe you and they let me see. It was *you*,' she said, swinging once more to Amaziga, 'who urged Shannow – pleaded with him – to come here and stop the Parson. It was you who sent him scaling that Peak and risking his life. So whose finger was on the trigger, you bitch?'

'It was not my fault,' shouted Amaziga. 'I didn't know!'

'And he did? Jon Shannow knew that if the Sword passed through the gate it would destroy two worlds? You make me sick. Carry your own guilt, like the rest of us. Don't seek to palm it off on the man who just saved all our lives.'

Amaziga backed away from Beth's anger and walked out into the sunlight.

Shannow followed her. 'I am sorry for your loss,' he said. 'Samuel Archer was a fine man. I don't know what else to say to you.'

Amaziga sighed. 'The woman is right in what she says and you are just part of the circle of history. Forgive me, Shannow. Nu-Khasisatra said he was sent to find the Sword of God. He found it.'

'No, he didn't,' said Shannow sadly. 'There was no Sword – only a foul instrument of mass death.'

She placed her hand on his arm. 'He found the Sword, Shannow, because he found you. You were the Sword of God.'

'I hope Nu survived,' said Shannow, changing the subject. 'I liked the man.'

Amaziga laughed. 'Oh, he survived, Jon Shannow. Be assured of that.'

'Is there something else in the scrolls then?'

'No.' She shook her head. 'Nu is the Arabic form, and Khasisatra the Assyrian name, for Noah. You remember what he said about the Circle of God? Nu-Khasisatra came to the future and read of Noah's survival in your Bible, Shannow. So he went home, rescued his family and, I should imagine, with the aid of the Sipstrassi, created a ship that was storm-proof. How's that for a Circle of God?' Her laughter was almost hysterical... then the weeping began.

'Come away,' said Beth McAdam, taking Shannow by the arm and leading him back towards the horses.

Some planes had already begun to land on the hardbaked sand of the desert. 'What are they?' asked Beth.

'Nothing that I would see,' he told her, as Flight 19 touched down four centuries after take-off.

Together Shannow and Beth rode from the desolated Pool.

'What will you do now, Shannow?' she asked. 'Now that you are young again, I mean? Will you still seek Jerusalem?'

'I have spent half a lifetime pursuing that dream, Beth. It was a mistake. You don't find God across a distant hill. There are no answers in stone.' Turning back in the saddle, he gazed at the broken Peak and the forlorn figure of Amaziga Archer. Reaching out he took Beth's hand, lifting it to his lips. 'If you'll have me, I'd like to come home.'

EPILOGUE

Under the leadership of Edric Scayse and the Committee, led by Josiah Broome, Pilgrim's Valley prospered. The church was rebuilt and, for the want of a preacher, a young bearded farmer named Jon Cade took the service. If any noted the resemblance between Cade and a legendary killer called Shannow, none mentioned it.

Far to the south a beautiful black woman walked with a golden, black-maned lion at her side and climbed the last hill before the ocean. There she stood staring out to sea, feeling the cool of the ocean breeze, watching the sun's broken reflection on the rippling waves.

Beside her the lion turned his head and focused on a herd of deer grazing on a distant hillside. He did not know why the woman had stopped here, but he was hungry and padded off in search of food.

Amaziga Archer watched him go, tears welling to her cheeks.

'Farewell, Oshere,' she said.

But the lion did not hear her . . .

Bloodstone

DEDICATION

Bloodstone is dedicated with love to Tim and Dorothy Lenton for the gift of friendship, and for shining a light on the narrow way at a time when all I could see was darkness.

ACKNOWLEDGEMENTS

My thanks to my editors John Jarrold at Random and Stella Graham in Hastings, and to my copy editor Jean Maund, and test reader Val Gemmell. I am also grateful for the help so freely offered from fellow writers Alan Fisher and Peter Ling. And to the many fans who have written during the years demanding more tales of Jon Shannow – my thanks!

Foreword

There is something about the character and personality of Jon Shannow that leaves people loving or loathing him. Sometimes both emotions are aroused simultaneously. It is hard to pin down the reasons.

There is an iron quality about Jon Shannow that is admirable and worthy in a lone knight riding through a savage world. The decisions he makes are based solely on what he sees and experiences. He lives with a code of honour that refuses to allow evil to rage unchecked. He will always seek to defend the weak against predators.

Offset against this is his capacity for violence, and his certainty that his actions are right. It is just such certainty that can lead to horrors like the Spanish Inquisition, the butchery of the Aztecs, the burning at the stake of Catholics and Protestants, and the vileness of the Holocaust. When ruthless men are *certain* then the gulags and the concentration camps follow.

I have tried to present Jon Shannow as a flawed man in a flawed world. There is more to him than the nature of his deeds, just as I hope there is more to the stories than simple adventures of good versus evil. The tales have a spiritual centre not based exclusively on any recognised religion or creed. For me the message is simple, though I know from conversation and correspondence with fans that the underlying sub-text is very often – though not always – misunderstood.

But what is of enormous value to me is that *Bloodstone* sprang from the inter-action between myself and the readers. For some years the weight of mail was light, and I was able to respond to every fan who took the trouble to write. Increasing letters meant I could reply only to first time writers. Now even that has become difficult. But every letter is read by me, and often the points made will find their way into subsequent stories. This is especially true of *Bloodstone*.

The questions from readers that prompted the novel were many. One young fan wrote to ask whether Shannow was a symbol for the way I thought society should behave, as Forrest Gump is said to be a symbol for America. Others talked of the nature of legends, or the lack of a spiritual centre in politics. One wrote saying that, while he enjoyed the novels, he hated Shannow because he was the epitome of men like the Ayatollah Khomeini. Can you imagine, he asked, what any society would be like if a man like Shannow ever had power?

Could I imagine that? Yes I could. *Bloodstone* is the result and concludes the story of Jon Shannow.

I do not believe there will be another. Though I don't doubt there's a fan in Liverpool who knows better.

David A. Gemmell   Hastings, 1995

Prologue

I have seen the fall of worlds and the death of nations. From a place in the clouds I watched the colossal tidal wave sweep towards the coastline, swallowing the cities, drowning the multitudes.

The day was calm at first, but I knew what was to be. The city by the sea was awakening, its roads choked with vehicles, its sidewalks full, the veins of its subways clotted with humanity.

The last day was painful, for we had a congregation I had grown to love, peopled with Godly folk, warm-hearted and generous. It is hard to look down upon a sea of such faces and know that within a day they will be standing before their Maker.

So I felt a great sadness as I walked across to the silver and blue craft that would carry us high towards the future. The sun was setting in glory as we waited for take-off. I buckled the seat-belt and took out my Bible. There was no solace to be found.

Saul was sitting beside me, gazing from the window. 'A beautiful evening, Deacon,' he said.

Indeed it was. But the winds of change were already stirring.

We rose smoothly into the air, the pilot informing us that the weather was changing for the worse, but that we would reach the Bahamas before the storm. I knew this would not be so.

Higher and higher we flew, and it was Saul who first saw the portent.

'How strange,' he said, tapping my arm. 'The sun appears to be rising again.'

'This is the last day, Saul,' I told him. Glancing down I saw that he had unfastened his seat-belt. I told him to buckle it. He had just done so when the first of those terrible winds struck the plane, almost flipping it. Cups, books, trays, bags all flew into the air, and there were screams of terror from our fellow passengers.

Saul's eyes were squeezed shut in prayer, but I was calm. I leaned to my right and stared from the window. The great wave had lifted now, and was hurtling towards the coast.

I thought of the people of the city. There were those who were even now merely observing what they saw to be a miracle, the setting sun rising again. They would smile perhaps, or clap their hands in wonder. Then their eyes would be drawn to the horizon. At first they would assume a low thundercloud was darkening the sky. But soon would come the terrible realisation that the sea had risen to meet the sky, and was bearing down upon them in a seething wall of death.

I turned my eyes away. The plane juddered, then rose and fell, twisting and helpless against the awesome power of the winds. All of the passengers believed that death would soon follow. Except me. I knew.

I took one last glance from the window. The city looked so small now, its mighty towers seemingly no longer than a child's finger. Lights shone at the windows of the towers, cars still thronged the freeways.

And then they were gone.

Saul opened his eyes, and his terror was very great. 'What is happening, Deacon?'

'The end of the world, Saul.'

'Are we to die?'

'No. Not yet. Soon you will see what the Lord has planned for us.'

Like a straw in a hurricane the plane hurtled through the sky.

And then the colours came, vivid reds and purples washing over the fuselage, masking the windows. As if we had been swallowed by a rainbow. Then they were gone. Four seconds perhaps. Yet in those four seconds I alone knew that several hundred years had passed.

'It has begun, Saul,' I said.

Chapter One

The pain was too great to ignore, and nausea threatened to swamp him as he rode. But the Preacher clung to the saddle and steered the stallion up towards the Gap. The full moon was high in the clear sky, the distant mountain peaks sharp and glistening white against the skyline. The sleeve of the rider's black coat was still smouldering, and a gust of wind brought a tongue of flame. Fresh pain seared through him and he beat at the cloth with a smoke-blackened hand.

Where were they now, he thought, pale eyes scanning the moonlit mountains and the lower passes? His mouth was dry and he reined in the stallion. A canteen hung from the pommel and the Preacher hefted it, unscrewing the brass cap. Lifting it to his lips, he found it was filled not with water but with a fiery spirit. He spat it out and hurled the canteen away.

Cowards! They needed the dark inspiration of alcohol to aid them on their road to murder. His anger flared, momentarily masking the pain. Far down the mountain, emerging from the timber line he saw a group of riders. His eyes narrowed. Five men. In the clear air of the mountains he heard the distant sound of laughter.

The rider groaned and swayed in the saddle, the pounding in his temple increasing. He touched the wound on the right side of his head. The blood was congealing now, but there was a groove in the skull where the bullet had struck, and the flesh around it was hot and swollen.

He felt consciousness slipping from him, but fought back using the power of his rage.

Tugging the reins he guided the stallion up through the Gap, then angled it to the right, down the long wooded slope towards the road. The slope was treacherous and the stallion slipped twice, dropping to its haunches. But the rider kept the animal's head up and it righted itself, coming at last to level ground and the hard-packed earth of the trade road.

The Preacher halted his mount, then looped the reins around the pommel and drew his pistols. Both were long-barrelled, the cylinders engraved with swirls of silver. He shivered and saw that his hands were trembling. How long had it been since these weapons of death were last in use. Fifteen years? Twenty? *I swore never to use them again. Never to take another life.*

And you were a fool!

Love your enemy. Do good to him that hates you.

And see your loved ones slain.

If he strikes you upon the right cheek, offer him the left.

And see your loved ones burn.

He saw again the roaring flames, heard the screams of the terrified and the dying . . . Nasha running for the blazing door as the roof timbers cracked and fell upon her, Dova kneeling beside the body of her husband Nolis, her fur ablaze, pulling open the burning door, only to be shot to ribbons by the jeering, drunken men outside . . .

The riders came into sight and saw the lone figure waiting for them. It was clear that they recognised him, but there was no fear in them. This he found strange, but then he realised they could not see the pistols, which were hidden by the high pommel of the saddle. Nor could they know the hidden secret of the man who faced them. The riders urged their horses forward and he waited, silently, as they approached. All trembling was gone now, and he felt a great calm descend upon him.

'Well, well,' said one of the riders, a huge man wearing a double-shouldered canvas coat. 'The Devil looks after his own, eh? You made a bad mistake following us, Preacher. It would have been easier for you to die back there.' The man produced a double-edged knife. 'Now I'm going to skin you alive!'

For a moment he did not reply, then he looked the man in the eyes. '*Were they ashamed when they had committed the abomination?*' he quoted. '*No, they were not ashamed, and could not blush.*' The pistol in his right hand came up, the movement smooth, unhurried. For a fraction of a second the huge raider froze, then he scrabbled for his own pistol. It was too late. He did not hear the thunderous roar, for the heavy-calibre bullet smashed into his skull ahead of the sound and catapulted him from the saddle. The explosion terrified the horses, and all was suddenly chaos. The Preacher's stallion reared but he re-adjusted his position and fired twice, the first bullet ripping through the throat of a lean, bearded man, the second punching into the back of a rider who had swung his horse in a vain bid to escape the sudden battle. A fourth man took a bullet in the chest and fell screaming to the ground, where he began to crawl towards the low undergrowth at the side of the road. The last raider, managing to control his panicked mount, drew a long pistol and fired; the bullet came close, tugging at the collar of the Preacher's coat. Twisting in the saddle, he fired his left-hand pistol twice, and his assailant's face disappeared as the bullets hammered into his head. Riderless horses galloped away into the night and he surveyed the bodies. Four men were dead; the fifth, wounded in the chest, was still trying to crawl away, and leaving a trail of blood behind him. Nudging the stallion forward, the rider came alongside the crawling man. '*I will surely consume them, saith the Lord.*' The crawling man rolled over.

'Jesus Christ, don't kill me! I didn't want to do it. I didn't kill any of them, I swear it!'

'*By their works shall ye judge them*,' said the rider.

The pistol levelled. The man on the ground threw up his hands, crossing them over his face. The bullet tore through his fingers and into his brain.

'It is over,' said the Preacher. Dropping the pistols into the scabbards at his hip, he turned the stallion and headed for home. Weariness and pain overtook him then, and he slumped forward over the horse's neck.

The stallion, with no guidance now from the man, halted. The rider had pointed him towards the south, but that was not the home the stallion knew. For a while it stood motionless, then it started to walk, heading east and out into the plains.

It plodded on for more than an hour, then caught the scent of wolves. Shapes moved to the right. The stallion whinnied and reared. The weight fell from its back . . . and then it galloped away.

*

Jeremiah knelt by the sleeping man, examining the wound in

the temple. He did not believe the skull to be cracked, but there was no way of being sure. The bleeding had stopped, but massive bruising extended up into the hairline and down across the cheekbone almost all the way to the jaw. Jeremiah gazed down at the man's face. It was lean and angular, the eyes deep-set. The mouth was thin-lipped, yet not, Jeremiah considered, cruel.

There was much to learn about a man by studying his face, Jeremiah knew, as if the experiences of life were mirrored there in code. Perhaps, he thought, every act of weakness or spite, bravery or kindness, made a tiny mark, added a line here and there, that could be read like script. Maybe this was God's way of allowing the holy to perceive wickedness in the handsome. It was a good thought. The sick man's face was strong, but there was little kindness there, Jeremiah decided, though equally there was no evil. Gently he bathed the head wound, then drew back the blanket. The burns to the man's arm and shoulder were healing well, though several blisters were still seeping pus.

Jeremiah turned his attention to the man's weapons. Revolvers made by the Hellborn, single-action pistols. Hefting the first he drew back the hammer into the half-cock position, then flipped the release, exposing the cylinder. Two shells had been fired. Jeremiah removed an empty cartridge case and examined it. The weapon was not new. In the years before the Second Satan Wars the Hellborn had produced double-action versions of the revolver, with slightly shorter barrels, and squat, rectangular automatic pistols and rifles that were far more accurate than these pieces. Such weapons had not saved them from annihilation. Jeremiah had seen the destruction of Babylon. The Deacon had ordered it razed, stone by stone, until nothing remained save a flat, barren plain. The old man shivered at the memory.

The injured man groaned and opened his eyes. Jeremiah felt the coldness of fear as he gazed into them. The eyes were the misty grey-blue of a winter sky, piercing and sharp, as if they could read his soul. 'How are you feeling?' he asked, as his heart hammered. The man blinked and tried to sit. 'Lie still, my friend. You have been badly wounded.'

'How did I get here?' The voice was low, the words softly spoken.

'My people found you on the plains. You fell from your horse. But before that you were in a fire, and were shot.'

The man took a deep breath and closed his eyes. 'I don't remember,' he said, at last.

'It happens,' said Jeremiah. 'The trauma from the pain of your wounds. Who are you?'

'I don't remem . . .' the man hesitated. 'Shannow. I am Jon Shannow.'

'An infamous name, my friend. Rest now and I will come back this evening with some food for you.'

The injured man opened his eyes and reached out, taking Jeremiah's arm. 'Who are you, friend?'

'I am Jeremiah. A *Wanderer*.'

The wounded man sank back to the bed. *'Go and cry in the ears of Jerusalem, Jeremiah,'* he whispered, then fell once more into a deep sleep.

Jeremiah climbed from the back of the wagon, pushing closed the wooden door. Isis had prepared a fire, and he could see her gathering herbs by the riverside, her short, blonde hair shining like new gold in the sunlight. He scratched at his white beard and wished he were twenty years younger. The other ten wagons had been drawn up in a half-circle around the riverbank and three other cook-fires were now lit. He saw Meredith kneeling by the first, slicing carrots into the pot that hung above it.

Jeremiah strolled across the grass and hunkered down opposite the lean, young academic. 'A life under the sun and stars agrees with you, doctor,' he said amiably. Meredith gave a shy smile, and pushed back a lock of sandy hair that had fallen into his eyes.

'Indeed it does, Meneer Jeremiah. I feel myself growing stronger with each passing day. If more people from the city could see this land there would be less savagery, I am sure.'

Jeremiah said nothing and transferred his gaze to the fire. In his experience savagery always dwelt in the shadow of Man, and where Man walked evil was never far behind. But Meredith was a gentle soul, and it did a young man no harm to nurse gentle dreams.

'How is the wounded man?' Meredith asked.

'Recovering, I think, though he claims to remember nothing of the fight that caused his injuries. He says his name is Jon Shannow.'

Anger shone briefly in Meredith's eyes. 'A curse on that name!' he said.

Jeremiah shrugged. 'It is only a name.'

*

Isis knelt by the river-bank and stared down at the long, sleek fish just below the glittering surface of the water. It was a beautiful fish, she thought, reaching out with her mind. Instantly her thoughts blurred, then merged with the fish. She felt the cool of the water along her flanks and was filled with a haunting restlessness, a need to move, to push against the currents, to swim for home.

Withdrawing, she lay back . . . and felt the approach of Jeremiah. Smiling, she sat up and turned towards the old man. 'How is he?' she asked, as Jeremiah eased himself down beside her.

'Getting stronger. I'd like you to sit with him.' The old man is troubled, but trying to hide it, she thought. Resisting the urge to flow into his mind, she waited for him to speak again. 'He is a fighter, perhaps even a brigand. I just don't know. It was our duty to help him, but the question is: Will he prove a danger to us as he grows stronger? Is he a killer? Is he wanted by the Crusaders? Could we find ourselves in trouble for harbouring him? Will you help me?'

'Oh, Jeremiah,' said Isis, softly. 'Of course I will help you. Did you doubt it?'

He reddened. 'I know you don't like to use your talent on people. I'm sorry I had to ask.'

'You're a sweet man,' she said, rising. Dizziness swept over her and she stumbled. Jeremiah caught her, and she felt swamped by his concern. Slowly strength returned to her, but the pain had now started in her chest and stomach. Jeremiah lifted her into his arms and walked back towards the wagons where Dr Meredith ran to them. Jeremiah sat her down in the wide rocking-chair by the fire, while Meredith took her pulse. 'I'm all right now,' she said. 'Truly.'

Meredith's slender hand rested on her brow, and it took all her concentration to blot out the intensity of his feelings for her. 'I'm all right!'

'And the pain?' he asked.

'Fading,' she lied. 'I just got up too quickly. It is nothing.'

'Get some salt,' Meredith told Jeremiah. When he returned Meredith poured it into her outstretched palm. 'Eat it,' he commanded.

'It makes me feel sick,' she protested, but he remained silent and she licked the salt from her hand. Jeremiah passed her a mug of water, and she rinsed her mouth.

'You should rest now,' said Meredith.

'I will, soon,' she promised. Slowly she stood. Her legs took her weight and she thanked both men. Anxious to be away from their caring glances she moved to Jeremiah's wagon and climbed inside, where the wounded man was still sleeping.

Isis pulled up a chair and sat down. Her illness was worsening, and she sensed the imminence of death.

Pushing such thoughts from her mind, she reached out, her small hand resting on the fingers of the sleeping man. Closing her eyes, she allowed herself to fall into his memories, floating down and down through the layers of manhood and adolescence, absorbing nothing until she reached childhood.

Two boys, brothers. One shy and sensitive, the other boisterous and rough. Caring parents, farmers. Then the brigands came. Bloodshed and murder, the boys escaping. Torment and tragedy affecting them both in different ways, the one becoming a brigand, the other . . .

Isis jerked back to reality, all thoughts of her illness forgotten now as she stared down at the sleeping man. 'I am staring into the face of a legend,' she thought. Once more she merged with the man.

The Jerusalem Man, haunted by the past, tormented by thoughts of the future, riding through the wild lands, seeking . . . a city? Yes, but much more. Seeking an answer, seeking a reason for being. And during his search stopping to fight brigands, tame towns, kill the ungodly. Riding endlessly through the lands, welcome only when his guns were needed, urged to move on when the killing was done.

Isis pulled back once more, dismayed and depressed – not just by the memories of constant death and battle, but by the anguish of the man himself. The shy, sensitive child had become the man of violence, feared and shunned, each killing adding yet another layer of ice upon his soul. Again she merged.

She/he was being attacked, men running from the shadows. Gunfire. A sound behind her/him. Cocking the pistol Isis/ Shannow spun and fired in one motion. A child flung back, his chest torn open. Oh God! Oh God! Oh God!

Isis clawed her way free of the memory, but did not fully withdraw. Instead she floated upwards, allowing time to pass, halting only when the Jerusalem Man rode up to the farm of Donna Taybard. This was different. Here was love.

The wagons were moving, and Isis/Shannow rode out from them, scouting the land, heart full of joy and the promise of a better tomorrow. No more savagery and death. Dreams of farming and quiet companionship. Then came the Hellborn!

Isis withdrew and stood. 'You poor, dear man,' she whispered, brushing her hand over the sleeping man's brow. 'I'll come back tomorrow.'

Outside the wagon Dr Meredith approached her. 'What did you find out?' he asked.

'He is no danger to us,' she answered.

*

The young man was tall and slender, a shock of unruly black hair cut short above the ears but growing long over the nape of his neck. He was riding an old, sway-backed mare up and over the Gap, and stared with the pleasure of youth at the distant horizons, where the mountains reared up to challenge the sky.

Nestor Garrity was seventeen, and this was an adventure. The Lord alone knew how rare adventures were in Pilgrim's Valley. His hand curled round the pistol butt at his hip, and he allowed the fantasies to sweep through his mind. He was no longer a clerk at the timber company. No, he was a Crusader hunting the legendary Laton Duke and his band of brigands. It didn't matter that Duke was feared as the deadliest pistoleer this side of the Plague Lands. For the hunter was Nestor

Garrity, lethal and fast, the bane of war-makers everywhere, adored by women, respected and admired by men.

Adored by women . . .

Nestor paused in his fantasy, wondering what it would be like to be adored by women. He'd walked out once with Ezra Feard's daughter, Mary, taken her to the Summer Dance. She'd led him outside into the moonlight and flirted with him.

'Should have kissed her,' he thought. 'Should have done some damn thing!' He blushed at the memory. The dance had turned into a nightmare when she walked off with Samuel Klares. They'd kissed. Nestor saw them down by the creek. Now she was married to him, and had just delivered her first child.

The old mare almost stumbled on the scree slope. Jerked from his thoughts, Nestor steered her down the incline.

The fantasies loomed back into his mind. He was no longer Nestor Garrity, the fearless Crusader, but Jon Shannow, the famed Jerusalem Man, seeking the fabled city, and with no time for women – much as they adored him. Nestor narrowed his eyes, and lifted his hat from where it hung at his back. Settling it into place, he turned up the collar of his coat and sat straighter in the saddle.

Jon Shannow would never slouch. He pictured two brigands riding from behind the boulders. In his mind's eye he could see the fear on their faces. They went for their guns. Nestor's hand snapped down. The pistol sight caught on the tip of his holster, twisting the weapon from his hands. It fell to the scree. Carefully Nestor dismounted and retrieved the weapon.

The mare, pleased to be relieved of the boy's weight, walked on. 'Hey, wait!' called Nestor, scrambling towards her. But she ambled on, and the dejected youngster followed her all the way to the bottom, where she stopped to crop at the dry grass. Then Nestor remounted.

One day I'll be a Crusader, he thought. I'll serve the Deacon and the Lord. He rode on.

Where was the Preacher? It shouldn't take this long to find him. The tracks were easy to follow to the Gap. But where was he going? Why did he ride out in the first place? Nestor liked the Preacher. He was a quiet man, and throughout Nestor's youth he had treated him with kindness and understanding. Especially when Nestor's parents had been killed that Summer ten years ago. Drowned in a flash flood. Nestor shivered at the memory. Seven years old – and an orphan. Frey McAdam had come to him then, the Preacher with her. He had sat at the bedside and taken Nestor's hand.

'Why did they die?' asked the bewildered child. 'Why did they leave me?'

'I guess it was their time, only they didn't know it.'

'I want to be dead too,' wailed the seven-year-old.

The Preacher had sat with him then, quietly talking about the boy's parents, of their goodness, and their lives. Just for a while the anguish and the numbing sense of loneliness had left Nestor, and he had fallen asleep.

Last night the Preacher had escaped out of the church, despite the flames and the bullets. And he had run away to hide. Nestor would find him, tell him that everything was all right now and it was safe to come home.

Then he saw the bodies, the flies buzzing around the terrible wounds. Nestor forced himself to dismount and approach them. Sweat broke out on his face, and the desert breeze felt cold upon his skin. He couldn't look directly at them, so he studied the ground for tracks.

One horse had headed back towards Pilgrim's Valley, then turned and walked out into the wild lands. Nestor risked a swift, stomach-churning glance at the dead men. He knew none of them. More importantly, none of them was the Preacher.

Remounting, he set off after the lone horseman.

*

People were moving on the main street of Pilgrim's Valley as Nestor Garrity rode in, leading the black stallion. It was almost noon and the children were leaving the two school buildings and heading out into the fields to eat the lunches their mothers had packed for them. The stores and the town's three restaurants were open, and the sun was shining down from a clear sky.

But a half-mile to the north smoke still spiralled lazily into the blue. Nestor could see Beth McAdam standing amid the blackened timbers as the undertakers moved around the debris, gathering the charred bodies of the Wolvers. Nestor didn't relish facing Beth with the news. She had been the headmistress of the Lower School when Nestor was a boy, and no one ever enjoyed the thought of being sent to her study. He grinned, remembering the day he had fought with Charlie Wills. They had been dragged apart and then taken to Mrs McAdam; she had stood in front of her desk, tapping her fingers with the three-foot bamboo cane.

'How many should you receive, Nestor?' she had asked him.

'I didn't start the fight,' the boy replied.

'That is no answer to my question.'

Nestor thought about it for a moment. 'Four,' he said.

'Why four?'

'Fighting in the yard is four strokes,' he told her. 'That's the rule.'

'But did you not also take a swing at Mr Carstairs when he dragged you off the hapless Charlie?'

'That was a mistake,' said Nestor.

'Such mistakes are costly, boy. It shall be six for you and four for Charlie. Does that sound fair?'

'Nothing is fair when you're thirteen,' said Nestor. But he had accepted the six strokes, three on each hand, and had made no sound.

He rode slowly towards the charred remains of the little church, the stallion meekly following his bay mare. Beth McAdam was standing with her hands on her ample hips, staring out towards the Wall. Her blonde hair was braided at the back, but a part of the braid had come loose and was fluttering in the wind at her cheek. She turned at the sound of the approaching horse and gazed up at Nestor, her face expressionless. He dismounted and removed his hat.

'I found the raiders,' he said. 'They was all dead.'

'I expected that,' she said. 'Where is the Preacher?'

'No sign of him. His horse headed east and I caught up with it; there was blood on the saddle. I backtracked and found signs of wolves and bears, but I couldn't find him.'

'He is not dead, Nestor,' she said. 'I would know. I would feel it here,' she told him, hitting her chest with a clenched fist.

'How did he manage to kill five men? They were all armed.

All killers. I mean, I never saw the Preacher ever carry a gun.'

'Five men, you say?' she replied, ignoring the question. 'There were more than twenty surrounding the church according to those who saw the massacre. But then I expect there were some from our own . . . loving . . . community.'

Nestor had no wish to become involved in the dispute. Wolvers in a church was hardly decent anyhow, and it was no surprise to the youngster that tempers had flared. Even so, if the Crusaders hadn't been called out to a brigand raid on Shem Jackson's farm there would have been no violence.

'Anything more you want me to do, Mrs McAdam?'

She shook her head. 'It was plain murder,' she said. 'Nothing short.'

'You can't murder Wolvers,' said Nestor, without thinking. 'I mean they ain't human, are they? They're animals.'

Anger shone in Beth's eyes, but she merely sniffed and turned aside. 'Thank you, Nestor, for your help. But I expect you have chores to do and I'll not keep you from them.'

Relieved, he turned away and remounted. 'What do you want me to do with this stallion?' he called.

'Give it to the Crusaders. It wasn't ours and I don't want it.'

Nestor rode away to the stone-built barracks at the south of town, dismounting and hitching both horses to the rail outside. The door was open and Captain Leon Evans was sitting at a rough-built desk.

'Good morning, sir,' said Nestor.

Evans looked up and grinned. He was a tall, broad-shouldered man with an easy smile. 'Still looking to sign up, boy?'

'Yes, sir.'

'Been reading your Bible?'

'I have, sir. Every day.'

'I'll put you in for the test on the first of next month. If you pass I'll make you a cadet.'

'I'll pass, sir. I promise.'

'You're a good lad, Nestor. I see you found the stallion. Any sign of the Preacher?'

'No, sir. But he killed five of the raiders.'

The smile faded from Captain Evans's face. 'Did he, by

God?' He shook his head. 'As they say, you can't judge a man by the coat he wears. Did you recognise any of the dead men?'

'Not a one, sir. But three of them had their faces shot away. Looks like he just rode down the hill and blasted 'em to Hell and gone. Five men!'

'Six,' said the Captain. 'I was checking the church this morning, there was a corpse there. It looks like when the fire was at its worst the Preacher managed to smash his way out at the rear. There was a man waiting. The Preacher must have surprised him, there was a fight and the Preacher managed to get the man's gun. Then he killed him and took his horse. Jack Shale says he saw the Preacher riding from town; said his coat and hair were ablaze.'

Nestor shivered. 'Who'd have thought it?' he said. 'All his sermons were about God's love and forgiveness. Then he guns down six raiders. Who'd have thought it?'

'I would, boy,' came a voice from the doorway and Nestor turned to see the old prophet making his slow way inside. Leaning on two sticks, his long white beard hanging to his chest, Daniel Cade inched his way to a seat by the wall. He was breathing heavily as he sank to the chair.

Captain Evans stood and filled a mug with water, passing it to the prophet. Cade thanked the man.

Nestor faded back to the far wall, but his eyes remained fixed to the ancient legend sipping the water. Daniel Cade, the former brigand turned prophet, who had fought off the Hellborn in the Great War. Everyone knew that God spoke to the old man, and Nestor's parents had been two of the many people saved when Cade's brigands took on the might of the Hellborn army.

'Who burned the church?' asked Cade, the voice still strong and firm, oddly in contrast to the arthritic and frail body.

'They were raiders from outside Pilgrim's Valley,' the captain told him.

'Not all of them,' said Cade. 'There were townsfolk among the crowd. Shem Jackson was seen. Now that disturbs me – for isn't that why the Crusaders were not here to protect the church? Weren't you called to Jackson's farm?'

'Aye, we were,' said the captain. 'Brigands stole some of his stock and he rode in to alert us.'

'And then stayed on to watch the murders. Curious.'

'I do not condone the burning of the church, sir,' said the captain. 'But it must be remembered that the Preacher was told – repeatedly – that Wolvers were not welcome in Pilgrim's Valley. They are not creatures of God, not made in his image, nor true creations. They are *things* of the Devil. They have no place in a church, nor in any habitat of decent folk. The Preacher ignored all warnings. It was inevitable that some . . . tragedy . . . would befall. I can only hope that the Preacher is still alive. It would be sad . . . if a good man – though misguided – were to die.'

'Oh, I reckon he's alive,' said Cade. 'So you'll be taking no action against the townspeople who helped the raiders?'

'I don't believe anyone *helped* them. They merely observed them.'

Cade nodded. 'Does it not strike you as strange that men from outside Pilgrim's Valley should choose to ride in to lance our boil?'

'The work of God is often mysterious,' said Evans, 'as you yourself well know, sir. But tell me, why were you not surprised that the Preacher should tackle – and destroy – six armed men? He shares your name and it is said he is your nephew, or was once one of your men in the Hellborn War? If the latter is true, he must have been very young indeed.'

Cade did not smile, but Nestor saw the humour in his eyes. 'He is older than he looks, Captain, and, no, he was never one of my men. Nor is he my nephew – despite his name.' With a grunt the prophet pushed himself to his feet. Captain Evans took his arm and Nestor ran forward to gather his sticks.

'I'm all right. Don't fuss about me!'

Slowly, and with great dignity, the old man left the room and climbed to the driving seat of a small wagon. Evans and Nestor watched as Cade flicked the reins.

'A great man,' said Evans. 'A legend. He knew the Jerusalem Man. Rode with him, some say.'

'I heard he *was* the Jerusalem Man,' said Nestor.

Evans shook his head. 'I heard that too. But it is not true. My father knew a man who fought alongside Cade. He was a brigand, a killer. But God shone the great light upon him.'

The Deacon stood on the wide balcony, his silver-white beard rippling in the morning breeze. From this high vantage point he gazed affectionately out over the high walls and down on the busy streets of Unity. Overhead a bi-plane lumbered across the blue sky, heading east towards the mining settlements, carrying letters and possibly the new Barta notes that were slowly replacing the large silver coins used to pay the miners.

The city was prospering. Crime was low and women could walk without risk, even at night, along the well-lit thoroughfares.

'I've done the best I could,' whispered the old man.

'What's that, Deacon?' asked a slender, round-shouldered man, with wispy white hair.

'Talking to myself, Geoffrey. Not a good sign.' Turning from the balcony he re-entered the study. 'Where were we?'

The thin man lifted a sheet of paper and peered at it. 'There is a petition here asking for mercy for Cameron Sikes. You may recall he's the man who found his wife in bed with a neighbour. He shot them both to death. He is due to hang tomorrow.'

The old man shook his head. 'I feel for him, Geoffrey, but you cannot make exceptions. Those who murder must die. What else?'

'The Apostle Saul would like to see you before setting off for Pilgrim's Valley.'

'Am I free this afternoon?'

Geoffrey consulted a black, leather-bound diary. 'Four-thirty to five is clear. Shall I arrange it?'

'Yes. I still don't know why he asked for that assignment. Perhaps he is tired of the city. Or perhaps the city is tired of him. What else?'

For half an hour the two men worked through the details of the day, until finally the Deacon called a halt and strolled through to the vast library beyond the study. There were armed guards on the doors, and the Deacon remembered with sadness the young man who had hidden here two years before. The shot had sounded like thunder within the domed building, striking the Deacon just above the right hip and spinning him to the floor. The assailant had screamed and charged across the huge room, firing as he ran. Bullets ricocheted from the stone floor. The Deacon had rolled over and drawn the small, two-shot pistol from his pocket. As the young man came closer the old man had fired, the bullet striking the assassin just above the bridge of the nose. The youngster stood for a moment, his own pistol dropping to the floor. Then he had fallen to his knees, and toppled on to his face.

The Deacon sighed at the memory. The boy's father had been hanged the day before, after shooting a man following an argument over a card game.

Now the library and the municipal buildings were patrolled by armed guards.

The Deacon sat at a long oak table and stared at the banks of shelves while he waited for the woman. Sixty-eight thousand books, or fragments of books, cross-indexed; the last remnants of the history of mankind, contained in novels, textbooks, philosophical tomes, instruction manuals, diaries and volumes of poetry. And what have we come to, he thought? A ruined world, bastardised by science and haunted by magic. His thoughts were dark and sombre, his mind weary. No one is right all the time, he told himself; you can only follow your heart. A guard ushered the woman in. Despite her great age she still walked with a straight back, her face showing more than a trace of the beauty she had possessed as a younger woman.

'Welcome, Frey Masters,' said the Deacon, rising. 'God's blessing to you, and to your family.' Her hair was silver, the lights from the ornate arched and stained-glass windows creating soft highlights of gold and red. Her eyes were blue, and startlingly clear. She smiled thinly and accepted his hand, then she sat opposite him.

'God's greeting to you also, Deacon,' she said. 'And I trust he will allow you to learn compassion before much longer.'

'Let us hope so,' said the Deacon. 'Now, what is the news?'

'The dreams remain the same, only they are more powerful,' she said. 'Betsy saw a man with crimson skin and black veins. His eyes were red. Thousands of corpses lay around him, and he was bathing in the blood of children. Samantha also dreamed of a demon from another world. She was hysterical upon wakening, and claimed that the Devil was about to be loosed upon us. What does it mean, Deacon? Are the visions symbolic?'

'No,' he said sadly. 'The Beast exists.'

The woman sighed. 'I too have been dreaming more of late. I saw a great wolf, walking upright. Its hands held hollow talons, and I watched as it sank them into a man, saw the blood drawn out of him. The Beast and the Wolf are linked, aren't they?' He nodded, but did not answer. 'And you know far more than you are telling me.'

'Has anyone else dreamed of wolves?' he asked, ignoring the comment.

'Alice has seen visions of them, Deacon,' said Frey Masters. 'She says she saw a crimson light bathing a camp of Wolvers. The little creatures began to writhe and scream; then they changed, becoming beasts like those in my dream.'

'I need to know *when*,' said the Deacon. 'And *where*.' From his pocket he took a small golden Stone, which he twirled against his fingertips.

'You should use the power on yourself,' said the woman sternly. 'You know that your heart is failing.'

'I've lived too long anyway. No, I'll save its power for the Beast. This is the last of them, you know. My little hoard. Soon the world will have to forget magic and concentrate once more on science and discovery.' His expression changed. 'If it survives.'

'It'll survive, Deacon,' she said. 'God must be stronger than any demon.'

'If He wants it to survive. We humans have hardly made the earth a garden now, have we?'

She shook her head and gave a weary smile. 'Yet there are still good people, even though we know that the path of evil offers many rewards. Don't give in to despair, Deacon. If the Beast comes, there will be those who will battle against it. Another Jerusalem Man, perhaps. Or a Daniel Cade.'

'Come the moment, come the man,' said the Deacon, with a dry chuckle.

Frey Masters rose. 'I'll go back to my Dreamers. What would you have me tell them?'

'Get them to memorise landscapes, seasons. When it comes, I need to be there to fight it. And I will need help.' Standing, he held out his hand and she shook it briefly. 'You have said nothing of your own dreams, Frey.'

'My powers have faded over the years. But, yes, I have seen the Beast. I fear you will not be strong enough to withstand it.'

He shrugged. 'I have fought many battles in my life. I'm still here.'

'But you're old now. *We* are old. Strength fails, Deacon. All things pass away . . . even legends.'

He sighed. 'You have done a wonderful job here,' he said. 'All these fragments of a lost civilisation. I would like to think that after I am dead men and women will come here and learn from the best of what the old ones left us.'

'Don't change the subject,' she admonished him.

'You want me to spare the man who killed his wife and her lover?'

'Of course – and you are still changing the subject.'

'Why should I spare him?'

'Because I ask it, Deacon,' she said, simply.

'I see. No moral arguments, no scriptural examples, no appeal to my better nature?'

She shook her head, and he smiled. 'Very well, he will live.'

'You're a strange man, Deacon. And you are still avoiding the point. Once you could have stood against the Beast. Not any longer.'

He grinned and winked at her. 'I may just surprise you yet,' he said.

'I'll grant you that. You are a surprising man.'

*

Shannow dreamed of the sea, the groaning of the ship's timbers almost human, the waves like moving mountains, beating against the hull. He awoke, and saw the lantern above his bed gently swaying on its hook. For a moment the dream and the reality seemed to blend. Then he realised he was in the cabin of a prairie wagon and he remembered the man . . . Jeremiah? . . . ancient and white-bearded, with but a single, long tooth in his upper mouth. Shannow took a deep, slow breath, and the pounding pain in his temples eased slightly. With a groan he sat up. His left forearm and his shoulder were bandaged, and he could feel the tightness of the burnt skin beneath.

A fire? He searched his memory, but could find nothing. It doesn't matter, he told himself; the memory will come back. What is important is that I know who I am.

Jon Shannow. The Jerusalem Man.

And yet . . . Even as the thought struck him he felt uneasy, as if the name was . . . what? Wrong? No. His guns were hanging from the headboard of the bed. Reaching out, he drew a pistol. It felt both familiar and yet strange in his hand. Flicking the release he broke open the pistol. Two shells had been fired.

Instantly, momentarily, he saw a man fall back from his horse, his throat erupting in a crimson spray. Then the memory vanished.

A fight with brigands? Yes, that must have been it, he thought. There was a small hand mirror on a shelf to his right. He took it down and examined the wound in his temple. The bruising was yellowing now, fading fast, and the groove in his skull was covered by a thick scab. His hair had been trimmed close to his head, but he could still see where the fire had scorched the scalp.

Fire.

Another flash of memory! Planks ablaze, and Shannow hurling his body at the timbers time and again until they gave. A man beyond with pistol raised. The shot, hitting his head like a hammer. Then that vision also faded.

He had been in a church. Why? Listening to a sermon perhaps.

Easing himself from the bed, he saw that his clothes were folded neatly on a chair by a small window, the burned coat having been cleaned and patched with black cloth. As he dressed he looked around the cabin of the wagon. The bed was narrow, but well made of polished pine, and there were two pine chairs and a small table by the window. The walls were painted green, there were elaborate carvings around the window in the shape of vine leaves, and a strange motif had been carved above the door – two overlapping triangles making a star. A bookshelf sat upon two brackets above the bed.

Buckling his gun scabbards to his hips Shannow scanned the books. There was a Bible, of course, and several fictions, but at the end was a tall, thin volume with dry, yellowed pages. Shannow pulled it clear and carried it to the window. The sun was setting and he could just make out the title in faded gold leaf. *The Chronicle of Western Costume* by John Peacock. With great care he turned the pages. Greek, Roman, Byzantine, Tudor, Stuart, Cromwellian . . . Every page showed men and women dressed in different clothing, and each page carried dates. It was fascinating. Until the coming of the planes many men had believed that only three hundred years had passed since the death of Christ. But the men and women travelling in those great ships of the sky had changed all that, consigning the previous theories to the dust of history. Shannow paused. *How do I know that?* He replaced the book, then moved to the rear of the cabin, opening the door and climbing unsteadily down the three steps to the ground.

A young woman with short blonde hair was walking towards him carrying a dish of stew. 'You should still be in bed,' she admonished him. In truth he felt weak and breathless, and sat back on the wagon steps, accepting the stew.

'Thank you, lady.' She was extraordinarily pretty, her eyes blue-green, her skin pale tan.

'Is your memory returning, Mr Shannow?'

'No,' he said, then began to eat.

'It will in time,' she assured him. The outside of the wagon was painted in shades of green and red, and from where he sat Shannow could see ten other wagons similarly decorated.

'Where are you all going?' he asked.

'Where we like,' said the girl. 'My name is Isis.' She held out her hand and Shannow took it. Her handshake was firm and strong.

'You are a good cook, Isis. The stew is very fine.'

Ignoring the compliment, she sat down beside him. 'Doctor Meredith thinks you may have a cracked skull. Do you remember nothing at all?'

'Nothing I wish to talk about,' he said. 'Tell me about you.'

'There is little to tell,' she told him. 'We are what you see, *Wanderers*. We follow the sun and the wind. In Summer we dance, in Winter we freeze. It is a good way to be.'

'It has a certain charm,' said Shannow. 'Yet is there no destination?'

She looked at him in silence for a moment, her large blue eyes holding his gaze. 'Life is a journey with only one destination, Mr Shannow. Or do you see it otherwise?'

'It doesn't pay to argue with Isis,' said Jeremiah, moving into sight. Shannow looked up into the old man's grizzled face.

'I think that is true,' he said, rising from the step. He felt unsteady and weak, and reached out to grasp the edge of the wagon. Taking a deep breath, Shannow moved into the open. Jeremiah stepped alongside, taking his arm.

'You are a tough man, Mr Shannow, but your wounds were severe.'

'Wounds heal, Jeremiah.' Shannow gazed at the mountains. The nearest were speckled with stands of timber, but further away, stretching into an infinite distance were other peaks, blue and indistinct. 'It is a beautiful land.' The sun was slowly sinking behind the western peaks, bathing them in golden light. Off to the right Shannow focused on a rearing butte, the sandstone seeming to glow from within.

'It is called Temple Mount,' said Jeremiah. 'Some say it is a holy place, where the old gods live. For myself I believe it to be a resting-place for eagles, nothing more.'

'I have not heard the name,' Shannow told him.

'The loss of memory must cause you some anguish?' said Jeremiah.

'Not tonight,' Shannow answered. 'I feel at peace. The memories you speak of hold only death and pain. They will come back all too soon, I know this. But for now I can look at the sunset with great joy.'

The two men walked towards the river-bank. 'I thank you for saving my life, Jeremiah. You are a good man. How long have you lived like this?'

'About twelve years. I was a tailor, but I longed for the freedom of the big sky. Then came the Unifier Wars, and city life became even more grotesque. So I made a wagon and journeyed out into the wilderness.'

There were ducks and geese on the river, and Shannow saw the tracks of a fox. 'How long have you nursed me?'

'Twelve days. For a while the others thought you were going to die. I told them you wouldn't; you have too many scars. You've been shot three times in your life: once over the hip, once in the upper chest and once in the back. There are also two knife wounds, one in the leg and a second in the shoulder. As I said, you are a tough man. You won't die easy.'

Shannow smiled. 'That is a comforting thought. And I remember the hip wound.' He had been riding close to the lands of the Wall, and had seen a group of raiders dragging two women into the open. He had ridden in and killed the raiders, but one of them had managed a shot that clipped Shannow's hip-bone and ripped through his lower back. He would have died but for the help of the Man-Beast, Shir-ran, who had found him in the blizzard.

'You are miles away, Mr Shannow. What are you thinking?'

'I was thinking of a lion, Jeremiah.'

They strolled back up the river-bank and towards the campfires in the circle of wagons. Shannow was weary now and asked Jeremiah to loan him some blankets so that he could sleep under the stars. 'I'll not hear of it, man. You'll stay in that bed for another day or two, then we'll see.'

Too tired to argue, Shannow pulled himself up into the wagon. Jeremiah followed him.

Fully clothed, Shannow stretched out on the narrow bed. The old man gathered some books and made to leave but Shannow called out to him, 'Why did you say I had an infamous name?'

Jeremiah turned. 'The same name as the Jerusalem Man. He rode these parts some twenty years ago – surely you have heard of him?'

Shannow closed his eyes.

Twenty years?

He heard the cabin door click shut, and lay for a while staring through the tiny window at the distant stars.

*

'How are you feeling – and do not lie to me!' said Dr Meredith. Isis smiled, but said nothing. If only, she thought, Meredith could be as assertive in his life as he was with his patients. Reaching up, she stroked his face. The young man blushed. 'I am still waiting for an answer,' he said, his voice softening.

'It is a beautiful night,' observed Isis, 'and I feel at peace.'

'That is no answer,' he scolded.

'It will have to suffice,' she said. 'I do not want to concentrate on my . . . debility. We both know where my journey will end. And there is nothing we can do to prevent it.'

Meredith sighed, his head dropping forward, a sandy lock of hair falling across his brow. Isis pushed it back. 'You are a gentle man,' she told him.

'A powerless man,' he said sadly. 'I know the name of your condition, as I know the names of the drugs that could overcome it. Hydro-cortisone, and Fludro-cortisone. I even know the amounts to be taken. What I do not know is how these steroids were constructed, or from what.'

'It doesn't matter,' she assured him. 'The sky is beautiful, and I am alive. Let's talk about something else. I want to ask you about our . . . guest.'

Meredith's face darkened. 'What about him? He is no farmer, that is for sure.'

'I know that,' she said. 'But why has his memory failed?'

Meredith shrugged. 'The blow to the head is the most likely cause, but there are many reasons for amnesia, Isis. To tell you more I would need to know the exact cause of the injury, and the events leading up to it.'

She nodded, and considered telling him all she had learned. 'First,' she said, 'tell me about the Jerusalem Man.'

He laughed, the sound harsh, his face hardening. 'I thank God that I never met him. He was a butchering savage who achieved some measure of fame vastly greater than he deserved. And this only because we are ruled by another merciless savage who reveres violence. Jon Shannow was a killer. Putting aside the ludicrous quasi-religious texts that are now being published, he was a wandering man who was drawn to violence as a fly is drawn to ox droppings. He built nothing, wrote nothing, sired nothing. He was like a wind blowing across a desert.'

'He fought the Hellborn,' said Isis, 'and destroyed the power of the Guardians.'

'Exactly,' said Meredith sharply. 'He *fought* and *destroyed*. And now he is seen as some kind of saviour – a dark angel sent by God. I wonder, sometimes, if we will ever be free of men like Shannow.'

'You perceive him as evil, then?'

Meredith stood and added several sticks to the dying fire, then returned to his seat opposite Isis. 'That is a difficult question to answer. From all I know of the man he was not a murderer; he never killed for gain. He fought and slew men he believed to be ungodly or wicked. But the point I would make Isis, is that *he* decided who was wicked, and *he* dispensed what he regarded as justice. In any civilised society such behaviour should be deemed abhorrent. It sets a precedent, you see, for other men to follow his line of argument and kill any who disagree. Once we revere a man like Shannow, we merely open the door to any other killer who wishes to follow his example. Men like the Deacon, for instance. When the Hellborn rose against us he destroyed not only their army, but their cities. He visited upon them a terrible destruction. And why? Because *he* decided they were an evil people. Thousands of ordinary Hellborn farmers and artisans were put to death. It was genocide, an entire race destroyed. That is the legacy of men like Jon Shannow. So tell me, what has this to do with our guest, as you call him?'

'I don't know,' she lied. 'He claims to be Shannow, so I wondered if it would have a bearing on his . . . What did you call it?'

'Amnesia.'

'Yes, his amnesia. You asked about the event that led to his being wounded.' Isis hesitated, preparing her story. 'He watched his friends being murdered, horribly murdered, some shot down, others burned alive. His . . . home . . . was set ablaze. He escaped and took up weapons that he had put aside many years before. He was once a warrior, but had decided this was wrong. But in his pain he tracked the killers and fought them, killing them all. Does that help?'

Meredith sat back and let out a long breath. 'Poor man,' he said. 'I fear I have misjudged him. I saw the guns and assumed him to be a brigand, or a hired man. Yes, indeed it helps, Isis.

The mind can be very delicate. I trust your talent and, taking everything you have told me as true, it means that our guest went to war against not only a vile enemy, but his own convictions. His mind has reeled from the enormity of anguish and loss, and closed itself against the memories. It is called protective amnesia.'

'Would it be wise for me to explain it to him?' she asked.

'Under no circumstances,' he told her. 'That is what is meant by protective. To tell him now could cause a complete disintegration. Let it come back slowly, in its own time. What is fascinating, however, is his choice of new identity. Why Jon Shannow? What was his occupation?'

'He was a preacher,' she said.

'That probably explains it,' said Meredith. 'A man of peace forced to become something he loathed. What better identity to choose than a man who purported to be religious, but was actually a battle-hardened killer? Look after him, Isis. He will need that special care only you can supply.'

*

'Everyone is wrong and you're right; is that what you're saying, Mother?' The young man's face was flushed with anger as he rose from the dinner table and strode to the window, pushing it open and staring out over the tilled fields. Beth McAdam took a deep breath, struggling for calm.

'I am right, Samuel. And I don't care what *everyone* says. What is being done is no less than evil.'

Samuel McAdam rounded on her then. 'Evil, is it? Evil to do the work of God? You have a strange idea of what constitutes evil. How can you argue against the word of the Lord?'

Now it was Beth who became angry, her pale blue eyes narrowing. 'You call murder the work of God? The Wolvers have never harmed anyone. And they didn't ask to be the way they are. God alone knows what caused them to be, but they have souls, Samuel. They are gentle, and they are kind.'

'They are an abomination,' shouted Samuel. 'And as the Book says, *Neither shalt thou bring an abomination into thine house, lest thou be a cursed thing like it.*'

'There is only one abomination in this house, Samuel. And I

bore it. Get out! Go back to your murdering friends. And tell them from me, if they ride on to my lands for one of their Wolver hunts I'll meet them with death and fire.'

The young man's jaw dropped. 'Have you taken leave of your senses? These are our neighbours you're talking of killing.'

Beth walked to the far wall and lifted down the long-barrelled Hellborn rifle. Then she looked at her son, seeing not the tall, wide-shouldered man he had become but the small boy who once feared the dark, and wept when thunder sounded. She sighed. He was a handsome man now, his fair hair close-cropped, his chin strong. But like the child he once had been he was still easily led, a natural follower.

'You tell them, Samuel, exactly what I said. And if there are any who doubt my word, you put them right. The first man to hunt down my friends dies.'

'You've been seduced by the Devil,' he said, then swung away and strode through the door. As Beth heard his horse galloping away into the night, a small form moved from the kitchen and stood behind her. Beth turned and forced a smile. Reaching out, she stroked the soft fur of the creature's shoulder.

'I am sorry you heard that, Pakia,' Beth sighed. 'He has always been malleable, like clay in the hands of the potter. I blame myself for that. I was too hard on him. Never let him win. Now he is like a reed that bends with every breeze.'

The little Wolver tilted her head to one side. Her face was almost human, yet fur-covered and elongated, her eyes wide and oval, the colour of mixed gold, tawny with red flecks. 'When will the Preacher come back?' she asked, her long tongue slurring the words.

'I don't know, Pakia. Maybe never. He tried so hard to be a Christian, suffering all the taunts and the jeers.' Beth moved to the table and sat down. Now it was the slender Pakia who laid her long fingers on the woman's shoulder. Beth reached up and covered the soft, warm hand. 'I loved him, you know, when he was a real man. But, I swear to God, you can't love a saint.' She shook her head. 'Wherever he is, he must be hurting. Twenty years of his life gone to dust and ashes.'

'It was not a waste,' said Pakia, 'and it is not dust and ashes.

He gave us pride, and showed us the reality of God's love. That is no small gift, Beth.'

'Maybe so,' said Beth, without conviction. 'Now you must tell your people to head deep into the mountains. I fear there will be terrible violence before the month is out. There's talk of more hunts.'

'God will protect us,' said Pakia.

'Trust in God – but keep your gun loaded,' said Beth softly.

'We do not have guns,' said Pakia.

'It's a quote, little one. It just means that . . . sometimes God requires us to look after ourselves.'

'Why do they hate us? Did not the Deacon say we were all God's children?' It was a simple question and Beth had no answer for it. Laying the gun on the table, she sat down and stared at the Wolver. No more than five feet tall, she was humanoid in shape, but her back was bent, her hands long and treble-jointed, ending in dark talons. Silver-grey fur covered her frame.

'I can't tell you why, Pakia, and I don't know why the Deacon changed his mind. The Unifiers now say you are abominations. I think they just mean "different". But, in my experience, men don't need too much of an excuse for hate. It just comes natural to them. You'd better go now. And don't come back for a time. I'll come into the mountains with some supplies in a little while, when things have cooled down a mite.'

'I wish the Preacher was here,' said Pakia.

'Amen to that. But I'd sooner have the man he once was.'

*

Nestor counted the last of the notes and slipped them into a paper packet, which he sealed and added to the pile. One hundred and forty-six lumber men and seven hauliers were to be paid today, and the Barta notes had only arrived late last night from Unity. Nestor glanced up at the armed guards outside the open doorway. 'I've finished,' he called.

Closing the account ledger, Nestor stood and straightened his back. The first of the guards, a round-shouldered former lumberjack named Leamis, stepped inside and leaned his rifle against the shack wall. Nestor placed the payment packets in a canvas sack and handed it to Leamis.

'A long night for you yongen,' said the guard. Nestor nodded. His eyes felt gritty and he yearned for sleep. 'The money was due yesterday morning,' he said wearily. 'We thought there'd been a raid.'

'They went the long way, up through the Gap,' Leamis told him. 'Thought they were being followed.'

'Were they?'

Leamis shrugged. 'Who knows? But Laton Duke is said to be in these parts, and that don't leave anyone feeling safe. Still, at least the money got here.'

Nestor moved to the doorway and pulled on his heavy topcoat. Outside the mountain air was chill, the wind picking up. There were three wagons beyond the shack, carrying trace chains to haul the timber. The drivers were standing in a group chatting, waiting for their pay. Turning to Leamis, Nestor said his farewells and strolled to the paddock where the company horses were held. Taking a bridle from the tack box, he warmed the bridle bar under his coat; pushing a chilled bridle into a horse's warm mouth was a sure way of riling the beast. Choosing a buckskin gelding he bridled and saddled him and set off down the mountain, passing several more wagons carrying loggers and lumber men to their day's labour.

The sun was bright as Nestor turned off the mountain path and headed down towards Pilgrim's Valley. Far to the north he could see the squat, ugly factory building where meat was canned for shipment to the growing cities, and a little to the east, beyond the peaks, smoke had already started to swirl up from the iron works – a dark spiral, like a distant cyclone, staining the sky.

He rode on, past the broken sign with its fading letters, welcoming travellers to *Pi. gr . . s Val . . y, pop. 827*. More than three thousand people now dwelt in the valley, and the demand for lumber for new homes meant stripping the mountainsides bare.

A low rumbling sound caused him to rein in the buckskin, and he glanced up to see the twin-winged flying machine moving ponderously through the air. It was canvas-coloured, with a heavy engine at the front and fixed wheels on wings and tail. Nestor hated it, loathed the noise and the intrusion on his thoughts. As the machine came closer the buckskin grew skittish. Nestor swiftly dismounted and took firm hold of the reins, stroking the gelding's head and blowing gently into its nostrils. The gelding began to tremble, but then the machine was past them, the sound disappearing over the valley.

Nestor remounted and headed for home.

As he rode into town Nestor tried not to look at the charred area where the little church had stood, but his eyes were drawn to it. The bodies had all been removed and workmen were busy clearing away the last of the blackened timbers. Nestor rode on, leaving his mount with the company ostler at the livery stable, and walking the last few hundred yards to his rooms above Josiah Broome's general store.

The rooms were small, a square lounge that led through to a tiny, windowless bedroom. Nestor peeled off his clothes and sat by the lounge window, too tired to sleep. Idly he picked up the book he had been studying. The cover was of cheap board, the title stamped in red: *The New Elijah* by Erskine Wright. The Crusader tests would be hard, he knew, and there was so little time to read. Rubbing his eyes, he leaned back and opened the book at the marked page and read of the travels of the Great Saint.

He fell asleep in the chair and awoke some three hours later. Yawning, he stood and rubbed his eyes. He heard sounds of shouting from the street below and moved to the window. A number of riders had drawn up and one of them was being helped from the saddle, blood seeping from a wound in his upper chest.

Dressing swiftly, Nestor ran down to the street in time to see Captain Leon Evans striding up to the group. The Crusader captain looked heroic in his grey, shield-fronted shirt and wide-brimmed black hat. He wore two guns, belted high at his waist, gun butts reversed.

'The bitch shot him!' shouted Shem Jackson, his face ugly with rage. 'What you going to do about it?'

Evans knelt by the wounded man. 'Get him to Doctor Shivers. And be damn quick about it, otherwise he'll bleed to death.' Several men lifted the groaning man and bore him along the sidewalk, past Broome's store. Everyone began to speak at once, but Leon Evans raised his hands for silence. 'Just one,' he said, pointing to Jackson. Nestor didn't like the man, who was known for his surly manner when sober and his violent streak when drunk.

Jackson hawked and spat. 'We spotted some Wolvers on the edge of my property,' he said, rubbing a grimy hand across his thin lips. 'And me and the boys here rode out after 'em. We come near the McAdam place when she ups and shoots. Jack went down, then Miller's horse was shot out from under him. What you going to do about it?'

'You were on her property?' asked Evans.

'What's that got to do with anything?' argued Jackson. 'You can't just go round shooting folks.'

'I'll talk to her,' promised Evans, 'but from now on you boys stay clear of Beth McAdam. You got that?'

'We want more than talk,' said Jackson. 'She's got to be dealt with. That's the law.'

Evans smiled, but there was no humour in his expression. 'Don't tell me the law, Shem,' he said quietly. 'I know the law. Beth McAdam gave fair warning that armed men were not to hunt on her property. She also let it be known that she would shoot any man who trespassed on her land in order to hunt Wolvers. You shouldn't have gone there. Now, as I said, I'll speak to her.'

'Yeah, you speak to her,' hissed Jackson. 'But I tell you this, woman or no woman, no one shoots at me and gets away with it.'

Evans ignored him. 'Get on back to your homes,' he said and the men moved away, but Nestor could see they were heading for the Mother of Pearl drinking-house. He stepped forward. The captain saw him and his dark eyes narrowed.

'I hope you weren't with those men,' said Evans.

'No, sir. I was sleeping up in my room. I just heard the commotion. I didn't think Mrs McAdam would shoot anybody.'

'She's one tough lady, Nestor. She was one of the first into Pilgrim's Valley; she fought the Lizard men, and since then there have been two brigand raids out on the farm. Five were killed in a gun battle there some ten years back.'

Nestor chuckled. 'She was certainly tough in school. I remember that.'

'So do I,' said Evans. 'How's the studying going?'

'Every time I try to read I fall asleep,' admitted Nestor.

'It must be done, Nestor. A man cannot follow God's path unless he studies God's word.'

'I get confused, sir. The Bible is so full of killing and revenging – hard to know what's right.'

'That why the Lord sends prophets like Daniel Cade and Jon Shannow. You must study their words. Then the ways that are hidden will become known to you. And don't concern yourself about the violence, Nestor. All life is violence. There is the violence of disease, the violence of hunger and poverty. Even birth is violent. A man must understand these things. Nothing good ever comes easy.'

Nestor was still confused, but he didn't want to look foolish before his hero. 'Yes, sir,' he said.

Evans smiled and patted the young man's shoulder. 'The Deacon is sending one of his Apostles to Pilgrim's Valley at the end of the month. Come and listen.'

'I will, sir. What will you do about Mrs McAdam?'

'She's under a lot of strain, what with the Preacher gone, and the burning. I think I'll just stop by and talk with her.'

'Samuel says he thinks the devil has got into her,' said Nestor. 'He told me she threw him out of the house and called him an abomination.'

'He's a weak man. Often happens to youngsters who have strong parents. But I hope he isn't right. Time will tell.'

'Is it true that Laton Duke and his men are near by?' asked Nestor.

'His gang were shot to pieces down near Pernum. So I doubt it,' said the Crusader. 'They tried to rob a Barta coach, heading for the mines.'

'Is he dead then?'

Evans laughed. 'Don't sound disappointed, boy. He's a brigand.'

Nestor reddened. 'Oh, I'm not disappointed, sir,' he lied. 'It's just that he's . . . you know . . . famous. And kind of romantic.'

Evans shook his head. 'I never found anything romantic about a thief. He's a man who hasn't the heart or the strength for work, and steals from other, better men. Set your sights on heroes a little bigger than Laton Duke, Nestor.'

'Yes, sir,' promised the youngster.

Chapter Two

It is often asked, How can the rights of the individual be balanced evenly with the needs of a society? Consider the farmer, my brothers. When he plants the seeds for his harvest of grain he knows that the crows will descend and eat of them. Too many birds and there will be no harvest. So the farmer will reach for his gun. This does not mean that he hates the crows, nor that the crows are evil.

The Wisdom of the Deacon
Chapter iv

* * *

Beth swung the axe. It was an ungainly stroke, but the power of her swing hammered the nine-pound blade deep into the wood, splitting it cleanly. Woodlice crawled from the bark and she brushed them away before lifting the severed chunks of firewood and adding them to the winter store.

Sweat ran freely on her face. Wiping it away with her sleeve, she rested the axe against the wood-store wall, then hefted her long rifle and walked to the well. Looking back at the axe and the tree round she used as a base, Beth pictured the Preacher standing there and the fluid poetry of his movements. She sighed.

The Preacher . . .

Even she had come to regard Shannow as the man of God in Pilgrim's Valley, almost forgetting the man's lethal past. But then he had changed. By God he had changed! The lion to the lamb. And it shamed Beth that she had found the change not to her liking.

Her back was aching and she longed for a rest. 'Never leave a job half done,' she chided herself. Lifting the copper ladle from the bucket she drank the cool water, then returned to the axe. The sound of a horse moving across the dry-baked ground made her curse. She had left the rifle by the well! Dropping the axe she turned and walked swiftly back across the open ground, not even looking at the horseman. Reaching the rifle, she leaned down. 'You won't need that, Beth, darlin',' said a familiar voice.

Clem Steiner lifted his leg over the saddle pommel and jumped to the ground. A wide grin showed on Beth's face and she stepped forward with arms outstretched. 'You're looking good, Clem,' she said, drawing him into a hug. Taking hold of his broad shoulders, she gently pushed him back from her and stared into his craggy features.

The eyes were a sparkling blue and the grin still made him look boyish, despite the grey at his temples and the weather-beaten lines around his eyes and mouth. His coat of black cloth seemed to have picked up little dust from his ride, and he wore a brocaded waistcoat of shining red above a polished black gunbelt.

Beth hugged him again. 'You're a welcome sight for old eyes,' she said, feeling an unaccustomed swelling in her throat.

'Old? By God, Beth, you're still the best-looking woman I ever saw!'

'Still the flatterer,' she grunted, trying to disguise the pleasure she felt.

'Would anyone dare lie to you, Beth?' His smile faded. 'I came as soon as I heard. Is there any news?'

She shook her head. 'See to your horse, Clem. I'll prepare some food for you.' Gathering her rifle, Beth walked to the house, noticing for the first time in days how untidy it was; how the dust had been allowed to settle on the timbered floor. Suddenly angry, she forgot the food and fetched the mop and bucket from the kitchen. 'It's a mess,' she said, as Clem entered. He grinned at her.

'It looks lived-in,' he agreed, removing his gunbelt and pulling up a chair at the table.

Beth chuckled and laid aside the mop. 'A man shouldn't surprise a woman this way – especially after all these years. Time has been good to you, Clem. You filled out some. Suits you.'

'I've lived the good life,' he told her, but he looked away as he spoke, glancing at the window set in the grey stone of the wall.

Clem smiled. 'Strong-built place, Beth. I saw the rifle slits at the upper windows, and the reinforced shutters on the ground floor. Like a goddamn fortress. Only the old houses now have rifle ports. Guess people think the world's getting safer.'

'Only the fools, Clem.' She told him about the raid on the church, and the bloody aftermath when the Preacher strapped on his guns. Clem listened in silence. When she had finished he stood and walked to the kitchen, pouring himself a mug of water. Here also there was a heavy door, a strong bar beside it. The window was narrow, the shutters reinforced by iron strips.

'It's been hard in Pernum,' he said. 'Most of us thought that with the War over we'd get back to farming and ordinary life. Didn't work out that way. I guess it was stupid to think it would, after all the killing in the north. And the war that wiped out the Hellborn. You had the Oathmen here yet?' She shook her head. Crossing the room, he stood outlined in the open doorway. 'It's not good, Beth. You have to swear your faith in front of three witnesses. And if you don't . . . well, at best, you lose your land.'

'I take it you swore the Oath?'

Returning to the table, he sat opposite her. 'Never been asked. But I guess I would. It's only words. So tell me, any sign of him since the killings?'

She shook her head. 'He's not dead, Clem. I know that.'

'And he's wearing guns again.'

Beth nodded. 'Killed six of the raiders – then vanished.'

'It will be a hell of a shock to the Righteous if they find out who he is. You know there's a statue to him in Pernum? Not a good likeness, especially with the brass halo around his head.'

'Don't joke about it, Clem. He tried to ignore it, and I think he was wrong. He never said or did one tenth of the things they claim. And as for being the new John the Baptist . . . well, it seems like blasphemy to me. You were there, Clem, when the Sword of God descended. You saw the machines from the sky. You *know* the truth.'

'You're wrong, Beth. I don't know anything. If the Deacon claims he comes direct from God, who am I to argue? Certainly seems that God's been with him, though. Won the Unifier War, didn't he? And when Batik died and the Hellborn invaded again he saw them wiped out. Scores of thousands dead. And the Crusaders have mostly cleaned out the brigands and the Carns. Took me six days to ride here, Beth, and I didn't need the gun. They got schools, hospitals, and no one starves. Ain't all bad.'

'There's lots here that would agree with you, Clem.'

'But you don't?'

'I've no argument with schools and the like,' she said, rising from the table and returning with bread, cheese and a section of smoked ham. 'But this talk of pagans and disbelievers needing killing, and the butchery of the Wolvers – it's wrong, Clem. Plain wrong.'

'What can I do?'

'Find him, Clem. Bring him home.'

'You don't want much, do you? That's a big country, Beth. There's deserts, and mountains that go on for ever.'

'Will you do it?'

'Can I eat first?'

*

Jeremiah enjoyed the wounded man's company, but there was much about Shannow that concerned him and he confided his worries to Dr Meredith. 'He is a very self-contained man, but I think he remembers far less than he admits. There seems to be a great gulf in his memory.'

'I have been trying to recall everything I read about protective amnesia,' Meredith told him. 'The trauma he suffered was so great that his conscious mind reels from it, blanking out vast areas. Give him time.'

Jeremiah smiled. 'Time is what we have, my friend.'

Meredith nodded and leaned back in his chair, staring up at the darkening sky. A gentle wind was drifting down across the mountains, and from here he could smell the cottonwood trees by the river, and the scent of grass from the hillsides. 'What are you thinking?' asked Jeremiah.

'It is beautiful here. It makes the evil of the cities seem far away, and somehow inconsequential.'

Jeremiah sighed. 'Evil is never inconsequential, doctor.'

'You know what I mean,' chided Meredith. Jeremiah nodded, and the two men sat for a while in companionable silence. The day's journey had been a good one, the wagons moving over the plains and halting in the shadows of a jagged mountain range. A little to the north was a slender waterfall and the *Wanderers* had camped beside the river that ran from it. The women and children were roaming a stand of trees on the mountainside, gathering dead wood for the evening fires, while most of the men had ridden off in search of meat. Shannow was resting in Jeremiah's wagon.

Isis came into sight, bearing a bundle of dry sticks which she let fall at Jeremiah's feet. 'It wouldn't do you any harm to work a little,' she said. Both men noticed her tired eyes, and the faintest touch of purple on the cheeks below them.

'Age has its privileges,' he told her, forcing a smile.

'Laziness more like,' she told him. She swung to face the sandy-haired young doctor. 'And what is your excuse?'

Meredith reddened and rose swiftly. 'I am sorry. I . . . wasn't thinking. What do you want me to do?'

'You could help Clara with the gathering. You could have cleaned and prepared the rabbits. You could be out hunting with the other men. Dear God, Meredith, you are a useless article.' Spinning on her heel she stalked away, back towards the wood.

'She is working too hard,' said Jeremiah.

'She's a fighter, Jeremiah,' answered Meredith sadly. 'But she's right. I spend too much time lost in thoughts, dreaming if you like.'

'Some men are dreamers,' said Jeremiah. 'It's no bad thing. Go and help Clara. She's a little too heavily pregnant to be carrying firewood.'

'Yes . . . yes, you're right,' Meredith agreed.

Alone now, Jeremiah made a circle of stone and carefully laid a fire. He did not hear Shannow approach, and glanced up only when he heard the creak of wood as the man sat in Meredith's chair. 'You're looking stronger,' said the old man. 'How do you feel?'

'I am healing,' said Shannow.

'And your memory?'

'Is there a town near here?'

'Why do you ask?'

'As we were travelling today I saw smoke in the distance.'

'I saw it too,' said Jeremiah, 'but with luck we'll be far away by tomorrow night.'

'With luck?'

'*Wanderers* are not viewed with great friendliness in these troubled times.'

'Why?'

'That's a hard question, Mr Shannow. Perhaps the man who is tied to a particular piece of land envies us our freedom. Perhaps we are viewed as a threat to the solidity of their existence. In short, I don't know why. You might just as well ask why men like to kill one another, or find hatred so easy and love so difficult.'

'It is probably territorial,' said Shannow. 'When men put down roots they look around them and assume that everything they can see is now theirs – the deer, the trees, the mountains. You come along and kill the deer and they see it as theft.'

'That too,' agreed Jeremiah. 'But you do not share that view, Mr Shannow?'

'I never put down roots.'

'You are a curious man, sir. You are knowledgeable, courteous, and yet you have the look of the warrior. I can see it in you. I think you are a . . . deadly man, Mr Shannow.'

Shannow nodded slowly and his deep blue eyes held Jeremiah's gaze. 'You have nothing to fear from me, old man. I am not a war-maker. I do not steal, and I do not lie.'

'Did you fight in the War, Mr Shannow?'

'I do not believe that I did.'

'Most men of your age fought in the Unifying War.'

'Tell me of it.'

Before the old man could begin, Isis came running into view. 'Riders!' she said. 'And they're armed.' Jeremiah rose and walked between the wagons. Isis moved alongside him, and several of the other women and children gathered round. Dr Meredith, his arms full of firewood, stood nervously beside a pregnant woman and her two young daughters. Jeremiah shaded his eyes against the setting sun and counted the horsemen. There were fifteen, and all carried rifles. In the lead was a slender young man, with shoulder-length white hair. The riders cantered up to the wagons and then drew rein. The white-haired man leaned forward on to the pommel of his saddle.

'Who are you?' he asked, his voice edged with contempt.

'I am Jeremiah, sir. These are my people.'

The man looked at the painted wagons and said something in a low voice to the rider on his right. 'Are you people of the Book?' asked White-hair, switching his gaze back to Jeremiah.

'Of course,' the old man answered.

'You have Oath papers?' The man's voice was soft, almost sibilant.

'We have never been asked to give Oaths, sir. We are *Wanderers* and are rarely in towns long enough to be questioned about our faith.'

'I am questioning it,' said the man. 'And I do not like your tone, *Mover*. I am Aaron Crane, the Oath Taker for the settlement of Purity. Do you know why I was given this office?' Jeremiah shook his head. 'Because I have the Gift of Discernment. I can smell a pagan at fifty paces. And there is no place in God's land for such people. They are a stain upon the earth, a cancer upon the flesh of the planet, and an abomination in the eyes of God. Recite for me now Psalm 22.'

Jeremiah took a deep breath. 'I am not a scholar, sir. My Bible is in my wagon – I shall fetch it.'

'You are a pagan!' screamed Crane, 'and your wagon shall burn!' Swinging in his saddle, he gestured to the riders. 'Make torches from their camp-fires. Burn the wagons.' The men dismounted and started foward, Crane leading them.

Jeremiah stepped into their path. 'Please sir, do not do . . .' A rider grabbed the old man, hurling him aside. Jeremiah fell heavily, but struggled to his feet as Isis ran at the man who had struck him, lashing out with her fist. The rider parried the blow easily and pushed her away.

And Jeremiah watched in helpless despair as the men converged on the fire.

*

Aaron Crane was exultant as he strode towards the fire. This was the work he had been born for, making the land holy and fit for the people of the Book. These *Movers* were trash of the worst kind, with no understanding of the demands of the Lord. The men were lazy and shiftless, the women no better than common whores. He glanced at the blonde woman who had struck at Leach. Her clothes were threadbare and her breasts jutted against the woollen shirt she wore. Worse than a whore, he decided, feeling his anger rise. He pictured the wagon aflame, the pagans pleading for mercy. But there should be no mercy for such as these, he resolved. Let them plead before the throne of the Almighty. Yes, they would die, he decided. Not the children, of course; he was not a savage.

Leach made the first torch and handed it to Aaron Crane. 'By this act,' shouted Crane, 'may the name of the Lord be glorified!'

'Amen!' said the men grouped about him. Crane moved towards the first red wagon . . . and stopped. A tall man had stepped into view; he said nothing, but merely stood watching Crane. The white-haired Oath Taker studied the man, noting two things instantly. The first was that the newcomer's eyes were looking directly into his own, and secondly he was armed. Crane glanced at the two pistols in their scabbards at the man's hips. Acutely aware that his men were waiting, he was suddenly at a loss. The newcomer had made no hostile move, but he was standing directly before the wagon. In order to burn it, Crane would have to push past him.

'Who are you?' asked Crane, buying time to think.

'*They have gaped upon me with their mouths, as a ravening and a roaring lion,*' quoted the man, his voice deep and low.

Crane was shocked. The quote was from the psalm he had asked the old *Mover* to recite, but the words seemed charged now with hidden meaning.

'Stand aside,' said Crane, 'and do not seek to interfere with the Lord's work.'

'You have two choices, live or die,' said the tall man, his voice still low, no trace of anger in his words.

Crane felt a sick sense of dread in his belly. The man would kill him, Crane knew that with an ice-cold certainty. If he tried to fire the wagon, the man would draw one of those pistols and shoot him. His throat was dry. A burning cinder fell from the torch, scorching the back of his hand, but Crane did not move . . . could not move. Behind him were fifteen armed men, but they might as well have been a hundred miles away, he knew, for all the good they could do him. Sweat dripped into his eyes.

'What's happening, Aaron?' called Leach.

Crane dropped the torch and backed away, his hands trembling. The tall man was walking towards him now, and the Oath Taker felt panic surging within him.

Turning, he ran to his horse, scrambling into the saddle. Hauling on the reins, he kicked the beast into a gallop for almost half a mile. Then he drew up and dismounted.

Kneeling on the hard-packed earth, he tasted bile in his mouth and began to vomit.

*

Shannow's head was pounding as he walked towards the group of men. The Oath Taker was riding away, but his soldiers remained, confused and uncertain.

'Your leader is gone,' said Shannow. 'Do you have other business here?' The thick-set man who had passed the burning torch to Crane was tense, and Shannow could see his anger growing. But Jeremiah stepped forward.

'You must all be thirsty after your long ride,' he said. 'Isis, fetch these men some water. Clara, bring the mugs from my wagon. Ah, my friends,' he said, 'in these troubled times such misunderstandings are so common. We are all people of the Book, and does it not tell us to love our neighbours, and to do good to those who hate us?'

Isis, her face flushed and angry, brought forward a copper jug, while the pregnant Clara moved to the group, passing tin mugs to the riders.

The thick-set man waved Isis away and stared hard at Shannow.

'What did you say to the Oath Taker?' he snarled.

'Ask him,' said Shannow.

'Damn right I will,' said the man. He swung on his comrades who were all drinking. 'Let's go!' he shouted.

As they rode away Shannow returned to the fire and slumped

down into Dr Meredith's chair. Jeremiah and the doctor approached him.

'I thank you, my friend,' said Jeremiah. 'I fear they would have killed us all.'

'It is not wise to stay here the night,' Shannow told him. 'They will return.'

*

'There are those among us,' said the Apostle Saul, the sunlight glinting on his long, golden hair, 'who shed tears for the thousands who fell fighting against us in the Great War. And I tell you, brothers, I am one of those. For those misguided souls gave their very lives in the cause of Darkness, while believing they were fighting for the Light.

'But as the good Lord told us, narrow is the path and few who will find it. But that Great War is over, my brothers. It was won for the Glory of God and his son, Jesus Christ. And it was won by you, and by me, and by the multitudes of believers who stood firm against the Satanic deeds of our enemies, both pagan and Hellborn.'

A great cheer went up, and Nestor Garrity found himself wishing he could have been one of those soldiers of Christ in the Great Wars. But he was only a child then, attending the lower school and living in fear of the formidable Beth McAdam. All around him the men and women of Pilgrim's Valley had flocked to the Long Meadow to hear the words of the Apostle. Some of the other people present could still remember the sleek white and silver flying machine that had passed over Pilgrim's Valley twenty years before, bringing the Deacon and his Apostles to the people. Nestor wished he could have seen it in the air. His father had taken him to Unity eight years ago, to the great Cathedral at the city centre. There, raised on a plinth of shining steel, was the flying machine. Nestor would never forget that moment.

'It may be over, my friends, but another battle awaits us,' said the Apostle, his words jerking Nestor back to the present. 'The forces of Satan are overthrown – but still there is peril in the land. For, as it is written, the Devil is the Great Deceiver, the son of the Morning Star. Do not be misled, my brothers and sisters. The Devil is not an ugly beast. He is handsome, and charming, and his words drip like honey. And many will be deceived by him. He is the voice of discontent whispering in your ears at night. He is the man – or woman – who speaks against the word of our Deacon, and his holy quest to bring this tortured world back to the Lord.

'For was it not written, *by their works shall ye judge them*? Then I ask you this, brethren: who brought the truth to this benighted world? Tell me!' Raising his arms, he stared down from the podium at the crowd.

'The Deacon!' they yelled.

'And who descended from the Heavens with the word of God?'

'THE DEACON!' Caught up in the hypnotic thrill of the moment, Nestor stood, his right fist punching the air with each answer. The voices of the crowd rolled like thunder and Nestor found it hard to see the Apostle through the sea of waving arms. But he could hear him.

'And who did God send through the vaults of Time?'

'THE DEACON!'

The Apostle Saul waited until the roar died down, then spread his hands for silence. 'My friends, by his work have you judged him. He has built hospitals and schools and great cities, and once more the knowledge of our ancestors is being used by the children of God. We have machines that will plough the land, and sail the seas, and fly through the air. We have medicines and trained doctors and nurses. And this tortured land is growing again, at one with the Lord. And He is with us, through His Servant in Unity.

'But everywhere sin waits to strike us down. That is why the Oath Takers move through the land. They are the gardeners of this new Eden, seeking out the weeds and the plants that do not bloom. No God-fearing family should fear the Oath Takers. Only those seduced by Satan should know the terror of discovery. Just as only brigands and lawbreakers should fear our new Crusaders – our fine young soldiers, like your own Captain Leon Evans.'

Nestor cheered at the top of his voice, but it was lost within an ocean of sound.

As it died down the Apostle Saul raised his voice one last time. 'My friends, Pilgrim's Valley was the first settlement over which we flew when the Lord brought us from the sky. And for that reason the Oath Taker's role shall be a special one. The Deacon has asked me to fulfil that role, and I shall do so, with your blessing. Now let us pray . . .'

As the prayers were concluded, and the last hymn sung, Nestor made his way back to the main street of Pilgrim's Valley, moving slowly within the crowd. Most of the people were returning to their homes but a select few, Nestor among them, had been invited to a reception at the Traveller's Rest, and the formal welcome for the new Oath Taker. Nestor felt especially privileged to be asked to attend, even though his role was only that of a waiter. History was being made here, and the young man could hardly believe that one of the Nine Apostles was actually going to live – if only for a month or two – among the people of Pilgrim's Valley. It was a great honour.

Josiah Broome, who now owned the Traveller's Rest, was waiting at the back of the inn as Nestor arrived. Broome was in his late sixties now, a slender, bird-boned man, balding and near-sighted. Despite his tendency towards pompous speech Broome was a man with a heart, and Nestor liked him.

'Is that you, young Garrity?' asked Broome, leaning in close.

'Yes, sir.'

'Good boy. There is a clean white shirt in the upper back room. And a new black necktie. Put them on and help Wallace prepare the tables.'

Nestor said that he would, and moved on through the rear of the inn, climbing the stairs to the staff quarters. Wallace Nash was pulling on his white shirt as Nestor entered the back room.

'Hi, Nes. What a day eh?' said the red-headed youngster. Two years younger than Nestor, he was an inch taller, standing almost six foot three, and as thin as a stick.

'You look like a strong wind could blow you down, Wallace.'

The red-head grinned. 'I'd outrun it afore it could.'

Nestor chuckled. Wallace Nash was the fastest runner he had ever seen. Last year on Resurrection Day, when he was just fifteen, Wallace had raced three times against Edric Scayse's prize stallion, Rimfire, winning both short sprints and losing only on a longer race. It had been a fine day. Nestor remembered it well, for it was his first time drunk – an experience he had pledged to himself he would never repeat.

'You want to carry the drinks or the eats?' Wallace asked.

'Doesn't matter,' said Nestor, pulling off his faded red shirt and lifting a clean white one from the dresser drawer.

'You take the drinks then,' said Wallace. 'My hands ain't too steady today. Lord, who would have believed that an Apostle would come to our town?'

Nestor pulled on his shirt and tucked it into his black trousers. For a minute or so he fumbled with the necktie, then he moved to the mirror to see if the knot was in place. 'You think he'll perform any miracles?' asked Wallace.

'Like what?'

'Well, I guess he could try to raise the Preacher from the dead.' The red-head laughed.

'That ain't funny, Wallace. The Preacher was a good man.'

'That's not so, Nes. He spoke out against the Deacon during one of his sermons. Can you believe that? Right there in a church. It's a wonder God didn't strike him dead there and then.'

'As I recall hearing it, he just said he thought it weren't necessary to have Oath Takers. That's all.'

'Are you saying the Apostle Saul ain't necessary?' asked Wallace.

Nestor was about to make a light-hearted remark, but then he saw the shining glint in Wallace's eyes.

'Of course I'm not. Wallace. He's a great man,' he said carefully. 'Now come on, we'd better get to work.'

*

The evening was long, and Nestor found his back aching as he stood against the wall holding the brass tray in his hands. Few were drinking now, and the Apostle Saul was sitting by the fire with Captain Leon Evans and Daniel Cade. The old prophet had been late arriving; most of the welcoming party had long since gone to their homes before the old man made his entrance. The Apostle had welcomed him warmly, but it seemed to Nestor that Daniel Cade was ill at ease.

'It is a privilege to meet you at last,' said Saul. 'Obviously I have read of your exploits against the Hellborn in the First War. Vile times, calling for men of iron – much as now. I am sorry to see that you have such difficulty with your movements. You should come to Unity; our Hospital is performing miracles daily, thanks to the discoveries of our medical teams.'

'The Daniel Stones, you mean,' said Cade.

'You are well informed, sir. Yes, the fragments have been most helpful. We are still seeking larger Stones.'

'Blood and death is all they'll bring,' Cade said. 'Just like before.'

'In the hands of the Godly all things are pure,' said Saul.

Excited as he had been earlier in the evening Nestor was now tired, and becoming bored. He was due at the lumber site soon after dawn to collate the orders for timber, and issue working instructions to the men at the sawmill. Uncle Joseph was not an easy man to serve, and one yawn from Nestor would earn an hour's lecture at the end of the day.

'You knew the Jersualem Man, I understand,' remarked Saul to Cade. Instantly Nestor's weariness was forgotten.

'I knew him,' grunted the old man. 'And I never heard him say a word of prophecy. I don't reckon he'd be pleased to read what's said of him now.'

'He was a holy man,' said Saul, showing no sign of irritation, 'and the words he spoke have been carefully gathered from sources all over the land. Men who knew him. Men who heard him. I regard it as a personal tragedy that I never met him.'

Cade nodded solemnly. 'Well, I did, Saul. He was a lonely man, heartsick and bitter, seeking a city he knew could not exist. As to his prophesying . . . as I said, I never heard it. But it's true to say that he brought you and the Deacon into this world, when he sent the Sword of God thundering through the Gates of Time. We all know that's true.'

'The ways of the Lord are sometimes mystifying,' said Saul, with a tight smile. 'The world we left was a cesspool, owned by the Devil. The world we found had the potential for Eden – if only men would return to God. And by His grace we have conquered. Tell me, sir, why you have refused all invitations to travel to Unity, and be honoured for your work in the Lord's name?'

'I don't need honours,' Cade told him. 'I lived most of my life, after the Hellborn War, in Rivervale. Had me a good woman and raised two tall sons. Both died in your Wars. Lisa was buried last Autumn and I came here to wait for death. Honours? What are they worth?'

Saul shrugged. 'A worthy point, from a worthy man, Mr Cade. Now tell me, do you think Pilgrim's Valley is a God-fearing community?'

'There are good people here, Saul. Some better than others. I don't think you can judge a man merely because three of his friends say he's a believer. We got farmers on the outskirts, newcomers who wouldn't be able to raise three men who know them that well. It doesn't make 'em pagans.'

'You also had a church that welcomed Wolvers,' Saul pointed out, 'And a preacher who offered them the word of God. That was an obscenity, Mr Cade. And it took outsiders to put an end to it. That does not reflect well on the community.'

'What have you got against Wolvers?' Cade asked.

Saul's eyes narrowed. 'They are not true creations, Mr Cade. In the world I came from, animals were being genetically engineered to resemble people. This was done for medical reasons; it was possible then for a man with a diseased heart, or lungs, to have them removed and replaced. That was an abomination, Mr Cade. Animals have no souls, not in the strictest sense of eternal life. These mutated creatures are like plague germs, reminding us all of the dangers and disasters of the past. We must not repeat the errors that led God to destroy the old world. Not ever. We are on the verge of a new Eden, Mr Cade. Nothing must be allowed to halt our progress.'

'And we're going to find this new Eden by hounding people from their homes, by killing Wolvers and anyone who doesn't agree with us?'

'Not the Deacon, nor any of his Apostles take any joy in killing, Mr Cade. But you know your Bible. The Lord God does not tolerate evil in the midst of his people.'

Cade reached for his sticks and slowly, painfully, pushed himself to his feet. 'And the next war, Saul? Who is that going to be with?'

'The ungodly wherever we find them,' answered Saul.

'It's late, and I'm tired,' said Cade. 'I'll bid you good night.'

'May God be with you,' said Saul, rising.

Cade did not reply as, leaning heavily on his sticks, he made his way to the door. Nestor stifled a yawn and was about to ask if he could be excused from his duties when Saul spoke to Captain Evans.

'A dangerous man, Captain. I fear we may have to deal with him.'

Nestor blinked in surprise. At that moment Leon Evans looked up and saw him and the captain grinned. 'Go on home, Nestor,' he said, 'otherwise you're going to keel over like a felled tree.'

Nestor thanked him, bowed to the Apostle and walked out into the night where the old prophet was leaning against his buggy, unable to mount the steps. Nestor moved alongside him and took his arm. With an effort, he half-lifted Cade to the seat. 'Thank you, boy,' grunted Cade, his face red from the exertion.

'It was a pleasure, sir.'

'Beware the words of brass and iron, boy,' whispered the prophet. He flicked the reins and Nestor watched as the buggy trundled off into the night.

*

Alone now, Shannow waited among the rocks, his horse tethered some fifty paces to the north in a small stand of trees. Glancing to the east, he could make out the last of the wagons as they travelled further into the mountains. The sky was lightening. Dawn was close.

Shannow settled down with his back against a rock and stared to the west. Maybe he had been wrong. Maybe the white-haired Oath Taker had decided against a punitive raid. He hoped so. The night was cool and he breathed deeply of the crisp mountain air. Glad to be alone, he let his mind wander.

Twenty years had passed since his name was feared among the ungodly. Twenty years! Where have I been, he wondered. How did I live? Idly he began to review what he remembered of his life, the gunfights and the battles, the towns and settlements.

Yes, I remember Allion, he thought, and saw again the day Daniel Cade led his brigands into the town. In the blaze of gunfire that had followed several of Cade's men had been shot from their saddles, while Cade himself took a bullet in the knee. Daniel Cade. Brother Daniel. For some reason that Shannow could never fathom, God had chosen Daniel to lead the war against the Hellborn.

But what then? Hazy pictures drifted into his mind, then vanished like mist in the breeze. A blonde woman, tall and strong, and a young fighter, lightning-fast with a pistol . . . Cram? Glen?

'No,' said Shannow aloud. 'Clem. Clem Steiner.'

It will all come back, he promised himself. Just give it time.

Then came the sound of horses moving slowly through the darkness, the creak of leather saddles, the soft clopping of hooves on the dry plain. Shannow drew his pistols and eased himself further down into the rocks as the horses came closer. Removing his wide-brimmed hat, he risked a glance to the west; he could see them now, but not well enough to count them.

I don't want to kill again.

Aiming high, he loosed a shot. Some of the horses reared in fright, several others stampeded. Shannow saw one man thrown from the saddle, and another jumped clear of his bucking mount. Several shots were fired in his direction, but the bullets struck the rocks and screamed off into the night.

Dropping to his belly, Shannow peered round the rocks. The riders had dismounted and were now advancing on his position. From the east he heard the distant sound of gunfire.

The wagons! In that instant he knew there were two groups, and the blood-letting had already begun. Anger surged within him.

Swiftly he pushed himself to his feet and stepped out from the rocks. A man reared up . . . Shannow shot him through the chest. Another moved to his right and again his pistol boomed.

He walked in amongst the men, guns blazing. Stunned by this sudden attack, the raiders broke and ran. A man to Shannow's right groaned as the Jerusalem Man strode past him. A bullet whipped by Shannow's face, so close he felt its passing, the sound ringing in his ears like an angry bee. Twisting, he triggered both pistols and a rifleman was punched from his feet.

Two horses were standing close by. Shannow strode to the

first and vaulted to the saddle. A man reared up from the undergrowth. Shannow shot him twice; then kicking the animal into a run, he headed east, reloading his pistols as the horse thundered across the plain. Anger was strong upon him now, a deep, boiling rage that threatened to engulf him. He did nothing to quell it.

Always it was the same, the evil strong preying on the weak, violence and death, lust and destruction. When will it end, he wondered? Dear God, when will it end?

The full moon bathed the land in silver, and in the distance the red of fire could be seen as one of the wagons blazed. The firing was sporadic now, but at least it suggested that some of the *Wanderers* were still fighting.

Closer still he came, and saw five men kneeling behind a group of boulders; one of them had long white hair. A rifleman rose up, aiming at the wagons. Shannow loosed a shot which missed the man but ricocheted from the boulder, making the rifleman jerk back. The white-haired Oath Taker swung round, saw Shannow and began to run. Ignoring him, Shannow trained his guns on the riflemen.

'Put down your weapons,' he ordered them. 'Do it now – or die!'

Three of the four remaining men did exactly as they were told, then raised their hands, but the last – the thick-set man he had spoken to earlier – suddenly swung his rifle to bear. Shannow put a bullet into his brain.

'Jeremiah! It's me, Shannow,' shouted the Jerusalem Man. 'Can you hear me?'

'He's been shot,' came the answering call. 'We've wounded here –three dead, two badly hit.'

Gesturing to the captured men, Shannow ordered them towards the wagons. Once inside he gazed around. The pregnant Clara was dead, half her head blown away. A burly man named Chalmers was lying beside her. By Jeremiah's wagon lay the body of a child in a faded blue dress: one of Clara's two daughters. Shannow dismounted and moved to where Dr Meredith was kneeling beside the wounded Jeremiah. The old man had taken two shots, one to the upper chest and a second to the thigh. His face was grey in the moonlight.

'I'll live,' the old man whispered.

The wagons had been formed into a rough circle, and several of the horses were down. Isis and two of the men were battling to put out a fire in the last wagon. Guns in hand, Shannow strode back to the captured men, who were standing together at the centre of the camp.

'*The bellows are burned, the land is consumed of the fire; the founder melteth in vain, for the wicked are not plucked away.*' His guns levelled and he eased back the hammers.

'Shannow, no!' screamed Jeremiah. 'Let them be! Christ, man, there's been enough killing already.'

Shannow took a deep, slow breath. 'Help put out the fire,' he ordered the men. They obeyed him instantly, and without another word he walked to his horse and stepped into the saddle.

'Where are you going?' called Dr Meredith.

Shannow did not answer.

*

Aaron Crane and the survivors of the raid galloped into Purity and drew up before the long stone meeting-hall. Crane, dust-covered and dishevelled, dismounted and ran inside. The hall was crowded, the prayer meeting under way. On the dais Padlock Wheeler was reaching the midpoint in his sermon, concerning the path of the righteous. He stopped as he saw Crane and inwardly he groaned, but it was not wise to incur the wrath of the Oath Taker. The black-bearded minister fell silent for a moment, then forced a smile.

'You seem distraught, brother,' he said. Heads turned then, among them Captain Seth Wheeler and the twelve men of Purity's Crusaders. Crane drew himself up and ran a slender hand through his long white hair.

'The forces of the Devil have been turned against us,' he said. 'The Lord's riders have been cut down.'

There was a gasp from the congregation and several of the women began to shout out questions concerning the fate of their husbands, brothers, or sons.

'Silence!' thundered Padlock Wheeler. 'Let the Oath Taker speak.'

'As you all know,' said Crane, 'we came upon a band of pagan *Wanderers*. With them was a demonic force: I recognised the power of Satan instantly. We tried, in vain, to overcome it. Many are dead. A few of us escaped, through the intervention of the Lord. We must have more men! I demand that the Crusaders ride out after these devils!'

Padlock Wheeler glanced down at his brother Seth. The captain rose from his seat. He was a tall, slim man with a long face and a dour expression. 'Let the women go to their homes,' he said. 'We'll discuss what's to be done.'

'Where's my boy?' screamed a woman, rushing at Crane. 'Where is Lemuel?'

'I fear he perished,' Crane told her, 'but he died in the Lord's work.' The woman's hand snaked out to slash across Crane's cheek. Two other women grabbed her, hauling her back.

'Stop this!' thundered Padlock Wheeler. 'This is a house of God!' The commotion died instantly. Slowly the women filed from the hall, the men gathering around Crane.

Seth Wheeler moved forward. 'Tell us of this demon,' he ordered Crane.

'It is in the guise of a man, but it is Satan-inspired. He is a killer. A terrible killer!' Crane shivered. 'He cast a spell upon me that took all the power I had to overcome.'

'How many are dead?' asked the Crusader captain.

'I don't know. We advanced on two fronts. The killer was waiting in the east and shot down four men: Lassiter, Pope, Carter and Lowris. Then he rode west and slew . . . everyone but me. I managed to escape.'

'You ran?'

'What else could I do?'

Seth Wheeler glanced at the men gathered in the hall. There were some twenty in all, plus his twelve Crusaders. 'How many *Wanderers* were there?'

'Eleven wagons,' Crane told him. 'Perhaps thirty people. They must be destroyed. Utterly destroyed!'

Still on the dais, Padlock Wheeler saw the door at the back of the hall open, and a tall man step inside. Dressed in a dust-stained black coat, patched on the left arm, he wore two long guns.

'Where are the lawmakers of this community?' he said – his voice, though not loud, cutting through the conversation at the centre of the hall.

Crane saw him and screamed. 'It's him! It's the Devil!' Backing away, the white-haired Oath Taker ducked down behind a line of benches.

'This is a house of the Lord,' said Padlock Wheeler. 'What do you want here?'

'Justice,' answered the man. 'You are sheltering a murderer, a killer of women and children.'

'He tells it differently,' said Padlock. 'He claims you are demon-possessed.'

The newcomer shook his head. 'Twenty miles from here they are burying a woman named Clara. She was pregnant; half her head was shot away. They will bury one of her daughters beside her. The man Crane rode up to the wagons yesterday and demanded to hear Psalm 22. I gave him to understand that I knew it. As indeed I do. But he is an evil man, and was determined upon murder. So tell me this: How will you judge him?'

Padlock looked down at where Crane was cowering. The minister felt exultant. All along he had believed Crane to be a dangerous man, and this was the opportunity to bring him down. He would ask Seth for an inquiry, and he had no doubt that the Oath Taker would be shown to be a lawbreaker. But just as he was about to speak he saw Crane draw a pistol from his belt and cock it.

Within a heartbeat all was chaos and confusion. 'You lie!' screamed Crane, rearing up and pointing his pistol. The shot splintered the wood of the door by the stranger's head. The gathered men dived for cover, but the stranger calmly drew one of his pistols and fired once. Crane's head exploded.

The Oath Taker's body stood for a moment, his black coat drenched in blood and brain. Then it crumpled to the floor.

'I am the Jerusalem Man,' said the stranger, 'and I do not lie.'

Sheathing his pistol, he left the hall.

One by one the watching men rose and moved back to view the body. Padlock Wheeler, his legs unsteady, climbed down from the dais. His brother Seth stood by the corpse and shook his head.

'What happens now?' asked Padlock.

'We'll send a message to Unity,' said Seth. 'They'll have to send another Oath Taker.'

Padlock took his brother's arm and led him away from the other men. 'He claimed to be Jon Shannow.'

'I heard him. That was blasphemy! I'll take some men to the *Wanderers* tomorrow. We'll speak to them, find out what really happened.'

'Crane was a wretch! I'll shed no tears for him. Why not let them go their way?'

Seth shook his head. 'He claimed to be the Jerusalem Man. He took the saint's name in vain. Everyone heard it; he's got to answer for that.'

'I don't want to see anyone else die for the sake of Crane's evil. Not even a blasphemer.'

Seth smiled thinly. 'I am a Crusader, Pad. What do you expect me to do?'

'Walk warily, brother. You saw him shoot. He was under fire, but he calmly aimed and blew Crane's soul to Hell. And if what the wretch said was true – and I don't doubt it was – he shot down a number of other armed men.'

'I've no choice, Pad. I'll try to take him alive.'

Chapter Three

In a small section of the garden a tiny weed spoke to the blooms that grew there. 'Why,' he asked, 'does the gardener seek to kill me? Do I not have a right to life? Are my leaves not green, as yours are? Is it too much to ask that I be allowed to grow and see the sun?' The blooms pondered on this, and decided to ask the gardener to spare the weed. He did so. Day by day the weed grew, stronger and stronger, taller and taller, its leaves covering the other plants, its roots spreading. One by one the flowers died, until only a rose was left. It gazed up at the enormous weed and asked: 'Why do you seek to kill me? Do I not have a right to life? Are my leaves not green, as yours? Is it too much to ask that I be allowed to grow and see the sun?'

'Yes, it is too much to ask,' said the weed.

The Wisdom of the Deacon
Chapter vii

* * *

They had buried Clara and her daughter by the time Shannow returned to the wagons. Jeremiah was in bed in his wagon, his chest bandaged, his face grey with sorrow and pain. Shannow climbed in to sit beside the old man.

'You killed him?' asked Jeremiah.

'I did. I would have had it otherwise, but he fired upon me.'

'That will not end it, Mr Shannow. Though I do not blame you. You did not inspire the evil. But you must go.'

'They will come again and you will need me.'

'No. I spoke to the men you captured before I let them go. Crane was the instigator.' Jeremiah sighed. 'There will always be men like Crane. Thankfully there will also always be men like Meredith, and men like you. It is a balance, Mr Shannow. God's balance, if you will.'

Shannow nodded. 'Evil will always thrive if men do not oppose it.'

'Evil thrives anyway. Greed, desire, jealousy. We all carry the seeds of evil. Some are stronger than others and can resist it, but men like Crane will feed the seed.' Jeremiah leaned back against his pillow, his eyes resting on Shannow's lean face. 'You are not evil, my boy. Go with God!'

'I am sorry, old man,' said Shannow, rising.

Back in the open he saw Isis coming towards him, carrying a bundle. 'I gathered some ammunition from the dead, and there is a little food here,' she said. He thanked her and turned away. 'Wait!' She handed him a small pouch. 'There are twelve Bartas here. You will need money.'

Jeremiah heard the creak of saddle leather as Shannow mounted, then the steady clopping of hooves as he headed away from the wagons. The pain from his wound was strong, but the old man flowed with it. He felt sick, and weaker than sin.

Isis brought him a herbal tisane, which settled his stomach. 'I am happier with him gone,' she said, 'though I liked him.'

They sat in companionable silence for a while, then Meredith joined them. 'Riders coming,' he said. 'Look like Crusaders.'

'Make them welcome, and bring the leader here,' said Jeremiah. Within minutes a tall, round-shouldered man with a long, dour face climbed into the wagon. 'Welcome to my home,' said Jeremiah. The man nodded, removed his wide-brimmed grey hat and sat alongside the bed.

'I'm Captain Seth Wheeler,' said the newcomer. 'I understand you have a man with you who calls himself Jon Shannow?'

'Will you not ask, sir, why there are fresh-dug graves outside, and why I am lying here with a bullet in my chest?'

'I know why,' muttered Wheeler, looking away. 'But that was not my doing, Meneer. Nor do I condone it. But there have been deaths on both sides, and the man who instigated them is among the dead.'

'Then why hunt Jon Shannow?'

'He is a blasphemer and a heretic. The Jerusalem Man – of blessed memory – left this earth twenty years ago, taken up by God like Elijah before him in a chariot of fire.'

'If God can lift him, which of course he can,' said Jeremiah carefully, 'then he can also bring him back.'

'I'll not argue that point with you, Meneer. What I will say is this, if the good Lord did choose to bring back the Jerusalem Man, I don't think he'd arrive with singed hair and a patched coat. However, enough of this – which direction did he take?'

'I cannot help you sir. I was in my wagon when he rode away. You will have to ask one of my people.'

Wheeler rose and moved to the door, then he turned. 'I have already said that I do not condone what happened here,' he said softly. 'But know this, *Mover*, I share Crane's view about the likes of you. You are a stain upon God's land. As the Deacon says, *There is no place for the scavenger among us. Only those who build the cities of the Lord are welcome*. Be gone from the lands of Purity by tomorrow night.'

*

Shannow rode towards the high country, angling north. The horse was a bay gelding and strong, but it was tired after the exertions of the night and breathing heavily. Shannow dismounted and led the horse into the trees, seeking a cave or a sheltered spot in the lee of the wind. He was cold, and his spirits were low.

The loss of memory was an irritation, but this he could bear. Something else was nagging at him from deep within the now shuttered recesses of his mind. He had killed men tonight, but that was nothing new for the Jerusalem Man. I did not seek the battle, he told himself. They rode out in search of blood, and they found it. And it was their own. Such is the price of violence. Yet the killings hung heavily upon him.

Shannow stumbled, his strength deserting him. His wounds were too recent for this kind of climb, he knew, but he pushed on. The trees were thicker now and he saw a cleft in the rockface to his left. It will have to do, he thought. Taking a deep breath, he walked on. As he neared the cleft he saw the flickering reflection of a fire on the rock-face, just inside the cleft.

'Hello, the camp!' he called. It was not wise in the wilderness to walk uninvited into a campsite. With the fear of brigands everywhere, a sudden appearance could lead to a volley of shots from frightened travellers.

'Come on in,' came a voice, which echoed eerily up through

the cleft. Shannow pushed his coat back over the butt of his right-hand pistol and, leading the horse with his left hand, approached the cleft. It was narrow only at the entrance, and widened into a pear-shaped cave within. An old man with a waist-length white beard was sitting before the fire, above which a hunk of meat had been spitted. At the back of the cave a mule had been hobbled. Shannow led his horse to the rear and looped the reins over the beast's head, trailing them to the ground. Then he joined the white-bearded man.

'Welcome to my fire,' said the man, his voice deep. He extended his hand. 'You can call me Jake.'

'Jon Shannow.'

'You're welcome, Mr Shannow. I kept looking at this meat and thinking, there's too much here for you, Jake. Now the Lord has supplied me with a dinner guest. Come far?'

Shannow shook his head. A great weariness settled on him and he leaned back against a rock and stretched out his legs. Jake filled a mug with a steaming brew and passed it to him. 'Here, drink this, boy. It's a great reviver and there's a ton of sugar in it.'

Shannow sipped the brew. It was rich and bitter-sweet. 'My thanks, Jake. This is good. Tell me, do I know you?'

'Could be, son, the world's a mighty small place. I've been here and there: Allion, Rivervale, Pilgrim's Valley, the Plague Lands. You name it, I've seen it.'

'Rivervale . . . yes, I seem to remember . . .' He saw a beautiful woman and a young boy. The memory faded like a dream upon wakening, but a name slipped through the shutters. 'Donna!' he said.

'You all right, boy?'

'Do you know me, Jake?'

'I've seen you. It's a fearsome name you carry. You sure it's yours?'

'I'm sure.'

'You seem a mite young – if you don't mind me saying so. What are you . . . thirty-five . . . six?'

'I think I'll sleep now,' said Shannow, stretching himself out beside the fire.

His dreams were fractured and anxious. He was wounded

and the Lion-man Shir-ran was tending to him. A creature with scaled skin ran into the cave, a jagged knife held in its hand. Shannow's guns thundered and the creature fell back, becoming a child with open, horrified eyes. 'Oh God, no! Not again!' cried Shannow.

His eyes opened and he saw Jake was kneeling beside him. 'Wake up, boy. It's just a dream.' Shannow groaned and pushed himself to a sitting position. The fire had died down, and the old man handed him a plate on which strips of cold roast meat had been carved. 'Eat a little. You'll feel better.'

Shannow took the plate and began to eat. Jake took a pot from the dying fire and filled a tin mug. Then he added sticks to the coals. New flames flickered as Shannow shivered.

'It will soon warm up.' Jake rose and walked to the rear of the cave, returning with a blanket which he wrapped around Shannow's shoulders.

'You were in that gun-battle last night,' he said. 'I can smell the powder on your coat. Was it a good fight?'

'Are there any good fights?' responded Shannow.

'It's a good fight when evil perishes,' said Jake.

'Evil does not usually die alone,' said Shannow. 'They killed a young woman and her daughter.'

'Sad times,' agreed Jake.

The meat was good and Shannow felt his strength returning. Unbuckling his gun-belt he laid it alongside him, then stretched his tired muscles. Jake was right. The heat from the fire was beginning to reflect back from the walls.

'What are you doing in the wilderness, Jake?'

'I like the solitude – generally speaking. And it is a good place to talk to God, don't you think? It's clean and open, and the wind carries your words to the Heavens. I take it you were with the *Movers*.'

'Yes. Good people.'

'That's as maybe, son, but they don't plant and they don't build,' said Jake.

'Neither does the sparrow,' responded Shannow.

'A nice Biblical reference, Mr Shannow, and I do enjoy a debate. But you are wrong. The sparrow eats many seeds, then he flies away. Not all the seeds are digested and he drops them in other places. All the great forests of the world were probably started by birds' droppings.'

Shannow smiled. 'Perhaps the *Wanderers* are like the birds. Perhaps they spread the seeds of knowledge.'

'That would make them really dangerous,' said Jake, his eyes glinting in the firelight. 'There's all kinds of knowledge, Mr Shannow. Knew a man once who could identify every poisonous plant there was. Wanted to write a book on it. That's dangerous knowledge – you agree?'

'People reading the book would be able to tell what plants not to eat,' said Shannow.

'Aye, and people wishing to learn of poisons would know what plants to feed their enemies.'

'Did he write the book?'

'No. He died in the Unity War. Left a widow and five children. Did you fight in the War?'

'No. At least I don't think so.'

Jake looked at him closely.

'You having trouble remembering things?'

'Some things,' said Shannow.

'Like what?'

'Like the last twenty years.'

'I saw the head wound. Happens sometimes. So, what will you do?'

'I'll wait. The Lord will show me my past when he's good and ready.'

'Anything I can do?'

'Tell me about the Deacon, and his War.'

The old man chuckled. 'That's a tall order, boy, for one night around the fire.' Leaning back, he stretched out his legs. 'Getting too old to enjoy sleeping on rock,' he said. 'Well then, where do we start? The Deacon.' He sniffed loudly and thought for a moment. 'If you are who you claim to be, Mr Shannow, then it was you who brought the Deacon into this world. He and his brethren were in a plane that took to the skies on the Day of Armageddon. It was then trapped, held by the power that also snared the Sword of God. You released them when you sent the Sword into the past to destroy Atlantis.'*

* As told in *The Last Guardian*.

Shannow closed his eyes. The memory was hazy, but he could see the Sword hovering in the sky, the Gateway of Time opening. And something else . . . the face of a beautiful black woman. No name would come to him, but he heard her voice: '*It is a missile, Shannow. A terrible weapon of death and destruction.*' Try as he would, Shannow could not pluck any more from his past. 'Go on,' he told Jake.

'The Deacon and his men landed near Rivervale. It was like the Second Coming. Nobody in this world knew about the decay and corruption that plagued the old cities, killers walking the streets, lust and depravity everywhere. The world, he said, was godless. The sins of Sodom and Gomorrah were multiplied a hundredfold in that old world. Before long the Deacon was a revered figure. His power grew. He said the new world must never be allowed to make the mistakes of the old; that the Bible contained the seeds of man's future prosperity. There were those who argued against him, saying that his plans were an affront to their views of personal freedom and liberty. That led to the Great War, and the Second Hellborn War. But the Deacon won both. Now he rules in Unity, and there is talk that he plans to build the new Jerusalem.' Jake lapsed into silence, and added more fuel to the fire. 'Ain't much else I can tell you, boy.'

'And the Jerusalem Man?' asked Shannow.

Jake grinned. 'Well, you, if indeed that is you, were John the Baptist reborn, or maybe Elijah, or both. You were the herald to announce the new coming of God's word to the world. Until, that is, you were taken by God in a fiery chariot to a new world that needed your talents. You still remember nothing?'

'Nothing about a fiery chariot,' said Shannow grimly. 'All I know is who I am. How I came to be here, or where I have been for the last twenty years, is a mystery to me. But I sense I was living under another name, and I did not use my pistols. Maybe I was a farmer. I don't know. I will find out, Jake. Fragments keep coming back to me. One day they will form a whole.'

'Have you told anybody who you are?'

Shannow nodded. 'I killed a man in the settlement of Purity. I told them then.'

'They'll come hunting you. You are a holy figure now, a

legend. It'll be said that you've taken the Jerusalem Man's name in vain. Personally I think they'd be wise to leave you alone. But that's not the way it will be. In fact there could even be a terrible irony in all this.'

'In what way?'

'The Deacon has a group of men close to him. One of them – Saul – has formed a group of riders called the Jerusalem Riders. They travel the land as judges and law-bringers. They are skilled with weapons and chosen from the very best – or perhaps it is the worst – of the Crusaders. Deadly men, Mr Shannow. Perhaps they will be sent after you.' Jake chuckled and shook his head.

'You seem to find the situation amusing,' said Shannon. 'Is it because you do not believe me?'

'On the contrary, it is amusing simply because I *do* believe you.'

*

Nestor Garrity took careful aim. The pistol bucked in his hand, and the rock he had set atop the boulder shivered as the bullet sliced the air above it. The sound echoed in the still mountain air and a hawk, surprised by the sudden noise, took off from a tree to Nestor's left. Sheepishly Nestor looked around. But there was no one close and he took aim again. This time he smashed fragments of stone from the boulder, low and to the right of the rock. He cursed softly, then angrily loosed the final four shots.

The rock was untouched. Nestor sat down, broke open the pistol and fed six more shells into the chambers. It had cost him eighteen Bartas, almost a month's wages at the logging camp, and Mr Bartholomew had assured him it was a fine, straight shooting-piece, created by the old Hellborn factory near Babylon.

'Is it as good as the Hellborn used to make?' Nestor had asked him.

The old man shrugged. 'I guess,' he said.

Nestor felt like taking it back and demanding the return of his money.

Sheathing the pistol, he opened the pack of sandwiches he had purchased from Mrs Broome and took out his Bible. Then he heard the horse approaching and turned to see a rider coming over the crest of the hill. He was a tall, handsome man, dark hair streaked with silver, and he was wearing a black coat and a brocaded red waistcoat. At his hip was a nickel-plated pistol in a polished leather scabbard.

The rider drew up a little way from the youth and dismounted. 'You'd be Nestor Garrity?' he asked.

'Yes, sir.'

'Clem Steiner. Mrs McAdam suggested I speak to you.'

'In connection with what, sir?'

'The Preacher. She has asked me to find him.'

'I fear he's dead, Mr Steiner. I looked mighty hard. I seen blood and wolf tracks.'

Steiner grinned. 'You don't know the man as well as I do, Nestor. His kind don't die so easy.' Nestor saw Steiner switch his gaze to the bullet-scarred boulder. 'Been practising?'

'Yes, sir. But I fear I am not skilled with the pistol. Safest place in these mountains is that rock yonder.'

In one smooth motion Steiner's gun seemed to leap to his hand. At the first shot the rock leapt several feet into the air, the second saw it smashed to powder. Steiner spun the pistol back into its scabbard. 'Forgive me, Nestor, I never could resist showing off. It's a bad vice. Now about the Preacher, were there any other tracks close by?'

Nestor was stunned by the display and fought to gather his thoughts. 'No, sir. Not of a man afoot, anyway.'

'Any tracks at all?'

'No . . . well, yes. There was wheel marks to the east. Big ones. I think they were *Wanderers*. The tracks were recent though, sharp-edged.'

'Which way were they heading?' Steiner asked.

'East.'

'Any towns out there?'

'There's a new settlement called Purity. It's run by Padlock Wheeler. He used to be one of the Deacon's generals. I ain't . . . haven't been there.'

Steiner walked to the boulder, selected another small rock and placed it on the top. Strolling back to Nestor, he said. 'Let's see how you shoot.'

Nestor took a long, deep breath, and wished he had the nerve to refuse. Drawing the pistol, he eased back the hammer and sighted along the barrel. 'Hold it,' said Steiner. 'You're tilting your head and sighting with your left eye.'

'The right is not as strong,' admitted Nestor.

'Put the gun away.' Nestor eased the hammer forward and holstered the pistol. 'All right, now point your finger at my saddle.'

'What?'

'Just point at my saddle. Do it!' Nestor reddened, but he lifted his right hand and pointed. 'Now point at the tree on your right. Good.'

'I never had much trouble pointing, Mr Steiner. It's the shooting that lets me down.'

Steiner chuckled. 'No, Nestor. It's the lack of pointing that lets you down. Now this time draw the pistol, cock it and point it at the rock. Don't aim. Just point and fire.'

Nestor knew what would happen and wished with all his heart that he had chosen to stay home today. Obediently he drew the long-barrelled pistol and pointed at the rock, firing almost instantly, desperate to get the embarrassing moment over and done with.

The rock exploded.

'Wow!' shouted Nestor. 'By damn I did it!'

'Yes,' agreed Steiner. 'That's one rock that will never threaten innocent folks again.'

Steiner moved to his horse and Nestor realised the man was about to leave. 'Wait!' he called. 'Will you join me in some lunch? I got sandwiches and some honey biscuits. It ain't much, but you're welcome.'

As they ate Nestor talked of his ambition to become a Crusader, and maybe even a Jerusalem Rider one day. Steiner listened politely, no hint of mockery in his expression. Nestor talked for longer than he ever had to one person at one time, and eventually stumbled to a halt. 'Gee, I'm sorry, Mr Steiner. I think I near bored you to death. It's just, nobody ever listened so good before.'

'I like ambition, son, it's a good thing. A man wants

something bad enough, and he'll generally get it if he works at it, and he's unlucky enough.'

'Unlucky?' queried Nestor.

Steiner nodded. 'In most cases the dream is better than the reality. Pity the man who fulfils all his dreams, Nestor.'

'Did you do that, sir?'

'Certainly did.' Steiner's face looked suddenly solemn and Nestor switched the subject.

'You ever been a Crusader, Mr Steiner?' he asked. 'I never seen anybody shoot that good.'

'No, not a Crusader.'

'Not . . . a brigand?'

Steiner laughed aloud. 'I could have been, son, but I wasn't. I was lucky. I had me a curious ambition, though. I wanted to be the man who killed the Jerusalem Man.'

Nestor's mouth dropped open. 'That's a terrible thing to say.'

'It is now. But back then he was just a man with a big, big name. I was working for Edric Scayse and he warned me to change that ambition. I said, "There's no way he can beat me, Mr Scayse." You know what he said? He told me, "He wouldn't beat you, Clem, he'd kill you." He was right. They broke the mould when they made Shannow. Deadliest man I ever knew.'

'You knew him? Lord, you're a lucky man, Mr Steiner.'

'Luck certainly has played a part in my life,' said Steiner. 'Now I'd best be on my way.'

'You're going to look for the Preacher?'

'I'll find him, son,' said Clem, easing himself to his feet. In that moment Nestor knew what he wanted to do; knew it with a certainty he had never before experienced.

'Could I come with you, Mr Steiner? I mean, if you wouldn't mind.'

'You've got a job here, boy, and a settled life. This could take some time.'

'I don't care. Since my folks died I've been working for my uncle. But I think I could learn more from you, Mr Steiner, than ever I could from him. And I'm sick of counting out Barta coin, and docking wages for lost hours. I'm tired of counting timber and writing out orders. Will you let me ride with you?'

'I'll be riding into town to buy supplies, Nestor. You'll need a blanket roll and a heavy coat. A rifle would be handy.'

'Yes, sir,' said Nestor happily. 'I've got a rifle. I'll get the other gear from Mr Broome.'

'How old are you, son?'

'Seventeen, sir.'

Clem Steiner smiled. 'I can just remember what it was like to be seventeen. Let's go.'

*

Josiah Broome pushed out his bare feet towards the hearth, trying to concentrate on the warmth of the flames, while ignoring the constant stream of words coming from the kitchen. It was not easy: Else Broome was not a woman to be ignored. Broome stared into the fire, his thoughts gloomy. He had helped build Pilgrim's Valley back in the old days, and then had been one of the leaders when the town was rebuilt after the invasion from Atlantis. Josiah Broome had survived the assault by the scaled Lizard warriors, known as Daggers, and had tried in his own small way to make Pilgrim's Valley a decent place for the families that settled there.

He abhorred men of violence, the hard-drinking, brawling warriors who once peopled this land. And he loathed men like Jon Shannow, whose idea of justice was to slaughter any who crossed their path. Now, in these enlightened days, Jon Shannow was considered a saint, a holy man of God. Else's voice droned on, and he noticed a lilt at the end of the sentence. 'I am sorry, my dear, I didn't catch that,' he said.

Else Broome eased her vast bulk through the doorway. 'I asked if you agreed that we should invite the Apostle Saul to the barbecue?'

'Yes, dear. Whatever you think best.'

'I was only saying to the Widow Scayse the other day . . .' The words rolled on as she retreated to the kitchen and Broome blanked them from his mind.

Jon Shannow, the saint.

The Preacher had laughed at it. Broome remembered their last evening together in the small vestry behind the church.

*

'It is not important, Josiah,' said Jon Cade. 'What I used to be is irrelevant now. What is important is that God's word should not be corrupted. The Book speaks of love as well as judgement. And I'll not be persuaded that the Wolvers are denied that love.'

'I don't disagree with you, Preacher. In fact of all men I hold you in the highest regard. You turned your back on the ways of violence, and have shown great courage during these last years. You are an inspiration to me. But the people of Pilgrim's Valley are being seduced by the Deacon's new teachings. And I fear for you, and the church. Could you not minister to the Wolvers outside town? Would that not allow the anger to die down?'

'I expect that it would,' agreed Cade. 'But to do so would be like admitting to the ignorant and the prejudiced that they have a right to deny my congregation a service within my church. I cannot allow that. Why is it so hard for them to see the truth? The Wolvers did not seek to be the way they are, even the Deacon admits to that. And there is no more evil in them than in any race.'

'I don't know what the Deacon thinks. But I have read the words of his Apostle Saul, and he claims they are not of God, and are therefore of the Devil. A pure land, he says, needs pure people.'

Cade nodded. 'I don't disagree with that, and there is much good in what the Deacon has said in the past. I respect the man. He came from a world gone mad, depravity and lust, corruption and disease of the body and the spirit. And he seeks to make this world a better place. But no one knows better than I the dangers of living by iron rules.'

'Come, come, my friend, are you not still living by those rules? This is but a building. If God – if there is a God – does care about the Wolvers, he will care about them in the mountains just as well as here. I fear there will be violence.'

'Then we shall turn the other cheek, Josiah. A soft answer turneth away wrath. Have you seen Beth lately?'

'She came in to the store with Bull Kovac and two of her riders. She looked well, Jon. It's a shame the two of you couldn't make a go of it – you were so well suited.'

Cade smiled ruefully. 'She was in love with the Jerusalem Man, not with the Preacher. It was hard for her – especially when the brigands raided, and I did nothing to stop them. She told me I was no longer a man.'

'*That must have hurt.*'

Cade nodded. '*I've known worse pain, Josiah. A long time ago I killed a child. I was being attacked, there were armed men all around me. I killed four of them, then heard a noise behind me and I swung and fired. It was a boy, out playing. He haunts me still. What might he have been? A surgeon? A minister? A loving father and husband? But, yes, losing Beth was a deep blow.*'

'*You must have been tempted to take up your pistols during the raid.*'

'*Not once. I sometimes dream that I am riding again, pistols by my side. Then I wake in a cold sweat.*' Cade stood and moved to a chest at the far end of the room. Flipping it open, he lifted clear a gun-belt. '*The weapons of the Thundermaker.*' Broome stood and walked across to stand beside the Preacher.

'*They look as they always did.*'

'*Aye. Sometimes at night I sit here and clean them. It helps to remind me of what once I was. And what, God willing, I will never become again.*'

*

'You're not listening to a word I say,' said Else Broome, stalking back into the living-room.

'What's that, my love?'

'What is the matter with you? I was asking if you would stand Oath for that McAdam woman.'

'Of course. Beth is an old friend.'

'Pah! She's a trouble-maker, and we'd all be better off if she were sent from the Valley.'

'In which way does she cause trouble, my dear?'

'Are you soft in the head?' she stormed. 'She shot at men hunting Wolvers. She speaks against the Deacon, and even her own son says she's been seduced by Satan. The woman is a disgrace.'

'She's a good Christian woman, Else. Just like you.'

'I take that as an insult,' snapped Else Broome, her multiple chins quivering. 'You have a store to run, and I don't think people will take it kindly if you are seen to support a woman of her kind. You'll lose business to Ezra Feard, you'll see. And I don't see why it should be you who gives Oath for her. Let her find someone else who doesn't mind being a laughing-stock.'

Broome turned his attention back to the fire.

'And another thing . . .' began Else Broome.

But her husband was not listening. He was thinking of five dead raiders on the road, and the tortured spirit of the man who had killed them.

Chapter Four

The world does not need more charismatic men. It does not need more intellectual men. No, and it does not need more caring men. What it cries out for is more holy men.
The Wisdom of the Deacon
Chapter ii

* * *

Seth Wheeler pulled the blanket up tight around his ears and settled his head against his saddle. The night air was cold and it had been two years since he had slept out in the open. The blanket was thin; either that or I'm getting old, he thought. No, it's the damn blanket. Sitting up, Seth held the blanket close to him as he moved to the fire. It was burning low now, just a tiny flicker of flame above the coals. There were four sticks left, and these would normally have been left for the morning. Casting a nervous glance at his four sleeping comrades, he added the wood to the fire. It blazed instantly to life and Seth shivered as the warmth touched him. God, he'd almost forgotten just how good it felt to be warm.

There were no clouds in the night sky, and a ground frost was sprinkling the grass with specks of silvered white. The wind gusted, scattering ash across Seth's boots. He stared down at the sticks. Why did they have to burn so damned fast?

This high in the mountains there was little dead wood, and his men had gathered what there was close by. Seth had two choices: return to his cold bed-roll, or gather more wood. Rising with a softly whispered curse, he stepped across one sleeping body and walked to the thin line of trees.

It had been a long ride in search of the killer. They had found his tracks soon enough, and followed him up into the mountains. But the pursuers had lost his trail twice after that and four fruitless days had followed. Then they'd picked up the wrong trail and come upon an old man and a mule. Strange old coot, thought Seth. Odd eyes, looked as if they could see right through you.

'We're hunting a man,' Seth had told him. 'We're Crusaders from Purity.'

'I know that,' the oldster had replied. 'Spent the night in a cave yonder with the man you're looking for.'

'Which way was he heading?'

'North. Into the wild lands.'

'We'll find him,' said Seth.

'Hope you don't, son. Strikes me you're good men. Shame to see such men die.'

'Is he a friend of yours, this man?' asked Seth. The old man shook his head.

'He only met me last night. But I'd say I like him. You best be careful, Crusader. Men like him don't offer second chances.' The old man had grinned at them and, without another word, had ridden off.

Short on food, and getting colder by the day, the Crusaders had finally found the killer's trail. Tomorrow they would have him.

Seth gathered an armful of sticks and a thick, broken branch and started back towards the fire. Something cold touched the back of his neck, and an even colder voice spoke. 'You are making a mistake that will lead you to your death.'

The Crusader swallowed hard. His legs felt shaky and the gun-barrel felt icy against his skin. But Seth was no coward, and he gathered himself.

'You are a blasphemer and a killer,' he said.

'Take your men back to Purity,' said the cold voice. 'I do not wish to kill any of you. But if you are on my trail come daylight, none of you will ever see your families again. Had I so chosen, I could have walked into your camp tonight and slain you all. Now go.'

The gun-barrel withdrew. Seth blinked back the sweat that was dripping into his eyes. Strangely he did not feel cold at all. He took a step, then another. Then he dropped the wood, threw aside the blanket, drew his pistol and swivelled.

There was no one there.

For a minute or more he remained where he was. The cold

came back into his bones. Sheathing the pistol, he gathered the fallen sticks and returned to the fire, banking it up until the flames were too hot to sit alongside. Returning to his bed-roll he thought of Elizabeth, and his sons Josh and Pad.

One of his men awoke with a cry. 'Hell's bells, Seth, you trying to set us all ablaze?' The edge of the man's blanket was smouldering and he beat at it with his palm.

The commotion woke the others.

'We're going home,' said Seth. 'We've no food and the wild lands are just beyond the ridge.'

'Are you all right, Seth?' asked Sam Drew, his lieutenant.

'Aye. But this man is too much for us, boys. Take my word on it. We'll send word to the Apostle Saul in Pilgrim's Valley. He can order out the Jerusalem Riders. Let them deal with him.'

'This isn't like you, Seth. What changed your mind?'

'It's a funny thing, Sam. A little while ago I was cold and hated it. Now it feels good. It tells me I'm alive. I'd kind of like to stay that way.'

*

It was near midnight and the main street of Pilgrim's Valley was almost deserted as the five riders made their way to the house behind the Crusader compound. The first of the men, tall and broad-shouldered and wearing a full-length, double-shouldered topcoat, dismounted and turned to the others. 'Get 'em stabled, then get some rest,' he said.

Removing his wide-brimmed leather hat, he climbed the three steps to the porchway of the house and tapped on the front door. It was opened by a young woman in a long white gown. She curtseyed.

'God's greetings, brother,' she said. 'Would you be Jacob Moon?'

'Aye. Where is the Apostle?'

'Would you follow me, sir?'

The dark-haired woman moved along the hallway, then opened a door on the right. Moon stepped past her and into the study beyond where the Apostle Saul was sitting in a wide leather chair, reading a large, gold-edged Bible. Putting it aside, he rose and smiled at the woman. 'That will be all, Ruth.

You may go.' Ruth curtseyed once more and pulled shut the door. 'God's greetings, Jacob.'

'A pox on this religious bullshit,' said Moon. 'It's bad enough having to mouth it when people are around. Damned if I'll take it in private!'

Saul chuckled. 'You are too impatient, Jacob. It is a bad failing in a man who seeks to rule.'

'I don't want to rule,' said the tall man. 'I just want to be rich. The old fool is dead – just like you ordered.'

Saul's smile faded and his eyes took on a dangerous glint. 'I chose you because you have talent. But understand this, Jacob, if you become a danger to me I will have you cut down. And nothing is more dangerous than a loose tongue.'

The tall man seemed unfazed by the threat. Tossing his hat to the floor, he removed his topcoat and draped it over the back of a chair. Unbuckling his gun-belt, he sat down and stretched out his legs. 'You have a drink here? It was a thirsty ride.'

Saul poured a glass of red wine and handed it to the man. Moon downed it in a single swallow, holding out the glass for a refill. 'Tell me of it!' Saul demanded.

Moon shrugged. 'It was as you said. He rode alone to his cabin in the mountains and I waited the twenty days, watching him all the time. Then a rider came from Unity. He saw the old man, then rode away. The following morning I shot the old man through the back of the head. Buried the body in the foothills. No one will find it.'

'You're sure it was him?'

'I guess it might have been the angel Gabriel,' sneered Moon. 'Course it was him. You can rest easy, Saul, the Deacon is dead. Question is: Who do you need dead now?'

Saul returned to his seat. 'No one *today*, Jacob. But there will be trouble, I'm sure of that. There is some fine land to the west, with good suggestions of silver – perhaps gold. The man who owns it is called Ishmael Kovac. There is also a farm which I believe has significant oil deposits; that is owned by a woman named Beth McAdam. Both will be refused the Oath; then we shall acquire the land legally.'

'Then why call us down here? Sounds like it's all sewn up.'

Saul sipped his wine. Then, 'There is a complication, Jacob.'

'There usually is.'

'The burning of the church. There was a Preacher who survived. He hunted down five of my men and killed them. Yesterday I had a long talk with a local man who knows the Preacher – has known him for twenty years.'

'Cut to the chase, Saul. I don't need the gift wrapping.'

'I think you do. The Preacher came here twenty years ago, just after the Blessed Coming of our sainted Deacon. He was a young man, maybe twenty. But this local man told me an interesting story. He said the Preacher was in fact much older, and that he'd regained his youth through a Daniel Stone in a tower.'

'Sounds like he's either drunk or an idiot,' said Moon, draining his wine and reaching for the bottle.

'He's neither. And I know the Daniel Stone was in that tower, because the Deacon and I went there fifteen years ago. We saw what was left of it, its power gone. It was huge, Jacob, big enough to hold planes and ships in stasis for hundreds of years. Now the man who took the last of its power, in order to become young again, was Jon Shannow.'

Moon froze. 'You've got to be joking!'

'Not at all, Jacob. The Jerusalem Man. The one and only. The new Elijah.'

'And you think this Preacher was Jon Shannow? Why the Hell would he stay in this lousy backwater if he was the Jerusalem Man? He could have been rich beyond his dreams.'

'I don't know his reasons, but I believe it to be the truth. He rode out and slew our comrades, and now he is somewhere out there.' Saul waved his hand towards the window.

Moon glanced up. 'Jesus, man, but couldn't he put the fox in the hen-house? He could finish the myth of the Deacon right enough, prove him to be a pompous old windbag and a liar to boot.'

'I don't think so,' said Saul. 'The Jerusalem Man is too much a part of myth now. People would expect to see the halo. No, that is only one part of the problem. Firstly, we don't want the Deacon discredited –since I am his heir. And I want the kingdom united behind me as it is behind him. But secondly, Beth McAdam was once the man's mistress. There could well be residual good feeling between them. When she is dispossessed, or killed, I don't want the likes of Jon Shannon hunting me.'

'What about this man who knows the truth?'

'Well, he is another matter. At the moment he is useful to me, but he has promised to stand Oath for Beth McAdam in ten days. The night before the Oath Taking you will kill him.'

'Has he got a pretty wife?'

Saul laughed aloud. 'Pretty? Else Broome? She looks like an overweight sow that's been squeezed into a dress.'

'Fat, eh? I like 'em fat,' said Jacob Moon.

*

Dr Meredith found the old stranger irritating beyond belief. Jeremiah, on the other hand, seemed amused, but then everyone knew that Jeremiah loved a good debate. Even Isis listened spellbound.

'How can you argue against the development of reason, or science?' pressed the doctor.

'Easily,' answered Jake. 'Centuries ago a man in Ancient Greece came up with the theory that all matter, however huge, from a planet down to a rock, is made up of tiny component parts. The tiniest of these he called *atoms*, which is Greek for *uncuttable*. Man being what he is, he just had to cut the uncuttable. And look where we are! Man is a hunting, killing animal. A predator. Every advance he makes is ultimately linked to destruction, either physical or moral.'

'What of medicine?' Dr Meredith persisted. 'The world before the Fall made magnificent advances in the controlling of disease.'

'Yes, they did,' agreed Jake, 'and they moved into genetic engineering, in order that animal parts could be used for transplant into humans. Hence the Wolvers and the other poor mutated creatures who stalk this planet. Hence the awful build-up of chemical weapons, bacteria and plague germs that were dumped into what was the Atlantic and have now poisoned vast areas of our present land.'

Jake stood and moved to the water barrel, filling his tin mug. 'You can pin it all on one example,' he said. 'Christ told people to love one another and to do good to them that hates you. He said all men were brothers and that we should love our neighbours as ourselves. Within a few hundred years men were arguing about what this meant. Then they went to war over it, and slaughtered one another in order to prove that their version of love thy neighbour was the best system.'

Jeremiah laughed aloud. 'Ah, Jake,' he said, 'you surely do have a way with words. You and the Deacon have a lot in common.'

'Yep,' said Jake. 'Him in his ivory tower and me on my mule. We know how the world works, the Deacon and me.'

'The Deacon is evil,' said Meredith. 'Plain and simple.'

Jake shook his head. 'Nothing in this God-forsaken world is plain and simple, boy. Except death. That's the only sure thing you can guarantee: we're all going to die. Apart from that it's just a sea of complexity. But I would disagree with you about the Deacon. He's just a man who likes to see firm lines drawn. I was in Unity when he was Chief Magistrate; he made some good calls, to my mind.'

'Ah, yes,' sneered Meredith. 'Like public murder. Dragging a man through the streets to be executed in front of his family.'

'You're twisting it just a mite,' said Jake. 'You're talking about the villain meeting his punishment at the scene of his crime. I don't think that is too bad; it lets folk see that justice is done.'

'That's not justice,' stormed Meredith. 'That's barbarity!'

'These are barbarous times, doctor. But you could argue that it comes down to values. What value do we place on a life? The Deacon says that back in his time a killer could be walking the streets within a couple of years, sometimes less. Even mass killers could be released at some time. So the value they put on a human life was two years. Life was awful cheap in those days. At least with the Deacon a killer knows he will get just what his victim got. No more, no less.'

'And what if the court is wrong?' asked Meredith. 'What if an innocent man is found guilty?'

'What about it?' replied Jake. 'It's sad, sure enough, but then mistakes happen, don't they? It doesn't mean the system is wrong. A doctor once told a man I knew he was getting too fat and needed to exercise. He went on a diet and dropped dead. What are we supposed to do? Encourage everybody to get fat just in case there's another lard-belly with a weak heart?'

'That's an outrageous view!'

Jake grinned, and Jeremiah stepped in. 'What about forgiveness, Jake? Didn't Christ talk about that too?'

'Well, you can forgive a man – and still hang him.'

'This is too much!' hissed Dr Meredith, rising from the fireside and stalking back to his wagon.

'Do you see everything so simply, Jake?' asked Isis. 'Is it all black and white for you? Truly?'

The old man gazed at her and his smile faded. 'Nothing is simple, Isis, no matter how hard we try to make it so. I wish it was. Young Doctor Meredith is not wrong. Life is the greatest gift, and every man and woman has infinite possibilities for good or evil. Sometimes for both.' The night breeze strengthened, fanning the flames of the fire. Jake shivered and pulled his old sheepskin coat more tightly around his shoulders. 'But I suppose the question is really one of focus. For a society to succeed it must have strong rules to protect the weak and yet inspire the strong. You agree?'

'Of course,' said Isis.

'Ah, but now the complications begin. In nature the weak perish, the strong survive. So then, if we protect the weak they will flourish, growing like weeds within the society, needing more and more protection, until finally the weak so outnumber the strong that – in a democracy – they rule, and make laws encouraging even more weakness. That society will sicken and die, slowly falling apart as it sows the seeds of its own destruction.'

'How do you define weakness, Jake?' asked Jeremiah. 'Do you mean the sick, or the lame?'

Jake laughed. 'As I said, this is where the complications begin. There are those who are weak in body, but strong in mind and heart. There are those who have the physical strength of lions, but who inside are cowardly and weak. Ultimately a society will judge its people on their ability to supply that society with what it needs to grow and be successful.'

'Ah!' said Jeremiah. 'But that brings us to the old, who have already worked for the society, but can do so no longer. They become weak and therefore, by your arguments, useless. You are arguing against yourself, old man. You would have no place in a strong society.'

'Not so,' said Jake. 'For if I have earned from my labours, and amassed some savings, then I will use my money to buy food and clothing, which continues to help the society. For I will pay the tailor for my coat, enabling him to earn money. I still contribute.'

'But what if you have amassed no savings?' asked Isis.

'Then, by my own definitions, I would be a fool – and therefore useless.'

'It is a harsh image you paint, Jake,' said Jeremiah.

'The world is a harsh place. But believe me, my friends, it is a lot less harsh than the one that the Deacon left behind. As I said, it all becomes a sea of complexity. Out here, however, under God's stars you can still find simplicity. You *Wanderers* understand that. You hunt deer and wild sheep in order to eat, and you journey into towns in order to work for Barta coin to support the life-style you have chosen. If there are no deer you will starve. Simple. And if there was one among you who refused to hunt, or was incapable of hunting or working, you would cast him out.'

'That's not true!' said Isis. 'We would support him.'

'For how long?' Jake asked. 'And what if there was not one, but three, or five, or twenty-five? You can only survive for as long as you work together. A society is no different, child.'

'But aren't you missing something, Jake, in all your equations?' insisted Isis. 'Man is, I will agree, a hunting, killing animal. But he is also capable of love, of compassion, of selflessness. A society must surely incorporate these values.'

'You're a wise woman, Isis,' Jake told her, 'but your point also leaves out a number of Man's vices – like the propensity for evil. Some men – and women – are just plain malicious. They wouldn't understand compassion or selflessness. They'd kill you for the price of a meal, or just because they felt like it. When it comes down to basics a society can only prosper as long as everyone in it is willing to work for its benefit. The word *weak* is a cover-all – maybe *parasites* would be a better description. But then I don't have all the answers. Neither does the Deacon.'

'Tell me, Jake,' said Isis, 'even if I accept all the points you have made so far, what about the slaughter of the Hellborn? Men, women and children were butchered by the Deacon's army. In their thousands. Were they all weak, Jake? Were the babies they murdered evil?'

Jake shook his head, and the smile faded from his face. 'No, girl, they weren't evil. The Deacon was wrong, in my view. But, in his defence, it was at the end of a terrible War and passions were running high. Two armies converged on Babylon . . .' He faded into silence, gazing into the fire.

'You were there?' whispered Jeremiah.

'I was there. I didn't go in when the city walls fell. I could hear, though. The screams! The Deacon heard them too. He ran from his tent, scrambling over the walls and the bodies of the dead defenders. There was no stopping the slaughter. When the dawn came the Deacon stumbled through the city, eyes red from weeping. And not a man in the Army of God failed to feel shame. But the war was over, right enough. And the Hellborn would never invade again.'

Jeremiah leaned forward, placing his hand on Jake's shoulder. 'I think that you, too, carry scars from that day.'

Jake nodded. 'The kind that never heal,' he said sadly.

*

Shannow rode down the hillside and into the valley. There were ploughed fields here, and trees planted in lines as windbreaks. To his right, about a half-mile distant, was a farmhouse, timber-built with a slate roof. There was a paddock beyond the two-storey house, and a barn beyond that. The setting was peaceful. Twisting in his saddle, Shannow glanced back. The mountains loomed high behind him, and there was no sign of pursuit.

The horse was tired and walked with a listless gait. 'Not much further, boy,' said the rider.

Shannow rode up to the paddock and dismounted. The door of the house opened and an elderly woman strode out into the yard. Tall and gaunt, her iron-hair tied in a tight bun, she marched out to face the rider with a long rifle cradled in her arms, her right hand on the action, her finger resting on the trigger.

'If ye're a brigand, be warned,' she said. 'I'll tolerate no ructions here. And I can neuter a gnat from fifty paces with this rifle.'

Shannow smiled. 'Though I may look less than holy, lady, I am not a war-maker, nor a brigand. But I would be grateful for some water, and to be allowed to rest my mount for a day. I'll chop wood, or attend to any chores you set me.'

Her eyes were bright, her face seamed with fine lines, her skin the texture of leather. She sniffed loudly, and did not return his smile. 'I'd turn no man away without a meal at least,' she said. 'Unsaddle the beast and come up to the house. But you can leave those pistols on the hook outside the front door. You'll have no use for them inside.' So saying, she turned and walked back to the house. Shannow unsaddled the horse and led him into the paddock.

The front door led into a long, rectangular room, elegantly furnished with carved wooden chairs, an elaborate folding table and a long horsehide-covered couch. Even the cupboards on the walls boasted flourishes in carved pine. As she had requested, Shannow hung up his guns and moved to a chair by the empty hearth. His neck and back were aching from the ride and he settled gratefully into the chair.

'I see you know how to make yourself at home,' she said, striding in from the kitchen and laying a tray on a small table before him. There was a hunk of bread and a slab of cheese laid on plates of fine china.

'You have a beautiful house, lady.'

'Aye, Zeb was a right handy man with wood and the like. And don't call me *lady*. My name is Wheeler. Zerah Wheeler.'

'The *rising of the light*,' said Shannow.

'What?'

'The woman who raised me was called Zerah. It means *the rising of the light* in one of the older tongues. Hebrew, I think.'

Zerah sat down opposite him. 'I kind of like that,' she said. 'You heading on for Domango?'

'How far is it?' asked Shannow.

'About three days west – if the weather is kind, and it usually is this time of year.'

'I may.' Shannow bit into the bread, but he was almost too tired to eat.

Zerah offered him a mug of cool water. 'You been riding long?' she asked.

'Yes. All my life.' Leaning back in his chair, he closed his eyes.

'Don't you go falling asleep in here!' she said, harshly. 'You're covered in dust. You go on out to the barn. There's a water-butt and you can wash the smell of travel and sweat from your body. If you're awake early enough, there'll be eggs and bacon. If not, it'll be stale bread. There's a fence out back you can mend in the morning, if you're of a mind to earn your food.'

Shannow pushed himself to his feet. 'My thanks to you, Zerah Wheeler. May God bless your house.'

'You got a name, young man?' she asked, as he reached the door and looped his gun-belt over his shoulder.

'Jon,' he said, and stepped out into the dusk.

The barn was warm, and he slept on a bed of straw. His dreams were many, but they ran together chaotically. He saw himself in a small church, and then on a ship, set on a mountain. Faces fled past his eyes, names danced in his mind.

He awoke with the dawn and washed in cold water. Locating a box of tools, he mended the broken fence, then replaced several tiles that had slipped from the slanting roof of the woodshed. The winter store was low, but there was a saw and an axe and he set about preparing logs for the fire. He had been working for an hour when Zerah called him for breakfast.

'I like a man who knows how to work,' she said, as he sat down at the table. 'I had three sons, and not one of them was lazy. How'd you get the wound to your head?'

'I was shot,' he told her, spooning fried eggs and bacon to his plate.

'Who by?'

'I don't know. I have no memory of it.'

'I expect you shot back,' she said. 'You don't look the kind of man to be set upon and not smite them hip and thigh.'

'Where are your sons?' countered Shannow.

'One died in the Unity War. Seth and Padlock are over in Purity. Seth's a Crusader now. It suits him, he's a man who likes order. You pass through there?'

'Yes.'

'You know, it's strange. I'm sure I've seen you someplace. Just can't put a finger on where.'

'If it comes to you I'd be glad to hear it,' said Shannow. Finishing the breakfast, he helped the old woman clear away the dishes and then returned to the wood-store. The labour was tiring, but his muscles felt good, and the mountain air was fresh in his lungs. Zerah came out just after noon, bringing a mug of a hot, sweet tisane.

'I've been thinking,' she said, 'and it wasn't you after all. There was a man back in Allion, where I grew up. He was a brigand-slayer named Shannow. You look a little like him. Not as tall or as big in the shoulders. But you've a similar shape to the face. You planning to keep that beard?'

'No. But I have no razor.'

'When you've finished what you're doing, come on over to the house. I still have Zeb's shaving blade. You're welcome to it.'

Chapter Five

There was a wolf who slew the lambs, the goats and the geese. One day a holy man went to see the wolf and said to him: 'My son, you are a wicked beast, and a long way from God.' The wolf thought about this for a while, and realised that the man was right. He asked how he could come nearer to Heaven. The holy man told him to change his ways and pray. The wolf did so, and became known for his purity and the sweetness of his prayers. One summer the wolf was walking by the riverside when a goose mocked him. The wolf turned and leapt, killing the goose with one bite from his terrible jaws. A sheep standing close by said: 'Why did you kill it?'

The wolf replied: 'Geese should not cackle at a holy wolf.'

The Wisdom of the Deacon
Chapter xi

* * *

Shannow stared into the oval mirror and wiped the last of the soap from his chin. He looked younger without the salt-and-pepper beard, but the sight of his clean-shaven face brought back no new memories. Disappointed, he stepped back, cleaned the razor and returned it to its carved wooden box.

He was tired. The journey through the mountains had been long and hard, for the land was unfamiliar to him. Once convinced that the pursuit had ended he had still to find a path through the peaks. He had tried many trails, but some of these had ended in box canyons, or had led up to treacherous, narrow ridges where only bighorn sheep or mountain-bred mules could walk with safety. City dwellers had no conception of the vastness of the wild lands, the endless mountains, ridges and hills stretching into eternity and beyond. On his journey Shannow had come across the rotted remains of a wagon, still packed with furniture and the beginnings of a home. It was in a boxed canyon, low down at the foot of a steep slope. Close to it he found a skull and a broken section of a thigh-bone. These people too had tried to cross the peaks, and had found only a lonely, unmarked grave beneath the sky.

Back in the main room Zerah Wheeler looked at him closely. 'Ye're not exactly a handsome lad,' she said, 'but it's a face that wouldn't curdle milk neither. Sit at the table and I'll bring ye some lunch. Cold ham and fresh onions.'

While he waited he looked around the room. Every piece of furniture was lovingly carved, giving the home a tranquil quality. There was a triangular corner cabinet, inset with leaded-glass windows, containing tiny cups and saucers beautifully painted and glazed. Shannow walked to the cabinet and peered inside. Zerah saw him there as she returned with the food.

'Zeb found them on a ship in the desert. Beautiful, ain't they?'

'Exquisite,' agreed Shannow.

'He liked beautiful things, did Zeb.'

'When did he die?'

'More than ten years ago now. We were sitting on the couch watching the sunset. It was Summer and we used to move the couch out on to the porch. He leaned back, put his arm round me, then rested his head on my shoulder. "Beautiful night," he said. Then he just died.' Zerah cleared her throat. 'Best tuck into that ham, Jon. I don't want to get all maudlin. Tell me about yourself.'

'There's not a great deal to tell,' he said. 'I was wounded and some *Wanderers* found me. I know my name, but precious little else. I can ride, and I can shoot, and I know my Bible. Apart from that . . .' he shrugged, and cut into the ham.

'You might have a wife somewhere, and children,' she said. 'Have you thought of that?'

'I don't think so, Zerah.' But as she spoke he saw in his mind a brief glimpse of a blonde woman, and two children, a boy and a girl . . . Samuel? Mary? Yes, that felt right. But they were not his children. He knew that.

'So what do you remember about the wound?' she asked.

'There was a fire. I was . . . trapped. I got out.' He shook his head. 'Gunshots. I remember riding up into the mountains. I think I found the men who caused the burning . . .'

Were they ashamed when they had committed the abomination?

'You killed them?'

'I believe so.' Finishing his meal, he made to rise.

'You sit there,' she said. 'I've got some cakes in the oven. Long time since I made cakes, and they may not be so grand. But we'll see.'

So many brief memories lying in the dust of his mind, like pearls without a string to hold them together. Zerah returned with the cakes; they were soft and moist, and filled with fruit preserve.

Shannow chuckled. 'You were wrong, Zerah. They are grand.'

She smiled, then her expression became thoughtful. 'If you're of a mind to stay awhile you'd be welcome,' she said. 'The Lord knows I need help here.'

'That is most kind,' he said, seeing her loneliness, 'but I must find out where I come from. I don't think it will come back to me here. But, if I may, I'd like to stay a few days more?'

'The stream that feeds my vegetable patch is silted up. That could be dug out,' she said, rising and clearing away the dishes.

'That would be my pleasure,' he told her.

*

As the dawn sun broke clear of the mountains, the Apostle Saul eased himself from the wide bed. One of the sisters stirred, the other remained deeply asleep. Saul rose and wrapped his robe about his shoulders. The golden Stone lay on the bedside table. Gathering it up, he moved quickly from the room.

Back in his own quarters he stood before the long, oval mirror, surveying his square-chinned, handsome face and the flowing golden hair that hung to his broad shoulders. A far cry from the balding, slight, stoop-shouldered Saul Wilkins who had landed with the Deacon twenty years before. But then Saul had almost forgotten *that* man. Now he stared hard at the tiny lines around the eyes, the almost imperceptible web marks of ageing upon his cheeks and throat. Gazing down at the coin-sized Stone, he saw there were now only four slender lines of gold in the black. Yesterday there had been five.

The sisters had not been worth it, he thought. Under the influence of the Daniel Stone they had obeyed his every desire, performing acts that would shame them to their souls could they but remember them. Inspiring their debauchery and then removing the memory had cost him a fifth of his power. Now in the dawn light it seemed a waste.

'Curse you, Deacon!' he hissed. Anger rose in him. The old fool knew where the Daniel Stones lay. Indeed, he had a score of them hidden in his palace in Unity. But did he use them for himself? No. What kind of an idiot could hold such power and not keep his body young and vibrant? It was unfair and unjust. Where would he have been without me, thought Saul? Who formed the Jerusalem Riders and led the final charge up Fairfax Hill? Me! Who organised the books and the laws? Me! Who created the great legend of the Deacon and made his dreams reality? Me. Always me. And what does he give me? One tiny Stone.

From his window he could see the blackened earth where the church had stood, and the sight eased his anger.

'Fetch me the Preacher from Pilgrim's Valley,' the Deacon had said.

'Why?'

'He's a very special man, Saul. The Wolvers respect him.'

'They're just beasts. Mutated creatures!'

'They have human genes. And they are not a threat. I have prayed long and hard about them, Saul, and every time I pray I see the Pillars of Fire. I believe the Wolvers could live in the lands beyond them. I believe that is where God intends them to be.'

'And you will empower this Preacher to lead them?'

'Yes. You and I are the only ones left now, Saul. I think this young man has a talent for leadership.'

'What does that mean, Deacon? I am your heir, you know that.'

The Deacon had shaken his head. 'I love you, Saul, like a son. But you are not the man to lead a people. You follow the devices and desires of your heart. Look at you! Where is Saul Wilkins now? Where is the little man who loved God? You have used the Stone on yourself.'

'And why not? With them we can be immortal, Deacon. Why should we not live for ever, rule for ever?'

'We are not Gods, Saul. And I am tired. Fetch me the Preacher.'

Saul looked at the charred wood and the singed earth. Did the Deacon know that the anonymous Bible mouther was the Jerusalem Man? Saul doubted it. The one man on this new earth who could destroy the myth of the Deacon.

Well, that myth will only grow now you are dead, you old bastard!

Saul would like to have seen the killing, the moment when the bullet smashed home. I wonder, he thought, what last thought went through your mind, Deacon? Was it a prayer? If it was, you finished it in person. How long, he wondered, before the Church realises that its blessed Deacon will not be returning? Another ten days? Twenty?

Then they will send for me, for I am the last of the men from beyond the Gates of Time.

The first three Apostles had died long before the Unity Wars, killed by the radiation and pestilential chemicals that filled the air of this new world. Then the Deacon had found the Stones, and given the eight survivors one each in order to strengthen their bodies against the poisons in the atmosphere. One each! Saul found his anger rising again, but fought it down. He had used his quite swiftly, not just making himself strong but also handsome. And why not? He had lived for forty-three years with an ugly face and a short, twisted frame. Did he not deserve a new life? Was he not one of the Chosen?

Then the War had started. He and Alan were given command of two sections of the Jerusalem Riders. Fairfax Hill had been the turning point. But Alan had died, shot to pieces as he neared the summit. Saul had been the first to find the dying man.

'Help me!' Alan had whispered. Two of the shots had shattered his spine, cutting through his belt and separating it from his body. His Stone was in a leather pouch; Saul had pulled it clear. It was almost totally gold, with only the thinnest of black strands. To heal Alan would probably have exhausted it all. Indeed, the wounds were probably too great for his life to be saved. Saul had pocketed the Stone and walked away. When he returned an hour later Alan was dead.

One month later Saul had met Jacob Moon, an old, grizzled former brigand. The man was a killer, and Saul had seen instantly the value of such a man. In giving him back his youth, he made an ally that would take him all the way to power.

Moon had killed the others, one by one. And Saul had gathered the Stones of power. Most were almost dry of magic.

Then only the Deacon was left . . .

Saul dressed and moved down to the ground floor. Moon was sitting at the breakfast table, finishing a meal of bacon and eggs.

'You had a good night, brother Saul,' said Moon, with a sly grin. 'Such noise!'

'What news of the Preacher, Jacob?'

Moon shrugged. 'Be patient. I have men scouring the wild lands for news. I've also sent Witchell to Domango. We'll find him.'

'He's a dangerous man.'

'He doesn't even know he's being hunted. That will make him careless.'

Saul poured a mug of fresh milk and was sipping it when he heard the sound of a walking horse in the yard outside. Going to the window, he saw a tall, square-bearded, broad-shouldered man in a long black coat dismount and walk towards the house. Moving to the door, Saul opened it.

'God's greetings, brother,' he said.

The man nodded. 'God's greetings to you, brother, and a blessing upon this fine house. I am Padlock Wheeler from Purity. Would you be the Apostle Saul?'

'Come in, brother,' said Saul, stepping aside. He remembered Wheeler as the Deacon's favourite general, a hard-riding martinet who drove his men to the edge of exhaustion and beyond. They followed him because he asked for nothing from them that he did not give himself. After the War, Saul recalled, Wheeler had returned to his own land and become a preacher. The man looked older, and two white streaks made a bright fork in his beard on either side of his chin. Wheeler removed his flat-crowned hat and stepped into the dining-room.

'You looked different the last time I saw you, sir,' said

Padlock Wheeler. 'You were thinner, I recall, and with less hair. Even your face seems now more . . . regular.'

Saul was irritated. He didn't like to be reminded of the man he once was – the man he could become again if ever he lost the power of the Stones.

'What brings you so far?' he asked, fighting to remain civil.

'Our Oath Taker has been shot dead,' said Wheeler. 'He was a verminous rascal, and by all accounts deserved his fate. But the man who shot him is a blasphemer and a heretic. You will forgive me, sir, for speaking bluntly, but he claimed to be the Jerusalem Man.'

Moon rose. 'You apprehended him?'

Wheeler glanced at Moon and said nothing, appraising the man. 'This is the Jerusalem Rider Jacob Moon,' said Saul.

Wheeler nodded, but his dark eyes remained fixed on Moon for a moment. Finally he spoke. 'No, we did not apprehend the man. Our Crusaders followed him, but lost him in the mountains. He appeared to be heading into the wild lands near Domango.'

Saul shook his head, his expression sorrowful. 'You bring dreadful news, brother Wheeler. But I am sure brother Moon will know what to do.'

'Indeed I do,' said Jacob Moon.

*

There were many things that twelve-year-old Oswald Hankin did not know, but of one he was sure: There was no God.

'I'm hungry, Oz,' said his little sister, Esther. 'When can we go home?'

Oz put his arm around the six-year-old's shoulder. 'Hush now, I'm trying to think.'

What could he tell her? She's watched father being shot down, the bullets smashing into his head and chest, the blood exploding from his frame. Oz shut his eyes against the memory, but it remained locked in place in his mind's eye, bleak and harsh, and terribly savage.

He and Esther had been playing in the long grass when the seven riders had come up to the house. There was no indication of the murder to follow. The sky was clear, the sun bright, and only this morning their father had read to them from an old leather-bound book with gold-edged pages. The tale of Lancelot and Guinevere.

For some reason Oz had decided to remain in the long grass, though Esther wanted to run out and see the riders close up. His father had walked from the house to greet them. He was wearing a white shirt, and his long fair hair was golden in the sunlight.

'We told ye once,' said the leading rider, a bald man with a black trident beard. 'We'll suffer no pagans around Domango.'

'By what right do you call me a pagan?' his father had replied. 'I do not accept your authority to judge me. I travelled far to buy this land, and where I came from I am well known as a man who loves the church. How can I be at fault here?'

'You were warned to leave,' said the rider. 'What follows be on your own head, pagan.'

'Get off my land!'

They were the last words his father spoke. The leading rider produced a pistol and fired a single shot that hammered into the unarmed man's chest. Father had staggered back. Then all the men began firing.

'Find the young'uns,' shouted the trident-bearded leader.

Esther was too shocked to cry, but Oswald virtually had to drag her back into the long grass. They crawled for some way, then cut into the pines and up along the mountain paths to the old cave. It was cold here, and they cowered together for warmth.

What will I do, thought Oz? Where can we go?

'I'm hungry, Oz,' said Esther again. She started to cry. He hugged her and kissed her hair. 'Where's Poppa?'

'He's dead, Esther. They killed him.'

'When will he come for us?'

'He's dead,' repeated Oz wearily. 'Come on, let's walk a little. It'll make you warmer and take your mind off your hunger.'

Taking Esther's hand, he walked to the mouth of the cave and peered out. Nothing moved on the mountain trails, and he listened for the sound of horses. Nothing. Nothing but the wind whispering through the trees.

Leading Esther, he began to walk towards the east, away from his home.

His mother had died back in Unity, just a year after Esther was born. Oz didn't remember much about her, save that she had red hair and a wide, happy smile. His one clear memory was of a picnic by a lake when he had fallen in, and swallowed some water. His mother had hurled herself in after him, dragging him back to the bank. He recalled her red hair, wet and dripping, and her green eyes so full of love and concern.

When she died he had cried a lot, and had asked his father why God had killed her.

'God didn't kill her, son. A cancer did that.'

'He's supposed to work miracles,' argued the seven-year-old Oswald.

'And he does, Oz. But they're His miracles. He chooses. Everybody dies. I'll die one day. It's wrong to blame God for death. Maybe we should be thanking Him for the gift of what life we have.'

Oz adored his father, and put his lack of faith on hold.

But today he knew the truth. There was no God – and his father was dead. Murdered.

Esther stumbled over a jutting tree-root, but Oz was holding her hand and hauled her up. She started to cry again, and refused to go on. Oz sat with her on a fallen tree. He had not been this far along the mountain path before, and had no idea where it led. But equally he had nowhere else to go. Behind them the killers would be searching.

After a while Esther calmed down and they walked on, coming to a steep trail that led down into a valley. In the distance Oz could see a house and a barn. He stopped and stared at the house.

What if trident-beard lived there? Or one of the others?

'I'm really *very* hungry, Oz,' said Esther.

Oz took a deep breath. 'Let's go down then,' he said.

*

Zerah Wheeler sat in the chair by the fire and thought about her sons. Not as men, but as the children they once had been. Oz Hankin and Esther were asleep now in the wide bed that Zeb had built more than forty years ago, their pain and their loss shrouded in the bliss of sleep. Zerah sighed as she thought of Zachariah. In her mind he was always the *laughing child*, full of pranks and mischief that no amount of scolding could forbid. Seth and Padlock had always been so serious. Just like me, she thought – gazing at the world through cynical, suspicious eyes, ever wary and watchful.

But not Zak. He gloried in the sunshine or the snow, and gazed about him with a wide-eyed sense of wonder at the beauty of it all. Zerah sniffed and cleared her throat. 'Did you believe them?' she asked her mysterious guest.

He nodded solemnly. 'Children can lie,' he said, 'but not this time. They saw what they saw.'

'I agree,' said Zerah. 'They witnessed a murder. You'll have to ride to Domango and inform the Crusaders. It was their territory. I'll keep the children here with me.'

Jon remained silent for a moment. 'You're a good woman, Frey Wheeler. But what if they come here when I'm gone?'

Zerah's grey eyes took on a frosty gleam. 'Son, I'm a known woman. There have been those who sought to take advantage. I buried them out back. Don't you worry none about this old girl.' She gave him directions to Domango, advising him of various landmarks he should watch out for.

'I'll ride out now,' he said, rising from his chair. 'I thank you for the meal.'

'You don't have to stay so formal, Jon,' she told him. 'I'd look on it kindly if you stopped calling me Frey and started to use my given name.'

He smiled then, and it was good to see, for his eyes seemed less cold. 'As you wish . . . Zerah. Good night.'

She rose and walked to the door, watching him gather his guns from the hook and stroll to the paddock. And, not for the first time, she wondered who he was. Turning back into the house, she extinguished one of the lamps. Oil was short now, and soon she would have to ride into Domango for supplies. There was a time when the farm had supported three hired men, when cattle had roamed in the pasture lands to the south. But those days were gone now, just like the cattle. Now Zerah

Wheeler survived by growing vegetables in the plot out back, and by breeding a few pigs and many chickens.

Twice a year Padlock would visit, arriving in a wagon laden with boxes, tins of peaches canned in Unity, sacks of flour, salt and sugar, and – most precious of all – books. Most of them were Bible studies, printed by the Deacon Press, but occasionally there were gems from the old world. One she had read a score of times, savouring every sentence over and over. It was the first part of a trilogy. Pad hadn't realised that when he bought it for her; to him it was just an antique tome his mother might enjoy. And she had. At first she had been irritated by the fact that there was no record of any of the other books in the series. But during the last seven years, she had thought and thought about the story, inventing her own endings, and this had given her immense pleasure in the long, lonely evenings.

She heard the soft sounds of sobbing begin in the bedroom and walked swiftly through to sit on the bed alongside the little girl. Esther was crying in her sleep. 'Hush now, child, all is safe. As is well,' she crooned, stroking the child's auburn hair. 'All is safe, all is well,' Esther murmured, then began sucking at her thumb. Zerah was not a great believer in thumb-sucking, but there was a time and a place for admonishments and this was not it.

'Always wanted a girl-child,' whispered Zerah, still stroking the child's head. Then she saw that Oswald was awake, his eyes wide and fearful. 'Come join me for a glass of milk,' she said. 'Always have one before sleeping. Move soft now, so as not to wake little Esther.'

Oswald padded out after her. He was a strongly-built boy, reminding her of Seth, with serious eyes and a good jaw. Pouring two glasses from the stone jug she passed one to Oswald, who hunkered down by the dying fire.

'Having trouble sleeping, boy?'

He nodded. 'I dreamed of Poppa. He was walking around the house calling for us. But he was all covered with blood, and his face wasn't there any more.'

'You've seen some hard, hard times, Oz. But you're safe here.'

'They'll come for us. You won't be able to stop them.'

Zerah forced a chuckle. 'Me and Betty will stop them, Oz. Count on it.' She walked to the fire and lifted the long rifle from its rack. 'She fires four shots, and every shell is thicker than your thumb. And I'll tell you a little secret – I ain't missed with this gun for nigh on seventeen years.'

'There was more than four of them,' said Oz.

'I'm glad you mentioned that, Oz,' she said, laying aside the rifle and moving to a handsomely carved chest of drawers. From it she produced a small, nickel-plated revolver and a box of shells. 'This here pistol belonged to my son, Zak. She's small, but she's got stopping power. It was made by the Hellborn thirty years ago.' Flipping open the breech she put the pistol on half-cock, freeing the cylinder, and fed in five shells, lowering the hammer on the empty chamber. 'I'm giving this to you, Oz. It is not to play with. This is a gun. It will kill people. You fool with it and it's likely to kill you or your sister. Are you man enough to deal with that?'

'Yes, Frey Wheeler. I am man enough.'

'I didn't doubt it. Now between us, Oz, we're going to look after little Esther. And we're going to see justice done. My man, Jon, is riding now to Domango to report the . . .' She hesitated as she saw the look of anguish in his eyes. 'To report the crime to the Crusaders.'

Oswald's face twisted then, and his eyes shone. 'The man who first shot Poppa *was* a Crusader,' he said.

Zerah's heart sank, but she kept her expression neutral. 'We'll work things out, Oz, you see if we don't. Now you best get back to bed. I'll need you fresh and clear of eye in the morning. Put the pistol by your bedside.'

The boy padded off and Zerah returned to the chest of drawers. From the third drawer she pulled a scabbard and belt, then a short-barrelled pistol. For some time she cleaned the weapon. Then she loaded it.

*

Despite the dangers Shannow loved night riding. The air was crisp and clean and the world slept. Moonlight gave the trees a shimmering quality, and every rock glistened with silver. He rode slowly, allowing the horse to pick its way carefully over the trail.

The loss of memory no longer caused him irritation. It would come back or it wouldn't. What did concern him was the problems such a loss could cause the Jerusalem Man. If his worst enemy of the last twenty years were to ride up in plain sight, Shannow feared he would not recognise the danger.

Then there was the question of ageing. According to Jeremiah, the Jerusalem Man had ridden through the Plague Lands twenty years before, and had then been a man in his late thirties or early forties. That would make him around sixty now. Yet his hair was still dark, his skin virtually unlined.

He rode for almost three hours, then made camp in a hollow. There was no water near by and Shannow did not bother with a fire but sat with his back to a tree, his blanket wrapped around his shoulders. The head wound gave him no pain now, but the scab itched.

Sitting in the moonlight, he traced over his life in his mind, piecing together tiny fragments as they came to him. *I am Jon Shannow.*

Then a face leapt to his memory, a thin, angular face with deep brooding eyes. A name came with it: Varey. Varey Shannow. Like a key slipping sweetly into a lock he saw again the brigand-slayer who had taken the young man under his wing. *I took his name when he was murdered.* And his own name slipped into his mind: Cade. Jon Cade. The name settled on his mind like water on a parched tongue.

The world had gone mad, preachers everywhere talking of Armageddon. But if Armageddon was true, then the new Jerusalem would exist somewhere. The new Jon Shannow had set out to find it. The journey had been long, with many perils. Varey Shannow had taught him never to back away from evil:

'Confront it wherever you find it, Jon. For it will thrive when men cease to fight it.'

Shannow closed his eyes and remembered the conversations around many camp-fires. '*You are a strong man, Jon, and you have tremendous hand-eye co-ordination. You have speed, and yet you are cool under fire. Use those skills, Jon. This land is full of brigands, men who would lie, steal and kill for gain. They must be fought. For they are evil.*' Shannow smiled at the memory. '*It used to be said that you can't stop a man who keeps* on going and knows he's right. It just ain't true, Jon. A bullet will stop any man. But that's not the point. Winning is not the point. If a man only fought when he believed there was a chance to win, then evil would beat him every time. The brigand relies on the fact that when he rides in with his men, all armed to the teeth, the victim will – realising he has no chance – just give in. Trust me, Jon, that's the moment to walk out with guns blazing.'

Just before the fateful day, as the two men rode into the small town, Varey Shannon had turned to the youngster beside him. 'Men will say many things about me when I'm gone. They could say I got angry too fast. They could say I wasn't none too bright. They'll certainly say that I was an ugly cuss. But no man ever will be able to say that I abused a woman, stole or lied, or backed down in the face of evil. Ain't too bad an epitaph, is it, Jon?'

Varey Shannon had been cut down in his prime, backshot by villains who feared he was hunting them.

Jon Shannon opened his eyes and gazed up at the stars. 'You were a good man, Varey,' he said.

'Talking to yourself is a sure sign of madness, they say,' said Jake, 'and I hope you don't fire that pistol.' Shannon eased back the hammer and holstered the gun. At the first sound he had drawn and cocked the weapon in one swift, fluid move. Despite the speed of his response, he was nettled by the old man's silent approach.

'A man could be killed approaching a camp that way,' he said.

'True, boy. But I reckoned you weren't the type to shoot before looking.' Jake moved opposite Shannon and hunkered down. 'Cold camp. You expecting trouble?'

'Trouble has a way of happening when you least expect it,' said Shannon.

'Ain't it the truth.' The old man's beard was shining silver in the moonlight. Shucking off his sheepskin topcoat, he gave a low whistle and his mule came trotting into the camp. Swiftly Jake removed the saddle and blanket roll, then patted the beast's rump. The mule moved out to stand alongside Shannon's horse. 'She's an obedient girl,' said Jake fondly.

'How did you find me?'

'I didn't. The mule must have picked up the scent of your stallion. You heading for Domango?'

Shannow nodded, but said nothing. 'A sight of activity there in the last few days,' continued Jake. 'Riders coming in from all over. Tough men, by the look of them. Ever heard of Jacob Moon?'

'No.'

'Jerusalem Rider. Killed fourteen men that I heard of. Can you guess who he's asking about?'

'Who are you, Jake?' countered Shannow.

'Just an old man, son. Nothing special. I take it you aren't interested in Moon?'

'At the moment I'm more interested in you. Where are you from?'

Jake chuckled. 'Here and there. Mostly there. I've been over the mountain a few times. You think I'm hunting you?'

Shannow shook his head. 'Perhaps. Perhaps not. But you are hunting something, Jake.'

'Nothing that need worry you, son.' Shaking loose his blanket, Jake wrapped it around his shoulders and stretched out on the earth. 'By the way, those *Wanderers* you helped – they're on the way to Domango too. You'll probably see them.'

'You do get around, old man,' said Shannow, closing his eyes.

*

Shannow awoke with the dawn to find that the old man had gone. He sat up and yawned. He had never known anyone who could move as quietly as Jake. Saddling his horse, he rode out on to a broad plain. There were ruins to his left, huge pillars of stone, shattered and fallen, and the horse's hooves clattered in the remains of a wide stone road. The city must have been vast, Shannow considered, stretching for several miles to the west.

He had seen many such on his travels, cold stone epitaphs to the glory that was once Atlantis.

Another memory came to him then, of a man with a golden beard and eyes the colour of a clear summer sky.

Pendarric. The King.

And he recalled with great clarity the day when the Sword of God had torn across the curtain of time. Reining in his horse, he gazed with fresh eyes on the ruins.

'I destroyed you,' he said aloud.

Time's portals had been opened by Pendarric, the ruler of Atlantis, and Shannow had closed them by sending a missile through the Gateway. The world had toppled, tidal waves roaring across the continent. The words of Amaziga Archer floated up from the hidden depths.

'You are not the Jerusalem Man any longer, Shannow. You're the Armageddon Man!'

Shannow turned his back on the ancient city and headed south-west. It was not long before he saw the Hankin house. There was no body outside, but there was fresh blood on the dust of the yard. As he rode in, a tall man with a sandy beard came walking from the house, a rifle cradled in his arms.

'What do you want here?' he asked.

'Nothing, friend. I am on my way to Domango and thought I'd stop for a little water, if it is not inconvenient to you.' Shannow could not see the second man at the window, but he saw a rifle barrel showing at the edge of the curtain.

'Well, be quick about it. We don't like *Movers* here.'

'Is that so? When last I stopped here, there was a man with two children. Has he moved on?'

The man's eyes narrowed. 'Yes,' he said, at last. 'He moved on.'

'Do you own the property now?'

'No, I just been told to watch over it. Now get your drink and be gone.'

Shannow dismounted and led his horse to a trough by the well. Loosening the saddle girth, he wandered back to where the man stood. 'It is a fine place,' he said. 'A man could raise a family here and never tire of looking at the mountains.'

The sandy-haired rifleman hawked and spat. 'One place is pretty much like another.'

'So where did he move on to . . . my friend with his children?' asked Shannow.

'I don't know anything about it,' said the rifleman, growing more uneasy.

Shannow glanced down at the dust, and the stains that peppered the ground. 'Slaughtered a pig,' said the man swiftly. The second man moved from the house. He was powerfully built, with a bull-like neck and massive shoulders.

'Who the Hell is he, Ben?' asked the newcomer, his right hand resting on the butt of his scabbarded pistol.

'Stranger riding for Domango. He's just watering his horse.'

'Well, you've done that,' he told Shannow. 'Now be on your way.'

Shannow stood silently for a moment, holding back his anger. There was no movement in the house now, and he guessed that these two men alone had been left to guard the property. All his life he had known such men – hard, cruel killers, with no understanding of love or compassion. 'Were either of you party to the murder?' he asked softly.

'What?' responded the rifleman, eyes widening. The bigshouldered man took a step back and made a grab for his pistol. Shannow shot him in the head; he stood for a moment, eyes wide in shock, then he toppled to the bloodstained earth. The Jerusalem Man's pistol swung, the black eye of the barrel halting directly before the other man's face.

'Jesus Christ!' said the rifleman, dropping his weapon and raising his hands.

'Answer the question,' said Shannow. 'Were you party to the murder of Meneer Hankin?'

'No . . . I never shot him, I swear to God. It was the others.'

'Who led the killers?'

'Jack Dillon. But Hankin, he never had no Oath papers and no one would stand up and speak for him. It was the law. He was told to leave, he brung it on himself. If he'd just gone, none of this would have happened. Don't you see?'

'And this Dillon has now laid claim to the property?'

'No. It's held for Jacob Moon. Please, you're not going to kill me, are you?' The man fell to his knees and began to weep.

'Did Meneer Hankin weep and beg?' asked Shannow. He knew he should kill this man. More than that, he knew that the old Jon Shannow would have done so without a second thought. Holstering his pistol, he moved to his horse.

'You son of a bitch!' screamed the man, and Shannow turned

to see that he had gathered up his rifle, which was now pointed in Shannow's direction. 'You bastard! Think you're so tough? Think you can just ride in here and do as you like? Let's see how tough you act with a bullet in your guts.'

Smoothly Shannow stepped to the right, palming his pistol as he moved. The rifle shot slashed past him on the left, cutting through his coat. Shannow fired and the rifleman pitched backwards, the weapon flying from his hands. Hitting the ground hard the man grunted once, then his leg twitched and he was still.

'You have become a fool, Shannow,' said the Jerusalem Man.

The land to the east was vast and empty, the plain dry, the grass yellow-brown. He could see where once there had been rivers and streams, but they were long gone now, evaporated by the searing heat of the sun. After an hour of riding he saw the broken hull of a rusted ship jutting from the desert that stretched away to the horizon and beyond, grim evidence that this had once been the ocean floor.

Shannow skirted the edge of the desert and, after another hour, began the long climb up into the higher country. Here there were green trees, and grass, and a wide, well-used road that angled down towards the distant town of Domango.

*

The sun was high in the sky, and Clem was enjoying the freedom of the ride. Meg was a gentle woman and a fine wife, but he had felt trapped at the ranch in Pernum. The thought made him feel guilty. His life at the ranch had brought him everything he thought he had ever wanted: security, status and love. So why had it not been enough? When the locusts had wiped out his crop five years ago he could have worked on, labouring through the long hours of daylight. The merchants in town all liked him and they would have extended his credit. Instead, he had run away and taken to the road.

The first robbery had been easy: two men carrying a shipment of Barta notes to Pernum. Clem had ambushed them on the mountain road, shooting the first through the shoulder. The second had thrown away his gun. Twelve thousand he had made that day.

After that everything had gone to Hell in a bucket. Half of the cash was sent to the banker in Pernum, who held the mortgage on the farm. The rest had gone to Meg.

Nothing had been easy from that moment on.

'What was he like?' asked Nestor, the words cutting through Clem's thoughts. They were no more than an hour's ride from the settlement of Purity, and Clem could already see the smoke from the town's factories drifting lazily into the blue sky.

'What's that lad? Did you say something?'

'The Jerusalem Man. What was he like?'

Clem thought about the question. 'He was grim, Nestor. Mighty grim. Unpredictable and deadly. Pilgrim's Valley was a new settlement then. There was no Deacon, no natural unified government. Settlers just headed out into uncharted lands and built their farms. Merchants followed them and soon there were towns. We stopped in Pilgrim's Valley just short of the Great Wall. Now that was a sight to behold.'

'I seen it,' said Nestor. 'But what about Jon Shannow?'

Clem laughed. 'By God, boy, I do so like the young. That wall was built twelve thousand years ago, and beyond it there was a city, where men became lions. And in the sky, shining bright, there was the Sword of God. Hell of a thing, Nestor. Anyways, the demons of the pit were released around then, walking Snake-men.'

'I seen one of those too,' said Nestor. 'They got one down in Unity, on display. And several skeletons.'

'I've seen that too,' mimicked Clem, growing irritated by the interruptions. 'But what you won't know is that the King of these demons sent three special men to kill Shannow. Great warriors, fearless and lightning-fast with pistols. Shannow killed the first, but the other two kidnapped Frey McAdam and took her to where the Sword was hanging in the sky.'

'Why'd they take the headmistress?'

'God's Blood, son, will you just listen?'

'I'm sorry, sir.'

'They kidnapped Beth because she was close to Shannow. They wanted to bring him to them. And they did just that. But it didn't take 'em long to wish they hadn't. I'd been wounded, but I followed them anyway. I come on the scene just as Shannow had give himself up. Suddenly there was guns blazing. I took down one, but the best of them was facing up to the Jerusalem Man. Shannow just stood there like he didn't have a care in the world – calm, powerful. Then it was over. I tell you, boy, I wouldn't want to face him.'

'He was that fast?'

'Oh, it wasn't the speed. I'm faster than ever he was. It's the sureness. Strange man – holds himself in chains of iron.' He glanced at Nestor. 'You know why he hates brigands and killers?' The boy shook his head. 'Because deep down he is one. A natural. You see, most men hesitate when it comes to killing. I think that's a good thing, generally. Life is precious, and you don't want to take it away from someone over a whim. I mean, even a brigand can change. Look at Daniel Cade. There wasn't a more murderous bastard than him, but he saw the Light, boy. And he fought the Hellborn. So, like I said, life is precious. But Shannow? Cross him and you die. It's that simple. That's why brigands fear him. He deals with them just like they deal with others.'

'You talk about him like he's alive. But he ain't, is he? He went up to Heaven years back.'

Clem hesitated, anxious to share the secret he had kept hidden for twenty years. 'He is alive to me,' he said. 'I never saw him die, and I never saw no fiery chariot neither. But I watched him tame a wild town. You've never seen the like.'

'Wish I had,' said Nestor. 'I'd love to have met him – just once.'

Clem laughed again. 'If wishes were fishes, poor men wouldn't starve. How long have you known the Preacher?'

'All my life. Quiet man. He used to live with Frey McAdam, but she threw him out. Then he had a little place behind the church. He gave some good sermons . . . always kept you awake in church. Well, until he started letting Wolvers in, that is. Most people stopped going then. If he'd been a stronger man he'd have kicked those Wolvers out. Then there would've still been a church.'

'What's strength got to do with it?'

'Well, everybody in town got mighty sick of it and they told him so. But I guess he just didn't have the nerve to order the Wolvers away. Some men just don't take to confrontation.'

'I guess not,' said Clem. 'Did you like him?'

Nestor shrugged. 'Didn't like him or dislike him. Felt sorry for him mostly. Shem Jackson hit him once, knocked him into the mud. The Preacher just got up and went on his way. I was ashamed for him then. I still can't believe how he shot down all them raiders. Guess he must have surprised them.'

'A surprising man,' agreed Clem.

Chapter Six

Evil will always rise, like scum to the surface. For an evil man will seek to impose his power on others. All the governments of history have seen evil men gain ascendancy. How then do we ensure that the rule of evil is for ever banished from this new land? We cannot. All that we can do is strive for holiness, and seek out, individually, the Will of God. And we can pray that when evil rises there will be men, aye and women, who will stand against it.

The Wisdom of the Deacon
Chapter xxii

* * *

Isis stood before the broad desk and stared at the Crusader, trying to hold on to her temper. The man had small, bright eyes and a face that seemed to her to show cruelty and arrogance. 'You have no reason to lock up our doctor,' she said.

'When the Oath Taker gets here we'll see what's right,' he said. 'We're not partial to *Movers* here. We don't like thieves and skulkers in Domango.'

'We are not thieves, sir. We came into town looking for work. I am a seamstress, our leader Jeremiah is a tailor, and Doctor Meredith is a physician.'

'Well, now he's a prisoner.'

'Of what is he accused?'

'Begging. Now be on your way – or I'll find a nice cell for you.' His eyes raked her figure. 'Maybe you'd like that,' he said, leering.

'I doubt that she would,' said a cold, deep voice, and Isis turned to see Jon Shannow standing in the doorway. Moving inside, he walked past her without a word and stood before the broad desk. 'I am here to report a murder,' he said.

The Crusader leaned back in his chair, linking his hands behind his head. 'A murder, you say? Where and when?'

'About three hours' ride north-east of here. A man named Hankin. Shot to death by a group of riders.'

Isis saw the change of expression on the Crusader's face. The man sat up straight. 'How do you know there was a murder?' he asked. 'Did you see it?'

'His children saw it,' said Shannow.

'And where are they now?'

'Safe,' Shannow told him.

'You saw the body?'

'No. But I believe the children.'

The man fell silent, but the fingers of his right hand began tapping nervously on the desk-top. 'All right,' he said at last, 'this'll have to wait until the captain gets back – some time this afternoon. Why not get yourself something to eat, and come back later?'

'Very well.' Shannow swung and left the office and Isis followed him.

'Wait!' she called, as he stepped off the boardwalk. 'They've got Doctor Meredith in there!'

'It would be better for you to avoid me,' said Shannow. 'There is evil here, and it will draw unto me.'

Isis was about to reply, but he walked away across the wide street towards an eating-house on the far side.

'You know that man?' asked the Crusader, moving alongside her.

'No,' she said. 'He rode by our wagons some days back, that's all.'

'Well, steer clear of him. He's trouble.'

'Yes, I will,' said Isis.

*

Inside the small eating-house Shannow sat with his back to the wall. There were three other diners; a thin, balding man who was reading a book, having finished his meal; a thick-set young miner with his left arm in a sling; and a slim, dark-eyed black man who was nursing a hot mug of Baker's. Dismissing the other two from his mind, Shannow concentrated on the young black man. He was wearing a coat of dark grey wool over a white shirt, and Shannow could see the enamelled butt of a revolver in a shoulder holster on his left side.

A tall black woman approached Shannow's table. 'We got good steaks, some fresh-laid eggs, and new bread from the oven this morning,' she said. 'Or else there's what's printed on the board.'

Shannow glanced up at the blackboard and the dishes and drinks scribbled in chalk. 'I'll have bread and cheese, and some warmed milk, if you please.'

'You want honey in the milk?' she asked him.

'That would be pleasant.'

As she walked away his thoughts returned to the meeting in the office. The Crusader's reactions had been wrong. There was no surprise when Shannow mentioned the murder, and the man's twin concerns had been the whereabouts of the children and whether Shannow had seen the body. When the waitress returned with a mug of sweetened milk, Shannow thanked her, then asked in a low voice, 'There is a man in this area named Jack Dillon. How will I know him?'

'Best if you don't,' answered the woman, walking away. As she passed the table of the slim black man Shannow saw her bend her head and whisper something to him. The man nodded, then rose and walked towards Shannow's table. Reversing a chair, he sat down opposite the Jerusalem Man.

'Dillon's big and he's bald and he sports a thick beard,' said the newcomer. 'Is that a help?'

'Where will I find him?'

'If you are looking for him, my friend, he will find you. Seeking to work for him, are you?'

'What would make you think so?'

'I know your kind,' said the black man. 'Predator.'

'If that is the case,' said Shannow, with the briefest of smiles, 'then are you not walking a perilous path by insulting me?'

The man chuckled. 'All life involves risk, friend. But I think it is minimal in this situation. For you see I am armed – and facing you.' His dark eyes were gleaming, and the fact that he held Shannow in contempt was all too obvious. 'What do you say to that?'

'*A fool uttereth all his mind, but a wise man keepeth it in,*'

Shannow told him. 'Beware, boy, it can be fatal to make hasty judgements.'

'You calling me a fool?' The black man's hand was hovering now over the enamelled pistol-butt beneath his jacket.

'I am stating a fact,' said Shannow, 'and if you listen very closely you will hear the sound of a pistol being cocked.' The double click of the drawn-back hammer sounded from below the table. 'You seem very anxious to cause trouble, young man,' continued Shannow. 'Could it be you have been sent to kill me?'

'No one sent me. I just despise your kind,' the man answered.

'The young are always so swift to judge. Did you know a farmer named Hankin?'

'I know him. Men like you forced him off his place. Couldn't find three people to give Oath for him.'

'He was murdered,' said Shannow. 'Shot to death, his children hunted like animals. I am waiting to see the Captain of the Crusaders; then I shall file a complaint against Jack Dillon.'

The black man leaned forward, elbows on the table. 'You really don't know anything about Dillon, do you?'

'I know that he – and other men – shot an unarmed man in cold blood. And I will see him brought to justice.'

The black man sighed, 'I guess I may have been wrong about you, friend. But I'm not the only one who's being foolish. I think you should just ride out now – far and fast.'

'Why would I wish to do that?'

The black man leaned in close. 'Jack Dillon *is* the Captain of the Crusaders. Appointed last month by the Apostle Saul himself.'

'What kind of settlement is this?' asked Shannow. 'Are there no honest men?'

The black man laughed. 'Where have you been living, friend? Who is going to speak against an anointed Crusader? There's forty of them – and Jacob Moon and his Riders. No one is going to go against them.'

Shannow fell silent, and the black man heard the welcome sound of the pistol hammer being eased forward. 'My name is Archer, Gareth Archer.' He extended his hand.

'Leave me, boy. I have much to think on.'

Archer moved away, and the waitress returned with a second mug of sweetened milk. This time she smiled. Shannow gazed out of the window at the settlement's main street. Beyond the buildings to the west he could see the mines on the distant hillsides, and beyond them the smoke from smelting houses and factories. So much dirt and darkness from the soot and smoke.

A face leapt unbidden to his mind, a slender man in late middle age, balding and sharp-featured with soft brown eyes.

'It's progress, Preacher. Ever since the planes landed and we found out what once we were, things changed. The planes carried engineers and surgeons, all sorts of skilled people. Most of them died within the year, but they passed on a lot of knowledge. We're building again. Soon we'll have good hospitals and fine schools, and factories that can manufacture machines to help us till the land and gather the harvest. Then there'll be roads and cities to those roads. It will be a paradise.'

'A paradise built on belching smoke and foul-smelling soot? I see the trees have all died around the canning plant, and there are no fish now in the Little River.'

Shannow sipped the sweetened milk, and sought a name for the face. Brown? Bream? Then it came to him: Broome. Josiah Broome. And with it came another face, strong female features surrounded by corn-blonde hair.

Beth.

The memory struck him like a knife in the heart.

'Jesus Christ! You used to be a man. Now you let scum like Shem Jackson strike you in front of a crowd. Knock you down in the dirt! God's teeth, Jon, what have you become?'

'The blow lessened him more than me. I have done with killing. Beth. I have done with the ways of violence. Can't you understand that there must be a better way for men to live?'

'What I understand is I don't want you here any more. I just don't want you!'

The sound of approaching horses jerked Shannow back to the present as four riders drew up in front of the Crusader offices. Shannow stood, left a half-silver on the table, then walked to the door.

Gareth Archer moved alongside him. 'Don't be a fool, man! Dillon is a dead shot, and those others with him are no angels.'

'If thou faint in the day of adversity, thy strength is small,' said Shannow. Stepping out, he moved from the wooden sidewalk, down the three short steps to the dusty street.

'Jack Dillon!' he called. The four men dismounted and the tallest of them, dark-bearded and powerfully-built, swung round to face him.

'Who wants me?' he replied. People who had been moving along the street stopped and watched the two men.

'I am Jon Shannow and I name you as a murderer and a brigand.' Shannow could hear the sharp intake of breath from the crowd, and he saw the bearded man redden.

Dillon blinked and licked his lips, then he recovered some of his bluster. 'What? This is nonsense!'

Shannow walked slowly towards him, and his voice carried to all the observers. 'You shot down a farmer named Hankin, murdered him in cold blood. Then you hunted his children. How do you answer this accusation, villain?'

'I don't answer to you!' The big man's hand swept down towards his pistol and the crowd scattered. Dillon drew first, a bullet slashing past Shannow's cheek. His own guns boomed in reply and Dillon, struck in the chest and belly, staggered back, triggering his revolver into the dust. A second man loosed a shot at Shannow, the bullet passing high and wide. Sighting his right-hand pistol, Shannow shot the man in the chest; he fell back over a guard-rail and did not move. The other two Crusaders were standing stock-still. Dillon was on his knees, blood drenching his vest.

Shannow strode to where the dying man waited. *'Whoso diggeth a pit shall fall therein, and he that rolleth a stone, it will return upon him.'*

'Who . . . are . . . you?' Dillon fell sideways, but his pain-filled eyes continued to stare up at his killer.

'I am retribution,' Shannow told him. Kicking away the man's pistol, he scanned the crowd. 'You have allowed evil to prosper here,' he said, 'and that is a shame upon you all.' To his left he saw Gareth Archer move into sight, leading Shannow's horse.

Keeping the two remaining Crusaders in sight, Shannow mounted.

'Ride south-east for an hour,' Archer whispered, 'then turn west by the fork in the stream.'

'She is there?'

Archer was shocked, but he nodded. 'You knew?'

'I see her in you,' said Shannow.

And turning the horse, he rode slowly from the town.

*

Amaziga Archer was waiting for him by the stream. The black woman had changed little since Shannow had last seen her and, like himself, she seemed untouched by the passage of the decades. Her hair was still jet-black, her face unlined, her almond-shaped eyes dark and lustrous. She was wearing a grey shield shirt and a riding skirt of leather. Her horse was a grey gelding of some sixteen hands.

'Follow me,' she ordered him, then headed up over rocky ground, her mount splashing along the shallow stream. They rode in the water for almost half an hour before she turned the gelding to the right, urging him up a steep bank. Shannow followed, his mount struggling on the greasy slope.

'They will see where we emerged,' he said. 'A skilled tracker will not be fooled by our route. The stream is not swift-running and the hoof-marks will be there for some days.'

'I am aware of that, Shannow,' she said. 'Grant me a little respect. I spent the last hour before your arrival moving back and forth in the water, emerging at no fewer than seven banks. Added to that, where we are about to go no man – save one – could follow.'

Without another word she rode on, heading towards a high wall of rock. The ground was hard, and glancing down Shannow saw that they were moving along an ancient road paved with slabs of granite.

'This was the road to Pisaecuris,' she told him, 'a major city of the Akkadians. They were descended from the peoples of the Atlantean empire, and flourished thousands of years ago.'

Ahead of them was a series of ruined buildings, and beyond that a circle of great stones. Amaziga Archer rode through the ruins and dismounted at the centre of the circle. Shannow stepped from the saddle. 'What now?' he asked.

'Now we go home,' she said. From a deep pocket in her skirt she took a small golden Stone. The air shimmered with violet light and Shannow's horse reared, but he calmed him swiftly. The light faded. Beyond the circle there was now a two-storey house built of red brick and painted timbers, with a slanted roof of black slate. Before it was a garishly painted and highly elaborate carriage; it had windows all around and rested on four thick, black wheels.

'This is home,' she said coldly, interrupting his examination of the object. 'I wish I could say you were welcome – but you are not. There is a paddock behind the house. Release the horses there. I will prepare some food.' Tossing him the reins to her grey, she walked into the house. Shannow led the horses to the rear of the building, unsaddled them and freed them in the paddock. Then he returned to the front door and tapped lightly on the wood. 'For God's sake,' she said, 'you don't need to observe the niceties here.'

Stepping inside, he saw the most remarkable room. It was fully carpeted in thick grey wool, upon which stood four padded armchairs and a couch covered with soft black leather. From the ceiling hung a curious lamp of glass, no larger than a wine goblet, from which came a light so bright it hurt his eyes to stare at it. There was a fire blazing in a stone hearth but the coals, though they glowed, did not burn. On a desk by the far wall was a curious contraption, a box, grey on three sides but with one black side facing towards a chair. Wires extended from the rear, running down to a small block set in the wall.

'What is this place?' asked Shannow.

'My study,' said Amaziga. 'You should be honoured, Shannow. You are only the third man to see it. The first was my second husband, the second was my son, Gareth.'

'You married again. That is good.'

'What would you know about it?' she snapped. 'My first husband died because of you. He was the love of my life, Shannow. I don't suppose you'd understand that, would you? And because of you and your demented faith my home was destroyed, and I lost my first son. I didn't think there was much more you could do to hurt me. Yet here you are, large as life. The new Elijah, no less, and your twisted values have become enshrined in the laws of your bizarre new world.'

'Is that why you brought me here, lady?' he asked softly. 'So that you could blame me for all the evils of Man? Your husband was killed by an evil man. But your people died because they followed Sarento, and he was behind the Hellborn War. It was he, not I, who turned the Daniel Stones to blood and brought destruction on the Guardians. But then you know all this. So unless you want to blame me for every storm and drought, every plague and pestilence, pray tell me why you asked your son to guide me to you.'

Amaziga closed her beautiful eyes and drew in a deep breath, which she released slowly. 'Sit down, Shannow,' she said at last, her voice more mellow. 'I'll make some coffee, then we'll talk.' She moved to a cupboard on the far wall and removed a brightly coloured packet. Shannow watched as she tipped the contents – small dark stones – into a glass jug. She flicked a switch and the jug whirred, grinding the stones to powder. This she poured into a paper container set atop a second, larger jug. Seeing him watching her, she smiled for the first time. 'It's a drink that is popular in this world,' she told him. 'You may prefer it sweetened with milk and sugar. It will take a little time.'

'Where are we?' he asked.

'Arizona,' she said, leaving him none the wiser.

Crossing the room, she sat opposite him. 'I am sorry,' she said, 'for my angry words. And I do know that you are not *wholly* at fault. But equally, had you not entered my life my first husband would still be alive and so would Luke. And I cannot forget that I saw you destroy a world – perhaps two worlds. Millions upon millions of people. But Beth was right. You were not seeking to detonate the Sword of God; you did not even fully know what it was.' Hot water began bubbling into the jug and Amaziga rose and stood by it. 'I am not religious, Shannow. If there is a God, then he is capricious and wilful and I want no part of him. So I find myself disliking you on too many counts to be able to handle.'

The bubbling noises from the jug abruptly ceased and Amaziga poured the black liquid into two ornate mugs. She passed one to Shannow, who sniffed it apprehensively. When he sipped it, the taste was acrid and bitter, similar to Baker's but with more body. 'I'll get the sugar,' said Amaziga.

Sweetened, the drink was almost bearable. 'Tell me what you want of me, lady,' he said, putting aside the mug.

'You are so sure I want something?'

He nodded. 'I am not seeking another angry dispute, but I already knew that you held me in contempt. You have made that clear on a number of occasions. So, the fact that I am here means you need me. The question is, for what purpose?'

'Perhaps it was just to save your life.'

He shook his head. 'No, lady. You despise me and all that you believe I stand for. Why would you save me?'

'All right!' she snapped. 'There is something.'

'Name it, and if it is possible I will attempt it.'

She rubbed her face and looked away. 'You give your promises so easily,' she said, her voice low.

'And when I do, I keep them, lady. I do not lie.'

'I know that!' she said, her voice rising. 'You are the Jerusalem Man! Oh, Christ . . .'

'Just tell me what you want,' he urged her.

'I will tell you what I need from you, Shannow. You will think I am mad, but you must hear me out. You promise that?' He nodded and for a moment she said nothing, then she looked directly into his eyes. 'All right. I want you to bring Sam back from the dead.'

He stared at her in silence.

'It is not as crazy as it sounds,' Amaziga went on. 'Trust me on that, Shannow. The past, the present and the future all co-exist, and we can visit them. You know that already, because Pendarric's legions crossed the vault of time to invade our lands. They crossed twelve thousand years. It can be done.'

'But Sam is dead, woman!'

'Can you only think in straight lines?' she stormed. 'Supposing you were to go back into the past and prevent them killing him?'

'But I didn't. I do not understand the principles behind such journeys, but I do know that Sam Archer died – because that is what happened. If I went back and changed that, then it would already have happened and we wouldn't be having this conversation.'

Suddenly she laughed and clapped her hands. 'Bravo,

Shannow. At last a little imagination! Good. Then think on this: If I journeyed back into the past and shot your father, before he met your mother, and then returned here, would I be alone? Would you have ceased to exist?'

'One would suppose so,' he said.

'No,' she said triumphantly. 'You would still be here. That is the great discovery.'

'And how would I be here without having had a father?'

'There are infinite universes existing alongside our own, perhaps in the same space. Infinite. Without number, in other words. There are thousands of Jon Shannows, perhaps millions. When we step through the ancient Gateways we cross into parallel universes. Some are identical to our own, some fractionally different. With an infinite number it means that anything the mind can conceive *must* exist somewhere. So somewhere Sam Archer did not die in Castlemine. You see what I am saying?'

'I hear the words, lady. Understanding is something else entirely.'

'Think of it in terms of the grains of sand in a desert. No two are exactly identical. The odds against finding twin grains would be, say, a hundred million to one. But then the number of grains is finite. It may be thirty trillion. But supposing there was no limit to the number of grains? Then a hundred million to one would be small odds. And within infinity there would be an infinite number of twins. That is a fact of life within the multiverse. I know. I have seen it.'

Shannow finished his coffee. 'So you are saying that in some world, somewhere, there is a Sam Archer waiting to be taken to Castlemine? Yes.'

'Exactly.'

'Then why do you not go back back and find him? Why is it necessary to send a messenger?'

Amaziga moved to the jug and refilled the mugs. This time Shannow sipped the brew appreciatively. She sat down and leaned back in the leather chair. 'I did go back,' she said, 'and I found Sam and brought him home. We lived together here for almost a year.'

'He died?'

She shook her head. 'I made a mistake. I told him everything and one morning he was gone, searching for what he termed *his* own life. What he didn't know was that I was already pregnant with Gareth. Perhaps that would have changed his mind. I don't know. But this time I'll get it right, Shannow. With your help.'

'Your son must be around twenty years old. How is it you have waited this long to try again?'

Amaziga sighed. 'He is eighteen. It took me two years to find Sam again, and even in that I was lucky. I have spent the last decade in research, studying clairvoyance and mysticism. It came to me that clairvoyants cannot *see* the future, for it does not exist yet. What they can do is to glimpse other *identical* worlds – which is why some of their visions are so ludicrously wrong. They see a future that exists on another world and predict that it will happen here. But all kinds of events can change the possible futures. Finally I found a man whose powers were incredible. He lived in a place called Sedona – one of the most beautiful lands I have ever seen, red rock buttes set in a magnificent desert. For a time I lived with him. I used my Sipstrassi Stones to duplicate his powers, and imprint them on a machine.' She stood and walked to the black-faced box on the desk by the wall. 'This machine. It resembles a computer, but it is very special.' Amaziga pressed a button and the screen flickered to life, becoming a face, a handsome man with red-gold hair and eyes of startling blue.

'Welcome home, Amaziga,' it said, the voice low and smooth, and infinitely human. 'I see you found the man you were seeking.'

'Yes, Lucas. This is Jon Shannow.'

Shannow rose and approached the box. 'You trapped the man in there?' he said, horrified.

'No, not the man. He died. I was away on research and he collapsed with a heart attack. Lucas is a creation which holds all of the man's memories. But he is also something different. He is self-aware in his own right. He operates as a kind of time-scope, using both the power of Sipstrassi and the magic of the ancient Gateways. Through his *talent* we can view alternate worlds. Show him, Lucas.'

'What would you like to see, Mr Shannow?' asked Lucas.

He wanted to say *Jerusalem*, but he could not. Shannow hesitated. 'You choose,' he told the machine.

The face disappeared and Shannow found himself staring at a city on a hill, a great temple at the centre. The sky above was deep blue, and the sun shone with unbearable brightness. A man was standing outside the temple, arms raised, and a great crowd was listening to him; he was dressed in golden armour, with a burnished helm upon his head. Sounds came from the machine, a language Shannow did not know, but the armoured man's voice was low and melodious. Lucas's voice cut in: 'The man is Solomon and he is consecrating the great temple of Jerusalem.' The scene faded, and was replaced instantly by another; this time the city was in ruins and a dark-bearded figure stood brooding over the broken stones. Again Lucas cut in: 'This is the King of the Assyrians. He has destroyed the city. Solomon was slain in a great battle. There is, as you can see, no temple. In this world he failed. Do you wish to see other variations?'

'No,' said Shannow. 'Show me the Sam Archer you wish me to find.'

The screen flickered and Shannow saw a mountainside and a collection of tents. Several people were gathering wood. One of them was the tall, broad-shouldered man he remembered so well: Sam Archer, archaeologist and Guardian. He had a rifle looped over his shoulder and was standing on a cliff-edge staring down over a plain. Upon the plain was an army.

'The day following this scene,' said Lucas, 'the army sweeps into the mountains, killing everyone.'

'What War is it?'

'It is the Hellborn. They have conquered and are now sweeping away the last remnants of the defeated army.'

The screen changed once more, becoming the handsome face with the clear blue eyes. 'Do I exist in this world?' asked Shannow.

'You did, as a farmer. You were killed in the first invasion. Sam Archer did not know you.'

'Who rules the Hellborn? Sarento? Welby?'

'Neither. The Bloodstone rules.'

'Someone must control it, surely?'

'No, Shannow,' said Amaziga. 'In this world the Bloodstone lives. Sarento drew it into himself, and in doing so created a demon with awesome powers. Thousands have died since to feed the Bloodstone.'

'Can it be killed?'

'No,' said Lucas. 'It is impervious to shot or shell, and can create a field around it of immense force. The Sword of God could have destroyed it, but in this world there is no missile waiting.'

'The Bloodstone is not your problem, Shannow,' put in Amaziga. 'All I want is for you to rescue Sam and bring him back. Will you do it?'

'I have a problem,' he said.

'Yes, with your memory. I can help you with that. But only when you get back.'

'Why wait?'

She hesitated before answering. 'I will tell you the truth, and ask you to accept it. You would not be the same man if I returned your memory to you. And the man you will become – though more acceptable to me – would have less chance of success. Will you take that on trust?'

Shannow sat silently, his pale gaze locked to her dark eyes. 'You need Shannow the killer.'

'Yes,' she whispered.

He nodded. 'It lessens us both.'

'I know,' she answered, her eyes downcast.

*

The main street of Purity was bustling with people as Nestor and Clem rode in; miners, their weekend pay burning holes in their pockets, were heading for the taverns and gambling-houses, while the locals moved along packed sidewalks to restaurants and eating-houses. Shops and stores were still open, although dusk was long since past, and three lamplighters were moving along the street carrying ladders and tapers. Behind them, in double lines, the huge oil-lamps gave off a yellow glow that made the mud of the main street shine as if it was streaked with gold.

Nestor had never been to Purity, though he had heard that

the silver mines had brought great prosperity to the community. The air stank of smoke and sulphur, and music was playing all along the street, discordant and brash as many melodies vied for the ear.

'Let's get a drink,' shouted Clem. 'My throat feels like I'm carrying half the desert caked around it.' Nestor nodded in reply and they drew up outside a large tavern with ornate stained-glass windows. Some twenty horses were hitched to the rail and Nestor had difficulty finding a place to leave their mounts. Clem ducked under the rail and strode into the tavern. Inside there were gaming tables, and a long bar served by five barmen. A band was playing brass instruments, a pianist accompanying them. Above the gaming hall a gallery ran around the room and Nestor saw gaudily-dressed women moving along it, arm-in-arm with miners or local men. The boy frowned. Such behaviour was immoral, and it surprised him that any Deacon township would tolerate such displays.

Clem eased his way to the bar and ordered two beers. Nestor did not like the taste of beer, but said nothing as the glass was pushed towards him.

The noise within the tavern was deafening, and Nestor drank in uncomfortable silence. What pleasure, he wondered, could men draw from such places? He wandered across to a card table, where men were pushing Barta notes into the centre of the table. He shook his head. Why work all week and then throw your money away in a single night? It was incomprehensible.

Nestor turned away – and collided with a burly man carrying a pint of beer. The liquid splashed down the man's shirt and the glass fell from his grasp to shatter on the sawdust-strewn floor.

'You clumsy bastard!' the man shouted.

'I'm sorry. Let me buy you another.' A fist hit Nestor square in the face, hurling him back over a card table, which toppled, spilling Barta notes to the floor. Nestor rolled and tried to come upright but, dizzy, he stumbled back to his knees. A booted foot cracked into his side and he rolled away from the blow, but came up against a table-leg. The man reached down and dragged him up by the lapels of his jacket.

'That will be enough,' Nestor heard Clem Steiner say.

The man glanced round. 'It will be enough when I say it is. Not before,' retorted his attacker.

'Let him go or I'll kill you,' said Clem.

The music had ceased when Nestor had been struck, but now the silence was almost unbearable. Slowly the man let him go, then pushed him away. He turned towards Clem, his hand hovering over the holstered gun at his hip. 'You'll kill me, dung-breath? You know who I am?'

'I know you're a lard-belly with all the speed of a sick turtle,' said Clem, with an easy smile. 'So before you make an attempt to pull that pistol, I should call on what friends you have to stand beside you.'

The man swore and made a grab for the gun, but even as his hand closed on the butt he found himself staring down the barrel of Clem's nickel-plated revolver. Clem walked forward until the barrel rested on the man's forehead. 'How did anyone as slow as you live to get so ugly?' he asked. As he finished speaking, he stepped forward and brought his knee up hard into the other's groin. With a groan the man slumped forward and Clem's pistol landed a sickening blow to the back of his neck. He hit the floor face first and did not move.

'Friendly place,' said Clem, holstering the pistol. 'You finished fooling around, Nestor?'

The boy nodded glumly. 'Then let's find somewhere to eat,' said Clem, clapping the younger man on the shoulder.

Nestor stumbled forward, still dizzy, and Clem caught him. 'By God, boy, you are a trouble to be around.'

An elderly man approached them. 'Son, take a little advice and leave Purity. Sachs won't forget that beating. He'll be looking for you.'

'Where's the best eating-house in town?' countered Clem.

'The Little Marie. Two blocks down towards the south. On the right.'

'Well, when he wakes up, you tell him where I've gone. And tell him to bring his own shovel. I'll bury him where he lands.'

Clem steered Nestor out of the tavern and half-lifted him to the saddle. 'Cling on there, boy,' he said. 'The pain'll pass.'

'Yes, sir,' mumbled Nestor. Clem mounted and led Nestor north. 'Ain't we going the wrong way, sir?'

Clem just chuckled. Several blocks further along the street they came to a small restaurant with a painted sign proclaiming, 'The Unity Restaurant'. 'This will do,' said Clem. 'How are you feeling?'

'Like a horse walked over me.'

'You'll survive. Let's eat.'

The restaurant boasted just five tables, only one of which was occupied. The diner was a tall man, wearing the grey shield shirt of a Crusader. Clem hung his hat on a rack by the door and walked to a table. A slender waitress with honey-blonde hair approached him. 'We got steak. We got chicken. We got ham. Make your choice.'

'I can see the reason for the restaurant's popularity,' said Clem. 'I hope the food is warmer than the welcome.'

'You won't find out till you make a choice,' she said, without a change of expression. 'We got steak. We got chicken. We got ham.'

'I'll have steak and eggs. So will he. Medium rare.'

'Er, I prefer mine well done,' said Nestor.

'He's young, but he'll learn,' put in Clem. 'Make it two, medium rare.'

'We got local wine. We got beer. We got Baker's. Make your choice.'

'How good is the wine?' She raised one eyebrow. 'Forget I asked. We'll take the beer.'

As she walked away Nestor leaned forward. 'What kind of a town is this?' he asked Clem. 'Did you see what they were doing in that tavern? Gambling, and consorting with . . . with . . .' the young man stumbled to a halt.

Clem chuckled. 'You mean the women? Ah, Nestor, you've got a lot to learn, boy.'

'But it's against the Deacon's laws.'

'There are some things you can't legislate against,' said Clem, his smile fading. 'Most men need the company of a woman from time to time. In a mining community, where men outnumber women maybe twenty to one, there's not enough to go round. That sort of situation leads to trouble, Nestor. A good whore can help keep the peace.'

'Your friend is a wise man,' said the Crusader, easing back his chair and wandering over to their table. He was tall and stoop-shouldered, with a drooping moustache. 'Welcome to Purity, boys,' he said. 'I'm Seth Wheeler, local Captain of Crusaders.'

'Those are the first pleasant words we've heard,' said Clem, offering his hand.

Wheeler shook it and pulled up a chair. 'Just visiting?' he asked.

'Passing through,' said Clem, before Nestor could speak.

Wheeler nodded. 'Don't judge us too harshly, young man,' he told Nestor. 'Your friend is right. Once the silver mines opened up we got every kind of villain here, and some four thousand miners. Hard men. At first we tried to uphold the laws regarding gambling and the like. But it went on just the same. Tricksters and conmen fleece the workers. That led to killings. So we opened up the gambling-houses and we tried to keep them fair. It ain't perfect, but we do our best to keep the peace. It ain't easy.'

'But what about the law?' said Nestor.

Wheeler gave a weary smile. 'I could make a law that says a man can only breathe on a Sunday. You think it would be obeyed? The only laws men will follow are those that they either agree with, or can be enforced by men like me. I can make the miners and the rogues stay away from the decent folk here. I can do that. But Unity needs silver, and this is the richest strike ever. So we got special dispensation from the Apostle Saul to operate our . . . places.' It was obvious that Wheeler didn't like the situation, and he struck Clem as a decent man. 'So where you heading?' he asked Nestor.

'We're looking for someone,' replied the youngster.

'Anyone in particular?'

'Yes, sir. The Preacher from Pilgrim's Valley.'

'Jon Cade? I heard he was killed after his church was burnt down.'

'You knew him?' asked Clem.

'Never seen him, but word spread that he was friendly to Wolvers – even had them in his church. No wonder it got blazed. He's alive then, you reckon?'

'Yes, sir, we think so,' said Nestor. 'He killed some of the raiders, but he was wounded bad.'

'Well, he's not been here, son. I can assure you of that. Still, give me a description and I'll see it's circulated.'

'He's around six feet two, dark hair – a little grey at the temples. And he was wearing a black coat and a white shirt, black trousers and shoes. He's sort of thin in the face, with deep-set eyes, and he don't smile much. I'd say he was around 35, maybe a little older.'

'This wound he took,' said Wheeler softly. 'Was it in the temple . . . here?' he added, tapping the right side of his head.

'Yes, sir, I believe so. Someone seen him riding out, said he was bleeding from the head.'

'How would you know that if you haven't seen him?' put in Clem.

'Oh, I've seen a man who answers that description. What else can you tell me about him?'

'He's a quiet man,' said Nestor, 'and he doesn't like violence.'

'You don't say? Well, for a man who doesn't like it he's mighty partial to it. He shot our Oath Taker to death. Right there in the church. I have to admit that Crane – the dead man – was an odious little runt, but that ain't hardly the point. He was also involved in an earlier gun-battle when Crane and some other men attacked a group of *Wanderers*. Several men – and a woman – were killed. I think the wound must have scrambled your Preacher's brains, son. You wouldn't believe who he's claiming to be.'

'Who?' asked Nestor.

'The Jerusalem Man.'

Nestor's mouth dropped open, and he swung a quick glance to Clem. The older man's face was expressionless. Wheeler leaned back in his chair. 'Don't seem to have surprised you none, friend?'

Clem shrugged. 'Head wounds can be very tricky,' he said. 'I take it you didn't catch him?'

'Nope. To be honest, I hope we don't. That's a very sick man. And he was provoked. I'll tell you this, though, he can surely handle a pistol. That's a surprising gift for a Preacher who don't like violence.'

'He's a surprising man,' said Clem.

*

Jacob Moon was thinking of other, more weighty matters as the mortally wounded man crawled painfully across the yard, trying to reach the fallen pistol. He was considering his prospects. The Apostle Saul had treated him fairly, giving him back his youth and supplying a plentiful share of wealth and women. But his day was passing.

Saul might think he could take the Deacon's place, but Moon knew it wouldn't happen. For all his bluster and his willingness to kill for power, there was a weakness in Saul. Others had not, apparently, noticed it. But then they were blinded by the brilliance of the Deacon, and failed to see the flaws in the man who stood beside him. Let's face it, thought Moon, Saul casts a mighty thin shadow.

The wounded man groaned. He was close to the pistol now; Moon waited until his hand closed over the butt, then shot him twice in the back. The last shot had severed the spine just above the hip, and the man's legs were useless. Moon's victim, the pistol in his hand, was trying to roll over in order to aim at his assailant. He couldn't. The legs were dead weight now.

Moon moved to the right. 'Over here, Kovac,' he said. 'Try this side.'

Gamely the injured Bull Kovac pushed against the ground, his powerful arms finally twisting him far enough to be able to see the tall assassin. With trembling fingers Bull eased back the hammer of his pistol. Moon drew and fired, the bullet entering Kovac's head just above the bridge of the nose.

'By God, he was game,' said one of the two Jerusalem Riders accompanying Moon.

'Game doesn't get it done,' said Moon. 'You boys get back to Pilgrim's Valley and report the attack on Kovac's farm. You can say that I'm out hunting the killers. If you need me, I'll be in Domango. And Jed,' he called as the riders turned their mounts.

'Yes, sir, Jacob?'

'I haven't the time to deal with the storekeeper. You handle it.'

'When?'

'In two days,' Moon told him. 'The night before the Oath Taking.'

As the men rode away Moon stepped across the corpse and strolled into the house. The log walls were well-crafted and neatly fitted, the dirt floor hard-packed and well-swept. Bull Kovac had traced a series of motifs into it, making it more homely. There were no pictures on the wall, and all the furniture was hand-made. Moon pulled up a chair and sat down. A jug of Baker's was still sitting on the old iron stove, gently steaming. Reaching out he filled a mug, his mind returning to the problem of Saul.

The Apostle was right. Land was the key to wealth. But why share it? Most of what they had gathered was already in Moon's name. With Saul dead I will be doubly rich, he thought.

A small black and white cat moved out of the shadows and rubbed against Moon's leg. It jumped to his lap and began to purr. Moon stroked its head and the animal gratefully curled up, its purrs increasing.

When to kill him was the question now.

Stroking the cat, Moon found his inner tension subsiding, and he remembered a line from the Old Testament. Something about, for every thing there is a season, a time to plant, a time to reap, a time to live, a time to die. That sounded right.

It wasn't the season on Saul just yet . . .

First there was the Jerusalem Man. Then the woman, Beth McAdam.

Moon finished his mug of Baker's and stood, the cat dropping to all fours on the floor. As he strode from the building, the cat followed, and stood in the doorway meowing.

Moon turned and fired in one flowing motion. Then reloading his pistol, he mounted his horse and set off for Domango.

Chapter Seven

People say we no longer live in an age of miracles. It is not so. What has been lost is our ability to see them.
The Wisdom of the Deacon
Introduction

* * *

Josiah Broome put aside his Bible. He had never been a believer, not in the fullest sense, but he valued those sections of the New Testament which dealt with love and forgiveness. It always amazed him how people could be so quick to hate and so slow to love. But then, he reasoned, the first seemed so much easier.

Else was out for the evening, at the Bible study group held every Friday at Frey Bailey's home on the outskirts of town, just beyond the meeting hall, and Josiah Broome was enjoying the unnatural silence. Friday night produced an oasis of calm within his tidy home. Replacing the Bible on the bookshelf, he moved to the kitchen and filled the kettle. One mug of Baker's before retiring, heavily sweetened with honey, was his one luxury on a Friday night. He would carry it out on to the porch and sip it while watching the distant stars.

Tomorrow he would give Oath for Beth McAdam, and Else would scold him for the entire evening. But tonight he would enjoy the silence. The kettle began to vibrate. Taking a cloth from a peg on the wall, he wrapped it around the handle and lifted the kettle from the range. Filling the mug, he added the powdered Baker brew and three heaped spoonfuls of honey. As he was stirring it he heard a tapping at his front door. Annoyed by the interruption, he carried the drink through the kitchen and across the main room. 'Come in!' he called, for the door was never locked.

Daniel Cade eased his way inside, leaning heavily on his sticks, his face red from exertion. Josiah Broome hurried to his side, taking hold of the Prophet's arm and guiding him to a deep chair. Cade sank down gratefully, laying his sticks on the floor.

Leaning his head back, the Prophet took several deep breaths. Broome laid the mug of Baker's on a table to his visitor's right. 'Drink that, sir,' he said. 'It will help restore your strength.' Hurrying back to the kitchen, he made a second mug and returned to the fireside. Cade's breathing had eased, but the old man looked tired, worn out, dark circles beneath his eyes and an unhealthy pallor replacing the fiery red of his cheeks.

'I'm about all done in, son,' he wheezed.

'What brings you to my home, sir . . . not that you are unwelcome, you understand!'

Cade smiled. Lifting the Baker's with a trembling hand, he sipped the brew. 'By God, that is sweet!' he said.

'I could make you another,' offered Broome.

Cade shook his head. 'It will do, son. I came to talk, not to drink. Have you been noticing the new arrivals?'

Broome nodded. More than a score of riders had come in to Pilgrim's Valley during the past week, all of them tough men, heavily armed. 'Jerusalem Riders,' he said. 'They serve the Deacon.'

Cade grunted. 'Saul, more like. I don't like it, Broome. I know their kind. God's Blood, *I am their kind*. Brigands, take my word for it. I don't know what game Saul is playing, but I don't like it, Broome.'

'I understand that Jacob Moon called them in after the murder of poor Bull Kovac,' said Broom.

Cade's pale eyes narrowed. 'Yes,' he said softly. 'The man you and Beth were to stand Oath for. Now two of those same Jerusalem Riders have moved in to Bull's house. There's something very wrong here. But no one else can see it.'

'What do you mean?'

'It started with the burning of the church. Why were no Crusaders present? And how did the raiders know that there would be no one to stand against them? There were at least twenty masked killers around that building, yet only five left the town. Take away the dead man outside the church, and that leaves fourteen unaccounted for in the raid. Curiously that is the same number of Crusaders who rode out to the supposed attack on Shem Jackson's farm.'

'You're not suggesting . . . ?'

'I'm suggesting something is beginning to smell bad in Pilgrim's Valley.'

'I think . . . if you'll pardon my directness . . . that you are over-reacting. I have spoken to the Apostle Saul, and he assures me that Jacob Moon and his Riders will soon apprehend the brigands who murdered poor Bull. These men are carefully chosen for their skills and their dedication, as indeed are the Crusaders. I have known Leon Evans since he was a boy; I cannot believe he would have taken part in such a . . . such a dreadful business.'

'You've more faith than I have,' said Cade wearily. 'Something is happening, and I don't like it. And I don't like that Saul – can't understand what the Deacon sees in him, save that he's the only one of the Apostles still living.'

'I'm sure he is a fine man. I have spoken to him on many occasions and always found him to be courteous and caring,' said Broome, beginning to be uncomfortable. 'He knows all the Scriptures by heart, and he spends his day in prayer and communion with the Lord.'

Cade chuckled. 'Come, come, Broome, you don't need to pull no wool over these old eyes. You ain't a Christian – though you're a damn sight closer to it than many others. But that's by the by. Jon told me that you were one of the few who knew of his past. He trusted you . . . and I will too. I'm heading for Unity tomorrow. I'm going to try to see the Deacon and find out just what the Hell is happening.'

'Why come to me?'

'I think Saul knows how I feel and he may try to stop me reaching the capital. If I don't make it, Broome, I want you to tell Jonnie what I said. You understand?'

'But . . . but he's dead. Lost in the desert.'

'He ain't dead. Don't you listen to the gossip? A man claiming to be the Jerusalem Man shot the Purity Oath Taker to death. He ain't dead, Broome. God damn, he's alive again! And he'll be back.'

A movement came from the doorway and Broome glanced

up to see a tall, wide-shouldered man standing there, a gun in his hand. 'What do you want?' he asked, rising.

'Been told to kill you,' said the man amiably, 'but no one said a God damn thing about this old fart. Still, orders is orders.' The gunman smiled. His pistol thundered and Broome was smashed back against the wall. He fell heavily, pain flaring in his chest, and collided with the small table by his chair. It tipped and he felt the mug of Baker's strike his back, the hot liquid soaking through his shirt. Despite the pain, he stayed conscious and stared up at the man who had shot him.

'Why?' he asked, his voice clear.

The gunman shrugged. 'I don't ask questions,' he said.

'Neither do I,' said Daniel Cade. Broome's eyes flickered to the Prophet. His voice sounded different, colder than the grave. The gunman swung his pistol – but he was too late and Cade shot him twice in the chest. The man fell back into the doorframe and tried to lift his weapon, but it fired into the floor. He sagged down, his fingers losing hold of the pistol.

'You're . . . supposed to . . . be a . . . man of God,' said the gunman, coughing blood.

'Amen to that,' said Cade. His gun came up and a third shot smashed through the man's skull. 'Rot in Hell,' said the Prophet. Broome struggled to his knees, blood staining his shirt, his left arm hanging uselessly at his side.

'Come on, Jed,' shouted a voice from outside, 'what the Hell is keeping you?'

'If you can walk, Broome,' whispered Cade, 'I suggest you get out back. You'll find my buggy. Make for Beth McAdam's place.'

'What about you?'

'Go now, son. There's no more time for talk.' Cade had broken open his pistol and was feeding shells into the cylinder. Broome stood, staggered, then backed away through the kitchen. The glass of the front window shattered, and a man pushed the curtains aside. Cade shot him. Another gunman leapt through the doorway. Broome saw him fire twice, both bullets hammering into the Prophet. Cade's gun boomed and the gunman flew back, blood spraying to the wall behind him.

Broome staggered out into the night, hauling himself up on to

Cade's buggy. Grabbing the reins with his good hand, he kicked free the brake and lashed the reins down on the horse's back. The beast lurched into the traces and the buggy picked up speed.

A shot sounded from behind him, then another. He heard a bullet thud into the wooden frame and ducked down. Then the buggy was clear and racing away into the night.

*

'I'd like to know what is going on,' Nestor Garrity told Clem Steiner, once the two men were alone. Clem looked away, and cut into his steak. 'Who is he? Really?' persisted Nestor.

Clem pushed away his plate and wiped his mouth with a napkin. 'He's who he says he is.'

'The Jerusalem Man? He can't be! I know him! He's the Preacher, for God's sake!'

'Times change, Nestor. Men change. He fought the Daggers and he'd had enough. Think of it, boy. He was a sad, bitter man, searching for a city that didn't exist. Then he sent the Sword of God through time and destroyed a world. Maybe two worlds. He was in love with Beth. He wanted a different life. The last ounce of power in the Daniel Stone gave him back his youth. It was a new start. As far as I know, only two people recognised him when he came back from the Wall: Josiah Broome and Edric Scayse. Scayse took the secret to the grave – and Broome? He's a peaceful man and a dreamer. He liked what Shannow was trying to become. That's all, Nestor.'

'But the books? The chariot to Heaven. Is it all lies?'

'Mostly,' said Clem, with a wry grin. 'But then legends are like that, son. We misremember them. We don't do it intentionally most of the time. Take me, for example. When I was a kid I had a teacher who told me that I would be a brigand or a war-maker. He expelled me from school and told my folks there was no good in me. Now I own three hundred thousand acres and I'm a rich, powerful man. I saw that teacher last year, he came to live in Pernum. Know what he said? "Clem, I always knew you had the seeds of greatness in you." He wasn't lying. Understand?'

The young man shook his head. 'I don't understand any of it.

It's all built on lies. The Deacon, everything. It's all lies! All that Bible shit. All the studying. Lies!'

'Whoa, son! Don't lump it all in together!' warned Clem. 'We all need heroes – and Shannow was . . . is . . . a good man. No matter what other people may write about him, he always did what he thought was right, and he would never pass by and let evil have its way. And some of the things he did can't be disputed. He fought the Hellborn, and he destroyed the Guardians who were behind the War. Nestor, he is a good man; it is not his fault that others – of a more political mind – chose to take his name in vain.'

'I want to go home,' said Nestor. 'I don't want to do this any more.'

'Sure, son,' said Clem. 'I understand that.'

Clem paid for the meal and stood. Nestor rose also, his shoulders hunched, his eyes distant. Clem felt for the boy. The iron hooves of reality had ground his dreams to dust. 'Let's go,' said the older man, and together they walked out on to the street. A shot sounded, and shards of wood exploded from the post beside Clem's head; he ducked, drew his pistol and dived forward. A rifleman stepped into sight and Clem fired, the bullet striking the man in the shoulder and spinning him, the rifle falling from his hands. Nestor stood transfixed; then he saw the man from the tavern.

Sachs was aiming a pistol at Clem's back. Without thinking Nestor drew his pistol and triggered it, the shell hammering home into Sachs' chest. Suddenly all of Nestor's anger welled up and, walking towards the wounded man, he fired again. And again. Each shot thundered home and Sachs was hurled back against the wall of a building.

'You bastard!' screamed Nestor, continuing to pull the trigger even after the gun was long empty and the lifeless would-be assassin was dead at his feet. Clem came alongside him, gently pulling the pistol clear. Nestor was crying, his body racked by deep, convulsive sobs. 'It's all lies!' he said.

'I know,' said Clem.

Seth Wheeler appeared, a long-barrelled pistol in his hands. 'What in Hades is happening here?' he asked Clem.

'We had an argument earlier with . . . him,' he said, pointing down at the corpse. 'When we left the eating-house they opened fire on us. There's a man back there with a busted shoulder; I guess he'll tell you more.'

'Well,' said Wheeler, 'it's for damned sure that Sachs ain't going to tell us anything. You boys better walk with me to the office. I'll need to make a report for the town elders.'

'He was a damn fool,' said Clem bitterly. 'He's dead over a spilled beer.'

'He's killed others for less, I reckon,' muttered Wheeler. 'But there was never any proof.'

Later, when Seth Wheeler had painstakingly written out his report, he put down his pen and looked up at Nestor. The young man's face had a ghostly pallor and his eyes were distant. 'You all right, son?' asked the Crusader. Nestor nodded, but said nothing and Wheeler looked at him closely. 'I guess you've never been in a killing fight before?' Nestor just stared at the floor. Wheeler turned his attention to Clem. 'I think you should both ride out. Sachs wasn't popular, but he had drinking friends. Tough men. They may feel the need to . . . well . . . you know.'

Clem nodded. 'We were leaving anyway in the morning. But now's as good a time as any.'

Wheeler nodded. 'I take it you'll be travelling towards Domango? It's where your friend was last seen.'

'I guess so,' agreed Clem.

'Then I'd take it as a kindness if you'd stop by and see that my mother is well. She has a farm just over the mountains. You take the Domango trail and you won't miss it. An old place in a valley east of the trail. She'll fix you a good meal and give you a roof for the night.'

'Any message?'

Wheeler shrugged, and gave a boyish grin. 'Just tell her that Seth and Pad are fine, and we'll be coming by at summer's end.'

Wheeler lifted Nestor's empty pistol and opened the side drawer of his desk, taking out a box of shells. Swiftly he loaded the revolver and handed it to Nestor. 'An empty gun is no good to anyone,' he said. 'And you might as well keep these,' he added, tossing the box to Clem.

'It might be better if all the guns were empty,' replied Clem, reaching out to shake the Crusader's hand.

'Amen to that,' said Seth Wheeler.

*

Shannow lay awake in the spare bedroom, staring out of the window at the bright stars. He and Amaziga had talked into the early hours, then she had shown him through to this curious room. The bed had a metal frame and a thick mattress, but instead of blankets there was a single, down-filled covering. Beside the bed was a small table, on which sat one of the strange lamps that burned brightly without oil. It was lit, and extinguished, by what appeared to be a coat button attached to the base. Beside this was a small box, which at first bore the glowing numbers 03.14. When Shannow next glanced at it the numbers had changed: 03.21. He watched it, and soon worked out that it changed at regular intervals. A timing device!

Climbing from his bed, he walked naked to the window and opened it. The night air was fresh, but not cool. Indeed, it was considerably warmer outside than in. A humming sound began, coming from the wall by his bed. There was a metal grille there and he moved to it. Cold air was spilling from the vent.

Shannow walked across the room and entered the second room Amaziga had shown him. Stepping inside the tall glass box, he turned the small steel wheel as she had demonstrated. Cold water streamed from a dish above him. Taking a tablet of soap, he began to scrub the dust of travel from his body. But the water grew steadily more hot until at last he had to leap from the box. Kneeling down, he examined the wheel. There were painted arrows upon it pointing to two coloured circles, one blue, one red. The coloured circles were repeated on the faucets at the sink beside the glass box. Shannow pressed each: one hot, the other cold.

Returning to the shower, he twisted the metal wheel back towards the blue. Gradually the steam subsided and the water cooled. Satisfied, he stepped back into the box and rinsed the soap from his body.

Refreshed, he towelled himself down and wandered back to his bed. The humming was still sounding from above him and he found the noise irritating, like making camp close to a beehive. Standing on the bed he stared into the vent, seeking some way of closing it. There was a lever, and just as he was about to press it he heard Lucas's voice echoing in the vent. '... too dangerous, Amaziga. It has already all but destroyed a world. Why take such a terrible risk?'

Shannow could not hear her response, but Lucas cut in swiftly, 'Nothing, as you know, is certain. But the probabilities are too high. Let me show you the data.'

Stepping down from the bed, Shannow walked to the door, easing it open and moving into the carpeted hallway. Now the voices were louder and he could hear Amaziga: '... probabilities are high; they are bound to be. But they would be high regardless of whatever action I take. Sarento has become the Bloodstone, and with the power it gives him, and with his extraordinary intelligence, he is almost bound to discover Gateways. Is that not so?'

'That is not the point,' came the reasoned voice of the machine-man. 'By your actions you will increase the probabilities.'

'By a fraction,' said Amaziga.

'And what of Shannow? The risks to him are great. He might die on this quest of yours.'

'Hardly the greatest loss to the culture of a planet,' sneered Amaziga. 'He is a killer, a man of violence. Whereas the rescue of Sam would mean so much. He was . . . is . . . a scientist, and a humanitarian. Together we may even be able to stop this world from falling. You understand? At least on this version of earth we might prevent the apocalypse. That alone is worth the risk to Shannow's life.'

The Jerusalem Man stepped back into his room and lay down.

There was truth in the harsh words he had heard. From somewhere deep in his memory he remembered Josiah Broome saying: '*I dread to think of people who look up to men like Jon Shannon. What do they give to the world? Nothing, I tell you.*'

His guns were hanging over the back of a chair. The weapons of the Thundermaker.

What peace have they ever brought, he wondered? What good have you ever done?

It was not a question he could answer, and he fell into an uneasy sleep.

*

'Lie back and rest,' the voice told him, but Josiah Broome could not obey it. His shoulder ached abominably, and he felt a painful throbbing in the fingers of his left hand. Nausea swept over him in waves, and tears squeezed through his closed eyelids, flowing to his thin cheeks. Opening his eyes, he saw an old man with a long white beard.

'I've been shot,' he said. 'They shot me!' Even as he spoke he realised how stupid it must sound. Of course the man knew he'd been shot. Broome could feel the bandage around his chest and up over his shoulder. 'I'm sorry,' said Broome, weeping, and not knowing what he was apologising for. The pain flared in his wound and he groaned.

'The bullet glanced up from a rib,' said the old man softly, 'then broke your collar-bone before digging deep to rest under your shoulder-blade. It's nasty – but not fatal.' Broome felt the man's warm hand on his brow. 'Now rest like I told you. We'll talk in the morning.'

Broome took a deep breath. 'Why did they do it?' he asked. 'I have no enemies.'

'If that's true,' said the old man, his voice dry, 'then at least one of your friends doesn't like you too much.'

The humour was lost on Josiah Broome and he drifted into a nervous and disturbed sleep, punctuated by appalling nightmares. He was being chased across a burning desert by riders with eyes of fire. They kept shooting at him, every bullet smashing into his frail body. But he did not die, and the pain was terrible. He awoke with a start, and fresh agony bloomed in the wound. Broome cried out and instantly the old man was beside him. 'Best you sit up, son,' he said. 'Here, I'll give you a hand.' The old man was stronger than he looked and Broome was hoisted to a sitting position, his back against the cave wall. There was a small fire, and meat was cooking in a black iron pot. 'How did I get here?' asked Broome.

'You fell off a buggy, son. You were lucky – the wheel just missed you.'

'Who are you?'

'You can call me Jake.'

Broome stared hard at the man. There was something familiar about him, but he could not find the connection. 'I am Josiah Broome. Tell me, do I know you, Jake?'

'You do now, Josiah Broome.' Jake moved to the cook-fire and stirred the broth with a long wooden spoon. 'Coming along nicely,' he said.

Broome gave a weak smile. 'You look like one of the Prophets,' he said. 'Moses. I had a book once, and there was a picture of Moses parting the Red Sea. You look just like him.'

'Well, I ain't Moses,' said Jake. As he shrugged off his coat, Broome saw the butts of two pistols scabbarded at the old man's hips. Jake glanced up. 'Did you recognise any of the men?'

'I think so . . . but I'd hate to be right.'

'Jerusalem Riders?'

Broome was surprised. 'How did you know?'

'They followed you and found the buggy. Then they back-tracked. I listened to them talking. They were mad fit to bust, I can tell you.'

'They didn't . . . see you?'

'Nobody sees me unless I want them to,' Jake told him. 'It's a talent I have. Also, you'll be relieved to hear, I know a little about healing. Where were you heading?'

'Heading?'

'Last night, in the buggy?'

'Oh, that was Daniel Cade's vehicle. He . . . Oh, dear God . . .'

'What is it?'

Broome sighed. 'He was killed last night. He saved me by shooting the . . . the assassin. But there were others. They rushed the house and killed him.'

Jake nodded. 'Daniel would have taken at least two of them with him. Tough man.' He chuckled. 'No one ever wants to leave this life, son, but old Daniel – given a choice – would have plumped for a fight against the ungodly.'

'You knew him?'

'Back in the old days,' said Jake. 'Not a man to cross.'

'He was a brigand and a killer,' said Broome sternly. 'Worthless scum. But he saw the Light.'

Jake laughed, the sound rich and merry. 'Indeed he did, Meneer Broome. A regular Damascus Road miracle.'

'Are you mocking him?' asked Broome, as Jake spooned the broth into a wooden bowl and passed it to the wounded man.

'I don't mock, son. But I don't judge either. Not any more. That's for the young. Now eat your broth. It'll help replace some of that lost fluid.'

'I must get word to Else,' said Broome. 'She'll be worried.'

'She certainly will,' agreed Jake. 'From what I heard of the riders' conversations, she thinks you killed the Prophet.'

'What?'

'That's the word, son. He was found dead in your house, and when the Jerusalem Riders went to find out what the shooting was about you shot two of them dead. You're a dangerous man.'

'But no one would believe that. I have stood against violence all my life.'

'You'd be amazed what people will believe. Now finish the broth.'

'I'll go back,' said Broome suddenly. 'I'll see the Apostle Saul. He knows me; he has the Gift of Discernment; he'll listen.'

Jake shook his head. 'You're not a fast learner, are you, Broome?'

*

The man called Jake sat quietly at the mouth of the cave as the wounded man groaned in his sleep. He was tired himself, but this was no time to enjoy the bliss of a dark, dreamless sleep. The killers were still out there, and a greater evil was waiting to seep into this tortured world. Jake felt a great sadness flow over him and rubbing his eyes, he stood and stretched his weary legs. A little to the left, on a stretch of open ground, the mule raised her head and glanced at him. An owl swooped overhead, banking and turning, seeking its rodent prey. Jake took a deep breath of the mountain air, then sat again, stretching out his long legs.

His mind wandered back over the long, long years, but his eyes remained alert, scanning the tree line for signs of movement. It was unlikely that the killers were closing in; they would be camped somewhere, waiting to follow the tracks in the morning. Jake drew one of his pistols and idly spun the chamber. How long since you fired it, he wondered? Thirty-eight years? Forty?

Returning the pistol to its scabbard, he dipped a hand into the wide pocket of his sheepskin coat and drew out a small golden Stone. With its power he could be young again. Flexing his knee, he felt the arthritic pain flare up. Use the Stone, you old fool, he told himself.

But he did not. The time was coming when the power would be needed, and it would need to serve a far greater purpose than to repair an age-eroded joint.

Could I have stopped the evil, he thought? Probably, if only I'd known how.

But I didn't – and I don't. All I can do is fight it when it arrives.

If you have the time!

It had been weeks since the last paralysing chest pain, the dull ache in his right bicep and the pins and needles in his fingertips. He should have used the Stone then, but he hadn't. Against the power that was coming, even this pure and perfect fragment of Sipstrassi might not be enough.

The night was cool. Josiah Broome was sleeping more peacefully now as Jake walked silently back into the cave and added fuel to the dying fire. Broome's face was wet with perspiration, and streaked with the grey lines of pain and shock.

You're a good man, Broome, thought Jake. The world deserves more like you, with your hatred of violence and your faith in the ultimate nobility of Man. Returning to his sentry post, Jake felt the sorrow growing. Glancing up at the velvet sky, he gave a rueful smile. 'What do you see in us, Lord?' he asked. 'We build nothing and smother everything. We kill and we torture. For every man like Broome there are hundreds of Jacob Moons, scores of Sauls.' He shook his head. 'Poor Saul,' he whispered. 'Treat him gently when you see him, Lord, for he was once a man of prayer and goodness.'

'Was he?'

Jake remembered the balding, stooped little man who had organised the church's finances, arranging fêtes and gatherings, fund-raisings and parties. There were thorns in his flesh even then, but he controlled them. Nature helped him there, for he was short and ugly. Not now! I should have seen it, thought Jake, when he used the Stone to make himself golden and handsome. I should have stopped it then. But he hadn't. In fact he had been pleased that Saul Wilkins had, at last, found a form that brought him happiness.

But the joy had been so transient, and Saul had gone searching for the bodily pleasures his life, his ugliness and his faith had denied him for so long.

'I can't hate him, Lord,' said Jake. 'It's just not in me. And I'm to blame for putting the power in his hands. I tried to make a holy world – and I failed.' Jake stopped talking to himself and listened. The night breeze was low, whispering through the leaves of the near by trees. Closing his eyes, he drew in a long slow breath through his nostrils. There was the scent of grass – and something else.

'Come out, little Pakia,' he said, 'for I know you are there.'

'How do you know me?' came a small voice from the undergrowth.

'I am old, and I know many things. Come out and sit with me.'

The little Wolver emerged and shuffled nervously forward, squatting down some ten feet from the old man. Her fur shone silver in the moonlight and her dark eyes scanned the weather-beaten face and the white beard. 'There are men with guns in the woods. They found the trail of your mule. They will be here at first light.'

'I know,' he said softly. 'It was good of you to seek me out.'

'Beth asked me to find Meneer Broome. I smell blood.'

'He is inside . . . sleeping. I will bring him to Beth. Go and tell her.'

'I know your scent,' she said, 'but I have no knowing of you.'

'But you know you can trust me, little one. Is that not so?'

The Wolver nodded. 'I can read your heart. It is not gentle, but you do not lie.'

Jake smiled. 'Sadly you are right. I am not a gentle man. When you have seen Beth, I want you to go to your people. Tell them to move away from here with all haste. There is an evil coming that will tear through the land like a burning fire. The Wolvers must be far away.'

'Our Holy One has told us this,' said Pakia. 'The Beast is coming from beyond the Wall. The Spiller of Blood, the Feaster of Souls. But we cannot desert our friend Beth.'

'Sometimes,' said Jake sadly, 'the best thing we can do is to desert our friends. The Beast has many powers, Pakia. But the worst of them is to change that which is good into that which is evil. Tell your holy man that the beast can turn a heart to darkness, and cause a friend to rip out the throat of his brother. He can do this. And he is coming soon.'

'Who shall I say has spoken these words?' asked Pakia.

'You tell him they are the words of the Deacon.'

*

Clem Steiner was worried about the youngster. Nestor had said little since they rode from Purity, and had seemed unconcerned at the prospect of pursuit. Twice Clem had swung off the trail, studying the moonlit land, but there was no sign that they were being followed. Nestor rode with his head down, obviously lost in thought, and Clem did not try to pierce the silence until they were camped in a natural hollow with a small fire burning. Nestor sat with his back against a thick pine, his knees drawn up.

'It wasn't your fault, boy,' said Clem, misunderstanding the youngster's anguish. 'He came looking for us.' Nestor nodded, but did not speak and Clem sighed. 'Speak to me, son. There's nothing to be gained by brooding.'

Nestor looked up. 'Didn't you ever believe in anything, Meneer Steiner?'

'I believe in the inevitability of death.'

'Yeah,' said Nestor, looking away. Clem cursed inwardly. 'Just tell me, Nestor. I never was much at guessing.'

'What's to tell? It's all just horse-shit.' Nestor laughed. 'I believed it all, you know. Jesus, what a fool! The Deacon was sent by God, the Jerusalem Man was a prophet like in the Book.

We were God's chosen people! I've lived my life chasing a lie. Don't that beat all?' Nestor took up his blanket and spread it on the ground.

Clem stayed silent for a moment, gathering his thoughts, before he spoke. 'If you need to hear something sage, Nestor, you're camped out with the wrong man. I'm too old to even remember what it was like to be young. When I was your age, I just wanted to be known as the greatest shootist in the known world. I didn't give a cuss about God or history. Never thought about anything much – except maybe getting a little faster. So I can't advise you. But that doesn't mean that I don't know you're wrong. You can't change the world, son. There'll always be serpents. All you can do is to live your own life in the way you feel is right.'

'And what about the truth?' asked Nestor, his eyes angry.

'The truth? What the Hell is the truth? We're born, we live and we die. Everything else is just shades of opinion.'

Nestor shook his head. 'You don't understand, do you? I guess your kind never will.'

The words stung Clem, but he tried to bite back his anger. 'Maybe you'd like to tell me what *my kind* is, boy?'

'Yeah, I'll do that. All your dreams have always been selfish. The fastest shootist. To make a name for yourself by killing the Jerusalem Man. To own land and be rich. So why would you care if the Deacon proves to be a fraud, or if hundreds of kids like me are lied to. It doesn't mean anything to you, does it? You just act like all the rest. You lied to me. You didn't tell me the Preacher was Shannow – not until you had to.'

'Put not your faith in princes, Nestor,' said Clem, all too aware of the bitter truth in the boy's words.

'What's that supposed to mean?'

Clem sighed. 'There was an old man used to work for Edric Scayse. He read old books all the time – some of them just fragments. He told me the line. And it's true, but we do it all the time. Some leader rises up and we swear to God that he's the best man since Jesus walked on water. It ain't so. Because he's human, and he makes mistakes, and we can't forgive that. I don't know the Deacon, but a lot of what he's done has been for the good. And maybe he truly believed Shannow was John the

Baptist. Seems to me a lot of would-be holy men gets led astray. It's got to be hard. You look up at the sky and you say, Lord, shall I go left or shall I go right? Then you see a bird flying left and you take it as a sign. The Deacon and his people were held in time for three hundred years. The Jerusalem Man released them. Maybe God did send him, I don't know. But then, Nestor, the sum of all I don't know could cover these mountains. But you're right about me. I won't deny it – I can't deny it. But what I'm saying is that the truth – whatever the Hell it is – doesn't exist outside of a man. It exists in his heart. Jon Shannow never lied. He never claimed to be anything other than what he was. He fought all his life to defend the Light. He never took a backward step in the face of evil. It didn't matter what men *said* was right. And there isn't a man alive who could have dented his faith. Because he didn't hand that faith over to men. It was his, his alone. You understand? And as for the truth, well . . . I once asked him about that. I said, "Supposing all that you believe in is just so much dust on the wind? Suppose it ain't true, how would you feel?" He just shrugged and smiled. You know what he said? "It wouldn't matter a damn – because it ought to be." '

'And I'm supposed to understand that?' stormed Nestor. 'All I know is that all my life I've been taught to believe something which was just made up by men. And I don't intend to be fooled again. Not by the Deacon, and not by you. Tomorrow I head for home. You can go to Hell in a bucket!'

Nestor lay down, turning his back on the fire. Clem felt old and tired and decided to let the matter rest. Tomorrow they would talk again.

Your kind never will!

The boy was sharp, no doubt about that. Over the years Clem had gathered a band of robbers to him, and their raids were daring and brilliantly executed. Exciting times! Yet men were killed or crippled – good men for the most part. Clem remembered the first of them, a young payroll guard who, against all the odds, had refused to lay down his rifle. Instead he had fired a shot that clipped the top of Clem's shoulder and killed the man behind him. The guard had gone down in a volley of fire. One shot had come from Clem's gun. The young man haunted him now; he was only doing his duty, earning an honest day's pay.

Your kind never will!

Clem sighed. You want to know *my kind*, boy? Weak men governed by their desires, yet without the strength of purpose to work for them.

When the ambush had come, the bullets ripping into the gang, Clem had spurred his horse over a high cliff-face and fallen a hundred feet into a raging torrent. He had survived, where all his men had died. With nowhere to go he had headed back to Pilgrim's Valley, where any who remembered him would recall a gallant young man by the name of Clem Steiner, not a brigand who rode under the name Laton Duke. By what right do you preach to this boy, he wondered? How could you tell him to live his life the way he thinks is right? When did you do that, Clem?

And what had the stolen money brought him? A fine red waistcoat and a nickel-plated pistol, several hundred faceless whores in scores of nameless towns. Oh yes, Clem, you're a fine teacher!

Picking up a handful of twigs, he leaned towards the fire. The ground trembled, the little blaze spitting cinders into the air. The hobbled horses whinnied in fear and a boulder dislodged from the slopes above them, rolling and bouncing down into the valley below. Nestor came to his knees and tried to stand, but the ground shifted under his feet, hurling him off balance. A bright light shone on the hollow. Clem glanced up. Two moons hung in the sky, one full, the other like a crescent. Nestor saw it too.

A jagged rip tore across a narrow hillside, swallowing trees. Then the full moon faded from sight, and an eerie silence settled on the land.

'What's happening?' asked Nestor.

Clem sat back, the fire forgotten. All he could think of was the last time he had seen such a vision, and felt the earth tremble beneath him, when the terror of the Lizard warriors had been unleashed upon the land.

Nestor scrambled across to him, grabbing his arm. 'What's happening?' he asked again.

'Someone just opened a door,' said Clem softly.

Chapter Eight

Two wise men and a fool were walking in the forest when a ravening lion leapt out at them. The first wise man estimated the size of the charging lion as some eight feet from nose to the tip of its tail. The second wise man noted that the beast was favouring its left front leg, indicating that it was lame and thus had, through hunger, been forced to become a man-eater. As the beast reared the fool shot it. But then he didn't know any better.
The Wisdom of the Deacon
Chapter xiv

* * *

Shannow awoke early and looked for his clothes. They were gone, but in their place he found a pair of black trousers of heavy twill and a thick woollen cream-coloured shirt. His own boots were beside them. Dressing swiftly, he swung his guns around his hips and walked through to the main room. Amaziga was not there, but the machine was switched on, the calm, handsome face of the red-headed Lucas pictured on the screen.

'Good morning,' said the face. 'Amaziga has driven into town to fetch some supplies. She should be back within the hour. There is coffee, should you desire it, or some cereal.' Shannow glanced suspiciously at the coffee-maker and decided to wait.

'Would you care to listen to music?' asked Lucas. 'I have over four thousand melodies on hand.'

'No, thank you.' Shannow sat down in a wide leather chair. 'It is cold in here,' he said.

'I'll adjust the A.C.,' said Lucas. The soft whirring ceased and within moments the room began to feel warmer. 'Are you comfortable with me here?' asked Lucas. 'I can remove this visual and leave the screen blank if you prefer. It does not matter to me. Amaziga created it, and finds it comforting, but I can understand how disconcerting it might be to a man from another time.'

'Yes,' agreed Shannow, 'it is disconcerting. Are you a ghost?'

'An interesting question. The man from whom my memory and thought patterns were duplicated is now dead. I am therefore a copy – if you like – of his innermost being, and one which can be seen, though not touched. I would think my credentials as a ghost would be quite considerable. But since we co-existed, he and I, I am therefore more like a cerebral twin.'

Shannow smiled. 'If you want me to understand you, Lucas, you'll have to speak more slowly. Tell me, are you content?'

'Contentment is a word I can describe, but that does not necessarily mean that I understand it. I have no sense of discontent. The memories of Lucas the man contain many examples of his discontent, but they do not touch me as I summon them. I think that Amaziga would be better equipped to answer such questions. It was she who created me. I believe she chose to limit the input, eliminating unnecessary emotional concepts. Love, hate, testosteronal drives, fears, jealousies, pride, anger – these things are neither helpful nor useful in a machine. You understand?'

'I believe that I do,' Shannow told him. 'Tell me of the Bloodstone and the world we are to enter.'

'What would you wish to know?'

'Start at the beginning. I usually find I can follow stories better that way.'

'The beginning? Very well. In your own world you fought the Guardian leader Sarento many years ago, destroying him in the catacombs beneath the mountains which held the broken ship. In the world to which Amaziga will take you there was no Jon Shannow. Sarento ruled. But then he was struck down with a crippling and terminal illness. Having corrupted the Sipstrassi boulder, creating a giant Bloodstone, he could no longer rely on its powers to heal him. He searched everywhere for a pure Stone that could take away the cancer. Time was against him and in desperation he turned to the Bloodstone; it could not heal, but it could reshape. He drew its power into himself, merging with the Stone, if you will. The energy flowed through his veins, changing him. His skin turned red, streaked with black veins. His power grew. The cancer shrivelled and died. There was no going back, the change was irrevocable. He could no longer take in food and drink; all that could feed him was contained in blood: the life force of living creatures. He hungered for it. Lusted for it. The Guardians saw what he had become and turned against him, but he destroyed them, for he was now a living Bloodstone with immense power. With the Guardians slain or fled, he needed to feed and journeyed to the lands of the Hellborn. You know their beliefs, Mr Shannow. They worship the Devil. What better Devil could they find? He strode into Babylon and took the throne from Abaddon. And he fed. How he fed! Are you a student of ancient history, Mr Shannow?'

'No.'

'But you know your Bible?'

'Indeed I do.'

'Then you will recall the tales of Molech, the god fed by souls upon the fire. Citizens of cities where Molech was worshipped would carry their first-born children to furnaces and hurl them alive into the searing depths. All for Molech. The Hellborn do that for Sarento. Though there are no flames. The children are slaughtered and, at first, Sarento would bathe in the blood of victims. Every citizen carried a small Bloodstone – a *demonseed*. These are corrupted Sipstrassi Stones, the pure power long used up. They are fed with blood and thereby acquire a different kind of power. They can no longer heal wounds, or create food. Instead they give great strength and speed to their bearers, while feeding the baser human instincts. An angry man, in possession of a Bloodstone becomes furious and psychopathic. Honest desire becomes lustful need. They are foul creations. Yet with them Sarento can control the people, swelling their lusts and desires, reducing their capacity for compassion and love. He rules a nation founded on hatred and selfishness. *Do as thou wilt is the whole of the law.* But his need for blood grows daily. Hence the War, where his legions sweep across the land. And before them go the Devourers. He has mutated the Wolvers, making them larger, more ferocious, huge beasts that move with great speed and kill without pity. He no longer needs to bathe in blood, Mr Shannow. Every time a Devourer feeds it swells a Bloodstone embedded in its skull. This transmits power to Sarento, the ultimate Bloodstone.

'Samuel Archer is – at the point you will enter the story – one of the few rebels still alive. But he and his people are trapped in the high country, surrounded. Soon the Devourers will stalk them.'

Shannow stood and stretched his back. 'Last night you and Amaziga spoke of probabilities. Would you explain them to me – in a way that I might understand?'

'I hardly think so, yet I will try. It is a question of mathematics. There are doorways we can use to cross what has been believed to be the thresholds of time. But it is not really time we cross. There are millions of worlds. An infinite number. In the world of the Bloodstone no one yet knows of the Gateways. By opening one, therefore, we increase the mathematical possibilities that our actions will alert the Bloodstone to their existence. You follow?'

'So far.'

'So then, by rescuing Sam Archer we risk the Bloodstone finding other worlds. And that would be a disaster of colossal proportions. Do you know anything about humming-birds, Mr Shannow?'

'They're small,' said the Jerusalem Man.

'Yes,' agreed the machine. 'They are small, and their metabolism works at an astonishing rate. The smallest weighs less than a tenth of an ounce. They have the highest energy output per body weight of any warm-blooded animal – and to survive they must consume half their body weight in nectar every day. Sixty meals a day, Mr Shannow, just to survive. The need for a plentiful supply of food makes them extraordinarily aggressive in defending their areas. The Bloodstone is identical. It needs to feed, it *lives* to feed. Every second of its existence, it suffers enormous pangs of hunger. And it is insatiable, Mr Shannow. Insatiable and ultimately unstoppable. Any world it finds it will ultimately devour.'

'You do not think that saving Sam is a risk worth taking,' observed Shannow.

'No, I do not. And neither do you. Amaziga points out that Sarento is a man with high intelligence, and that intelligence is now boosted by corrupted Sipstrassi power. She maintains, perhaps rightly, that he will discover the Gateways regardless of any action on our part. Therefore she is adamant that the quest will continue. But I fear she is guided by emotion, and not by reason. Why are you helping her?'

'She would go without me. It may be arrogance on my part, but I believe she will have a better chance of success with me. When do we set out?'

'As soon as Amaziga returns. Are your pistols fully loaded?'

'Yes.'

'Good. I fear they will need to be.'

The roar of angry lions came from outside and Shannow moved from the chair, his right-hand pistol pointing towards the door. 'It is only Amaziga,' said Lucas, but the Jerusalem Man was already moving out on to the porch. There he saw the bright-red four-wheeled carriage swing from the dirt track to draw up outside the house in a trail of dust and noise. The noise subsided, then died.

Amaziga pushed open a side door and stepped out. 'Help me with these boxes, Shannow!' she called, moving to the rear of the vehicle and opening another door. This one swung out and up, and Shannow watched her lean inside. Holstering the pistol, he walked towards her. A strange and unpleasant smell came from the vehicle, acrid and poisonous. It made his nostrils itch.

Amaziga was pulling a large box towards her and Shannow leaned in to help. 'Be careful. It's heavy,' she said. Shannow lifted it and turned towards the house, happy to be clear of the fumes from the vehicle. Once inside, he laid the box on the table and waited for the black woman.

The voice of Lucas sounded: 'It may interest you to know, Mr Shannow, that your reflexes are five point seven per cent higher than normal.'

'What?'

'The speed at which you drew the pistol shows that you are faster than the average man,' explained Lucas.

Amaziga entered and heaved a second box alongside the first. 'There's one more,' she told Shannow, who left reluctantly to fetch it. This was lighter and, with no room on the table-top, he set it down alongside the table.

'Did you sleep well?' she asked him. He nodded. She was wearing a soft, long-sleeved shirt with no collar. It was dark blue and a portrait of a leaping black man had been painted on the chest.

'Is that Sam?' he asked.

Amaziga laughed, the sound good-humoured. 'No, it's a basketball player. A sportsman in this world.' She laughed again. 'I'll explain it later,' she said, 'But now let's unpack the shopping.' Glancing at a dial on her wrist, she turned to Lucas. 'Six and a half hours, yes?'

'An adequate approximation,' responded the machine.

Amaziga pulled a small folding knife from her pocket and opened the blade. Swiftly she ran it along the top of the first box, then placed it on the table. Opening the flaps, she lifted clear a squat black weapon, shaped, to Shannow's eyes at least, like the letter T. More weapons followed, two automatic pistols and twelve clips of ammunition. Discarding the empty box she opened the second, drawing from it a short rifle with a pistol grip and two barrels. 'This is for you, Shannow,' she said. 'I think you'll like it.' Shannow didn't, but he said nothing as she laid boxes of shells alongside the gun.

Leaving her to unpack the other box, he walked to the door and stared out over the landscape. The sun was high, the temperature soaring. Heat shimmers were rising from the front of the vehicle. To the left he saw a movement from within a giant cactus. Narrowing his eyes he stared at the hole in the central stem. A tiny buff-coloured owl appeared, launched into the air and flew in a tight circle around the cactus, before disappearing back into the hole. Shannow guessed the bird to be around six inches in height, with a wingspan of around fourteen inches. He had never seen an owl so small.

Amaziga moved out alongside him, handing Shannow the ugly rifle with the pistol grip. 'It's a shotgun, and it takes six shells,' she said. 'It is operated by a pump under the barrels. Try it out on that cactus.'

'There's a nest there,' said Shannow.

'I don't see a nest.'

'A small owl, in that hole. Let's move further out.' Shannow strode away. The desert sun was riding high now, the temperature searing. Some way to the right he saw what could have been a small lake, but was more likely to be a mirage. He pointed it out to Amaziga.

'There's nothing there,' she said. 'During the last century scores of settlers died here, taking their tired oxen down into the valley, expecting water. It's a harsh country.'

'It is one of the greenest deserts I've seen,' observed Shannow.

'Most of the plants here can live for up to five years without rainfall. Now, how about that saguaro? See any nests?'

Shannow ignored the sarcasm and hefted the weapon, aiming from the hip at a small barrel cactus close by. He pulled the trigger and the cactus exploded; the sound of the shot hung in the air for several seconds. 'It's grotesque,' said the Jersualem Man. 'It would tear a man's arm off.'

'I would have thought you would have loved that,' put in Amaziga.

'You have never understood me, woman, and you never will.'

The words were not spoken with anger, but Amaziga reacted as if struck. 'I understand you well enough!' she stormed. 'And I'll not debate my thoughts with the likes of you.' Swinging, she aimed her own squat weapon at a saguaro and pulled the trigger. A thunderous wall of sound erupted from the gun, and Shannow was peppered with bright brass shell-cases. The saguaro leaned drunkenly to one side, its thick body showing gaping holes half-way up the central stem, then it fell to the desert floor.

Shannow turned and headed back for the house. He heard Amaziga ram another clip home, and a second burst followed the first. Inside, he dropped the shotgun to the table.

'What did she shoot?' asked the machine.

'A tall cactus.'

'A saguaro,' the machine told him. 'How many arms did it have?'

'Two.'

'It takes around eighty years before a saguaro grows an arm. And less than a second to destroy it.'

'Is that regret?' Shannow asked.

'It is an observation,' answered the machine. 'The bird you

saw is called an Elf Owl; they are quite common here. The desert is home to many interesting birds. The man, Lucas, used to spend many long hours studying them. His favourite was the Gilded Flicker. It probably made the nest hole the Elf Owl now inhabits.'

Shannow said nothing, but his eyes strayed to the shotgun. It was an obscene weapon.

'You will need it,' said Lucas.

'You read minds?'

'Of course. My clairvoyant abilities are what caused Amaziga to create me. The Devourers are powerful creatures. Only a shot to the heart with a powerful rifle or pistol will stop them. The skulls are thick and will resist your weapons. What are they, thirty-eights?'

'Yes.'

'Amaziga has purchased two forty-fours. Smith and Wesson, double-action. They are in the box on the floor.' Shannow knelt by it and opened the flaps. The guns were long-barrelled and finished in metallic blue, the butts white and smooth. Lifting them clear, he hefted them for weight and balance. 'Each weighs just under two and a half pounds,' Lucas told him. 'The barrels are seven inches long. There are three boxes of shells on the table.'

Shannow loaded the weapons and stepped out into the sunlight to see Amaziga walking back towards the house. There was a small sack hanging on a fence post some thirty feet from the Jerusalem Man. Moving to it, she pulled out four empty cans which she stood on the fence rail, around two feet apart. Stepping aside, she called to Shannow to try out the pistols.

His right arm came up. The pistol thundered and a can disappeared. The left arm rose, but this time his shot missed. 'Put them close together,' he ordered Amaziga. She did so and he fired again. The can on the left flew from the rail. 'More cans,' he called. Reloading the pistols, he waited as she set out another six.

This time he fired swiftly, left and right. All the targets were smashed from the fence.

'What do you think of them?' asked Amaziga, approaching him.

'Fine weapons. This one pulls a fraction to the left. But they'll do.'

'The salesman assured me they would stop a charging rhino . . . a very large animal,' she added, seeing his look of puzzlement.

He tried to drop the pistols into his scabbards, but they were too bulky. 'Don't worry about that,' Amaziga told him. 'I picked up a set of holsters for you at Rawhide.' She chuckled, but Shannow could not see the reason for humour.

Back inside the house she unwrapped a brown parcel, handing Shannow a black, hand-tooled gun-belt with two scabbards. The leather was thick, and of high quality, the buckle highly-polished brass. There were loops all around it, filled with shells. 'It is very handsome,' he said, swinging it around his hips. 'Yes, very handsome. My thanks to you, lady.'

She nodded. 'They do suit you, Shannow. Now I must leave you again. We'll be back at dusk. Lucas will brief you.'

'*We'll* be back?' queried Shannow.

'Yes, I'm going to meet Gareth. He'll be coming with us.'

Without another word she left the house. Shannow watched her move to the circle of broken stones. There was no bright light; she merely faded, and disappeared from sight.

Inside once more, Shannow gazed at the calm, tranquil face on the screen. 'What did she mean, *brief* me?'

'I shall show you the route you will travel, and the landmarks you must memorise. Sit down, Mr Shannow, and observe.'

The screen flickered, and Shannow found himself staring out over a range of mountains, thickly covered with pine.

*

Jacob Moon watched as the painted wagons moved slowly out of sight, the tall, slender blonde woman riding the last of them. He hawked and spat. On another day he would have extracted a price for freeing the sandy-haired young man . . . Meredith? And the price would have been the woman, Isis. Mostly Jacob Moon liked his women fat, but there was something about this girl that excited him. And he knew what it was. Innocence, and a fragile softness. He wondered if she was consumptive, for her skin was unnaturally pale and she had, he noticed, difficulty climbing to the wagon. Turning away, he focused on more important matters.

Dillon's body lay in the undertaker's parlour, and the Jerusalem Man rode free somewhere in the mountains. The trackers had followed him, but lost the trail in the desert. Shannow and a companion had ridden their horses into a circle of stones – and vanished. Moon shivered.

Could the man be an angel? Could the whole sorry Bible fairy tale be fact? No. He couldn't believe that. If God existed, then why does he not strike me down? Christ alive, I've killed enough people! He was quick enough to strike down Jenny, and she never harmed anyone.

It's all random, he thought. A game of chance.

The strong survive, the weak die.

Bullshit! We all die some day.

The town was unnaturally quiet today. Yesterday's shooting had astonished them. True, Dillon had been a feared man, but more than that he had been full of life. A loud, powerful, bull of a man radiating strength and certainty. Yet in the space of a few heartbeats he had been cut down by a stranger who had stood in the street and named their sins.

Jacob Moon had arrived in Domango three hours after the killing, when the hunters were just returning. Then a rider had come in from the Hankin farm. Two more men dead. The Jerusalem Man? Probably, thought Moon.

Still, sooner or later he would have Shannow in his sights. Then that problem would be over.

Moon smiled, and recalled the woman. With Dillon's blood still staining the street, she had walked into the Crusader office and approached him. 'I understand, sir, that you are a Jerusalem Rider.' Moon had nodded, his hooded eyes raking the slender lines of her body. 'My name is Isis. I have come to you for justice, sir. Our doctor, Meredith, has been wrongly imprisoned. Would you release him?'

Moon had leaned back in his chair and thrown a glance at the stocky Crusader standing by the gun-rack. The man cleared his throat. 'They're *Movers*,' he said. 'They come in beggin'.'

'That is not true,' said Isis. 'Dr Meredith merely erected a sign saying that he was a doctor, and inviting people to visit him.'

'We already got a doctor,' snapped the Crusader.

'Let him go,' said Moon. The Crusader stood silent for a moment, then lifted a ring of keys from a hook by the gun-rack and moved back through to the rear of the building.

'I thank you, sir,' said Isis. 'You are a good man.'

Moon had smiled then, but he said nothing. He glanced up as the Crusader brought out Meredith – a tall young man with sandy hair and a weak face. Moon wondered if he was the girl's lover, and idly pictured them coupling. 'They knew Dillon's killer,' said the Crusader. 'That's a fact.'

Moon turned his stare to the woman. 'He was wounded,' she said. 'We found him near to death and nursed him. Then, later, when we were attacked he fought off the raiders.' Moon nodded, but remained silent. 'Then he killed the Oath Taker from Purity. After that he rode away. I don't know where.'

'Did he say his name?' asked Moon.

'Yes. He said he was Jon Shannow. Our leader Jeremiah thinks the wound to his head has confused him. He has no memory, you see. He cannot remember who shot him, or why. Jeremiah believes he has taken refuge in the identity of the Jerusalem Man.'

The sandy-haired young man stepped alongside Isis, putting his arm around her shoulder. The action annoyed Moon, but he remained silent. 'The mind is very complex,' said Meredith. 'It is likely that his memories of childhood included many stories about Shannow. Now that he is an amnesiac, the mind is trying to piece together those memories. Hence his belief that he is the fabled Jerusalem Man.'

'So,' said Moon softly, 'he does not remember where he is from?'

'No,' said Isis. 'He struck me as a lonely man. Will you treat him with understanding when you find him?'

'You can rely on that,' promised Jacob Moon.

*

Shannow watched the screen, noting landmarks and listening as Lucas talked of the lands of the Bloodstone. Mostly the terrain was unfamiliar to Shannow, but occasionally he would see, in the distance, the shape of a mountain that seemed to strike a chord in his memory.

'You must remember, Mr Shannow, that this is a world gone mad. Those disciples who follow the Bloodstone receive great gifts, but for the vast majority the future is only to die to serve his hunger. We will not have long to find Samuel Archer. The jeep will get us within range within a day. We will have, then, perhaps another twenty-four hours to save him.'

'Jeep?' queried Shannow.

'The vehicle outside. It can travel at around sixty miles per hour over difficult terrain. And no Devourer or horseman will catch it.'

Shannow said nothing for a moment. Then: 'You can see many places and many people.'

'Yes, I have extensive files,' agreed Lucas.

'Then show me Jon Shannow.'

'Amaziga does not wish you to see your past, Mr Shannow.'

'The lady's wishes are not at issue. I am asking *you* to show me.'

'What would you like to see?'

'I know who I was twenty years ago, when I fought the Lizard-men and sent the Sword of God through to destroy Atlantis. But what happened then? How did I use those years? And why am I still relatively young?'

'Wait for a moment,' said Lucas. 'I will assemble the information.' Shannow immediately felt a sensation he had long forgotten and it surprised him. His stomach trembled and he could feel his heart beating wildly. In that moment nameless terrors seemed to be clawing at him from deep within his mind, and he realised with a sickening certainty that he did not want to know. His mouth was dry and he found himself breathing too quickly, becoming dizzy. The desire rose in him to stop the machine, to command it to silence. 'I will not be a coward,' he whispered. Gripping the arms of the chair, he sat rigid as the screen flickered and he saw himself on a tower of rock, the Sword of God blazing across the sky. The man on the rock slumped down, his black and silver beard darkening. 'That,' came Lucas's voice, 'is the moment when you regained youth. The last fractions of Sipstrassi power seeping through the tower, regenerating ageing tissue.' The scene shifted to Pilgrim's Valley and Shannow watched as the preacher Jon

Cade gave his first sermon, listened to the words and the message of hope and peace. Beth McAdam was sitting in the front row, her eyes upon the speaker, the light of love shining in them.

Sadness engulfed the Jerusalem Man . . . the sadness of love, the grief of bereavement. His love for Beth came roaring from his subconscious to rip at his heart. Forcing himself to stare at the screen he watched the passing of the years, saw himself struck down by Shem Jackson and felt again the numbing shame that came from having the strength to walk away. He heard once more the man's scornful laughter behind him.

At the last he saw the burning of the church and the murder of the Wolvers. 'Enough,' he said softly. 'I want to see no more.'

'You remember it?' asked the machine.

'I remember it.'

'You are a man of extremes, Mr Shannow, and great inner strength. You cannot walk the middle ground and you have never learned how to compromise. You became a preacher, and you preached of love and understanding – at its best a gentle doctrine. You could not be a man of violence and preach such a doctrine, therefore you put aside your guns and *lived* it, using the same iron control that you enjoyed as a brigand-slayer.'

'But it was a fraud,' said Shannow. 'I was living a lie.'

'I doubt that. You gave it everything you could – even to losing the woman you loved. That is a commitment beyond most men. Even iron, however, can be ripped apart. When the raiders burned the church the iron gave way. You pursued them and slew them. The mind is a very sensitive creature, Mr Shannow. To all intents and purposes, you had betrayed everything you had stood for during those twenty years. So the mind, in self-protection, threw the memories of those years into a box and held it from your view. The question is, now that the box has been opened, who are you? Are you Jon Cade, preacher and man of God, or are you Jon Shannow, fearless killer?'

Shannow ignored the question and rose. 'Thank you, Lucas. You have been of great service to me.'

'It was my pleasure, Mr Shannow.'

Outside the light was beginning to fade, the desert heat

abating. Shannow wandered to the paddock and climbed to the fence, watching the four horses cropping grass. They were standing in two pairs, nose to tail, protecting each other's faces from the swarms of flies that surrounded them.

He drew one of the long, blue-barrelled pistols.

The question is, now that the box has been opened, who are you? Are you Jon Cade, preacher and man of God, or are you Jon Shannow, fearless killer?'

*

As Nestor Garrity and Clem Steiner were riding towards Purity, and Jon Shannow stood alone on the streets of Domango, the Apostle Saul urged his tired mount towards the ruined city.

Saul was seething with suppressed fury. Word had reached him yesterday that the Deacon had survived Moon's attack, that the man killed had been Geoffrey, the Deacon's secretary. The council in Unity was in turmoil. The Deacon was missing.

Missing! My God, thought Saul, what if he knows it was me?

A mosquito stung Saul's right leg and angrily he slapped it, the sound causing the horse to shy. He swore. The heat was unbearable, and stinking horse sweat had seeped through his trousers. His back ached from hours in the saddle and the ancient city seemed no closer. He swore again.

The Deacon was alive! Josiah Broome was alive! Jon Shannow was alive! It was all coming to nothing; all the years of careful planning unravelling before his eyes.

I've always been cursed, he thought, remembering his childhood in Chicago, the taunts he had taken from his fellow schoolchildren over his lack of size and his weasel features, the mockery from girls who would not be seen dead with a 'runt like you'. And always in his work there were others who would succeed, moving past him on the promotional ladder, men and women with far less talent. Always it was Saul Wilkins who was overlooked. Little Saul.

It wasn't as if he didn't play the game. He sucked up to those above him, laughed at their jokes, supported their endeavours and worked hard to be as good as anyone. Yet never did he gain the recognition he craved.

Now it was happening again, this time to the tall, handsome, golden-haired Apostle Saul. Overlooked by the Deacon he had, for the first time in his life, planned for the great gamble. And he was failing.

As he had always failed . . .

No, not always, he thought. There was the golden time at the Tabernacle, when he had first found God. Laid off from his job in the north, Saul had moved to Florida. One Thursday afternoon late in February, he had been driving along I-4 West and had pulled in for a coffee at a fast-food outlet. There was a trailer parked there, and several young people were handing out leaflets. A girl offered one to Saul. It was an invitation to a Bible picnic being held near Kissimmee the following Sunday. The girl's smile had been radiant, and she called him 'brother'.

That Sunday Saul had attended the picnic with some three hundred other people. He had enjoyed himself, and the sermon from the fat preacher had touched a chord in him, with its emphasis on the meek and the lowly. God's love was very special for them.

Short of friends, his lay-off money holding out, Saul had joined the small church. It was the happiest time of his life – especially after the Deacon arrived and appointed him as full-time church treasurer. Jason had been set for the role, had coveted it – and he was tall and handsome. Saul was convinced that yet again he would be overlooked. But no. The Deacon had called him in and calmly offered him the post. Jason, bitter and vengeful, had quit the church.

Good days. Great days, Saul realised.

Then came the fateful flight and the end of the world he knew. Even then there were joys ahead, the gifts of the Sipstrassi, a handsome body, endless women.

I had it all, thought Saul. But the Sipstrassi was running out, the Deacon was getting older, and soon it would all end. Without the Sipstrassi I would be little Saul Wilkins again, bald and bent, peering at the world through watery eyes. Who would take me seriously? What would I do?

The answer was simple. Become rich in this new world. Take control like the hard, ruthless men of the old world. Control land and resources, oil, silver, gold. And all the while search for Sipstrassi.

The Deacon had found his hoard soon after arriving. He had ridden off into the wild lands and returned with a bag of Stones.

Oh God, thought Saul, there must have been thirty of them! He had asked him where he found them.

'On my travels,' the Deacon answered, with a smile.

Then last year a man came to Unity who claimed to know the Deacon. He had been ushered into Saul's office. He was an old prospector, who said he had met the Deacon during his wanderings in the land beyond the Wall. 'Whereabouts?' Saul had asked.

'Near Pilgrim's Valley – you know,' said the man, 'where the Lord guided your flying-machine to land.'

Somewhere near here the Deacon had discovered the Stones of power.

There must be more! Please God let there be more!

With enough Sipstrassi he could still gain power. Just five Stones! Three. Dear God, help me to find them!

He was close enough now to see the towering columns of stone that marked the southern gate of the Atlantean city. One was taller than the other, reaching almost sixty feet. Once there had been a lintel stone between them, but it had fallen to the paved area below, shattering into fragments.

For several moments Saul forgot his mission, as he gazed over the miles and miles of what had once been a magnificent city. There were statues in marble, mostly toppled and broken, but some remaining still on their plinths, stone eyes staring at this latest intruder to observe their silent grief. Many of the buildings were still standing, seemingly untouched by the thousands of years on the ocean floor. Saul rode on, his horse's hooves clattering on the paved streets, the sound echoing eerily.

The Deacon had told him that there was an ancient King of Atlantis, named Pendarric. It was he who had brought about the doom of his people, the earth toppling, drowning the empire under a tidal wave of colossal proportion.

Saul rode his tired mount up a long hill, towards a multi-turreted palace. The horse was breathing heavily now, its flanks white with foaming sweat. At the top he dismounted, and tethered the poor creature in the sunshine. The horse stood with head hung low. Ignoring the beast's discomfort, Saul strode into the palace. The floor was covered in thick dry dust that had once been silt. Close to the windows, where the wind had blown away the dust Saul could see evidence of an elaborate mosaic on the floor, deep blues and reds in shifting patterns. There was no furniture here, nor any sign of wood. That had long since been destroyed – probably adding to the dust. But there were statues, of warriors in breastplate and helm, reminding Saul of pictures he had seen of Greek soldiers during the battle for Troy.

He walked on through many doorways until he came to a vast, round hall, at the centre of which stood a circle of beautifully crafted rectangular stones, standing vertically. The dust was everywhere, and as he walked it rose up around him, drying his throat and causing him to cough.

Slowly he searched the hall, but found nothing save the golden hilt of a ceremonial dagger, which he dropped into the pocket of his coat. Returning to the horse, he took a drink from his canteen. From here he could see even more powerfully the vastness of this ancient city. Ruins as far as the eye could see, stretching in all directions.

Despair touched him. Even if the Stones are here, how will I find them?

Then an idea came to him. It was brilliant in its simplicity and, did he but know it, Saul Wilkins had arrived at a conclusion that had evaded thousands of brilliant men in the past. He licked his lips, and fought to control his rising excitement.

Sipstrassi power could do anything! Could it not therefore be used like a magnet, calling upon other Stones, drawing them to it or, at the very least, guiding him to where they lay hidden?

Saul delved into his pocket, pulling clear the Stone. Only three threads of gold remained now. Would they be enough? And where to try his theory?

The Stones were too powerful to have been owned by many people in the city. Only the rich would have had access – and the man who owned this palace must have been rich indeed.

The circular hall was at the very centre of the building. That is where to begin, thought Saul. Hurrying back through the empty palace, he made his way to the centre of the circle of stones. Here he paused. How to use the power? Think, man!

Clenching the Stone tightly in his fist, he pictured a full golden Stone and willed it to come to him. Nothing happened. The Stone in his fist did not grow warm, as was usual when power was drawn from it. What he could not know was that there was no Sipstrassi left in this ancient ruin. He tightened his grip. A small, sharp fragment of the Stone bit into his palm. Saul swore and opened his fingers. A tiny bead of blood swelled there, touching the Stone. The bright yellow threads darkened, turning red-gold in the dim light.

But now the Stone was warm. Saul tried again. Holding up his fist, he willed the Stone to seek out its fellows. And the new Bloodstone obeyed, sending its power through the gateway of the circle.

Violet light filled the air around him. Saul was exultant: it was working! The light was blinding and when it cleared he saw a strange scene. Some thirty yards away a powerful man was sitting on a huge golden throne, staring directly at Saul. The man's skin was deep red and seemed to be decorated with thin black lines. Saul glanced over his shoulder. Behind him everything was as it should be, the stone circle and the dust-covered hall. But ahead was this curious man.

'Who are you?' asked the tattooed man, his voice rich and deep.

'Saul Wilkins.'

'Saul . . . Wilkins,' echoed the man. 'Let me read your mind, Saul Wilkins.' Saul felt a curious warmth creep into his head, flowing through him. When it finally receded he felt lost and alone. 'I don't need you, Saul Wilkins,' said the tattooed man. 'I need Jacob Moon.'

A shape reared up before Saul, obscuring his view. He had a fraction of a second to register sleek grey fur, blood-red eyes, and yellow-stained fangs in a gaping maw. There was no time to scream. Talons ripped into his chest, and the terrible mouth opened before him, the fangs closing on his face.

Chapter Nine

A wise man and a fool were lost in the desert. The one knew nothing of desert life, and soon became thirsty and disorientated. The other grew up in the desert. He knew that often a man could find water by digging at the lowest point of the outside bend of a dry stream-bed. This he did, and the two drank.

The one who found the water said to his companion, 'Which of us is the wise man now?'

'I am,' said the other. 'For I brought you with me into the desert, whereas you chose to travel with a fool.'

The Wisdom of the Deacon
Chapter vi

* * *

Amaziga met her son at the cross-roads outside Domango. She smiled as he rode up and waved. He was a handsome man, more slender than his father, but with a natural grace and confidence that filled Amaziga's heart with pride.

'You have him safe?' asked Gareth, leaning across his saddle to kiss Amaziga's cheek.

'Yes. And ready.'

'You should have seen him, Mother, striding out on to the street and calling out Dillon. Amazing!'

'He's a killer. A savage,' snapped Amaziga, irritated by the admiration she saw in Gareth.

Gareth shrugged. 'Dillon was the savage. Now he's dead. Do not expect me to mourn for him.'

'I don't. What I also do not expect is for a son of mine to hero-worship a man like Jon Shannow. But then you are a strange boy, Gareth. Why, with your education in the *modern* world, would you choose to live here of all places?'

'It is exciting.'

She shook her head in exasperation and swung her horse. 'There's not much time,' she said. 'We had better be moving.'

They rode swiftly back to the stone circle. Amaziga lifted her Stone and violet light flared around them.

The house appeared, and the two riders moved down towards the paddock. Shannow was sitting on the fence as they approached. He looked up and nodded a greeting. Amaziga swung down and opened the paddock gate. 'Unsaddle the horses,' she ordered Gareth. 'I'll load up the jeep.'

'No jeep,' said Shannow, climbing down from the fence.

'What?'

'We will ride through.'

'That jeep can move three times as fast as the horses. Nothing in the world of the Bloodstone can catch it.'

'Even so, we don't take it,' said the Jerusalem Man.

Amaziga's fury broke clear. 'Who the Hell do you think you are? I am in command here, and you will do as I say.'

Shannow shook his head. 'No,' he said softly, 'you are not in command here. If you wish me to accompany you, then saddle fresh horses. Otherwise be so kind as to return me to the world I know.'

Amaziga bit back an angry retort. She was no fool, she heard the iron in his voice and swiftly she changed tack. 'Listen, Shannow, I know you do not understand the workings of the . . . vehicle, but trust me. We will be far safer with it than on horseback. And our mission is too vital to take unnecessary risks.'

Shannow stepped closer and gazed down into her dark brown eyes. 'This entire enterprise is an unnecessary risk,' he said, his voice cold, 'and were I not bound by my word I would leave you to it without a moment's hesitation. But understand this, woman. I will lead, you and your son will follow that lead. You will obey without question . . . and that begins now. Choose your horses.'

Before Amaziga could respond Gareth spoke up. 'Is it all right if I keep this mount, Mr Shannow?' he asked. 'She's a stayer, and is still fresh.'

Shannow's eyes raked the buckskin, then he nodded. 'As you will,' he said, and without another word he moved away, walking towards the open desert.

Amaziga swung on her son. 'How could you side with him?'

'Why keep a dog if you are going to bark yourself?' answered Gareth, stepping down from the saddle. 'You say he is a killer and a savage. Everything I know about the Jerusalem Man tells me that he is a survivor. Yes, he is hard and ruthless, but where we are going we will need a man like that. No disrespect, Mother. You are a fine scientist and a wonderful dinner companion. But on this venture I guess I would sooner follow the tall man. Okay?'

Amaziga masked her anger and forced a smile. 'He's wrong about the jeep.'

'I'd sooner ride anyway,' said Gareth.

Amaziga strode into the house and on to her room. From a closet by the far wall she removed a shoulder rig to which two small silver and black boxes were attached. Swinging it over her shoulder she clipped it to her black leather belt, then attached two leads to the first box, which nestled against her waist on the left-hand side. Connecting the other ends of the leads into the second box, she clipped this to the back of her belt, alongside a leather scabbard containing four clips of ammunition for the nine-shot Beretta holstered at her hip. Returning to the outer room, she pulled a fresh set of leads from the drawer beneath the computer and attached them first to the back of the machine, then to the small box at her belt.

'You are angry,' said Lucas.

'The batteries should last around five days. Long enough, I think,' she said, ignoring the question. 'Are you ready for transfer?'

'Yes. You are, of course, aware that I cannot load all my files into your portable? I will be of limited use.'

'I like your company,' she said, with a wide smile. 'Now, are you ready?'

'Of course. And you have not connected the microphone.'

'It's like living with a maiden aunt,' said Amaziga, looping a set of headphones around her neck. The transfer of files took just under two minutes. Lifting the headphones into place, she flipped out the curved stick of the microphone. 'Can you hear me?' she asked.

'I dislike not being able to see,' came Lucas's voice, as if from a great distance.

Amaziga adjusted the volume. 'One thing at a time, dear heart,' she said. The fibre-optic camera had been designed to fit neatly into a black headband, the leads connected to a set of tiny batteries contained in the shoulder rig. Settling it into place, she engaged the batteries.

'Better,' said Lucas. 'Move your head to left and right.' Amaziga did so. 'Excellent. Now will you tell me why you are angry?'

'Why should I tell you something you already know.'

'Gareth was correct,' said Lucas. 'Shannow is a survivor. He is an untutored clairvoyant. His gift is in reading signs of danger before that danger has materialised.'

'I know about his skills, Lucas. That's why I am using him.'

'Look down,' Lucas told her.

'What? Why?'

'I want to see your feet.'

Amaziga chuckled and bent her head low. 'Aha,' said Lucas. 'As I thought, trainers. You would be advised to wear boots.'

'I am already hip-deep in wires and leads. The trainers are comfortable. Now, do you have any other requests?'

'It would be nice if you were to walk to the saguaro where the Elf Owl is nesting. The camera on the roof cannot quite traverse far enough for a good study.'

'When we get back,' she promised. 'For now I'd like you to concentrate on the lands of the Bloodstone – if it is not too much trouble? You'll need to re-think the route and the place and time of entry. Without the jeep it'll take a damn sight longer.'

'I never liked jeeps,' said Lucas.

*

Josiah Broome awoke to see the old man cleaning two long-barrelled pistols. Pain lanced through Broome's chest and he groaned.

Jake glanced up. 'Despite how you feel, you will live, Josiah,' he said.

'It wasn't a dream?' whispered Broome.

'It surely wasn't. Jersualem Riders tried to kill you, and shot Daniel Cade in the process. Now you are a wanted man. Shoot on sight, they've been told.' Broome struggled to a sitting position. Dizziness swamped him. 'Don't do too much now, Josiah,' insisted Jake. 'You've lost a lot of blood. Take it slow and easy. Here . . .' Jake laid aside the pistol and lifted a steaming jug from the coals of the fire. Filling a tin mug he passed it to Broome, who took it with his left hand. The old man returned to his place and lifted the pistol, flipping out the cylinder and loading it.

'What am I going to do?' asked Broome. 'Who will believe me?'

'It won't matter, son,' said Jake. 'Trust me on that.'

'How can you say that?' asked Broome, astonished. Jake returned the pistols to two deep shoulder holsters and reached for a short-barrelled rifle which he also began to load, pressing shell after shell into the side gate. When he had finished he pumped the action and laid the weapon aside.

'Sometime soon,' he said, his voice low, 'people will forget all about the shooting; they'll be too concerned with just staying alive. And against what's coming that won't be easy. You were there when the Daggers invaded. But they were an army of soldiers. They had orders. They were disciplined. But a terror is about to be unleashed that is almost beyond understanding. That's why I'm here, Josiah. To fight it.'

Josiah Broome understood none of it. All he could think of was the terrible events of yesterday, the murder of Daniel Cade and the pain-filled flight into the night. Was the old man insane, he wondered? He seemed rational. The pain in his chest settled to a dull, throbbing ache and the dawn breeze chilled his upper body. He shivered. The bandages around his thin chest were caked with dried blood, and any movement of his right arm sent waves of nausea through him.

'Who are you?' he asked the old man.

'I am the Deacon,' said Jake, emptying out the jug and stowing it in a cavernous pack.

For a moment all Broome's pain was forgotten, and he stared at the man with undisguised astonishment. 'You can't be,' was all he could say, taking in the man's threadbare trousers and worn boots, the ragged sheepskin coat and the matted white hair and beard.

Jake smiled. 'Don't be deceived by appearances, son. I am

who I say I am. Now, we've got to get you to Beth McAdam's place. I need to speak to the lady.' Jake hoisted the pack to his shoulders, hefted his rifle, then moved over to Broome and helped him to his feet. Wrapping a blanket around the wounded man's upper body, Jake steered him out into the open where the mule was hobbled. 'You ride, I'll lead,' said the old man. With great difficulty Broome climbed to the saddle.

An eerie howl echoed in the trees and Jake stiffened. It was answered by another some way to the east . . . then another.

Broome noted the sound, but compared with the pain from his chest wound and the pounding that had begun in his head, it seemed unimportant. Then he heard two gunshots in the distance, followed by a piercing scream of terror, and he jerked in the saddle. 'What was that?' he asked.

Jake did not reply. Slipping the hobble from the mule's forelegs, he took the reins in his left hand and began the long descent down into the wooded valley.

*

The Deacon moved on warily, leading the mule and glancing back often at the wounded man. Broome was semi-delirious now, and the man called Jake had lashed his wrists to the pommel of the saddle. The day was bright and clear, and there was no discernible breeze. The Deacon was thankful for that. The pack was heavy, as was the rifle, and he was mortally tired. The descent into the valley was slow and he paused often, listening, scanning the trees.

Death stalked these mountains now, and he knew the Devourers were fast and lethal. He would have little time to bring the rifle to bear. Every now and then the Deacon glanced at the mule. She was a canny beast and would pick up their scent much faster than he. At the moment she was moving easily, head down, ears up, contentedly following his lead.

With luck they would make Beth McAdam's farm by sunset. But what then?

How do you defeat a god of blood?

The Deacon didn't know. What he did know was that the pain in his chest was intense, and that his old and weary body was operating at the outer edge of its limits. For the first time in years he was tempted to use the Stone on himself, rejuvenating his ancient muscles, repairing the time-damaged heart.

It would be so good to feel young again, full of energy and purpose, infused with the passion and belief of youth. And the speed, he realised. That could be vital.

The mule stopped suddenly, jerking the Deacon back. He swung and saw her head come up, her eyes widen in fear. Slipping the pack from his shoulders, he hefted the rifle and moved back to stand beside the mule's head. 'It's all right, girl,' he said, his voice soft and soothing. 'Steady, now!'

He noticed that an easterly breeze had picked up. The mule had caught the scent of the man-wolves. Leaving the pack where it lay, the Deacon scrambled up behind Broome and kicked the mule into a run. She needed no further encouragement and set off down the slope at breakneck speed. As Broome swayed to his left, the Deacon's left arm caught him, hauling him upright.

The mule thundered on. When a grey shape reared from the right of the trail, the Deacon lifted the rifle like a pistol and loosed a shot which caught the beast high on the shoulder, spinning it. Then the mule was past and on to level ground, racing out into the valley.

*

They crossed the Gateway at midnight, the air cool, the stars glittering above them, and emerged seconds later into the bright sunshine of an Autumn morning. The stone circle into which they had travelled was almost completely overgrown by dense bush, and the trio were forced to dismount and force a way through to open ground some fifty yards to the left.

Amaziga spoke softly into the microphone. Shannow could not hear the words, but he saw her lift the time-piece on her wrist and make adjustments. She saw him watching her. 'Lucas says it is 8.45 a.m., and we have two days to reach the Mardikh mountains where Sam and his group are holding out. It is forty-two miles from here, but the ground is mostly level.'

Shannow nodded and stepped into the saddle. Gareth rode alongside him. 'I am grateful to you, Mr Shannow,' he said. 'It is not every day that a man is given the opportunity to bring his father back from the dead.'

'As I understand it,' said Shannow, 'he is not your father, merely a man who carries the same face and name.'

'And an identical genetic structure. Why did you come?'

Shannow ignored the question and rode towards the north, Amaziga and Gareth falling in behind. They pushed on through the day, stopping only once to eat a cold meal. The land was vast and empty, the distant blue mountains seeming no nearer. Twice they passed deserted homes, and in the distance, towards dusk, Shannow saw a cluster of buildings that had once made up a small town on the eastern slopes of a narrow valley. There was no sign of life, no lanterns burning, no movement.

As the light began to fail Shannow turned off the trail and up into a stand of pine, seeking a place to camp. The land rose sharply, and ahead of them a cliff face ran south to north. A narrow waterfall gushed over basaltic rock, the fading sunlight casting rainbows through the spray and a rippling stream flowing on towards the plain.

Shannow dismounted and loosened the saddle cinch. 'We could make at least another five miles,' said Amaziga but he ignored her, his keen eyes picking up a flash of red in the undergrowth some sixty yards beyond the falls. Leaving the horse with trailing reins, he waded across the narrow stream and climbed the steep bank beyond. Gareth followed him.

'Jesus Christ!' whispered Gareth as he saw the crushed and ruined remains of a red jeep.

'Do not take His name in vain,' said Shannow. 'I do not like profanity.' The jeep was lying on its back, the roof twisted and bent. One door had been ripped clear, and Shannow could see the marks of talons scoring through the red paint and the thin steel beneath. He glanced up. Torn and broken foliage on the cliff above the jeep showed that it had fallen from the cliff-top and bounced several times against sharp outcrops before landing here. Ducking down, he pulled aside the bracken and peered into the interior. Gareth knelt alongside him.

Inside the jeep was a crushed and twisted body. All that could be seen was an outflung arm, half severed. The arm was black, the blood-soaked shirt sleeve olive-green with a thin grey stripe. Gareth's shirt was identical. 'It's me,' said Gareth. 'It's me!'

Shannow rose and moved to the other side of the wreck.

Glancing down, he saw huge paw-prints in the soft earth, and a trail of dried blood leading into the undergrowth. Drawing a pistol and cocking it, he followed the trail and twenty yards further on found the remains of a grisly feast. Lying to the left was a small box, twisted, torn wires leading from it. Easing the hammer forward, he holstered his pistol, then he picked up the blood-spattered box and walked back to where Gareth was still staring down at the body.

'Let's go,' said the Jerusalem Man.

'We've got to bury him.'

'No.'

'I can't just leave him there!'

Hearing the anguish in the young man's voice, Shannow moved alongside him, laying a hand on his shoulder. 'There are hoof-marks around the vehicle, as well as signs of the Devourers. If any of the riders return and find the corpses buried, they will know that others have passed this way. You understand? We must leave them as they are.'

Gareth nodded, then his head flicked up. 'Corpses? There is only one, surely?'

Shannow shook his head and showed Gareth the blood-spattered box. 'I don't understand . . .' the young man whispered.

'Your mother will,' said Shannow, as Amaziga strode to join them. He watched her as she examined the jeep, her face impassive. Then she saw the box, identical to the one she had strapped to her belt, and her dark eyes met Shannow's gaze.

'Where is her body?' she asked.

'There is not much of a body left. The Devourers lived up to their name. A part of the head remains, enough to identify it.'

'Is it safe to remain here?'

'Nowhere in this land is safe, lady. But it offers concealment for the night.'

'I take it the twin of your body is not here, Mr Shannow?'

'No,' he said.

She nodded. 'Then she chose to undertake the mission without you – obviously a mistake which she paid for dearly.'

Amaziga turned away and returned to the horses as Gareth approached Shannow. 'That's the closest she'll ever come to saying you were right about the jeep,' said the young man, attempting a smile. 'You're a wise man, Shannow.'

The Jerusalem Man shook his head. 'The wise man was the Jon Shannow who *didn't* travel with them.'

*

Gareth took the first watch, a thick blanket round his shoulders against the cool night breeze. He was sitting on a wide branch that must have snapped in a recent storm. The sight of the body in the jeep had unnerved him as nothing else had in his young life. He *knew* the dead man better than he knew anyone, understood the hopes and dreams and fears the man had entertained or endured. And he couldn't help but wonder what had gone through his twin's mind as the jeep had crashed over the cliff. Despair? Terror? Anger? Had he been alive after the fall? Had the Devourers forced their way in and torn at his helpless body?

The young black man shivered and glanced to where Shannow slept peacefully beneath a spreading elm. This quest had seemed like an adventure to Gareth Archer, yet another exciting experience in his rich, full young life. The prospect of danger had been enticing. But to see his own corpse! Death was something that happened to other people . . . not to him. Nervously he glanced across at the ruined jeep.

The night was cold, and he noticed that his hands were trembling. He glanced at his watch: two more hours before he woke his mother. She had seemed unfazed by the tragedy that had befallen their twins and, just for a moment, Gareth found himself envious of her calm. Amaziga had spread out her blanket, removed the boxes and headphones and passed them to her son. 'Lucas's camera has an infra-red capacity,' she said. 'Don't leave it on for long. We must conserve the batteries. Two minutes every half-hour should be sufficient.' Now she too seemed to be sleeping.

Gareth pressed the button on the box. 'You are troubled,' whispered Lucas's voice, sounding tinny and small through the earphones. Gareth flipped the microphone into place.

'What can you see?' he asked, turning his head slowly, allowing the tiny camera on the headband a view of the plain below.

'Move your head to the right – about an inch,' ordered Lucas.

'What is it?' Gareth's heart began to pound, and he slipped his Desert Eagle automatic from its shoulder holster.

'A beautiful spotted owl,' said Lucas. 'It's just caught a small lizard,' Gareth swore. 'There is nothing on the plain to concern you,' the machine chided him. 'Calm yourself.'

'Easy for you to say, Lucas. You haven't seen your own corpse.'

'As a matter of fact, I have. I watched the original Lucas collapse with a heart attack. However, that is beside the point. Your resting heartbeat is currently one hundred and thirty-three beats per minute. That is very close to panic, Gareth. Take some long, slow, deep breaths.'

'It is a hundred and thirty-three beats faster than the poor son of a bitch in the jeep,' snapped the young man. 'And it is not panic. I've never panicked in my life. I won't start now.'

A hand touched his shoulder and Gareth lurched upright. 'One hundred and sixty-five beats,' he heard Lucas whisper, and he spun round to see Amaziga standing calmly behind him.

'I said use the machine,' she told him, 'not get into an argument with it.' She held out her hand. 'Let me have Lucas, and then you can get some sleep.'

'I've another two hours yet.'

'I'm not tired. Now do as you're told.' He grinned sheepishly and carefully removed the headband and boxes. Amaziga laid aside her Uzi and clipped the machine to her shoulder rig. Gareth moved to his blanket and lay down. The Desert Eagle dug into his waist and, easing it clear, he laid it alongside him.

Amaziga turned off the machine and walked to the edge of the trees, staring out over the moonlit landscape. Nothing moved, and there were no sounds save for the rustling of leaves in the trees above her. She waited until Gareth was asleep and then waded back across the stream, past the ruined jeep and on to the scene of the feast. The body – or what was left of it – was in three parts. The head and neck were resting against a boulder, the face – thankfully – turned away. Amaziga flicked on the machine.

'What are we looking for?' asked Lucas.

'I am carrying a Sipstrassi Stone. There is little power left. She should have an identical Stone. Scan the ground.'

Slowly she turned her head. 'Can you see anything?'

'No. Nothing of interest. Traverse to the left . . . no . . . more slowly. Was it in the trouser pocket or the shirt?'

'Trouser.'

'There's not much left of the legs. Perhaps one of the beasts ate the Stone.'

'Just keep looking!' snapped Amaziga.

'All right. Move to the right . . . . *Amaziga!*' The tone in his voice made her blood grow cold.

'Yes?'

'I hope the weapon you are holding is primed and ready. There is a beast some fifteen metres to your right. He is around eight feet tall . . .' Amaziga flipped the Uzi into position and spun. As a huge, grey form hurtled towards her the Uzi fired, a long thunderous roar of sound exploding into the silence of the night. Bullets smashed into the grey chest, blood sprayed from the wounds, but still it came on. Amaziga's finger tightened on the trigger, emptying the long clip. The Devourer was flung backwards, its chest torn open. '*Amaziga!*' shouted Lucas. 'There are two more!'

The Uzi was empty and Amaziga scrabbled for the Beretta at her hip. Even as she did so the beasts charged.

And she knew she was too slow . . .

'Down, woman!' bellowed Shannow. Amaziga dived to her right. The booming sound of Shannow's pistol was followed by a piercing howl from the first Devourer which pitched backwards with half its head blown away. The second swerved past Amaziga and ran directly at the tall man at the edge of the trees. Shannow fired once; the creature slowed. A second shot ripped into its skull and Amaziga was showered with blood and brains.

Shannow stepped forward, pistols raised.

Amaziga turned her head. 'Are there any more of them?' she whispered to Lucas. There was no answer, and she saw that one of the leads had pulled clear of the right-hand box. She swore softly and pressed it home.

'Are you all right?' Lucas asked.

'Yes. What can you see?' asked Amaziga, turning slowly through a full circle.

'There are riders some four kilometres to the north, heading away from us. I can see no beasts. But the cliff face is high; there may be others on the higher ground. Might I suggest you reload your weapon?'

Switching off the machine Amaziga rose unsteadily to her feet. Shannow handed her the Uzi just as Gareth came running on to the scene, his Desert Eagle automatic in his hand.

'Thank you, Shannow,' said Amaziga. 'You got here very fast.'

'I was here all the time,' he told her. 'I followed you across the stream.'

'Why?'

He shrugged. 'I felt uneasy. And now, if you'll excuse me, I'll leave you to your watch.'

'Son of a bitch,' said Gareth, staring down at the three dead beasts. 'They're huge!'

'And dead,' pointed out Shannow as he strode past.

Gareth moved alongside Amaziga, who was pressing a full clip into the butt of the Uzi. 'Jesus, but he's like an iceman . . .' He stopped speaking, and Amaziga saw his gaze fall on the moonlit head of the other Amaziga. 'Oh, my God! Sweet Jesus!'

His mother took him by the arm, leading him away. 'I'm alive, Gareth. So are you. Hold to that! You hear me?'

He nodded. 'I hear you. But, Christ . . .'

'No buts, my son! They are dead – we are not. They came to rescue Sam. They failed; we will not. You understand?'

He took a long, deep breath. 'I won't let you down, Mother. You can trust me on that.'

'I know. Now go and get some sleep. I'll resume the watch.'

*

Samuel Archer was not a religious man. If there was a God, he had long ago decided, he was either wilful or incompetent. Perhaps both. Yet Sam stood now on the crest of the hill and prayed. Not for himself, though survival would be more than pleasant, but for the last survivors of those who had followed him in the War against the Bloodstone. Behind him were the remaining rebels, twenty-two in all, counting the women. Before and below them on the plain were the Hellborn elite.

Two hundred warriors, their skills enhanced by the *demonseeds* embedded in their foreheads. Killers all! Sam glanced around him. The rebels had picked a fine setting for their last stand, high above the plain, the tree line and thick undergrowth forming a rough stockade. The Hellborn would be forced to advance up a steep slope in the face of withering volleys. With enough ammunition we might even have held, thought Sam. He glanced down at the twin ammunition belts draped across his broad chest; there were more empty loops than full. Idly he counted the remaining shells. From the breast pocket of his torn grey shirt he drew a strip of dried beef, the last of his rations.

There would be no retreat from here, Sam knew. Two hundred yards behind them the mountains fell away into a deep gorge that opened out on to the edge of the Mardikh desert. Even if they could climb down, without horses they would die of thirst long before reaching the distant river.

Sam sighed and rubbed his tired eyes. For four years now he had fought the Bloodstone, gathering fighters, battling against Hellborn warriors and Devourers. All for nothing. His own small store of Sipstrassi was used up now, and without it they could not hope to hold off the killers. An ant crawled on to Sam's hand. He brushed it away.

That's what we are, he thought, ants standing defiantly before an avalanche.

Despair was a potent force, and one which Sam had resisted for most of these four years. It was not hard back at the beginning. The remnants of the Guardians had gathered against Sarento, and won three battles against the Hellborn. None had proved decisive. Then the Bloodstone had mutated the Wolvers and a new, terrible force was unleashed against the human race. Whole communities fled into the mountains to escape the beasts. The flight meant that the Guardian army, always small, was now without supplies as farming communities disappeared in the face of the Devourers. Ammunition became in short supply, and many fighters left the army in order to travel to their homes in a vain bid to protect their families.

Now twenty-two were left. Tomorrow there would be none.

A young, beautiful olive-skinned woman approached Sam. She was tall and wore two pistols in shoulder holsters over a faded red shirt. Her jet-black hair was drawn tightly into a bun at the nape of her neck. He smiled as he saw her. 'I guess we've come to the end of a long, sorrowful road, Shammy. I'm sorry I brought you to this.'

Shamshad Singh merely shrugged. 'Here or at home . . . what difference? You fight or you die.'

'Or do both,' said Sam wearily. She sat down beside him on the boulder, her short-barrelled shotgun resting on her slim thighs.

'Tell me of a happy time,' she said suddenly.

'Any particular theme?' he asked. 'I've lived for three hundred and fifty-six years, so there is a lot to choose from.'

'Tell me about Amaziga.'

He gazed at her fondly. She was in love with him, and had made it plain for the two years she had been with the rebels. Yet Sam had never responded to her overtures. In all his long life there was only one woman who had opened the doors to his soul – and she was dead, shot down by the Hellborn in the first months of the War.

'You are an extraordinary woman, Shammy. I should have done better by you.'

'Bullshit,' she said, with a wide smile. 'Now tell me about Amaziga.'

'Why?'

'Because it always cheers you up. And you need cheering.'

He shook his head. 'It has always struck me as particularly sad that there will come a point in a man's life where he has no second chances. When Napoleon saw his forces in full retreat at Waterloo, he knew there would never be another day when he would march out at the head of a great force. It was over. I always thought that must be hard to take. Now I know that it is. We have fought against a great evil, and we have been unable to defeat it. And tomorrow we die. It is not a time for happy stories, Shammy.'

'You're wrong,' she said. 'At this moment I can still see the sky, feel the mountain breeze, smell the perfume of the pines. I am alive! And I luxuriate in that fact. Tomorrow is another day, Sam. We'll fight them. Who knows, maybe we'll win? Maybe God will open up a hole in the sky and send his thunderbolts down upon our enemies.'

He chuckled then. 'Most likely he'd miss and hit us.'

'Don't mock, Sam,' she chided him. 'It is not for us to know what God intends.'

'It baffles me, after all you've seen, how you can still believe in Him.'

'It baffles me how you can't,' she responded. The sun was dropping low on the horizon, bathing the mountains in crimson and gold.

Down in the valley the Hellborn had begun their camp-fires, and the sound of raucous songs echoed up in the mountains.

'Jered has scouted the gorge,' said Shamshad. 'The cliff face extends for around four miles. He thinks some of us could make the descent.'

'That's desert down there. We'd have no way of surviving,' said Sam.

'I agree. But it is an option.'

'At least there are no Devourers,' he said, returning his stare to the Hellborn camp.

'Yes, that is curious,' she replied. 'They all padded off late yesterday. I wonder where to?'

'I don't care, as long as it's not here,' he told her, with feeling. 'How many shells do you have?'

'Around thirty. Another twenty for the pistol.'

'I guess it will be enough,' said Sam.

'I guess it will have to be,' she agreed.

*

Amaziga watched as Gareth lifted the coils of rope from his saddle. The cliff face was sheer and some six hundred feet high, but it rose in a series of three ledges – the first around eighty feet above them, its glistening edge shining silver in the bright moonlight.

'What do you think?' asked Amaziga.

Gareth smiled. 'Easy, Mother. Good hand and foot-holds all the way. The only problem area is that high overhang above the top ledge, but I don't doubt I can traverse it. Don't worry. I've soloed climbs that are ten times more difficult than this.' He turned to Shannow. 'I'll go for the first ledge, then lower a rope to you. We'll climb in stages. How is your head for heights, Mr Shannow?'

'I have no fear of heights,' said the Jerusalem Man.

Gareth looped two coils of rope over his head and shoulder and stepped up to the face. The climb was reasonably simple until he reached a point just below the ledge, where the rock was worn away by falling water. He considered traversing to the right, then saw a narrow vertical crack in the face some six feet to his left. Easing his way to it, Gareth pushed his right hand high into the crack, then made a fist, wedging his hand against the rock. Tensing his arm, he pulled himself up another few feet. There was a good handhold to the left and he hauled himself higher. Releasing the hand-jam hold, he reached over the edge of the ledge and levered himself up. Swinging, he sat on the edge staring down at the small figures below. He waved.

Climbing was always so exhilarating. His first experience of it had been in Europe, in the Triffyn mountains of Wales. Lisa had taught him to climb, shown him friction holds and hand-jams, and he had marvelled at her ability to climb what appeared to be surfaces as smooth as polished marble. He remembered her with great affection, and sometimes wondered why he had left her for Eve.

Lisa wanted marriage, Eve wanted pleasure. The thought was absurd. Are you really so shallow, he wondered? Lisa would have been a fine wife, strong, loyal, supportive. But her love for him had been obsessive and, worse, possessive. Gareth had seen what such love could do, for he had watched his mother and lived with her single-minded determination all his life. I don't want that kind of love, he thought. Not ever!

Pushing such thoughts from his mind, Gareth stood and moved along the ledge. There was no jutting of rock to which he could belay the rope, allowing friction to assist him in helping Shannow make the climb, but there was a small vertical crack. From his belt he unclipped a small claw-like object in shining steel. Pushing it into the crevice, he pulled the knob at its centre. The claw flashed open, locking to the walls of the crack. Lifting one coil of rope clear, he slid the end through a ring of steel in the claw and lowered it to the waiting Shannow. Once the Jerusalem Man had begun the climb, Gareth looped the rope across his left shoulder and took in the slack.

But Shannow made the climb without incident and levered himself over the ledge. 'How did you find it?' whispered Gareth.

Shannow shrugged. 'I don't like the look of those clouds,' he replied, keeping his voice low. Gareth tied the rope to his waist. Shannow was right. The sky was darkening, and they had still a fair way to go.

Lowering the rope once more, Gareth helped his mother make the climb. She was breathing heavily by the time she pushed herself up alongside them.

During the next hour the three climbers inched their way up to the last ledge. They were only forty feet from the top now, but darkness had closed in around them and a light drizzle had begun, making the rock-face slick and greasy. Gareth was worried now. It had not been possible to see from the ground the slight overhang at this point. Climbing it would be difficult at the best of times, but in darkness, with the rain increasing?

For the third time Gareth prowled along the ledge, gazing up, trying to judge the best route. Nothing he could see filled him with encouragement. The rain slowed. He glanced down at the tiny, insect-sized shapes of the hobbled horses. To come this far and not be able to complete his mission – Jesus, Amaziga would never forgive him. He had long known that his mother did not love him, and he accepted her pride in him as a reasonable substitute. She would – could – never love anyone as she did her husband. That love was all-encompassing, all-consuming. As a child this had hurt Gareth, but in manhood he had come to understand the complexities and the bewildering brilliance of the woman who had borne him. If her pride was all he could have, then it would have to suffice. He stepped up to the face and reached up for the first hand-hold; it was no more than a groove in the rock but he found a small foot-hold and levered himself up. Friction holds were vital on an overhang, but the young man's fingers were tired now, the rock-face slippery. Gareth's mouth was dry as he struggled to climb another fifteen feet. His foot slipped! He locked the fingers of his right hand to a small jutting section of rock, and swung out over the six-hundred-foot drop. Panic touched him. He was hanging by one hand, and unable to reach a second hold. Worse, he had moved out on to the overhang – and if he fell now he would miss the first ledge. The drop to the second was more than eighty feet . . . he would be smashed to pulp. Gareth's heart was pounding so hard he could feel the pulse thudding at his temple. Twisting his body, he looked up at the face. There was a small hold around eighteen inches above the tiny jut of rock to which he clung. Taking a long, deep breath he prepared himself for the surge of effort needed to reach it.

If you miss you will be dislodged! Christ! Don't think like that! But he couldn't help it. His mind flew back to the other Gareth, dead in a crushed jeep.

And he knew he didn't have the courage to make that last effort.

Oh, God, he thought. I'm going to die here!

Suddenly something pressed hard against the underside of his foot, taking the weight. Gareth looked down and saw that Shannow had climbed out on to the overhang. Now the two of them were out on the face, and if Gareth fell he would carry the Jerusalem Man to his death.

Shannow's voice drifted up to him, calm and steady. 'I can't hold you like this all night, boy. So I suggest you make a move.'

Gareth lunged up, catching the hold and swinging his foot to a small ridge in the stone. Above this the holds were infinitely easier and he gratefully hauled himself over the summit.

For a moment he lay back with eyes closed, feeling the rain on his face. Then he sat up, looped the rope over his shoulder and tugged it twice, signalling Shannow to start the climb. The rope went tight. Gareth leaned back to take the strain.

Something cold touched his temple.

It was a pistol . . .

A hand moved into sight. It held a razor-sharp knife, which sliced through the rope.

*

Shem Jackson was sitting in the front room of his house, his booted feet resting on a table. His brother, Micah, idly shuffled a pack of dog-eared cards. 'You wanna game, Shem?'

'For what?' responded the older man, lifting a jug of spirit and swigging from it. 'You lost everything you got.'

'You could lend me some,' said Micah, reproachfully.

Shem slammed the jug down on the table-top. 'What the Hell is the point of that? You play cards when you got money – it's that simple. Can't you get it into your head?'

'Well, what else is there to do?' whined Micah.

'And whose fault is that?' snapped Shem, pushing a dirty hand through his greasy hair. 'She wasn't much to look at, but you had to go and thrash her, didn't you?'

'She asked for it!' replied Micah. 'Called me names.'

'Well, now she's run off. And this time it's for good, I'll bet. You know the trouble with you, Micah? You never know when you're well-off.' Shem stood and stretched his lean frame. Rain couldn't be far away; his back was beginning to ache. Walking to the window, he stared out at the yard and the moonlit barn beyond. A flash of movement caught his eye and, leaning forward, he rubbed at the grimy glass. It merely smeared and Shem swore.

'What is it?' asked Micah. Shem shrugged.

'Thought I saw something out by the barn. It was probably nothing.' He squinted, caught a flash of silver-grey fur. 'It's Wolvers,' he said. 'God damn Wolvers!' Striding across the room, he lifted the long rifle down from its pegs over the mantel and, grinning, swung on Micah. 'Damn sight more fun than playing cards with a loser like you,' he said, pumping a shell into the breech. 'Come on, get your weapon, man, there's hunting to be had.'

Good humour flowed back to him. Little bastards, he thought. They won't get away this time. No Beth McAdam to save you now!

Stepping to the front door, he wrenched it open and walked out into the moonlight. 'Come on, you little beggars, show yourselves!' he called. The night was quiet, the moon unbearably bright to the eye. A hunter's moon! Shem crept forward with gun raised. He heard Micah move out behind him and stumble on the porch. Clumsy son of a bitch!

On open ground now Shem angled to the right, towards the vegetable patch and the corral. 'Show yourselves!' he shouted. 'Old Uncle Shem's got a little present for you!'

Behind him Micah made a gurgling sound, and Shem heard the clump of something striking the ground. Probably his rifle, thought Shem as he turned.

But it was not a rifle. Micah's head bounced twice on the hard-packed earth, the neck completely severed by a savage sweep of a long-taloned hand. Micah's body toppled forward, but Shem was not looking at it. He was staring in paralysed horror at the creature towering before him, its silver fur shining, its eyes golden, a bright red stone embedded in its forehead.

Shem Jackson's rifle came up and he pulled the trigger. The bullet smashed into the creature's chest, sending up a puff of dust. But it didn't go down; it howled and leapt forward, its talons flashing down. Shem felt the blow on his shoulder and staggered back. The rifle was on the ground. He blinked and then felt a rush of blood from his shoulder. There was no pain – not even when his arm fell clear, thumping against the ground and draping across his boot.

The Devourer lashed out once more . . .

Shem Jackson's face disappeared.

From the shadows, scores more of the beasts moved forward. Several stopped to feed.

Most loped on towards the sleeping town of Pilgrim's Valley.

Chapter Ten

The greatest folly is to believe that evil can be overcome by reason. Evil is like gravity, a force that is beyond argument.
The Wisdom of the Deacon
Chapter xxvii

* * *

Jacob Moon was not given to hearing voices. Such gifts were for other men. No visions, no prophecies, no mystic dreams or revelations. Jacob Moon had only one real gift, if such it could be called: he could kill without emotion. So when the voice did come Moon was utterly astonished. He was sitting by his campfire in the lee of the Great Wall some twenty miles from Pilgrim's Valley. Having heard nothing from the Apostle Saul, Moon had left Domango and made the long ride across the mountains. A flash flood had diverted him from his course, delaying him, but he was now less than three hours' ride from the town. His horse was exhausted and Moon made camp beside the Wall.

The voice came to him just before midnight, as he was settling down to sleep. At first it was a whisper, like a breath of night winds. But then it grew. *'Jacob Moon! Jacob Moon!'*

Moon sat up, pistol in hand. 'Who's there?'

'Behind you,' came the response and Moon spun. One of the great rectangular blocks had apparently disappeared and he found himself facing a red-skinned man, with what appeared to be painted black lines across his face and upper body. The man was seated on an ebony throne. Moon cocked his pistol. 'You will not need that,' said the man on the throne. The image drifted closer, until the strange face filled the hole in the wall: the eyes were the red of rubies, the whites bloodshot. 'I need you, Moon,' said the vision.

'Well, I don't need you,' was Moon's response as the pistol bucked in his hand, the bullet lancing through the red face.

There was no mark to show its passing and a wide smile appeared on the face.

'Save your ammunition, Moon, and listen to what I offer you – riches beyond your dreams, and life eternal. I can make you immortal, Moon. I can fulfil your wildest desires.'

Moon sat back and sheathed his pistol. 'This is a dream, isn't it? God damn it, I'm dreaming!'

'No dream, Moon,' the red man told him. 'Would you like to live for ever?'

'I'm listening.'

'My world is dying. I need another. A man known to you as Saul opened the Gateway for me, and I have now seen your world. It is to my liking. But it would help me to have a lieutenant here, to direct my . . . troops. From the few thoughts I could extract from the dying Saul, I gathered that you were that man. Is that so?'

'Tell me about the life eternal,' said Moon, ignoring the question.

'That can begin now, Moon. Is it what you desire?'

'Aye.' Moon reeled back as a terrible burning sensation erupted on his forehead. He cried out and lifted his hand to his head. The pain subsided as suddenly as it had appeared, and now Moon could feel a small stone embedded in his brow.

'As long as you serve me, Moon, you will be immortal. Can you feel the new strength in your limbs, the power . . . the life?'

Jacob Moon felt more than that. His long-held bitterness was unleashed, his anger primal. As the vision promised he felt strong, no longer tired from his journey, no longer aching from long hours in the saddle. 'I feel it,' he admitted. 'What do you want from me?'

'Ride to the ruined city north of Pilgrim's Valley. There I shall greet you.'

'I asked what you wanted from me,' said Moon.

'Blood,' responded the vision. 'Rivers of blood. Violence and death, hatred and war.'

'Are you the Devil?' asked Moon.

'I am better than the Devil, Moon. For I have won.'

*

Unbeknown to Gareth it was his mother who had chosen to climb next, leaving Shannow on the ledge. When the rope suddenly gave she was dislodged from the face. Many people faced with such a moment would have panicked, screamed and fallen to their deaths. Amaziga was different.

She lived for only one prize – finding Sam.

In the moment the rope gave way and she slipped, her hand snaked out, fingers scrabbling against the wet stone. The first hold she grasped was not large enough to hold her and she slipped again. Her fingers scraped down the rock, one fingernail tearing away, then her hand clamped over a firm hold and the descent ceased. She was hanging now on the lower part of the overhang, her legs dangling below the curve of the rock. Her arm was tiring fast, and she could feel her grip loosening.

'Shannow!' she called. 'Help me!'

A hand grabbed at her belt just as her fingers lost their grip and she fell, but he dragged her back to the ledge. Slumping to her haunches, she leaned her head against the rock face and closed her eyes. The pain from her damaged hand was almost welcome: it told her she was alive.

Shannow hauled in the rope and examined the end.

'Someone cut it,' he said.

Fear coursed through her. 'Gareth!' she whispered.

'Maybe they took him alive,' said Shannow, keeping his voice low. 'The question is, what do we do now? We have enemies above and horses below.'

'If they look over the edge they will not be able to see us,' she said. 'They will assume we have fallen. I think we should make the climb.' She saw Shannow smile.

'I don't know if I can, Lady. I know you cannot – not with that injured hand.'

'We can't just leave Gareth.' She glanced at her watch. 'And there is only an hour left before they will kill Sam. We have no time to climb down and go round.'

Shannow stood and prowled along the ledge. There was nowhere that he could climb. Amaziga joined him, and together they examined the face. Long minutes passed; then the sound of gunfire came from above them, heavy and sustained.

'You are right,' she said at last, her voice heavy with despair. 'There is nothing we can do.'

'Wait,' said Shannow. Lifting a pistol from his belt, he pushed the end of the rope through the trigger guard and tied it in place. Stepping to the edge of the ledge he let out the rope, then began to swing it round and round. Amaziga looked up. Some twenty-five feet above them, at the narrowest point of the overhang, there was a jutting finger of stone. Shannow let out more rope and continued to swing the weighted end. Finally he sent it sailing up; the pistol clattered against the rock face, then dropped, looping the rope over the stone. Shannow lowered it, removed the pistol and holstered it.

'You think it will take your weight?' asked Amaziga.

Shannow hauled down on the doubled rope three times. 'Let us hope so,' he said.

And he began to climb.

*

Gareth's anger was mounting. The olive-skinned woman had cut the rope and then ordered him to rise, with his hands on his head. 'Listen to me,' he said, 'I am here to—'

'Shut it!' she snapped, and he heard the pistol being cocked. 'Walk forward, and be aware I'm right behind you and I have killed before.' She did not rob him of his weapons, which spoke either of confidence or stupidity. Gareth guessed it to be confidence. He obeyed her and walked towards the clearing, where he could see around a score of men and women kneeling behind rocks or fallen trees, rifles in their hands. A tall black man turned as they approached.

'I found this *creature*,' sneered the woman, 'climbing the cliff-face behind us. There were others, but I cut the rope.'

'Indeed she did,' said Gareth, 'and probably killed one of the few friends you had in this world, Sam.'

The black man's eyes widened. 'Do I know you, boy?'

'In a manner of speaking.' The sky was lightening with the pre-dawn, and the rain had cleared. 'Look at me closely, Sam. Who do I remind you of?'

'Who are you?' asked Samuel Archer. 'Speak plainly.'

Gareth could tell by his surprised expression that he had, at least in part, guessed the truth. 'My mother's name is Amaziga,' he said.

'You lie!' shouted Sam. 'I've known Amaziga all her life. She had no other sons.'

'My mother is stuck back there on that rock face. She crossed a world to find you, Sam. Ask her yourself.'

At that moment a volley of shots came from Gareth's right. Several men and a woman fell screaming. Then the Hellborn rushed the camp, firing as they came, tall men in tunics of black leather and ram-horned helms. Sam swung away, reaching for his pistol. Gareth flipped the Uzi into position and the sound of rolling thunder exploded in the clearing. The first line of Hellborn warriors went down as if scythed. Gareth ran towards the rest with the machine pistol juddering in his hands. Other shots sounded from all around him as the rebels opened fire. He snapped clear the empty clip and rammed home another. But the first attack having failed, the Hellborn had faded back into the trees and were firing from cover. A bullet slashed past Gareth's head, another kicked up dirt at his feet. Ducking, he sprinted to a boulder and crouched down behind it. A dead young woman lay to his left, a small dark hole oozing blood from her temple. A shot glanced from the boulder above Gareth's head. Risking a glance, he saw a rifleman in the upper branches of a nearby tree. Lifting the Uzi, he squeezed off a quick burst. The sniper tipped back and fell through the tree, crashing into the undergrowth below.

Across the clearing Sam was lying behind a fallen log. He cursed himself for a fool for not realising that the Hellborn would try a sneak attack under cover of the dawn mists. The young man's arrival with the multi-firing rifle had saved them. He glanced at Gareth. In profile he could see even more clearly the resemblance to Amaziga, the fine high cheekbones, the pure sleek brow. Gareth saw him and grinned – and that was the final proof. Sam did not understand how such a thing was possible, but it was true!

A volley came from the left and some thirty Hellborn leapt from cover, firing as they came. Sam saw several of his rebels fall. The Uzi thundered, but the charge continued. Raising his pistol, Sam shot into the charging group. Bullets ripped the air around him, one grazing his skull and knocking him from his feet. He rolled and saw Shammy, a pistol in each hand, running towards the invaders. Her life seemed charmed – until a shot caught her in the upper thigh, spinning her to the floor. Jered, firing his shotgun from the hip, leapt to her aid. Just as he reached her his face disappeared in a spray of crimson.

Sam came to his knees and emptied his pistol into the last of the attackers. Gareth's Uzi fired again, and the clearing was still. Shammy crawled to where he lay. Blood was soaking her leggings. 'I'll get a tourniquet on that,' said Sam.

'No point,' answered Shammy. Sam looked around. There were maybe forty Hellborn dead, leaving at least another 150. But of the rebels only he and Shammy were still alive. And the young stranger.

Gareth joined them, moving across the ground in a commando crawl. 'My rope is still back there,' he said. 'We'd at least have a chance if we pulled back.'

'No time,' answered Shammy, lifting her reloaded pistols just as the next wave of Hellborn rushed them. Gareth rolled to his knees and emptied the last clip into the warriors. At least ten of them were hurled from their feet, but the others came on.

Then a second roll of thunder scythed through the attackers and Gareth saw Amaziga run forward, her own Uzi blazing. Behind her was Shannow, his long pistols firing steadily. The Hellborn broke and fled back into the undergrowth.

'Let's get out of here!' said Gareth. He and Sam lifted the injured Shamshad and staggered across the clearing. Shots sounded around them, but then they were into the cover of the trees. Swiftly Gareth tied his last rope to a slender tree-trunk. 'You first, Sam,' he said. 'There's a ledge below and you'll find another rope. There are horses at the foot of the cliff.' Sam seemed not to hear. He was staring at Amaziga. 'Questions later, okay?' said Gareth, grabbing the man's arm. 'For now . . . the rope! When you are on the ledge, flick the rope twice. Then the next to come will follow you.'

Sam grabbed the rope and slithered over the edge as Gareth moved alongside his mother. 'You have any more clips for the Uzi?'

'One more,' she said, handing it to him.

A Hellborn moved into sight with rifle aimed. Shannow shot him twice through the body. Gareth glanced back at the rope. 'Come on, man!' he whispered. As if obedient to his thoughts, the unseen Sam reached the ledge and the rope flicked twice. 'You next, Mother,' he said. 'Give the Uzi to Shannow.' Tossing the weapon to the Jerusalem Man, she moved to the rope and disappeared from sight.

Shots sliced the air around them. Shannow fired the Uzi and all was suddenly silent.

The rope flicked. 'Now you, Shannow!'

'I'll come last,' he said. 'Get yourself down.' Gareth handed his Uzi to Shammy and moved to the edge.

There was a silence for a while, then Shannow saw the rope jerk twice. 'Better join them,' he told the young woman.

She smiled and shrugged. 'Lost too much blood, friend. No strength left. You go. I'll hold them for a while.'

'I'll carry you,' he announced.

'No. The artery is cut in the groin, I'm bleeding to death. I've probably only minutes left. Save yourself – and Sam. Get Sam away.'

Two Hellborn reared up. A bullet ricocheted from the tree by Shannow's head. Twisting, he emptied the Uzi, then cast it aside. Shammy was lying down now, a second wound in her chest. Shannow crawled to her.

'Well,' she whispered, 'that one took the pain away.'

'You are a brave woman. You deserved better.'

'You'd better go,' she said. 'Sit me up first. I may yet get off another few rounds.' Shannow lifted her to a sitting position with her back to a tree, the Uzi in her hands. Then he slithered back to the edge and dropped from sight.

As he reached the ledge he heard a burst of firing.

Then silence . . .

*

Sam sat on the hillside above the small cluster of deserted buildings, his mind still reeling from the shocks of the day. Shammy was dead. They were all dead: Jered, Marcia, Caleb . . . And Amaziga was alive. He was filled with a sense of unreality, a pervading numbness that blocked all emotion.

They had climbed down to the foot of the cliff, the Hellborn firing down upon them, the bullets kicking up puffs of dust but none coming near. He and Amaziga had shared the lead horse, the young black man and the grim warrior following behind. They had ridden for hours, stopping at last at this deserted hamlet, its residents long since slain by the forces of the Bloodstone – the few homes empty, dust-filled reminders of a community that had vanished for ever.

Amaziga had led him into one of the houses, sitting him down and kneeling before him. There she had explained it all. But her words drifted around in his mind without meaning. He had reached out and touched her face; she had leaned in to him and kissed his fingers, just as she had always done. His tears flowed then, and he rose and staggered from the house, brushing past the young man and breaking into a run that carried him far up the hill.

Shammy was dead. Loyal, steadfast Shammy, who asked for nothing save to fight beside him.

Yet where was the grief? Amaziga, whom he had loved more than life, was back. Not his Amaziga, she said, but another woman from another world. It made no sense, and it made no difference. On the ride he had sat behind her, the scent of her hair filling his nostrils, the feel of her body against him.

Samuel Archer struggled to marshal his thoughts. He had studied the principle of multiple universes back at the Guardian Centre, had indeed theorised that other Samuel Archers might exist. Then Sarento had mutated into the Blood Beast and all Sam's studies had been forgotten in the savage Wars that followed.

Amaziga had died, cut down by a hail of bullets, her beautiful face shattered and torn.

Amaziga was alive!

Oh, God!

It was all too much. Sam stared up at the sky. Not a single bird flew, and as far as the eye could see not one living creature roamed the land. The Bloodstone had sucked the world dry. The sun was shining, the sky powder-blue and dappled with clouds. Sam lay back on the grass, his thoughts haphazard, chaotic. Amaziga came walking up towards him and his eyes drank in her lithe movements, the swaying, unself-conscious sexuality, the lightness of step. God, she was the most beautiful woman he had ever known!

I don't know her!

'We need to talk, Sam,' she said softly, sitting beside him.

'Let's talk about our shared memories,' he said, more harshly than he intended. 'You recall the summer in Lost Hawk, near the lake?'

She shook her head sadly. 'You and I have shared no summers, though I don't doubt that some of our memories will be linked. That's not the point, Sam. I crossed the universe to find you and save you from death. I could not save my own Sam, any more than you could protect the Amaziga you knew. But we are each the identical copies of the originals. Everything I loved about my Sam you share, and that is why I can say – without fear of contradiction – that I love you, Sam. I love you and I need you.'

'Who is the boy?' asked Sam, knowing the answer but needing the confirmation.

'Your son – the son you would have sired. Whichever.'

'He's a fine man, brave and steady. I could be proud of a son like that.'

'Then *be* proud, Sam,' she urged him. 'Come with us. Together we can try to stop a world falling. It won't be our own, but it will be a world just like the one that almost died. We can save it, Sam. We can fulfil the dream of the Guardians.'

'And what of the Bloodstone?'

She spread her hands. 'What of him, Sam? He has killed a world. He will not be able to feed. He is finished anyway.'

Sam shook his head. 'Sarento was no fool. What is to stop him from finding other worlds? No, I have pledged myself to destroy him, and that I must do.'

Amaziga was silent for a moment. 'This is foolish, Sam; we both know it. His powers are beyond us. You have a plan? Or is this just a quixotic impulse that will not allow you to know when you are beaten?'

'*My* Amaziga would not have asked that,' he said.

'Yes, she would, Sam, and you know it. You are a romantic and an idealist. She never was. Was she?'

He sighed and turned his face away from her, staring down at the small cluster of buildings and the two men who waited there. 'Who is the cold killer?' he asked, avoiding the question.

'His name is Shannow. In his own world they call him the Jerusalem Man. He too had an impossible dream – but he learned the folly of such fantasies.'

'He does not look like a dreamer. Nor does he look like a man who has lost hope.' Swinging back towards her, he smiled. 'You are right, my Ziga would have asked the same question. What interests me is how you will react to what I am about to say. Or can you predict it?'

'Oh, I can predict it, Sam,' she told him. 'You are going to say that running away would destroy you, for it would mean turning your back on everything you believe in. Or something like it. You are going to tell me that you will continue the battle against the Bloodstone, even if I say we will leave without you. Am I right?'

'I can't deny it.'

'And you are wrong, Sam. Oh, I admire you for your courage, but you are wrong. Before coming here we studied the Bloodstone. Sarento cannot be harmed by any weapon in our possession. He is invulnerable. We cannot shoot him, starve him or burn him. We could pack him in a thousand tons of ice, and it would have no effect upon him. So tell me, Sam, how will you fight this monster?'

Sam looked away. 'There has to be a way. God knows there has to be.'

'If there is, my love, we will not find it here. Perhaps in the world before the Fall we can find something – and then come back.'

Sam thought about it for a while, then slowly nodded. 'You are right – as always. How do we get to your world?'

Amaziga laughed. 'Don't look so crestfallen. There is so much we can do together for the good of all mankind. You are alive, Sam! And we are together.'

'And the Bloodstone is triumphant,' he whispered.

'Only for now,' she assured him.

*

Shannow glanced up at the two of them, watching their embrace.

Gareth moved alongside him. 'Well, we did it, Mr Shannow. We brought the lovers back together.'

Shannow nodded, but said nothing, turning his gaze to the distant mountains and the fringe of the desert to the north. 'You think they will follow us?' asked Gareth.

'Count on it,' Shannow told him. 'According to Lucas, it would take them most of a day to find a path down for their horses. Even so, I don't like the idea of sitting here and waiting. Four people with three tired horses? We won't outrun them, that's for sure.' He stood and wandered back to a brick-built well to the rear of the first house. Lowering the bucket, he dunked it below the surface, then hauled it back to the top. The water was cool and clear and he drank deeply. The death of the olive-skinned girl had touched him: she was so young, with untold paths lying before her. Now she would walk none of them, her life snuffed out by a murdering band of killers, serving an abomination.

Not for the first time he wondered how men could descend to such barbarism. He remembered the words of Varey Shannow: *'Jon, Man is capable of greatness, love, nobility, compassion. Yet never forget that his capacity for evil is infinite. It is a sad truth, boy, that if you sit now and think of the worst tortures that could ever be inflicted on another human being, they will already have been practised somewhere. If there is one sound that follows the march of humanity, it is the scream.'*

Gareth led the horses to the well and filled a second bucket. 'You look far away, Mr Shannow,' said the young man. 'What were you thinking?'

Shannow did not reply. Turning, he saw Amaziga and Sam approaching hand in hand.

'We're ready to go,' she said.

'The horses will need to rest for tonight,' said Shannow. 'They're worn out. We'll make use of one of these houses and leave at first light. I'll take the first watch.'

To his surprise, Amaziga offered no argument. Removing the headband and silver boxes that contained Lucas, she handed them to him, pointing out how to engage the machine, and warning him of the need to limit the use so as to conserve the energy.

Sam and Amaziga went into the first house. Gareth remained for a moment with Shannow; he grinned. 'I think I'll sleep in the next house,' he said. 'I'll relieve you in four hours.'

Removing his hat, Shannow slid the headband into place and then looped the shoulder rig across his right shoulder and pressed the button on the first box. Seconds later he heard Lucas's soft voice. 'Is everyone safe?'

'Yes,' said Shannow.

'I can't hear you, Mr Shannow. Engage the microphone. It eases from the headband. Once in position it will activate automatically.'

Shannow twisted the slender rod into place. 'Yes, we are safe. Amaziga has Sam.'

'There is sadness in your voice. I take it there was some tragedy?'

'Many people died, Lucas.'

'Ah yes . . . I see her now. Young and beautiful. You did not want to leave her. Oh, Mr Shannow. The world can be so savage.' Lucas was silent for a moment. 'What a lonely place this is,' he said at last. 'No birds, no animals. Nothing. Would you turn your head, Mr Shannow? There is a camera in the headband. I will scan the countryside.' Shannow did as he was bid. 'Nothing,' said Lucas. 'Not even an insect. Truly this is a dead place. Wait . . . I am picking up something. . .'

'What? Riders?'

'Shhh. Wait, please.' Shannow scanned the distant mountains, seeking any sign of movement, but there was nothing that he could see in the fading light. Finally the voice of Lucas drifted back. 'Tell Amaziga that we will be travelling back through the stone circle in Babylon; it is closer.'

'You want us to ride to the Hellborn city?' asked Shannow, astonished.

'It will save half a day.'

'There is the matter of an enemy nation to consider,' observed Shannow.

'Trust me,' said Lucas. 'Ride north-east tomorrow. Now, Mr Shannow, please cut the power. I have seen all I want to see.'

Shannow flicked the switch, then removed the headband.

*

Else Broome could not sleep. Her enormous body tossed and turned on the rickety bed, the springs creaking in protest at the weight. She was angry. Her husband had lost his mind and shot down the Prophet, ending in one miserable moment all her dreams of status and respect. He had always been useless, weak and spineless, she thought. I should never have married him. And she wouldn't have, had Edric Scayse not rejected her. Men! Scayse would have been a considerable catch – rich, handsome, respected. He had also died young, which would have left Else as the grieving widow, heir to his fortune and able to live a life of luxury, perhaps even in Unity. The Widow Scayse. It was a delicious thought. Yet despite every inducement she could offer, Scayse had remained immune to her advances, and she had been forced to settle for second-best. Second-best? She almost laughed at the thought. Josiah Broome was the runt of the litter. But through good fortune – and the benefit of a sensible wife – he had risen to a place of eminence among the people of Pilgrim's Valley.

Now even that small gain was gone for good. Today, on the main street, in front of everyone, several women had crossed the road to avoid Else Broome. Eyes were downcast as she passed – all except for Ezra Feard, Josiah's main competitor. He had smiled broadly and his thin witch of a wife had hurried out to stand beside him, gloating in Else's downfall.

And it would get worse. The Jerusalem Riders would bring her husband back, probably snivelling and crying, and lock him up in the Crusader jail, before the public trial which would see him hang. Oh, the shame of it!

Squeezing shut her eyes, she said a prayer. 'Oh, Lord, you know what trials I have been through with that wretched man. It is said that he was shot trying to escape. Let him die in the mountains. Let his body be devoured and never found.'

Maybe, after a few years, the memory of her mad husband would diminish in the eyes of the townsfolk. Or she could marry again.

A sudden noise downstairs caused her eyes to jerk open.

Someone was moving around the house. 'Dear God, don't let it be Josiah! Anything but that!' she whispered.

There was a small pistol in the bedside table. Else sat up. If she crept down and killed him she would become a hero, all her status restored. Opening the drawer, she pulled out the weapon. It seemed tiny in her fat fist. Flicking open the revolver's side gate, she checked that it was loaded; then, easing her vast bulk from the bed, she moved out to the doorway and the stairs beyond. The belt of her cavernous white flannel nightgown caught on the door handle. Shaking it loose, she stepped on to the first stair which creaked loudly.

'Is that you, Josiah, dear?' she called, as she moved down into the darkness. Then she caught a flicker of movement to the left. Cocking the pistol, she stepped from the stairs. The moon emerged from behind the clouds, silver light streaming through the window and the open door. A huge shape reared up before her.

Else Broome had time for one piercing scream . . .

It was heard by the Crusader Captain Leon Evans as he made his nightly rounds. The sound chilled him. A figure moved from the shadows and Leon spun, his gun flashing into his hand.

'It's only me, sir,' said Samuel McAdam, stepping out to join him. 'Did you hear it?'

'Damn right. It came from West Street.'

'You want me to come with you?'

Leon smiled and clapped the boy on the shoulder. 'You're not a Crusader yet, Sam. Wait until you get paid for it.' Holstering his pistol, he moved along the street. A silver shape ran at him from the shadows, but Leon was moving past the alleyway and failed to see it. Samuel blinked. He couldn't believe his eyes. No Wolver could possibly be that big!

'Captain!' he shouted, at the same time dragging out his pistol. His first shot missed the beast. But Leon Evans swung, drew and fired in one smooth motion. Samuel saw the beast stagger, its head snapping back as blood sprayed from a cut to the scalp. Samuel fired again. Dust kicked up from the beast's hide, just above the hip, and blood pumped from the wound. Leon Evans stepped in close and triggered two shots into the Devourer's chest. With a terrible howl it sank to its haunches.

Movement came from the far end of the street and screaming began in several of the houses to Samuel's right. High above a window smashed and a man's body hurtled down, smashing through the slanting wooden roof that protected the sidewalk. He landed head-first. Leon ran to the body, Samuel following. It was Ezra Feard, his chest ripped open.

People came running from their homes, converging at the centre of the main street. A huge beast climbed from Ezra Feard's window and leapt down among them. Samuel saw a woman dragged screaming to the ground. A man ran to her aid but talons ripped into his chest. Panic swept through the crowd and they began to run. From the far end of the street came a score more of the creatures, their howls echoing above the screams of the crowd.

'Get to the Crusader building!' yelled Leon Evans, trying to make himself heard above the sounds of terror that rent the night. Pistol in hand, Samuel forced his way through the crowd, trying to reach the law officer. The Crusader Captain was standing his ground with arm extended, coolly firing at the charging beasts. The hammer clicked down on an empty chamber, Leon Evans broke open the pistol and began to reload, but a beast bore down on him and leapt. Samuel was some yards back. He fired – and missed. Talons ripped into Leon Evans' cheek, tearing his face away. The Crusader Captain fell back, dropping his pistol. As the creature leapt again, the mortally wounded man drew a hunting-knife and lunged out, but the blade did not even pierce the hide. Talons tore into his body and he fell in a spray of blood. Samuel backed away, trembling, then turned and ran for his life.

Many people were crowding into the stone-built Crusader building, while others continued to run along the main street. As a horse came bolting from a side street Sam jumped at it, grabbing the mane, trying to vault to the animal's bare back. He missed and was dragged for some thirty yards before falling to the dust. Scrambling up, he gazed around him. A huge Wolver was running at him. When Samuel's hand swept down to his holster . . . it was empty.

A shotgun blast came from the right and above. Hit full in the chest the creature staggered back, letting out a bellow of pain.

Samuel glanced up to see the youngster Wallace Nash leaning out of a window above him. 'Better get in here, Sam!' shouted Wallace. Samuel ran up the three short steps to the main door and swiftly moved inside. Out on the street the wounded beast bounded forward to hurl itself at the door, which broke into two pieces as it burst open. Samuel fled for the stairs, taking them two at a time, the beast just behind him. Wallace Nash appeared at the top. 'Drop, Sam!' shouted the youngster.

Samuel threw himself down as the shotgun blasted, and he heard the body of the beast tumbling back behind him. Scrambling up, he joined the red-headed youngster at the top of the stairs. He did not know Wallace well, and remembered the boy was a sprinter who had once outrun Edric Scayse's racing horse, Rimfire.

'Thanks, Wallace,' he said, as the youngster thumbed two shells into the double-barrelled gun.

'We got to get out of here,' said Wallace. 'This old bird gun ain't going to hold them, that's for damn sure. Where's your pistol?' he asked, glancing down at the empty scabbard.

Samuel was embarrassed. 'Dropped it out on the street. I panicked.' Wallace nodded, then reached into his belt to pull clear an old, single-action Hellborn pistol.

Fresh screaming erupted from the street and the two young men ran through to the upper front room and looked out of the window. A young woman carrying a baby was hammering on the door of the Crusader building, but the people inside were too frightened to let her in.

A beast loped towards her.

'Over here!' shouted Samuel. The woman spun, and Samuel could see her gauging the distance against the speed of the Wolver. She would never make it . . .

But she tried.

Wallace levelled the shotgun and let fly with both barrels, taking the beast high in the shoulder and spinning it. Regaining its balance, it lurched after the woman. Samuel pushed open the window and climbed out. To the eternal regret of his mother, Beth, he had never been blessed with great courage or stamina. Samuel believed he had failed her in almost everything. Taking a deep breath he jumped, landing heavily and twisting his ankle. The woman was almost at the steps – the beast just behind her – as Samuel moved left and fired, his first bullet smashing into the creature's open mouth. His second took it in the throat and blood sprayed from the exit wound. Still it came on.

In that instant Samuel McAdam knew he was going to die, and an icy calm settled on him.

The woman ran by him without a glance, her baby screaming. Other beasts were gathering now. The first creature loomed above Samuel and he fired twice more, straight into the heart. The Wolver slumped – then its taloned hand slashed out.

'Get back, Sam!' he heard Wallace shout. The beast fell dead. Something hot and sticky was drenching Sam's shirt. He glanced down. It was blood, gushing from a gaping wound in his throat.

Samuel fell to his knees, all strength seeping from him. Toppling sideways, his face struck the hard-packed dirt of the street. There was no pain. 'I'm dying,' he thought dispassionately. 'This is it.' A great weariness settled over him, and an old nursery prayer drifted into his mind. Samuel tried to say it, but there was no time.

*

This was the day that Dr Julian Meredith had long dreaded. Isis lay in the wagon, unconscious, her pulse weak and fluttering erratically, her eyelids tinged with blue, her cheeks sunken. With hindsight he knew this day had been coming for several weeks. Her energy was low, and it was becoming an effort even to talk.

Meredith sat by the bedside as Jeremiah drove the wagon. How long, he wondered, before the end? Leaning forward, he kissed her cold brow. His eyes misted and a warm tear splashed to the pale cheek below him. When the wagon creaked to a stop, Meredith rose and opened the rear door, climbing down to the ground. Jeremiah looped the reins around the brake handle and joined him.

'Is she any better?' asked the old man.

Meredith shook his head. 'I think it will be tonight.'

'Oh dear,' whispered Jeremiah. 'She's such a sweet lass. There's no justice, is there, Doctor?'

'Not in cases like hers,' Meredith agreed.

Jeremiah built a fire and carried two chairs down from the wagon. 'I still don't understand what's killing her,' he said. 'Cancer I can understand, or a weak heart. Not this.'

'It's very rare,' explained Meredith. 'In the old world it used to be called Addison's Disease. We all have a defence system inside our bodies, which can isolate germs and destroy them. In the case of Isis the system malfunctioned and began to turn on itself, destroying the adrenal glands among others.'

'Then she is killing herself,' said Jeremiah.

'Yes. The old race found cortisonal substitutes and these kept Addisonians alive. These days we do not know how they were manufactured.'

Jeremiah sighed and glanced around at the vast, empty prairie. They had left the other wagons outside Domango when Isis fell sick, and were heading now for Pilgrim's Valley, searching for a miracle. The Apostle Saul was the last of the Deacon's disciples, and it was said that he had performed miracles in Unity years ago. When they heard he was in Pilgrim's Valley, Jeremiah had left the others and headed the wagon across the prairie.

They were only two days from the Valley now, but those two days might just as well be two centuries. For Isis was dying before their eyes.

Jeremiah lapsed into silence and fed the blaze as Meredith returned to the wagon. Isis lay so still he thought she had passed away, but he held a small mirror beneath her nostrils and the merest ghost of vapour appeared on the surface. Taking her hand he began to talk to her, saying the words he had longed to speak. 'I love you, Isis. Almost from the first day I saw you. You had a basket of flowers and you were walking down the main street offering them for sale. The sun was shining, and your hair was like a cap of gold. I bought three bunches. They were daffodils, I think.' He fell silent and squeezed her fingers; there was no answering pressure and he sighed. 'And now you are going to leave me, and journey where I cannot follow.' His voice broke and the tears flowed. 'I find that hard to take. Terribly hard.'

When Meredith climbed down from the wagon, Jeremiah

had a pot of stew upon the fire and was stirring it with a wooden spoon. 'Thought I saw a Wolver,' said the old man, 'over there in the trees.' Meredith squinted, but could see nothing save the breeze flickering over the top of the grass, causing the stems to imitate the actions of waves upon an ocean.

From the distance came an eerie howling. 'Do you have a gun?' asked Meredith.

'Nope. Gave it to Malcolm. Said I'd pick it up when next we met.'

Meredith sat down and extended his fingers to the blaze. Camped in the open there was little heat to be felt, for the breeze dispersed it swiftly. Normally they would have found a sheltered place to set the fire, against a rock or even a fallen tree. But the oxen were tired, and there was good grass here.

'I don't suppose we'll need a weapon,' said Meredith. 'I have never heard of a single instance of Wolvers attacking humans.'

'What will you do, Doctor, when . . . ?' Jeremiah stumbled to silence, unable to finish the sentence.

'When she dies?' Meredith rubbed his hand over his face. His eyes were tired, his heart heavy. 'I shall leave the *Wanderers*, Jeremiah. I'll find a little town that has no doctor, and I'll settle there. I only joined you to be close to Isis. You?'

'Oh, I'll keep travelling. I like to see new land, fresh scenery. I love to bathe in forgotten streams, and watch the sun rise over un-named mountains.'

A silver-grey form moved out from the grass and stood, unnoticed, some twenty yards from the wagon. Meredith was the first to see the Wolver and he tapped Jeremiah on the shoulder. The old man looked up. 'Come join us, little friend,' he said.

The Wolver hesitated, then loped forward to squat by the fire. 'I am Pakia,' it said, head tilting to one side, long tongue lolling from its mouth.

'Welcome, Pakia,' said Jeremiah. 'Are you hungry? The stew is almost ready.'

'No hunger. But very frightened.'

Jeremiah chuckled. 'You have nothing to fear from us. I am Jeremiah, and this is my friend, Doctor Meredith. We do not hunt your people.'

'I fear you not,' said the Wolver. 'Where do you go?'

'Pilgrim's Valley,' answered the old man.

The Wolver shook her head vehemently. 'No go there. Much evil. Much death. All dead.'

'A plague?' asked Meredith. Pakia tilted her head, her eyes questioning the word. 'A great sickness?'

'Not sickness. The blood beasts come, kill everyone. I smell them now,' she added, lifting her long snout into the air. 'Far way, but coming closer. You have guns?'

'No,' said Meredith.

'Then you will die,' said Pakia, 'and my Beth will die.'

'Who is Beth?' asked Jeremiah.

'Good friend. Farms land south of here. You go to her, she has guns. Maybe then you live. She live.'

Pakia stood and loped away without another word. 'Curious creature,' said Meredith. 'Was it a male or female?'

'Female,' said Jeremiah, 'and she was jumpy. I've travelled these lands for years, and I know of no blood beasts. Maybe she meant lions, or bears. I shouldn't have given Malcolm my rifle.'

'What do you think we should do?'

Jeremiah shrugged. 'We'll finish the stew and then head for the farm.' The howling came again and Jeremiah shivered. 'Let's forget the stew,' he said.

*

Beth McAdam was dozing when Toby Harris tapped lightly on the door-frame. She came awake instantly and rubbed her eyes. 'Been a long day, Tobe,' she said.

The workman doffed his cap and grinned. 'There's still some old bulls up in the thickets. Take a sight of work to move 'em out.'

Beth stretched her back and rose. Toby Harris had arrived two weeks before, on a worn-out horse that was in better condition than he was. A small wiry man, with a stoop, he had worked as a miner in Purity, a horse-breaker on a ranch near Unity, and had been a sailor for four years before that. On an impulse he had decided to ride into what used to be termed the wild lands and make his fortune. When he had arrived at Beth McAdam's farm he was out of food, out of Barta coin, and just about out of luck. Beth had taken an instant liking to the little man; he had a cheeky grin that took years from his weather-beaten face, and bright blue eyes that sparkled with humour.

Tobe ran a hand through his thinning black hair. 'I seen a wagon heading this way,' he said. '*Wanderers*, most like. Guess they'll stop by and beg a little food.'

'How many?' asked Beth.

'One wagon, all bright painted. Ox-drawn. Two men riding it.'

'Let's hope one of them's a tinker. I've some pots that need repairing, and some knives that are long overdue for a sharpening. Tell them they're welcome to camp in the south meadow – there's a good stream there.'

Tobe nodded and backed out of the door as Beth took a long, deep breath. With winter coming she had needed a good workman. Her few cattle had wandered high into the hills, deep into the thickets and the woods. Driving them out was at least a four-man job, but Tobe worked as hard as any three workmen she had employed before. Samuel used to help, but he now spent all of his time in the settlement, studying to be a Crusader. Beth sighed, they couldn't meet now without harsh words.

'I raised him too hard,' she said aloud.

Tobe reappeared. 'Begging your pardon, Frey McAdam, but there's a rider coming. Two to be precise. Riding double on an old mule. I think one of them's ill – or drunk.'

Beth nodded, then moved to the mantel, lifting down the old rifle. Levering a shell into the breech, she stepped out into the fading light. The riders were coming down from the mountains, and even from here she could see the sweat-streaked flanks of the mule. In the waning light she could just make out a white beard on one of the riders; the other looked familiar, but his head and upper body were bent low across the mule's neck, the old man holding him steady. The mule pounded up and the old man slid from its back, turning to support his companion. Beth saw that it was Josiah Broome and, laying the rifle aside, she ran forward to help.

'He's been shot,' said white-beard.

'Tobe!' yelled Beth. The wiry workman came forward, and together they lowered the wounded man. Broome was unconscious, his face pale, the gleam of fever sweat on his brow. 'Get him to my room,' said Beth, leaving the two men to carry Broome into the house.

'Pick up your rifle, Frey McAdam,' said white-beard. 'There's killers close by.'

They laid Broome in Beth's wide bed and covered him with a thick blanket. White-beard moved outside. 'What killers?' she asked.

'The most terrible creatures you'll ever see,' he told her. 'Huge Wolvers. Right about now they'll be moving in on Pilgrim's Valley. I hope the Crusaders there are good, steady men.'

'Wolvers would never attack anyone,' said Beth suspiciously.

'I agree with you, but these aren't just Wolvers. Is that rifle fully loaded?'

'Be pretty useless if it wasn't!' she snapped. The old man was tall and commanding, but there was about him an unconscious arrogance that needled Beth McAdam. If there were such beasts as he described, she'd certainly never seen one and she'd lived near Pilgrim's Valley for twenty years. 'How did Josiah get his wound?' she asked, changing the subject.

'Shot down in his home. They killed Daniel Cade too.'

'The Prophet? My God! Why?'

'The same reason Bull Kovac was killed. Broome was going to give Oath for you.'

'That makes no sense,' she said. 'What difference could it make?'

'This is rich land, Frey McAdam. Saul has taken to gathering such land to himself, through Jacob Moon and his men. I should have seen what was happening. But I had other, more pressing, problems on my mind. I'll deal with Saul – if we survive what is coming.'

'*You'll* deal with Saul. By what right?'

White-beard turned, his gaze locking to hers. 'I made him, Beth, he is my responsibility. I am the Deacon.'

'This is insane,' stormed Beth. 'Giant Wolvers and supposed murders are bad enough. You're obviously deranged.'

'Begging your pardon, Frey McAdam,' said Tobe, 'but he *is* the Deacon. I seen him at the Unity Cathedral last year – it's him all right.'

The Deacon smiled at Tobe. 'I remember you,' he said. 'You worked with horses, and you brought in the young rider with the broken back. He was healed, I recall.'

'Yes, sir, Deacon. Then he got killed in a flash flood.'

Beth's anger flared. 'If you are the Deacon, then you are not welcome in my house,' she said icily. 'Because of you a good man saw his church burned, his people slaughtered. And he's out there now suffering. By God, you should be ashamed of yourself.'

'And I am, lady,' he said softly. 'I gave orders that the Wolvers should be moved back away from human settlements. My reasons will be all too clear within days. There is an enemy coming with powers you could not dream of – he has mutated Wolvers into creatures of colossal power. But, yes, I am ashamed. It does not matter that I did what I thought was right. Whatever evil was done in my name is my responsibility and I will live with that. As to not being welcome . . .' He spread his hands, 'I can do nothing about that, save to ask you to bear with me. Only I can fight what is coming.'

'Why should I believe that?' countered Beth. 'Everything you have is built on lies. The Jerusalem Man never predicted your coming. Shall I tell you how I know?'

'I'll tell you,' he said mildly. 'Because Jon Shannow, after sending the Sword of God through to destroy Atlantis, came back here to live a life as Jon Cade, a Preacher. He lived with you for many years, but you tired of his purity and cast him out. Now understand this: Nothing was built on lies. Shannow brought me down from the sky, but more than that. He is my reason for being! He is why I am here, at this time, to fight this enemy. It is not necessary that you believe me, Beth. It is only necessary that you put aside your disbelief.'

'I have a friend out looking for him,' she said, her words cold. 'He'll come back. Then you can explain it to him!'

An eerie howl echoed in the valley. It was answered by several others.

'I saw a wagon to the north,' said the Deacon. 'I suggest you invite the occupants to join you. They may not survive the night if you don't.'

Chapter Eleven

When the farmer seeds his field with corn he knows that the weeds will grow also. They will grow faster than his crop, the roots digging deep, drawing the nutrients from the land. Therefore, if he is wise, he patrols his field, uprooting the weeds. Every human heart is like that farmer's field. Evil lurks there, and a wise man will search out the weeds of evil. Beware the man who says, 'My heart is pure', for evil is growing within him unchecked.
The Wisdom of the Deacon
Chapter xiv

* * *

The city was vast and silent, the shutters on open windows flapping in the early morning breeze, open doors yawning and creaking. The only other sound to break the silence was the steady clopping of the horses. Shannow was in the lead, Amaziga and Sam sharing the horse behind, with Gareth bringing up the rear.

The great south gate of Babylon was open, but there were no guards, no sentries patrolling the high walls. The silence was eerie, almost threatening.

The streets were wide and elegantly paved, the houses built of white rock, many boasting colourful mosaics. Statues lined the avenues, heroic figures in the armour of Atlantis. Although Babylon was a relatively new city, many of the statues and ornaments had been looted from an Atlantean site, as had much of the stone used in the buildings. The riders moved on through an open market square with rotting fruit displayed on the stalls – brown, partly-collapsed apples, oranges covered with blue-grey mould. Slowly they rode on, passing a tavern. Several bench tables were set outside the main doors, and upon these were goblets and plates of mildewed bread and cheese.

Not a dog or a cat moved in the silence, and no flies buzzed around the decomposing food. In the clear sky above them no bird flew.

Gareth eased his horse alongside the mount carrying his mother and Sam. 'I don't understand,' he said.

'You will,' she promised him.

On they rode, through narrow streets and out on to broad avenues, the hoofbeats echoing through the city. Shannow loosened his pistols in their scabbards, his eyes scanning the deserted homes. Ahead of them was a huge colosseum five storeys high – colossal, demonic statues surrounding it, images of demons, horned and scaled. Shannow drew back on the reins. 'Where now?' he asked Amaziga.

'Lucas says that beyond the colosseum's arena is a wide tunnel leading into the palace. The grounds beyond that contain the remnants of the stone circle.'

Shannow gazed up at the enormous building. 'It must hold thousands,' he said.

'Forty-two thousand,' said Amaziga. 'Let's go on.'

The central avenue led directly to the bronze gates of the main entrance; these were open, and Shannow rode through into an arched tunnel. Many doorways opened on to stairs to left and right, but the trio rode on, and down, emerging at last into what had been a sand-covered arena.

Now it boasted a new carpet. Corpses lay everywhere, dried husks that had once been human. Shannow's horse was reluctant to move on, but he urged it forward. The gelding stepped out gingerly, its hoof striking a corpse just below the knee; the leg snapped and fell away.

Shannow looked around him as the horse slowly picked its way across the centre of the arena. Row upon row of seats, in tier upon tier, ringed the circle. Corpses filled every seat.

'My God!' whispered Gareth Archer.

'No,' said Shannow, '*their* god.'

'Why would he kill them all? All his people?'

'He had no more use for them,' said Amaziga, her voice flat, cold and emotionless. 'He found a gateway to a land of plenty. What you see here is the result of his last supper.'

'Sweet Jesus!'

With great care they moved across the arena of death, and

Gareth kept his eyes fixed on the distant entrance to yet another tunnel, wincing as dried bones broke beneath his mount's hooves. At last they reached the far side and Gareth swung in his saddle, looking back over the colosseum and its silent audience.

Forty-two thousand people, their bodies drained of moisture. He shuddered and followed the others down into the second tunnel.

*

The palace gardens were overgrown with weeds and bracken and only three of the old stones were still standing. One of these had slipped to the right, showing a jagged crack on its side. Shannow dismounted and forced his way through the undergrowth. 'Will the circle still . . . work?' he asked, as Amaziga joined him.

'The stones are not important in themselves,' she told him. 'They were merely placed by the Ancients at points of great natural power.' Amaziga flicked the microphone into place and switched on the computer. Shannow wandered away, eyes raking the wall surrounding the garden and the balconies that overlooked what was once a series of rose-beds. He felt uncomfortable here, exposed. One rifleman creeping along behind those balcony walls could kill them all.

Samuel Archer approached him. 'I have had no time to thank you properly, Mr Shannow. I am grateful for your courage.'

Shannow smiled at the tall black man. 'I knew another Sam Archer once,' he said. 'I could not save him and I have always regretted that.' He glanced to the left, where Gareth Archer was sitting quietly lost in thought, his face a mask of sorrow. 'I think you should speak to him,' said the Jerusalem Man. Archer nodded.

Gareth looked up as the older man sat down on the marble bench beside him. 'Soon be home,' said Gareth. 'You'll like Arizona. No Bloodstone.'

'It is always hard to gaze upon the fruits of evil,' said Sam softly.

Gareth nodded agreement. 'Forty-two thousand people. Son of a bitch!'

'Do you study history, Gareth?'

'Battle of Hastings, 1066 AD; Second World War, 1939 AD; War of Liberation, 2016 AD,' said Gareth. 'Yes, I studied history.'

'I didn't mean the dates, son. You've just seen a multitude of the dead. Yet Genghis Khan killed ten times as many people, and Stalin murdered a hundred times more. Man's history is hip-deep in Bloodstones. The dead that you saw *chose* to worship Sarento. They fed him their children, and the children of other races. Lastly they fed him themselves. I mourn for their stupidity, but there is nothing new about a leader who leads his people to destruction.'

'There's a cheering thought,' said Gareth.

Amaziga joined them. 'Lucas says that we must wait four hours for a window home. It's almost over, Sam.'

Samuel Archer stared at her intently, noting the lines of anguish on her beautiful face. 'There is something else,' he said. She nodded and glanced round to look for Shannow, but the Jerusalem Man was gone.

'The Bloodstone is now in Shannow's world,' she said.

Gareth swore. 'Did we open the Gate?' he asked bitterly.

'Lucas says not. Yet the fact remains that it is free to reduce another world to dust and death.'

'You once told me about Sarento,' said Gareth, anger in his voice. 'You told me he wanted to see a return to the old world, hospitals and schools, care, love and peace. How could you be deceived by such a monster?'

Sam cut in. 'He did want all those things,' he said. 'He was a man in love with the past. He adored all aspects of twentieth- and twenty-first-century life. And he *did* care. Thirty years ago there was a plague. The Guardians went out among the people with medicines and vaccines we hoped would eradicate it. We were wrong. Many of us died. Yet still Sarento went out, until he himself succumbed. He almost died, Gareth, trying to help others. It was the Bloodstone that corrupted him. He is no longer the human Sarento we knew.'

'I don't believe that,' snapped Gareth. 'There must have been evil in him to begin with. You just couldn't see it.'

'Of course there was,' said Amaziga. 'As there is in all of us, in our arrogance, in our belief that we know best. But the Bloodstone enhances such feelings, at the same time as drowning the impulses for good. You have no idea of the influence of such Stones. Even a small *demonseed* will drive a bearer to violence, unleashing the full force of the beast within Man. Sarento took into himself the power of an entire *boulder*.'

Gareth rose and shook his head. 'He knew the Bloodstone was evil, even before he did that. I'll not listen to excuses for him. I just want to know how we can kill him.'

'We can't,' said Sam, 'not while he has power. I used to believe that if we could deprive him of blood until he was weak and then attack him, we would have a chance to destroy him. Yet how would it have been possible? Whoever approached him would only feed him. You understand? He is invulnerable. He might have died here, on a planet drained of life. But now he is free to wander the universe, growing in power.'

'There must be a way,' urged Gareth.

'If there is we'll find it, Gareth,' said Amaziga. 'I promise you that.'

*

Jon Shannow wandered through the deserted halls of Babylon, past columns fashioned from human bones and mosaics depicting scenes of torture, rape and murder. His footsteps echoed and he came out, at last, on to a balcony overlooking the garden. From here could be seen the original layout of the grounds, the walkways shaped like intertwined serpents, forming the number of the Beast. Nature had conspired to cover most of the walkways, and vines grew up over repulsive statues that ringed the six small pools. Even these were stagnant, and the fountains silent.

Shannow felt burdened by it all, the evidence of Man's stupidity laid out before him like an ancient map. Why is it, he thought, that men can be inspired to evil more swiftly and powerfully than they can be inspired to good?

His heaviness of heart deepened. Look at yourself, Jon Shannow, before you ask such questions. Was it not you who put away the guns, pledging yourself to a life of pacifism and religion? Was it not you who took to the pulpit, and reached out your mind to the King of Heaven?

And what happened when evil men brought death and flames?

'I gunned them down,' he said aloud.

It was always thus. From his earliest days, when he and Daniel had seen their parents slain, he had been filled with a great anger, a burning need to confront evil head to head, gun to gun. Through many settlements and towns, villages and communities the Jerusalem Man had passed. Always behind him there were bodies to be buried.

Did it make the world a better place, Shannow? he asked himself. Has anything you have done ensured a future of peace and prosperity? These were hard questions, but he faced them as he faced all dangers. With honesty.

No, he told himself. I have made no difference.

Twice he had tried to put aside the mantle of the Jerusalem Man, once with the widow Donna Taybard, and then with Beth McAdam. Believing him to be dead, Donna had married another man. Beth had grown tired of Jon Cade's holiness.

You are a man of straw, Shannow, he chided himself. A year before, when Daniel Cade first moved to Pilgrim's Valley he had visited the Preacher in the small vestry behind the church.

'Good morning, brother Jon,' he said, 'you are looking well for a man of your years.'

'They do not know me here, Daniel. Everything has changed.'

Daniel shook his head. 'Men don't change, brother. All that happens is that they learn how best to disguise the lack of change. Me, I'm still a brigand at heart, but I'm held to goodness by the weight of public opinion and the fading strength of an age-weakened body.'

'I have changed,' said the Preacher. 'I abhor violence, and will never kill again.'

'Is that so, Jonnie? Answer me this then, where are your guns? In a pit somewhere, rusted and useless? Sold?' His eyes twinkled and he grinned. 'Or are they here? Hidden away somewhere, cleaned and oiled.'

'They are here,' admitted the Preacher. 'I keep them as a reminder of what once I was.'

'We'll see,' said Cade. 'I hope you are right, Jon. Such a life is good for you.'

Now the sun broke clear of the clouds above Babylon and Jon Shannow felt the weight of the pistols at his side. 'You were right,' Daniel,' he said softly. 'Men don't change.'

Gazing down on the garden he saw Amaziga, Gareth and Sam sitting together. The first Samuel Archer had been a man of peace, interested only in researching the ruins of Atlantis. He had been beaten to death in the caverns of Castlemine. In this world the black man was a fighter. In neither had he won.

Amaziga said there existed an infinity of universes. Perhaps in one of them Samuel Archer was still an archaeologist who would slowly, and with great dignity, grow old among his family. Perhaps in that world, or another, Jon Shannow did not see his family gunned down. He was a farmer maybe, or a teacher, his own sons playing around him, happy in the sunshine, a loving wife beside him.

A whisper of movement came from behind and Shannon hurled himself to the left as a bullet ricocheted from the balcony, screaming off into the air. Spinning as he fell, Shannow drew his right-hand pistol and fired. The Hellborn warrior staggered, then tipped over the balcony wall. Drawing his left-hand gun, Shannow rose and ran back to the hall entrance.

Two Hellborn warriors were crouching behind pillars. The first, shocked by his sudden appearance, fired too swiftly, the bullet slashing past Shannow's face. His own left-handed gun boomed and the man was flung back. The second warrior reared up, a knife in his hand. Shannow's pistol slammed down, the barrel cracking home against the man's cheekbone, and the warrior fell heavily.

Shots sounded now from the garden. As Shannow ran through the hall, a rifleman leaned over the gallery rail above him. Shannow fired – but missed, the bullet chipping wood from the rail. He ducked into a corridor, turned left down a stairway and right into another corridor. Here he stopped and waited, listening for sounds of pursuit.

Footsteps sounded on the stairs and two men ran down. Stepping out, Shannow shot them both, then ran for the garden. Halting in a shadowed archway, he re-loaded his pistols. There were no sounds now from the garden.

Guns in hand, he moved swiftly out into the sunshine, scanning the balconies.

No one was in sight.

Creeping silently through the undergrowth, he approached the circle of stone. The sound of voices came to him as he neared the circle.

'The Lord has left us,' said a deep voice, 'and you are to blame. We were ordered to kill you and we failed. Now that we have you, he will come back for us.'

'He's not coming back,' Shannow heard Amaziga tell them. 'Can't you understand what has happened? He's not a god, he's a man – a corrupted, ruined man who feeds on life. Have you not seen the colosseum? He's killed everyone!'

'Silence, woman! What do you know? The Lord has returned to his home in the Valleys of Hell, and there he has taken our people to enjoy the rewards of service. This is what he promised. This is what he has done. But my comrades and I were left here because we failed him. When your bodies bleed upon the High Altar he will return for us, and we shall know the joy of everlasting death-life.'

Sam's strong, steady voice cut in. 'I understand that you *need* to believe. Yet I also see that the *demonseeds* embedded in your brows are black now and powerless. You are men again, with free will and intelligence. And deep down you are already questioning your beliefs. Is that not true?'

Shannow heard the sound of a vicious slap. 'You black bastard! Yes, it is true – and all part of the test we face because of you. We will not be seduced from the true path.'

Shannow edged to the right to a break in the undergrowth and stepped out on to the walkway some fifteen yards from the Hellborn group. There were five in all, and each of them held a weapon pointed at his three companions. The Hellborn leader was still speaking. 'Tonight we shall be in Hell, with servants and women, and fine food and drink. Your souls will carry us there.'

'Why wait for tonight?' asked Shannow. The Hellborn swung to face him and Shannow's guns thundered. The Hellborn leader was hurled back, his face blown away; another man spun back, his shoulder shattered. Shannow stepped to his right and continued to fire. Only one answering shot came his way; it passed some feet to his left, smashing into the stone head of a statue demon, shearing away a horn.

The last echoes faded away. Shannow cocked his pistols and moved to join the trio. Amaziga was kneeling beside Gareth. Blood was staining the olive-green shirt he wore as Shannow knelt beside him.

'Jesus wept, Shannow!' whispered the young man. 'You really are death on wheels.' Blood frothed at his lips and he choked and coughed. Amaziga pulled out her Sipstrassi Stone, but Gareth's head sagged back.

'No!' screamed Amaziga. 'Please God, no!'

'He's gone,' said Shannow. Amaziga reached out and stroked the dead boy's brow, then she turned her angry eyes upon the Jerusalem Man.

'Where were you when we needed you?' she stormed.

'Close by,' he said wearily, 'but not close enough.'

'May God curse you, Shannow!' she screamed, her hand lashing out across his face.

'That's enough!' roared Sam, reaching down and hauling her away from him. 'It is not his fault. How could it be? And if not for him we would all be dead.' He glanced at Shannow. 'Are there more, do you think?'

'There were two inside I did not kill.' He shrugged. 'There may be others.'

Sam took Amaziga by the shoulders. 'Listen to me, Ziga. We must leave. What will happen if we activate the Gateway early?'

'Nothing, save that it uses more Sipstrassi power. And I have little left.'

'Is there enough to get us back?'

She nodded. A shot ricocheted from the walkway and Sam ducked, dragging Amaziga down with him. Shannow returned the fire, his bullets clipping stone from a balcony.

'Let's go,' said Shannow calmly. Amaziga reached down to touch her son's face for the last time, then she stood and ran for the stone circle. Sam followed. Shannow backed after them, eyes scanning the balconies. A rifleman reared up; Shannow fired and the man ducked down.

Inside the circle Amaziga knelt behind one of the stones and engaged the computer. Shots peppered the ground around them. 'They're circling us,' said Shannow.

Violet light flickered around them . . .

Shannow holstered his pistols and strode out on to the hillside above Amaziga's Arizona home.

*

Shannow sat on the paddock fence for more than an hour, oblivious to the blazing sunshine. The desert here was peaceful upon the eye, the giant saguaros seemingly set in place by a master sculptor. His thoughts swung back to the rescue of Samuel Archer. So much death! The girl, Shammy, and all the other nameless heroes who had followed Sam. And Gareth. Shannow had liked the young black man; he had a zest for life, and the courage to live it to the full. Even the sight of his twin's corpse had not kept him from his path – a path that led to a bullet fired by a Hellborn warrior who had seen the destruction of his race and not understood its meaning.

Amaziga's unjust anger was hard to take, but Shannow understood it. Every time they met it seemed that someone she loved had to die.

Sam strolled out. 'Come inside, my friend. You need to rest.'

'What I need is to go home,' Shannow told him.

'Let's talk,' said Sam, avoiding Shannow's gaze. The Jerusalem Man climbed down from the fence and followed the black man into the house. It was cool inside, and the face of Lucas shone from the computer screen. Amaziga was nowhere in sight. 'Sit down, Mr Shannow. Amaziga will be with us shortly.'

Unbuckling his guns, Shannow let the belt fall to the floor. He was mortally tired, his mind weary beyond words. 'Perhaps you should clean up first,' suggested Sam, 'and refresh yourself.' Shannow nodded, and leaving Sam he walked through the corridor to his own room and removed his clothes. Turning on the faucets he stepped under the shower, turning his face up to the cascading water. After some minutes he stepped out and moved to the bed where he sat down, intending to gather his thoughts, but fell asleep almost instantly.

When Sam woke him it was dark, the moon glinting through

the clouds. Shannow sat up. 'I didn't realise how tired I was,' he said.

Sam sat down alongside him. 'I have spoken to Ziga. She is distraught, Shannow, but even so she knows that Gareth's death could not be laid at your door. She is a wonderful woman, you know, but headstrong. She always was incapable of being wrong – I think you know that, from past experience. But she is not malicious.'

'Why are you telling me this?'

Sam shrugged. 'I just wanted you to know.'

'There is something else, Sam.'

'That's for her to tell you. I brought some clean clothes. Amaziga will be in the lounge when you are ready.' Sam stood and left the room.

Rested and refreshed, Shannow rose and walked to the chair where Sam had laid the fresh clothes. There was a blue plaid shirt, a pair of heavy cotton trousers and a pair of black socks. The chest of the shirt was over-large, the sleeves too short, but the trousers fitted him well. Pulling on his boots, he walked out into the main room where Amaziga was sitting at the computer speaking to Lucas. Sam was nowhere in sight.

'He went for a walk,' said Amaziga, rising. Slowly she approached him. 'I am very sorry,' she said, her eyes brimming with tears. Instinctively he opened his arms and she stepped into his embrace. 'I sacrificed Gareth for Sam,' she said. 'It was my fault.'

'He was a brave lad,' was all Shannow could think to say.

Amaziga nodded and drew away from him, brushing her sleeve across her eyes. 'Yes, he was brave. He was everything I could have wished for. Are you hungry?'

'A little.'

'I'll prepare you some food.'

'If it is all the same to you, lady, I would like to go home.'

'Food first,' she said. 'I'll leave you with Lucas for a moment.'

When she had left the room Shannow sat down before the machine. 'What is happening?' he asked. 'Sam out for a walk, Amaziga playing hostess. Something is wrong.'

'You came through the window earlier than anticipated,' said Lucas. 'It drained her Stone.'

'She has others, surely?'

'No. Not at the moment.'

'Then how will she send me back?'

'She can't, Mr Shannow. I have the capacity to hack into . . . to enter the memory banks of other computers. I have done so, and in the next few days papers will begin to arrive giving you a new identity in this world. I will also instruct you into the habits and laws of the United States. These are many and varied.'

'I cannot stay here.'

'Will it be so bad, Mr Shannow? Through my . . . contacts, if you like . . . I have amassed a large fortune for Amaziga. You will have access to those funds. And what is there left behind you? You have no family, and few friends. You could be happy in America.'

'Happy?' Shannow's eyes narrowed. 'Everything I love is lost to me, and you speak of happiness? Damn you, Lucas!'

'I fear I am already damned,' said the machine. 'Perhaps we all are for what we have done.'

'And what is that?' asked Shannow, his voice hardening. 'What is there that is still unsaid?'

Amaziga returned at that moment carrying two cups of coffee. 'I have some food in the oven. It will not take long,' she said. 'Has Lucas spoken to you?'

'He has. Now you tell me.'

'Tell you what?'

'No games, lady. Just the truth.'

'I don't know what you mean. The power is gone. Until I find more Sipstrassi we are trapped in this version of the old world.'

'Tell him,' said Sam, from the doorway. 'You owe him that.'

'I owe him nothing!' stormed Amaziga. 'Don't you understand?'

'No, I don't understand, but I know how you feel, Ziga. Tell him.'

Amaziga moved to an armchair and sat, not looking at Shannow or Sam but staring down at the floor. 'The Bloodstone found a Gateway through to your world, Shannow. That's where he is now. It wasn't our fault. Truly it wasn't. Someone else opened a Gateway – Lucas will vouch for that.'

'Indeed I will,' said the machine. 'Amaziga transferred the

files from the portable. I know everything that happened back in Babylon. Sarento passed through the Gateway while we were in the hills, camping at that deserted town. All I can tell you is that the Bloodstone is in the time of the Deacon. Your time.'

Shannow slumped down in a chair. 'And I can't get back there, to Beth?'

'Not yet,' said Lucas.

The Jerusalem Man looked up at Amaziga. 'What will I do here in the meantime, lady, in this world of machines? How will I live?'

Amaziga sighed. 'We have thought of that, Shannow. Lucas has arranged papers for you, under a new name. And you will stay here while we teach you the ways of this world. There are many wonders for you to see. There is Jerusalem. For this world is still twenty-one years from the Fall.'

'Twenty years, four months and eleven days,' said Lucas.

'We have that amount of time to try to prevent it happening,' said Amaziga. 'Sam and I will search for Sipstrassi. You will do what you did in Pilgrim's Valley – become a preacher. There is a church in Florida, a small church. I have friends there, who will make you welcome.'

Shannow's eyes widened. 'A church in Florida? Is that not where the Deacon is from?'

Amaziga nodded.

'And my new name?' he said, his voice harsh.

'John Deacon,' she told him, her voice barely above a whisper.

'Dear God!' said Shannow, pushing himself from the chair.

'We did not know, Shannow,' said Amaziga, 'and it won't be the same. Sam and I will find Sipstrassi, then you will be able to return.'

'And if you don't?'

Amaziga was silent for a moment, then she looked up into his angry eyes. 'Then you must take your disciples and be on that plane on the day the earth falls.'

*

The Deacon stood outside the farm building and watched as Beth McAdam and Toby Harris led the horses from the paddock into the barn. You are still beautiful, Beth, he thought. And you did not know me. That hurt him. But then why should she, he asked himself. Only weeks before she had seen a relatively young man giving sermons. Now a long-haired ancient stood in her home, his features obscured by a thick white beard. Understanding did nothing to help the pain.

Shannow felt alone in that moment, and terribly weak.

Amaziga and Sam had kept in touch with him, keeping him up to date with their journeys and their search for the Stones. Sometimes they had believed themselves to be close, only to face terrible disappointment. With eleven days left before the Fall, they had telephoned Shannow.

'Have you arranged the tickets?' asked Sam.

'Yes. Why don't you come also?'

'Ziga has found evidence of a Circle in Brazil. The architecture of the surrounding ruin is different from other Aztec finds. We will journey there, and see what is to be found.'

'May God go with you, Samuel.'

'And with you, Deacon.'

Shannow remembered the day the plane had emerged from time's dungeon and soared above the ruined tower of Pendarric. He had looked down, trying to make out the tiny figures below, hoping to see himself and Beth and Clem Steiner. The plane was too high and it flew on, making a landing near Pilgrim's Valley.

The temptation had been great in those early years to seek out Beth. But the shadow of the Bloodstone remained with him, and he gathered to himself clairvoyants and seers in a bid to pierce the veils of time.

Shannow had grown used to leadership during his days in Kissimmee, but the demands of forming rules and laws for a world took their toll. Every decision seemed to lead to discord and disharmony. Nothing was simple. Banning the carrying of weapons in Unity led to protests and violent disagreements. Every community had evolved its own laws, and unifying the people proved a long and bloody affair. The Unifier Wars had begun when three communities in the west had refused to pay the new taxes. Worse, they had killed the tax collectors. The Deacon had sent a force of Crusaders to arrest the offenders.

Other communities joined the rebels and the War spread, growing more bloody with each passing month. Then, after two savage years, with the War almost over, the Hellborn had invaded. Shannow remembered his reaction with deep regret. He and Padlock Wheeler had routed the enemy in three pitched battles, then entered the lands of the Hellborn, burning settlements and slaughtering civilians. Babylon was razed to the ground. No surrender was accepted. The enemy were butchered to a man – not just to a man, Shannow remembered.

The Deacon had won. In doing so he had become a mass murderer.

Estimates of the dead in the two Wars reached more than eighty thousand. Shannow sighed. What was it Amaziga called you once, 'The Armageddon Man'?

Following the Wars the Deacon's laws grew more harsh, Shannow's rule being governed more by fear than love. He felt increasingly alone. All but one of the men who had travelled with him through time were dead. He alone knew of the terrible evil waiting to be unleashed on the world; it was an awful burden, dominating his mind and blinding him to the beginnings of Saul's betrayal. It would have been so different if Alan had survived.

Alan had been the best of his disciples – calm, steady, his faith a rock. He had died on Fairfax Hill in one of the bloodiest battles of the Unity War. Saul had been with him. They never recovered Alan's Stone. One by one they died, three from diseases and radiation sickness left over from the Fall, but the others cut down in battles or skirmishes.

Until only Saul was left. All those years of wondering where the Bloodstone would strike and, had he but known it, the answer lay with Saul.

Who else in this area had the use of Sipstrassi? Who else could have opened the Gateway?

'You were a fool, Shannow,' he told himself.

Something moved beyond the fence! The Deacon's rifle came up and he found himself aiming at a hare which had emerged from a hole in the ground. Slowly he scanned the valley and the distant hillsides. The moon was bright, but there was no sign of movement.

They will come, though, he told himself. Tobe Harris moved

alongside him. 'All the animals is locked away, Deacon. Save for my horse, like you ordered. What now?'

'I want you to ride for Purity,' Shannow told him. 'Padlock Wheeler is the man to see. Tell him the Deacon needs him, and every man with a rifle he can bring. Miners, farmers, Crusaders – as many as can be gathered. Tell him not to ride into the town, but to meet us here.'

'Yes, sir.'

'Go now, Tobe.'

Beth McAdam, her rifle cradled in her arms, came alongside in time to hear the order. 'We've seen nothing yet,' she said. 'What makes you so sure they are coming?'

'I've seen them, lady. Not here, I'll grant you. But I've seen them.'

The Deacon had been leaning on the fence rail. Now he straightened and staggered, weariness flowing over him. As he almost fell, Beth caught his arm. 'You're all in,' she said. 'Go and get some rest. I'll stand watch.'

'No time for rest,' he said. Tobe galloped away into the night. The Deacon drew a deep breath, then climbed to the fence and sat, resting his rifle on a post.

'Someone coming,' said Beth. The Deacon followed her pointing finger, but his old eyes could see nothing.

'Is it silver-grey?' he asked.

'No, it's a young man leading a woman. She's carrying a baby.'

They waited together as the two approached. As they neared, Beth said, 'It's Wallace Nash and Ezra Feard's daughter. What the Hell are they doing walking out here at this time of night?'

The Deacon did not answer. Instead he said, 'Look beyond them. Is anything following?'

'No . . . Yes. Christ! It's a monster! Run, Wallace!' she screamed.

Shannow felt helpless, but he watched as Beth's long rifle came up. She sighted and fired. 'Did you hit it?' he asked. Beth sighted again and the rifle boomed.

'Son of a bitch,' whispered Beth. 'Got it twice, but it's still coming!'

Jumping from the fence, the Deacon stumbled towards the fleeing couple, straining to see the creature beyond them. His chest was tight and pain flared in his left arm as, heart pounding, he ran on. He saw the young man release his hold on the woman's arm and swing round to face whatever was chasing them. Shannow saw it at the same time as Wallace Nash. It was huge, over seven feet tall, with blood flowing from two wounds in its chest. Nash fired his shotgun. The creature fell back. A second lunged out of the darkness and Shannow fired three times, smashing it from its feet.

'Get back!' yelled Beth. 'There are more of them!'

Shannow's legs felt like lead, and all energy seemed to vanish. Wallace grabbed his arm. 'Come on, old man! You can make it!'

With the young man's help he backed away to the fence as Beth's rifle thundered. 'Into the house,' he wheezed. 'The house!'

Something hard struck him in the side. His body hit the fence rail, snapping the wood. Hitting the ground hard, he lost hold of his rifle but instinctively drew a pistol and rolled. A huge form bore down on him and he could feel hot, fetid breath on his face. Thrusting up with all his strength, he pushed the gun-barrel into the creature's mouth and pulled the trigger. The head snapped back as the bullet passed through the skull. Beth took hold of his arm, dragging him clear of the dead beast.

All was quiet now.

The Deacon gathered up his fallen rifle and, together, they backed to the house.

The woman with the baby was sitting slumped in an armchair. Shannow pushed shut the door, dropping a thick bar into place to lock it. 'Check the windows upstairs,' he told the red-headed youngster. 'Make sure the shutters are in place.'

'Yes, sir,' said the boy. Shannow glanced around.

'Where are the people from the wagon?'

'Oh, my God, I forgot them,' said Beth.

*

Jeremiah's wagon was some two hundred yards from the farm buildings when the shots broke. The old man ducked, thinking at first that the shots were aimed at them. Meredith stood up on the driver's seat. 'I think they must be shooting rabbits,' he said. 'I can see a blonde woman with a rifle and an old man . . . damn, I think it's that reprobate Jake.'

'I like the old boy,' said Jeremiah. 'Lively company.'

Meredith said nothing. The four oxen were tired now, and moving slowly, heads low. The ground beneath the wheels was soft from heavy overnight rain, and they were making little headway. Isis was still clinging to life, but she couldn't last much longer now, he knew, and he dreaded the moment when she was gone forever.

He saw Jake jump from the fence and run off, but his view was masked by the stone-built farm building. More shots followed. The wagon entered the yard, then one wheel sank into a deep mud hole. Jeremiah swore. 'I guess we're close enough,' he said.

A young woman came into sight, carrying a baby. She ducked behind the fence rails and ran on towards the house. A red-headed youngster came next, supporting Jake. Meredith would never forget the next sight. A huge beast reared up alongside Jake, an enormous arm clubbing the old man against the fence which shattered under his weight. As he fell Jake drew a pistol, but the creature leapt on him. In the fading light Meredith heard the muffled shot, and saw blood spray up like a crimson mushroom from the creature's head. The woman pulled Jake clear of the corpse and they made it to the house. The door slammed shut.

Several more of the creatures came into sight.

Only in that moment did Meredith realise the seriousness of their plight. It had been like watching a tableau, a piece of theatre. 'Get back inside,' hissed Jeremiah, twisting in his seat and opening the front hatch to the inner cabin. The old man scrambled back, Meredith followed him. The hatch lock was a small brass hook.

'It won't hold them,' Meredith whispered.

'Stay silent,' urged Jeremiah.

A terrible scream rose from the oxen and the wagon rocked from side to side, the air filled with the sounds of howling and snarling. Meredith risked a glance through the narrow slit in the hatch – and wished that he hadn't. The still-struggling oxen were engulfed in a writhing mass of blood-spattered, silver-grey fur.

The rocking of the wagon continued for several minutes, then the two men sat quietly listening to the beasts feed. Meredith began to tremble, jerking with every snap of bone. Jeremiah put his hand on the doctor's shoulder. 'Be calm now,' he whispered.

Moonlight shone through the cabin's wide windows.

Meredith and Jeremiah crouched on the floor beneath the left window, listening to the sounds of their own breaths. Meredith glanced up. Moonlight was shining directly on to the still, pale face of Isis as she lay upon the bed, one arm outside the coverlet.

A grotesque face appeared at the window above her. Steam clouded the glass, but Meredith could see the long fangs and the oval eyes, and what appeared to be a red stone on the creature's brow. The snout pressed against the window, and both men heard the snuffling as it sought out the smell of flesh.

The wagon rocked again as a second beast came up on the right, pushing at the wood.

Meredith's mouth was dry, and his hands continued to tremble so badly that he felt the movement must be obvious.

Suddenly the window was smashed to shards, glass peppering the cabin. A taloned hand gripped the frame, hauling on it as slowly the creature pulled itself half into the cabin, directly over Isis. Its snout lowered, its nose snuffled over the face of the unconscious woman. A low growl sounded, then it dropped back to the yard.

A shot sounded, making both men jerk. The creatures outside howled, and Meredith heard the padding of their paws as they moved away from the wagon.

'What are we going to do?' whispered Meredith.

'Stay still, boy. Wait.'

'They'll come back. They'll tear us apart.'

Jeremiah eased himself to his knees and looked through the hatch. With great care he moved back alongside the panic-stricken doctor. 'They've gorged on the oxen, Doctor. I think that's why it left Isis.' Stepping over his companion, Jeremiah risked a glance from the right window. Meredith rose alongside him. The yard was empty.

'We've got to try for the house,' said Jeremiah.

'No!' The thought of going out into the open was more than Meredith could consider.

'Listen to me, son. I know you are frightened. So am I. But you said it yourself, to stay here is to die. The house looks solid, and there are people with guns inside. We have to risk it.'

Meredith looked down at the comatose woman. 'We can't leave her!'

'We surely can't carry her, Meredith. And she is beyond this world now. Come on, my boy. Just follow me, eh?'

Jeremiah moved silently to the rear of the cabin and unfastened the door latch. As usual it gave out with a creak as it opened. Gingerly he lowered himself to the ground and Meredith scrambled after him.

'Don't make any noise,' warned Jeremiah. 'We'll walk across, and hope to God the people inside are watching for us. You understand?' Meredith nodded.

The night was silent, and there was no sign of the creatures as Jeremiah drew in a deep breath and began to make his way across the thirty yards of open space that separated the wagon from the house. Meredith was behind him. Then the young doctor started to run and Jeremiah set off after him.

'Open the door!' screamed Meredith.

A creature emerged from behind the barn, howled and set off after them, covering the ground with immense speed. Meredith managed to reach the raised walkway around the house, then stumbled and fell on the steps. Jeremiah came up behind him and grabbed for his arm, trying to haul him upright.

The creature was close, but Jeremiah did not look back.

The door opened.

Jake stepped into sight with two pistols in his hands. Meredith lunged upright, colliding with Jake and knocking the old man aside. Jeremiah was just behind him. Something struck him in the back and a terrible pain tore through him.

Recovering his balance, Jake fired twice. The creature was smashed back from the walkway. Jake hauled Jeremiah inside, and a woman slammed the door behind him. Meredith swung to see Jeremiah lying face down on the dirt floor with blood streaming from a terrible wound in his back. 'Why the Hell did you shout, boy?' stormed Jake, grabbing Meredith by his shirt.

'I'm sorry! I'm sorry!' Meredith pulled himself clear and knelt by Jeremiah, his hands trying to cover the gaping wound.

Jeremiah sighed and rolled to his side. Reaching up, he took hold of the doctor's blood-drenched hand. 'Don't . . . blame . . . yourself. You're a good . . . man.'

And then he was gone. 'You pitiful son of a bitch!' said Jake.

Chapter Twelve

Nothing that lives is without fear. It is a gift against recklessness, a servant against complacency in the face of danger. But like all servants it makes a bad master. Fear is a small fire in the belly to warm a man in the coldness of conflict. Let loose, it becomes an inferno within the walls which no fortress can withstand.

The Wisdom of the Deacon
Chapter xxi

* * *

Esther had fallen asleep and Oz was manfully trying to hold her steady in the saddle. Zerah Wheeler glanced back, and smiled at the boy. 'We'll rest soon,' she promised, leading the horse higher into the hills and cutting towards the west. There were many caves close by, hidden in the trees, and only a very good tracker could follow the trail she had left. The rifle was heavy in her hands, and the holstered pistol was beginning to chafe her leg. It's been too long since I strolled these hills, thought Zerah. I'm getting old and useless.

A cave-mouth beckoned, but it was narrow and south-facing, the wind whistling into the opening, stirring up dust. Zerah moved on, leading the old buckskin along a narrow ledge that widened into a deep, pear-shaped cave. At first the buckskin was reluctant to enter the dark, but Zerah coaxed her in with soft words and a firm pull of the rein. Inside it was as large as the biggest room back at the house, with a long, natural chimney opening out on to the stars. Zerah looped the reins over the buckskin's head, leaned the rifle against the rock wall and moved back to lift Esther. The little girl moaned in her sleep, then looped her arms around Zerah's neck.

'You get down by yourself, boy. Untie the blanket roll before you do.'

Oz untied the rawhide strips that held the roll, then lifted his leg over the saddle and jumped to the ground. 'You think they'll find us?' he asked.

'They'll wish they hadn't if they do,' said Zerah. 'You still got that pistol safe?'

'Yes, Frey,' he answered, patting the pocket of his black broadcloth jacket.

Zerah ruffled his fair hair. 'You're a good boy, Oz. Your father would be proud of you. Now you wait here with Esther while I gather some wood for a fire.' Oz spread the blanket roll and Zerah knelt and laid Esther upon it. The six-year-old turned to her side, her thumb in her mouth. She did not wake.

'Want for me to come with you, Frey?'

'No, son. You stay here. Look after your sister.'

Gathering up the rifle, she passed it to the boy. 'It's a mite long for you, Oz, but it'll do no harm to get used to the feel.'

Zerah left the cave and walked back along the ledge. From this height, more than a thousand feet, she could see vast area of the plains below. There was no sign of pursuit. But then, she reasoned, they could be in the trees, beneath the vast dense carpet of green below and stretching far away to the east.

Leaning back, she stretched the muscles around her lower spine. They ached like the devil, but she took a good deep breath and walked back into the shadows of the trees. Night was falling fast, and the temperature would soon drop. Zerah gathered an armful of dead wood and walked back to the cave, returning for five more loads before weariness called a halt. From the pocket of her old sheepskin coat she took a pouch of tinder and carefully built a small fire.

Oz moved in close to her. 'They won't find us, will they, Frey?' he asked again.

'I don't know,' she told him, putting her thin arm around his shoulders and drawing him to her.

One of the men who had killed Oz's father had ridden up to the house and stopped at the well for water. He had seen Oz and Esther playing by the back fence. Zerah, not knowing the man, had walked from the house to greet the newcomer.

'Nice kids,' he said. 'Your grandchildren?'

'They surely are,' she told him. 'You passing through?'

'Yep. Well, thank you for the water, Frey,' he said, reaching for the pommel of his saddle.

Esther, looking up and seeing him, screamed and jumped to her feet. 'He shot my daddy!'

The man dropped to the ground, but in that moment Zerah had dragged her pistol clear and pulled the trigger, the shell hammering into his thigh. His horse had reared and run, he grabbed for the pommel and was dragged for thirty yards. Zerah fired twice more, but missed. She had watched him haul himself into the saddle and ride off.

Knowing he would return, Zerah had packed some food and supplies and taken the children back into the mountains, heading for Purity. But the pursuers had cut her off and were camped across the trail as she reached the last rise. Luckily Zerah had not ridden over the rise, but had left the buckskin with Oz and had crawled to the lip to check the road.

Now they were deep in the mountains and, Zerah was pretty sure, they had lost their pursuers.

With the fire blazing Zerah rose and moved outside the cavemouth, checking to see if any reflected light was flickering there. A carelessly laid camp-fire could be seen for miles. However, once outside the cave no light could be seen, and high above what little smoke there was had been dissipated by the undergrowth and trees on the cliff-top.

Satisfied, Zerah walked back inside. Oz was curled up alongside Esther, and both were fast asleep.

'Makes you feel young again, woman,' said Zerah, covering the two children. And she felt a sense of pride. She had saved them from killers. 'You're not so useless,' she whispered.

Tomorrow they would be safe in town, and the Crusaders would be hunting the villains.

It had been a long time since she had visited Pilgrim's Valley, and she wondered what changes she would see.

In the distance a wolf howled. Zerah settled down to sleep alongside the children.

*

Sarento strolled through the wooded hills above the Atlantean ruin, enjoying the cloudless blue sky and the sounds of early morning birdsong. The wind was cool upon his red-gold skin, and for the first time in years he had no sense of hunger. With a thrill of intense pleasure, he recalled the gathering in the colosseum, the anticipation and, at the last, the inflow of life. Rich and fulfilling and infinitely warming . . .

Below him was the camp of his elite, the five hundred Hellborn warriors he had sent through ahead of him. With them, and men like Jacob Moon, he would feed in this new world, and dream.

The Gateway was a desperately needed boon. His hunger in the old world had been painful, agonising, its clawing demands dominating his days. But here he could appreciate once more the beauty of a blue sky. His golden eyes focused on the ruined city. This was no fit place for a god, he thought as he gazed upon the derelict palace. Before it was two fallen pillars and a smashed lintel.

'Up!' he said. The distant stones groaned and raised themselves, powdered sections re-forming into shaped stone, the shards of the lintel flowing back into one whole and rising through the air to settle into place. Tiny remnants of paint grew, spreading out over the motifs on the lintel – fierce reds, vibrant blues, golden yellows. Golden tiles reappeared on the roof of the palace, catching the sunlight.

Trees flowered in the palace gardens, rose-bushes sprouted. Cracked and broken walkways repaired themselves, fallen statues climbing back to their plinths, their stone limbs as supple as the warriors who in ages past inspired them.

Gold leaf decorated the windows of the palace, and long-dry fountains sent sprays of water high into the air in the gardens.

Sarento gazed down on the city and smiled . . . Then the smile faded.

The hunger had returned. Not great, as yet, but a gnawing need. Glancing down at his naked torso, he saw that the thin black lines across his skin had thickened, the red-gold was fading. Raising his arms, he reached out with his mind.

The birds of the forest flew around him, foxes awoke and emerged from their holes, squirrels ran down from their tree-top homes. A huge bear let forth a roar and padded from his cave. Sarento was almost hidden from sight by the fluttering birds and the scrambling mass of furred creatures scurrying around his feet.

Then, in an instant, all was silence. The birds fell lifeless to the ground, the bear collapsing in on itself to crumble like ancient parchment.

Sarento walked across the corpses, which cracked underfoot like long-dead twigs.

His hunger was almost gone.

But the seed of it remained.

His Devourers were roaming the countryside, and he could feel the steady trickle of sustenance. Not enough to satisfy, yet adequate for the present. Reaching out he sought other Wolvers, ready to draw them to him for the *change*. But there were none within the range of his power. Curious, he thought, for he knew such beasts existed in this world; he had plucked their image from the dying memories of Saul Wilkins, and read them again in the sadistic mind of Jacob Moon. A tiny flicker of concern touched him. Without new Devourers his task in this new world would be made the more difficult. Then he thought again of the Gateway. If there was one, there must be more.

He pictured the teeming cities of the old world: Los Angeles, New York, London, Paris.

In such places he would never know hunger again.

*

Beth covered the dead man with a blanket and took hold of the weeping Meredith's shoulders. 'Come on,' she said gently. 'Come away.'

'It's my fault,' he said. 'I don't know why I shouted. I just . . . panicked.'

'Damn right!' said the Deacon.

'Leave it alone,' Beth told him icily. 'Not everyone is like you – and thank God for it. Yes, he panicked. He was frightened. But even his friend told him not to blame himself.' She patted Meredith's shoulder and stepped in closer to the Deacon. 'Blood and death is all you know, Deacon. Murder and pain. Now leave it be!'

At that moment there was a splintering of wood upstairs,

and the sound of a rifle booming. 'Are you all right, Wallace?' shouted Beth.

The young man appeared at the head of the stairs. 'One of them jumped up to the window. It's all right now. There's more coming across the meadows, Frey McAdam. Maybe fifty of them.'

'The shutters won't hold them,' said the Deacon. He drew a pistol, then winced and fell against the wall. Beth moved alongside him. His face was grey with exhaustion and pain. Reaching out, she put her arm around him and led him to a chair. As he sat she saw that her hand was smeared with blood.

'You're hurt,' she said.

'I've been hurt before.'

'Let me see it.' He half-turned in the chair. The back of his old sheepskin coat was ripped open, the flesh beneath it gashed and torn, and she remembered the snapping of the fence rail as his frail body was hurled against it. 'You may have broken a rib or two,' she said.

'I'll live. I have to.'

Meredith leaned over her. 'Let me look to it,' he said. 'I am a doctor.' Together they helped the Deacon to rise, removing his coat and torn shirt. Gently Meredith probed the wound. The old man made no sound. 'Two ribs at least,' said Meredith. In the background the baby began to cry.

'Needs feeding,' said Beth, but the young woman slouched in the chair made no movement. Beth moved to her and saw that her eyes were vacant. She undid the buttons of the girl's sweat-stained blouse, then lifted the baby to the swollen breast. As it began to suck the girl moaned and began to cry. 'There, there,' said Beth. 'Everything is all right now. Look at her feed. She was real hungry.'

'He's a boy,' whispered the mother.

'Of course he is. What a fool I am!' Beth told her. 'And a handsome boy he is. Strong, too.'

'My Josh was strong,' said the girl. 'They tore his head off.' Tears welled in her eyes and she began to tremble.

'You just think of the babe,' said Beth swiftly. 'He's all that matters now. You understand?' The girl nodded, but Beth saw that she was once more drifting away and with a sigh she returned to Meredith and the Deacon. The young doctor had cut up a tablecloth to make bandages. The old man reached up as Meredith completed his work.

'I am sorry, son,' he said. 'I hope you'll forgive my harsh words.'

Meredith nodded wearily. 'It's easier to forgive you, than to forgive myself. I have never been more frightened, and I am ashamed of my actions.'

'It's in the past, boy. You've been to the edge, and looked in the pit. Now you can be either stronger or weaker. It's a choice – but it's your choice. In life a man has to learn to be strong in the broken places.'

'They're moving on the barn,' Wallace shouted.

'Keep your voice down!' ordered Beth.

From across the yard came the sound of wood being splintered and broken, followed by the terrified neighing of horses. In the chair by the fire the young mother began to weep.

Beth lit two more lanterns, hanging them on hooks by the wall. 'It is going to be a long night,' she said. The screaming of the trapped animals went on for some minutes, then there was a silence. Beth sent Meredith through to the back room to check on Josiah Broome. The girl in the chair had fallen asleep, and Beth lifted the babe from her arms and sat with it on the old rocker.

Wallace Nash came down the stairs and stood in front of her. 'What is it, Wallace?' The red-headed youngster was ill at ease.

'I'm sorry, Frey McAdam. There's no other way to tell, but to go at it straight out. Samuel, well, he died saving the girl yonder and the child. Jumped from a window as one of them creatures was bearing down on her. Calm as you like. He killed it sure enough, but it got him too. I'm terrible sorry, Frey.'

'Best get back upstairs, Wallace,' she said, hugging the baby to her. 'Best keep a good watch.'

'I'll do that,' he said softly. 'You can rely on me, Frey.'

Beth closed her eyes. She could smell the burning oil in the lamps, the seasoned cedar-wood on the fire and the milky, newborn scent of the child in her arms.

Outside a beast howled.

*

Shannow reached into his pocket, his arthritic fingers curling around the golden Stone. I don't want to live for ever, he thought. I don't want to be young again. The pain in his chest was intensifying, linking and merging with the agony of his fractured ribs. You have no choice, he told himself. Gripping the Stone, he willed away the pain in his heart and felt new strength and vitality pounding through his veins. The ribs too he healed, drawing on the strength of the Stone.

Opening his hand, he gazed down at the golden pebble. Only the faintest thread of black showed where the power had been leached. Rising, he moved to the window. The aching pain was gone now from his shoulder and knees, and he moved with a spring in his step. Glancing through the gap in the shutters, he saw Devourers clambering over Jeremiah's wagon, moving into the cabin and up through the hatches. The barn was silent now, but he could see grey shapes lying on the hard-baked dirt of the yard or squatting near the fence.

Stepping back, he looked at the shutters. The wood was less than an inch thick; it could not withstand the explosive power in the taloned arms of the Devourers. Delving into his coat, he produced a box of shells which he tipped out on to the table-top. Twenty-three remained, plus the twelve in his pistols.

Meredith returned. 'The wounded man is sleeping,' said the doctor. 'His colour is good, and his pulse is steady.'

'He's tougher than he knows,' said Shannow.

'Where did these creatures come from?' Meredith asked. 'I have never heard of anything like them.'

'They're Wolvers,' answered Shannow, 'but they've been changed by . . . sorcery, if you will.' He started to speak, but then became aware that the young man was staring at him with what Shannow took to be blank disbelief. 'I know it is hard to understand,' he said. 'Just take me on trust, son. There is a creature . . .'

'Beth called you Deacon,' Meredith said, interrupting him, and Shannow realised that the young man had not been listening to a word of explanation.

'Yes,' he said, his voice weary. 'I am the Deacon.'

'I have always hated you,' said Meredith. 'You have been the cause of great evil.'

Shannow nodded. 'I don't argue with that, son. The butchery in the lands of the Hellborn was unforgivable.'

'Then why did you do it?'

'Because he's a killer and a savage,' said Beth, her voice flat and without anger. 'Some men are like that, Doctor. He came to power by deceit, and held on to it by fear. All who opposed him were killed – it was all he knew.'

Meredith swung to Shannow. 'Is that how it was?'

Shannow did not answer. Rising, he moved back through the house, pausing at Josiah Broome's bedside.

Is that how it was?

Broome stirred and opened his eyes. 'Hello, Jake,' he said sleepily.

Shannow sat on the edge of the bed. 'How are you feeling?'

'Better,' said the wounded man.

'That's good. You rest now.' Broome closed his eyes. Shannow remained where he was, remembering the two armies converging on the lands of the Hellborn, remembering his fury at the Hellborn betrayal and his fears about the coming of the Bloodstone. Many of the men who fought under him had lost family and friends to the Hellborn, and hatred ran strong in their veins. And in mine, he thought sadly.

Padlock Wheeler and the other officers had come to him on that fateful morning outside Babylon, when the Hellborn leaders were begging to be allowed to surrender.

'What orders, Deacon?'

There were many things he could have said in that moment, about the nature of evil, or the wisdom of forgiveness. As he stared at them he could think only of the terror that was coming, and the fact that in his previous world the Bloodstone had used the Hellborn to wreak destruction and death. And in the space of a single heartbeat he made a decision that still haunted him.

'Well, Deacon?'

'Kill them all.'

*

Zerah awoke before the dawn, and groaned. A small stone was digging into her hip and her shoulders ached abominably.

Another groan followed her attempt to sit up, and she swore bitterly.

'That's not nice,' said little Esther.

'Neither is the rheumatics,' grunted Zerah. 'How long you been awake, child?'

'Ever since the howling,' said Esther, sitting up and rubbing her eyes. 'There's lots of wolves about.'

Zerah had heard nothing. Pushing herself to her feet she stretched, then walked to the buckskin, lifting her water canteen from the saddle pommel. After a long drink she returned to the children and the dead fire. 'Wolves won't attack us,' she said. 'Now you see if you can find a spark in them ashes, and I'll cook us up some breakfast.'

With a yawn she stepped outside. The air was fresh and cool, and Zerah could smell the dew on the leaves and the musky scents of the forest. The sky was lightening in the east, and early bird-song greeted her as she walked under the trees. Despite the rheumatic pain in her back and shoulders, she felt good, glad to be alive.

It's the youngsters, she thought; they make everything seem fresh and new again. Zerah hadn't realised how much she missed company until the stranger had arrived. It saddened her that he hadn't come back. Jon was a good man, and quiet company. But the young ones were a joy, even when they squabbled. It brought back memories of her own children, back in the days of her youth, when the sky was more blue and the future was a golden mystery yet to be discovered.

Zeb had been a handsome man, with a ready wit that endeared him to everyone. And he was kind and loving. Everybody liked Zeb, because Zeb liked everybody. 'Never knew a man could see so much good in people,' she said, aloud.

When he died she remembered Padlock coming home. He put his arms around her and said, 'You know, Ma, there's no one in this world that he would ever need to say sorry to.'

Seemed like that was a good epitaph for a kind man.

Folks had come from far and wide for the funeral, and that pleased Zerah. But after he died the visitors had stopped coming. I never was the popular one, she thought. Old Zerah with her sharp tongue and her sharper ways.

She glanced up at the sky. 'Sometimes wonder what you saw in me, Zeb,' she said.

Turning to go back to the cave, she saw a paw-print in the soft earth. Kneeling, she ran her hand over it, opening her fingers to measure the span. It was enormous. Not a bear, though it was the right size. Nor yet a lion. Her mouth was dry as she stood. It was a wolf print – but larger than any she had ever seen.

Zerah hurried back to the cave. 'What's for breakfast?' asked Oz. 'Esther's got the fire going.'

'I think we'll wait until we reach town,' said Zerah. 'I think we should move on.'

'But I'm hungry,' complained Esther. 'Really starving!'

Zerah chuckled. Good God, woman, she thought, why the panic? You have a fire and a good pistol. 'All right,' she agreed. 'We'll eat first, and then travel.'

Walking to the back of the cave, she approached the buckskin. The horse was trembling, its ears tucked flat against its skull. 'It's only me, girl,' said Zerah. 'Calm down, now.' As she spoke Esther screamed, and Zerah spun round.

In the mouth of the cave stood a monstrosity. Eight feet tall, with huge shoulders and long arms, the fingers ending in curved talons, the beast was covered with silver-grey fur. Its massive head was lowered, its tawny eyes fixed on the two children cowering by the small fire. The buckskin reared and whinnied, catching the creature's attention.

Zerah Wheeler drew her old pistol, and wondered whether a bullet could bring the giant Wolver down. 'You stay calm, now, kids,' she said, her voice steady. Cocking the pistol she walked forward. 'I don't know if you can understand me,' she said, keeping her eyes on the beast, 'but this here pistol has six charges. And I hit what I god damn aim at. So back off and we'll all be happier.'

The beast howled, the sound reverberating like thunder in the cave. Zerah glanced at the fire. Beside it lay a thick branch festooned with long-dead leaves. Keeping the pistol steady, she reached down with her left hand and lifted the branch, touching the leaves to the little blaze. They caught instantly, flames searing out. Zerah stood and walked towards the creature. 'Back off, you son of a bitch!' she said.

The beast backed up – then sprang forward. Zerah did not give an inch, but thrusting the flames into its face she shot it in the throat. The huge Wolver went down and rolled. Zerah jumped to the mouth of the cave and shot it again as it tried to stand.

'Jesus wept!' she whispered.

Outside the cave were more of the beasts. 'Kids,' she called, 'I want you to climb that chimney at the back. I want you to do it *now*.'

Still holding the branch, she backed into the cave. A creature sprang at her, but calmly she shot it in the chest. Another ran from the right; a shot came from the back of the cave, shearing half the beast's head away. Zerah glanced back to see that Oz had her rifle in his hands and was standing his ground.

Pride flared in her then, but her voice was sharp and commanding. 'Get up that God damn chimney!' she ordered.

The beasts were advancing cautiously. With only three shells left, Zerah knew she could not hold them all – nor would she have time to turn and climb out of their reach. 'Are you climbing?' she called, not daring to glance back.

'Yes, Frey,' she heard Oz shout, his voice echoing from within the chimney.

'Good boy.'

Suddenly the buckskin bolted past her, scattering the beasts as it made a dash for the transient freedom of the forest. In that moment Zerah turned and sprinted for the chimney. Slamming the pistol in her holster, she grabbed a thin ledge of rock and levered herself up, her boots scrabbling on the stone. Swiftly she climbed until she could see Oz just above her, helping Esther. It was narrow in the chimney, but there was just room for the children to squeeze up on to a wider ledge below the cliff-top.

Pain flashed through her foot. Zerah screamed, and felt herself being dragged down. Oz pushed the rifle over the edge, barrel down, and fired. Zerah dragged out her pistol and put two shots into the Wolver below. It fell, its talons tearing off Zerah's boot. Oz grabbed her, and with the boy's help she eased her skinny body through the gap. Blood was seeping from a wound in her ankle, and a six-inch talon was embedded in her calf. Zerah prised it loose. 'You are brave kids,' she said. 'By God, I'm proud of you!'

From the pocket of her coat Zerah took a folding knife and opened the blade. 'If you'd be so good as to give me your shirt, Oz, I'll make some bandages and try to stop this bleeding.'

'Yes, Frey,' he said, pulling off his coat and shirt. As she worked she told the boy to count the shells left in the rifle. It didn't take long: there were two.

'I still have the little gun you gave me,' said Oz.

She shook her head. 'That'll do you no good against these creatures. Still, the noise might frighten 'em, eh?' The boy forced a smile and nodded. Zerah bandaged her ankle and then delved into the pocket of her coat, producing a strip of dried beef. 'It's not much of a breakfast,' she said, 'but it will have to do.'

'I'm not hungry,' said Esther. 'Are we going to die?'

'You listen to me, child,' said Zerah. 'We're alive, and I aim for us to stay that way. Now let's climb out of here.'

'Is that wise, Frey?' asked Oz. 'They can't get us here.'

'That's true, boy. But I don't think that strip of beef is going to hold us for the rest of our lives, do you? Now we can't be more than six, maybe seven, miles from Pilgrim's Valley. We'll be safe there. I'll go first, you follow.'

Zerah forced herself to her feet and climbed towards the patch of blue some twenty feet above her.

*

Shannow climbed the stairs to the second level and found the young red-headed youngster kneeling by a window, staring out over the yard. 'What are they doing now?' he asked the boy.

Wallace put down his rifle and stood. 'Just sitting. Can't understand it, Meneer. One minute they're tearing up everything in sight, the next they're lying like hounds in the moonlight.'

'They fed,' explained Shannow. 'The question is, how long before their hunger brings them against us? You be ready now.'

'This is a strong-built house, Meneer, but the windows and doors ain't gonna hold 'em – I can tell you that. Back in town they was ripping them apart like they was paper. And they can jump too, by God! I saw one spring maybe fifteen feet up on to the side of a building.'

'They can jump,' agreed Shannow, 'and they can die too.'

Wallace grinned. 'They can that.' As Shannow turned to move away, the boy reached out and took hold of his arm. 'You saved my life. I didn't even know that thing was close. I won't forget it.'

Shannow smiled. 'You settled that debt when you half-carried me back. I was all finished. You're a good man, Wallace. I'm proud to know you.' The two men shook hands and Shannow walked back to the narrow hallway, checking the other two adjoining rooms on this upper floor. Both were bedrooms, one decorated with lace curtains, yellowed now with age. Children's drawings and sketches were still pinned to the walls, stick men in front of box houses, with smoke curling from chimneys. In the corner, by the closed window, was a stuffed toy dog with floppy ears. Shannow remembered when little Mary carried it everywhere. The other room was Samuel's. The walls were lined with shelves which carried many books, including a special gold-edged edition of *The New Elijah*. Shannow sighed. Another of Saul's little vanities. When it was published Shannow had read the first chapter, outlining God's call to the young Jerusalem Man, then sent for Saul.

'What is this . . . garbage?'

'It's not garbage, Deacon. Everything in that book is fact. We got most of it from primary sources, men who knew the Jerusalem Man, who heard his words. I would have thought you would have been pleased. He predicted your coming.'

'He did no such thing, Saul. And half of the names in the first chapter never came within a hundred miles of Shannow. Several others have let their imaginations run riot.'

'But . . . how would you know that, Deacon?'

'I know. How is no concern of yours. How many have been printed?'

Saul smiled. 'Forty thousand, Deacon. And they've sold so fast we're going for a second printing.'

'No, we are not! Let it go, Saul.'

Shannow lifted the book from the shelf and flipped it open. In the centre was a black and white engraving showing a handsome man on a rearing black stallion, silver pistols in the rider's hands, and upon his head a sleek black hat. All around him were dead Hellborn. 'At least they didn't say I killed ten thousand with the jawbone of an ass,' whispered Shannow, tossing the book to the pine bed.

Carefully he opened the shutter and leaned out. Below him was Jeremiah's wagon, the roof ripped apart. Several Wolvers were asleep within it, others were stretched out by the ruined barn.

What are you going to do, Shannow? he asked himself.

How do you plan to stop the Beast?

Fear touched him then, but he fought it down.

'What are you doing here?' asked Beth. 'This is my son's room.'

Shannow sat upon the bed, remembering the times he had read to the boy. 'I don't need your hatred, Beth,' he said softly.

'I don't hate you, Deacon. I despise you. There is a difference.'

Wearily he stood. 'You ought to make up your mind, woman. You despise me because I gave no ground and saw my enemies slain; you despised your lover, Jon Cade, because he wouldn't slay his enemies. What exactly do you require from the men in your life?'

'I don't need to debate with you,' she said stonily.

'Really? Then why did you follow me here?'

'I don't know. Wish I hadn't.' But she made no move to leave. Instead she walked further into the room and sat down on an old wicker chair by the window. 'How come you knew about me and Jon? You have spies here?'

'No . . . no spies. I knew because I was here, Beth. I was here.'

'I never saw you.'

'You still don't see me,' he said sadly, rising and walking past her. The pine steps creaked under his weight and Dr Meredith turned as Shannow approached.

'It's terribly quiet,' said the younger man.

'It won't stay that way, Doctor. You should ask if Frey McAdam has a spare weapon for you.'

'I am not very good with guns, Deacon. I never wanted to be, either.'

'That's fine, Doctor, as long as there is someone else to do your hunting for you. However, you won't need to be good. The targets will be close enough to rip off your face. Get a gun.'

'What does it take to make a man like you, Deacon?' asked Meredith, his face reddening.

'Pain, boy. Suffering, sorrow and loss.' Shannow pointed at Jeremiah's blanket-covered corpse. 'Today you had a tiny taste of it. By tomorrow you'll know more. I don't mind you judging me, boy. You couldn't be harder on me than I am on myself. For now, though, I suggest we work together to survive.'

Meredith nodded. 'I guess that is true,' he said. 'You were starting to tell me about the Gateways. Who made them, and why?'

Shannow moved to the armchair and gazed down at the sleeping woman. Beth had found a small, beautifully carved crib and had placed the babe in it, beside the chair. 'No one knows,' he said, keeping his voice soft. 'A long time ago I met a man who claimed they were created in Atlantis, twelve thousand years before the Second Fall. But they may be older. The old world was full of stories about Gateways, and old straight paths, dragon trails and ley lines. There are few facts, but scores of speculative theories.'

'How are they opened?'

Shannow moved silently away from the mother and child and stood by the door. 'I couldn't tell you. I knew a woman who was adept at such matters. But she remained behind on the day of the Fall, and I guess was killed with the rest of the world. She once took me through to her home in a place called Arizona. Beautiful land. But how she did it . . . ?' He shrugged. 'She had a piece of Sipstrassi, a Daniel Stone. There was a burst of violet light, and then we were there.'

'Ah, yes,' said Meredith, 'the Stones. I've heard of them but never seen one. A hospital in Unity used them to cure cancer and the like. Astonishing.'

'Amen to that,' said Shannow. 'They can make an old man young, or heal the sick, or create food from molecules in the air. It is my belief that Moses used them to part the Red Sea – but I cannot prove it.'

'God had no hand in it, then?' asked Meredith, with a smile.

'I don't try to second-guess God, young man. If He created the Sipstrassi in the first place, then they are still miracles. If He gave one to Moses, you could still say that God's power parted the waves. However, this is not the time for Biblical debate. The Stones make imagination reality. That's all I know.'

'Be nice to have one or two at this moment,' said Meredith. 'With one thought we could kill all the wolves.'

'Sipstrassi cannot kill,' Shannow told him.

Meredith laughed. 'That's your problem, Deacon. You lack the very imagination you say the Stones need.'

'What do you mean?'

Meredith stood. 'Take this chair. It is of wood. Surely a Stone could transform it into a bow and arrows? Then you could shoot something and kill it. Sipstrassi would have killed it, albeit once removed. And these Gateways you speak of, well, perhaps there is no technique. Perhaps the woman you knew was not adept at all – merely imaginative.'

Shannow thought about it. 'You think she merely *wished* herself home?'

'Quite possibly. However, it is all academic now.'

'Yes,' agreed Shannow absently. 'Thank you, Doctor.'

'It is a pleasure, Deacon.' Meredith moved to the window and leaned down to peer through the gap in the shutters. 'Oh, God!' he said suddenly. 'Oh, my dear God!'

*

Isis floated back to consciousness on a warm sea of dreams, memories of childhood on the farm near Unity – her dog, Misha, unsuccessfully chasing rabbits across the meadow, barking furiously in his excitement. His enjoyment was so total that when Isis gently merged with his feelings tears of joy flowed from her eyes. Misha knew a happiness no human – bar Isis – could ever share. He was a mongrel, and his heritage could be seen in every line of his huge body. His head was wolf-like, with wide tawny eyes. But his ears were long and floppy, his chest powerful. According to Isis's father, Misha was quite possibly the worst guard-dog ever born; when strangers approached he would rush up to them with tail wagging, and wait to be petted.

Isis loved him.

She was almost grown when he died. Isis had been walking by the stream when the bear erupted out of the thicket. Isis stood her ground and mentally reached out to the beast, using all her powers to calm its rage. She was failing, for the pain within it was colossal. The young girl even had time to note the cancerous growth that was sending flames of agony through the bear's belly, even as it bore down on her.

Misha had charged the bear, leaping to fasten his powerful jaws on the furred throat. The bear had been surprised by the ferocity of the attack but had recovered swiftly, turning on the hound and lashing out with its talons.

A shot rang out, then another, and another. The bear had staggered and tried to lumber back into the thicket. A fourth shot saw it slump to the ground and Isis's father had run up, dropping his rifle and throwing his arms around his daughter. 'My God, I thought you were going to die,' he said, hugging her to him.

Misha had whimpered then. Isis tore herself loose from her father's embrace, and threw herself down alongside the dying hound, stroking its head, trying to draw away its pain. Misha's tail had wagged weakly, even as he died.

Isis had wept, but her father drew her upright. 'He did his job, girl. And he did it well,' he said gently.

'I know,' answered Isis. 'Misha knew it too. He was happy as he died.'

The sadness was still with her as she opened her eyes in the wagon. She blinked and found herself staring at the stars. Half of the roof was missing, and she could see great tears in the wooden canopy. Her right side was warm and she reached out, her hand touching fur. 'Oh, Misha,' she said, 'you mustn't get on the bed. Daddy will scold me.'

A low rumbling growl sounded, but Isis drifted off to sleep again, the terrible strength-sapping power of her illness draining her of energy. A weight came down over her chest, her eyes opened and she saw a huge face above hers, a long lolling tongue and sharp fangs. Her hand was still touching the fur, and she could feel the warmth of flesh beneath it. 'I can't stroke you,' she whispered. 'I'm too tired.'

She sighed and tried to turn to her side. At least the pain is gone, she thought. Maybe death will not be so very bad after all. Isis wanted to sit up, but she didn't have the strength. Opening her eyes again she saw that the side of the wagon was also partially destroyed. Something had happened! Some calamity.

'I must get up,' she said and lifting her hand, she looped her arm over Misha's neck and pulled. He growled, but she succeeded in raising her body. Dizziness swamped her and she fell in towards Misha, resting her head on his shoulder.

A second growl came from below the bed and a monstrous creature loomed up from the floor of the cabin. Isis looked at it, and yawned. Her head was spinning, her thoughts fragmented. Misha felt so warm. Reaching out, she touched his mind. There was anger there, a poisonous fury held in check only by . . . by what? Memories of a hollow by a lake, young Wolvers running around his feet. A . . . wife?

'You're not my Misha,' said Isis, 'and you are in pain.' Softly she stroked the fur.

The second beast lunged at her. The first hit it with a backhand blow, sending it smashing against the cabin wall.

'Stop it! Stop it!' said Isis wearily. 'You mustn't fight.' She sagged against the beast. 'I'm thirsty,' she said. 'Help me up.' Pulling once more she rose on trembling legs, pushing past the Devourer and stumbling to the rear of the cabin where she almost fell down the steps and out into the yard.

The moon was high, and she was almost at the end of her strength. There was no sign of Jeremiah, Meredith or the others. No wagons camped in a circle. No fires burning. Her vision swam and she swayed, catching hold of the left rear wheel.

The yard was full of hounds, big hounds.

She saw the house, bars of golden light showing through the closed shutters. Everyone must be there, she thought. But I can't reach it.

I must! I don't want to die here, alone. Drawing in a deep breath, she let go of the wheel and took two faltering steps.

Then she fell.

*

The Deacon saw Meredith stumble away from the window.

Shannow stepped up to the shutters, peering out through the crack. He saw a young woman in a dress of faded blue, her blonde hair shining white in the moonlight, lying stretched out on the ground. Before he could speak he heard the door open. 'No!' he hissed.

But Meredith was already moving out into the yard.

With a muttered curse Shannow followed him, drawing his pistols. The beasts were everywhere, most lying quietly under the stars, their bellies full, but a few prowling now at the edge of the barn, or gnawing on the bloody bones of the butchered horses, milk cows and oxen. Shannow cocked the pistols and stood in the doorway, watching the young doctor make his way across to the fallen girl. Meredith was moving slowly, and for the moment the beasts seemed to be ignoring him.

A Devourer moved from the rear of the wagon and saw the walking man. A deep growl sounded and it ambled forward. Several others looked up. One stretched and howled, the sound chilling. Meredith faltered, but then walked on and knelt beside Isis. Reaching down, he took hold of her wrist. The pulse was weak and fluttering. Pushing his hands under her shoulders he hauled her into an upright position, then twisted down to lift her legs. Her head fell to his shoulder.

A Devourer reared above him, saliva dripping from its fangs. Isis moaned as Meredith backed away, the beast following.

In the doorway Shannow aimed his pistol, but now other beasts were closing in on the doctor. Meredith turned his back on them and started to walk back towards the house. Shannow's mouth was dry, his palms greasy with sweat. The doctor stumbled, but righted himself and walked on. Shannow stepped aside as he climbed the porch steps and entered the house. Swiftly Shannow followed him, slamming shut the door and dropping the bar into place.

Outside a great howl went up. The shutters on the window exploded inwards and a beast thrust its upper body through the frame. Shannow shot it through the head. Another clambered over the body of the first; Shannow fired twice into its huge chest and it slumped forward, leaking blood to the dirt floor.

The young mother lurched to her feet, screaming, 'Don't let them get me! Don't let them get me!'

Talons raked at the door, splintering the wood. Wallace Nash ran half-way down the stairs and levelled his shotgun. A section of timber on the door was torn away as a taloned arm lunged through. Wallace fired both barrels. The arm jerked as blood sprayed from it. Shannow shot through the door.

The sounds of gunfire echoed away. Shannow moved to the window, seeing that the beasts had pulled back.

'I've never seen anything like it,' said Wallace Nash. 'Son of a bitch! Man, that took some nerve.'

Meredith wasn't listening. He was kneeling over the unconscious Isis, his tears falling to her face.

Shannow pushed closed the shutters. The locking bar had been snapped in half, but he wedged them by ramming a knife down into the window-sill. It would not hold against a Devourer, but it gave the illusion of security.

He could scarcely believe what he had seen. Meredith, the man whose panic had killed Jeremiah, had just performed an act of complete heroism. Beth came downstairs. The baby was crying now, and she lifted it from the crib. When the young mother snatched it away and fled upstairs, Beth moved alongside Meredith. There were no signs of wounds on the body of the young blonde girl he was attending. 'What's the matter with her, Doctor?' Beth asked.

'She has an illness which has corrupted her immune system. It is very rare; even in the old world it affected only a handful in every million.' He glanced up and saw that Beth did not understand him. Meredith sighed. 'Our bodies are equipped with a . . . defence mechanism. When illness strikes we make antibodies to fight it. Like measles, a child generally will succumb only once, because the body identifies the invading organism, then makes defences to stop it happening again. You understand? Well, in the case of Isis, her defence mechanism has targeted organs in her own body, and is slowly destroying them. It was called Addison's Disease.'

'And there is nothing that can be done?' asked Wallace.

'Nothing. The elders used medicines called steroids, but we don't know how they were made.'

'Where did she come from?' asked Wallace. 'How did she get here, through all them creatures?'

'We brought her with us,' said Meredith. 'She was in the wagon. We thought she was on the verge of death and . . . to my eternal shame . . . I left her there.'

'Jesus!' said Wallace. 'But why didn't they kill her? They was all over the wagon.'

Meredith shrugged. 'I have no answer to that.'

'No, but she does,' said the Deacon softly and, kneeling beside her, he laid his hand on her brow. 'Come back to us, Isis,' he said. Meredith watched amazed as colour seeped back into the pale face. Beneath his fingers the pulse became steadier, stronger.

Isis opened her eyes and smiled. 'Hello, Jake,' she said.

'How are you feeling?'

'Wonderful. Rested.' She sat up and looked around. 'Where is this place?'

'It's a farm near Pilgrim's Valley,' said Shannow.

'Where's Jeremiah?'

Shannow helped her to her feet. 'Do you remember the beasts in the wagon?' he asked, ignoring her question.

'Yes. Big, aren't they? Are they yours, Jake?'

'No. They are savage. They killed Jeremiah, and many others. The question is, why did they not kill you?'

'Jeremiah is dead?' Then she saw the blanket-covered body. 'Oh no, Jake!' Isis moved to the body, pulling back the blanket and gazing down on the old man's face.

Meredith moved alongside Shannow. 'Is she . . . healed?'

Shannow nodded. 'Completely. But I must know about the beasts.'

'Let it rest, for God's sake,' protested Beth. 'She's been through enough.'

'We cannot let it rest,' said Shannow. 'When those beasts make a concerted attack, we will be dead. If Isis knows a way to control them or render them harmless, I must know it. You hear me, child?' he asked the weeping Isis. She nodded, and covered Jeremiah's face once more. Rising, she faced the Deacon.

'I don't know why they didn't harm me,' she said. 'I can't help you.'

'I think you can, my love,' said Meredith. 'Animals never attack you, do they? You once told me it was because you liked them. But it is more than that, isn't it? You can . . . communicate with them. Remember when you told Jeremiah about the lung disease that was crippling his lead oxen?'

'I . . . can't talk to them, or anything,' Isis told him. 'I just . . . merge with their minds.'

'What do you remember of *their* minds?' asked the Deacon, pointing towards the window.

'It's very hazy. It's like their thoughts are full of angry wasps, stinging them all the time.'

'Here they come!' yelled Wallace.

*

Oz Hankin was more tired than frightened as they crossed the ridge and began the long descent into Pilgrim's Valley. They had walked for most of the day and there had been no sign of the wolf creatures. The wind had been at their backs for most of the journey, and it seemed now that they would escape the beasts. Esther was being carried by Frey Wheeler, which annoyed Oz. Little girls always got the best treatment. It was the same back at the farm with Dad; if their room was a mess, or if the chores weren't completed, it was Oz who got it in the neck.

Now it was Esther who was being carried. The fact that he was ten pounds heavier than Esther, and three inches taller, made little difference to the twelve-year-old. Life just wasn't fair!

And he was hungry. As he walked he remembered the taste of apple pie, and powdered sugar, and the sweet honey-cakes his father had made after they found the hive in the woods.

Frey Wheeler halted and swung Esther to the ground. 'Need to rest a mite, child,' she said. The woods were close and Oz saw Zerah studying them. She sniffed, then spat. It surprised Oz; ladies weren't supposed to spit. Esther immediately copied her and Zerah laughed. 'Don't imitate me, Esther,' she warned. 'There's things people will tolerate in the old that they won't in the young.'

'Why?' Esther asked.

'It just ain't done, child.' She turned towards Oz. 'You got sharp eyes, young Oz. What can you see in the trees yonder?'

'Nothing, Frey. Looks clear.'

'Then we'll chance it,' she said, hefting her rifle. Slowly the trio set off across the last stretch of open ground. The land dropped sharply to their right, and as they walked they saw a trail leading west across the mountains. 'Logging road,' said Zerah, as they scrambled down it. At the foot Zerah stopped again, her ancient face showing purple streaks under the eyes and beside the mouth. She was breathing heavily and Oz became concerned.

'You feeling okay, Frey?' asked Oz. The old lady was sweating now, and her eyes seemed more sunken than usual, lacking their normal brightness. She smiled, but Oz could see the effort behind it.

'Just tired, boy. But I ain't done yet. Just give me a minute to catch my breath.'

Oz sat back on a rock, while Esther ran off into the bushes at the side of the road.

The sound of horses' hooves came to him. Oz was about to warn Esther, but the riders appeared around a bend in the road. At first Oz was pleased, for if they were men from Pilgrim's Valley it would mean a pleasant ride in comparative safety. His joy was short-lived as he recognised the man on the lead horse: he was one of those who had shot his father. The men saw them and spurred their horses forward. There were seven in the group, but Oz recognised only the first as they reined in before Zerah.

'Well, well, what have we here?' asked the lead rider, a thin man with long side-burns and deep-set dark eyes. In his hands was a squat, black pistol which was pointed at Zerah. Oz saw that Zerah's rifle was still resting against the rock. There would be no time to lift it and fire. And even if she could, there were only two shots left.

'Don't harm these children,' said the old lady wearily.

'Where's the girl?' asked the leader.

Oz slipped his hand in his pocket, curling it round the butt of the little pistol. Only the lead rider had a gun in his hand, the rest were merely sitting on their horses, watching the exchange.

'You should just ride on,' said Zerah. 'Killing children is no work for grown men.'

'Don't lecture me, you hag! We was told to find them and get rid of them. That's what we aim to do. Now tell me where the girl is and I'll kill you clean. One shot. Otherwise I'll blow away your kneecaps and make you scream for an hour or two.'

'You always was a low creature, Bell,' said a voice. 'But, by God, I swear you could walk under a door without bending your knees.'

Oz looked to the right, where two riders had arrived unnoticed. The man who spoke was wide-shouldered, wearing a dust-stained black coat and a red brocade waistcoat. His hair was dark, though silver at the temples. Beside him was a younger man.

'By Heaven,' said Bell, 'you're a long way from home, aren't you, Laton? Heard they butchered your gang and that you ran off with your tail between your legs. I always knew you weren't so salty. Now be on your way, we've business here.'

'Threatening women?' taunted the rider. 'That's about all you're worth, Bell.'

Bell laughed and shook his head. 'Always one for words, Laton,' he said. Oz saw the killer suddenly swing the black pistol towards the rider. Laton swayed to the side, a nickel-plated pistol seeming to leap into his hand. Bell fired – and missed. Laton returned the shot, and Bell pitched from his saddle. Seizing the chance, Oz pulled the little pistol clear and fired at the closest man. He saw the shot strike home as a puff of dust came from the man's jacket and he sagged in the saddle. Horses reared and shots exploded all around him. Oz tried to aim but Zerah dived at him, dragging him down and covering him with her body.

He heard the thunder of hooves and saw the three remaining hunters fleeing. One horse was down and there were four bodies lying on the logging road. The other three horses had run off a little way and were now standing some fifty yards distant. 'It's all right, Frey, they've gone,' he said.

The man in the brocade waistcoat knelt by them, lifting Zerah from him. 'Are you hurt, lady?' he asked.

'Only my pride,' she said, allowing Laton to help her rise. 'Don't know how I let them get so close.'

Laton grinned. A groan came from the left where Bell was pushing himself to his knees, his right hand gripping his belly, blood pouring through his fingers. Oz watched as the rescuer approached the wounded man.

'By damn, Bell, you are a hard man to kill,' he said. His pistol came up and fired, and Bell pitched backwards and lay still.

'He was one that needed killing,' said Zerah, struggling to rise. Oz helped her, then recovered his pistol from the road.

'I should have done it a long time ago,' said Laton. Turning away, he called out to his friend, 'Hey, Nestor, catch those horses yonder and we'll offer these folks company on the road.'

Esther peeped out from the bushes. Zerah called to her and she scampered across to the old lady, hugging at her leg. Zerah leaned down and kissed the top of the child's head.

As the younger man rode off for the riderless horses, the older one turned to Oz. 'You did right well there, son. I like a lad with spirit.'

'Are you Laton Duke, sir?' asked Oz.

The man grinned and extended his hand. 'The name is Clem. Clem Steiner.'

'But he called you . . .'

'Just a case of mistaken identity. I never saw him before,' he said, with a wink.

Oz shook the man's hand as Zerah gathered up her rifle. 'I don't much care who you are,' she said. 'I'd have welcomed the Devil himself, with open arms, just to see that piece of scum go to Hell.'

'Your grandma is one tough lady,' observed Clem.

'Yes sir!' agreed Oz. 'You don't know the half of it.'

*

The attack was short-lived, only four of the creatures charging at the house. Wallace took out the first with a double-barrelled blast while it was still in the yard, Shannow shot down two others as they tore the shutters away from the window. The last leapt to the porch awning and tried to enter an upstairs window. Beth ran into the room and fired three shots into the beast's chest, catapulting it back to the yard, where Wallace killed it as it tried to rise.

The downstairs rooms stank of cordite and a haze of blue smoke hung in the air. Dr Meredith approached the Deacon. 'You have a Stone, don't you?' he said, as the Deacon reloaded his pistols.

'Yes. One small Stone.'

'Surely, with its power, you could block all the windows and the doors?'

'I could,' the Deacon agreed, 'but I don't know how long the power would last, and I need that Stone, Doctor, for when the real evil shows up.'

Meredith's eyes widened. 'The real evil? These beasts are not the *real* evil?' Quietly Shannow told him about the Bloodstone, and how it had destroyed its own world. He told him of the colosseum, and the forty thousand dead, of the absence of birds, animals and insects.

'Oh, God . . . you really saw this?' asked Meredith.

'I saw it, Doctor. Trust me. I wish I hadn't.'

'Then what can stop him?'

The Deacon gave a weary smile. 'That is a problem that has haunted me for twenty years. I still have no answer.'

Isis joined them. Leaning forward, she kissed the Deacon's cheek and the old man smiled up at her. 'A kiss from a beautiful girl is a wonderful tonic.'

'It must be working,' said Isis, 'for I'm sure your beard is darker, Jake, than when first I saw you.'

'That's true,' agreed Meredith. 'How is your wound?'

'I healed it,' said Shannow.

'I think you did more than that,' said Meredith. 'Isis is right – your skin is looking less wrinkled and ancient. You're getting younger.' He sighed. 'Good Lord, what wonders could be achieved if we had more of those Stones!'

The Deacon shook his head. 'The Guardians had them, but the Stones were corrupted – just like everything man touches. Sipstrassi has its dark side, Doctor. When fed with blood the result is terrifying. Look at the creatures yonder, the Bloodstones in their brows. Once they were Wolvers, gentle and shy. Look at them now. Consider the Bloodstone himself: once he was a man with a mission, to bring back the earth to a Garden of Eden. Now he is a destroyer. No, I think we would all be better off without any Stones of power.'

Beth called out to Meredith, to come and help her prepare food. The doctor moved away and Isis sat beside Shannow.

'You are sad,' she said.

'You see too much,' he told her, with a smile.

'I see more than you think,' she said, her voice low. 'I know who you are.'

'Best to say nothing, child.'

'I felt as if I was floating on a dark sea. Then you came to me. We merged when you drew me back. We were one – as we are one now.' She took his hand and squeezed it, and he felt a sudden warmth within his mind, a loss of loneliness and sorrow. He heard her voice inside his head. 'I know all of your thoughts and concerns. Your memories are now mine. That's why I can tell that you are not an evil man, Jake.'

'I am responsible for the deaths of thousands, Isis. By their fruits shall ye judge them. Women, children – an entire race. All dead by my order.' Harsh memories erupted into his mind, but Isis flowed over them, forcing them back.

'That cannot be changed . . . Deacon. But an evil man would not concern himself with guilt. He would have no conception of it. Putting that aside for a moment, I also share, now, your fears about the Bloodstone. You don't know what to do, but in your memories there is one who could help. A man with great imagination and the powers of a seer.'

'Who?' As swiftly as she had merged with him, she was gone, and Shannow felt the pain of withdrawal, a return to the solitary cell of his own being.

'Lucas,' she said, aloud.

He looked into her beautiful face and sighed. 'He went down with the Fall of the world hundreds of years ago.'

'You are not thinking,' she said. 'What are the Gateways, if not doorways through time? Amaziga took you back to Arizona. Could you not travel the same route? You must get Lucas.'

'I have no horse, and even if I did it's a three-day ride to Domango. I haven't the time.'

'Why go to Domango? Did not Amaziga tell you that the stone circles were placed where the earth energy was strongest? There must be other places where they did not place stones, yet the energy is still there.'

'How would I find one?'

'Ah, Deacon, you lack the very quality that the Stones need. You do not have imagination.'

'Meredith has already pointed that out,' he said testily.

'Give me the Stone,' she ordered him. Fishing it from his pocket, he placed it in her hand. 'Come with me,' she said, and he followed her upstairs into Mary's old room. She opened the shutter. 'Look out and tell me what you see.'

'Hills, the slope of the valley, woods. The night sky. What would you have me see?'

Placing the Stone against his brow, she said, 'I want you to see the land and its power. Where would a circle of stone be placed? Think of it, Deacon. The men who erected the stone circles must have been able to identify the power points. Draw from the Sipstrassi. See!'

His vision swam and the dark grey of the night landscape began to swirl with colour – deep reds and purples, yellows and greens, constantly shifting, flowing, blending. Rivers of colour, streams and lakes, never still, always surging and vibrant. 'What is the colour of power?' he heard her ask, as if from a great distance.

'Power is everywhere,' he told her. 'Healing, mending, growing.'

'Close your eyes and picture the stone circle at Domango.' He did so, seeing again the hillside and Amaziga's Arizona house, and the distant San Francisco Peaks.

'I can see it,' he told her.

'Now gaze upon it with the eyes of Sipstrassi. See the colours.'

The desert was blue-green, the mountains pink and grey. The rivers of power were lessened here, sluggish and tired. Shannow gazed upon the old stone circle. The hillside was bathed in a gentle gold, flickering and pulsing. Opening his eyes, he turned to Isis. 'It is a golden yellow,' he said.

'Can you see such a point from here, Jake?' she asked, pointing out of the window.

Chapter Thirteen

When will we have peace? That is the cry upon the lips of the multitude. I hear it. I understand it. The answer is not easy to voice, and it is harder to hear. Peace does not come when the brigands are slain. It is not born with the end of a current War. It does not arrive with the beauty of the Spring. Peace is a gift of the grave, and is found only in the silence of the tomb.
From the Deacon's last letter to the Church of Unity

* * *

Isis moved out into the yard, enjoying the freshness of the pre-dawn air. Several of the wolf creatures were stretched out asleep, but she sensed the presence of others within the ruined barn. She could feel them now, their pain and anguish, and as she crossed the lines of power that stretched back from them to the Bloodstone her limbs tingled and stung.

Concentrating hard, she narrowed her eyes. Now she could see the lines, tiny and red, like stretched wire, pulsing between the servants and the master, passing through the house, burrowing through the hillsides. Her body aglow with Sipstrassi power, she stared intently at the lines – severing them, watching them wither and fail. An instant later they were gone, snuffed out like candle flames.

Walking steadily forward, she approached the first sleeping beast. Reaching down she touched its brow, her index finger and thumb taking hold of the Bloodstone shard embedded there. The evil contained in the shard swept back over her and, for the merest moment, she felt a surge of hatred. It was an emotion she had never experienced and she faltered. The Bloodstone turned black and fell away from the wolf.

'I do not hate,' she said aloud. 'I will not hate.' The feeling passed, and Isis knew she was stronger now. 'Come to me!' she called. 'Come!'

The beasts rose up, growling. Others poured from the barn.

Now she felt the hatred coming at her like a tidal wave. Isis absorbed it all, draining it of energy and purpose.

A creature lunged forward, rearing up before her, but Isis reached out swiftly to touch its huge chest. Instantly she merged. Its Wolver memories were buried deep, but she found them, drawing them up into the beast's upper mind. With a cry it fell back from her.

Isis let her power swell, enveloping the mutated animals like a healing mist and sending the power out over the mountains and hills. One by one the beasts dropped to the ground, and she watched as their great size dwindled, the dead Stones falling from their brows.

Then the power left her, drifting away as the dawn light crept over the eastern mountains. Tired now, Isis sat down. A little Wolver padded across to her, taking her hand.

The Deacon strode across the yard, holstering his pistols. The Wolvers scattered and ran, heading away into the distant hills.

'I felt him, Deacon,' she whispered. 'I felt the Bloodstone.'

The Deacon helped her to rise. 'Where is he?'

'He has rebuilt a ruined city a day's ride from Pilgrim's Valley. He has warriors with him, black-garbed men with horned helmets. And the Jerusalem Rider, Jacob Moon.'

'Evil will always gather evil,' said the Deacon.

'The wolf creatures were linked to him, feeding him. Now the supply has stopped,' she said.

'Then he'll have to go hungry.'

She shook her head. 'The horned riders will come, Deacon. The war is only just beginning.'

*

Jon Shannow stood on the brow of the hill, the Sipstrassi Stone in his hand. There was no circle of stones here, and no indication that there ever had been. Yet he knew this was a point of power, mystically linked to others throughout time. What he did not know was how to harness that power, how to travel to a given destination.

Was it just imagination, or were there sets of co-ordinates needed by the users?

Back in Babylon he had learned that there were certain

windows in time that would enable travellers to move across the Gateways with minimum energy from Sipstrassi. How did one know when such a window was open?

Closing his fist around the Stone he pictured the house in Arizona, the paddock, and the red jeep, the sun over the desert. The Stone grew warm in his hand. 'Take me to the world before the Fall,' he said.

Violet light flared around him, then faded.

There was the house. There was no red jeep there now. The paddock was gone, replaced by a tarmac square and two tennis courts. Beyond the house he could see a swimming-pool. Shannow stepped out of the circle and strolled down to the building.

The front door was locked. Leaning back he kicked hard at the wood, which splintered but did not give. Twice more he thundered his boot against the lock, then the door swung inwards.

Swiftly he moved across the living-room. It was sweltering hot inside, and airless. Out of habit he wandered through to the lounge, flicking on the air-conditioning unit. He grinned. So long away, yet as soon as he returned he thought of the wonderful comforts of this old, doomed world.

Moving back to the main room he plugged in the computer leads, engaged the electricity and watched the screen flicker to life. Lucas's face appeared.

'Good day, Mr Shannow,' said Lucas.

'I need you, my friend,' said the Deacon.

'Is Amaziga with you?'

'No. I have not seen her in twenty years or more.' Shannow pulled up a swivel seat and sat before the screen.

'She left here some time ago for Brazil. My dates are confused. I think there must have been an electrical storm. What is today's date?'

'I don't know. Listen to me, Lucas. The Bloodstone is in my world. I need your help to destroy it.'

'There is nothing in your world to destroy it, Mr Shannow. As long as it lives it will feed. If you deny it blood, it will go dormant and wait – go into hibernation, if you will. But there is no weapon capable of causing it harm.'

'The Sword of God could have destroyed it,' said Shannow.

'Ah yes, but the Sword of God was a nuclear missile, Mr Shannow. Do you really want to see such a weapon descend on your land? It will wipe out countless thousands and further poison the land for centuries.'

'Of course not. But what I am saying is that there are weapons which could destroy him.'

'How can I help you? You can have access to all of my files, but few of them have any direct bearing on your world, save those which Amaziga supplied.'

'I want to know everything about Sarento. Everything.'

'The question, surely, is *which* Sarento. I know little about the man who became the Bloodstone.'

'Then tell me about the Sarento you know, his dreams, his vanities, his ambitions.'

'Very well, Mr Shannow, I will assemble the files. The refrigerator is still working and you will find some cool drinks there. When you return we will go over the information.'

Shannow strolled through to the kitchen, fetching a carton of Florida orange juice and a glass. Sitting before the machine he listened as Lucas outlined Sarento's life. He was not a primary survivor of the Fall, though he sometimes pretended to be, but was born one hundred and twelve years later. A mathematical genius, he had been in the first team to discover Sipstrassi fragments, and use them for the benefit of the people who became known as the Guardians. While he listened Shannow remembered the struggle on board the restored *Titanic*, and the disaster in the cave of the original Bloodstone. Sarento had died there, Shannow barely escaping with his life.[1] There was little new to be learned. Sarento had been obsessed with the thought of returning the world to the status and lifestyle enjoyed in the twentieth and twenty-first centuries. It was his life's work.

'Has that helped, Mr Shannow?'

Shannow sighed. 'Perhaps. Tell me now of the Gateways, and the points of power on which they were built.'

'You have me at a disadvantage there, Mr Shannow. The Gateways were *used* by the Atlanteans until the time of

---

[1] *Wolf in Shadow.*

Pendarric and the first Fall of the world. Whether they were built by them, or not, is another matter entirely. Most of the ancient races are lost to us. It could even be that the world has Fallen many times, wiping out great civilisations. As to the power sites, they are many. There are three near here, and one is certainly as powerful as that upon which the ancients erected the stones. The earth is peppered with them. In Europe most of the sites have churches built upon them. Here in the United States some have been covered with mounds, others bearing ancient ruins. The people known as the Anasazi erected cities around the energy centres.'

'Do you have maps in your files?' asked Shannow.

'Of course. What would you like to see?'

'Show me the deserts of Arizona, New Mexico, Nevada.'

'Do you have more specific instructions?'

'I want to see all the energy centres, as you call them.'

For more than an hour Shannow pored over the maps, Lucas highlighting sites of power. 'More detail on this one,' said Shannow. 'Bring it up closer.' Lucas did so.

'I see what you are getting at, Mr Shannow. I will access other data that may be relevant to this line of enquiry. While I am doing so, would you mind if I activate the television? It annoys me that my date and time sections are down.'

'Of course,' said Shannow.

The wall-mounted unit flickered to life, the picture switching to a news text. The date and time were outlined in yellow at the top right-hand side of the screen.

'Mr Shannow!'

'What is it?'

'You have chosen a strange time to pass through the Gateway. We are only twelve minutes from the Fall.'

*

Shannow knew instantly how it had occurred. The last thought in his mind as the violet light had flared around him was to get to Arizona before the Fall. And he had remembered that awful morning as the plane lifted off – as indeed it was even now lifting off on that far coast.

'I need you with me, Lucas,' he said. 'Where is the portable Amaziga used?'

'She took one with her, Mr Shannow. There is a second, in the back bedroom – a small cupboard beneath the television and video units.' Shannow moved swiftly through to the room. The portable unit was even smaller than that which Amaziga had carried through to the world of the Bloodstone; Shannow almost missed it, believing it to be a stereo headset.

'Eight minutes, Mr Shannow,' came the calm voice of Lucas as the Jerusalem Man strode back into the main room.

'How do I hook up these leads?' he asked.

Lucas told him. Then: 'Take the blue lead and attach it to the point at the rear of the machine immediately above the main power socket.' Shannow did so. 'Transferring files,' said Lucas. 'We have five minutes and forty seconds.'

'How long will the transfer take?'

'Three minutes.'

Shannow moved to the doorway, staring out over the desert. It was still, and hot, the sky a searing blue. A huge jet passed overhead, gliding west towards the runways of Los Angeles Airport – runways that would be under billions of tons of roaring ocean long before the plane touched down.

The earth trembled beneath Shannow's feet and he reached out, taking hold of the door-frame.

'Almost there, Mr Shannow,' said Lucas. 'I managed to save forty-two seconds. Unhook me – and put on the headset.'

Shannow unplugged the lead and clipped the portable to his gun-belt. There was no ON/OFF switch and Lucas's voice sounded tinny through the headphones. 'I think you had better run, Mr Shannow,' he said, his voice eerily calm.

The Jerusalem Man moved swiftly out of the house, leaping the porch steps and sprinting towards the old stone circle. 'One minute twelve seconds,' said Lucas.

The ground juddered . . . Shannow stumbled. Righting himself, he ran up the hill and into the circle.

'Get us back,' he said.

'What are the co-ordinates?' Lucas asked.

'Co-ordinates? What do you mean?'

'A trace. A date and a place. We must know where we are going?'

'Beth McAdam's farm . . . but I don't know exactly *when*.' The wind began to build, clouds racing across the sky.

'Twenty-eight seconds,' said Lucas. 'Hold tightly to the Stone, Mr Shannow.'

Violet light flared around them, as the wind shrieked and rose. 'Where are we going?' shouted Shannow.

'Trust me,' said Lucas softly.

*

Clem Steiner eased back from the brow of the hill, keeping his body low as he clambered down to join the others. Zerah and the children had dismounted, Nestor still sat in the saddle.

'What did you see?' asked Zerah.

'Kids, you hold on to the horses,' said Clem, with a smile to Oz.

'I want to see!' Esther complained, in a high voice.

Clem lifted a finger to his lips. 'Best stay quiet, girl, for there are bad men close by.'

'Sorry,' whispered Esther, putting her hand over her mouth.

Nestor dismounted and, together with Clem and Zerah, walked to just below the hilltop before dropping down to his belly and removing his hat. The others crawled alongside. On the plain below, no more than two hundred yards away, Nestor could see a dozen riders in horned helms and black breastplates, holding rifles in their hands. They were riding slowly alongside a walking group of men, women and children – maybe seventy of them, guessed Nestor.

'What are they doing?' asked Nestor. 'Who are they?'

'Hellborn.'

'There aren't any Hellborn,' snapped the boy. 'They was all wiped out.'

'Then this is obviously just a dream,' responded Clem testily.

'Oh, they're Hellborn all right,' said Zerah. 'Zeb and I were with Daniel Cade during the First Hellborn War. And those people with them are being treated as prisoners.'

Nestor saw that she was right. The Hellborn – if that's what they were – were riding with their rifles pointed in at the group. 'They're moving towards Pilgrim's Valley,' said Nestor, thinking of the quiet strength of Captain Leon Evans and his Crusaders. They'd know how to deal with the situation.

As if reading the youngster's mind, Clem spoke. 'They can already see the buildings in the distance, but it don't seem to worry them none,' he whispered.

'What does that mean?'

The old woman cut in. 'It means that the town is already taken – or everyone has gone.'

Nestor, whose eyes were sharper than his companions', spotted a rider in the distance galloping out from the settlement. As he neared, Nestor squinted to see better, but he did not know the man.

Clem Steiner swore softly. 'Well, I'll be a monkey's uncle,' he said. 'Damned if that isn't Jacob Moon.'

Nestor had heard the name of the fearsome Jerusalem Rider. 'We have to help him,' he said. 'He can't take them alone!' He started to rise, but Clem dragged him down.

'Let's just watch, boy. I don't think Moon has come for a fight.'

Nestor swung on him, his face twisted in anger. 'Yes, I can believe you don't want to see Jacob Moon,' he hissed. 'He'd make short work of a thieving brigand named Laton Duke.'

The rider closed on the Hellborn and raised his hand in greeting. One of the prisoners, a woman in a flowing blue skirt, ran to Moon, grabbing at his leg. The Jerusalem Rider kicked out to send her sprawling to the dust. A young man shouted and leapt at the rider. The gunshot echoed across the plain, and the man fell back screaming and clutching his shoulder.

'My God,' said Nestor, 'Moon is with them!'

'I'd say that was a pretty accurate assessment,' muttered Zerah. 'What I don't understand is why the Hellborn are taking prisoners. They didn't in the old days. Just blood and slaughter. It makes no sense. There can't be that many of them, so why waste time and men guarding prisoners? You understand it, Meneer Steiner?'

'No. But if Moon is involved there must be a profit in it. The man is a thief and a murderer – and possibly the fastest man with a pistol I ever knew.'

'As fast as you?' sneered Nestor.

Steiner appeared to ignore the sarcasm. 'I'd say faster. Let's hope it doesn't need to be put to the test.'

'Scared, are you?'

'Oh, for God's sake grow up!' snapped Clem. 'You think you're the first *boy* who ever learned that the world isn't made up of knights and damsels? Yes, I was . . . am . . . Laton Duke. And no, I'm not proud of it. I was weak where I should have been strong, and too damn strong where I should have been weak. But I don't owe you anything, son, and you have no right to take out your bitterness on me. Now I've taken it so far, because you're a nice lad, and learning about the Deacon's lies was a bitter blow for you. But you'd better shape up, son, because we're in deep water here and I fear we'll be lucky to get out with our lives.'

'You heed those words, young man,' said Zerah. 'I got two children to take care of and the forces of evil seem mighty strong in these parts right now. I don't believe it would be smart to war amongst ourselves.' Turning to Clem, she smiled. 'Where to now, Meneer Brigand?'

'There's a woman I know lives near by . . . if she's still alive. We'll make for her place. You agreed on that, Nestor, or do you want to ride your own road?'

Nestor fought down a cutting response and took a deep breath. 'I'll ride with you that far,' he said.

*

Amaziga Archer's mind was calm as the wind screamed above the old Aztec temple, tearing rocks from the ancient walls, hurling them through the air as if they were made of paper. Uprooted trees smashed against the walls and the noise was deafening as she and Sam cowered in the underground chamber. The storm wind was still increasing – close to 600 miles an hour, she remembered from her studies of the Fall of the world. As the earth toppled on its axis the setting sun rose in the west, the winds howled across the earth, to be followed by a tidal wave the like of which no man or woman had ever seen – and lived.

What strange beings we are, thought Amaziga, as she sheltered from the terrible storm. Why are we hiding, when the tidal wave will destroy us both? Why not stand outside and let the demon winds carry us up to the Heavens? She knew the answer. The instinct for survival – to cling to those precious last seconds of life.

As suddenly as it had come the wind died.

Amaziga stumbled outside, Sam following, and ran up the hill – scrambling over fallen trees, clambering up on to the steps of the pyramid, higher and higher, all the time watching the west for the gigantic wall of death that would soon be bearing down upon them. What was it the Prophet Isaiah had predicted? *And the seas shall tip from their bowls, and not one stone be left upon another.*

Wise old man, she thought, as she climbed the last steps to the summit.

'Look!' shouted Sam.

Amaziga swung to the west. The sight was incredible beyond belief and, just for a second, she felt privileged to see it. The oncoming wall was black and filled the sky. A thousand feet high. More. Much more, she realised, for here, in this remote jungle they were already two thousand feet above sea level.

'Oh, God!' whispered Sam. 'Dear God!'

They clung to one another as the wall raced towards them. 'I love you, Sam. Always have – always will.'

Glancing down at her, he smiled. Then he kissed her lightly upon the lips.

Violet light flared around them, and a great roaring filled their ears . . .

As the light faded they found themselves standing on an island, no more than sixty yards in diameter, the ocean all around them as far as the eye could see. Jon Shannow was standing some ten feet away, but he was so much older than when last they said their farewells, his beard long and white, streaked with shades of darker grey. He was wearing the portable computer.

Amaziga grinned at him. 'I don't know how you did it, but I'm grateful,' she said.

'It wasn't me, lady,' he told her, unclipping the machine and removing the headphones, which he passed to her. Amaziga slipped them into place, and heard the soft sweet sound of Lucas's voice.

'Electronic cavalry, darling,' he said.

'What did you do?'

'I moved us forward six days. The tidal wave has passed, the sea receding.'

'How did you find me?'

'Ah, Amaziga, I am always linked with you. I need no co-ordinates. The man Lucas loved you until the moment he died. Beyond, perhaps – I don't know. Therefore I love you too. Is that so strange?'

'No,' she said, humbled. 'Where can we go?'

'Under normal circumstances,' he said, 'anywhere you desired. But the Stone is Mr Shannow's, and he is fighting the Bloodstone. I need co-ordinates to bring him home. A date I can home in on.'

Amaziga called out to Shannow, who came across and sat beside her. For some time she questioned him about the events leading up to his journey through the Gateway, but there was nothing she could use. Sam joined in, asking about the positions of the stars, the cycles of the moon, the seasons. At last Amaziga gave up. 'We have to think of something else,' she said.

Shannow leaned back, weary and fighting back despair.

'You look more human as an old man,' said Amaziga, 'less fearsome.'

Shannow smiled. 'I know. I met . . . myself . . . Not a happy encounter. To see such youth, and to know where he was headed, yet being able to say nothing. Strange, as a young man newly wounded with no memory, I saw an ancient man who looked close to death. He said I could call him Jake. I recognised nothing of myself in him. And then to meet him again, as Jake, and see a face without lines and wrinkles, a body possessing the strength and suppleness I had long forgotten. He looked like a boy to me.'

Amaziga leaned forward. 'You met him in the mountains? Before he went to Domango?'

'One day before,' said Shannow.

'And how long after the meeting did you travel through the Gateway?'

'Eight . . . nine days, I think. Why?'

'Because I met you on the outskirts of Domango. Lucas *knows* that date. If we move forward . . . say ten days, we should get you back in the same time line. What do you think, Lucas?'

'Yes, I can do that,' Lucas told her. 'The question is where. I have no files on the power point Shannow used. We will have to come through elsewhere. You know the area. Where do you suggest?'

'There's a strong power centre close to Pilgrim's Valley. I used it myself twice,' she said.

'Then that will be our destination,' said Lucas. 'But I cannot guarantee to arrive at the same time, or on the same day. Erring on the side of caution, the margin of error could be as much as a week after he left.'

*

Four days had passed. Wallace Nash and Beth had repaired the damaged window shutters as best they could, while Isis and Dr Meredith had cut what meat remained from the slaughtered farm animals. On the third day the Deacon's mule had trotted back into the yard. Beth clapped her hands when she saw it. 'You son of a gun!' she said, smiling and walking forward to rub the mule's nose. 'You got away!' With ropes from the barn they hauled away the corpses of the Wolvers and the slaughtered oxen. Beth dug up vegetables from the small plot at the rear of the barn and stored them in the kitchen of the main building. She also filled several buckets of water from the well, and left them inside the house. On the fourth day, Dr Meredith helped Beth carry Jeremiah's body out to the ground behind the ruined barn. Wallace and the doctor dug a deep grave. Isis stood beside Beth as the earth was shovelled on to the blanket-wrapped corpse.

'He was a good man,' said Isis, holding on to Beth's hand.

'Even good men die. We all die,' said Beth. 'Let's hope this is an end to the terror.'

'It isn't,' said Isis. 'Men with horned helms and black armour will be riding here soon. The Bloodstone cannot be stopped, Beth. I felt him, and his power, his lust for blood and his terrible determination. And now the Deacon is gone. I think we are all going to die.'

Beth hefted her rifle and said nothing.

Meredith stood beside the grave and laid down his shovel. His slender face was bathed in sweat and his eyes were downcast, his sorrow evident. 'I'm sorry, Jeremiah,' he said. 'You were kind to me – and I killed you.'

'Don't dwell on it,' said Beth. 'You made a mistake. We all make mistakes. You just have to learn to live with them.' She turned to the red-headed youngster. 'As I recall, Wallace, you have a fine voice. Why don't you sing for us? "Rock of Ages" ought to be just fine.'

'Riders coming,' said Wallace. Beth cocked the rifle as she swung.

Clem Steiner rode into the yard and dismounted; Nestor Garrity sat on his horse, hands on the saddle pommel. The boy looked older, thought Beth, his face gaunt, his eyes tired. Behind him came two more horses, one bearing a stick-thin old woman with leathered skin and bright blue eyes, the other carrying two children.

'Didn't find him, Beth,' said Clem, 'but he's alive.'

She nodded absently and walked to where the old woman was dismounting. 'Welcome to my home,' said Beth, introducing herself.

The old woman gave a weary smile. 'Good to be here, child. I'm Zerah Wheeler and it's been quite a journey. I see you're burying someone. Don't let me interfere with the words of farewell.'

'There's food and drink in the house,' Beth told her. Together the two women lifted the youngsters from the horse, and Zerah led them inside. 'All right, Wallace,' said Beth. 'Let's hear the hymn!'

His voice was strong and surprisingly deep and the words of the old hymn rolled out over the hillsides, with Clem, Beth and Nestor joining in. Isis wept, and remembered the many kindnesses she had enjoyed from Jeremiah.

At last the song ended and Beth walked away from the grave, linking arms with Clem. He told her of their travels, and how Nestor had been forced to kill. She listened gravely. 'Poor Nestor,' she said. 'He always was a romantically inclined boy. But he's strong, Clem, he'll get over it. I wish Jon was here. There's more trouble coming.'

'I know,' he said, and told her of the horned riders herding prisoners towards the town. In turn she explained about the Deacon and the Bloodstone, and the spell of changing he had placed over the Wolvers.

'Maybe we should get away from here,' said Clem. 'Far and fast.'

'I don't think so, Clem. First, we've only four horses and ten people – and one of those is badly wounded. You remember Josiah Broome?'

'Sure. Inoffensive man, hated violence.'

'He still does. He was shot down, Clem – by Jerusalem Riders.'

Clem nodded. 'Never did trust that bunch – especially with Jacob Moon in the lead. The man's rotten through to the core. I saw him with the Hellborn.' Clem grinned at her. 'So we stay here then?'

'It's my home, Clem. And you said yourself it's built like a fortress. No one's been able to drive me off it so far.'

Clem swore. 'Looks like that's going to be put to the test, Beth darlin',' he said.

Beth looked up. On the far hillside to the north she saw a line of riders, sitting on their horses and staring down at the farmhouse. 'I think we had better get inside,' she said.

Arm in arm they walked slowly towards the house. The riders were some two hundred yards distant. Beth counted them as she walked; there were around fifty men, all wearing horned helms and carrying rifles.

Inside the house she sent Wallace and Nestor upstairs to watch from the bedroom windows, while Zerah took up a rifle and positioned herself at the downstairs window. Dr Meredith sat on the floor by the fire, beside Isis, and the young mother and her baby. Clem glanced at the sandy-haired man. 'You need a spare weapon, Meneer?' he asked.

Meredith shook his head. 'I can't kill,' he said.

Josiah Broome, his thin chest bandaged, a bloodstain showing through it, moved into the main room. 'What's happening?' His eyes were feverish, and cold sweat bathed his face. He saw Clem and smiled. 'Well, well, if it isn't young Steiner. Good to see you, my boy.' Suddenly he sagged against the door-frame. 'Damn,' he whispered. 'Weaker than I thought.'

Clem took his arm and led him back into the bedroom, laying the wounded man on the bed. 'I think you should stay here, Meneer. You are in no condition to fight.'

'Who are we fighting, Clem?'

'Bad men, Josiah, but don't you worry. I'm still pretty good with a pistol.'

'Too good,' said Josiah sadly, his eyes closing.

Clem rejoined the others. The Hellborn had left the hillside and were riding slowly towards the building. Beth stepped outside. Clem grabbed her arm. 'What the Hell. . . ?'

'Let's hear what they've got to say,' said Beth.

'Why?' asked Clem. 'You think they've stopped by for Baker's and biscuits?'

Beth ignored him and waited on the porch, her rifle cradled in her arms. Clem took off his jacket and stood beside her, hand resting on the butt of his pistol.

*

Beth stood quietly watching the riders. They were grim men, hard-eyed and wary, their faces sharp, their eyes stern. The look of fanatics, she thought, ungiving, unbending. They wore black breastplates engraved with swirls of silver, and black horned helms buckled under the chin. In their hands were short-barrelled rifles, and pistols were strapped to their hips. Yet the most disturbing feature for Beth was that each of them had a Bloodstone in the centre of their foreheads. Like the wolves, she thought. The Hellborn rode into the yard, fanning out before the house. A lean-faced warrior kneed his horse forward and sat before her. His eyes were the grey of a winter sky, and there was no warmth in the gaze. His helmet was also horned, but the tips had been dipped in gold.

'I am Shorak,' he said, 'First Lieutenant of the Second Corps. This land is now the property of the Lord of Hell.' Beth said nothing as Shorak's gaze raked the building, noting the riflemen at the slits in the upper windows. 'I am here,' he said, returning his stare to Beth, 'to escort you to the Lord Sarento, so that you may pay homage and learn of his greatness at first hand. You will need no possessions, nor weapons of any kind, though you may bring food for the journey.'

Beth looked up at the man, then at the others who sat on their horses silently. 'Never heard of the Lord Sarento,' she told the leader.

He leaned forward, the sun glinting on the golden horns of his helmet. 'That is your loss, woman, for he is the Living God, the Lord of All. Those who serve him well gain eternal life, and joy beyond imagining.'

'This is my home,' Beth told him. 'I have fought for it, and killed those who would take it from me. I raised children here, and I guess I'll die here. If the Lord Sarento wants me to pay homage he can come here himself. I'll bake him a cake. Now, if that's all you wanted to tell me I suggest you ride off. I've work to do.'

Shorak seemed unconcerned by her refusal. He sat quietly for a moment, then spoke again. 'You do not understand me, woman. I shall make it plain. Gather food and we will escort you to the Lord. Refuse and we will kill you all. And the manner of your passing will be painful. Now, there are others within the house and I suggest you speak to them. Not all of them will wish to die. You have until noon to make a decision. We will return then.'

Wheeling his horse, Shorak led the riders back out to the hillside.

'Polite, wasn't he?' said Clem.

Beth ignored the humour and strode inside. The first person to speak was the young mother, Ruth. 'I want to go with them, Frey McAdam,' she said. 'I don't want any more fear and fighting.'

'It would seem the only course,' agreed Dr Meredith. 'We can't outfight them.'

Wallace and Nestor came downstairs to join in the discussion. Beth poured herself a mug of water and sipped it, saying nothing. 'How much ammunition we got?' Wallace asked.

Beth smiled. 'A hundred rounds for the rifles. Twenty for my pistol.'

'I've got thirty,' Clem said.

'We mustn't fight them,' said Ruth. 'We mustn't! I've got my baby to think of. What's so hard about paying homage to someone? I mean, it's only words.'

'Speaking of which,' remarked Zerah Wheeler, 'we only have *their* word for it that paying homage is all they want. Once outside and unarmed, they can do as they damn well please with us.'

'Why would they want to harm us?' asked Dr Meredith. 'It would make no sense.'

'They are Hellborn,' put in Isis, 'and it was their master who sent the wolves against us.'

'I don't care about that!' shouted Ruth. 'I just don't want to die!'

'Nobody wants to die,' snapped Beth. 'Wallace, get back upstairs and watch them. I don't want them sneaking up on us.'

'Yes, Frey,' he said, and returned to his post.

Nestor spoke. 'When we saw them heading towards the town they were leading a group of prisoners. They didn't kill none of them. Maybe it's just like the man said – just paying homage to their leader.'

Beth turned to Clem. 'You're not saying much?'

Clem shrugged. 'I don't think there's much to say. I don't know where these Hellborn came from, but if they're anything like the warriors of the First War they're murdering savages: they'll rape and torture the women and mutilate the men. And I'm not surrendering my weapons to the likes of them.'

'You're crazy!' screamed Ruth. 'You'll condemn us all to death!'

'Shut your mouth!' stormed Beth. 'I won't have it! This is no time for hysterics. What do you think, Zerah?'

Zerah put her arms around Esther's shoulder, Oz moved in close and she ruffled his hair. 'I got less to lose than the rest of you, being old and worn out. But I've also been trying to keep these children alive, and I'm kind of torn. You look to me, Frey McAdam, like a woman who's been over the mountain a few times. What do you think?'

'I don't like threats,' said Beth, 'and I don't like men who make them. They want us alive. I don't know why; I don't much care.'

'I can tell you why,' said Isis softly. 'When I went out to the wolf-beasts I felt the power of the Bloodstone. He is hungry, and he feeds on souls. To go to him would mean death.'

'What do you mean, feeds on souls?' sneered Ruth. 'That's insane. You're making it up!'

Isis shook her head. 'He was linked to the wolves. Every time they killed, part of the life was fed back through the Stones in their heads. He is a creature of blood and death. All we are to him is food. The Deacon knew that.'

'And where is he?' hissed Ruth. 'Gone and left us days ago. Run away! Well, I'm not dying here. No matter what any of you say.'

'I think we should vote on it,' said Clem. 'It's getting close to noon.'

Beth called out to Wallace and he stood at the top of the stairs, rifle in hand. 'You called the vote, Clem, so what's your view?' she asked.

'Fight,' said Clem.

'Wallace?'

'I ain't going with them,' said the red-headed youngster.

'Nestor?'

The young man hesitated. 'Fight,' he said.

'Isis?'

'I'm not going with them.'

'Doctor?'

Meredith shrugged. 'I'll go with the majority view,' he said.

'Zerah?'

The old woman kissed Esther on the cheek. 'Fight,' she said.

'I think that about settles it,' said Beth.

Ruth stared at them all. 'You are all crazy!'

'They're coming back,' shouted Wallace.

Beth moved to the dresser and pulled clear three boxes of shells. 'Help yourselves,' she said. 'You youngsters stay down low on the floor.' Esther and Oz scrambled down below the table. Zerah stood and took up her rifle as Beth walked to the door.

'You're not going out there again?' asked Clem.

Beth pulled open the door and stood leaning against the frame, her rifle cocked and ready, and held across her body.

The Hellborn rode, fanning out as before.

Ruth ran across the room, brushing past Beth and sprinting out into the yard. 'I'll pay homage,' she shouted. 'Let me go with you!'

Shorak ignored her and looked at Beth. 'What is your decision, woman?' he asked.

'We stay here,' she said.

'It is all of you or none,' said Shorak. Smoothly he drew his pistol and shot Ruth in the head. The young woman was pole-axed to the ground. Beth swung her rifle and fired, the bullet screaming past Shorak to punch into the chest of the rider beside him and pitch him from the saddle. Clem grabbed Beth, hauling her back inside as bullets smashed into the door-frame and screamed through the room. Nestor kicked shut the door and Clem dropped the bar into place.

Zerah fired three shots through the window, then a bullet took her high in the shoulder, spinning her to the floor. A Hellborn warrior ran to the window. Clem shot him through the face. The door juddered as men hurled themselves against it.

Beth scrambled to her feet. Several more Hellborn reached the window, firing into the room. Zerah, blood drenching her shirt, rolled against the wall beneath the sill. Beth fired, taking a man in the chest. He pitched forward. Another warrior hurled himself against the window, smashing the frame and rolling into the room. Nestor shot him twice. The Hellborn hit the floor face first, twitched, then was still.

Clem ran across the room, tipping the pine table to its side. Shots ripped into the walls of the house, and ricocheted around the room. The door began to splinter. Beth pumped three shots through it, and heard a man scream and fall to the porch.

Nestor ran for the stairs, climbing them two at a time. Bullets struck the wall around him, but he made it to the top and moved to help Wallace. Meredith lay on the floor, holding tightly to Isis, trying to shield her with his body. The two children were crouched down behind the upturned table. In the back of the house the baby started to cry, the sound thin and piercing.

'They're at the back of the house!' bellowed Wallace from upstairs.

Beth looked at Clem and pointed to Josiah Broome's room. 'The back window!' she shouted.

Clem ducked down and crawled across the floor. As he reached the doorway he saw the shutters of the window explode inwards. Rearing up he shot the first man through the throat, catapulting him back into his comrades. Broome was unconscious, but lying directly in the line of fire. Clem dived across to the bed, dragging the wounded man to the floor. Shots exploded all around him, searing through the down-filled quilt and sending feathers into the air. A shot scorched across Clem's neck, tearing the skin. He fired, his bullet entering under the man's chin and up through the brain.

Ducking below the level of the bed, Clem re-loaded. A bullet slashed through the mattress to smash into his thigh, glancing from the bone and ripping across the flesh. Clem hurled himself back and fired three quick shots into the bodies massed at the window. The Hellborn ducked from sight. Clem glanced down at his leg to see blood pouring from the wound. He swore softly.

A man leapt at the window. Clem shot him as he was clambering through, and the body fell across the frame, the dead man's pistol clattering to the floor. Rolling to his belly, Clem crawled across to the weapon, snatching it up.

Then all was silence.

*

Josiah Broome came awake, his mind floating above the fever dream. He was lying on the floor of the bedroom and young Clem Steiner was sitting some four feet away, two pistols in his hands, blood staining his leg.

'What's happening, Clem?' he whispered.

'Hellborn,' answered the shootist.

I'm still dreaming, thought Broome. The Hellborn are all gone, destroyed by the Deacon in the bloodiest massacre ever seen in this new world. A shot clipped wood from the window-frame and smashed into a framed embroidery on the far wall. Josiah Broome chuckled. It was the damnedest dream. The embroidery tilted, the centre ripped away. Broome could still read the words: *The works of man shall perish, the love of the Lord abideth always.*

He tried to stand. 'Get down!' ordered Steiner.

'Just a dream, Clem,' said Josiah, getting his knees under him. Steiner launched himself across the floor, his shoulder cannoning into Broome's legs as the older man straightened. Shots smashed into the far wall and the embroidery fell to the floor, the pine frame splitting.

'No dream. You understand? This is no dream!'

Josiah felt the breath forced from his lungs, and his chest wound flared, pain ripping through him.

'But . . . but they can't be Hellborn!'

'Maybe so,' agreed Clem, 'but trust me, Josiah, if they're not originals they are giving a passable fair impression.' The younger man groaned as he twisted up into a sitting position, guns cocked. 'If you feel strong enough, you might think of getting a tourniquet on this wound of mine. Don't want to bleed to death and miss all the fun.'

A shadow crossed the window. Clem's guns roared and Josiah saw a man smashed from his feet. 'Why are they doing this?' Josiah asked.

'I don't feel up to asking them,' Clem told him. 'Rip up a sheet and make some bandages.' Josiah glanced down at the wound in Clem's thigh. Blood was flowing steadily, drenching the black broadcloth pants. His own clothes were laid over the back of a chair. Crawling to them, Josiah pulled the belt clear and returned to Clem. Then he broke off a section of the pine frame that had encased the embroidery. Clem wrapped the belt around his thigh above the wound, stretching the leather tight against the skin. He tried to use the pine to twist the belt tighter, but the wood snapped. The bleeding slowed, but did not stop.

'You better take one of these pistols, Josiah,' said Clem. 'I might pass out.'

Broome shook his head. 'I couldn't kill – not even to save my life. I don't believe in violence.'

'I do so like to meet a man of principle at times like these,' said Clem wearily. Shots sounded from above, and outside a man screamed.

Clem crawled across to the doorway, and glanced into the main room. Beth was behind the table, rifle in hand. The old woman, Zerah, was below the window, a pistol in her fist. Dr Meredith was lying by the western wall, the children and Isis close to him. 'Everyone all right?' called Clem.

'Bastards broke my shoulder,' Zerah told him. 'Hurts like Hell.'

Meredith left the children and crawled across to Zerah. Swiftly he examined her. 'The bullet broke your collar-bone and ripped up and out through the top of your shoulder. It's bleeding freely, but no vital organs were hit. I'll get some bandages.'

'What can you see upstairs?' shouted Beth.

Nestor Garrity's voice floated down to them. 'They've taken shelter at the barn and behind the trough. We downed fourteen of them. Some crawled back to safety, but there's nine bodies that ain't moving. And I think Clem hit two more that we can't see from up here.'

'You keep watch now,' Beth called, 'and let us know when they move.'

'Yes, Frey.'

The baby began to cry, a thin pitiful sound that echoed in the building. Beth turned to Isis. 'There's a little milk left in the kitchen, girl. Be careful as you get it.'

Isis kept low as she crossed the room and went through the kitchen. The back door was barred, the shutters on the window closed tight. The milk was in a tall jug on the top shelf. Isis stood and lifted it down; then moving back to the baby, she sat beside the crib. 'How do I feed her?' she asked Beth.

Beth swore and moved from the table to a chest of drawers, laying down her rifle and removing a pair of fine leather gloves from the second drawer. They were the only gloves she'd ever owned, given to her by her first husband, Sean, just before they were married. Never even worn them, thought Beth. From a sewing box on top of the chest she took a needle and made three small holes through the longest finger of the left-hand glove. Gathering up her rifle, she made her way to the crib. The baby was wailing now and she ordered Isis to lift the infant boy and hold him close. Beth half-filled the glove, then waited until milk began to seep through the needle-holes. At first the baby had difficulty sucking on the glove, and choked. Isis supported the back of his head and he began to feed.

'They're sneaking round the back!' shouted Nestor. 'Can't get a good shot!'

Clem lurched back into the rear bedroom and waited to the right of the window. Shadows moved on the ground outside, and Clem could make out the horns of a Hellborn helmet on the hard-baked earth. There was no way he could tell how many men were outside, and the only way to stop them was to frame himself in the window and open fire. Clem's mouth was dry.

'Do it now,' he told himself, 'or you'll never have the nerve to do it at all.'

Swiftly he spun round, guns blazing through the shattered window. Two men went down, the third returned fire and Clem was hit hard in the chest, but he coolly put a shell through the Hellborn's head. Then he slumped down and fell against the bed.

Josiah Broome crawled alongside him. 'How bad is it?' asked the older man.

'I've had better days,' Clem told him as he struggled to reload. The Hellborn pistol took a larger calibre of shell than his own pistol, and it was empty now. Angrily he cast it aside. 'God damn,' he said bitterly. 'Those sons of bitches are really starting to get my goat!' His gun loaded, he leaned back, too frightened to check the chest wound. Broome moved out into the main room and called for Dr Meredith. The sandy-haired young man made his way to Clem, and the shootist felt the man's fingers probing.

Meredith said nothing and Clem opened his eyes. 'You want to tell me the good news?' he asked.

'It isn't good,' said Meredith softly.

'There's a surprise.' Clem was feeling light-headed and faint, but he clung on. There weren't enough defenders and he wasn't going to die just yet. He coughed. Blood rose in his throat and sprayed out on to Meredith's pale shirt. Clem sank back. The sun was setting, the sky the colour of burning copper. Clem levered himself to his feet, staggered and righted himself by gripping the window-frame.

'What are you doing?' asked Josiah Broome, reaching out to grab Clem's arm. Meredith took hold of Broome's shoulder, drawing him back.

'He's dying,' whispered Meredith. 'He has only minutes left.'

Clem fell across the ruined window, then lifted his leg over the sill. The air was fresh and cool outside, not filled with the acrid smell of black powder. It was a good evening, the sky bright. Clem dropped to the ground and half-fell. Blood filled his throat and he thought he was suffocating, but he swallowed it down and staggered to the corpses, relieving them of their pistols and tossing the weapons through the window. One of the Hellborn was wearing a bandolier of shells. With difficulty, Clem tugged it loose and passed it to Broome.

'Come back inside!' urged Broome.

'I like . . . it . . . here,' whispered Clem, the effort of speaking bringing a fresh bout of coughing.

Clem staggered to the edge of the building. From here he could see the horse trough, and the two men hiding behind it. As he stepped into sight, they saw him and tried to bring their rifles to bear. Clem shot them both. A third man rose from behind the paddock fence and a bullet punched into Clem's body, half spinning him. He returned the fire – but missed.

Falling to his knees, Clem reached into the pocket of his coat, pulling clear his last few shells. Another bullet struck him. The ground was hard against his cheek, and all pain floated away from him. Three Hellborn ran from hiding. Clem heard the pounding of their boots on the earth.

With the last of his strength Clem rolled. There were two shots left in the pistol and he triggered them both, the first shell slamming into the belly of the leading Hellborn, pitching him from his feet, the second tearing into an unprotected throat.

A rifle boomed and Clem saw the last Hellborn stagger to a stop, the top of his head blown away. The body crumpled to the ground.

Clem lay on his back and stared up at the sky. It was unbearably bright for a moment, then the darkness closed in from the sides, until, at last, he was staring at a tiny circle of light at the end of a long, dark tunnel.

Then there was nothing.

*

Nestor and Wallace watched him die. 'He was a tough one,' said Wallace.

'He was Laton Duke,' said Nestor softly.

'Yeah? Well, don't that beat all!' Wallace lifted his rifle to his shoulder and sighted on a man creeping along beneath the paddock fence. He fired, the bullet splintering wood above the man and causing him to dive for cover. 'Damn it! Missed him. Laton Duke, you say? He was sure good with that pistol.'

'He was good,' agreed Nestor sadly. Glancing up at the red-headed youngster, he asked, 'You frightened, Wal?'

'Yep.'

'You don't look it.'

The youngster shrugged. 'My folks were never much on showing stuff . . . you know, emotions and the like. Busted my arm once and cried. My dad set the bone, then whacked me alongside the head for blubbing.' He sniffed and chuckled. 'I did love that old goat!' Wallace fired again. 'Got him, by God!'

Nestor glanced out to see the Hellborn warrior lying still in the gathering dusk.

'You think they'll attack us after dark?'

'Bet on it,' said Wallace. 'Let's hope there's a good clear sky and plenty of moonlight.'

Movement in the distance caught Nestor's eye. 'Oh, no!' he whispered. Wallace saw them too. Scores of Hellborn were riding down the hillside.

Jacob Moon was with them.

As they neared, Wallace tried a shot at the Jerusalem Rider – but missed, his shot thumping into the shoulder of a rider to Moon's left. The Hellborn dismounted and ran to the shelter of the barn. Wallace spat through the rifle slit, but said nothing.

Nestor backed from the room and called down the news to Beth McAdam.

'We saw them,' she called back. 'Clem threw in some pistols. Better come down here and help yourself, son.' Nestor moved swiftly downstairs. Isis and Meredith held pistols now, but Josiah Broome sat defiantly on the floor, his hands across his knees.

'Are you some sort of coward?' asked Nestor. 'Haven't you even got the guts to fight for your life?'

'That's enough of that!' stormed Beth. 'Sometimes it takes more courage to stick by what you believe in. Now get back upstairs and stay with Wallace.'

'Yes, Frey,' he said meekly.

Beth knelt by Josiah Broome, resting her hand on his shoulder. 'How are you feeling?' she asked.

'Sad, Beth,' he told her, patting her hand. 'We never learn, do we? We never change. Always killing and causing pain.'

'Not all of us. Some of us just fight to stay alive. When it starts, stay low.'

'I'm ashamed to admit that I wish he was here now,' said Josiah. Beth nodded, remembering Shannow in his prime. There was a force and a power about him that made him appear unbeatable, unstoppable.

'So do I, Josiah. So do I.' Beth called the children to her, and told them to sit with Josiah. Esther snuggled down and buried her face in the old man's shoulder. Broome put his arm around her.

Oz pulled clear his small pistol. 'I'm going to fight,' said the child.

Beth nodded. 'Wait till they're inside,' she said.

'They're coming!' Nestor yelled.

Beth ran to the window. Zerah, blood seeping from her shoulder wound, stood to the left of the window with her pistol ready. Beth risked a glance. The Hellborn were coming in a solid wedge of men, racing across the yard.

The few defenders could never stop them.

There was no need to aim and Beth and Zerah triggered their pistols into the advancing wedge of attackers. Bullets smashed into the room, ricocheting around the walls.

Upstairs Nestor levered shells into the rifle, sending shot after shot into the charging Hellborn.

They were half-way to the house when Wallace gave a whoop. 'Son of a bitch!' he yelled.

More riders were thundering down the hillside. But they were not Hellborn. Many wore the grey shield shirts of the Crusaders.

As they rode they opened fire, a volley of shots ripping through the ranks of the charging men. The Hellborn slowed, then swung to meet their attackers. Nestor saw several horses go down, but the rest came on, surging into the yard.

'Son of a bitch!' yelled Wallace again.

The Hellborn scattered, but were shot down as they ran.

Wallace and Nestor continued to fire until their bullets ran out. Then they raced downstairs.

Beth staggered to a chair and sat down, the pistol suddenly heavy in her tired hand. A face appeared at the window. It was Tobe Harris.

'Good to see you, Tobe,' said Beth. 'I swear to God you have the handsomest face I ever did see.'

*

Nestor gathered up Beth's pistol and ran out into the yard where bodies lay everywhere, twisted in death. The Crusaders from Purity had moved on into the fields, chasing down the fleeing Hellborn. Nestor couldn't believe it. He was going to live! Death had seemed so certain. Unavoidable and inevitable. The sun was sinking behind the mountains and Nestor felt tears well into his eyes. He could smell the gun-smoke, and through it the fresh, sweet scent of the moisture on the grass.

'Oh, God!' he whispered.

Horsemen came riding back into the yard, led by a tall, square-shouldered man in a black coat. The man lifted his flat-crowned hat from his head and produced a handkerchief from his pocket, wiping his face and beard.

'By the Lord, you fought well here, boy,' he said. 'I am Padlock Wheeler. The Deacon sent for me.'

'I'm Nestor Garrity, sir.'

'You look all in, son,' said Wheeler, dismounting and tethering his horse to a rail. Around him other Crusaders moved among the dead. Occasionally a pistol shot would sound as they found wounded Hellborn. Nestor looked away; it was so cold, so merciless. Padlock Wheeler moved alongside him, patting his shoulder. 'I need to know what is happening here, son. The man, Tobe, told us of the giant Wolvers, but we've now had two run-ins with Hellborn warriors. Where are they from?'

Isis walked from the doorway. Padlock Wheeler bowed and the blonde girl smiled wearily. 'They are from beyond the Gates of Time, Meneer. The Deacon told me that. And their leader is a soul-stealer, a taker of life.'

Wheeler nodded. 'We'll deal with him, young lady. But where is the Deacon?'

'He vanished through one of the Gateways. He has gone seeking help.'

Nestor stood silently by, his thoughts confused. The Deacon was a liar and a fraud. It was all lies; lies and death and violence.

His mouth tasted of bile and he found himself shivering, his stomach churning with nausea.

One of the Crusaders shouted to Wheeler, and pointed to the east. Three riders were coming. Nestor leaned against the porch rail and watched them approach. In the lead was a white-bearded old man, behind him came a black woman, her head bandaged. Beside her rode a black man, blood staining his white shirt.

'The Deacon!' said Padlock Wheeler, his voice exultant. Leaving the porch, Wheeler stepped down to the yard, raising his arm in greeting.

At that moment a body moved beside his feet, springing up with gun in hand. An arm encircled Wheeler's neck and a pistol barrel was thrust under his chin. No one moved.

The gunman was Jacob Moon. 'Stay back, you bastards!' shouted the Jerusalem Rider. All was still, save for the slow walking horse which the Deacon rode. Nestor's gaze flicked from the rider to Moon and his victim, and back again. The Deacon wore a long black coat and a pale shirt. His beard shone silver in the moonlight, and his deep-set eyes were focused on Moon. Slowly he dismounted. The black woman and her companion remained where they were, sitting motionless on their horses.

'Let him go,' said the Deacon, his voice deep and steady.

'I want a horse and a chance to ride free from here,' said Moon.

'No,' said the Deacon simply. 'What I will give you is an opportunity to live. Let Padlock go free and you may face me, man to man. Should you triumph, not a man here will stop you.'

'In a pig's eye!' stormed Moon. 'As soon as I let him go, you'll gun me down.'

'I am the Deacon, and I do not lie!'

Moon dragged Padlock further back towards the wall. 'You're not the Deacon!' he screamed. 'I killed him at his summer cabin.'

'You killed an old man who served me well. The man you are holding is Padlock Wheeler, one of my generals in the Unity Wars. He knows me – as do several of these riders. Now, do you have the nerve to face me?'

'Nerve?' snorted Moon. 'You think it takes nerve to shoot down an old goat?'

Nestor blinked. The old man couldn't know who he was threatening. It was madness. 'He's Jacob Moon!' he shouted. 'Don't do it!'

Darkness had fallen now, and the moon was bright in the sky. The Deacon appeared not to hear the youngster's words. 'Well?' he said, removing his coat. Nestor saw he was wearing two guns.

'I'll go free?' asked Moon. 'I have your word on that? Your oath?'

'Let every man here understand,' said the Deacon. 'Should I die, this man rides free.'

Moon threw Padlock Wheeler aside and stood for a moment, gun in hand. Then he laughed and moved out into the open. Behind him men opened up a space, spreading out of the line of fire.

'I don't know why you want to die, old man, but I'll oblige you. You should have listened to the boy. I am Jacob Moon, the Jerusalem Rider, and I've never been beat.' He holstered his pistol.

'And I,' said the Deacon, 'am Jon Shannow, the Jerusalem Man.' As he spoke the Deacon smoothly palmed his pistol. There was no sudden jerk, no indication of tension or drama. The words froze Moon momentarily, but his hand flashed for his pistol. He was fast, infinitely faster than the old man, but his reaction time was dulled by the words the Deacon had spoken. A bullet smashed into his belly and he staggered back a pace. His own gun boomed, but then three shots thundered into him, spinning him from his feet.

The world continued to spin as Moon struggled to his knees. He tried to raise his pistol, but his hand was empty. He blinked sweat from his eyes and stared up at the deadly old man, who was now walking towards him.

'The wages of sin is death, Moon,' were the last words he heard.

Padlock Wheeler rushed to the Deacon's side. The old man fell into his arms. Nestor saw the blood then on the Deacon's shirt. Two men ran forward, and they half-carried the Deacon into the house. Nestor followed them.

The first person he saw was Beth. Her face was unnaturally pale and she stood with eyes wide, hand over her mouth, as they laid the Deacon on the floor.

'Oh, Christ!' she whispered. 'Oh, dear Christ!' Falling to her knees beside him, she stroked a hand through his grey hair. 'How can it be you, Jon? You are so old?'

The man smiled weakly, his head resting in Padlock Wheeler's lap. 'Long story,' he said, his voice distant.

The black woman entered the room and knelt by Shannow. 'Use the Stone,' she commanded.

'Not enough power.'

'Of course there is!'

'Not for me . . . and the Bloodstone. Don't worry about me, lady. I'll live long enough to do what must be done. Where is Meredith?'

'I'm here, sir,' said the sandy-haired young man.

'Get me into the back room. Check the wound. Strap it. Whatever.'

Wheeler and Meredith carried him through the house. Beth rose and turned to face the black woman. 'It's been a long time, Amaziga.'

'Three hundred years and more,' said Amaziga. 'This is my husband, Sam.' The black man smiled and offered his left hand; the right was strapped to his chest.

Beth shook hands. 'You've been in the wars too, I see.'

Amaziga nodded. 'We came through a Gateway north of here. We walked for a while, but we were surprised by some Hellborn warriors. There were four of them. Sam took a bullet in the shoulder. I got this graze,' she said, lightly touching the bandage on her brow. 'Shannow killed them. It's what he's good at.'

'He's good at a damn sight more than that,' said Beth, reddening, 'but then that's something you've never been capable of understanding.'

Turning on her heel, she followed the others into the bedroom. Shannow was in the bed, Meredith examining the wound, while Josiah Broome sat to the left, holding Shannow's hand. Wheeler stood at the foot of the bed. Beth moved alongside the doctor. The wound was low, and had ripped through the flesh above the hip-bone to emerge in a jagged tear on Shannow's side. Blood was flowing freely and Shannow's face was grey, his eyes closed.

'I need to stop the flow,' said Meredith. 'Get me needle and thread.'

Outside Nestor introduced himself to Amaziga Archer and her husband. The woman was astonishingly beautiful, he thought, despite the grey steaks in her hair. 'Is he really the Jerusalem Man?' asked Nestor.

'Really,' said Amaziga, moving away to the kitchen. Sam smiled at the boy.

'A living legend, Nestor.'

'I can't believe he beat Jacob Moon. I just can't believe it! And him so old.'

'I expect Moon found it even harder to believe. Now excuse me, son, but I'm weary, and I need to rest. Is there a bed somewhere?'

'Yes, sir. Upstairs. I'll show you.'

'No need, son. I may be wounded, but I believe I still have the strength to find a bed.'

As Sam moved away Nestor saw Wallace sitting by the window with Zerah Wheeler. The red-head was chatting to the children. Esther was giggling and young Oz was staring at Wallace with undisguised admiration.

Nestor walked from the house.

Outside the Crusaders were clearing away the corpses, dragging them to the field beyond the buildings. Several campfires had been lit in the lee of the barn, and men were sitting quietly talking in groups.

Isis was sitting by the paddock fence, staring out over the moonlit hills. When Nestor joined her she looked up and smiled. 'It is a wonderful night,' she said.

Nestor glanced up at the glittering stars. 'Yes,' he agreed. 'It's good to be alive.'

*

Beth sat beside Shannow's bed, Padlock Wheeler standing beside her. 'By God, Deacon, I never thought to hear you lie,' said Wheeler. 'But it did the trick; it threw him, right enough.'

Shannow smiled weakly. 'It was no lie, Pad.' Slowly, and with great effort, he told the story of his travels, beginning with the attack on his church, his rescue by the *Wanderers*, the fight with Aaron Crane and his men, and finally his meeting with Amaziga beyond the town of Domango.

'It really was you then, in my church!' said Wheeler. 'By Heaven, Deacon, you never cease to amaze me.'

'There's more, Pad,' said Shannow. He closed his eyes and spoke of the Bloodstone, and the ruined world from which it came.

'How do we fight such a beast?' asked Padlock Wheeler.

'I have a plan,' said Shannow. 'Not much of one, I'll grant you, but, with the grace of God, it'll give us a chance.'

Zerah Wheeler entered the room, her shoulder bandaged and her arm bound across her chest. 'Leave the wounded man be,' she said, 'and say hello to your mother.'

Padlock spun, jaw agape. 'Jesus wept, Mother! I did not know you were here. And you're wounded!' Moving to her side, he threw his arm around her shoulder.

'Whisht, you lummox! You'll set it bleeding again,' she scolded, knocking his hand away. 'Now come outside and leave the man to rest. You too, Beth.'

'I'll be with you soon,' said Beth quietly as Zerah led her son from the room. Josiah Broome rose and patted Shannow's arm. 'It is good to see you, my friend,' he said, and left the wounded man alone with Beth. She took his hand and sighed.

'Why did you not tell me who you were?' she asked.

'Why did you not recognise me?' he countered.

She shrugged. 'I should have. I should have done so many things, Jon. And now it's all wasted and gone. I couldn't take it, you see. You changed – from man of action to preacher. It was such a change. Why did it have to be so drastic, so radical?'

He smiled wearily. 'I can't tell you, Beth. Except that I have never understood compromise. For me, it is all or nothing. Yet despite my efforts, I failed – in everything. I didn't find Jerusalem and, as a preacher, I couldn't remain a pacifist.' He sighed. 'When the church was burning I felt a terrible rage. It engulfed me. And then as the Deacon . . . I thought I could make a difference. Bring God in to the world . . . establish discipline. I failed at that too.'

'History alone judges success or failure, Shannow,' said Amaziga, moving into the room.

Beth glanced up, ready to tell the woman to leave, but she felt Shannow's hand squeeze hers and saw him shake his head. Amaziga sat down on the other side of the bed. 'Lucas tells me you have a plan, but he won't share it with me.'

'Let me speak with him.' Amaziga passed him the headphones and the portable. Shannow winced as he tried to raise his arm. Amaziga leaned forward and settled the headphones into place, slipping the microphone from its groove and twisting it into position. 'Leave me,' he said.

Beth rose first. Amaziga seemed reluctant to go, but at last she too stood up and followed Beth from the room.

Outside, Padlock and his brother Seth were sitting with Zerah, Wallace and the children. Beth walked out into the moonlight, past Samuel Archer who was sitting on the porch, watching the stars; Amaziga sat beside him. Beth walked out, breathing the night air. Nestor and Isis came towards her, both smiling as they passed.

Dr Meredith was standing by the paddock fence, looking out over the hills.

'All alone, Doctor?' she said, moving to stand beside him.

He grinned boyishly. 'Lots to think about, Frey McAdam. So much has happened these past few days. I loved that old man; Jeremiah was good to me. It hurts that I caused his death; I would do anything to bring him back.'

'There's things we can't change,' said Beth softly, 'no matter how much we might want to. Life goes on. That's what separates the strong from the weak. The strong move on.'

'You think it will ever change?' he asked suddenly.

'What will change?'

'The world. People. Do you think there'll ever come a day when there are no wars, no needless killing?'

'No,' she said simply. 'I don't.'

'Neither do I. But it's something to strive for, isn't it?'

'Amen to that!'

*

Sarento's hunger was intense, a yawning chasm within him filled with tongues of fire. He strode from the rebuilt palace and out into the wide courtyard. Four Hellborn warriors were sitting together by an archway; they stood as he approached, and bowed. Without thinking he drew their life forces from them, watching them topple to the ground.

His hunger was untouched.

An edge of panic flickered in his soul. For a while, in the late afternoon, he had felt the flow of blood from the men he had sent out to the farm. Since then, nothing.

Walking on, he came out on to a ruined avenue. He could hear the sound of men singing, and on the edge of what had once been a lake garden he saw a group of his men sitting around camp-fires. Beyond them were a score of prisoners.

The hunger tore at him . . .

He approached silently. Men toppled to the ground as he passed. The prisoners, seeing what was happening, began to scream and run. Not one escaped. Sarento's hunger was momentarily appeased. Moving past the dried-out corpses, he walked to the picket line and mounted a tall stallion. There were around thirty horses here, standing quietly, half-asleep. One by one they died.

All save the stallion . . .

Sarento took a deep breath, then reached out with his mind.

Sustenance. I need sustenance, he thought. Already the hunger was returning, and it took all his willpower not to devour the life force of the horse he was riding. Closing his eyes, he allowed his mind to float out over the moonlit land, seeking the soul-scent of living flesh.

Finding it, he kicked the horse into a run. And headed out towards Pilgrim's Valley.

*

Shannow, his side strapped, blood seeping through the bandages, sat at the wide, bullet-ripped table, Padlock Wheeler standing alongside. At the table sat Amaziga Archer and her husband; beside Sam were Seth Wheeler and Beth McAdam. Amaziga spoke, telling them all of the Bloodstone, and the terrible powers he possessed.

'Then what can we do?' asked Seth. 'Sounds like he's invincible.'

Sam shook his head. 'Not quite. His hunger is his Achilles heel: it grows at a geometric rate. Without blood – or life if you prefer – he will weaken and literally starve.'

'So we just keep out of his way? Is that it?' asked Padlock.

'Not quite,' admitted Amaziga. 'We none of us know how long he could survive. He could move from active life into a suspended state, being re-activated only when another life force approaches. But what we hope for is that, in a depleted state, his body will be less immune to gunfire. Every shot that strikes him will leach power from him as he struggles to protect himself. It may be that if we can corner him we can destroy him.'

Seth Wheeler glanced at the beautiful black woman. 'You don't seem too confident,' he said shrewdly.

'I'm not.'

'You said you had a plan,' said Beth, looking at Shannow. His face was grey with pain and weariness, but he nodded. His voice, when he spoke, was barely above a whisper.

'I don't know if I'll have the strength for it, and would be happier should Amaziga's . . . theory . . . prove accurate. Whatever happens we must stop Sarento from reaching Unity, or any major settlement. I have seen the extent of his power.' They were hushed as he told them of the amphitheatre in the other world, with its rank upon rank of dried-out corpses. 'His power can reach for more than a hundred yards. I don't know the limits. What I do know is that when we find him we must hit him with rifle shot, and make sure the riflemen stay well back from him.'

Nestor ran into the room. 'Rider coming,' he said. 'Weirdest-looking man you ever saw.'

'Weird? In what way?' Shannow asked.

'Appears to be painted all in red and black lines.'

'It's him!' shouted Amaziga, lurching to her feet.

Padlock Wheeler gathered up his rifle and ran from the building, shouting for his Crusaders to gather at the paddock fence. The rider was still some two hundred yards distant. Wheeler's mouth was dry. Levering a shell into the breech, he levelled the weapon and fired. The shot missed, and the rider kicked his mount into a gallop.

'Stop the son of a bitch!' yelled Wheeler. Instantly a volley of shots sounded from all around him. The horse went down, spilling the rider to the grass, but he rose and walked steadily towards the farm. Three shots struck him in the chest, slowing him. A shell hammered against his forehead, snapping his head back. Another cannoned against his right knee. Sarento stumbled and fell, but rose again.

Sixty rifles came to bear, bullet after bullet hammering into the man – glancing from his skin, flattening against bone and falling to the grass. Infinitely slowly he pushed forward against the wall of shells. Closer and closer to the men lining the paddock fence.

One hundred and fifty yards. One hundred and forty yards . . .

*

Even through the terrible and debilitating hunger Sarento began to feel pain. At first the bullets struck him almost without notice, like insects brushing his skin, then like hailstones, then like fingers jabbing at him. Now they made him grunt as they slammed home against increasingly bruised skin. A shot hit him in the eye and he fell back with a scream as blood welled under the lid. Lifting his hand to protect his eyes he stumbled forward, the sweet promise of sustenance driving him on.

He was so close now, the scent so strong that he began to salivate.

They could not stop him.

'Sarento!' Above the sound of the gunfire he heard a voice calling his name. Turning his head he saw an old man being supported by a black woman, moving slowly out to his left away from the line of fire. Surprised, he halted. He knew the woman: Amaziga Archer. But she was dead long since. He blinked, his injured eye making it difficult to focus. 'Cease fire!' bellowed the old man and the thunder of guns faded away. Sarento stood upright and stared hard at him, reaching out with his power to read his thoughts. They were blocked from him.

'Sarento!' he called again.

'Speak,' said the Bloodstone. He saw that the old man was wounded; his hunger was so intense that he had to steel himself not to drag the life force from the two as they approached. What helped was that he was intrigued. 'What do you want?'

The old man sagged against the woman. Amaziga took the weight, while at no time taking her eyes from the Bloodstone. He tasted her hatred and laughed. 'I could give you immortality, Amaziga,' he said softly. 'Why not join me?'

'You are a mass murderer, Sarento,' she hissed. 'I despise you!'

'Murder? I have murdered no one,' he said, with genuine surprise. 'They're all alive. In here,' he added, tapping his chest. 'Every one, every soul. I know their thoughts, their dreams, their ambitions. With me they have eternal life. We speak all the time. And they are happy, Amaziga, dwelling with their god. That is paradise.'

'You lie!'

'Gods do not lie,' he said. 'I will show you.' He closed his eyes, and spoke. The voice was not Sarento's.

'Oh, dear God!' whispered Amaziga.

'Get back from him, Mother,' came the voice of her son, Gareth. 'Get back from him!'

'Gareth!' she screamed.

'He's the Devil!' shouted the familiar voice. 'Don't bel—' Sarento's eyes opened, and his own deep voice sounded. 'He has yet to appreciate his good fortune. However, I think my point is made. No one is dead; they merely changed their place of habitation. Now what do you want, for I hunger?'

The old man pushed himself upright. 'I am here to offer you . . . your greatest desire,' he said, his voice faltering.

'My desire is to feed,' said Sarento. 'And this conversation prevents me from so doing.'

'I can open the Gateways to other worlds,' the old man said.

'If that is true,' responded Sarento, 'then all I have to do is draw you into myself and I will have that knowledge.'

'Not so,' said the other, his voice stronger now. 'You used to understand computers, Sarento, but you will not have seen one like this,' he went on, tapping the box clipped to his belt. 'It is a portable. And it is self-aware. Through this machine I can control the Gateways. Should I die, it has instructions to self-destruct. You want to feed? Look around you. How many are here?' Sarento transferred his gaze to the farm buildings. He could see around fifty, perhaps sixty riflemen. 'Not enough, are there?' said the old man. 'But I can take you where there are millions.'

'Why would you do this?'

'To save my friends.'

'You would sacrifice a world to me, for these few?'

'I will take you wherever you choose.'

'And I am to trust you?'

'I am Jon Shannow, and I never lie.'

'You can't, Shannow!' screamed Amaziga, lunging at the portable. Shannow backhanded her across the face, spinning her to the ground. The effort caused him to stagger and his hand moved to his side, where blood oozed through the bandages. Amaziga looked up from the ground. 'How could you, Shannow? What kind of a man are you?'

Sarento reached out and touched Amaziga's mind. She felt it and recoiled. 'So,' said Sarento, 'you are a truth speaker. And wherever I name you will take me?'

'Yes.'

'The twentieth century on earth?'

'Where in the twentieth century?' responded the old man.

'The United States. Los Angeles would be pleasant.'

'I cannot promise you an arrival inside a city. The points of power are usually found in less crowded areas.'

'No matter, Jon Shannow. You, of course, will travel with me.'

'As you wish. We need to make our way to the crest of that hill,' said Shannow. Sarento's eyes followed where he pointed, then swung back to the group by the paddock fence. 'Kill even one of them and you will never see the twentieth century,' warned Shannow.

'How long will this take? I hunger!'

'As soon as we reach the crest.' The man turned and walked slowly towards the hillside. Sarento strode alongside him, lifting him from his feet. He began to run, effortlessly covering the ground. The old man was light, and Sarento felt his life draining away.

'Don't die, old man,' he said. Reaching the summit, he lowered Shannow to the ground. 'Now your promise!'

Shannow swung the microphone into place. 'Do it!' he whispered.

Violet light flared – and then they were gone . . .

Amaziga staggered to her feet. Behind her the riflemen were cheering and hugging one another, but all Amaziga could feel was shame. Turning from the hillside, she walked back to the farmhouse. How could he have done it? How could he?

Beth came out to greet her. 'He succeeded then,' she said.

'If you can call it success.'

'We're still alive, Amaziga. I call that success.'

'Was the cost worth it? Why did I help him? He's doomed a world.' When the Bloodstone had appeared Shannow had called her to him.

'*I have to get close to him,*' *he said.* '*I need you!*'

'*I don't think I can take your weight. Let Sam help!*'

'*No. It must be you!*'

Sam came out to join them now. Laying his hand on Amaziga's shoulder, he leaned down and kissed her brow. 'What have I done, Sam?' she asked.

'What you had to do,' he assured her. Together and hand in hand they walked away to the far fields. Beth stayed for some time, staring at the hillside. Zerah Wheeler and the children joined her.

'Never seen the like,' said Zerah. 'Gone, just like that!'

'Just like that,' echoed Beth, holding firm against the yawning emptiness within. She remembered Shannow as she had first seen him, more than two decades before – a harsh, lonely man, driven to search for a city he knew could not exist. I loved you then, she thought, as I could never love you since.

'Has the bad man gone?' asked Esther suddenly.

'He's gone,' Zerah told her.

'Will he come back?'

'I don't think so, child.'

'What will happen to us, to Oz and me?'

Zerah chuckled. 'You're going to stay with old Zerah. Isn't that a terrible punishment? You're going to have to do chores, and wash and clean. I suspect you'll run away from the sheer torment of it all.'

'I'd never run away from you, Zerah,' Esther promised, her face suddenly serious. 'Not ever.'

'Me neither,' said Oz. Lifting the little pistol from his coat pocket, he offered it to Zerah. 'You'd better keep this for me, Frey,' he said. 'I don't want to shoot nobody.'

Zerah smiled as she took the gun. 'Let's go get some breakfast,' she said.

Beth stood alone. Her son was dead. Clem was dead. Shannow was gone. What was it all for, she wondered? To the left she saw Padlock Wheeler talking to a group of his men, Nestor Garrity among them. Isis was standing close by, and Beth saw Meredith take her hand and raise it to his lips.

Young love . . .

God, what was it all for?

Tobe Harris moved alongside her. 'Sorry to bother you, Frey,' he said, 'but the baby is getting fractious and the last of the milk's gone bad. Not to mention the little fellow is beginning to stink the place out, if you take my meaning?'

'You never cleaned up an infant, Tobe?'

'Nope. You want me to learn?'

She met his eyes and caught his infectious grin. 'Maybe I should teach you.'

'I'd like that, Beth.' It was the first time he'd used her name, and Beth realised she liked it. Turning towards the house, she saw Amaziga and Sam coming down the hillside. The black woman approached her.

'I was wrong about Shannow,' she said, her voice soft. 'Before he asked me to help him from the house, he gave this to Sam.' From her pocket she took a torn scrap of paper and passed it to Beth. On it was scrawled a single word: **Trinity**.

'What does it mean?' asked Beth.

Amaziga told her.

Trinity

New Mexico, July 16, 5.20 a.m.

The storm was disappearing over the mountains, jagged spears of lightning lashing the sky over the distant peaks. The rain had passed now, but the desert was wet and cool. Shannow fell forward as the violet light faded. Sarento grabbed him, hauling him close.

'If you have tricked me . . .' he began. But then he picked up the soul scents, so dense and rich that they almost overwhelmed him. Millions of them. Scores of millions. Sarento released Shannow and spun round and round, the heady mind aroma so dizzying that it almost quelled his hunger just to experience it. 'Where are we?' he asked the old man.

Shannow sat down by a rock and looked around him at the lightning-lit desert. The sky was brightening in the east. 'New Mexico,' he said.

Sarento walked away from the wounded man, climbing a low hill and staring out over the desert. Glancing to his left he saw a metal lattice tower, like a drilling rig, and below it a tent, its open flaps rippling in the wind.

The twentieth century! His dream. Here he could feed for an eternity. He laughed aloud and swung round on Shannow. The old man limped up behind him and was standing staring at the tower.

'We are a long way from the nearest settlement,' said Sarento, 'but I have all the time in the world to find it. How does it feel, Shannow, to have condemned the entire planet?'

'Today I am become death,' said Shannow. Wearily, the old man turned away and walked back down the hillside. Sarento sensed his despair; it only served to heighten the joy he felt. The sky was clearing, the dawn approaching.

He looked again at the metal tower, which was around one

hundred feet high. Something had been wedged beneath it, but from here Sarento could not see what it was.

Who cares, he thought. The largest concentration of people was away to the north. I will go there, he decided. Shannow's words came back to him, tugging at his memory.

Today I am become death.

It was a quote from an old book. He struggled to find the memory. Ah, yes ... The *Bhagavad Ghita*. I am become death, the shatterer of worlds. How apt.

There was something else, but he couldn't think of it. He sat down to await the dawn, and to exult in his new-found freedom. Atop the metal lattice tower was a galvanised iron box, as large as a shed. As the sun rose it made the box gleam, and light shone down on the tower itself. Now Sarento could see what was wedged below it.

Mattresses. Scores of them. He smiled and shook his head. Someone had laid mattresses twenty feet deep under the tower. How ridiculous!

The quote continued to haunt him.

Today I am become death.

Knowledge flew into his mind with every bit as much power as the distant lightning. With the knowledge came a numbing panic, and he knew without doubt where he was – and when.

The Alamogordo bombing range, New Mexico, 180 miles south of Los Alamos. Now that his memory was open, all the facts came flashing to his mind. The mattresses had been placed beneath the atomic bomb as servicemen hauled it into place with ropes. They had feared dropping it and triggering a premature explosion.

Swinging round, he sought the old man. There was no sign of him.

Sarento started to run. The facts would not stop flowing into his mind.

The plutonium bomb resulted in an explosion equal to 20,000 tons of TNT. The detonation of an atomic bomb releases enormous amounts of heat, achieving temperatures of several million degrees in the bomb itself. This creates a large fireball.

On wings of fear Sarento ran.

Convection currents created by the explosion suck dust and other matter up into the fireball, creating a characteristic mushroom cloud. The detonation also produces a shock wave that goes outward for several miles, destroying buildings in the way. Large quantities of neutrons and gamma rays are emitted – lethal radiation bathes the scene.

I can't die! I can't die!

He was one hundred and seventy-seven yards from the tower at 5.30 a.m. on July 16 1945. One second later the tower was vaporised. For hundreds of yards around the zero point, that Oppenheimer had christened *Trinity*, the desert sand was fused to glass. The ball of incandescent air formed by the explosion rose rapidly to a height of 35,000 feet.

Several miles away, J. Robert Oppenheimer watched the mushroom cloud form. All around him men began cheering. 'Today I am become death,' he said.